All the Dear Faces

The two older men had been flinging insults at one another for the past ten minutes, each blaming the other's child for the catastrophe, not knowing what else to do to ease the despair, the bitterness, the shame which had befallen each family, and yet aware now that it did no good. It was too late. What did it matter who was the instigator in this since the outcome was the same. A decent Catholic girl had been disgraced. A young and blameless boy had been seduced, and so the men fell away from one another, hopeless and helpless before the inevitability of it all.

About the author

Audrey Howard was born in Liverpool in 1929 and it is from that once-great seaport that many of the ideas for her books come. Before she began to write she had a variety of jobs, among them hairdresser, model, shop assistant, cleaner and civil servant. In 1981, out of work and living in Australia, she wrote the first of her novels. She was fifty-two. Her fourth novel, *The Juniper Bush*, won the Romantic Novel of the Year Award in 1988. She now lives in her childhood home, St Anne's on Sea, Lancashire.

All the Dear Faces

Audrey Howard

CORONET BOOKS
Hodder and Stoughton

First published in Great Britain in 1992
by Hodder and Stoughton
A division of Hodder Headline PLC
First published in paperback in 1993
by Hodder & Stoughton
A Coronet Paperback

10

A CIP catalogue record for this book is available from
the British Library

ISBN 0 340 58627 3

Photoset by Rowland Phototypesetting Ltd.,
Bury St Edmunds, Suffolk
Printed and bound in Great Britain by
Mackays of Chatham PLC, Chatham, Kent

Hodder and Stoughton
A division of Hodder Headline PLC
338 Euston Road
London NW1 3BH

For Pam Storrie, who sat beside me in school:
A dear friend and still is.

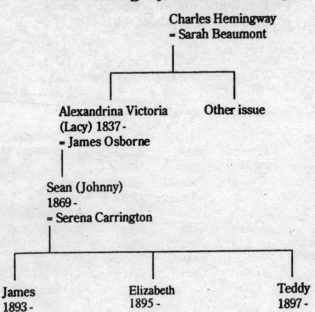

The Hemingway/Osborne Family

Charles Hemingway
= Sarah Beaumont

Alexandrina Victoria
(Lacy) 1837 -
= James Osborne

Other issue

Sean (Johnny)
1869 -
= Serena Carrington

James
1893 -

Elizabeth
1895 -

Teddy
1897 -

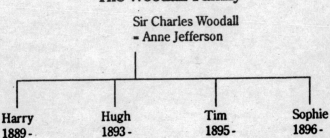

The Woodall Family

Sir Charles Woodall
= Anne Jefferson

Harry
1889 -

Hugh
1893 -

Tim
1895 -

Sophie
1896 -

The O'Shaughnessy Family

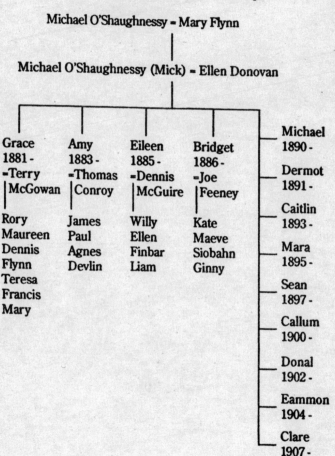

Michael O'Shaughnessy = Mary Flynn

Michael O'Shaughnessy (Mick) = Ellen Donovan

Grace 1881 - =Terry McGowan	Amy 1883 - =Thomas Conroy	Eileen 1885 - =Dennis McGuire	Bridget 1886 - =Joe Feeney	Michael 1890 -
Rory Maureen Dennis Flynn Teresa Francis Mary	James Paul Agnes Devlin	Willy Ellen Finbar Liam	Kate Maeve Siobahn Ginny	Dermot 1891 -
				Caitlin 1893 -
				Mara 1895 -
				Sean 1897 -
				Callum 1900 -
				Donal 1902 -
				Eammon 1904 -
				Clare 1907 -

1

The gathering of the O'Shaughnessy family for the first meal of the day could only be likened to some earth-shattering celebration, a great and noisy reunion at which an outsider might be forgiven for thinking that they hadn't seen one another for a month at the very least instead of the previous evening. Voices were raised to such a pitch it was difficult to hear what was being said which didn't matter in the least since everyone round the table spoke at the same time anyway. There were seldom less than fifteen of them crammed together about the sturdy, rectangular table with its scoured pine top and substantial turned legs. Not that any other meal of the day was different to this one. Kitchen or dining room, it was all the same to them, and whether it be breakfast, dinner or supper, Ellen O'Shaughnessy as a matter of course always prepared a meal as though she was expecting a battalion of the Lancashire Fusiliers since she said her family ate like one.

Of the eighteen children Ellen had borne, thirteen had lived and of those thirteen, eight still remained at home though that wasn't the end of it by any means. The four eldest, all girls and married now, were as fertile as their mother. Being a close-knit and loving family and with them living no more than a stone's throw from Edge Lane and their childhood home, one or more of Ellen's girls was usually to be found in her kitchen at some time of the day. With children at the knee or the breast it was not surprising that a handful should now and again be overlooked when Gracie or Amy, Eileen or Bridget departed reluctantly for their own kitchens at the end of the day. And what did it matter, Ellen asked carelessly. They were accommodated good naturedly around the enormous table or put to bed in haphazard fashion with Ellen's own to be called for the next day or the next. Five or six or a dozen, it was all the same to her.

Ellen could boast to being a grandmother sixteen times over. That is if it had been her nature to boast, which it wasn't, for what was clever or even unusual in bearing children? It was as natural as the grass coming through the fertile soil in the spring, and as regular. What the Good Lord sent must be accepted and usually was but Ellen was forty-six now and she prayed nightly to the Holy Mother to let their Clare, three years old a week since, be her last. She loved every one of them, children and grandchildren alike, and would gladly have died to save them from a moment's hurt but, praise be to the Holy Virgin from whom all goodness came, she really had had enough. She'd 'seen' nothing now for over six months so perhaps that time which comes to all women was upon her and if that was the case there would be no need for her Mick to hold back in their marriage bed as he had taken to doing recently, since, like her, he wanted no more children. It was against all the teachings of Holy Mother Church, of course, what Michael did – or did not do, to be more precise – in their intimate moments and she herself didn't much care for it either since he was forced to pull away before she was ready, but surely now they could 'go at it' as they had joyously done in the early years of their marriage, taking a chance there'd be no more babies.

She looked along the length of the table at the results of her and Mick 'going at it' for the best part of thirty years, smothering the fond smile which creased her rosy Irish face at the memory of it. A lusty man was Mick O'Shaughnessy and despite their age she and himself still found a great deal of satisfaction in their loving. He was there at the head of the table, the baby, as Clare was still called, on his lap and about him, clustered as thickly as buds on the branch of a

2

fruitful tree, were the O'Shaughnessy family. Down both sides of the laden table, seated on benches shoulder to shoulder and forced by lack of space to keep their elbows well into their sides and each one, even Clare, talking sixteen to the dozen. It didn't stop them eating, mind, since it was something they had learned to do, copying their elders, from an early age. Now and again, more from force of habit than a need to chastise, Ellen beseeched them not to talk with their mouths full but with airy cries of 'sorry Mammy' they still continued to do so.

There was not one among them who had seen the green hills of Ireland but they all spoke with a rich and lilting Irish brogue. Mick's father had come over during the potato famine of 1845, as had Ellen's own forebears, leaving behind the sod cottages in which they and generations of their people had existed, living at the best of times only just above subsistence level. For many the move to Liverpool had barely improved their poverty-stricken circumstances since the starvation and death they had thought to leave behind in County Clare or Tipperary or Cork had followed them across the water. The men had dreams of finding work as navvies in the building of railways, as dock labourers or bricklayers in the construction of the houses which sprawled across the fields and pastures at the back of the dockland; the women dreamed of no more than filling their children's bellies with something other than dock leaves and nettles.

They had clung together, as exiles often will, forming colonies where they lived in dangerously close proximity to one another, ten, fifteen, twenty families stuffed cheek by jowl into one house, in crooked narrow streets no wider than a man's outstretched arms, in courts consisting of back to back houses measuring overall eleven feet by eleven, rising out of a sea of stench into dense and dirty masses in the areas of Brook Alley, Naylors Yard and Addison Close, from Scotland Road down to the river. It was said that 66,000 people lived in one square mile of that teeming region of squalor and that on one acre of land alone it was possible to build 130 hovels to accommodate them.

Lacy Hemingway, daughter of the great shipping house of Hemingway, who had become Mrs James Osborne, had changed all that for the O'Shaughnessy family on a fine summer day over fifty years ago when Michael O'Shaughnessy, Ellen's father-in-law, had come to her attention as he worked by the dockside. A fine, well-set-up man he had been, despite his poor beginnings, with an air of authority about him which Miss Hemingway, newly starting up on her own in the business of shipping, had admired. She had offered him the job of manager in her warehouse and within the year Michael and his wife Mary had moved to the grand, recently-built house in Edge Lane. Out in the country it had been, Edge Lane no more than a meandering track off Mount Vernon leading to a sandstone quarry. Fields stretched away to Knotty Ash and West Derby, dotted with farms and the well-tended homes of the wealthy of which there were a good many in the growing industrial affluence of Liverpool, and at the back of the row of houses, all detached and set in a quarter of an acre of long garden, was the Corporation Water Works reservoir giving the family clean, disease-free water for the first time since they had left the old country.

Mick, Michael O'Shaughnessy the second, was born there in 1859, the middle child between two sisters and two brothers. The children Mary had borne before the move to Edge Lane, thirteen in all, lay buried in the land of their birth or in St Mary's Churchyard, Everton, their father's good fortune coming too late to be of any use to them.

Ellen had been brought to this house as a sixteen-year-old bride, sharing the kitchen with her mother-in-law for six years before the old lady had herself gone, outliving her husband by a bare six months. Ellen had Gracie then, and Amy and Eileen, and under her apron was Bridget and though she had been fond of her husband's mother it had been grand to have the spacious kitchen and house all to

4

herself and her growing family. A large house it was, three storeys high, tall and sturdy, sitting foursquare in the centre of its strip of land with a bit of a lawn in the front and the flowerbeds old Mary had planted well established by then. At the back the first Michael had grown potatoes and carrots and cabbage. With his deep rooted Irish love of the land and his bitter memories of death and destruction in the old country he was unable to tolerate the squandering of earth which could produce food for his children. He could never forget the harrowing images of the famine and in his opinion it was only prudent, despite his well-settled position in the Hemingway warehouse, to provide for the future when his circumstances might not be so rosy.

But his son, Ellen's husband, was as different to his father as a cheerful family pet is to a hard-working wiry gundog. Both fine animals and useful in their way but where his father was ambitious, wary and far thinking, perhaps because of his hard and desperate past, his son was easy going and though possessing a quick Irish temper was, on the whole, a peaceable man. Not that Ellen's father-in-law had been grim, or without humour, or that her husband was not hard-working, but like the gundog whose nature it is to seek what it has been trained to, the first Michael O'Shaughnessy could not seem to put aside the past and enjoy his good fortune but must always strive towards better things. He worked hard, long hours, unable to settle unless he had seen to the final shipment of a cargo, the supervision of the unloading of another, neither of them his concern since he had men to do the job and though he got on and was the envy of his compatriots, he was dead at the age of fifty-five.

The second Michael O'Shaughnessy, born when the first was in his late twenties, took over the management of the warehouse when his father died. Mick did the job with the same steady application to work as his father but though he had been brought up, as Ellen had, on terrible tales of the

5

troubles, he had not suffered them and neither had his children and the absence of hunger and want made for a contented man and a peaceful existence. The vegetable garden at the rear of the house grew wild and abundant, with long grass and tall wide-spreading trees, a grand haven for hordes of children and grandchildren to run riot in, and he would sit at the window and smile at them, his pipe in his mouth and the *Echo* in his lap, for was that not the purpose of a garden?

Not that peace was much in evidence in the house in Edge Lane. They were Irish, after all, and volatile. Self-willed, the lot of them, and tempers are easily lit when more than a dozen people, all bent on their own way, live under the same roof. They were a decent, hard-working family of comfortable means but the house had no more than five bedrooms which, with Michael and Ellen in one, the two servants in another, left three for the eight remaining children and the assorted grandchildren who somehow found their way there. Michael O'Shaughnessy the third, the eldest of Mick and Ellen's boys, had a fine, live-in job in the stables at Woodall Park, but it was still a tight squeeze on occasion.

The kitchen-cum-living room was spacious and warm and though the house was fifty years old Ellen had one of the latest closed ranges to cook on. It had a flat hotplate over the fire and an efficiently controlled oven beside it, replacing the open range which had been considered quite sufficient in her mother-in-law's day. Ellen could remember it well, a big cast-iron monster which must be lit every morning after it had been swept out and the ashes sifted. It had to be cleaned with black lead which was rubbed in, then brushed and buffed with a pad. The brass fender round the range was polished until it sparkled and it had been her job as a new bride, sickly in the mornings with her first pregnancy, to do it. Holy Mother, but she'd hated it and had been glad to see the back of it. Mind you, she'd insisted on keeping the lovely red, stone-flagged floor. When it was scrubbed and polished you could see the warmth of the fire in it. The white, lime-washed walls, the gleaming rows of copper pans, graduating from the tiniest milk-pan to the largest, a heavy preserving pan, gave to Ellen a deep and primitive satisfaction she could explain to no one.

There were rows of preserve jars, flat-lidded, salt-glazed stoneware in shades from a creamy buttercup yellow to a dark chocolate brown, with fawn, bronze and caramel shades in between. In them were her jams and apple rings, plums, mushrooms, pineapple pieces crystallised in sugar syrup, pickled meats and chutneys. There was an enormous dresser against the whole of one wall crammed on each shelf with every imaginable plate and dish, cups and saucers, soup tureens and gravy boats, pie dishes and cake stands, all of earthenware since a family as large and careless as hers could not be safely trusted to use for everyday the 'good' dinner and tea service she had tucked lovingly away in her dining room sideboard for special occasions.

Simmering on the range was a heavy, cast-iron stock pot, filled up with meat and vegetables the night before to ensure a constant supply of soups and broths, for Ellen scorned the manufactured tins of 'rubbish' which the lazy housewife could purchase to feed her family.

There were shelves on which decorative biscuit tins crouched beside bottles of ketchup and Cadbury's Cocoa Essence, Patersons Extract of Malt and Quaker Rolled Oats, and high in the ceiling was her airing pulley, a long contraption made of slats of strong wood over which she hung her family's freshly ironed shirts, bodices, drawers, vests and petticoats to air in the warm draught which rose from the range.

This morning was no different to any other Monday morning. Lifting the heavy frying pan from the range Ellen turned, still as light on her feet as her own daughters, pushing unceremoniously between young Michael and Dermot, her second son, brandishing the pan and the fork she held in her right hand as though she would stand no nonsense from either of them.

'You'll have some more sausage, son?' It was not a question but a statement directed at both her boys. 'And another egg? Sure an' it's a cold day an' the pair of you to be out in it before the streets are aired. Now I'll not take no for an answer for only the Blessed Mother herself knows what you'll get to eat up at that place,' this last directed at young Michael, just as though he was off to the Borough gaol instead of the comfortable kitchen at Woodall Park. 'Growing boys, the pair of you,' she went on, 'an' you'll be needing a decent breakfast inside of you. See, Matty...' to the middle-aged maidservant who was clattering about the range with a second frying pan '... pass Michael some of that fried bread, an' will yer look at that? Eammon's plate's empty an' him off to school in a minute. Jesus, Joseph and Mary, can you not see to him, Lucy...' to the second maid '... before the spalpeen starves an' fetch me some more bacon from the pantry while you're at it. Now don't be pulling a face at me, Donal O'Shaughnessy. I'll not have it said that any son of mine goes hungry to school, and what's the matter with you, Mara? D'you not like your Mammy's cooking, is that it? Well, perhaps if you got off your behind and helped Matty instead of daydreaming the live long day, and Caitlin, will you get your nose out of that paper and pass Dermot the marmalade. Holy Mother, d'you really need to read at the table, girl? No, don't tell me what it is, for sure, don't I already know and how you can believe in such nonsense is beyond me. Decent women parading themselves when they should be in their own homes seeing to their family, and I'll have no arguments, d'you hear? Clare, darlin', let Daddy up now. He's to be off to work in a minute and by the beard on him not even shaved yet. Sure an' will you look at Flynn with his bootlaces not tied and his jacket buttoned up all wrong and what his Mammy'll be saying...' referring to her eldest daughter, Gracie, whose son Flynn

8

was '.. I don't know, when Sister Angela asks who got him ready today. Michael, darlin', do him up, will you, there's a good lad, or Gracie'll die of shame when next she meets the good Sister. Now, Donal, will you not try another egg? Matty's cooked it just as you like it . . .'

'Ma, I haven't time to be seeing to Flynn and shouldn't he be able to dress himself by now, for God's sake? How old is he? How old are you, Flynn?' turning to the boy, his own nephew 'Six, is it, an' can't tie your own bootlaces! For shame. Look, go to Caitlin, she'll do them up for you, won't you, Caitlin? I've hardly time to tie me own bootlaces, never mind yours. You know I've to be up at the park by seventhirty at the latest or Mr Jackson'll not let me stop overnight again and he'll report me to Sir Charles, so he will, an' I'll be getting the bloody sack.'

'Language, Michael!'

'Sorry, Ma, but I'll have to go. What's Flynn doing here anyway? He's got his own home to go to, hasn't he? Our Gracie's got a bloody nerve . . . sorry Ma . . . landing you with him as if you haven't got enough to do with your own. She's .. '

'Now Michael, I'll not have you calling your own sister. A good girl and a good mother and if Flynn wants to stay the night, sure an' what's one more amongst you lot? See, darlin', will you not have a bit more bacon? Matty's cooked another rasher or two an' I'll not have them goin' beggin'.'

'I'll have one, acushla, an' if there's a bit of fried bread left over ?' Her husband's voice, though quiet and patient, was heard quite clearly above the babble of voices which flowed about him and just as though her ears were tuned in to this one which seldom complained or demanded, his wife flew at once, full of contrition, to his end of the table. Ladling the hot, crispy bacon and fried bread on to the plate he was sharing with his youngest daughter, her manner was one of penitence at having missed him. Passing the frying pan to Matty she whisked the child from his knee and squeezed her in between her two brothers, kissing her soundly on her rosy cheek. Recovering the frying pan from the hovering maid she circled the table again in the manner of a preacher searching out wrong-doers, ready to fill an empty plate or indeed any need her family might have of her. She was not satisfied until every hand was lifting food steadily to every mouth, irrespective of age and sex, and her voice as she urged them to eat up was as lilting and enduring as the rushing waters of the River Shannon besides which her forebears had lived.

Michael, her son, was the first to leave. He was just twenty years of age and the first boy to be born alive to herself and Mick O'Shaughnessy. Ten years they had been married when he came and if she was honest with herself, and she rarely was where her family was concerned since she felt no mother should have favourites, he was hers. Tall and supple, lean as a young sapling he was, the replica of his father at the same age, though with twice his impudence, Ellen admitted fondly. Dark-haired as all her children were, his lifted from his forehead in a mass of tumbled waves, falling across his brow and shading the startling blue of his laughing eyes. His sun-darkened face was arresting and aggressive and yet there was a certain vulnerability about his mouth which she knew captivated the opposite sex. He could be grave at times, her bold Irish son, and at others high-spirited and merry. A true Irish nature, even if he had never seen the rolling green land of his forefathers, and she loved him for it.

'Mind how you go on that infernal thing, darlin',' she said, referring to the bicycle which leaned against the wall by the back kitchen door. 'Why you can't walk on the two good legs the Lord gave you I'll never know. Tell him, Mick,' appealing to his father who still sat placidly by the kitchen table despite the uproar which rose to a crescendo as those about it prepared to leave. His manner said that he would start the day in his own good time despite the fact that he had yet to shave and put on his tie and jacket. He would catch the tram at the corner of Jubilee Drive and Edge Lane and be down at the Pier Head, a distance of no more than two miles, by eight-thirty. He liked to sit quietly with his wife and a fourth cup of tea after his family had gone on their way, taking his daughter on his knee again whilst their Mara, fifteen now, and Caitlin, who was two years older and kept at home to help her mother, supervised the maids in the clearing of the table.

'To be sure the boy's old enough to please himself, Ellen,' he said mildly, belching on the last bit of fat bacon he had eaten. 'I'd ride one of the dratted things meself if it wasn't for that hill at Mount Pleasant. Anyway, I'm too old for them new-fangled things now,' and he reached for his daughter, a little scrap of a dark-haired, pink-cheeked, blue-eyed creature who, as though he knew she would be the last fruit of his loins, was extra dear to him.

'Well, I don't like them, son and that's a fact, but if you must then you must. See now, wrap up well. Holy Mother of God, you're not going out without your scarf?' She was aghast. 'Are you mad in this weather? There's a wind to cut you like a knife, so there is. And where d'you think you're off to, Eammon O'Shaughnessy?' whirling to catch by his jacket collar her youngest son who was attempting to escape his Mammy's notice. Little good it did him for where her children were concerned Ellen had eyes in the back of her head. 'I asked you to wait for Callum, didn't I? I'll not have a wee scrap of a lad like yourself going off to school on your own, so I won't.'

'Aw Mammy, will you stop it now. I'm six years old and not a baby and I said I'd meet . . .'

'To be sure you're meeting no one . . .'

'Let the boy go, Ellen. He's a man, so he is . . .'

Ellen turned distractedly to her husband, ready to lay about him with her tongue for encouraging the boy. Taking advantage of their mother's wandering attention,

11

Sean, Callum, Donal and Eammon, her four youngest sons, along with her grandson Flynn, raced out of the kitchen and round the back of the house. Headlong down the path they bounded, out of the gate and into Edge Lane, all five yelling like dervishes as they indulged in some masculine game of their own devising.

'Now see what you've done,' Ellen admonished her husband, settling herself nevertheless on the bench at his side. She poured a cup of tea from the enormous pot and sipping with deep pleasure fell into the companionable silence which was so rare and therefore so precious to herself and Mick. The contrast to the hullabaloo which had gone before was quite startling and but for the irrepressible crashing of pots and pans as Lucy and Matty prepared to wash the dirty dishes, all was quiet. The little girl leaned against her father, playing with a tattered rag doll which had evidently been much loved by more than one child before her.

'I'm off now, Ma.'

'Jesus and all his Angels, I thought you'd gone, son ' In a moment Ellen was up again, fussing about their Dermot, a year younger than his brother Michael and the scholar of the family. Worked in a bank, did Dermot, and great things were expected of him and Ellen was so proud she could not help but boast of him to her friends. He was the first of her boys to follow in his Daddy's footsteps and work with his head and not with his hands and the grand suit he had on this morning testified to the fact. A good navy blue serge, a sparklingly white shirt with a stiff wing collar and a shine on his boots you could see your face in. Dermot had things inside his brain none of them could understand and would be manager of the bank one day, he told them, and they believed him.

'Now keep that coat buttoned up, son, and promise you'll not go hanging about at the Pier Head at dinner time. Stay in the office where it's warm.'

Dermot sighed. His mother still thought he was six years

old and like a six-year-old would be drawn down to the river to see the boats. 'I will, Ma.' He pulled away from her loving hand impatiently. His father saw it and his own genial face hardened, though he said nothing. On the quiet he thought his second son was a cold fish but his Mammy loved him and as long as Dermot did not trouble his Mammy his father was prepared to overlook his somewhat high opinion of himself. He wasn't a bad lad, just a bit too big for his boots and life would cure that, his father told himself. They were none of them bad. Some were more wayward than others though when he got right down to it he'd be hard pressed to say who, for they were all somewhat headstrong. Would you listen to Mara now, giving what for to Matty as though she was the mistress of the house and not her Mammy, and squabbling with Caitlin over who should run up the stairs and make their and Clare's beds. Ellen, despite having two live-in maids, was not having her daughters brought up in idle ways, she said a dozen times a day, and the two girls took it in turns to see to their own room. But each morning it was the same, the pair of them spitting like a couple of tabby cats, swearing it was the turn of the other. And it was usually Mara who was the culprit. She'd be a handful, that one, if Ellen didn't keep a tight rein on her with her big ideas and abomination of anything which might spoil her white hands which could be anything and everything from kneading the dough for the bread to sewing on a button! A beautiful girl, his Mara, as was Caitlin, both with an abundance of thick, dark hair rippling in shining profusion down their straight backs, eyes as blue as the Madonna's robe and Mara with skin on her as white and pure as the petal on a daisy. But Mara was haughty, thinking herself a cut above all the good Irish Catholic boys her Mammy had to the house, saying she would marry a gentleman, if you please, and a rich one at that, or go to be a nun. A *nun*, her! If ever a girl was cut out to be a nun, it certainly wasn't their Mara.

13

And Caitlin, her head filled with nothing but women's rights and the Women's Social and Political Union, worrying her poor mother into an early grave and for what? But Caitlin could give you an answer, more than you bargained for, sometimes, her eyes flashing dangerously, her gift of words tying her brothers into bewildered knots when they argued with her. She didn't give a damn if Mammy had been a mother at her age, she cried defiantly, tossing her provocative head, for there were other things in the world for a woman to do than bear children and tend to the fire, dodging the outraged slap her Mammy aimed at her. A clever girl was Caitlin, frustrated by her enforced life of domesticity beneath her mother's watchful eye for none of *her* girls would go out to work whatever Caitlin said, she told her. Pity she hadn't been born a lad, his Caitlin, he sighed, for she'd have made something of herself with that bright and enquiring mind of hers.

'The boy should let me make him some soup for his carrying out, Mick,' his wife fretfully reproached herself as she came back into the kitchen. ''Tis as cold as charity out there and a good hot bowl of oxtail would see him through the day. And did you see young Michael on that dratted machine of his? He'll go under a horse's hooves one of these days, so he will,' crossing herself hastily. 'Like a bird he was, going up towards Dorothy Street as though he had wings under him instead of wheels. It's such a long way, darlin', all those miles to Woodall Park. I wish he'd chosen to do something in town, like you an' Dermot, then he could have lived at home. Horses, he said, and now it's motor cars! Why's he so set on motor cars, will you tell me that? They'll not last the year out, I shouldn't wonder. Dreadful contraptions, so they are. He'd have been grand in the warehouse with you, but no, he must go all that way, working all hours God sends and what will he be at the end of the day? No more than a handyman up at Woodall.'

Her voice was plaintive and to distract her Mick lifted the

little girl and placed her on her mother's lap. Give Ellen a child to nurse, to feed and comfort and she forgot her woes in a trice and he was relieved to see her relax into the posture of fulfilled motherhood which was her role.

'Now then, darlin',' he heard her say as he moved out of the warmth of the kitchen into the bone-chilling cold of the hallway and the stairs which led up to the first floor. 'Say the rosary with Mammy and when we've finished here you an' me'll go down to St Mary's to hear Mass.'

Michael O'Shaughnessy felt his strong legs surge with power as he pumped the pedals of what his mother called his 'dratted machine'. It was only a second-hand safety built almost twenty years ago but it was light and simple to mount and because of this had been a great favourite with the ladies. It had a sprung saddle and a plunger brake and though he would have preferred something a bit more dashing like the Rudge Whitworth Racer, this had cost him only five shillings from a pawn shop at the back of the General Post Office and at least it wasn't a boneshaker or an ordinary which was what the working-class man usually rode. An unredeemed pledge it had been but with a bit of polish and a touch of oil here and there, a few minor adjustments to pedals and brakes it had proved to be a bargain and got him to Woodall Park where he worked as a groom to Sir Charles Woodall's horses, and back to Liverpool on his day off. Every other Sunday, that was, taking turn and turn about with Fred Renshaw, the second stable lad, and if Mr Jackson was in a good mood, sometimes Saturday afternoon as well. Ten miles he had to cycle but he was young, fit, lean and graceful as a greyhound and with the stamina of an athlete. Ten miles was nothing to him, he told himself, whistling cheerfully as he followed the road out of Liverpool and on to Childwall, skimming along country lanes, taking sharp bends and crossing shallow fords with a skill and speed he had perfected in six years of doing the same journey every second weekend.

He passed mile after mile of farmland, rattling through villages, in at one end and out of the other in no more than thirty seconds. There was a sharp ground frost and the air was clear and pure and cold as a mountain spring. There was little traffic; a milk cart pulled by an ancient horse, a fruiterer's van coming back from the market, a man on horseback who glared and shook his riding crop as Michael's machine overtook him, and a sluggish cart loaded with bricks.

He'd had a grand weekend helped by the attentions of the pretty young parlourmaid he'd met at the music hall in Bold Street on Saturday night. She'd been there in the threepenny stalls with her friend, another parlourmaid, and he and Dennis Conron, his pal since schooldays, had 'clicked' right away. Vesta Tilley had been the star turn, a male impersonator, and what a show she'd put on. They'd laughed and sung along with her, their faces flushed with their intense enjoyment and when it was over the girls had not taken much persuading to join him and Dennis in a port wine at the bar. And he'd had a promise from her, Molly, she was called, that she'd meet him in two weeks' time and her bright and knowing eyes had told him it would be well worth the journey. She could borrow a bicycle from a friend, she'd confided, and if she could get a Sunday off and he could escape his mother's insistence that he attend Communion and Mass, she'd be quite willing to take a ride out with him, she'd said.

His narrowed eyes dwelled on the picture of himself and Molly riding side by side up to Woolfall Heath, perhaps having a few drinks in The Horns and afterwards ... well, he knew of a snug little place right off the beaten track where walkers never went and if Molly was as impressed with him as he was with her, who knew what she might allow. He considered pleasurably what that might be, sighing as he pictured himself showing off his prowess on his dashing machine, then the image faded to be replaced with another and in it was himself and Molly but this time they were sitting side by side in Sir Charles Woodall's brand new Vauxhall motor car. Holy Mother, now wouldn't that dazzle her? She'd be so awestruck he'd have his hand up the leg of her drawers before she could say, 'Now then, Michael!'

He shook his head, almost tipping himself and his bicycle into the ditch at the side of the lane but the picture stayed with him. Not just of the girl who would be putty in his hands but the sweet idea of Michael O'Shaughnessy driving one of those grand machines which were appearing more and more often on the roads. There were two now in the old stable at Woodall Park, not only the Vauxhall belonging to his employer but a wicked little Austin Seven two-seater Sir Charles had recently bought for his eldest son, Harry. Hell's teeth, he was a lucky bastard, was Master Harry, dashing about the countryside with a different girl tucked in next to him every day of the week, he shouldn't wonder. Most of them actresses or shop girls, young ladies who were not of his own class and he'd have no trouble persuading them to allow him a liberty or two.

Still an' all, Michael O'Shaughnessy envied no man. He was supremely content in his work, in his carefree, unencumbered existence which allowed him to enjoy an open air life which, though it was a hard one, was not a lot different to that of the young gentlemen he served: exercising the horses, grooming them, riding at the back of the hunt in season in case he was needed, walking the moor with Sir Charles' guns across his arm should an extra man be necessary. This was what his master's sons did when they were not away at school and though Michael worked long hours he was well satisfied with it. He would marry one day, one of the good Catholic girls his mother had earmarked for him, perhaps, and raise a family in one of the estate cottages provided by Sir Charles, continuing to do exactly as he did now. He was not ambitious and had no urge to get on, to be somebody, as his brother Dermot did. The only thing he would like to do which he wasn't doing now was to drive his employer's smart Vauxhall motor car and there was no reason why it should not happen, for he was well thought of by Sir Charles. If he minded his manners and things went as he hoped, and if Lady Woodall got her way, which she usually did, a splendid Rolls-Royce Silver Ghost, the queen of motor cars, was soon to be delivered to Woodall Park. Many grooms, as the motor car became increasingly popular with the upper classes who were the only ones able to afford them, were becoming mechanics and chauffeurs and what was to stop him doing the same? He was clever with machinery, he knew he was and he'd soon get the hang of it. The Rolls-Royce was a family car with a spacious enclosed back seat and a rack on the back for her ladyship's luggage and at the front was a double seat for a chauffeur and another servant, and if Michael Patrick O'Shaughnessy had his way, he was to be that chauffeur!

He was almost at the park now, cutting across the railway which lay between Liverpool and St Helens, his bicycle wheels sounding a swift clackety-clack as they passed over the lines. Through Farnworth and along the narrow lane from Bold Hill to Tibbs Cross and there was the lodge which guarded the south gate into the estate of Sir Charles Woodall. It was not quite twenty-five minutes past seven.

'Morning Tommy,' he shouted to the lodgekeeper. 'You only just got out of bed then?' standing up on the pedals as Tommy Perks wandered down the bit of garden which led to the privy behind the hedge.

'Cheeky bugger,' Tommy threw good-naturedly after him, taking no offence. Michael O'Shaughnessy was well liked by his fellow servants. A great favourite with the lasses, of course, since he had a knack of making each and every one of them, from the youngest skivvy in the scullery right up to Mrs Blythe, the housekeeper, feel she was a bit special.

Tommy supposed it to be something to do with being Irish for were they not known to have the gift to charm the very devil himself?

'Only just in time, O'Shaughnessy,' Mr Jackson said, looking at his watch as Michael slithered to a stop in the cobbled stable-yard.

'Not late though, Mr Jackson,' grinning. 'I'll just put me bicycle away and then I'll begin mucking out.'

'Aye, do that lad, an' then get yerself a bite of breakfast. You'll be peckish after that ride.'

'I will, Mr Jackson,' wondering what his Mammy would say if she heard himself described as peckish after what she had stuffed into him less than an hour since.

As Michael, whistling softly, began the mucking out of the stables, Caitlin was folding the corner of the sheet neatly under the mattress of her bed, making a good job of it, for if a job was worth doing it was worth doing well, in her opinion, a belief instilled into her by her Mammy, even if it was only making a damned bed. She smoothed the sheet before replacing the soft woollen blankets, then turned them down beneath the pillows. Next came the plain white bedspread made by her grandmother and as it was winter, the pink eiderdown on top.

She sighed as she turned to do Mara's bed and for perhaps the thousandth time in the last three years, in fact every morning since she was fourteen years of age and had left school, wished with all her heart that she was dashing off to catch the tram to some interesting, fulfilling, brain-taxing job as so many men were doing. To work in an office, or a warehouse, as her father did, or even a shop, anything was better than this continual round of household duties, Church, Church meetings, sewing circles and all the other tedious female things her mother enjoyed so much and which she expected her daughters to enjoy too. If it were not for the activities of the WSPU, the Women's Social and

Political Union, which she had somehow – only the Blessed Mother in Heaven herself knew how – managed to persuade Mammy and Daddy to let her attend, she would go out of her mind with boredom. Twice a week if Mammy was in an indulgent mood, or if she could slip out unnoticed, she took the tram to the WSPU office, helping in any way she could to further the cause of the suffragist movement in which she believed so passionately. After all, why should women not have exactly the same rights as men? Just because a brain was in a female head did not mean it could not think or reason as well as a man's. But try telling that to a man, or even to many women, for that matter. Take Mara, for instance. She attacked her sister's pillow ferociously before replacing it on the smooth undersheet. All *she* wanted from life, to hear her talk, was some chap to take over where Daddy left off. Of course he must be rich and handsome, that went without saying, charming and witty and be madly in love with Mara O'Shaughnessy, but all she would finish up with in the end was exactly the life their own Mammy had. Ten children in as many years and nothing in her brain but the best way to make a light egg custard.

Caitlin tossed the eiderdown high in the air before laying it neatly on her sister's bed then, standing back, surveyed the room with the keen eye of one who will allow not even the faintest speck of dust to escape her notice, in exact imitation of her mother, had she but known it.

She moved to the window and tweaked the curtains into a more becoming line, straightened the clean towels on the washstand and satisfied in her methodical mind that all was in order turned to peer through the window on which crystals of ice were still patterned. She breathed on the glass and rubbed it with her fist, making a round, clear space to look through. Her father was just closing the gate behind him, warmly wrapped in his scarf and greatcoat, no doubt by her mother's loving hand, and Caitlin smiled. Was there ever a woman like her Mammy and really who was she,

Caitlin O'Shaughnessy, to say her mother lived a useless meaningless life just because she didn't have the rights that men enjoyed? Was there ever a woman more loved, more fulfilled, more perfectly content with her life than Ellen O'Shaughnessy? There were thousands upon thousands like her up and down the land who were just the same and wouldn't give a blessed thank you for Caitlin's determined belief that she was to get them the right to vote. In fact they would probably tell her to mind her own damned business!

She smiled ruefully as she left the room.

2

James Osborne tightened the girth beneath his horse's belly. He patted the fine, arching neck and smoothed the polished coat of chestnut, then holding the rein loosely walked round the mare soothing her with soft, murmuring sounds in the back of his throat. The groom watched him, his own eyes fond as Master James studied the lovely animal.

'She looks grand, sir,' he offered proudly, taking some of the credit for the mare's splendour since he himself had looked after her welfare whilst the boy was away at school ever since Master James' father had given her to him on his twelfth birthday. The animal turned her head, nudging the groom's shoulder affectionately.

'She does indeed, George. You've done well with her. She'll be the best-looking mount at the Sutton Meet to-morrow despite Harry Woodall's new hunter which he promises I shall see this morning. I really can't believe the beast can be finer than Lady here no matter how much Harry paid for him. Come from Leicestershire, he says, where there are some damned fine hunters bred so I suppose he'll be good but I'll put my money on this little beauty any day of the week.'

'I'm sure you're right, Master James. There's not a mare to touch her in my opinion. She's got a heart as big as herself an' she's a brave little jumper an' all. By God, you should have seen her take that gate down Sandy Lane End, t'other day. Like a bloody bird, she were.'

James patted the mare's neck approvingly, ready to put his foot in the stirrup and spring into the saddle, but the sound of a door opening from the direction of the house made him turn and his mouth curled down in an expression of intense irritation.

'Oh God, I'd thought I'd got away before these two were up. They must have heard me come downstairs. Talk about having ears like a lynx. Well, I've had it now, George, because if they've decided to come with me there is no way I can get away without them. Damn and blast the pair of them.'

'Yes, sir.' The groom's voice was sympathetic.

'Hell's teeth, there's nothing I can do about it either, short of strangling the two of them and then they'd make such a bloody commotion they'd have the whole household rushing from their beds to see what all the fuss was about. In no time at all Mother would be begging to be told what was wrong with a chap taking his brother and sister to Woodall and before I knew it she would make me feel I was the most confounded bounder who ever wore shoe leather. Damn it to hell,' he swore softly.

The two figures who had emerged from the side entrance of the house came towards him. One was a boy in his early teens, tall and rangy with that look of being all elbows and pointed shoulders that the adolescent has. He was dark, his tangled hair sticking out from his head in uncombed abandon and he was still shrugging into a tweed jacket with leather patches at the elbow. His riding breeches curved above boots which had the mud of a previous day's ride

22

still upon them. His shirt collar was unbuttoned and the cap in his hand was, in James' opinion, completely unsuitable for riding. Only the working classes wore cloth caps unless it was to shoot in. James shuddered violently, wondering if he had been as unprepossessing at the same age.

Striding beside the boy was a girl. In complete contrast and despite the early hour she was immaculately turned out and James' expression changed to one of fond approval. She wore a dark blue riding habit consisting of a well-fitting jacket and an apron skirt over her breeches and a small but very becoming bowler hat with a veil which neatly secured her hair. Her stock was snowy at her neck and deftly tied and her riding boots gleamed. He had to admire her, he really did even if she was his younger sister for no matter what the occasion or the time of day somehow she always took your breath away with her instinctive flair for doing the right thing. She was as dark as the boy, her hair, what could be seen of it, a rich chestnut brown and her back was as straight as a ruler. Her face was heart-shaped, broad of brow, pointed of chin and her skin was as smooth and pale as ivory. Her long, tilted green eyes looked as though a sooty finger had outlined them, so thick and black were her eyelashes and her mouth was as red and as full as a field poppy. She was tall and slender, her waist no more than a man's two hands could encompass.

She looked at him, smiling a little, a secret female smile, and her brother groaned for he knew she was about to challenge him in that way a female had and which he, as a gentleman, must not oppose.

'Wait for us, James,' the boy called, galloping like some unschooled colt across the yard, his long legs badly out of control in his eagerness not to be left behind. He rammed his cap on his unruly hair as he ran towards the open door-way where his own horse was stabled. 'George, be a good fellow and get High Jinks up for me, will you? Promise you'll wait, James. I'll only be a minute.' He grinned disarmingly

23

over his shoulder and his brother's groan deepened.

'Dear God, have I any choice?' There was resignation in James' voice.

'Not a lot, James,' his sister said sweetly, turning her head in the direction of a second groom who had come running from another open stable door, still apparently eating his breakfast, his expression one of dismay since it was only seven-thirty and the young mistress had not been expected. Knowing exactly what she wanted he moved even faster to obey her unspoken command. A calm and unruffled young lady, was Miss Elizabeth, but it was still his job to jump to her bidding.

'And it was very mean of you to try and slip away without Teddy and me,' she continued whilst she waited for her mare to be saddled. 'You know we wanted to see Harry's hunter just as much as you.'

'I'm not only going to see Harry's hunter, Elizabeth. Hugh and I have some business of our own to attend to. We mean to ride to ... well, never you mind where we are going. That is our affair, mine and Hugh's, and it is nothing to do with ...'

'I know exactly where you and Hugh Woodall are off to, James, so there is no need for that high and mighty tone with me. And that sheepish expression doesn't suit you, either.'

'Sheepish! Now look here, Elizabeth ...'

His sister raised a delicate eyebrow. 'My maid Minty is friendly with Betty who is the sister of the girl you and Hugh have been ... calling on recently ...'

'That's enough of that, Elizabeth. You know far too much for your own good and far more than you should, a well-brought-up young girl like yourself. I don't know who's been talking to you but I can assure you that what Hugh and I do ... really, there is no need to grin like that. I'm shocked, really I am ...' Her brother did his best to maintain his veneer of sophisticated maturity but he was only

24

seventeen years old and the sexuality of which he and Hugh Woodall were so proud was new and somewhat unwieldy. His manner became conciliatory. 'Look here, Elizabeth, anything you might have heard, and I'm not admitting there *is* anything, but I'd be obliged if you wouldn't mention it to father. I wouldn't like him to . . . well, you know how stories get about and he is a bit of a stickler for the proprieties. I mean, Hugh and I are doing no harm to . . . well, you understand how he would be if it came to his ears.' He kicked at the cobblestones moodily. 'Not that he was a saint in his youth from all I hear. A reputation as a bit of a lad, or so Hugh told me. He had it from Sir Charles that he and father often used to . . .'

Conscious suddenly of his sister's fascinated interest and aware that he had been about to speak to a gently reared and sheltered girl on a subject about which she should have no knowledge and in front of a servant as well, he stopped abruptly. His father would skin him if he knew but Elizabeth seemed to have this talent for saying absolutely nothing which somehow led a fellow to divulge confidences he had no intention of divulging in the first place which was most unnerving. 'Anyway, you and Teddy would only be in the way at Woodall,' he said hopefully, 'especially you, Elizabeth. Sophie won't be there. Only Harry, Hugh and Tim . . .'

'I'm coming, James, and if you try to stop me I shall tell father about you and Hugh and Betty whatsit's sister,' which of course, she wouldn't and really James knew it, but best not to take the slightest chance.

Elizabeth's smile deepened and the two men, her brother and the groom who still hung about to see which way the wind blew, were struck quite speechless by the artfulness of woman.

'Do we have a bargain?' she continued. 'Can I come?'

'What about Teddy? I'll look such an ass in front of the others turning up with my kid brother and sister,' he pleaded, but he was already beaten and he knew it. He was

25

saddled not only with Elizabeth but with Teddy as well who would probably demand to go wherever he and Hugh went which was not at all convenient, today of all days. Elly Fielding, the dairymaid in question might not take kindly to three young men jostling one another for her favours, besides which Teddy was far too young for that sort of thing.

'I won't let Teddy follow you and Hugh,' Elizabeth said, just as though she had read his mind. She smiled serenely. 'That is if you'll let me come.'

He hesitated, then, 'Promise?'

'I promise,' and he knew she meant it. She was a good sport really and could be trusted with a fellow's life once she had given her word on it, or his secrets, which was much more important.

Teddy came tumbling through the stable door leading the handsome bay which had been a gift from his father on his twelfth birthday a year ago and behind him Alfie held the reins of Elizabeth's sorrel mare, a dainty little animal, gentle but brave and considered by Johnny Osborne to be a suitable mount for a young lady. Elizabeth turned to study her as the groom led the mare towards her. She frowned.

'I'm not sure I want to take Holly today,' she declared coolly. 'I had a fancy to try out Princess to see if she is fit enough to take the gate out of High Meadow. As it's the meet tomorrow I want to be absolutely certain which of the two is best. I know Princess is mother's horse but I'm sure she wouldn't mind if I rode her since she scarcely goes out herself now. And you know what swaggering fools some of those friends of Harry's are. They think they are the best huntsmen in the country just because they have been out with the Quorn a time or two and I'll not be shown up by . . .'

'Elizabeth. I haven't the time to stand about here while you agonise over whether to take Holly or Princess . . .'

'No, James, I won't be hurried. It is most important that I have the proper mount for tomorrow.'

'Goddammit, Elizabeth, I am in a hurry...'

'I'm sure Betty whatsit's sister will wait for...'

'Elizabeth, get on your bloody mare.' James spoke through gritted teeth and Teddy grinned delightedly. The patient grooms stood to one side, though on George's face was the gritty, pugnacious look of a northcountryman who was ready to argue if these two didn't stop wasting his damned time. Master James had been as pleasant as you please fifteen minutes ago and but for Miss Elizabeth and Master Teddy would have been halfway to Woodall by now and himself and Alfie tucking into a good, hot breakfast in the kitchen of the big house before starting on the tack room. Women! They really were the most awkward and contrary of God's creatures and if he had his way would have been kept in the nursery, the schoolroom, the kitchen and the bedroom where they could do no harm. He stared over Miss Elizabeth's shoulder and waited grimly.

'Please don't swear at me, James, and I would remind you that we have a bargain over the matter of...'

'Don't push me too far, Elizabeth. You can take your damned bargain and ride that to hounds tomorrow for all I care but if you and Teddy want to come with me today, and it seems I have no choice in the matter, then you will get on your mare, the one Alfred is holding and follow me now.'

'James Osborne...'

'*Now*, Elizabeth,' and his sister who knew exactly when to back down, unlike many women, did so, fully aware that she had won one victory today and could not really be expected to win a second.

The ride from Beechwood, home of the Osborne family ever since the railway had encroached across their original property on the shores of the River Mersey, took no more than twenty minutes to Woodall Park. The Osbornes had once lived at Highcross, a lovely estate to the south of the dockland area of Liverpool, just a stone's throw from the two great shipping concerns of Hemingways and Osbornes which through marriage had merged and made the families amongst the wealthiest in Lancashire.

But as the industrial growth of Liverpool began to spread out from the city, impinging on the privacy and peace of what had once been pastureland, Lacy and James Osborne, the grandparents of the three youngsters in the stable-yard, had sold up and moved out to Beechwood Hall, another house they owned, and had lived in it until the death of James in 1905. His widow, now in her seventies, lived in what was grandly called the dower house, surrounded by a coppice wood in a corner of the thousand-acre estate. Her only son, her only child, christened somewhat unusually Sean but always called Johnny, now lived with his wife Serena, and their three children, James, Elizabeth and Edward, in the more isolated but equally luxurious splendour of Beechwood Hall.

The three Woodall brothers were in the stable-yard admiring Harry's new hunter when the Osbornes clattered in through the yard gate and if Harry was surprised that James had brought his younger brother and sister he was too well mannered to let it show. He was the eldest of Sir Charles Woodall's sons, the future baronet, and with an obligation to take his father's place as host in his absence, particularly to a lady. He was only twenty years of age but in him was the unconscious gallantry and courtesy which generations of pedigree and the customs of the English rul-ing class had produced. A well-bred, well-polished young gentleman, he greeted a young lady of the same class as himself with the good-humoured and impeccable manners bred in him since his days in the nursery.

He helped Elizabeth to dismount, asking after her health and her mother's health in that charming and lazy drawl all the gentlemen of his station in life adopted. She might have been an honoured, invited, indeed a welcome guest, his manner implied, and not an awkward and unlooked for annoyance to them all. He was well aware that Hugh and James were off to try their luck with some dairymaid on one of his father's farms and would probably succeed since she was known to be obliging in that direction. Indeed he himself had learned his first lesson in the delights of the flesh in her lusty arms. But he and Tim, his younger brother, had planned to put Monarch through his paces and Teddy would be no problem, for he could go with them, but it was not an outing for a young lady in a fashionable riding habit mounted on a dainty mare.

He sighed inwardly, wondering if he should draw O'Shaughnessy to one side and tell him to run up to the house with a message for his sister Sophie to come and keep Elizabeth company, thinking, like George before him, that women were the very devil sometimes, insisting on going where they were not intended to go. She was a beautiful girl, there was no doubt about it, and young as she was he had to admit that his own eyes were inclined to linger on that luscious red mouth of hers. When she came out in a year or two she would be much sought after since not only was she damned attractive but would be wealthy into the bargain. Still, that was then and this was now and it was deuced inconvenient of James to have brought her.

'Now Harry,' she was saying, smiling up at him, 'don't look like that. I've had enough of it with James.' The Woodall boys were almost like three more brothers to her. She had grown up with them, ridden with them and, when she was allowed, larked about in childish adventures with them in the surrounding woodlands, open fields and parkland of Beechwood and Woodall. She and Sophie were almost the same age and had shared a dancing teacher. Harry was five years her senior but he was as familiar to her as James or Teddy and though he was too well mannered to let it show, sometimes just as impatient.

'I shall look at your hunter and then I shall go and beg a cup of chocolate from Sophie, whilst you and Tim and

Teddy...' remembering her promise to James, '...put Monarch through his paces. You thought you were to be burdened with me, didn't you? No, don't argue, I can see it in your face despite your smiling politeness, but don't despair. I shall let the gentlemen go off on whatever adventures you have planned...' with a mischievous look at James. 'No, there's no need to protest since I am quite certain you are up to something, the lot of you,' smiling as James and Hugh both blushed a deep and furious red. 'Your gallantry does you credit, Harry, and I wish you could teach my two dreadful brothers some manners. Now then, lead me to the...'

She stopped speaking suddenly as the skin which lay beneath the net holding her heavy hair began to prickle. She was conscious of someone looking at her, of eyes boring into the back of her neck, or was it at the base of her spine where feathers of disquiet had begun to brush? It was none of the five young men who stood restively about her, wondering, she was perfectly aware, how soon they could decently get rid of her. It was someone she couldn't see but who she knew was there behind her. Harry was waiting politely for her to go on, his expression courteous, and somehow, without appearing awkward or strange, she must turn round and find out who was watching her. As far as she was aware there had been no one in the yard but the usual grooms and stable boys going about their normal duties.

Smiling at Harry in quite the most inane way, she was well aware, she turned, doing her best to appear casual, the smile stretching her mouth into a curious shape, more of a grimace really, pretending an unconcern she did not feel and there he was, one hand on the neck of a roan, the other holding a curry comb, his arresting blue eyes looking directly into hers.

It was as though five years fell away and instead of the composed young lady she aspired to be and usually was, she became a pink-cheeked, tongue-tied child again straight from the schoolroom and thrown amongst a group of young men whose presence, or so it seemed, had seriously startled her. She didn't know what to do or where to look. She could feel the sudden thump of her heart in her breast and the flush which reddened her cheeks began to spread down inside her bodice and the awful thing was that James and Teddy were staring at her too, just as if she'd gone mad. James even turned his head to see where she was looking expecting to be confronted with some frightful apparition but there was nothing there, only a stable boy grooming a horse.

'What's the matter?' he asked. 'You look as though you've seen a ghost,' and at the sound of his perplexed voice she came out of her trance. She turned quite violently and Harry put out his hand to steady her and without thinking she took it gratefully. It was warm, firm and surprisingly strong and she clung to it gratefully. Harry began to smile, raising his eyebrows, surprised and pleased somehow, since Elizabeth Osborne, who had been no more than a child to him, a friend of his young sister, had suddenly become a woman, with the delightful female tendency to sway in the direction of a gentleman for support. And she looked quite devastatingly pretty with her cheeks as pink as a hedge rose and the green of her eyes soft and confused, and he was a man after all.

'Show me your hunter, Harry,' she begged breathlessly, holding his hand tightly, her voice unusually high, and he was only too eager to oblige. James and Teddy turned to look at one another, then back at her, shrugging their male shoulders at the complexity of the female mind and the group moved slowly across the stable-yard to where the hunter stamped and whirled under the restraining hand of Mr Jackson. The groom watched them, his eyes unreadable. The sound of their drawling, cultured voices drifted back to him and he returned to his task of grooming the roan just as though nothing had happened between himself and Elizabeth Osborne.

She had admired the hunter, a tall black beast with wild eyes, standing with the young men as the animal was walked round in the frosted morning sunshine. The park beyond the open gates of the stable-yard was still shrouded in a purple blue mist of early morning, the skeletal outline of black winter trees standing mysteriously in deep, shadowed haze. The rough grass was stiff and spiked, with crisp mounds of frozen moss clustered at the foot of each rough tree trunk. A thin, patterned film of ice lay over the pools of water which had collected and the sun above the mist turned them to silver and muted gold. The woodland was hushed, expectant almost, as though it was waiting with drawn breath for the wild riding explosion of young gentlemen who disturbed its peace moments later, thundering off on their animals with the enthusiasm of carefree youth. For several minutes Elizabeth could still hear the excited cries of Teddy and Tim Woodall as they shouted their admiration of Harry's new mount. There were sharp reports like the crack of a rifle as frozen branches strewn about the thinly wooded ground snapped beneath the horses' hooves and the two young hound dogs Harry was 'walking on' for a friend yelped in the fading distance. They were all young animals, the well-bred youths, the horses and dogs, mettlesome and high-spirited and as she listened to the sound of them die away into the curling mist, she shivered as though at some premonition of what was to come.

'Tis a cold day, to be sure, and not one for hanging about. Will I fetch your mare for you? I've given her a wee bit of a rub down and a handful of oats an' she's rarin' to go. Sure an' isn't she the fine one as well she knows it.'

The voice was at her back, lilting and soft with the music of Ireland in it, but deep nonetheless and she knew at once that it belonged to the groom who had been watching her and she also knew with that deeply buried instinct with which all females are born that the last few words he spoke so admiringly were directed not at her mare but at Elizabeth herself.

She felt a strange reluctance to turn and face him just as though to do so would commit her to a course of action she was not at all sure she wanted to take. It was absurd, she knew it, for what possible influence could an Irish stable boy have on Elizabeth Osborne's life, but in that last moment when there was still time to escape it, when she might have said with the loftiness of her kind, 'Leave her here, if you please and I'll send for her when I'm ready to go,' she knew that this was to be a moment of immense importance in her life.

She did her best to avoid it as she began to walk away from him. She did not turn to look back but strode briskly across the yard towards the door which led into a side passage of the house. It was the one through which estate workers who wished to see Sir Charles might enter. The passage went beyond Sir Charles' estate office, through a green baize door and into the main hallway of the old house. There would be servants about, housemaids and footmen who would curtsey or bow as her familiar figure went by and within minutes Elizabeth would be safely ensconced in her friend's bedroom where they would drink hot chocolate and while away a pleasant hour or two in the chatter so dear to the heart of a young girl. Since that was what she was. A young girl still in the schoolroom who, though she had been trained to be unruffled and moderate in all the things she did, was badly frightened by the strength and fierceness of this strange desire she had to turn round and look at Sir Charles Woodall's groom.

'When you're ready to go I'll take you home. I'll saddle a horse and wait for you,' the groom continued. The voice was stern. There was no disrespect in it and had it been Mr Jackson or Sir Charles' old Frederick who had looked after his master's carriages for thirty years she would have thought no more about it, throwing a careless word of thanks over her shoulder. It was perfectly natural for a servant to concern himself with the safety of the young lady of the house or the young lady's friend, and had it been Sophie calling on her at Beechwood, George or Alfred would do the same. She and Sophie were the carefully reared daughters of the upper class and did not ride about willy-nilly without a chaperone.

Something in her over which she had no control made her hesitate. The door to the side entrance was directly ahead of her and she knew she had but to open it and return to the safe world of her childhood which she had shared with Sophie in the Woodall nursery and schoolroom. Nanny would be there and Miss Atkinson, Sophie's old governess, their faces placid and ready to smile. The atmosphere of the everyday familiarity would calm her and disperse this unease which the man at her back had caused in her. Her hand reached out to the handle ready to open the door and as she did so the delicate balance between girlhood and womanhood was reached. She could go inside the house, race up the stairs as she had done a thousand times before and remain a girl for a little while longer or she could turn about and face the challenge which, it seemed to her, the man had flung at her though in what way she could not have said. She had naturally seen the admiring glances of men's faces before and had understood what they meant since she was not the ninny many of the girls of her class were brought up to be. She was aware that within the next five years, probably before she was twenty-one, she would have not just a husband but a child of her own for that was the way of her class but it had not concerned her for there was still a part of her childhood to be lived and, like a child, she believed five years to be a lifetime away. But this man at her back, whoever he was, seemed to be capable of taking that from her if she let him. If she turned about and looked into his face and those incredible blue eyes which had disturbed her so dreadfully a little while ago, a decision, her decision must be made and she didn't want to make it. Not yet. But what was it, her feverish mind demanded to know? What was it that had her in this dither of foolish, wavering indecision on whether to go or whether to stay? Good God, he was only a groom, asking respectfully to accompany her to her father's house, after all. Which was only right and proper so why was she in this state of fluttering palpitation? She had not even had a good look at his face, only his eyes which had seemed to probe right into the heart of her and . . .

This was ridiculous, was her last irritated thought as she whirled about to face him and as she did so she wished with all her heart, as she was to wish a hundred times in the future, that she had trusted her instinct and continued on through the side door and up to Sophie Woodall's room where safety lay. She knew at once that she had made a mistake, that in him, and in herself, some folly lay, but it was too late. It had always been too late.

He simply looked at her, his eyes brooding and troubled. He was not smiling nor was there anything in his manner, in his expression, which could be called insulting, impolite or even disrespectful. He was not bold nor overtly admiring, just a young man with tumbling, dark brown hair, a mouth which was curled up at the corners though he was not smiling, a lean, dark grace and strong hands which held her mare in a steady grip. Not handsome really, in the accepted sense of the word. Not handsome like Harry Woodall was handsome but immensely appealing; dressed in riding breeches and boots, a working man's shirt and jacket, with a bright red kerchief tied about his brown throat. A groom, a man employed by her father's friend, a man she had never seen, or at least noticed before. Had she?

'Who are you?' Though she did her best to keep it steady her voice trembled and Michael O'Shaughnessy knew she was badly frightened and that he was to blame. She was only a girl and even had they been of the same class was not ready for the involvement of any sort which takes place between man and woman. She was staring at him with those amazing green eyes as though he was Lucifer himself and he knew he must take that look of dread away from her. He was quite bewildered by his own response to her, an emotion which had seized him as she rode into the yard. Used as he was to the admiration of many a pretty girl, her young beauty had moved something inside him which he had never felt before. It was not as though this was the first time he had seen her. She had been about the place, in the stable-yard and riding about the parkland with Miss Sophie ever since he had first started work here six years ago but for some reason it was as if this was the first time they had encountered one another.

'Michael,' he said as though they were of the same social standing, then remembering, 'Michael O'Shaughnessy.' He could not bring himself to call her by the impersonal and respectful 'Miss'. 'Groom to Sir Charles,' he added, then he smiled, the impish, endearing smile his Mammy loved since it had none of the sexuality in it he used to charm others of the female gender. He could see her relax a little.

'I have not seen you before.'

'Aah well, 'tis six years since I started here but I'm a divil for work, though me Mammy would give you an argument over that.'

'Would she?' and she had begun to smile as well.

'When there's work to be done sure an' aren't I the one who's missing, or so she says, an' she's probably right but then when you've twelve brothers and sisters doesn't it make sense to keep out of the way?'

'Twelve! Really?' She was clearly amazed and she took a step towards him, her interest growing, her eyes brightening with curiosity.

'To be sure. Four of me sisters are married with children

of their own. Then there's me an' our Dermot who's in the bank in Liverpool. An' doesn't he think he's the fine one because of it.'

She laughed and relaxed even further. 'Who else?'

'Well, next there's Caitlin. The serious one, we call her, but that's only because Mara, who's two years younger, is as flighty as a butterfly and giddy as a two-year-old. Thinks she's as grand as the Queen of England, so she does.'

'Really?' she said again.

'Indeed she does and after Mara it's all boys. Sean, Callum, Donal and Eammon and then there's the baby who's three and she's Clare for the county me Daddy's Daddy came from.'

'Heavens, what a houseful. It must be very crowded when you're all at home.'

'Begod, you should see us at Christmas. Like sardines in a tin with not a bit of space between us. That's why I live in here.' He nodded his head vaguely in the direction of the stables over which he had a room of his own. 'Six years now and I'm always about in the yard or the paddock, me head down behind one of these owd fellows so that's why you'd not see me. I've seen you, though,' and his voice deepened, the tone of it that of a man admiring a pretty girl.

It was a mistake. Elizabeth took a step backwards. She had begun to think she had imagined the strong attraction which had drawn her to this man. He was just an ordinary working man, pleasant, with a whimsical Irish brogue and a friendly smile but those four words and all they implied, which was not the relationship of a lady and a servant, brought it back with the sharpness of a blow.

'I must get home,' she babbled, looking about her desperately.

'I'll take you. You can't go alone.'

'No ... really ... or perhaps Mr Jackson ...?'

'He's in the paddock with ...'

'Then ... I'll just wait for ...'

37

'Who...? Bejasus, I'm sorry. I didn't mean to...'

But she had turned and with the swiftness of a small animal fleeing from a predator ran towards the side entrance of the house. She fumbled at the door handle, unable to open it in her panic – at what, at *what*? her practical mind asked her foolishly beating heart – then, her hand steadier now, she turned it and ran inside the house.

They drank hot chocolate, she and Sophie, gossiping carelessly in the small and feminine sitting room which Sophie, now at fifteen, and out of the schoolroom and considered to be a young woman, had been given as her own. Elizabeth had her booted feet to the fire, the skirt of her riding habit thrown back to reveal the breeches underneath, her eyes narrowed and unfocused, her smooth young face flushed, and not just with the heat from the fire.

'Are you to hunt tomorrow, Elizabeth?' Sophie was saying. 'Algie Winters is over from Leicestershire and has brought a delicious friend with him called Chris Sinclair. They were both at school with Harry so Mama has asked them to spend the weekend. We've known Algie for ages, you've met him, haven't you...?'

'Mmm...'

'...but Chris is absolutely divine and I'm warning you now that I have great designs on him so don't you dare flash those green eyes of yours at him. You know how they devastate every gentleman in the room when you enter so I'd be obliged if you would keep them to yourself when Chris is about.'

Even at fifteen Sophie was physically if not emotionally prepared for marriage and had already begun to worry that she might be left on the shelf since the role of wife was the one she had been trained for ever since she could walk or speak. To be a spinster was the most dreadful fate that could befall any female. Though she knew the final decision would be her parents', it would be 'divine' – a word Sophie was extremely fond of – if it could be a gentleman she was ready to fall in love with, one like the dashingly good-looking Sir Christopher Sinclair.

'I wouldn't dream of it.' Elizabeth scarcely heard her as she contemplated eyes of a rich and vivid blue as they smiled indolently at her from the fire flames.

'And at the Hunt Ball I shall wear my new Worth gown for Mama says that as I am nearly sixteen now I may attend, at least until midnight. Did I tell you about my gown?'

'Mmm . . .'

'Did I? When? It only came this morning.' Sophie looked suspiciously at her friend, studying the soft . . . well, one could only call it bemused look on her face, and she tutted irritably

'Elizabeth Osborne, you're not even listening to me. Here am I telling you all the loveliest things about Algie and Chris, the Hunt Ball and my new ballgown and you're miles away in a world of your own. You've hardly said a word since you came in and if you're going to be as boring as Miss Atkinson, who is *very* boring, then you might as well go home, or join her and Nanny in the nursery.' Sophie pouted crossly.

'I've heard every word, Sophie, honestly and I'd love to see your gown. Go and get it,' and as Elizabeth had known she would be, Sophie was instantly diverted. She smiled at once and rang the bell for her maid since it would not have occurred to either girl that she was perfectly capable of opening the wardrobe in her bedroom and lifting out the gown herself. That was the job of her personal maid. Anything to do with clothes, with jewellery, with hair or shoes, fans or gloves or the mending and cleaning which went with any of these was performed by a lady's own personal maid.

For half an hour the white gown, full length, simple as a young, unmarried lady's should be, was admired, but somehow, though the time was long past when she should make her farewells, Elizabeth seemed reluctant to leave. She exclaimed over the quality of the sheer lace from which the gown was made, the satin slippers which had been fashioned to match it and the small tiara, a family heirloom, which Sophie was to be allowed to wear, echoing again and again her own longing to be sixteen and allowed to attend the Hunt Ball. Finally, when there seemed nothing else to admire, when the maid had begun to fidget, eager to put away the finery and get back to her other duties, when Sophie glanced surreptitiously at the clock above the fireplace since it was almost time for lunch and doubtless Elizabeth would be expected at home, Elizabeth stood up and moved towards the muslin-framed window.

'I suppose I had better be off,' she said reluctantly, peering into the garden, wishing foolishly that the window overlooked the stable-yard. If it had done she could have made sure that the groom was not about before dashing down and calling for Frederick or Jackson to fetch her mare.

'You are to ride with us tomorrow then?' Sophie's voice was casual and friendly.

'Oh yes. I'll come over with James and Teddy.'

'And meet the splendid Christopher.'

'Of course,' laughing.

'And you promise to let me have him. To do nothing to distract him from me.'

'Sophie, you are funny. Anyone would think you had the right to choose for yourself.'

'Well, I can pretend, can't I? And he is a baronet and quite suitable.' Sophie had opened the door and Elizabeth knew she must go. She took a deep breath, feeling the apprehensive excitement begin to swell in her breast ready to choke her, for what would she do if he was there? She could hardly refuse his help and escort home, could she, or say she would prefer Frederick or Mr Jackson or one of the other grooms, not without giving some reason, and what reason was there?

'Until tomorrow, then.' Sophie smiled, looking at the tiny

watch pinned on her bodice. Her mother *did* have guests for lunch and she really *must* go down, her glance said.

There was a drumming of booted feet on the stairs and the sound of men's laughter then, as she and Sophie turned in their direction, Harry and Tim turned the corner of the wide hallway. It was dark, opulent and spacious, richly carpeted and lined with portraits of dead and buried Woodalls, ladies and gentlemen all staring down at Elizabeth with apparent disapproval. There was carved oak panelling and wrought-iron candle sconces which were now lit by electricity and along its length were chests from Elizabethan days, heavy and black with age. There were many doors for Woodall Park was large and grand. From one, which was partially open, a small maid peeped, caught by the presence of her master's sons and, as she had been trained to do by Mrs Blythe who was somewhat old-fashioned in her ways, she would remain there until they had gone since it simply would not do to meet her superiors face to face.

The hallway seemed suddenly full of young men though there were only two, superb and self-commanding, mud spattered and spurred, their boots leaving imprints on the fine carpet which did not matter in the least since it was not their task to clean it nor were they concerned with cost since they had not been brought up to do so. They were hatless and flushed with their morning's exercise. They were already unbuttoning their jackets ready to fling them off wherever they might fall and change into outfits more suitable to their mother's dining room.

'Elizabeth! You're still here,' Harry called as he came towards her, his eyes for some reason softening as they looked into the confused and what could almost be described as fearful expression on the face of his sister's friend, though what she had to be fearful about he could not imagine. 'James and Teddy have gone but of course you must not go home alone.'

Already he was re-buttoning his jacket. 'Come on, I'll take

you ... no ...' as Elizabeth would have politely objected, '... would you deny me the pleasure of escorting a beautiful young lady to her own front door?' He was grinning that endearing, somewhat lopsided grin of his, the perfect gentleman but making mock of it in a light-hearted way. 'Make my apologies to mother and the rest, will you, Sophie. She'll understand,' and taking Elizabeth's hand he began to run with her down the hallway in the direction of the servants' staircase, just as though she was some delightful child he had encountered. He was making an adventure, a sense of playing truant out of a simple, well-mannered act, and Elizabeth was immensely grateful to him for it and for shielding her from the disconcerting presence of the groom in the stable-yard.

She began to laugh breathlessly as she clung to his hand.

3

It was in May when the King died and everyone from the lowliest skivvy in the kitchen to the highest in the land was plunged into the deepest black of mourning. Good King Teddy, loved and respected by all his people, was gone and they were shocked and grieved since his illness had scarcely been reported. They had thought him to be in splendid health for was he not tireless in his duties, so energetic, a strong and vigorous man, or so they had been led to believe. Sixty-nine he might have been but one had only to see him striding about the enclosure at the race course, on a shoot or one of the numerous sporting parties he attended to realise that his years meant nothing to him.

On Thursday the sixth of May an official bulletin had informed the people that His Majesty was suffering from an attack of bronchitis and anxious crowds had begun to gather outside the palace. On the following day they were told that the King's condition was giving rise to great anxiety.

Men and women of all ranks passed to and fro in front of the palace railings all that day. Even carriages going about their business were drawn to a halt, their occupants alighting to read the bulletins before moving sorrowfully and silently away.

The day passed and the press of people around the bulletin board was so great that a police inspector walked along behind the railings carrying a notice-board on which the medical news was pinned so that those who could not get near might read the latest bulletin.

Just before midnight Edward the Peacemaker passed peacefully away but it was not until thirty minutes later that the uneasy crowd at his gate were informed of it. A member of the Royal household came across the palace square and in a low and impressive tone said the simple words, 'The King is dead.'

Ellen cried sharply when the news came to them at breakfast, crossing herself vigorously and reaching for her beads. Catholic he might not have been and a bit of a lad in his time if all the tales about him were true but he had been a good king, once he had been allowed, much loved by his people. He deserved a moment of anyone's prayer.

'Well, I don't know what all the fuss is about,' Mara said sulkily, since he was an old man after all. 'We all have to die one day and to be sure I hope the Blessed Mother doesn't keep me until I'm sixty-nine. Can you imagine what it must feel like to be that age?' She shuddered dramatically, stopping for a moment to peer anxiously at her own fifteen-year-old face in the kitchen mirror and was amazed and outraged when a blow from behind nearly lifted her from her feet. It was so heavy her tip-tilted nose struck the mirror with a force which brought tears to her eyes. She whirled about to face her infuriated mother whose hand was still raised to fetch her another box on the ears, but Mara ducked nimbly out of her reach.

'Don't you dare speak of the dear old man like that, you wicked girl,' her mother hissed, 'and may the Blessed Virgin forgive you your cruel tongue. He was a good king and did his duty to the end and to be spoken of like that by a chit of a girl who hasn't a sensible thought in her head is beyond belief. I'm ashamed of you, so I am. Your own Daddy's only fifty-one but would you have him taken from us, God forbid . . .' crossing herself hastily '. . . just because he's a grey hair or two? I never heard such a thing. You'll go to Confession this afternoon and tell the good Father your sins, so you will, d'you hear me? Now off to your room to pray for forgiveness and you shall stay there until I say you can come out.'

Her room! When had it ever been *her* room, Mara asked herself moodily as she stared out of the bedroom window. It was on the first floor above the hallway and in it were four narrow brass beds, one in each corner, covered by a white counterpane. It was a pretty room, light and airy, the heavy Victorian furniture of her grandmother's day done away with after the birth of Ellen's four eldest daughters. The curtains of rose pink muslin were drawn back with swags of matching ribbon. The wallpaper was patterned in a simple stripe with pink rosebuds scattered across it and at the top of the wall just below the ceiling was a frieze of full blown pink roses. There were several pictures hanging from the picture rail. Prettily posed kittens and puppy dogs, two samplers and, of course, the Holy Mother and Her Son above a crucifix. A square of carpet, so worn the pattern and colour were barely distinguishable, covered the centre of the floor. It was surrounded by severely scrubbed, fiercely polished linoleum. The fireplace was tiled in rose pink to match the wallpaper and in it stood a pleated fan of paper since a fire was never lit unless one of the girls was ill. Two pine chests of drawers stood against the wall and opposite

44

the fireplace was an enormous pine wardrobe.

On a marble-topped washstand beneath the window was a basin and jug all done in white and pale pink roses with containers to match which held soap and a sponge. There were towels hanging to the side of it on a rail, as white and clean as summer clouds, for Ellen was fussy about such things and the laundress she employed each Monday to do the family's wash had been well trained in her trade.

The room was very crowded despite its size. Once it had slept four of the seven daughters Ellen had borne and even now Mara was never sure when one or more of her nieces might not be carelessly overlooked and left to spend a night or two there. There were a couple of them in the garden right now, racing round with Eammon and Clare and several of Bridget's – or was it Amy's, they all looked the same to Mara – racing with them. It was always the way and with all her heart Mara wished she had been born into a family with fewer children. There must be hundreds of them in hers, for as well as those her sisters dragged round here every day there was a great multitude of cousins, the offspring of Mammy and Daddy's brothers and sisters, and it seemed to Mara that the house and particularly this room in which she, Caitlin and Clare slept was always bursting at the seams with them.

At the age of twelve months and considered old enough to leave the cradle at the side of her Mammy and Daddy's bed, young Clare had been shoved in here with Caitlin and her and Mara still burned with resentment at the infamy of it. Caitlin was seventeen and herself fifteen, well, fourteen then, but still a young woman in her own eyes and for herself and her older sister – but mostly for herself, if she were honest – to be forced to put up with the indignity of a baby's cot and baby's toys, baby teething and the often appalling stench of the contents of her little sister's napkins was scarcely to be borne. Caitlin suffered it all with, in Mara's scornful opinion, saintly equanimity, seeming not to care

45

but Clare was not *their* baby, after all, as Mara pointed out indignantly and if the Holy Mother had seen fit to give Mammy and Daddy another child why in Heaven's name could She not have made it a boy? Her brothers, the four younger ones, shared the largest bedroom, next to Mammy and Daddy's and one more would have made little difference to them, would it? Dermot had taken himself off to the tiny attic in the roof when Michael left home, swearing he would rather leave home as well if he was to be forced to continue sharing with 'those four little divils' so there was a bed empty which could easily accommodate another. She had said so to Mammy and earned herself a box on the ears for it and her protestations at the unfairness of it had been to no avail.

'Where in Heaven's name is she to go then?' her mother had asked tartly of her at the time. 'Tell me that, if you can. Will I put her in with Dermot just to please you, or in a room with four rowdy lads, and yourself and Caitlin in a room with two empty beds? Don't be daft, girl. It's in here with her and I'll have no more nonsense from you.'

'Well, it's not fair.'

'Sure an' life's not fair, me girl. You'll learn that soon enough.'

And so she had. She and Caitlin were the only girls left, not counting the baby, in a great family of boys and it soon became very noticeable that though her older brothers might go about with their friends, even those younger than herself, having interests and experiences outside of the family home, it was a different matter altogether when it came to Caitlin and herself. She and her sister had no need to go out to work, a circumstance of great pride to her Mammy and Daddy, but she and her sister were expected to help their mother about the house with the lighter duties and were each given, in her opinion, a pitifully small allowance. When she had broached the subject of an increase to her father he had asked indulgently what did his little girls

46

want with more money? Did they need a new frock each and if so they had only to ask, or was it some other female frippery he could buy them? They were lucky girls to be so favoured, he told them. Hadn't they the comfortable home with plenty of good food in their bellies, pretty dresses by the score – 'no more than half a dozen,' Mara mumbled hopelessly – and there were hundreds, thousands of girls who would give their good right arm to be in their shoes, weren't there, Mammy, turning to the real head of the household and the minder of the family purse strings.

Caitlin had said nothing in the midst of all this turmoil. She was like that, was Caitlin. She had a way of lowering her eyes and standing penitently whilst Daddy spoke, just as though she agreed with his every word but the minute she got the chance, when nobody's eye was on her she was off about her stupid suffragette business, not caring a jot whether she had a new frock or not, or even a few shillings more to buy whatever took her fancy. She was as sly as a fox, that one, doubling back on herself a couple of times a week to evade Mammy's restraining hand as she crept out to attend her old meetings and getting away with it too, which was worse. What a bore, what a tedious, dry as dust bore she was, and why the Holy Mother had seen fit to give Mara a sister like Caitlin who was not the slightest bit interested in fashion or meeting young men or even having a good laugh, she would never know.

She sighed disconsolately and leaned her head against the window frame. It was a dismal sort of a day with a dark, iron grey arch of clouds above the roofs of the houses. Not at all spring-like. Though the may-apple and wildflowers her grandmother had planted showed their brave heads amongst the mass of primroses, and the greening sycamore trees promised better things to come, it was cold, heralding rain or even sleet. The weather matched her mood exactly and when she saw her mother appear below the window, calling to the children to 'come in at once and stop making

47

all that noise, today of all days', it brought back to her why she was up here and her melancholy deepened. Even the newspapers had been edged with black this morning and she'd be the next to be made to observe the formalities of mourning, she was convinced. Mammy was a divil for the conventions and she'd be certain to make all of the family wear their darkest, most sombre clothes. No pretty spring colours for Mara but blacks and browns and dark blues, at least until after the King's funeral. And she looked so awful in black. With her dark brown curling hair and rich butter-milk skin, the deep and vivid colour of her eyes which were somewhere between blue and green, she looked her best in bold colours, or in the palest of cream or ivory. She read the Fashion Magazine which Katy Murphy's mother allowed her to buy, not being as strict as her own Mammy, and was well acquainted with what the wealthy and fashion-conscious lady was wearing. Only fifteen she might be but already she was aware of her own glowing good looks and knew exactly what suited her best. It was all she concerned herself with from morning until night, her life's work you might say, and she was well versed in it. There was one thing she knew and that was how to dress and that know-ledge informed her that she was far too young for black.

She sauntered over to the mirror above the chest of drawers and studied her own reflection in it. She and Katy had been hoping to walk across to Sefton Park this afternoon but it seemed there was not much hope of that in the cir-cumstances which was a pity because every Saturday a band played on the stand in the centre of the park. This week it was to have been that of the Lancashire Fusiliers which would have been most exciting. All those handsome young soldiers in their impressive uniforms, brightly coloured and tight-fitting and every one more than willing to admire two pretty, unattached young ladies who might just stop to listen to them play. She and Katy would have had a fine old time of it, smiling and flirting a little bit but now it was all spoilt just because some old man had died and himself not even a relative of the O'Shaughnessy family.

Her mutinous face frowned back at her from the mirror and instantly she pulled it straight, smoothing out the creases formed by the scowl since that was a sure way to a wrinkled skin. She pouted her full pink lips and lifted her chin to admire the effect, then turned, smoothing down the lines of her bodice to accentuate the curve of her young breasts. She cupped them with her hands, her head on one side as she studied their shape. They were high and round and underneath the material of her dress she felt her nipples harden. She drew in a deep breath, imagining what it would be like if her hands were those of a man and low in her belly something fluttered with delight, beginning to spread up and then down the inside of her thighs.

She was deep in absorbed contemplation of the wicked pictures in her mind when the sound of her mother's voice at the foot of the stairs made her jump guiltily. Sweet Mother of God, if Mammy found her looking at her own body in the mirror and could read the thoughts which swarmed delightfully in her head she'd take the switch to her.

'Mara,' her mother shouted. 'You can come down now, pet. Caitlin and me are going to Church to light a candle for himself. Will you be after coming with us or shall I be leaving the baby with you?'

Mara ran lightly down the stairs, an expression of acute indecision on her face. Should she take the opportunity to get out of the house, even if it was only to Church, or should she stay at home and enjoy the absence of her mother? There might be all kinds of things to see on the journey from Edge Lane to St Mary's, to do with the King dying an' all, though what they might be she hadn't any idea, but on the other hand it was not often she had the house to herself without Mammy at her back finding her something to do. Even though they had two housemaids and a woman who came in to do the heavy scrubbing and another to see to

49

the family's laundry, Mammy had a knack of keeping 'idle fingers out of mischief' as she put it. What should she do, Mara considered frantically as her mother waited for her answer. She did not stop for a moment to wonder what her mother might want of her for with the selfishness of youth her own needs were the most important to her and instantly she decided she would stay at home.

Scarcely before Ellen and Caitlin were out of the gate Mara was comfortably settled on the sofa before the parlour fire. Her little sister was told curtly to 'be quiet and play with your dolls' as Mara took up the latest copy of *Lady's Realm* lent to her by Katy Murphy and hidden in Mara's drawer for a moment such as this. She sighed contentedly as she studied exactly how a lady should behave at a dinner party since she knew without a shadow of a doubt that some day she would be giving one of her own.

It was to be nearly a fortnight before King Edward VII was finally laid to rest in the crypt beneath St George's Chapel, Windsor, and Mara could honestly say it was the most tedious fortnight she had ever spent. The whole of England, or so it appeared to her, virtually closed down. Shops were shut and church bells were forever tolling. So impressive was the total mourning of the nation Mammy and Daddy took them all down the length of London Road and Dale Street to the Pier Head to see it after Mass on that first Sunday morning. There had been a vast congregation at Church with many who were not regular churchgoers crammed into the pews and it was said they were standing on one another's head in the two cathedrals, every last man, woman and child in some kind of mourning. She had never seen so much black and was vastly intrigued as to where all the material for it came from. Whole buildings draped in it and when they got to the dock area every single ship, foreign as well as British, flew their flags at half mast. People walked about, numbed and silent so that even Mara was impressed, shivering in the warm wool of her good coat and it had nothing to do with the inclemency of the weather.

The public lying-in-state of the King at Westminster began on May 16th lasting for three days and Ellen wept again as she read an account of it out loud to Matty, Lucy and Mrs Clegg, the daily, as they sat about the kitchen table sharing a pot of tea. The tragedy of it all had mellowed Ellen's usual determined application to work, allowing the servants to stop for ten minutes as she described to them the scenes of sorrow up in London.

Mara was sure that if she heard one more word about it from her mother who acted as though it were a member of the family who had gone, she would scream. She would sit on the floor and drum her heels and scream with sheer boredom.

'Is that the last of it, then?' she was unwise enough to ask.

'The last of what?' Mammy asked suspiciously and all those about the breakfast table on the day after the funeral looked up expectantly. Only young Michael wasn't there. Sir Charles and his family had gone up to London with other notable personages of Liverpool, to attend the funeral, and Michael had missed his day off because of it. Mara didn't know why, nor did she care, nor even ask since what did not affect Mara O'Shaughnessy did not interest her.

'Well, my girl, the last of what?' Ellen repeated ominously and Mick put out his hand to her. She was having what women called a 'bad change', was his Ellen and the smallest most inoffensive remark seemed to set her alight when she was that way out.

'I only meant will I . . . will we be able to go out now?' Mara offered contritely.

'Go out! Is that all you ever think about, Mara O'Shaughnessy?' and she would have been away on a hot swell of outrage had not her husband put a warm, restraining hand on hers.

'Now then, darlin', don't be cross with the girl. Sure an' has it not been difficult for her in the past fortnight, as it

51

has for them all. They're only young, Ellen, and all this talk of death and funerals and the whole country in mourning is hard on them. 'Tis over now, acushla, an' they've all been as good as gold. Let them out today, shall we? What d'you say?'

'We should be going to Mass to pray for the poor man's soul, God rest him . . .'

'An' so we will on Sunday but 'tis over for now and a change'll do them all good, so it will.'

And so it was that when a picnic was planned on Whitsuntide Monday at the end of May to Colton Wood, just south of Rainhill, Mara was allowed to go. It was Katy's brother who arranged it. Billy Murphy was a keen member of The Wavertree Cycling Club and he and a score of other young men and several young women were very keen to escape every weekend into the countryside about Liverpool on their exciting Safety cycling machines. Sometimes they went further afield, at least the young men did, staying overnight at the inns which accommodated cheaply the growing multitude of young people who had taken the new sport to heart. When Billy and his fellow club members went off on one of their madcap escapades, as his mother called them, it was not uncommon for them to send back a telegram from the furthest point of their achievement, firstly to report their safe arrival and secondly to prove just how many amazing miles they had covered. And of course, so that those at home could marvel at their daring. They loved the fresh air, the exhilarating exercise, the joys of collecting wildflowers or watching birds and butterflies which were not to be seen in great numbers in the city. They would picnic in a field or have a bite in a pub and could count on a hearty meal in a pleasant setting. They even had their own song, 'A Bicycle Made for Two', sung by Miss Katie Lawrence, and another, 'Ta ra ra boom de ay', performed by Miss Lottie Collins.

'We'll take the train to Rainhill, Mammy, me an' Katy . . .'

'On your own?' Ellen was horrified. 'Just you an' Katy Murphy? What about Caitlin? Is she not to go?'

'You can exclude me from this excursion, so you can. I've other things to do with my time than jaunt about the countryside with the likes of Billy Murphy.'

Mara was instantly on the defensive as she swung about, hands on her hips to face her sister.

'And what's wrong with Billy Murphy?'

'He's brainless, that's what!'

'And I suppose the ladies in your circle are as clever as college professors?' Mara's voice was sneering but half-hearted for this was old ground, gone over a hundred times before and nothing at all to do with the matter under discussion. She turned back to her mother, her face earnest.

'Mammy, it's quite safe ...'

'The train may be, but what about you?'

' 'Tis only a few miles, Mammy, and Billy'll meet us at the station with the rest of the club members.'

'All men, I suppose?' Ellen sniffed.

'No, there are some girls as well ...'

'And what sort of girls, may I ask, that'd dash about the roads on one of them infernal machines, showing their ankles and God only knows what else. I'm not happy about it, I'm not happy at all,' turning desperately to her husband who shushed her soothingly.

'Will we ask Dermot and Michael to go with them, darlin'?' he asked. 'Would it make you feel better if the boys went along to mind their sister?'

'Oh no, Daddy,' Mara wailed at the vision of herself and Katy amongst all those unattached young men with their Dermot like the spectre at the feast watching her every move. Michael would be more agreeable being a chap who liked a bit of fun and would probably find someone to flirt with himself, but Dermot, Holy Mother, she might as well take her Mammy along with her.

'Don't expect me to take part in this fascinating

expedition, Daddy.' Dermot's voice came from behind the financial newspaper he was reading. 'I've better things to do with my time than act as nursemaid to our Mara. Besides, on Whit Monday I've promised to join a colleague on an outing of me own.'

Ellen turned to her son, her expression fond and marvelling. A colleague! Her Dermot had a colleague. Everyone in their world had friends but Dermot had a colleague and his mother was vastly impressed. Even the way he spoke was different to the rest of them. It must be working in that bank, she supposed, but Mara's voice brought her back from her admiring contemplation of her second son.

'Please, Daddy, please. You can put us on the train, if you really must, but Billy's a...a responsible chap...'

'Billy Murphy! A responsible chap!' Ellen's voice was scathing but Mara knew by now that her mother was really only arguing for the sake of it. That was her way. She aired her opposition for several minutes just to let them know that she could put a stop to the whole sorry nonsense if it suited her, but she'd promised Mara a treat for being so good during the period of mourning for the King and she'd not go back on her word.

'Is it all right then, Mammy?' appeasing the one who made the rules. 'I promise to behave myself and stay close to Katy.'

'You'll not go in one of those public houses, will you, darlin'?'

'There aren't any where we're going, Mammy. Colton Woods is out in the country and...'

'How will you get there from the railway station?' Again Ellen was alarmed, visualising her beautiful and innocent daughter wandering the country lanes with no more protection than Katy Murphy who was half-witted anyway, in Ellen's opinion, prey to any vagrant or tinker who happened along, but Mara smiled and kissed her cheek, confident now that she was to go.

'There's a dog cart which'll take us from the station, Billy

54

says, to the picnic, an' it will come an' pick us up at the end of the day. Sure an' we'll be as safe as houses, Mammy.'

'You'll be home before dark or he'll have me to answer to, tell Billy Murphy.'

'I will, Mammy, I promise.'

The bluebells were out in Colton Wood, a drifting sea of hazed azure stretching away beneath the trees as far as the eye could see, so thick and glorious Mara was reluctant to step on them. She stood for several minutes just inside the trees whilst around her Billy and Katy and the members of the cycling club arranged bicycles and ground sheets, rugs and picnic baskets to their noisy satisfaction. They were young people away from the restraints and disciplines of their upbringing and class. The young ladies wore the latest cycling skirts with an inverted pleat at the back, long, serviceable woollen cardigans and completely unsuitable broad-brimmed hats or boaters, tied beneath the chin with a veil. The young men had Norfolk jackets, knickerbockers, flat caps, gloves and bright knee socks. They all thought themselves to be very dashing. They were high-spirited, carried gloriously away with their own emancipation, especially the young women, independent and unshackled by convention, or so they told themselves as this new dawn of what they thought of as 'bohemian' life stretched out before them. And the bicycle was responsible for it. Their parents had been no further than a walk down to the Pier Head under their own steam, perhaps a day's outing to Blackpool on a charabanc or a train excursion if they were lucky but with the advent of the bicycle their children were enjoying a freedom never before known by those of their class. The exhilaration of it quite went to their heads.

The wood was hushed and still but as Mara stepped carefully through the abundant undergrowth which sprang about her skirt she could hear small sounds as though the animals and birds of the woods, after a moment of caution caused by her arrival amongst them, were resuming their busy activities. The grasses rustled and something squeaked behind a mass of cow parsley. The pink of a stand of ragged robin shivered as some small creature whispered by and the great spread of bluebells nodded their heads as though to draw her further into the woods. There were elms flowering lightly above her head and the evergreen magnificence of yew. The leaves of a tall, grey-barked aspen turned and twisted in the light breeze, hitting each other and making a sound like rain.

'Where you going, Mara?' Katy's voice from behind startled her and she jumped.

'Nowhere, just for a walk.'

'You'll get lost,' Katy said fearfully, staring into the sunlit stand of trees as though demons lurked behind every leaf.

'No I won't. Look, there's a little stream over there. Sure an' why don't we walk along it then when we turn round we only have to follow the thing to get back here.'

'What for?'

'Sweet Mother of God. Did we come all the way out here just to sit on a rug and stare at the same bit of field all day? I want to have a look round, so I do, and besides, Mammy'd love some of those bluebells and I'm going to pick some for her.'

'Well . . .' Katy was undecided but Mara tutted impatiently and when Mara became impatient it was best to get a move on. Sometimes she wondered why she put up with Mara O'Shaughnessy's high-handed ways, not realising in her simple naivety that it was precisely her friend's absolute and lofty belief in herself and in the rightness of all she did that attracted Katy to her. Katy herself was easy-going and somewhat timid but Mara made the most ordinary outing, even if it was only a walk along the Marine Parade after Mass on a Sunday, seem as exciting as a trek through an African jungle. She was so commanding, so positive and though they had never really done anything which their respective Mammys could object to, there was always the feeling that any moment they were about to do so.

'Are you coming or not?'

'Well, I'd best tell our Billy.'

'Tell him, for Heaven's sake, and let's get on. It'll be dark before we even set off at this rate.'

It really was a delight. The little stream slipped musically beside them, shallow and sparkling where the sunlight caught it. Old willow trees hung across it, their heads almost touching the water but before they had gone more than a hundred yards or so Katy began to complain that she was getting her boots wet and her Mammy'd kill her if she saw the state of her skirt.

'I'm taking mine off.'

'What! Your skirt?' Katy's face was a picture of horror and Mara shook her head in exasperation.

'No, you eejit, me boots. I'm going to paddle.'

'Oh sweet Mary, will you look at the state of me, Mara. I've mud up me stockings...'

'Well, take them off as well, Katy. They'll soon dry if we hang them on the branches of this tree an' if you tie your boots together by the laces and sling them up too so that they're in the sunshine .. see, put them up here beside mine. Now watch how you step in the water. Them stones are slippery.'

Katy screamed as her shrinking flesh met the ice cold water of the stream, and clung frantically to Mara's arm.

'Blessed Mother, me foot's gone numb. See, the blood's frozen in me veins ... and *what's that*? Oh dear Mother, 'tis a frog and ... and ... Oh Mara, don't let the divil jump on me. Run an' fetch our Billy or one of the other chaps to kill it ...'

'What for? It'll not hurt you. See, 'tis gone now an' stop hanging on to me as if we were drowning in six feet of water, will you. You'll have us both down if you don't watch out. That's it, now just follow me an' we'll explore a bit along the stream. Will you look at those flowers,' pointing to a floating mass of delicate celandine which was growing along the bank. There were beech trees and holly, oak and larch and growing snugly in the enormous spread roots of the trees were colonies of mushrooms, wood anemones, heartsease and the lacy greenery of fern. Finding no threat in the presence of the two girls wood pigeons called to each other in throaty voices and running directly across the rough track to the right of the stream a cock pheasant caused Katy to almost die of fright, or so she said.

They were both absorbed in what was to them, as city girls, a new and fascinating environment. Now that Katy had overcome her alarm and was reassured by her braver friend that some dreadful wild creature was not about to leap out from behind a tree and devour her, or worse, she trailed along dreamily behind Mara, her feet accustomed to the cold of the water now, her skirt hitched up and securely fastened in the waistband. They had picked dozens of wild-flowers but with the careless ignorance of those who are not country bred had already abandoned them as too bulky to carry. After all there were so many and they'd pick some more on the way back, they told one another.

Mara had tucked an ivory butterfly orchid in the dark tangle of her hair which was tied at the back of her head with a crisp ribbon of enormous proportions. She had discarded her straw boater along with her boots and stockings and when James Osborne drew his chestnut mare to an amazed halt in the clearing beside the stream he thought she was the most enchanting creature he had ever seen.

The two girls recoiled sharply at the sight of the horse and rider, almost falling backwards into the silky ripple of the water and even Mara felt her heart trip frantically in ready alarm for she had thought Katy and herself to be completely alone and isolated in this magical place. It was another world to the one in which she lived day after mundane day and her bewitchment had made her smooth and relaxed, her guard down, less inclined to the sharpness of mind and tongue she usually employed. 'Prickly pear' her brothers called her because of her tendency to take offence where none was meant, but here, even with the exasperating Katy at her back, she had dreamed softly for an hour, losing the spikiness which characterised her normal state of mind. Her eyes were a depthless blue, limpid and unruffled and her full, pink mouth curled tenderly under the tranquil spell of the woodland.

She was the first to recover. Another young man had followed the first, crashing through the undergrowth, his horse's hooves trampling on the lovely bluebells without the slightest concern for their delicacy and it was this more than anything which incensed her.

'Watch where you're putting those damned great feet,' she exploded. 'Could you not keep that blessed animal off the bluebells. It's trampling them into the ground. Sure an' does it not matter to you that you're spoiling the lovely things?'

'Bloody hell,' Hugh Woodall said, his mouth hanging open, his eyes on Katy Murphy's white legs, bare to the knee and as shapely as any he had ever seen. Not that he'd seen many in his young life. He had been too busy with other delights when Elly Fielding had leaned back in the hay barn for him. The shape of her legs had escaped his notice completely as they spread out obligingly to accommodate him.

'Indeed,' James drawled in what he hoped was a sophisticated and worldly manner, but it was not at Katy Murphy's legs he looked.

'Who are you gawking at?' Mara flared, though she knew very well what it was the young gentlemen were eyeing so appreciatively for her own legs were as bare as Katy's and twice as shapely, in her opinion, and if her Mammy could see her she'd commit her to a convent and never let her out again.

James patted the neck of his restive mount, then throwing one leg over her rump, slid down to the spongy ground.

He knotted the reins over a branch, then turned for a better look at this vivid beauty who stood like some dazzling woodland nymph in the water. It sparkled about her slender feet, making sounds of evident pleasure as it caressed her ankles and, by God, could you blame it? He'd die happy if he were only allowed to do the same. She had put her hands on her hips now, surveying him haughtily, though the other one, fair and insipid beside her, was inclined to hang her head and weep. She could be Hugh's, he decided jubilantly. The dark one for him and the fair one for Hugh and the anticipation of the fun, and perhaps more, they would have with these two pretty little creatures put an arrogant spring in his already jaunty step and a smile about the corners of his good-humoured mouth. Not for a moment did he doubt that they were girls from a lower class than his own. He grinned and put out a hand, completely at his ease as he would not have been with a young lady of his own class.

'Let me help you out,' he offered gallantly, 'before you become even wetter than you already are.' Both Mara and Katy had hastily dropped their skirts as the first shock of seeing these two young men had lessened somewhat and they trailed limply in the water, wet up to the knee. 'Come on, Hugh, give a hand to the young lady. Can you not see she is about to drown? See,' he said to Mara, 'take my hand and step up on to the bank. Be careful now, it's slippery . . ' and somehow his hand became an arm about her waist as he hauled her out and her flushed rose and cream face was no more than an inch or two from his own. He held her to him for a laughing moment whilst beside them Katy giggled with Hugh, but Mara O'Shaughnessy was not a girl to be handled by any impudent chap who had a fancy for her and the lovely rose of her cheek became a fiery, outraged red. Her eyes which James had been just about to liken to the bluebells at their feet flashed as steely bright as a sword and raising her hands she pushed him away from her with all her strength.

'Don't you be putting your hands on me, you spalpeen,' she declared hotly. 'Help me out, you said, not help yourself to whatever you fancied, so get back on that dratted animal and take yourself off to wherever you came from. Me friend an' I are having a nice peaceful walk through this bit of old wood, so we are, and we want no company, do we Katy?'

Katy stared with the same bewilderment as the two young men since was this not exactly what they had hoped for today? A bit of fun, Katy had thought. Perhaps a mild flirtation with a couple of their Billy's pals, some cheeky back-chat, a laugh or two but nothing serious and now, just like magic, the magic these woods seemed to produce, here were two handsome young gentlemen ready for just that and Mara was screeching at them like an Irish washerwoman. Neither of them had done anything a girl could take offence at and yet Mara was seriously offended. Oh yes, Katy always knew when Mara was offended. Indeed the whole world knew when Mara was offended. This was one of those times and Katy couldn't understand it.

'Go on,' Mara ordered, 'take yourself off, the pair of you before I send for a constable. We're a couple of decent girls, so we are, and . . .'

'We never for a moment intimated that you weren't, Miss . . . Miss . . . may we know your name . . . ?'

'Never mind me name. Just go about your business and let me friend an' me do the same.'

'Well, as a matter of fact we were going about our business,' James Osborne observed pleasantly. 'We promised Hugh's father we'd try and get a look at the game in the . . .'

'Game! We know your game, don't we, Katy?'

'Really, I'm telling the truth, aren't I, Hugh?' James, laughing, turned an exasperated face to his friend.

'You are indeed, James, and . . .'

'Never mind that blarney. The pair of you are up to something and me and Katy are going to report you to whoever owns this bit of land when we get back, aren't we, Katy?'

Mara was at her most imperious and James promised himself at that moment, that one way or another, he was not sure how or when, he would make it his business to get to know this glorious girl more intimately, much more intimately.

'Then you will have to speak to my father,' Hugh Woodall pronounced somewhat pompously. 'You don't seem to be aware of it but you are trespassing on private land. This is Woodall Park...'

'Steady on, Hugh,' James appealed, reaching again for Mara's hand. 'I'm sure there's no need for that,' and without either girl seeing it he winked at his friend. There was a bit of fun to be had here, the wink said and Hugh, realising at once what James was up to, subsided immediately.

Mara was momentarily nonplussed. Trespassing was a frightening word. One which conjured up pictures of the high and mighty Sir Charles Woodall, who employed her brother, invading this patch of woodland with a force of police constables. Of herself and Katy manacled to one another as they were bustled off to Walton gaol and of Mammy hanging her head in shame at the disgrace of it all. Her inherited Irish love of the dramatic had her in thrall, exciting and frightening her at the same time but James Osborne's hand holding hers and the warm and admiring expression in his eyes told her that she'd nothing to fear from the constables. In a second she was herself again.

'Well, we'll just untrespass ourselves, will we not, Katy?' she flung at her friend who looked almost ready to faint. 'And let go of me hand or I'll scream so loud the police from three counties will hear me and it won't be me they'll arrest.' When James did so reluctantly she turned gracefully. With a disdainful lift of her head she beckoned to Katy. Holding her skirt up from her bare feet she strode away along the path beside the stream, with Katy sniffling behind her. The two young men watched, fascinated by her splendour, until both girls had vanished among the trees.

'Bloody hell, Hugh!' James came suddenly to life. 'Bloody hell, what a woman and what a temper. Come on, my lad, we've got to find out who she is. By God, she makes Elly Fielding look like a plank of wood.'

Mara smiled in the darkness. She stretched luxuriously, then turned on to her side to stare at the slit of navy blue sky which showed through the drawn curtains. She could hear Caitlin's light breathing, and from the small bed in the corner Clare laughed in her sleep and murmured something unintelligible. A prowling tom-cat lifted its lovelorn head in the garden at the back of the house and howled its longing for the pretty tabby which was at this moment curled up on the mat before the kitchen fire, supremely indifferent to its yearning.

Mara was scarcely aware of the feline caterwauling as she went over every detail of the thrilling events of the day. She had known it would happen, of course, for hadn't every story she read in the forbidden *Peg's Paper* told her it would. And wasn't she the special and unique person to whom such dreams as she dreamed always came true? The rich and handsome prince would ride up on his white charger, the stories went, and sweep the beautiful princess off her feet, adoring and revering her, and though James Osborne's horse had been a quite ordinary brown it didn't matter at all because it was the dream and its realisation that counted. It had happened, and what could be more real than that? He had come, the gentleman her young heart had longed for. Mara O'Shaughnessy was not meant for the life her Mammy led. Not for her the mundane, everyday existence of the housewife and mother, with a husband who came home every evening to his slippers and his pipe and her on one side of their fireplace, no doubt mending his shirt, and him on the other reading the *Liverpool Echo*. Oh no, Mara would wear silk dresses and have a carriage pulled by a pair of matched grey horses. She would have servants to do her bidding and go to endless parties and balls and winter in the South of France with the rest of the gentry. And the man who could give her all this had arrived at last. The gentleman who could give her all this, and what fun she was going to have convincing James Osborne, the son of one of the wealthiest men in Liverpool, that Mara O'Shaughnessy was, as the song said, the only girl in the world for him.

4

'What does James get up to these days, Elizabeth? We've scarcely seen him since he came home from school and every time some outing is suggested he always finds an excuse why he should not be included. Some girl, I've no doubt, knowing how young men are at that age ...'

'Really, Harry, anyone would think you were at least forty years old and not a young man who is about to celebrate his twenty-first birthday. And as for girls, he certainly doesn't confide in me but then I'm only his sister, after all. Anyway, whatever it is, I'm sure it will all blow over and Hugh will have his accomplice back again.'

As Elizabeth Osborne continued to speak Harry Woodall slowly sat up in the deck-chair in which he had been sprawling. He pushed the old panama hat shading his eyes from the afternoon sun to the back of his head and shouted with laughter.

'Elizabeth Osborne!' he declared, his chestnut brown eyes gleaming in delight. 'You wicked girl, you. You're not supposed to know such behaviour exists amongst young men, let alone talk about it to one of them. What would your Mama say if she heard you?'

'Faint first, I believe, and when she had regained her senses, command Nanny to wash out my mouth with soap and water, then confine me to my room until a suitable husband could be found for me since I am obviously beyond her control. One who would curb my unladylike spirit and be prepared to remove me from her sight at the first opportunity so that I could not embarrass her in front of her friends.'

'You've never done that, I'm sure.'

'No, you're right, Harry. I wouldn't dare, but I can say things to you that I would say to no one else. Except James, of course, since he's the one from whom I learn them. Having brothers does give one an education which is not usually included in a young lady's curriculum.'

'James should be careful of what he says, Elizabeth. I'm not awfully sure I approve of such ... things ... being discussed with one's sister.'

'Oh, he does not discuss them with me, Harry. He is too much the gentleman, as you are.' She smiled impishly. 'But one cannot help overhearing conversations ...'

'Eavesdropping, Elizabeth. Another misdemeanour of which your mother would not approve,' but Harry Woodall was smiling as he leaned forward to take her hand between his and on the far side of the wide lawn Elizabeth Osborne's Mama exchanged a gratified smile with her friend, Lady Anne Woodall.

The two ladies were sitting beneath the shade of an enormous oak tree, said to be four hundred years old. Between them was a large, lace covered table and seated about it were a dozen ladies and several gentlemen. They were the guests of Sir Charles and Lady Woodall, just a few of those invited to celebrate the coming of age of their son and heir whose birthday it was the following day. Out of sight and to the side of the house an enormous striped marquee had been set up on the lawn. There was to be a dinner party in the evening to which close friends and relatives had been invited, followed by what Lady Woodall called, in the new way, a dance in the marquee. On the day after that the tenant farmers and estate workers, the house and outdoor servants were to have their own celebration of their young master attaining his majority. The family and those of the guests who remained after the dinner party would, of course, be expected to join this festive occasion, dancing awkwardly with the workers, conscious, as they had been brought up to be, that it was their duty. Servants who had been with the family, some for as long as twenty or thirty years, were considered to be a part of it and naturally would wish to share in the rejoicing at this important event in the life of its heir.

Lady Woodall, the silver teapot poised in her hand, asked the eternal question of Sir Roger Fenton: 'One lump or two, Sir Roger?' pouring a pale and delicate stream of expensively perfumed tea into the paper-thin china teacup. On the table was an enormous display of food brought out by a procession of footmen and parlourmaids, preceded by the Woodall butler. Set out daintily for the guests' consumption were triangles of brown and white sandwiches plump with egg and cress, cucumber and smoked salmon. There was seed cake, fruit cake, rock cake, gingerbread and freshly baked scones luscious with strawberry jam and whipped cream, and though it was a bare three hours since they had arisen from the luncheon table and would be no more than another three before they sat down to dinner, their hostess, and indeed all hostesses of their class, believed in following the tradition of afternoon tea as it had been followed for as far back as any of them could remember. It was by such customs that their lives were ruled. Lady Anne was of the rank and generation which believed in setting her guests at their ease in the overwhelming luxury and comfort which, had their roles been reversed, they would have provided for her.

Maidservants hovered discreetly within call whilst Wilson,

the butler, kept an eye on everything and everyone at once, from the smallest infant on Nanny's lap, the grandson of Lady Woodall's sister, on the far edge of the company, to Lady Woodall herself. Several children, as decorous and well behaved as miniature adults, played decorous and well-behaved games beneath Nanny's daunting gaze. Each child, whether it be girl or boy, wore a Breton sailor hat. The boys were dressed in identical sailor suits and the girls in mid-calf dresses tied just below the waist with broad sashes. They were all severely restricted beneath the critical attention of their respective nannies from doing much beyond waiting for afternoon tea to be over so that they might retire thankfully to their own domain. They would normally have tea in the nursery, well away from the languid elegance of their elders, but today being a special occasion they had been allowed down as a treat.

There was a hammock strung between two trees and in it Hugh Woodall dozed with his hat over his eyes, his indolent demeanour speaking loudly of his boredom. A wasp buzzed close to his chin. He swatted at it lazily and the hammock swayed with the movement. The sun shone from a vivid blue sky patterned with one or two cauliflower clouds, rounded and fluffy. They had built up that morning but most had dissolved, showing no threat to Lady Woodall's afternoon tea party.

On the stretch of lawn beyond the terrace and the shaded spot where the guests were seated, croquet was being played by several of the Woodall brothers' friends. A few of the young ladies, despite the difficulty they had in moving about, wore the very newest of fashions, the 'hobble' skirt, in pale shades of summer. It was seen by many of those women agitating for more freedom as a device to ensure that they did not obtain too much. The tight, tube-like skirt necessitated, of course, a reduction in the bulk of undergarments still worn by their Mamas and the revelation of the anatomical outline of some of the 'gels' was shocking, in the opinion of the older ladies. The bodices were high-necked and boned and, in all, extremely unsuitable for games of any sort, but fashion was fashion and must be followed.

There was a genteel game of doubles taking place on the grass tennis court beyond the croquet lawn. Tim Woodall and Teddy Osborne, dressed in white flannels and shirts with the sleeves rolled up, partnered Sophie Woodall and Penelope Fenton, the daughter of Sir Roger and Lady Eleanor Fenton, come over from Cheshire for the forthcoming celebration and who were to be overnight guests. The two young ladies were also in white and, in the view of their Mamas, suitably dressed for their age and station in life: dresses of crisp holland reaching to just above the instep, neat and sportsmanlike, high at the neck and with long sleeves. Each girl wore a straw boater pinned firmly to her long, flowing hair, decorated in Sophie's case with a wide blue ribbon and in Penelope's, with pink. The gentlemen were, naturally, in honour bound never to serve with strength at a lady opponent and always endeavoured to return balls as near to their feet as possible but as she hit the ball her brother had just sent across the net to her Sophie threw up her tennis racquet in wild exasperation, though it did not quite leave her hand.

Lady Woodall carefully put her cup and saucer on the table, though nothing in her expression revealed her acute displeasure at the appalling lack of good manners in her daughter.

'Tim, will you please stop treating me to this quite unnecessary show of gentlemanly behaviour,' Sophie called out. 'Penelope and I want a decent game of tennis, don't we, Penny, but if you and Teddy continue this asinine...'

'Sophie, my dear, is something wrong?' her mother asked graciously.

Sophie raised her eyes to heaven and sighed hugely. 'No, mother.'

'Then what is happening, dear? Is there some reason why you have stopped playing?'

'No, mother.'

'Then do carry on, darling. We are all enjoying it so much, are we not?' smiling at the circle of her friends, most of whom had growing daughters of their own and who surely must sympathise with her. The young were really becoming quite unmanageable these days with their eternal quest for freedom, especially the girls, and one was really quite relieved when one's daughter was safely married and became the responsibility of her husband. Sophie was no worse than the rest of their circle but Lady Woodall did deplore a show of bad manners, particularly before one's friends, and Sophie must be made to realise it.

Several of the gentlemen got up and excused themselves gallantly, saying they would take a turn about the garden which the ladies knew meant they were about to light their cigars or cigarettes though the gentlemen did not of course say so. They strolled across the smooth green lawn which was faintly marked with the felted hoof-prints of the mowing-pony, stopping for a moment or two to watch the resumed tennis game before going on down to the lake. It was quite a walk across the deer park but it was somewhat of a relief to get away from the ladies' gossip, though this was not voiced.

Elizabeth watched them go. Her father was among them. She leaned back in the deck-chair and putting her hands unselfconsciously behind her head, closed her eyes, unaware of the young man's sudden interest beside her. His own eyes, despite his determined and gentlemanly resolution not to do so, were drawn to the soft swell of her young breasts. He was even certain he could see the peaks of her nipples through the fine cotton of her blouse and his breath caught uncomfortably in his throat. Elizabeth Osborne had grown up quite dramatically in the past year and though she was only fifteen, no . . . she was sixteen now, having had a birthday in March, she had become, almost overnight, it seemed, a young woman. She really didn't look any different. She had always been a pretty child but it was something in her manner, something he could not quite put a name to. There was a boldness of colouring and carriage which he had never noticed before, a dazzling contrast of dark, chestnut hair, pure white skin and her long, incredibly green eyes. It was fashionable to have a fine porcelain complexion, blue eyes and a dainty figure but Elizabeth's beauty could only be described as flamboyant, foreign even, and he wondered where it had come from. Her father had green eyes but her mother was pale and grey eyed, a true image of traditional English beauty. Harry was well aware that the female matured much more quickly than the male of their own age, that they were ready for marriage at sixteen or seventeen whereas a young man would enjoy his freedom for another ten or even fifteen years. A young man sowed his wild oats, if he had any to sow, and a young lady got married. A girl needed marriage since there was little else available to her and she must succeed in it. He liked Elizabeth, despite the difference in their ages, which at this age, was quite a lot. She was good fun, entirely natural with him and though she treated him as she would one of her own brothers, he knew lately that there had been a change in her attitude towards him. They were all growing up, he and his brothers and sisters, James and Elizabeth and even young Teddy, but really, Elizabeth was ... well ... quite delightful! Her sense of humour enchanted him and though she was never less than the perfect lady he believed that, given freedom from her Mama which was well nigh impossible in a girl of her rank, she would make a refreshingly engaging companion. Her candour regarding her brother's activities proved it.

'Oh, good shot, Sophie,' she was saying, her sea green eyes shaded beneath her hand as she watched a particularly daring service from his sister. There was some polite applause from the ladies who were not awfully certain they approved of such ... such ... enthusiasm in one so young, then she leaned back again, sighing in deep contentment. She closed her eyes. 'It's strange about James,' she went on. 'I hadn't realised he was going off without Hugh until you told me. I thought they were up to the usual tricks which occupy their school holidays but if he's on his own somewhere...' Her voice died away, then, 'Father was shouting for him only this morning saying he'd promised to go down to the shipping office with him. If he's to take an interest in the business he has to start sometime, though I can't quite see James busy with columns of figures and shipping manifests. Not that he need concern himself with it unduly since Father says the managers, or whatever it is they are called, can manage at whatever it is they do, very nicely without anyone to watch over them though of course Grandmama wouldn't agree. She's the one who built it up, or so they say, and if she knew of it would certainly not approve of James playing truant. But James is like Father. He would rather concern himself in the affairs of the estate and will not take kindly to going to the city each day.'

'I don't blame him.' Harry lounged back in the deck-chair again, speaking lazily from beneath the brim of the panama. 'Can you imagine having to waste one's time in a stuffy office on a glorious day such as this.'

'I know.' There was a pause. 'But I wonder where it is he has got to?'

'Lord knows, but wherever it is and whoever he's with,' which, in Harry's opinion, would be some pretty and obliging parlourmaid or shop girl, 'it's his own business, Elizabeth. He is eighteen, you know, and no longer a schoolboy.'

'That's what Father says to him, meaning he should find some worthwhile occupation but I'm sure he only says it because he thinks he should. I always get the impression that Father does not quite like being a businessman which

71

he is forced to do now and again. Directors' meetings and such. He would much rather Grandmama went in his place but ... well, since Grandfather died they say she has not been the same. She loved him very much, you know.'

'Really?' Harry lifted the brim of his panama again and his eyes turned to the girl beside him.

'Oh yes. They were absolutely devoted to one another. Father says even he, as their son, felt as though he was an intruder in their lives at times. Quite embarrassing he said, but I thought it was lovely, the way they were with one another. Do you know, just before grandfather died ... I was only ten at the time ... I can remember seeing them walk hand in hand through the garden and once, though they knew they could be seen not only by me but the gardeners as well, they turned to one another and ... embraced. With their arms about one another for everyone to see, they simply kissed as though they were alone. She must have been over seventy then and yet ...' she paused, her face soft and wondering. 'Even I, young as I was, could sense their ... it's a strange word to use ... their passion. Do I sound foolish, Harry?'

Harry felt something touch him deep inside. It unsteadied him and for a moment he could not answer her. She was looking at him expectantly, hopefully, begging him not to laugh for if he did some insubstantial thing which was growing between them would be shattered. He found he wanted to take her hand again, this time not in friendship but in that certain flowing way a man will with a woman who is dear to him.

'No, Elizabeth, you don't. There is nothing foolish in a man and woman loving one another as your grandparents did.' His voice had more feeling in it than was usual but she did not appear to notice. 'I hope one day you find . .'

She smiled at him, gently and utterly without guile.

'Yes, Harry?'

'I should like to love and be loved like that, Elizabeth.'

'It must be ... rather splendid.' She was somewhat breathless.

'Yes, splendid.'

His smiling expression was so familiar to her. It was possible, because of it, and because of their long relationship in childhood, just to smile as they were doing, almost intimately, though she did not recognise it as such. He was Harry, dear and trusted, her brother's friend and her own and what was in his eyes was not identified for what it was. The hint of complexity in him, concealed by the boyish air he assumed, hid his man's mind, and the thoughts which he himself had scarcely acknowledged as yet.

'You must come with me when I visit her next.'

'I would like that, Elizabeth.'

'She is still beautiful.'

'So that is where you get your looks?' and he grinned endearingly to let her think he was not serious.

The night of Harry Woodall's coming-of-age party was quite splendid with guests arriving all through the day and from distances as far south as London and from north of the border in Scotland. Sir Charles and Lady Woodall were both well connected and had many friends and every bedroom in the house was in use. Not only their guests but their guests' servants must be accommodated. Ladies' maids and valets, chauffeurs and even a coachman or two since not every gentleman amongst those who could afford one had seen fit to purchase himself a motor car.

Woodall Park was a lovely old house constructed like so many in Lancashire of stone. It was peaceful and dignified as it looked across the vast acres of the deer park towards the bustling cities which had grown up around it ever since the industrial age had begun. To the north was St Helens and its great glass factories and coal mines. West was Liverpool with the restless tumult of the river and its shipping, south was Warrington and Runcorn and in the centre lay

73

the serene two thousand acres of rural beauty which was Woodall Park and its three farms.

There were trees about the house and wide stretches of gardens, the beds at this time of the year gloriously massed with summer flowers. Arbours and bowers were overspread with creepers, vines and climbing roses, intermingling, or so it seemed, in a quite haphazard way, but in reality carefully controlled by the dozen gardeners who Sir Charles employed. The terrace at the back of the house was wide with steps cut out to the lawn where a sundial in the centre had the initials JW inscribed on it with the date 1648 testifying to the antiquity and pedigree of the Woodall family. There were fountains and rose gardens, ponds and rockeries, a garden maze with the hedges clipped to the smoothness of a billiard table, a laburnum tunnel and an orangery and at its roughest outskirts, a wild azalea dell.

The dinner party for a chosen fifty guests, close friends and relatives of the Woodall family was a great success and the skill and ingenuity of Sir Charles and Lady Woodall's cook appeared to confirm the rumour that she had once served with the great chef, Cézar Ritz, up in London. There was caviare, lobster consommé, salmon in a rich Médoc sauce, pâté of liver, succulent lamb, and sorbet au champagne. There were salads with asparagus followed by every known gâteau, ice cream and almonds, whipped cream and fruits. The dishes on which they were served were silver, family silver used only on special occasions and the table, when fully laid, was exquisite since Lady Woodall was known to be not only creative but a martinet in the name of perfection.

Woodall Park had recently been wired for the new electric light, a great inconvenience and terror to the servants who were still inclined to approach the light switches with utmost caution. Sir Charles and his wife had travelled to London for the season in June and had taken the opportunity whilst they were absent to have the work done since the noise and the confusion involved was bound to be frightful. But though the elegant dining room was lit by electricity, Lady Woodall had placed candles in elaborate silver candelabra down the centre of the long table since they were so kind to the colouring and complexion of many of her older female guests. There were silver epergnes holding beautifully arranged flowers cut only that day from the gardens and hothouses, trailing with ivy. Silver card holders informed each guest where he or she should sit. There were five wine glasses at each place setting and the damask napkins were fluted into the shape of a fan.

Elizabeth found herself, to her surprise, seated next to Harry, almost the place of honour since it was his coming of age and her entry into the adult world of society. She wore white, as did all the young unmarried girls present, but instead of the froth of girlish frills and ruffles which were usual in one so young she had persuaded her mother to allow her a simple dress of white chiffon studded at the front in a narrow line from the neckline to the hem with tiny seed pearls. A white satin underdress was edged at her ankles with a narrow, pearl-encrusted border. It was demure for though it showed her ankle-bone and the slim elegance of her white satin evening slippers, the neckline was very modest and the sleeves were almost to her elbow. She shimmered as she walked, the dress a filmy sheath which, though her mother had thought it decorous and even plain at the fittings, made her seem older than her sixteen years. She had been allowed to put up her hair and it was arranged in a loose and shining knot at the back of her head with a scattering of seed pearls, like dewdrops amidst the darkness.

But her demeanour, as always, was impeccable and her Mama, after that first anxious moment of wondering if she had allowed the child too much licence, relaxed and entered into conversation with the gentleman to her right. Every lady had removed her gloves and unfolded her napkin as soon as she was seated, as was correct. The soup was eaten with a soup spoon and the fish with two silver forks. A knife and fork must be used for the asparagus and salads and a fork with the sweets. The principle, as every lady knew, was that one used the implement most likely to convey the least possible quantity of food from the plate to one's mouth. Only the poor, the greedy or the ill-mannered spooned their food up in large and disgusting amounts. There were many pitfalls for a lady to avoid when first she entered society and many hideous gaffes which could be made but Elizabeth made none, passing all tests with flying colours. She would be allowed to stay for a dance or two in the marquee after dinner and then, with Teddy, would be taken home in her father's four-year-old Renault motor car, driven by Gibson, the chauffeur, who would then return to pick up his master and mistress. Sophie would be allowed to stay until midnight as she was slightly older than Elizabeth and it was, after all, her brother's coming of age celebration, but James and Hugh, two years older again, would stay on until the end of the somewhat decorous dancing, doing their duty as well brought up young gentlemen, partnering those ladies Lady Woodall, graciously and tirelessly circling the dance floor as a hostess should, found sitting alone.

The next day dawned bright and clear with a hint in the air of the warmth to come. The sky was a solid gleaming summer dome of cumulus, shading from pale lemon to a deep umber at the horizon. Across the park a haze of mist lay three feet deep above which the proud heads of the deer seemed to float then vanish as they bent to nibble at the grass. The marquee had been cleared of its elegant furbishings of the night before, its small tables and dainty gilt chairs, and in their place were arranged the long trestle tables and benches which were considered more suitable for the hundred or so people, tenants of Sir Charles' and the household servants. There would be, naturally, a certain segregation: the upper servants, the tenant farmers and their families all in their Sunday best, keeping themselves apart

76

from the lower servants, the labourers and gardeners. The Woodall family and their friends remained somewhat aloof from the servants. Sir Charles and Master Harry strolled about in their midst though, as was proper, the heir shaking every hand which was held out to him. Elizabeth, today dressed in a gown more appropriate to her age – at least in her mother's view – was again in white. Her dress was plain and collarless, of muslin and delicate French lace, the skirt three inches from the ground and just below her waist was a satin sash of palest blue. Her hair had been arranged by Minty, her maid, into a style which was somehow Grecian and a shining tendril or two had escaped to curl enchantingly about her ears and at the back of her neck and the man who watched her from amongst the other servants as she walked down the terrace steps towards the marquee felt a curious and distinctly tender desire to go to her and smooth them away. Tuck them behind her ears and then perhaps bend his head and ... His vivid blue eyes grew unfocused as his thoughts dwelled on her smooth young beauty.

The family table was smothered with plants and hothouse blooms in copper bowls and those who sat about it were ready to enter into the spirit of enjoyment. Sir Charles and Lady Woodall and their three handsome sons, the eldest who had yesterday become twenty-one years of age, and their daughter who, though not as striking as her brothers was lively and bonny enough to please any man's eye. There were the Osbornes, the Woodalls' closest friends: Mr Sean and Mrs Serena Osborne, their own sons and their quite breathtakingly lovely daughter and a multitude of local families from among the upper classes come to see young Harry observe this happy occasion with those who would one day be his people. There was to be a gargantuan banquet, a spread the likes of which many of those who were to share it had never before seen. Five hindquarters of beef, it was rumoured, a hundred and fifty legs of mutton, hams

and tongues, chickens and ducks and pork pies, with pud-
dings and cakes, fruit and nuts to follow and all to be washed
down with as much wine and ale as every man and woman
could decently hold.

Lady Woodall, collecting her daughter and younger sons,
began to circulate amongst them, beckoning Elizabeth to
come too.

'You will know most of them, my dear,' which was true
since from the day she had first been put on a pony and
learned to ride it, accompanied by either George the groom
or her brothers, she had spent almost as much time at
Woodall Park as at her own home. She and Sophie had
roamed the woods and farmlands belonging to Sir Charles,
a familiar sight to the gamekeepers, the farm labourers, and
groundsmen and gardeners and their wives and when they
had returned, sometimes like two 'drownded kittens' as Mrs
Barney, the cook, put it, it was the Woodall kitchen servants
who had squeezed them cosily in a chimney corner near
the fire and stuffed them with Mrs Barney's fresh made
biscuits and hot chocolate.

Unlike the rest who were too concerned with the disposal
of as much food and wine as they could decently consume
during the evening, Michael O'Shaughnessy stood up as
Lady Woodall and the two young ladies approached. For
an exquisite moment as their eyes met Elizabeth felt the
compelling maleness of him strike her like a blow in the
middle of her chest and she was certain she had gasped out
loud. He was dressed in brown cord trousers known as
'peg-tops' and a corduroy jacket the colour of dark honey.
His shirt was cream, beautifully laundered and his tie was
of the four in hand style, neat and fashionable in shades of
beige and brown. He could have passed for one of Lady
Woodall's own sons and was as different to his fellows in
his dress and manner as they were.

'Good evening, my lady,' he said politely. Lady Woodall
knew him to be one of her husband's grooms but not being

a horsewoman herself could not bring his name to mind.

'Good evening ... er.. '

'O'Shaughnessy, my lady.'

'You are enjoying yourself, O'Shaughnessy?' her ladyship asked, somewhat startled by the man's self-assurance and complete failure to look like any groom she had ever known. Of course, it was an informal affair, this celebration with the estate workers and servants, not at all like the previous evening, but most of those about the table were dressed as one would expect a servant to dress. Good dark suits and stiff wing collars on the men, the women in day dresses of sensible materials and colours which were brought out only on Sunday and for special occasions such as this. A hat, of course, large, with a wide, turned up brim, some of straw but most in a dark plush. One or two, those of a more daring nature, had a bit of tulle, a feather or some ribbon as decoration. They all bobbed their heads in her ladyship's direction, their eyes bright with the unaccustomed wine and ale, their faces flushed, some freely sweating.

Michael O'Shaughnessy continued to stand as Lady Woodall moved on. Miss Sophie smiled at him and followed her mother but Elizabeth remained rooted to the wooden flooring on which she had come to rest when his eyes met hers.

She had not seen him since that winter day at the end of last year when he had spoken of his family and though she had not admitted it, even to herself, she knew now that in all that time, well over nine months, she had deliberately avoided the Woodall stable-yard and the reason for it stood before her. She could feel the exact same sense of trembling, breathless agitation he had aroused in her then. Inside her chest her heart felt too big for the cage which held it, banging away dreadfully so that she could scarcely breathe. She wanted to run after Sophie but her feet would not let her and she was certain she looked exactly like a rabbit confronted by a stoat which was absolutely ridiculous because this young man, this servant who presented no threat to Elizabeth Osborne, was anything but stoat-like. He was tall and finely built, graceful as he leaned, one hand on the back of the chair he had just vacated, waiting for her to speak, or not, as she chose. There was as yet no urgency in him as there had been the last time they had met, only what seemed to be a quiet resignation, an acceptance of what was to come, whatever that might be. He studied her, his eyes a brilliant, almost a turquoise blue, warm and admiring in the youthful smoothness of his tanned face and over his forehead fell an uncontrolled tumble of dark brown hair. What was this fascination this man held for her? Whatever it was it frightened her but it enchanted her too, which was worse. It made her feel weak and dizzy with a ridiculous happiness and at the same time filled her with a dreadful terror of the unknown for that was what he was. Unknown. From another world.

His eyes locked with hers. He wanted her badly, he knew it, with none of the transient desire he had felt for other women, but he did not let her see it, of course. But he could not seem to drag his eyes away from hers and she was the same, which told him all he wanted to know. There was a perilous tension between them, even here among her own people and his, an intense disturbance of the air about them which he knew he must dispel before it was noticed.

He smiled, just a slight turning up of the corners of his mouth, still watching her, waiting for her to move, to speak, to smile in return, perhaps, asking nothing of her, telling her nothing except the absolute certainty that he was dangerous, as he had when they last met. Those around him were beginning to stare and nudge one another and she knew she must move on, follow Sophie. Oh dear God, she must follow Sophie, if only she knew how. If she could just get her feet to unglue themselves from the floor and take those necessary steps away from this ... this bewitchment the man seemed to have the ability to cast over her but she was stuck fast . . .

'Elizabeth, come and meet someone who swears you are the loveliest creature he has ever seen but don't tell him I told you so or he will never forgive me since I am sure he will want to tell you himself.'

A hand on her arm, warm, strong, safe: Harry's hand, and when she turned to him her radiantly shining eyes, the dazzling look of pleasure on her face which he did not recognise as relief made him smile in delight. She took his arm, holding it desperately to her with both hands, smiling up at him as she turned away from Michael O'Shaughnessy.

Her voice was high and strange. 'You're teasing me, Harry Woodall,' she said breathlessly. 'You're making all this up. I don't believe a word of it.'

'It's true, really it is. I went to school with him years ago. He couldn't get here for the party last night as he only arrived in Liverpool from America this morning but he is here now and has declared that when the band starts playing he has every intention of dancing every dance with you.'

The man who took care of Harry Woodall's horses was still there, standing quietly beside his chair, his face impassive, no sign of emotion of any kind in his expression. He might have been one of the pillars which held up the roof of the marquee for all the notice Harry and Elizabeth took of him and neither he, nor Harry, was aware of the great banging drum which beat in Elizabeth's breast and ears.

'Is that so?' she managed to say. 'Well you can tell your friend that I am determined to have at least some of those dances with my friend, Harry Woodall, if he will allow it.' She was babbling and she knew it but what did it matter if it got her away from the danger of . . . of . . . *him*. 'You are positively the most splendid dancer here. I should know for I've danced a lively polka or two with you in the past. Do you remember when we used to put the Victrola on in your Mama's conservatory? Those Sunday afternoons when it poured with rain and we couldn't play croquet? You and Sophie, Tim and Hugh, Teddy and James and I. We danced all afternoon and James and Hugh danced together. Do you remember how we laughed, they were so comical? Now promise you will dance with me tonight or I shall be forced to press James or Hugh into service and after their performance together I shudder to think how I will fare with either one. Please Harry, I had only two or three dances last night but mother says I may stay until midnight and I intend to wear my slippers right through by then. Oh, I do love dancing, Harry.'

Harry looked down at her with a growing warmth she failed entirely to comprehend. She was as fond of him as carelessly, as devotedly as she was her brothers. He represented the secure happiness of her childhood, the peace and tranquillity of those familiar days when the seven of them had wandered in the summer woods, she and Sophie only barely tolerated, in the masculine pursuits of their brothers. The excitement of hours hunting across Sir Charles' and her father's land, family parties, Christmas gatherings, the closeness of friendship which linked their two families. He was what she knew, with no dismaying alarms, no unease, no shrinking fears of what was in his eyes for they looked at her with a gentle regard, an interest and admiration she found infinitely satisfying. He was Harry who spoke with the same lazy accent of privilege as her brothers, and the man they had left behind, the man whose lilting Irish brogue still sang in her heart, was pushed firmly as far as he would go to the back of her mind.

She did dance with Harry. Far more than she really should, friends of their parents remarked, which must signify that Charles and Anne Woodall, Johnny and Serena Osborne had no objection to it. So that was the way the wind blew, was it, they said to one another privately, but then it really was a most suitable match. The Osbornes were an old family related by marriage to the Hemingways who were known to have an aristocrat or two in their background and the Woodalls had generations behind them of landed gentlemen of the noble sort. Wealth in both families, of course, some of it made by trade but then this was a new century, a new era and the word was not as obnoxious as once it had been. They made a handsome couple, Elizabeth Osborne and Harry Woodall, obviously liking each other well enough, laughing and talking animatedly and even when they were apart it was noticed that Harry Woodall's eyes followed her when she danced with another. Harry, as the heir whose coming of age was being celebrated by his people, must of necessity take a turn or two about the dance floor with the women servants, putting an arm about the ample waist of his mother's cook, Mrs Barney, who had known him since he was born, a parlourmaid or two who stared frozen-faced over his shoulder no matter how he joked with them, and several wives of the estate workers. His father did the same, as did his brother and sister, even Lady Woodall unbending sufficiently to engage in an achingly awkward waltz with her own butler.

'May I have the honour of this dance?'

The words, spoken with that soft Irish lilt she dreaded so desperately, came at her from behind. They might have been a sentence of death, so great was her fear, and Elizabeth indeed felt that if she turned round to face the man who asked her she would be led, if not to her death, then to her downfall. But how could she refuse? Her mother was there, nodding as though to say it was Elizabeth's duty, as it was the duty of them all, to dance with the Woodall servants on such an extraordinary occasion. Sophie giggled for Michael O'Shaughnessy was a good-looking young man and she would not have objected to taking a turn around the floor in his arms herself. James, who stood behind his mother's chair, frowned for some reason and seemed about to make a gesture of refusal on Elizabeth's behalf but his father shook his head at him warningly.

She put her right hand in his left, her other lightly touching his shoulder. She felt his hand in the small of her back, the delicacy of its touch burning through her gown and undergarments right to her skin. She stared over his shoulder, her face wooden; so frozen and disdainful it seemed, Serena Osborne remarked to her husband on it, saying that he must speak to his daughter on the need for good manners, even with those of a lower class.

Elizabeth swallowed and her eyes blinked furiously as she fought to keep her composure. Her heart beat so erratically, so absolutely out of control she was sure he could feel it beneath his hand on her back. She thought she would suffocate and when he spoke she jumped violently.

'Don't be afraid,' he said gently. ' 'Tis only a bit of an old dance.'

'I'm not . . .'

'Yes you are, but I mean you no harm, you know that.'

Did she? Then why did her heart thud and her breath shorten at the very sound of his voice and the closeness of his masculine body delight and appall her at the same time?

'Can you not look at me?' he asked her softly.

'Why . . .'

'So that you can see what . . . I feel. I . . . wouldn't hurt you, ever.'

There was a long silence in which even the music seemed to come from some far and distant place so that only the echo of it beat in their ears. His hand was warm and firm, holding hers and she could feel his breath on her cheek though they danced a proper foot at least away from one another. It was sweet and fresh and when she turned her head at last to look into his face, drawn by something she could no longer fight, his lips were curved in a rueful smile over strong white teeth. His eyes looked into hers and in them was the truth of what was between them though he said nothing more.

She could feel her body begin to surge joyously towards

his, young, eager, knowing exactly what it wanted, but her mind stampeded in terror and when the music stopped she snatched herself from his grasp with a force that propelled her into the couple behind her. Without any apology to them, or gracious thanks to him, she hurried away across the floor of the marquee and when Harry Woodall stepped into her path at the entrance she grasped his hand as though she was drowning.

'Oh Harry ... Harry ... I'm so warm ... dancing so long...a walk by the lake would be nice...' and those about them were not surprised when Harry began to run with her, she laughing somewhat hysterically, they were inclined to think, down the long slope of the lawn and across the deer park in the direction of the lake. They were not to know that this was the second time Harry Woodall had rescued her from Michael O'Shaughnessy.

Harry Woodall smoked a last cigarette before he went to bed. He had already undressed and dismissed his valet, and he leaned by the open window wearing only the bottom half of his silk pyjamas. The muted light of the bedside lamp shaded his lithe, finely boned body to amber, picking out the scattering of pale gold hairs which ran from his chest and down his flat stomach. There was not an ounce of surplus flesh on him but though he was lean the muscles were outlined strongly beneath his skin. He had boxed at school and in his last year had been champion of his weight and the grace and suppleness it had given him were apparent in the way he stood and moved. There was about him a beauty, utterly male, and yet his warm brown eyes with their long, silken eyelashes would not have gone amiss in the face of a girl. His mouth, though firm, was good-humoured with a hint of sensuality about it which augured well for the woman he would love.

His unfocused eyes stared out into the shaded black of the summer night. The stars pricked its density and he looked upwards to the zenith of the sky, the highest point above his head, studying them. They all had names, he knew, but he was no astronomer, recognising only the Great Bear and the cup shape of the Corona Borealis. The Marriage Crown, or wreath, the Greeks had called it, the wreath which Dionysus had placed on the young head of his wife Ariadne, the wreath of jewels and gold which the same Dionysus had been given by Aphrodite, the goddess of love.

He drew deeply on his cigarette, the smoke wisping about his fair, tousled head. He narrowed his long, brown eyes and noticed with great interest that as his thoughts turned quite naturally towards Elizabeth, his heart gave a great and what seemed to him a joyous leap. He had almost kissed her tonight. She had been inclined to cling to him, he had thought, as they had strolled by the side of the moon-shimmered lake and had it not been for the need to return to his party guests he might have done so. But it was not something he wished to hurry, that kiss which he was certain would be her first. A girl's first kiss should be soft, warm, sweet, an unhurried brushing together of two willing mouths which might, if carried out by a considerate man, which he hoped he was, be a pleasing experience to them both. God, but she was superb all of a sudden, this girl he had known all his life. Her bold, almost gypsy loveliness was in such complete contrast to her well-bred and subtle mind, to the patrician blood which ran in her veins, it had quite taken his breath away on the last few occasions he had been in her company and he was convinced he had acted like some callow youth. Her vivid green eyes had smiled at him with an intriguing depth in them as though they carried secrets which, when revealed, would enchant him, and yet her innocent mind was unaware that she sent any messages at all! She was still a girl, a virginal, untried girl but her face and body were that of a beautiful woman. She was an enigma, a complexity of woman and child, uncertain and vulnerable with no more than a thin veneer as yet of her pedigreed upbringing to protect her.

He sighed speculatively, reaching for another cigarette. One thing was certain. They would all be round Elizabeth Osborne like bees to honey before long.

5

James Osborne's square brown hand slipped smoothly down the front of Mara O'Shaughnessy's bodice and for a delicious moment was allowed to fondle the high peaked firmness of her naked breast. It was warm and round and had a softness which seemed to nestle in his cupped palm but before he could become more intimately acquainted with the lovely sensation and the hot desire which raged through him, she stiffened indignantly, slapping his hand away. She sat up, pulling at her bodice, rigid affront in every line of her body, her face set with that expression he had come to know so well in the past five months and he sighed despondently.

It was always the same. He would hold her hand, its smallness and fineness burdening his heart with his need. The smooth white nakedness of it delighted him when she was sometimes willing to let him remove her glove. Just the sight of it lying defencelessly in his own palm excited him. The delicacy of her fingers laced with the firmness of his own made him want to bend his lips to them, to rub his face against them, to kiss the pulse on the inside of her wrist and when he did he could feel her tremble.

Oh yes, inexperienced as he himself was, he knew she wanted to do it as much as he did. He sensed in her a great dammed passion matching his own and which he was certain was unusual in a girl of her age, or indeed of any age, since he had been led to believe that ladies, at least of his class, did not greatly care for that sort of thing. Perhaps that was the difference between Mara and the young ladies with whom he had previously been acquainted. Willingly she would sit in a patch of sunlight with her back against a tree trunk, his arm about her shoulders, her head thrown back to stare up into the sun-hazed leaves. She would smile her witch's smile and listen as he spoke of his love. She was ready to tell him all the things he was eager to hear, which were how she had missed him and looked forward to this moment. She would remove her hat, sighing and languid, letting the sun streak her dark brown hair with polished chestnut and russet and when he kissed it her mouth would open eagerly beneath his. He would ease her down on a bed of lush summer fern and mosses with wood violets for a pillow, lay his body against hers, the tension and need in him so great it was unbearable. She was the loveliest, softest, most sweet-smelling creature he had ever known and yet her complex woman's nature was as much a paradox to him as on the day they had met. All he wanted of her was to bury himself in her, not just the demanding hunger of his body, but his will, his own simple masculine uniqueness which had nothing to do with the physical and had never before been given to a woman. His hands would enfold her face and of their own volition would flutter about her arching throat in an agony of desire and her eyes begged him to go on, it seemed to him, their brilliantly blue-green depths mysterious and challenging. But when he did, when his hands moved to the next progression in their lovemaking, when one slipped inside her dress to caress the flesh which he was sure yearned for his touch, she would turn on him like a cat, spitting and slapping, just as though he had insulted her, dared to take a serious liberty and one to which she had given him not the slightest encouragement.

Once, driven beyond endurance by her fluctuating accessibility, he had thrust his hand up her skirt, had actually pulled her drawers down over her hips, brushed his hand across the thick curling mound of her pubic hair and had for an enchanted moment believed that she was going to let him slip his fingers inside that moist heaven he was ready to die for, but the crack across the head she gave him almost stunned him.

She had refused to see him for three whole weeks after that and had been as cool as ice on a pond for three more even though he had treated her as though she was made of spun glass and had promised never, never to do it again.

Jesus God, how he loved her.

'Why do you do it, Mara?' he asked simply, the eternal male question to the woman he believed teased him.

'Do what?' Her voice was innocent and haughty and she tossed her head in the way he had become familiar with.

'Lead me on like that and then when . . .'

'*Lead you on*! Bejasus, you've a cheek on you, James Osborne, an' I've a good mind to say to the divil with you, so I have, in fact I'm away right now so I'd be obliged if you'd fetch that damned motor car an' take me back to Liverpool.'

She stood up. Her face was a bright rose of indignation and her body positively bristled but if James had caught the expression in her eyes he might have wondered at the cause of it.

They had, in her vernacular if not his, been walking out ever since the day, Whitsuntide Monday, it had been, when he had met her in these very woods. No one knew of it, of course, except Katy Murphy and Hugh, though James sometimes had the feeling that one or two of the servants, particularly those in the stable-yard, were whispering amongst themselves about his abrupt neglect of the mare he loved and his astonishing and sudden interest in and decision to drive the motor car. He had learned the rudiments of it when his father did, though he had been only fourteen at the time, both of them taking a lesson or two from the mechanic who had delivered it. 'Not for me,' he had declared when his father, who was an easy-going sort of a chap in some respects, had told him he might drive it when he was eighteen, since in James' opinion there was nothing like the feel of a splendid mount beneath you. To go like a bird across the park, the sun in your eyes, the wind in your face, the scent of growing things in your nostrils, the sound of Lady's hooves pounding up the turf. The elation of it sang in his veins and when he slowed the mare to a gentle walk as he entered his father's wood, the great beech wood from which the house got its name, the communion between her flesh and his, the gentle rhythm of their shared breathing was something he had loved since he had first been put on a horse's back.

Now, for a reason not apparent to those who knew him and of his love for his mare, he would declare he felt like motoring today, if his father could spare the rather stately Renault, four years old now but under the meticulous care of Gibson still as shining and immaculate as on the day Johnny Osborne had bought it. Mara loved it, of course. She would whip into the back when he picked her up by the cemetery gates in Deane Road, closing the door smartly behind her and drawing the curtains so that no one could see her. He would be in the front, of course, where Gibson usually sat, open to the elements but for the roof, but the weather was mostly kind that summer, favouring lovers who must court one another in the open. Twice, when it had been wet, he had driven to a secluded stretch of lane at the back of Stanley Park and parking the car beneath the trees, had climbed into the back with her and that was where he had made the horrible mistake of – as she put it – 'going too far' and forgetting that not only was he a gentleman but that Mara O'Shaughnessy was a lady and not to be trifled with.

And that was all he wanted to do, trifle with her, at least at first. But for some reason she had been carelessly indifferent to his overtures which naturally made the chasing of her all the more thrilling.

'No, I will not meet you tomorrow, or any other day,' she had said loftily when he and Hugh had hurried after her and her friend, 'so be off the pair of you or I'll set Katy's brother on you, so I will,' but he knew by the turn of her curling pink mouth and the brightness of those incredible aquamarine eyes that she was enjoying this moment of power over him enormously. He wanted to see her again, he said, and though Mara knew it was quite impossible it was delightful to play the game the rules of which were decided entirely by her. He was not exactly handsome. His jaw was too pugnacious and his nose too jutting. He was not as tall as she had dreamed her hero – she never used the word lover – should be. He was somewhat stocky but he had a boyish humour about him which was attractive and his gold flecked brown eyes were deep and admiring. And he was a gentleman and she, Mara O'Shaughnessy, though she came from a class inferior to his, was being pursued by him.

'Don't say that,' he pleaded, his own eyes laughing and merry. He placed his hand on his heart in an endearing gesture of undying love, walking backwards in front of her as she strode to where she and Katy had left their boots and stockings. Hugh and Katy trailed behind, Katy still sniffing dolefully, Hugh somewhat perplexed by his friend's behaviour for though the girl he was doing his best to convince should meet him again was not of their class, she was obviously a decent girl. Not like Elly Fielding who sometimes wore no shoes when she worked in the dairy, and certainly no bloomers. This one was a girl who fell between two stools, so to speak. Neither the sort one could marry nor tumble in a haystack!

'Come for a ride in my motor car next Sunday,' James beseeched her. The idea came to him from somewhere in his masculine mind as though he knew instinctively what

91

would impress this high-toned young girl with the soft brogue of Ireland in her speech. 'I'll pick you up wherever you want and we can drive over to Blundell Sands. Have lunch at the Royal, a stroll along the front and be back into Liverpool by eight. Dinner at the Adelphi and I'll have you home by ten-thirty. What d'you say?'

She was dazzled. Jesus, Joseph and Mary, what wouldn't she give to be able to say, 'Very well. As it happens I have no other engagements on that day so you may pick me up at number 11 Edge Lane at ten-thirty.' To be casual and uncaring just as though this sort of thing happened to her all the time. That her engagement book was filled with such invitations and she was perplexed only with which one to take up. Without knowing it, though, her face gave her away and James, quick to take advantage and realising that such a girl as this, with, he presumed, parents at home who would be careful with her, would find it difficult to do what he had suggested, instantly changed his tactics.

'But if you're otherwise engaged perhaps just a short spin out to Newsham Park, or West Derby for afternoon tea one day. I'm sure you are a young lady with many admirers. How could you be anything else, but I would be honoured if you could spare an hour for me.'

Mara was enchanted for this was how a gentleman always spoke to a lady and of course the divil of it was she would be hard pressed to get out of the house on her own without some good excuse for doing so even for half an hour, let alone half a day. Naturally, she did not say so since she was reluctant to drop her pose, which was of a sophisticated woman overwhelmed with more invitations than she knew what to do with!

'I couldn't possibly,' she said high-handedly whilst her sharp mind juggled with one idea after another trying to find some reasonable excuse which Mammy would accept – if such a thing existed – to get her out of the house. She was allowed on a Saturday to go to the park to listen to the band with Katy Murphy but if she wasn't back within an hour or two Mammy would send Dermot or Sean to look for her. The need to go to God's Holy Mass was a possibility but as Mammy had to coax her to attend now it would look distinctly suspicious if she suddenly developed a religious streak, besides which it took only half an hour to walk to St Mary's church, take Holy Communion and walk back again and where could she and himself get to in half an hour? Katy was her best bet, her busy mind decided. Perhaps they could arrange to take up some hobby, something which would require her to be out of the house, some art or craft class at one of the technical colleges for the young men and women of Liverpool. There were such places, she knew, for didn't their Dermot go to one of them to improve his knowledge of mathematics, but the chance of Mammy and Daddy allowing her to do the same were very slim. There was the Liverpool Academy in Church Street where lectures on subjects dear to the hearts of ladies were given, ranging from travels in Africa, with slides, to flower arranging, the art of painting on china, and talks on the fascinating plight of the poor heathen native of South Africa. None of it was of interest to Mara but if it gave her a reason to get out and one which Mammy and Daddy would accept, what did it matter since she wouldn't be attending anyway. She would have to put her brain to work to find something but in the meanwhile Katy would have to do.

'Please try,' the young man was saying entreatingly. 'Just for an hour or two next Sunday afternoon.' He turned winningly to Katy, at the same time throwing a look of appeal at Hugh since he was well aware that the other girl would have to be included in the outing if his one was to come and though Hugh seemed singularly unimpressed, dragging reluctantly behind, he would just have to make up the foursome.

'Your friend is welcome as well, you know. Tell you what, the four of us could motor over to Thatto Heath. There is a splendid place for afternoon tea there and it would take no more than half an hour. How about it, Hugh?' and his expression told Hugh that should he refuse Hugh's future would not be worth a farthing piece.

It was Katy who answered. 'It would be more than me life's worth to get into one of them motor cars, especially with someone I don't know,' she said fearfully. 'Me Pa would have a fit...'

'He'd not know, Katy, and ... well ... I can see no harm in a ride out to Thatto Heath in the company of...' Mara turned her cool, enquiring gaze on James and he sprang eagerly to attention, bowing in the courtly fashion of a true gentleman.

'James Osborne, at your service, ma'am, and this is Hugh Woodall.'

James Osborne and Hugh Woodall! Sweet Jesus, the two most respected and wealthy families in the whole of Liverpool and these were their eligible sons and they were begging her and Katy to take a ride with them in their motor car. *A motor car!* Holy Mother, she'd be the first in the family to ride in one, a wonder and a bloody marvel to them all since even Michael who worked for the Woodall family who owned two such machines had never actually been in one. But they must never know, that's if she went, of course, which was a great shame since there was nothing she'd like more than to brag to the rest of them about her grand experience as she drove about the countryside beside the splendid person of James Osborne himself.

'May I know your name?' he was saying engagingly.

'Mara O'Shaughnessy an' this is me friend, Katy Murphy.'

And so it had begun. It had been surprisingly easy to convince her Mammy and Daddy that she should really be trying to improve herself by doing something other than helping her mother at home, though naturally, she would still continue to do that, she promised angelically. She had a fancy to attend the lectures at the Liverpool Academy which were conducted for the education of the ladies of Liverpool twice a week during the summer. The real ladies, she hastened to assure them, knowing that would impress her mother. Oh yes, she said to Mammy, the lectures were of a perfectly proper nature and if Mammy would allow her to take the tram into town she would obtain a programme of what was to be put on, starting next Tuesday, she'd been told, so that Mammy would know exactly what Mara was to be lectured on. She and Katy and another girl ... who? ... well, she was a friend of a friend of Katy's, daughter of a bank manager ... no, Mammy didn't know them ... Catholic, of course, who attended St Xavier's in town and the three of them, she and Katy and Mary ... now then, hadn't she the girl's surname on the tip of her tongue but she'd let Daddy know of it when it came to her ... would attend on Tuesdays and Thursdays. No, it cost nothing though she'd been told there was often a collection for the betterment of the poor heathens, may the Holy Virgin bless them ...

She thought it rather clever of her to have invented the non-existent Mary, whose surname she didn't know. If there ever came a time when her mother spoke to Katy's mother about the lectures and it was discovered Katy did not attend, Mary was there to take Katy's place, Mary who was vague and unknown to the O'Shaughnessys but was the good Catholic daughter of a bank manager.

Katy and Hugh were included in that first outing to Thatto Heath which took place on Saturday afternoon when she and Mara were supposedly strolling in the park and listening to the band. Two hours, no more, since Mara was afraid to stay out longer but though Katy was not unattractive she was so terrified that someone her Pa knew might see her, that the motor car James drove which was really quite magnificent might blow up, that Hugh might be inflamed by her closeness and the absence of a chaperone and take liberties, that she made a poor companion, constantly looking over her shoulder, haunted and white-faced. She did not have

Mara's love of danger, nor did she share her friend's zest for doing what she shouldn't. The fearful and yet exciting knowledge Mara relished that should she be found out in this escapade she would no doubt be committed to a convent held no charm for Katy and the first time in the Renault was to be her last.

But Mara and James met at least once a week – not on a Sunday since that was a day crammed with churchgoing – motoring out of Liverpool for an hour to two, sometimes three if there was an extra lecture at the Academy. Mara would leave the house in Edge Lane and walk briskly in the direction of the tram stop where she was to meet Katy. Round the corner into Jubilee Drive and then a furtive dart into Kensington Gardens, her heart thudding with excitement as she hurried round the smooth green lawns keeping to the shelter of the bushes as best she could. Out at the far side into Kensington Road towards the cemetery where James would be waiting for her. She always had an excuse ready just in case she met one of her mother's friends. She had missed the tram in Jubilee Drive, she would say, and had cut across to Kensington Road to catch the one to the Pier Head which ran down from Prescot Road but she had been lucky so far and had been seen by no one. She had made James wait for a moment or two so that she could have a good look about her from between a chink in the car curtains, to see if anyone was showing an interest in the fashionably dressed young lady who had just darted into the splendid motor car which idled at the side of the road, but it seemed no one did.

Describing what she had learned at the 'lectures' had been the most taxing thing, but her mother and father, though not illiterate, were uneducated and knew very little about what did not impinge on their own lives. Mick had a vast store of knowledge regarding the ports of the world since did he not work for a shipping line? He knew the cargoes which went to them and those that came back to Liverpool, the ships that carried them and the conditions under which they travelled but ask him about the people of those countries and he was woefully ignorant. And as for Ellen, what did not take place in her own home, at Church or Church gatherings, in the small orbit of her children's lives, or a national event such as the old king's death and the new king's coronation, did not, in a way, really take place at all. So Mara was able to use her wide and vivid imagination without the slightest fear of contradiction, holding her mother and father and the youngest members of the family enthralled by her tales. She did get a book or two out of the library, all about the nomadic Bushmen of Southern Africa who were said to speak in a strange language consisting of nothing but a series of clicks and hisses. Mammy was quite fascinated, begging to know how any man could possibly speak to another in such a way and would Mara, the next time she went to the Academy, ask the learned gentleman who knew about such things to give her a demonstration!

It was October now and this day had been identical to all the others James and Mara had spent together during the summer. The quick dash from Kensington Road out to Colton Wood where for half an hour they had lain on a bed of moss beneath a canopy of tawny autumn leaves, at peace with one another. She had described to him her latest 'lecture' amazing him with the skilfulness of her mind which was capable of painting a picture of something she knew nothing about. From a book taken from the library she had devised a series of images with which to deceive her family and he had wondered in the arrogant and overbearing way of the class to which he belonged what might have been made of this girl if she had known a different upbringing, the upbringing of a girl in the society he knew, but when she had turned and smiled at him, it had all been swept away in the urgent passion of their kisses. Until she jerked herself out of his arms, that is.

'Take me home if you please, and we'd best be saying

goodbye,' she continued, 'since all you seem to want of me is what you've been doin' your best to get for the past six months and we might as well be savin' you the bother of tryin' any more. I'm not one of your shop girls or dairymaids who'd do anythin' for a man as long as he gave her a good time, an' if you think a ride in your old motor car is enough to buy my favours, then you'd best think again, so you had. Week in an' week out you've brought me to places where no one will see us. None of your grand friends, nor your blessed family an' sure don't we all know what a chap wants when he treats a lady like that?' She smoothed her gloves over her hands then thrust them behind her back so that he would not see them tremble.

'You've been just as glad to keep out of sight, Mara, you know you have, afraid your mother would get to know. What about the lectures you go to and the tales you make up to convince them you've been?'

'That's different. My mother and father only want to protect me, just as yours would protect your sister, and bejasus, they wouldn't allow me to go out alone with the Prince of Wales himself, not unless he was Irish, Catholic an' had a weddin' ring in his pocket. I'm only savin' them the worry of it, so I am.'

'Then tell me why you are here with me.'

'Sure an' you're enjoyable company, James Osborne, so you are, an' why shouldn't I enjoy meself? I'm sixteen an' quite old enough to go out alone and to take care of meself, but Mammy and Daddy don't understand. They're old an' still livin' in the past century but I don't see why I should do the same. I like you an' we have a good time together but it's no fun fightin' you off every time we meet. Like one of those sea things with a dozen hands, so you are, and none of them kept to yourself an' there was me thinkin' you were a gentleman an' could be trusted. But you're not so there's no more to be said. I'll just have to take up with one of the young men Mammy's got lined up for me.'

She lifted her chin in a gesture of bold disdain, not caring one way or the other, or so she would have him believe. She adjusted her straw boater to a more becoming angle on the shining knot of her hair. The hat pins were not quite to her satisfaction and it took her several moments to get them just right. She arched her back, knowing her breasts were lifted, round and tempting above the neat curve of her waist and hips and she also knew James' eyes were on them. She thrust them forward provocatively and heard the hiss of his indrawn breath.

'Mara, don't let's quarrel,' he said thickly.

'Quarrel is it? And what d'you expect me to do when all you can think of is getting inside me ... well, I'll not say it since it only shames me, just as you shame me with your ...'

'I don't mean to, Mara, you must know that. It's just that you're so damn beautiful I can't resist reaching out for you.'

'Well, you'll just have to learn not to and to make up your mind that you can't have everything you take a fancy for, so you will.'

'God in Heaven, I do fancy you, Mara. I'd do anything if you'd only love me.'

'Don't talk daft, James,' but she had lowered herself again to the bed of sun-warmed moss on which he sat. She drew in a deep breath, letting her fear ebb away a little since the conversation was turning in a direction which seemed promising.

'Is it daft, as you quaintly put it, for a man to love a woman, Mara? To want her as I want you? Jesus, I've been seeing you once or twice a week for nearly six months and if I don't ... if you won't let me love you I'll go mad.'

James' breathing was laboured and he felt the hard knot of need tangle in his guts. God, she fascinated him, this impudent, boldly fearless Irish girl who was like nobody he'd ever known before. He had met dozens of pretty girls in the homes of his schoolboy friends, their sisters and cousins who even at the age of twelve, thirteen, fourteen, were on display for the future marriage markets. Well bred and charmingly shy, trained in all the qualities needed to be good wives and mothers. When they were of an age for it they would be an asset to their husband, knowing exactly how to run his home, bear and rear his children, entertain his friends and, if he were fortunate, add to the wealth he already had with the magnificence of their dowries. They knew exactly their function in life and their place in the society in which he and they had been brought up. They knew what was expected of them. They knew the customs and cultures of their class. They thought like him, admired what he admired, knew how he would react in any given situation and how to deal with it. They *were* him, in a way, except in the obvious biological one and when he married one of them he would know exactly what to expect. What each day would bring for the rest of their married life together. He might take a mistress providing he was discreet about it and be thought none the worse for it by his friends who did exactly the same. His wife would pretend she knew nothing about it or perhaps take a lover herself when she had fulfilled her duties as a childbearer. They would be friends, amiable and unexcited with one another and, as he watched Mara preen herself in the bit of sunlight which lit her hair to fiery russet and her eyes to a brilliance which was hard to describe, he felt the despair of it settle on his eighteen-year-old shoulders. There would be no such boredom with this one. Hell's teeth, she'd keep him on his toes every minute of the day, exciting him, teasing him, plaguing him, fighting him, challenging him to endeavours which he would achieve with no one else. It would be like living with a bomb which could explode at the slightest provocation, but by Christ, the uncertainty of it, the exhilaration of not knowing what the devil she would do and say next would make life bloody well worth living.

And the nights! His loins ached unbearably and he

groaned as he put a hand on the back of her neck where lively springing tendrils of hair lay.

'Mara, I'm quite, quite possessed by you, did you know that?'

'And what does that mean?' She did not pull away from him though, sensing some change in him which instinct told her needed care at this important moment.

'I can't do without you, that's what it means. I must have you and bugger those grand Irish boyos your mother has in her sights for you. You're mine, Mara, and I'll be damned if I'll let some witless oaf enjoy the sweetness and beauty of that fine body of yours.'

'Fiddlesticks, James Osborne. This is just another of your tricks to persuade me to let you ... well, you know what I mean. But it won't work. I'm sorry, James, really I am because ... well, you may not believe this but ... you're a fine man, so you are, and ... I like you ... more than like you, but I'm a decent girl an' I'll be treated as one. I'll go to me marriage bed virgin, so I will.'

There was a pride in her now, a dignity which was not assumed and her lovely eyes were clear and, perhaps for the first time, honest with him. The words she spoke were meant to show him that not only the ruling classes, of which he was one, had an honour, a code to which a man, or woman, must be true. If her father knew she was associating with James Osborne, despite James' privileged position in society, Mick O'Shaughnessy, taking his big, angry sons with him, would be round at Beechwood Hall demanding to see James' father and ready to fight anyone who stood in his way. There was no doubt in her mind that, in spite of the difference in their positions and the fact that Daddy worked for Mr Osborne, he would make it clear to him and his family that nobody, not even Mr Osborne's fine son, would be allowed to tamper with Mick O'Shaughnessy's lovely, decent girl, and get away with it! Just as virginity was prized amongst James' people, so it was in hers. Working class she might be but her husband would not be dishonoured, nor her family shamed, by sending her to her marriage bed sullied by another man. She had teased and promised James Osborne all kind of things with her eyes and her tricky woman's body but she would never have given it to him, and they both knew it now.

He smiled gently, no longer a boy but a man who had made a decision which nothing could alter. He was an Osborne, a Hemingway, come from men and women who had greatness in them, and honesty and though the last fragment of youth in him quailed at the thought of what was to come he did not flinch from it.

'You're a witch, Mara. A bloody witch but I love you and no one is to have you but me.'

'Well, we'll see about that ...'

'Indeed we will, my darling, but as for going to your marriage bed a virgin, I wouldn't count on it.'

'Sure an' I don't know what you mean and I'd be obliged if you'd take that hand off my ...'

'Be quiet, Mara. Jesus, I've never known a woman like you for talking and just when it's not needed.'

'James, stop it! What the divil d'you think you're doing? Didn't I just say ...?'

'Aah ... Mara ... my love ... kiss me ... no, just there and there and when I've got the hang of these damned buttons ...'

'James ...'

'I love you, Mara, and I mean to be your husband as soon as we can manage it. Accept that, and me, since there's nothing going to change it. But in the meanwhile show me how to undo these bloody buttons ... Oh Lord ... Oh dear Lord ...'

6

The Osborne family were at breakfast when the letter came. Johnny Osborne sat at the head of the table with his wife at its foot. On his left was his daughter Elizabeth and opposite her was his younger son Teddy.

The breakfast room was an annexe of the dining room, in comparison quite small, but bright and informal, and used when the family was alone. Its proximity to the dining room was important as this meant that food could be served efficiently and unobtrusively from the kitchens which were placed only a short corridor-length away. Between the kitchen and the dining room was a service room where the servants arranged the trays and the butler's mahogany trolley. In the service room was much of the apparatus necessary to facilitate the serving of hot meals, to the family and their guests. Cruets, toast racks, jam pots, muffineers and tea urns, a breakfast service and serving implements, egg cup cruets and all the paraphernalia with which the servants ministered to the needs of the five members of the family, sometimes six if old Mrs Osborne was present.

The room was quiet. Serena Osborne, unlike many of her friends who breakfasted in the seclusion of their own boudoirs, felt it her duty to share this first meal of the day with her family but she did insist upon a tranquil atmosphere. Johnny would read *The Times* and she would question her children on their plans for the day, quietly and peacefully. She felt it was beneficial to them all to have these calm moments with one another, moderating the spirit and sending them all off to wherever they were going in an even-tempered state of mind. Teddy, at fourteen, was of course inclined to be boisterous but he respected her wishes and ate his breakfast in comparative silence. He was long accustomed to her unruffled composure and her insistence upon it in others when they were in her company. She had been christened Serena just as though her parents had been able to instantly see the characteristics nature had given their daughter. The name suited her to perfection. She had always kept herself somewhat aloof from others, elusive, private and separate and asking only these things of them: that they be restful in her presence, polite and in all things true to the code of the society in which she and they moved. She was a beautiful woman with dark, glossy hair, a perfect oval face and smoky grey eyes, elegant at all times, even now in her morning gown which would be worn, naturally, only when she was alone with her family. It was full and floating and had bishop sleeves with a tight band at the wrist and a high neckline. It was delightfully feminine but completely modest. Her long hair, brushed until it glowed by her maid, was arranged in a simple knot at the back of her neck. She was quite exquisite and absolutely expressionless. There was a portrait of her in the large drawing room, painted just after her marriage to Johnny Osborne, when she had been eighteen and but for a slightly fuller figure and a certain look of maturity which spoke of experience of life, she looked exactly as she had then. Her children were all somewhat in awe of her. She smelled of lavender and was soft and eternally gracious but her daughter had decided long ago that though her mother did nothing to inflict hurt or distress on any of them, neither did she bestow affection. She was unknown, a calm and unhurried presence in their lives who was as easy to grasp as smoke.

'I suppose we should think of going upstairs to dress, Elizabeth,' she said to her daughter. 'The shoot is to begin at nine-thirty and the ladies are to join it at noon for luncheon, though I doubt more than three or four will be there. Noon is so early and yet I know if it runs later the light will be gone and the gentlemen will grumble. They say the pheasant are to be good this year, Johnny,' turning politely to her husband.

'So I heard, my dear. Charles was telling me his game-keeper is delighted with them and there will be no need to import birds on to the estate as they were forced to do last year. Ours have done well, too, so Warren tells me.'

'That is good news, dearest.'

'Yes, isn't it. I am hoping to beat our own record the weekend after next when the Fentons are over. Do you remember, three days' shooting bagged us just over four thousand last year but it really looks as though the extra game Warren reared over the last twelve months will be well worth it.'

'Splendid, darling.'

There was silence again and after waiting a courteous moment to see if his wife had anything further to add, Johnny Osborne returned to his newspaper, indicating to Eaton that he would take another cup of coffee.

There was enough food keeping hot beneath the covered silver dishes on the sideboard to feed not only those about the table but almost every servant in Johnny Osborne's employ. Kidneys, bacon, kedgeree, eggs, sausages, kept warm on their dishes which were heated by methylated spirit burners and watched over by Eaton, the Osbornes' butler, Jackson, the upper footman and Betty, the head parlourmaid. Toast was brought from the kitchen, carefully wrapped in a snowy damask napkin to keep it warm before it was placed in the silver toast rack. There was porridge and ham and muffins, and over all the fragrant aroma of fresh coffee which had previously been brewed in a cafe-tière before being transferred to the silver coffee pot.

It was the servants' task to see at once should anything be needed at the breakfast table and to supply it immediately. The family, should they choose to, might help themselves but the self-effacing and competent service they received made such a chore unnecessary. Nevertheless Serena kept a watchful eye on them as was her duty as mistress of the house. She was very good at what she did. She was a perfect wife, mother and hostess and was assiduous in her social duties. She would no more allow herself to be late, to be impolite or lacking in good taste than she would appear unclothed before her husband. She had been born and bred in the traditions of the upper class and what she did in life she did with a perfection which had been ingrained in her since she was in the nursery, and she had seen to it that her children were the same.

It was a bright and sunny morning, one of those which occur just when it is thought the summer was gone for good and the winter cannot be far behind. Already the sunshine streamed in a soft haze through the long bay windows which lined two walls of the room which was set at the corner of the house. The golden rays had placed oblongs of warmth on the thick, patterned carpet and in each one a dog lay curled and dozing. A black labrador and two golden retrievers, all three to join the shoot presently and strictly supposed to be kept to the stable-yard, but Johnny Osborne was somewhat easy-going where they were concerned and one or the other of the gun animals, or all three, usually found their way to where the family congregated. Serena did not care for it but since she had her way on most things to do with the household and was herself country bred, she was prepared to allow her husband this one indulgence. Each time one of the servants circled the table, removing plates that had been emptied, refilling coffee cups or just unobtrusively hovering to see if anything further was required by the family, they were forced to step over each of the animals in turn but not by a flicker of an eyelash or the clenching of a muscle did any of them show irritation.

The sunshine, clear and autumn bright, touched the glowing mahogany of the sideboard and the long oval dining table. It was reflected in the silver which was used so casually and it brushed to creamy rose the exquisite silk damask which lined the walls. The light muslin curtains, white and crisp, drifted in the small breeze from an open window, and beyond the window, leading from the terrace, gardeners worked down the long sloping lawn. It was formed into a series of wide steps, each one edged with a flowerbed and neatly clipped shrubs. Beyond it were small conifers, grouped together, in several shades of green, and clusters of pitted rocks arranged so that alpine plants might grow amongst them and from their shallow crevices. The sharp green, the yellow and white petals of the delicate flowers almost covered the stone. The grass had been mown right up to them but tufts grew round their bases awaiting the gardeners' shears. Tall pine trees and junipers had been planted years ago to form a protective half circle at the bottom of the last grassy slope and a bench had been placed in their shade. There was a small lake edged with chickweed, comfrey and willowherb and gliding effortlessly across the placid water were two swans.

The house was old and lovely, built of local stone, honey-coloured in the golden light of the late autumn sun. James Osborne, Johnny Osborne's father, had bought it fifty years ago and the ivy which had been well advanced even then had grown up to the roof tiles. There were dozens of chimneys, big bay windows and elegantly turned turrets at each corner of the green slate roof. It had a look of patient endurance, comfortable and protective, like a woman approaching her middle years, her maturity giving her an added beauty and wisdom.

'I expect the ladies will attend Church this morning,' Serena remarked. 'One should really put in an appearance and the vicar does like to see us there. Anne is so punctilious about such things it would only be good manners to accompany her. What do you think, Johnny?'

'Mmm?' Her husband had reached for his post, studying

the envelopes one by one and his attention was no longer given exclusively to his wife.

'I was saying that perhaps we should go to Church before . . '

'There's one here in James' hand,' her husband interrupted her, his voice bewildered.

'One what, dear?'

'A letter.' He was holding an envelope up to the light as though trying to guess at its contents, the expression on his face becoming more and more puzzled. He reached for the pearl handled letter opener beside his plate and slit the envelope reluctantly as though he was not awfully sure he wanted to know what was within it.

'A letter from James?' His wife smiled in disbelief. 'How can that be, Johnny? Why should James send you a letter? He is upstairs in his bed at this moment, no doubt sleeping like a log and completely oblivious to time and the fact that the shoot is to start at nine-thirty. Which reminds me, Elizabeth, did you remember to ask Minty to put out your tweed skirt and stout walking shoes? We shall need them, apparently, as the rain we had yesterday has made heavy going of the ground. Lady Woodall told me when she telephoned last night. Oh Eaton,' she turned to the butler, 'would you send someone to awaken Master James and tell him he is to be down here in no less than fifteen minutes. He really is a naughty boy and I shall tell him so when . . when . . .'

Her attention was suddenly caught by something in her husband's manner and her voice faltered and then stopped completely. The first stirring of unease prickled through her and she replaced her coffee cup carefully in its saucer.

'Johnny . . .' she questioned tentatively.

'Dear sweet Jesus . . . oh dear sweet Jesus . .'

'Johnny . . . what is it . . . ?'

The three servants, Elizabeth and Teddy all turned to look at her and then at Johnny Osborne, their heads moving in unison as though pulled by the same piece of string. They waited for him to speak.

'Johnny . . . Dear Lord, what is it?' his wife repeated. 'You look quite ill. Johnny, darling, please, what is in your letter? Oh darling, please . . . Eaton . . . Jackson . . .'

Serena Osborne could feel her usual self-control slipping badly away from her. Her sharp cries of distress brought back the footman who had been just about to leave the room, and he, Eaton and Betty moved in some confusion towards the table.

Serena stood up and her nervous hands knocked over her half filled coffee cup and instantly Betty, relieved to have some concrete task on which to concentrate, began to mop at the stain on the table with a fresh napkin, wondering impassively as she did so what all the damn fuss was about. Eaton, calm and unperturbed as a well trained person of his standing should be, frowned and waved her away. Like her he had no idea what was going on but it had nothing to do with the spilled coffee, of that he was certain. More like spilled milk, if you asked him, over which it was said there was no use in crying.

Johnny Osborne stared at the opened letter which was in his hand. His face had drained of all the normal healthy colour which his love of the outdoors put there, leaving it grey and dragged down. He was a man of forty-one, in the prime of his life, tall and handsome with the dark charm which had a look of the Irish about it and his eyes were the vivid green his daughter had inherited. Forty-one and at that moment he could have been twenty years older. His hand which held the letter shook badly and the notepaper fluttered as though in a stiff wind. He sagged back in his chair and when he lifted his eyes to his wife there was despair in them.

'Johnny.' His wife's voice was almost a scream. 'If you don't tell me what is in that letter I swear I shall lose my reason.' In the background Betty gasped. 'Johnny,' Serena moaned but though she begged to know there was a look about her which said she would give anything, really, not to be told.

Her husband stared at her sightlessly and his children, though less susceptible to fear than their mother, felt a thrill of excited dread run through them as they exchanged glances.

Their father spoke. 'It's from James,' he said at last.

'It can't be, Johnny. How can it? He is upstairs in ...'

'No, he is not, Serena. He is not upstairs. Our son is not here at all.'

'Please, Johnny ...'

'It seems he is in Scotland.'

'*Scotland* ...?'

'To be more precise, in Gretna Green.'

'Gretna Green, Johnny? Heavens, what can he be doing there?' Her voice was high, amused, she would have him believe, but knowing all the same.

'Getting married, Serena. That is what he is doing there. He is getting married,' her husband answered and as he stood up, ready to savagely vent his rage and fear and dashed hopes on anything to hand, ready to throw his breakfast, indeed everything which was on the table to the far corners of the room, his wife slipped silently down between the chair and the table, fainting for the first time in her placid and uneventful life, eluding the now fearful grasp of her second son who tried to save her.

'The postman's just been, Daddy. Will I be seeing if he's left us a letter?'

'There's a good girl, darlin'.'

It was Sunday morning and the eight-fifteen delivery, the first of three that would be made that day, had left only one letter at number 11, Edge Lane. It was picked up by the baby, Clare O'Shaughnessy, who carried it into the kitchen where the usual pandemonium of Sunday morning, or

110

indeed any morning, reigned as the family got ready for Mass. Unable to catch her father's eye as he re-arranged several small McGowans, Maguires and Feeneys amongst the O'Shaughnessys on the bench, Clare placed it beside his plate before squeezing in amongst them. Matty poured out a dozen cups of strong tea, then in the careless manner her mistress deplored, placed the teapot on the letter and tossed the crocheted tea-cosy over the pot.

There were at the very least a dozen of the family around the kitchen table. Ellen, with her husband and Caitlin, had already been to early Communion. The rest would attend Mass at some time during the day. Ellen insisted upon it and they all knew there would be no getting out of it. During the week, though she herself went every day, dragging Mara when she could, she was not quite as zealous with her children though she would not have admitted it for the world. A great one for self-deception, was Ellen, though only in small and well intentioned ways. They were all good children at heart, with no badness in them and though Father Paul sometimes asked after young Michael or Dermot or Sean in that whimsical – but serious – way he had she was quick to make excuses for them, begging forgiveness of the Blessed Virgin, herself a mother who must surely understand the young. Providing they said their rosary morning and night and went once to Mass on Sunday, taking communion, and to Confession when they had sinned – small sins, she was sure – she was satisfied that their souls were in order.

It was just the same on this morning as it was on every other; noisy, cheerful, crowded. There was a delicious smell of bacon and sausages frying for those who were not to take Holy Communion or who had already participated in the Sacrament of the Eucharist. Bread freshly baked by Matty was brought straight from the oven for Ellen believed that though it was Sunday it was no reason to starve her family. They ate and they talked, they laughed and they quarrelled, just as they always did, and every few minutes Ellen begged one of them to run up and get Mara out of her bed.

'She'll be late for Mass, so she will, the wicked girl and what's keepin' her only the Holy Mother knows. She'll be preening in front of that dratted mirror deciding which hat she should wear, I'll be bound, for no girl could sleep as long as she does. Jaysus, she was in her bed before eight last night, dead to the world for I saw her tucked in meself.'

'She was fast asleep when I got up, Mammy,' Caitlin said absent-mindedly as she knelt to tie the bootlaces of one of her small nephews.

Round and round the table Ellen circled, piling bacon and fried bread on to plates as fast as they were emptied, impervious to the pleas of her family that they had had enough, pleas which they made purely out of habit, knowing their mother would take not the slightest notice.

It was young Michael who knocked on Mara's door. Once on his way to his own bedroom to shave before going to Mass, and again fifteen minutes later on his way back. When the door remained firmly closed he shouted, 'I'm coming in, Mara, whether you're decent or not.'

Ellen's face changed colour, just as Johnny Osborne's was doing at almost the exact same moment, when Michael re-entered the kitchen. The frying pan in her hand tipped slowly, her weakened wrist unable to hold it. Its contents dripped to the clean red surface of her tiled kitchen floor and under her feet the tabby cat began to lap daintily at the congealing fat which spread at her skirt. Her son's eyes had gone straight to hers, of course, and the message in them was appallingly clear, though he had not yet spoken. Her mother's heart began to pound as he moved towards her across the threshold of the kitchen with the hesitancy and reluctance of the bearer of bad news. One who would give anything not to have to divulge it and one of her flushes began, spreading most distressingly all over her body beneath her clothing, up to her neck and face, bringing beads of sweat which slid across her skin and dampened her clean bodice under the arms and in the small of her back.

'Mammy, look what you're doin',' Eammon yelled. 'Sure an' you've spilled bacon fat on me best jacket an' me off to Mass in a minute.' But slowly those about the table, sensing some fearful thing which had just invaded their cheerful, carefree world, became silent until a dropped pin could have been clearly heard.

'Son?' Ellen's voice was no more than a whisper. Oh, Blessed Virgin, you who are a mother like me, spare me the pain I am about to suffer, her fearful mind jabbered. My Mara, my beautiful girl, my sweet baby who is the light of my life must be dead for it was in her son's eyes, the horror of it. His usual merry young face was set and rigid, the muscles in his strong jaw clenched hard in his remorse at being the carrier of such dreadful news, and her own became stiff and awkward since she did not wish to hear it and only by clamping her teeth together could she hold back the wail of despair within her.

'She's ... not there, Mammy,' Michael said quietly.

For a moment the relief was so great Ellen wanted to throw the heavy iron frying pan into the air and scream her joy since it seemed her girl was not dead after all but in Michael's face was something which told her not to rejoice just yet.

'There's a ... couple of pillows in her bed...'

'Pillows, son?' Mick asked, bewildered and not yet as terrified as his wife.

'To make it look as though she's ... sleeping, Daddy,' Michael explained apologetically.

'But...?'

'Oh dear sweet Mary Mother of God bless us now and in the hour of our need...' Ellen had begun to gabble, crossing herself frantically and backing away from this terrible thing which had come into her kitchen. She didn't know what it was. Her mind could not cope with any rational explanation of what was happening. It went round and round on a treadmill, just the one dreadful sentence telling her that Mara, who should have been in her bed or here, safely at the kitchen table eating her breakfast with her family, was in neither place. That she was ... gone! That she, Ellen O'Shaughnessy, did not know the whereabouts of her innocent and lovely, her vulnerable sixteen-year-old daughter and that she had no idea what to do about it. They were all running about, the children screaming, mostly with laughter for this was a splendid excuse not to go to Mass. Search for Mara, young Michael had said. Look in every cupboard and under every bed, just as if they were playing hide and seek. They vied with one another to find her as they raced about the house and garden, shouting her name whilst in the kitchen Ellen and Mick O'Shaughnessy stared at one another in growing terror.

The children had all returned, crestfallen and without Mara, standing about the kitchen not knowing whether to go to Mass or not for Mammy and Daddy looked so strange it frightened them.

'Will I wet you some fresh tea, Mrs O'Shaughnessy?' Matty said, for wasn't a pot of tea just the thing when a body was distressed? She picked up the teapot and the letter lay there and when Mick opened it, not even recognising his daughter's handwriting in his confused anguish and began to read it out loud Ellen's scream could be heard in the next street.

It took them half an hour in a hired taxi-cab to get to Beechwood Hall. Mick and young Michael, Dermot and Sean who was fourteen and considered old enough to be involved in this man's work. They had left Ellen in the care of her daughters who had been hastily summoned by Caitlin. Their mother had sat quietly at the table after that first scream, her eyes dry and staring, her face quite expressionless, a death mask of sunken cheeks and eyesockets, so little like their dear, hot-tempered, volatile Mammy they were all silenced and fearful. The letter was still in her hands, crushed and re-crushed between them and the ecstatic message it contained which her daughter had written, of love and the splendid future which was to be Mara's as Mrs James Osborne was barely readable. Not that Ellen wanted to read it ever again. Its contents were engraved on her broken heart, her unforgiving broken heart which the girl who had been her daughter had shattered irretrievably. It no longer mattered how, or why, or when. She was gone. Ellen's little girl, the daughter she had loved and fussed over, reproved and reprimanded was gone. It did not matter where for as far as Ellen was concerned Mara O'Shaughnessy was lost to her forever. She was dead. Dead and in her coffin, buried without the sins she had committed washed from her wicked soul by the last rites. Unshriven. She had gone to purgatory, the best place for her, in Ellen's opinion, and she could see no reason for the menfolk to go raving up to Beechwood demanding satisfaction for was it not too late for that? Mara was past redemption now so what was the point? The bird-twitterings of the others were scarcely heard as they crowded about her.

If Eaton was surprised to see the four broad-shouldered, black-visaged men, working men, at the front door to Beechwood Hall, he gave no sign of it. Anything that happened on this quite dreadful day would not surprise him and so, though he was inclined to order them round to the back door and would have done so had he not known who they were and why they were here, he restrained himself. It was no more than an hour since the letter had come which had sent his mistress fainting and distraught to her bed and produced in his master a white-faced, rage-filled frustration which was threatening to explode into a savagery they had none of them known he possessed, but already the servants were all aware that the son of the house, the heir to the noble name of Osborne, the eldest son in whom all great families have such hopes. had run away to Gretna Green to marry an Irish trollop from the back streets of Liverpool.

So these men, collarless and dishevelled, must be her people, for who else as Irish looking and as explosive looking would call at nine-fifteen on a Sunday morning at the front door of his master's house?

'We'll see himself, if you please,' Mick said grimly, 'and at once.' His normally peaceable and good-humoured face was rigid, white and drawn with pain since, like Ellen, he had doted on his beautiful daughter. The shock of it still showed in the blankness of his eyes and the obvious tremors which shook his ageing body, but he was dignified, held in to himself. His heart was breaking over the loss of his daughter but he was a fair man and conceded that what Mara and this man's son had done was not this man's fault. He would like what had happened as little as Mick did, so Mick was prepared, for now, to speak low and bear himself with restraint.

Not so his sons who flung themselves about the small drawing room into which Eaton had shown them with all the madness of freshly caged beasts.

'You are the ... the girl's father?' Johnny Osborne said baldly as he entered the room. No greeting, no sign of the usual engaging courtesy with which he greeted those who came to his door whatever their rank. His hair, still as thick and as dark as when he was a young man, was disordered as though he had in the last hour run his hands through it a dozen or more times. He had loosened his tie and he had the air of a man who is teetering on the edge of something which could prove to be dangerous. He was, like Mick, mild-mannered and inclined to be cheerful, allowing others to do as they liked as long as they did not interfere with him. His children had been brought up to be the same. They were well mannered, respectful of their elders and of the traditions of their class. They had been taught to be dutiful, aware of their responsibilities, to be thoughtful of others and to care for those who were not as well placed as they They were young still, and sometimes rebellious though not unduly so, which was natural in the young but on the whole they were sweet-tempered and obedient. This bitter blow his son had dealt him would never be forgiven and as he stared in arrogant loathing at the four truculent Irish faces which crowded together in his wife's dainty drawing room he wished he could hang the lot of them for what they had done to him and to his dreams of a splendid marriage for his son. To the continuing of the fine breeding which had run in his family for generations. Like marrying like, as it should, and now, with the taste of bile in his throat, he viewed the men who had spawned the Irish biddy his son had taken as a bride.

'That I am and these are her brothers. We've come to fetch her home...' since Mara's jumbled note had made no mention of Gretna Green. 'There'll be no marriage to one of your family so I'd be obliged if you'd tell her her Daddy's here. Sure an' I'd look lively if I were you for these lads o' mine are hot-headed and short-tempered.'

Johnny Osborne, incensed at the Irishman's tone and at being ordered about in his own home, clenched his fists ominously. 'I can see that but I'm afraid they are just going to have to control their tempers since your daughter is not here, so I'd be obliged if you would get out of my house right now.'

There was a threatening movement behind Mick's back as the three young men surged in menacing disbelief. Johnny moved lightly from one foot to the other. He was pitched into an anguish which he could do nothing about. His pain was almost too much for him to bear and his own violent feelings frightened him and he longed for one of these rough men to do something which would give him a reason to unleash it on them.

'I don't believe you.'

'It is a matter of supreme indifference to me what you

117

believe. You must do as you please, O'Shaughnessy. I know you are employed in one of my warehouses, as was your father before you, and I take it you know I am a man of my word. If I say she is not here, then she is not here and if you don't go peaceably I shall call my men to remove the lot of you, believe me.'

Mick took no notice. 'Then where is she, and that black-guard who has dishonoured her?'

'Be very careful what you say, man. I believe my son to be innocent in this affair.'

'Innocent, when he has ... has persuaded my daughter to leave her good home, to desert her family and break her Mammy's heart, so she has, rushing into a marriage which is no marriage at all in the eyes of Holy Mother Church.'

'I have no knowledge of that. I am aware that a man of ... of your faith would believe so but in the eyes of the law they will be man and wife by now and I can assure you I like it no better than you ... and I repeat, I cannot believe my son would enter into this ... this misalliance without a good deal of persuasion on your daughter's part. Taking into account the ... the dissimilarity between our two families I would say she had the most to gain, wouldn't you?'

There was a cold and disdainful sneer on Johnny Osborne's contorted face and young Michael's fists were seen to clench dangerously. He moved restlessly, swaying in the manner of a pugilist and his father, sensing it behind him, put out a warning hand.

'My girl is decent and beautiful, Mr Osborne, and worthy of any man's love, even your son who you seem to think is not to blame in this affair. What I want to know is where she is and what has been done to her?'

'What has presumably been done to girls such as her from the beginning of time,' Johnny Osborne taunted coarsely, pleased when Mick O'Shaughnessy's grey face became even greyer, the pain in the man, though it did not lessen his own, feeding something in him which was joyless. 'Perhaps if you had kept a closer watch on her this would not have happened.' His voice was vicious. 'I am not intimately acquainted with the customs of . . . of your people regarding your girl children but we keep ours sheltered and safe, not allowing them to roam about unaccompanied associating with any man who crosses their path. Can you blame my son if he was seduced into . . .'

'My daughter was as innocent and decent as any girl in this land until she was wronged by your son. She was brought up to respect her family, to love God and to keep herself pure . . .'

'Pure! Jesus Christ, that's a good one, that is. She knew enough to trap my boy into proposing marriage to her. Pure, was she? Well, whatever she was, whatever she had she used it to good effect. One can only wonder how many more she was pure with before she got her claws into my son. Eighteen he is, eighteen years old and tied for life to some Irish peasant girl who will drag him down to her level . . .'

He was nearly weeping and for a strange moment Mick felt a surge of pity for him, knowing exactly how he felt. They were both of them fighting on the same side in a way, completely in accord with one another – except over which of their children was at fault – over this disaster which had scythed through their families. For the same reason they were both devastated by it, knowing that their children were headed on a path which was right for neither of them, which could bring neither of them happiness. Their worlds could not be further apart, coming as they did from a different culture, religion and class, and only heartache could follow. The man did not care what he said in his hurt, wanting to hurt others just as badly. He himself desired nothing more than to smash his fist into Johnny Osborne's contemptuous face but fisticuffs would do no good here.

His sons thought otherwise and young Michael's roar of outrage could be heard in every corner of the house. In her bedroom Serena Osborne turned a white and senseless face towards her daughter who sat beside her bed and began to weep again, something she had not allowed herself to do for many years. Though she had told herself only an hour earlier that whatever had happened to James she would overcome it, as she had been taught to overcome all of life's trials, she really did not think she could face up to this. To the disgrace, to the pity of her friends, to the ostracism she might face with a daughter-in-law such as James was to bring home. She would rather he was dead, really she would.

'Who is it?' she whispered. 'Who is downstairs?'

'I believe it is ... her family, mother. Do you want me to go down and find out?' Elizabeth, only sixteen herself, bewildered and anxious, was not quite sure how to behave with this strange and weakened mother who seemed to be stupefied by her son's perfidy. Her mother's maid hovered discreetly with smelling salts and cologne, ready to run down to the kitchen for hot tea or a cold compress and Elizabeth felt she herself was really not needed in this daintily feminine room which was Serena Osborne's, remaining only from a sense of duty. She felt uncomfortable with the woman her mother had become and longed to be down in the paddock where Teddy had gone to escape the melancholy atmosphere of the house. Any excuse would be gratefully seized upon to get away from it, even the awful prospect of confronting a father who would, no doubt, be as devastated as her own.

'I can see no reason for it, Elizabeth, the damage is done,' her mother replied in her strange new manner, 'but go by all means if you must.'

Eaton who, though he tried to go about his butling business just as usual, setting an example to the rest of the servants who were inclined to hang about waiting to see what was to happen next, hovered by the green baize door which separated the kitchens from the hallway. At the sound of the uproar he turned swiftly, beckoning to a pair of sturdy footmen who stood beside him and with a ragged order to

Betty to 'run like the wind, girl, and fetch some lads from outside' he headed towards the small drawing room. There was the sound of a crash and he and the footmen began to run. They and Miss Elizabeth reached the closed door together, jostling quite foolishly against one another in an effort to get it open.

Elizabeth was the first to enter. The incredible scene which met her eyes was difficult to take in at first since the only thing amongst the noisy confusion she seemed able to focus on was the familiar and good-humoured face of the groom from Woodall Park. The man who, for the past twelve months, she had done her best to avoid in any way she could.

His face was not good-humoured now as it snarled its rage into that of her father's. They were not exactly grappling with one another since an older man held the groom's arms. Two younger men, one no more than a boy, really, were circling about them like two dogs longing to get into a fight.

'You bastard, you foul-mouthed bastard . . .' the groom, Michael, that was his name, her cool, uninvolved brain told her, was yelling into her father's face. 'That randy bugger you call a son is well known for it . . . a seducer of young girls with his hand up the skirt of any female who gets within a yard of him. They're none of them safe with him, the servants and farm women, him and that bastard of Woodall's. Riding off on their bloody horses looking for girls to prey on . . . a couple of tom-cats an' now the bugger's got my sister. I'll kill him when I get hold of him, the rutting sod. Don't you lay your filthy tongue round my sister's good name . . . an innocent girl . . .'

His face was distorted with fury and grief and savage pride which had been seriously wounded and his spittle sprayed in a fine mist over Johnny Osborne but the force of their shared anguish was beginning to lessen. The two older men had been flinging insults at one another for the past ten minutes, each blaming the other's child for the catastrophe, not knowing what else to do to ease the despair, the bitterness, the shame which had befallen each family, and yet aware now that it did no good. It was too late. What did it matter who was the instigator in this since the outcome was the same. A decent Catholic girl had been disgraced. A young and blameless boy had been seduced, and so the men fell away from one another, hopeless and helpless before the inevitability of it all.

A dull, heavy silence fell and Eaton, beckoning to the two eagerly curious footmen, backed from the room, recognising that the violence was over though he was not prepared to leave the hall and return to his pantry, not yet. He and the footmen and a couple of gardeners who had been summoned and who had hurried, cap in hand, through the side entrance, stood awkwardly just beyond the drawing room door.

'So there's nothing to be done,' Johnny Osborne said heavily. 'It seems your girl and my son have run away together. They are in Scotland, I have been informed. You will no doubt have heard that marriages are performed in a place called Gretna Green?'

'Yes . . .' Mick turned away, now that the danger of murder was over, his shoulders slumped, wondering how he was to ease Ellen's despair, knowing he never would since nothing could bring her child back, not as she had been this time yesterday.

'Mrs James Osborne by now, I suppose.' Johnny Osborne's voice was ragged but suddenly there came to his eye a strange gleam and he lifted his head. What if James had not married her. What if this was no more than a seduction, a game, a pursuit on his son's part which was to lead only to his own gratification. What if James, as all young men did at some time in their lives, especially young gentlemen, had done no more than bed her, then . . . Sweet Jesus . . . then there was still a chance for him. The girl paid off. Any unfortunate outcome of the liaison taken care of and James still free and, though not entirely blameless, ready to marry, eventually, a well-bred, eminently suitable, preferably wealthy young lady of his own class. Boys will be boys, after all and though he would be strictly dealt with did they not all go through the stage of falling in love with a parlourmaid or an actress? He had done so himself but he had not married her.

But the prowling, snapping anger in the faces of the four Irishmen, decent men and not of the order to be paid off and told to keep their mouths shut, had made it quite plain that any hopes he might have had in that direction were to be consumed and turned to ashes in his mouth. They would not allow it. No amount of money would buy their silence, their acceptance of what, in the old days, would have been considered quite usual. It would not restore the virtue of the girl his son had tarnished and they would settle for nothing less than marriage. Female virginity was enormously valuable, in this man's daughter as it was in his own, and damaged goods were difficult to get rid of.

For the first time he noticed Elizabeth standing with her back to the door. She was transfixed, it appeared to him, her eyes on the fierce, knife-edged anger in the face of one of the younger men. There was a strangeness in her, a tearing expression of indecision in her eyes as though something inside her was fighting a battle. She was white-faced and somehow unsteady, frightened, he was sure, of the violence in this room and could you blame her? His little girl who he had protected all her life and to whom he had shown nothing but kindness and affection. He was not sure how she had got here but it was no place for her and he must get her away before she was hurt by it.

'Darling,' he murmured gently, taking her hand, ready to lead her to her mother. 'Come away before . . .'

'Aye, take her away, Mr Osborne,' a bitter voice said. 'She's no more than a child, as my girl was. But your son changed all that and I mean to see he treats her with respect. It will

123

be marriage, by God, if not in this Gretna Green place then in Holy Mother Church right here in...'

Elizabeth's voice cut through Mick's words like a knife.

'They cannot be married in Gretna Green, father,' she said and slowly every man in the room turned to look at her.

'What...?' and the narrowed, sharp-daggered eyes of the groom from Woodall Park cut into her shrinking flesh.

'One of the parties involved must reside there for three weeks before they are allowed to marry.' She sounded like a child who is repeating, parrot-fashion, something which it has been taught. 'James and ... and ... this gentleman's daughter have ... it has only been a day since ... They will not yet be married, father...' and for some strange reason which Johnny Osborne could not even begin to understand, she began to weep.

7

She had ridden to Woodall Park at first, had even got as far as the stable-yard gate, drawn there by a bewildering but urgent need to talk to Harry about the devastating events of the previous day for if anyone could help her to put it into some kind of order Elizabeth knew it would be he. Though she was young and inexperienced in the ways of men she was not a fool and she had become increasingly aware since last August and Harry's coming-of-age party, as the months had drawn out in the pleasant way of life her class led, that Harry's affectionate, one could only call it brotherly welcome of her to his home, had undergone a subtle change. It had become warmer somehow; less casual is how she would have described it. She was a young woman now, his manner seemed to say, and one he was delighted to see and when he smiled at her in that lazy way he had there was a glow in his eyes which was decidedly agreeable. Her own response to it surprised her somewhat since after all it was only Harry, the older brother of her brother's friend, the boy, the youth, the young man she had known for as long as she could remember. But there was something in him that was altered. He looked for her in any room he entered. When their eyes met she knew he felt the same pleasure she did and he seemed to find more and more reasons to spend time in her company. He did not commit himself in any way but there was something between them, he appeared to be telling her, and if it was left to grow naturally and slowly, if she allowed it to grow slowly and naturally it would gain a meaning which would be worthwhile and a pleasure to them both.

They understood one another, she and Harry, she had decided. They were alike. Their minds matched and their senses were in harmony. She had seen it in his face, that spark of awakening desire, quickly controlled since she was a young lady of breeding and he was a gentleman. She knew the rules only too well. She had been brought up on them, accepted them and so had he and no matter what his male body told him it wanted he would not compromise her, would not flout convention with improper behaviour unless he wanted to take the next step in the pattern of courtship.

She was at ease with him always. They had no need of words at times for there was a symmetry in their thoughts which linked them. They were of the same class and had been brought up in exactly the same way, allowing for the difference in their gender. Harry was a man now, no longer a high-spirited boy like her brother James, or his brother Hugh. He was learning to manage the estate which would one day be his. He would be expected to settle down and marry, get himself a son to carry on the line just as generations of Woodalls had done before him.

But she was not yet ready to declare, even to herself, that she felt anything other than friendship towards him, that what she did feel was no more than the strong and affectionate warmth one feels for a friend. She was young yet, and perhaps, who could tell, some other man might walk into her life and positively enthrall her. With Harry it was warmth and safety, familiarity, deep satisfying silences and moments of compatible humour, a shared interest in country life and country pursuits, a shared belief in the rightness of their privileged existence and the knowledge that it would go on forever, the inbred arrogance of their class both of them had but which neither were aware of. Harry was simply Harry. Always there, trustworthy and understanding, his strength, which was not of the forceful kind, ready for her to lean on should she need it and though even he had not yet considered it through to its natural conclusion, since he perhaps thought her to be young yet, it would come if she wanted it.

This being so on the day after the dreadful confrontation which had taken place between her father and the Irish family, and not only that but the shock of seeing *him* in her mother's drawing room, she could think of no one she would rather unburden herself to than Harry.

Teddy had vanished without a word, as young men will do at a time of crisis, she had thought bitterly, unconcerned with his mother's collapse, or perhaps, Elizabeth decided more kindly, unable to deal with it and the appalling circumstances which had caused it. She tried to imagine him in her mother's bedroom, as she herself had been, holding her hand as she herself had done, doing her best to calm her back to her normal serenity. The smelling salts, the cologne, the endless cups of fragrant tea, the drawn curtains and the atmosphere of disaster which pervaded not only her mother's room but the whole house had dragged down Elizabeth's loyal and dutiful spirit.

She had done her best, understanding her mother's devastation for she loved James too, and like her mother and father was appalled at the thought of him married to some working-class Irish girl. How could he do this to them? What had happened to lead him into such a mad alliance? Was the girl to have his child or had she some other hold on him? Pretty she must be since all men liked a pretty face but surely that was no reason to marry her? No wonder mother was swooning and distraught in her darkened room, so distraught the doctor had had to be called to administer a draught which had put her to sleep.

Elizabeth had refused George's offer to ride with her and though he had been vexed, telling her in the way of an old family servant to whom a certain amount of familiarity was allowed that her father would give her 'what for', riding out alone, he had let her go. The whole house, and even the stable was in a state of turmoil for unusual circumstances such as these knocked all the conventions on the head. George had obviously thought so as he returned to the tack room.

The day was mild for late October and the stretch of continuous woodland between Beechwood and Woodall was a gold and copper carpet of autumn leaves crunching beneath her mare's hooves. The trees were almost bare, just a few tenacious drifts of bronze clinging in the misted tree-tops, one or two leaves still falling, featherlike, as she passed beneath the branches. The tranquil emptiness of the familiar woods, the well-trodden path between the browning ferns which she had ridden a thousand times in the past, the old gate she had jumped in contest with her brothers, the pungent smell of the decaying season, soothed her and it was not until she was at the Woodall stable-yard did the appalling thought occur to her that in her agitated state she had quite forgotten that *he* would most likely be working about the yard today. Just because his sister had run off with her brother ... Oh dear God, they would be related if ... if ... he would be her brother-in-law, and could she face him now, at this treacherous moment, if he should be there? Could she ride in and hand him the reins, take his proffered hand to help her dismount, look into his eyes as she had not done for three months just as though yesterday had not happened? Could she? When at this very moment her father and his were doing their best to get to Gretna Green before James and this ... this girl he vowed he was to marry, actually got into bed together, which seemed unlikely. Forty-eight hours since James and ... the girl had left Liverpool and by the end of that first day they would have discovered, James and ... her, that they could not be married immediately and Elizabeth knew her brother well enough to be aware that he would not be slow in taking advantage of the situation even if he meant the girl no harm nor insult. And the rugged old Irishman who had faced up to her father yesterday would have nothing less than marriage for his despoiled daughter, if that was the case, he had said, and the groom, his son, Michael O'Shaughnessy, whose name was branded into her brain, had violently agreed with him.

She drew in her mare, stopping just short of the gateway. Her breath quickened in panic. Was that him leading a bay from the stable? Were those his legs she could see beneath the belly of Tim Woodall's roan? She had not been in this yard for a long time, avoiding it and him by simply throwing the reins over the gatepost and calling out, knowing one of the grooms would come running to see to her mare. She could, of course, ride round to the front of the house and tether the animal to a convenient rosebush but if she did Lady Woodall would think her mad and Harry would ask why. Really, she could not cope with all the wondering and bemusement and for two pins she'd ride home again. It had seemed a good idea in the darkened cloister of her mother's bedroom to come out here, let the fresh air blow through the cobwebbed confusion of her mind, talk to Harry, have the calm and reasonable quality of his disposition put the matter into perspective for her, but now, suddenly, as though Michael O'Shaughnessy's shadow had fallen across her, she could not get away quickly enough.

She turned and with a clatter of iron-shod hooves on the cobblestones, galloped away madly in the direction from which she had just come.

He was leading Monarch, Master Harry's restive hunter, from his stable when he heard her mare's hooves and as he stared, frozen into stillness by the sight of her, he was just in time to see her go like an arrow in a straight and frenzied flight across the park towards the woodland. He didn't stop to think, or to consider the consequences not only to his employment here with the Woodall family, particularly when Sir Charles heard of his encounter with Mr Osborne the previous day, but to the expensive animal he had been about to rub down and which could be injured in a wild ride such as he was about to undertake.

Graceful and swift as a bird he leaped on to the hunter's bare back and gripping his mane with strong brown fingers rode full tilt for the stable-yard gate. He was vaguely aware of Fred Renshaw's startled face, gawping open-mouthed from under the belly of the roan he was currying, and if he heard Mr Jackson's shout of outrage from the stable door he took no notice. The horse's hooves crashed like a hammer attacking an anvil and Fred could swear he saw sparks fly from the cobblestones as Michael, who had evidently lost his mind, steered the hunter across them and on through the open gate. There the animal, excited to be free of the confines of the stable-yard, fresh and eager to go, stretched his long, fine legs across the rough turf of the park, great clods of earth flying up and away from him as he gathered speed.

Suddenly he was in the trees and the man on his back, after letting him run free across the park, took control, steering him expertly through the golden-hazed trunks of the autumn woodland. His knees pressed mercilessly into the hunter's sides and with superb horsemanship, since he had no saddle and only a bridle, kept him to the rough but well-defined path Elizabeth Osborne had taken. He could hear her ahead of him and he was certain she knew he was behind her. Her mare could almost be said to have bolted for surely no rider would go deliberately at such headlong speed and in this difficult terrain. There were trees and young saplings springing up in front of her, undergrowth still thick with summer foliage, low branches, hazardous and ready to whip an unwary horseman from his mount's back.

He gained on her. Her mare was young, frightened and of slighter build than his own mount and when, in a small but welcome patch of clearing, he drew alongside her she let him lean across and take the reins from her and into his own firm grasp.

'Whoa ... hold on, whoa, Monarch ... Slow down, slow ... steady, boy. Hold, old fellow, hold ...' The two animals, his and the terrified mare on whose back Elizabeth clung blindly, were strong and though the mare was tired, plunged and pulled and nearly had him over. He could see the ground tilt dangerously close to his face which appeared to be on a level with Elizabeth's knee but gradually, responding to his familiar voice, the hunter slowed to a walk and the smaller animal had no choice but to do the same.

They could not speak at first, either of them, Elizabeth Osborne and Michael O'Shaughnessy, and it had nothing at all to do with the wild ride they had just endured. Their breathing was laboured and both sat for several long moments, their heads hanging, their chests heaving, then, throwing a leg over the hunter's back, Michael slid to the ground. Moving round the animal's tossing head to Elizabeth, he looked up at her, his face expressionless.

'Get down,' he ordered and she did. She stood meekly whilst he led the horses to a tree from which several low branches sprang and tethering them to one of them he turned to face her.

'What the hell d'you think you're doing?' he asked harshly.

130

'I don't know what you mean. I was merely riding home and there was no need for you to chase after me as though my mare was bolting.'

'She was, but 'tis not that I'm talking about. I'm talking about your damned interference in what doesn't concern you. I'm talking about you meddling in the affairs of my family . . .'

'Really, you have no right to . . .'

'What the divil did you speak up for yesterday? It was nothing at all to do with you. Do you not want your fine brother to marry my sister, is that it? Is that why you told your father about the marriage laws in Scotland, so that he and my Pa could get up there and bring them back before she could take your hallowed name?'

'What difference does it make? They will be married anyway.' Her voice was low and weary. 'Whether my father and yours get to them before they . . .' She paused delicately.

'Before your brother deflowers her, is that what you're tryin' to say? We have another, more earthy word than that, us working-class lads, an' d'you know what it is?' He told her and felt a great sense of satisfaction at the appalled look on her face. She had never heard the word before, of that he was certain but she knew what it meant and it had nothing to do with the discreetly modest lovemaking she would share with Harry Woodall. Oh yes, he'd seen it, the tender look of love his master's son had directed at this beautiful girl and he'd hated him for it. He'd heard the gossip in the servants' hall as well and the speculation on when the betrothal would be announced and had been relieved in some insane way by the reassurance of Mrs Blythe that it would not be until after Miss Elizabeth had been presented at court when she was eighteen. It made not the slightest difference to him, Jesus and all His Angels knew that, but he'd been glad, glad that there were two years before that took place. And he was not unaware that for the past year almost, she had been avoiding him. Not once had she come into the yard though she still rode over regularly to Woodall to visit Miss Sophie and so what conclusion could he draw from that, he had asked himself.

'You have a vile tongue,' she said even more quietly and he felt a spasm of shame run through him. She could not be blamed for what had happened, nor for her upbringing which had made her, like his good Catholic mother, appalled at the thought of a union between their two families, though for different reasons.

He took a step towards her and she did not move away from him. 'I'm sorry,' he said. 'I don't know what the divil got into me. Sure an' I shouldn't have spoken to you like that.'

'We are all ... upset.'

'Upset, is it?' He laughed harshly and she looked at him steadily, catching his sudden pain. She felt surprise since it had not occurred to her that a man of his background and standing would object, could object to one of his people moving up to hers. It seemed to Elizabeth that this man's sister had done well for herself. She had bettered her own situation by forming a relationship with Elizabeth's brother and when she married him, which there was no doubt in Elizabeth's mind she would do, and was accepted, if she was, by her new social peers, she would become a member of the most privileged class in the county. What more could a girl from a working-class Irish family ask? She would find it hard to adjust, Elizabeth was aware of that, but if she had half the boldness and strength of will her brother obviously possessed she would overcome that obstacle in time. But he seemed to be saying his family were against it as much as Elizabeth's own.

'This is surely a fine marriage for her. Are you not pleased that your sister has done so well for herself?' she asked, not meaning to patronise, but his face darkened ominously.

'You high-toned bitch! You condescending, supercilious bitch! Who the hell d'you think you are to speak of my sister

132

as though she was some crawling biddy from the stews of Liverpool? As though your bloody, high and mighty brother was doing her a favour by sticking his...' Here he spoke so obscenely she flinched away from him again, shuddering and in a moment he was beside her, his expression appalled.

'Holy Mother of God, forgive me. I've done it again. Sure an' it's me wild Irish temper ... Jesus, I don't know what comes over me...' He passed his hand over his sweated face, his eyes haunted, ''tis just the Mammy...'

'The ... the Mammy...?'

'My mother. Begod, she'll never get over it. It tears me heart right out of me to see her grieving so and then to hear you talk as though we should be glad. Mara was...'

'Mara?'

'Jesus, Joseph an' Mary! You don't even know her name, do you? All this trouble an' my mother ... and yours ... their worlds upside down and you don't even know the name of the girl ... Christ, she's to be your ... God almighty, you people! You care for nothing but your own position, your own wounded pride and the names of those you ... you spoil are not even known to you.'

'I'm sure your sister wasn't ... spoiled against her will. I know my own brother and though he has his faults he would certainly not force a girl to ... do anything she was not willing to do.'

All the while she spoke and as she listened to Michael O'Shaughnessy, Elizabeth was acutely conscious of him, of his physical presence so close to her. She tried hard to be calm, to be as serene and moderate as her mother would be, and had always been until this terrible trouble struck her, but his nearness did something to her which she had no control over. She could barely speak her mouth was so dry and her tongue performed awkwardly, making the words sound strange when she did. She was breathless and edgy, afraid he would see the trembling of her limbs and yet at the same time she was filled with a strange and subtle joy which was wicked in the face of so much unhappiness. She tried hard to listen to what he was saying. She wanted to be reasonable, to see this from his side, from the viewpoint of his family but it was very hard to concentrate on it, whatever it might be, when her senses were so curiously, acutely winging towards him. She could see a pulse beating just beneath the smooth brown surface of his skin where his throat dipped into the open neck of his shirt. She found herself watching his mouth as he talked, fascinated by the way it curled at the corners, giving him a whimsical air of humour, despite the anger in him. His hair was uncombed, springing and vigorous, as dark as her own, but where a streak of sunlight touched it, lit to a deep chestnut. His eyes had narrowed as he looked at her and the pupils, a dramatic black in the centre of the deep and lovely blue, were dilating in the most curious way. His eyelashes tangled together at the corner of his eyes, long and fine and tipped with gold, like a child's. She could see the fine dark shadow on his chin where he had not yet shaved and smell the scent of his skin. Was it lemon, she wondered idly, bemusedly, and with it was the familiar and pleasant smell of the horses he worked with, the musky odour of male sweat and the sweetness of his breath which she remembered from the night she had danced with him.

She was not aware as she watched him that he had stopped snarling at her, that he had become quite still and was studying her openly in just the same way she was studying him. They were several feet apart, facing one another in the sun-dappled clearing, not close but near enough to be aware of the other's pulse beat and heart beat, skin odour and skin texture. It was making them both dangerously weak and dizzy with the strength of the curiosity they had about one another and yet it was more than just idle curiosity and they both knew it. This was not the scrutiny with which one class views another, nor the physical interest shown

134

between man and woman. It was more, much more and both were afraid to name it.

The silence which had fallen was warm like velvet and Elizabeth felt an overpowering and languid desire to move closer to him, to put up a questing hand to the smoothness of his cheek, to take a closer, more searching look at the shape of his mouth which was undoubtedly the most fascinating she had ever seen.

Their eyes locked and neither could look away and neither knew quite what to do next. They were both aware of what they wanted since the strong physical attraction which had flared up instantaneously a year ago like a match striking tinder drew them towards one another. It was strong and wilful, that feeling, and would get out of hand if one of them did not step back from it, but which one? Certainly not Michael who was snared in the trap of his masculine need to have her body against his and not Elizabeth who had no experience of such things, nor how to evade them. They were young and healthy. Their bodies were ready to mate in the natural way of young animals but their minds were worlds apart and each one was screaming soundlessly its warning of the danger they were so carelessly playing with, but it seemed to make no difference.

'This is how it was with James,' Elizabeth remembered thinking as Michael's hand drifted to her cheek and her own rose and closed over his. At the same moment she could see the thought was in him too, and the understanding.

'We can blame neither of them,' he said softly and she knew what he meant.

His hand still cupped her cheek and when it slid round to the nape of her neck and pulled her gently nearer she was unable to stop herself from stepping close to him. She watched his mouth curve in that captivating smile, then the sunlight was blotted out as his lips came to rest, light as a butterfly, on her own.

135

'You're the most beautiful girl I've ever met,' he murmured, his lips still against hers. 'You dazzle me. I've seen no one since you came into the stable-yard last year,' which was not strictly true but his heart meant it if his body lied. 'Elizabeth.' Her name, for the first time on his lips, was like honey. She could not speak, nor even tried. 'Elizabeth ... Elizabeth ...' and his mouth moved on hers until, quite naturally, her lips parted. She breathed into his open mouth and he returned it, sweet and warm and enchanting her.

Michael knew he must be very careful with her. Her response to him excited him, delighted him, but he was wise enough to know he must not alarm her. This would be her first sexual encounter and though his own more experienced body demanded to move on, to crush her against him, to explore and caress, he held himself back. He was bewildered by his own concern for her since in the past he had always taken joyfully any pleasure offered to him but though he tried to ignore the feeling, to take what she seemed to be saying might be his, he found he could not do so.

Regretfully he stood away from her. He kept both his hands on her shoulders and when he looked into her eyes he was not surprised to see, mixed with her unconscious sexuality, a soft relief.

He smiled. 'Sure an' you're lovely, Lizzie Osborne.'

'No one has ever called me that,' she said, just as though what had happened between them was the most natural thing in the world and nothing to remark on.

'Do you like it?' he teased.

'I don't know. I would have to get used to it.' Her voice was grave and still she made no move to step away from him.

' 'Tis an Irish name. At least my grandmother was called Lizzie and a grand old lady she was. Do you know, you have a look of the Irish about you.'

'Have I?' She began to laugh.

'Oh indeed. 'Tis in the shape of your face and the green of your eyes. The colour of Ireland, they say, though I've not been after seein' it meself.'

'My father's are the same but no one else in the family. Strangely, he is called Sean, which is Irish, I believe.'

As she said his name the ghost of Johnny Osborne stepped instantly between them and in some confusion his daughter moved away from Sir Charles Woodall's groom. The smiling magic which had enveloped them was sharply dispersed like mist in a breeze, leaving them exposed and vulnerable to the pulling drag of their separate classes, culture and customs and his voice was harsh when he spoke.

'It is that and haven't I a brother of the very same name, bejasus. But you'd best be getting home now, Elizabeth Osborne, or your Papa will be lookin' for you.'

'Hardly. He has gone to Scotland on urgent family business,' she managed to say, her face smooth and untroubled, as she was, she would have him believe.

'So he has, to be sure, an' what will be the outcome, d'you think?'

'Oh, I would imagine you and I will become related, wouldn't you?'

'Will you enjoy having a wild Irish mick for a brother-in-law, then? Will you invite him to join the hunt and to dine at your table afterwards? Will he bring his eleven brothers and sisters and his fifteen nieces and nephews and will you introduce them all to your fine friends, will you? These are my relations by marriage, will you say, or will you pretend we don't exist? Will your family make up some tale about Mara, pretending she's from the Irish gentry with a bob or two to her name? She'll not disgrace you, you know. Always wanted to be a lady, did Mara. Sure an' she always thought she was one an' she'll have no trouble fittin' in to the role at all, at all. A cut above the rest of us an' always was, or so she believes, so you've no need to think she'll bring shame to that fine brother of yours.'

His face jerked with the depth of his bitterness and she knew with utter certainty that it was not his sister's affair with her brother which was eating him up but something else entirely. He was a light-hearted, carefree young man, she imagined, who would make no objection to any man his sister married, up or down the social scale, providing her husband was good to her and could provide her with what she had always had. Even the difference in their religion would not worry him unduly, she suspected, since there were good men and evil men of all creeds and their belief or disbelief in a particular God did not change their character. She could visualise him moving blithely through life, good-natured, good-humoured, accepting cheerfully what came his way, shrugging his shoulders jauntily if it was not as splendid as the other fellow's. But this outrage he seemed to be telling her he suffered was not on his sister's account but for another reason altogether. It appeared to her that, like herself, he was practical enough to accept what had happened; had accepted it after his initial shock and natural affront. The girl would marry James and the ripple of astonishment in both their worlds would soon pass. They would never meet, of course, the Irish family and hers, but it would all be smoothed over, made to seem quite suitable by her father, for James' sake, who was, after all, the heir, and the influence Johnny Osborne had in Liverpool would silence the whispers. And this man, the girl's brother, was well aware of it and yet he was snarling and ugly again, glaring at her with eyes which were like blue glittering ice between his tangled lashes.

She must get away. She must get on her mare and ride away to the safety of her home. She was suddenly terrified of what had just taken place between them, appalled, since it had seemed so easy and so natural, so right, and of course, it was not right at all and she wondered, agonised on how it had happened. She had allowed him for some reason she could not even remember now to touch her, to kiss her, to treat her as though they were equals. She was Elizabeth Osborne, daughter of a great house, and he was a groom. Dear God, it was like some penny novelette and she was ashamed, ashamed. How had it happened? Wasn't one misfortune in the family enough with James carrying on – was that the term – with an Irish maidservant, without herself taking up with the maidservant's brother? She must be mad . . . mad . . .

She turned away, blindly reaching out to her mare. She stumbled over the root of the tree to which the animal was tethered and almost fell but when, instinctively, he put out a hand to steady her she flinched away from him.

'Please don't . . .'

'Of course. I beg your pardon.' His face was a mask of rigid pallor and his eyes were mocking.

'Thank you . . . for catching my mare.' She was mouthing the conventional words and assuming the conventional and proper role any lady would assume with a groom, treating the whole matter as though they were no more than that since it seemed the safest and only way to treat it. He had stopped her horse from bolting and quite properly she was thanking him.

' 'Twas no trouble at all. Any man would have done the same.'

'What . . . what will you tell Jackson?' She turned back for a moment, concerned as any lady would be that her rescuer would not be punished for what he had done since Monarch was a thoroughbred, expensive and irreplaceable. He . . . the groom . . . would have to account somehow for his astonishing action.

'Now then, Miss Osborne.' His voice was as mocking as his expression. 'There'll be no trouble to me, begorra. Wasn't I doin' just what you said? Wasn't meself in the yard and didn't I see your little mare take off like a greyhound an' with yourself clinging on for dear life. Lost the reins, so you had, an' could I do anything else but leap on this owd horse's back an' come after you? I may not be a gentleman, but bejasus I know when a lady needs a helping hand, so I do.' He grinned as he deliberately thickened his Irish brogue.

'Well then...'

'Aye, well then, you'd best be off. They'll be needing you at home, I shouldn't wonder, an' when you meet me sister as you surely will today or tomorrow, since the Mammy won't have her in the house, tell her I'll see her in church. They won't be there, of course, you can be sure of that, but by God, I will, if only to make sure that spalpeen of a brother of yours does the right thing by her. Now, I'll get you on your horse an' be away. Sure an' haven't I the muckin' out to do before me dinner and with Lady Woodall's new Rolls-Royce motor car arriving this afternoon an' me to have lessons to drive it, I've not a minute to spare. Oh aye, indeed, Miss Osborne, me sister's not the only one to be going up in the world, begorra. I'm to be the Woodall chauffeur an' only the Blessed Mother herself knows where that might lead. A grand uniform they're puttin' me in, I've been told. To be sure you'll not know me the next time we meet, Miss Osborne, what with me cap an' me gaiters, which can only be for the best, I'm after thinkin'. Well, I'll be off now or I'll not see the wonder of it arrive so the top o' the mornin' to you, Miss Osborne.'

Gripping the hunter's mane he leaped nimbly on to its back and with a wild, almost desperate shout broke into a full gallop through the trees. She watched him go, the leaden lump within her breast hurting her badly and when he had gone and the peaceful woodland sounds had returned she was surprised to find her face wet with tears for the second time in twenty-four hours.

8

Mara O'Shaughnessy was just three months pregnant when she married James Osborne though naturally no one would ever guess, Elizabeth thought, as Mara smoothed the pure silk of her wedding gown over her flat stomach. The dress was of ivory, fitting to her splendid figure like a glove on a hand, high-necked and with long, tight-fitting sleeves. Over the silk was a second skin of figured lace and at the hem and neck was a thick scatter of tiny seed pearls. On her smoothly brushed, intricately arranged hair was a crown of ivory rosebuds gathered only that morning from the hothouses at the back of the Hall and skilfully fashioned by Serena Osborne's milliner. Over it floated a diaphanous veil traced with lovers' knots, so fine it was like a cobweb, reaching to just below her knees. She wore a pair of ivory silk gloves and it would be Elizabeth's task to unbutton the left one at the door of the church so that Mara's finger would be free to receive her wedding ring without in any way revealing an immodest amount of bare flesh to her bridegroom which in the circumstances, Elizabeth told herself, was really quite amusing.

She watched as Mara turned with perfect composure to pick up her bridal posy which lay on the bed. It consisted of ivory and pale pink rosebuds set in fern and lace and tied with white satin ribbon and was the last fabrication in the Osbornes' challenge to society that this marriage had their approval and that this bride was in no way different to any lady of their own class their son might have chosen to marry The make-believe was complete.

'You look lovely,' Elizabeth's well-bred voice told Mara.

'Quite the most beautiful bride I have ever seen. James will be proud of you.'

'Sure an' he already is,' Mara declared loftily to her future sister-in-law and Elizabeth felt a stirring of the admiration she could not suppress for this girl, no older than herself, who was to become her brother's wife in an hour's time. From the first Mara had shown no inclination to be shy or overwhelmed in any way by the grandness of her new surroundings nor the family to which she was to belong. She had stepped from the motor car which had brought her and James and Elizabeth's father from Lime Street railway station just as though she had been accustomed to such things all her life, looking about her and smiling secretively at her husband-to-be, ignoring the curious servants who would very soon run to do her bidding or she'd know the reason why.

She had been taken, of course, directly to the dower house where she had been greeted, in Serena's absence, by Elizabeth since Serena had not yet regained the strength and authority which she was certain she would need to put her son's bride-to-be in her proper place. There was no doubt she would do just that but for now she really had not the heart to even try. She'd keep to her room, she'd told her daughter, her face still ethereal in its pale suffering and Elizabeth must 'see to the girl' for the time being. On that first day Serena still had hopes that this dreadful thing which had befallen them might blow over. That James might come to his senses, the girl be bought off, perhaps. That she would wake up and find that it had all been a nightmare, or failing that, given a few days away from her home and her own people, the girl would take fright and run home to them. Until then she was to stay with Grandmama Osborne who was as giddy as a butterfly herself and perhaps, God willing, Serena would have no need to meet her at all.

'Sure an' 'tis a lovely wee house you have,' Mara had remarked blithely, unrepentant and unbowed as James led her towards his sister and grandmother who stood in the warm, lighted doorway. Her manner said that though it was lovely, and very grand compared to what she had previously been used to, it would be nothing compared to the splendid manor house in which she expected to reside.

Behind her Johnny Osborne was seen to blanch and his proud shoulders slumped even further for if this was to be her usual manner and it seemed it was, how in God's name was he to introduce her into his circle? His mother's house-keeper was instructing the waiting footman in the placing of the cheap and bulging suitcase which appeared to be the only luggage the future Mrs Osborne had brought with her and the father of the groom beat a hasty and despairing retreat, leaving 'the girl' to his mother and daughter.

They had not been easy, those few weeks before the wedding, the arrangements hurried and almost furtive as the need to get it over and done with before the bride showed became urgent. Elizabeth did her best to make a friend of, or at least be courteous to her brother's fiancée. Mara herself had a tendency towards pride, a certain prickliness which could easily lead to offence being taken. A way with her which said she would not be patronised and every attempt on Elizabeth's part to make Mara's way easier was viewed with suspicion. She was in no way inferior to James' people and could see no reason to humble herself and if she considered Elizabeth, or indeed any member of the family, was in any way condescending to her she would toss her head, stick her pert nose in the air and strut away in search of James to whom complaints would certainly be made. Oh yes, the mother of the next generation of Osbornes, one of whom grew already within her, was prepared to be slighted by no one.

She got on best with old Mrs Osborne who, for some reason, had a fondness for the Irish and the pair of them would be heard laughing and chattering in some corner of the house in what Serena, when she finally consented to be in the girl's company, considered to be a most unladylike way, and what did they find to laugh at, she asked her husband, but he didn't know either.

'Well, I find it appallingly bad-mannered and I shall have a word with James about it. I really do not know how I shall introduce her to my friends, not with that dreadful voice of hers. And must she be included when I receive callers? The courtesies of society must still be observed even if one does have a future daughter-in-law who sounds as though she has just disembarked from the Irish ferryboat and is about to take up a post as a scullerymaid in my own kitchen. She has not the faintest idea how to conduct herself in good circles and one can only hope that our friends will continue to entertain us. Merciful heaven, what was James thinking about, putting us in such a terrible situation?' she moaned. 'Could he not have ... managed . without marrying the creature? Other gentlemen do. I grant you she is a good-looking girl if you care for that flamboyant and colourful type, which I don't ..'

Mara did look beautiful on her wedding day and had she not known it Elizabeth would have found it hard to believe that James' wife-to-be came from peasant stock. She had chosen her wedding outfit and her trousseau herself, taking no one's advice, not even Serena Osborne's dressmaker or milliner, knowing exactly what she wanted down to the last button, and what was more extraordinary, exactly what suited her. She was so vivid. Her hair was rich and abundant, somewhere between black and chestnut – *like his* Elizabeth's wilful mind whispered – gleaming in any ray of light which caught it. Her skin was as fine and white as porcelain, her lips rosy and full and her eyes a brilliant, devastating blue-green, *like his*. Exotic, Serena called her; though she would dearly have liked to use a word more derogatory, and exotic she might be, almost foreign-looking, but she dressed instinctively to enhance her colouring, in the whites and creams, the ivorys and pale misted greys, the lemons and golden honey, all shades which set off her dark beauty. She dressed simply but elegantly, the years of devouring the ladies' fashion magazines finally coming into use. She chose gowns with the minimum of embellishment but in the very latest style, ordering them by the dozen as though to make up for the thrifty, no nonsense economy her mother had imposed on her for as long as she could remember. A tailor-made, button-through dress of fine cream wool with an underbodice of cream lace which showed at the wrist and neckline, high waisted and ankle length. An afternoon gown in ivory valencia in the princess robe style with the lower part of the straight skirt pleated, the bodice fitted to her lovely breasts and over it a dashing waistcoat patterned in ivory and black. An evening gown of tawny velvet, cut daringly low at the neckline and shoulders, tight fitting to the knee where it flared into a fish-tail at the back. A cross-over tunic dress in the palest dove grey, almost white, and a flared and flounced dress with a three-tiered skirt in cinammon-coloured panne velvet. Coats reaching to the knee, double breasted, with collars and cuffs of sable. A ballgown of lace and peach satin worn with long gloves of silk and a dog-collar necklet of seed pearls, a wedding gift from her bridegroom. Fox stoles and muffs, a fan of ostrich feathers and another of Spanish lace.

Despite the season she had chiffon parasols and undergarments of pure lace organdie and taffeta which rustled when she walked though she refused absolutely to wear a corset. Gowns of chiffon and Venice lace, of cashmere and mohair, for the weather had turned cold as November became December. Silk gowns with fancy names, tussore, soft faille and ninon. Her hats were enormous cartwheels of velvet and lace, festooned with flowers and feathers and she wore high cut, high-heeled kid boots in shades to match exactly her outfits and which made her two inches taller than her stocky bridegroom.

It seemed incredible to Elizabeth, remembering that day

in October when it had all begun, that this day had ever been reached and when it came right down to it, it was this seventeen-year-old girl who had brought it about. Elizabeth, naturally, had not been included in that wild dash from Liverpool to Carlisle and onwards across the border into Scotland and the tiny village of Gretna Green. It had been almost midnight when her father and Mick O'Shaughnessy had thundered up to the door of the only hotel where, seeing no reason to wait out the three weeks necessary before they could be married, Mara and James were occupying the best bedroom and the most comfortable bed. They had been naked, beautiful and vulnerable in their young and, at that moment, terrified love. Like two trapped animals caught in the glare of the lamp the startled landlord had provided, held up by Johnny Osborne to reveal his son's and Mick O'Shaughnessy's daughter's shame.

But they had not been ashamed, it seemed, they had been defiant. James Osborne had tasted at last the sweetness and passion of Mara O'Shaughnessy's ripe body and was not at all prepared to give it up, he told his father and her father, though not, of course, in those exact words and if they would both be kind enough to leave the room and give himself and Mara a chance to get dressed he would discuss it with them in a civilised manner.

'How much will it cost me?' Johnny Osborne had asked, not prepared to give in no matter what the price, looking not at James but at the lovely, tousled and no longer frightened young girl who sat up beside his son in the bed, her nakedness modestly concealed by the bedcovers.

'There'll be none of that,' Mick had said beside him, his voice flat and tired. 'That boyo'll marry my girl an' that's an end to it. Will you look at the pair of them an' tell me it shouldn't be so?'

'I can see no reason for it. We must be realistic, clear-headed,' Johnny Osborne had argued, willing to fight Mick O'Shaughnessy, his daughter and even his own son to the

146

bitter end for what he saw as his son's future, whatever it might cost him and to free the boy from these predatory Irish clutches.

'Is that so? Well, I'll tell you this, Mr Osborne, either me daughter an' your fine son are wed before the year's out or your name will be on the tongue of every decent man in Lancashire. To be sure, don't I know you as a gentleman of some influence and meself only a man in your employ but I swear by the Blessed Mother that . .'

'Don't threaten me, you Irish bastard,' and they would have gone on raging over the couple in the bed for the rest of the night had not Mara threatened to get out of it, Elizabeth had heard later, naked as she was, if they did not give over and leave the room and Mick at least, and possibly James, knew she meant it.

' 'Tis no good the two of you fightin' like dogs over a bone,' she said loftily, 'tryin' to decide what's to be done with us since it's too late for that by at least a month. Sure an' aren't I that far gone with the child me an' James have made so you might as well both hold your tongues,' so certain was she that already she was pregnant, which proved to be true, and speechlessly they did as they were told. 'We're quite prepared to stay here for three weeks, aren't we, James?' she went on, 'an' get married in the village, just the two of us, but if you want it differently, we don't mind, do we, James?' and the besotted James had a great deal of trouble in preventing himself from bending his head to kiss her naked shoulder in the most shameless fashion, right there in front of his father and Mick O'Shaughnessy.

It was at that moment Johnny Osborne began to acknowledge the possibility of defeat.

They were brought home the next day, unrepentant, it seemed, for when they thought themselves to be unobserved they were seen to smile and whisper together, their eyes bright with secrets they shared, memories of the past month in which time, apparently, they had been lovers

147

and if everything they said was to be believed, they intended to go on being so until they were allowed to marry. They were under age, both of them, but they loved one another and they were prepared to wait, if parental consent was not given, and since James had an income of his own from a trust set up by his maternal grandfather there was nothing to stop them from doing just that. She loved James with her whole heart, Mara told her father, and would have no other. She was already his wife and the mother of his unborn child, James told his father and there was absolutely no more to be said.

The engagement was announced the next week in the best London newspapers as well as the *Liverpool Illustrated News*, causing a sensation amongst those people who moved in the same society as Johnny and Serena Osborne since no one had ever heard of the girl, or her family, nor that James, who was surely too young anyway for marriage, had favoured any particular young lady. Who was she? With a name like that she must be some great Irish heiress brought over from one of those vast and wealthy horse-owning, land-owning estates. A shy but well-bred, convent-reared child come to mix her blood with the pedigreed stuff which ran in the Osbornes' veins and when the truth came out, or at least part of it, since Serena was adamant that the coming child was not to be mentioned, the shock of it rippled like the waters of a lake into which a rock has been flung, through the *beau monde* of the north.

'You can't come home, child,' Mara's father had told her sadly. 'Your Mammy won't have it,' reluctant to tell her of her mother's steely refusal to even have her daughter's name spoken. Ellen moved about her house like a mechanical doll which has been wound up and will perform what it has been designed for until the mechanism runs down. She would recover from this terrible blow, she told her husband woodenly, her face cut into anguished, hollowed stone, but he must not expect her to ever be the same again, nor to forgive the girl who had brought this shameful disaster on them all.

Michael had been frightened. Ellen was a lovely bright star in the firmament of his life and in that of her family, but not cold and distant as a star is. She was the hub of the wheel around which they all turned, loving, warm, voluble, patient and impatient, excitable and calm and always, always there whenever they came home. She was their life and they were hers, often irritating them in her absolute devotion to their needs, in her interest and unhesitating belief that she should be the vessel into which their every thought and secret should be poured. She was eternally female, the motherly embrace, the loving kiss, the unstinting approval, the rock on which their lives were steadied. And now would you look at her! It was as though the very life had been drained from her, not leaking away bit by bit, but rushing and gushing out overnight, going God knows where and would it ever be replaced, he agonised? She moved from her bed to the kitchen each morning, quiet and restrained after that first anguished scream of agony when she had been told her girl was gone, clean and neat as she had always been, cooking and baking and stuffing her family with an overflowing abundance of food as she had always done, cleaning and washing and ironing, taking the work out of Mrs Clegg's and Mrs Dixon's very hands on the days they came in to help her as they had always done, and when she had the house gleaming and stiff with polish she would put on her black hat and coat, the one she had worn for the mourning of old King Teddy, and go down to St Mary's where she spent the rest of the day on her knees.

'The wedding is on Saturday, acushla,' he said diffidently to her and was horrified when her answer had been, 'Whose wedding?'

'You know who, Ellen O'Shaughnessy. Will you not come with me and see our daughter wed?' For Mick, if he had not exactly forgiven Mara for what she had done, was ready to

149

accept it and be thankful that the girl was to be married decently, even splendidly, though not in Holy Mother Church, of course. It was no marriage at all in the eyes of Rome, he knew that, but Mick who had not the devout faith of his wife, comforted himself with the thought that perhaps his God would be prepared to cooperate with theirs on the matter, and bless the union.

'I'll not put me foot in a Protestant church to see anyone wed, Mick O'Shaughnessy, you should know that.' Ellen's voice was cold and implacable.

'This is our girl, Ellen.' His was despairing.

'No, Mick, not *my* girl. No girl of mine would shame her family as that one did. She was deceitful and scheming, a liar and a whore . . .'

'Ellen!' Mick's cry was terrible to hear.

'A whore, Mick, and now she's a heathen and may her soul burn forever in purgatory as she deserves.'

'Don't, Ellen. The Holy Mother of God would weep to hear you speak so of your own flesh and blood. You must accept what has happened and forgive her . . .'

'Must, is it? Not in this life, Mick O'Shaughnessy, nor the next.' She was inexorable in her bitterness, just as she had been in her devotion.

'They want to go, Ellen. Not in to the church, of course, nor to the reception afterwards since they've not been invited but they want to see her come out a bride and . . . wish her well.'

'Who?'

'Her sisters.'

'They must do what their conscience tells them. 'Tis nothin' to do with me.'

'Michael is to . . . give her away.'

He thought she would break then. She leaned forward in her chair, her arms wrapped about herself, her head bowed. She began to rock, her pain almost physical, and he wanted to weep and he wanted her to weep for perhaps then she would be eased, perhaps even accepting and with accept-ance in time there might be forgiveness. She knew Mara was to have a child in six or seven months' time for he had told her immediately he got back from Gretna Green, thinking it might resign her to the inevitability of the union, but she had turned her face to the wall, terrifying them all as they crouched about the kitchen table. She had not wept then and she did not weep now.

'He must do what he thinks is right,' she said at last, her voice muffled, 'though I didn't think I'd see the day when ... when me own son would take the side of a woman who's not fit to walk the same earth as him. She will live in sin for the rest of her life, unwed and unblessed, you know that, Mick, and her children will be doomed to purgatory, and he's to lead her to it. I'll not forget it nor forgive him ...'

'Ellen, Ellen, I'll not have this. *I'll not have it!*' but she had simply stood up, straightening herself like a rusty bit of bent wire, painfully and creakingly, an old, old woman, and walked from the room.

Mick took his bewildered little daughter from where she crouched by the fire and lifted her on to his lap, holding her to him, comforting her and himself, and in the scullery Matty and Lucy shook their heads sorrowfully, wondering where the bright and lovely glow which had once resided in this house had gone.

There were white roses, for chastity, Elizabeth supposed, massed about the altar, and a carpet of white petals for the glorious bride to walk on as she floated up the aisle on her brother's arm to where her groom waited. Michael was stiff and unfamiliar but looking exactly like the rest of the gentle-men in his frock coat and pale grey waistcoat, his striped trousers and bow tie, and Elizabeth wondered wildly where he might have acquired such an outfit as he handed his sister from the carriage. She had walked behind him and Mara, the only bridesmaid since Mara had no friends who were considered suitable – or indeed would have offered their services – on this grand occasion, and her unmarried sister had declined in consideration for her mother. And what did it matter if she had one bridesmaid or ten, Serena had asked somewhat hysterically, since the whole event would make the Osbornes, particularly James, the laughing stock of the county.

Elizabeth studied the back of Michael's head and the smooth brown skin of his neck as she followed in solitary splendour. It was obvious that he had had his hair cut for the occasion and it was brushed carefully back from his forehead but several capricious strands had sprung up, spoiling the exact symmetry in which he had arranged it. In the nape of his neck it curled wilfully over his collar and again, disturbingly, it moved her heart. A great deal had been written, in plays and in novels, of hearts sinking or shifting at the onset of some great emotion and Elizabeth had viewed it with some scepticism but in the last year, ever since she had met this man, hers had done nothing else at the sight of him, plunging and bucketing in the most dreadful way. Now even the shape of his head and the strong line of his neck, moved her quite terrifyingly.

The church was full for by this time everyone knew exactly who Johnny and Serena Osborne's boy was marrying and not one wanted to miss the chance of getting a better look at this girl who came from some bog-Irish family from Scotland Road. There were ladies and gentlemen from the landed society of Lancashire, Cheshire, Yorkshire and some from further south where Serena Osborne's family lived. The Woodalls were there, naturally, since they were the Osbornes' closest friends, ready to rally round and put up a good front, should it be needed, to support poor Johnny and Serena in this their hour of adversity. The Fentons, Sir Roger and Lady Eleanor and their daughter Penelope came from Chester, the Ponsonbys who had estates near Sheffield and Durham and a villa in Nice, the Robertsons and the

Kennards and even, it was whispered, a member or two of that great Liverpool family, the Derbys.

Elizabeth, paler than usual but as beautiful as the bride in her own delicate white rosebud-crowned hat watched Sir Charles Woodall's groom – or was he chauffeur now? – holding his sister's hand for a moment longer than was necessary, carefully place it in James' then step back to stand, not in the pew where the bride's family should have been, but next to herself. He turned to her, his guard down, his affection and pride in his sister apparent in the softness of his mouth and the brightness of his eyes. He smiled at her, not at all overawed by the mass of the gentry and aristocracy who stood at his back and she felt her wayward heart swell again. It took courage to do what he was doing, she thought, sustaining his sister on this day which must be an ordeal of enormous proportions to them both. The eyes of the illustrious and fashionably dressed throng behind him were fixed avidly on him, and on his sister, their faces frigid, some of them, in case they might have to take his hand or speak to the Irish biddy who was to become Mrs James Osborne. Yet he was calm and self-contained, doing what was needed, standing by his sister who, Elizabeth thought privately, did not really need it and but for him would be alone today.

Mara Osborne was quite simply magnificent as she returned down the aisle on her husband's arm, nodding and even smiling at those who had come to see her triumph, none of whom she knew. The church bells pealed and the organ played and the congregation were astounded by her apparent lack of awareness of her new position in their society. She was smiling more broadly the further she journeyed towards the church porch, her happiness and that of her bridegroom shining about them in a great bursting explosion. One or two found they wanted to smile back at her and several remarked that she certainly looked all right so perhaps Serena and Johnny might be able to make something of her, and the marriage, after all.

Elizabeth's hand trembled on Michael's black arm as he led her from the church and he felt it. He was very conscious of her now that his duty was done and his sister was safe in the protection of her new husband and her new family. He could go home now if he wanted. Get out of this fancy dress suit which, determined as he was not to let Mara down on this special day of hers, and for his own pride's sake also, had cost him four whole guineas from H. J. & D. Nicoll, a tailoring house in Liverpool of a very expensive and superior kind. He could retrieve his bicycle which leaned at the back of the dower house in the grounds of Beechwood and ride up to Edge Lane and tell the Mammy that her daughter was married. Perhaps when she knew that it was now a matter of fact and could not be altered she would begin to accept. He hoped so. Her suffering, and because of it her family's, had been terrible these last two months and in all that time she had not spoken her daughter's name, nor even asked where she was. He himself had visited Mara in the small but elegant home in which old Mrs Osborne lived and had been made welcome by the dainty, almost fairy-like little lady who had, so they said, been a target of gossip herself in her girlhood, perhaps the reason she had been so tolerant with Mara. She was still beautiful, like a bit of crumpled velvet and lace, frail and delicate as a cobweb. A bit vague and tending, like most of the elderly, to drift back into the past where, Michael supposed, she had known her greatest happiness. She liked Mara, she told him on his first visit, because she reminded her of someone she had once known. Except for the colour of her eyes ... Her own had misted like great silvery pools as she'd told him that her greatest friend had been Irish, so what did he think of that? Surprised, he'd said, grinning, and was even more surprised when she'd ordered him to sit down on a soft velvet-backed chair in her little drawing room and drink Madeira with her and Mara.

'She'll be good for that grandson of mine,' she'd confided,

patting Mara's arm. 'He looks a little like my own James but not as handsome, of course, no matter what this girl says. None of them are,' wistfully, 'but you look more promising,' and though he hadn't known what she'd meant he had smiled at her.

And there she was on the arm of her second grandson as they all flooded out of the church into the pale December sunshine, smiling and yes, winking at him as though she approved of the occasion and him, unconditionally, no matter what her family thought. Elizabeth's hand still clung to his arm and he was tempted to close his own over it since she seemed so fragile and defenceless, as pale and tall as a lily, and why he should think her defenceless he didn't know since her brother, the one they called Teddy, and Harry Woodall were ready and eager to take her off his hands now that his part was done.

The carriage, lined with white silk and drawn by four white horses, which was to take the bride and bridegroom to the wedding breakfast was drawn up at the church gates and there was a certain amount of respectful cheering from Mr Osborne's tenants and farm workers, the throwing of confetti and rice and rose petals as the bridegroom drew his new wife towards it.

But something caught Mara Osborne's eye and she stopped. For a moment only she hesitated, like a wary animal which is not sure of its own safety, then, still holding her husband's arm, she drew him off the path towards a group of decently dressed people who stood unobtrusively to one side. They looked slightly out of place, fitting into no category, neither servant nor farm labourer nor of the rank of the Osbornes' guests.

'Glory be, 'tis Bridget,' Michael said out loud, 'with our Grace and Amy and Eileen, and there's Caitlin as well. Will you look at the lot of them, and there's Dermot and Sean and Callum outside the gate. 'Tis me brothers and sisters come to see Mara wed,' and he grinned delightedly.

Mara was embracing them one by one and with the emotional exuberance with which they greeted each day and each event in it, great and small, there were tears and sniffles, kisses and begorras by the score.

'Sure an' it's grand you look, alannah. A great lady now...'

'Will you look at her, as lovely as the Blessed Mother in Heaven...'

'An' himself so handsome...'

'We peeped in at you, pet, but didn't come in...' since not one of them had ever set foot in a church that was not of their faith and would be afraid to do so.

'A honeymoon in Rome, is it...?'

'Will you visit the Holy Father, darlin'...?'

'See, give us a kiss...'

'And one for James...'

'James, 'tis a fine name, a saint's name, begorra...'

'Is the Mammy not here...?' from Mara, a shadow of sadness falling about the chattering group momentarily

'No pet. She and Daddy felt that   well   'twouldn't be fitting in the circumstances but here's a kiss for you from them.'

'I'll see them when I come home.'

'To be sure you will. God and the Holy Father bless you, acushla

The grand guests who had come to watch Mara O'Shaughnessy make a fool of herself were not disappointed, though Mara herself would not have considered she had done so They had also come to commiserate with Johnny and Serena in their misfortune which seemed to be falling woefully about their ears at this very moment as their new daughter-in-law and her family gave vent to their joy with all the vulgar gusto and unconfined zest of their race. Poor Serena Poor Johnny. Would they ever live it down? It seemed not, for even their own daughter appeared to be infused with the same boisterous clamour and inclination towards skittishness as her brother's bride and with none other than her new brother-in-law who, it was said, was a groom in the stable of Sir Charles Woodall.

Elizabeth was smiling now, ready to laugh out loud and her hand steadied on Michael O'Shaughnessy's arm. She looked up at him in delight, unaware of the warm expression on her face and the softening of her vivid green eyes as they smiled into his. This time he did put his hand over hers, pulling her with him towards the noisy group by the church gate and Serena Osborne was treated to the sight of her well-mannered daughter, always composed and self-possessed despite her youth, picking up her skirts and running, one might almost say skipping, hand in hand down the church path with Sir Charles Woodall's stable lad.

At last James handed his glowing bride into the wedding carriage. Bridget and Callum, Caitlin and the rest of them, rubbing shoulders enthusiastically with those who considered themselves to be their betters, as they jostled to throw confetti at the departing bride and groom. Now that the religious aspect of the day was over and the question of the Church's teaching on the subject could be put to one side they evidently felt they had as much right to wish their sister and her new husband well as anybody here. Eileen even went so far as to remark to Lady Fenton in confidential tones that she'd never seen a lovelier bride and would anyone believe that the darlin' was nearly three months gone already!

James tucked Mara into the nest of velvet cushions, wrapping her about tenderly with lavish fur rugs, himself quite swept out of the usually correct and well-controlled manners which had been bullied into him at the famous public school he had attended. He was kissing her hand and her cheek, to his mother's mortification since such a vulgar display of affection was confined, surely, to the working classes, but what could one expect when one's son was marrying into them. He was even turning with Mara to wave cheerfully at her awful relatives and what was Eleanor Fenton thinking of, engaging one of them in conversation? Dear God, would this day never end and when it did would they ever be the same again?

The church bells continued to ring and a scatter of snow-flakes were mixed with the rice and rose petals James' new relatives flung with the exhilaration of folk at a country fair taking a shy at a coconut stand, as Serena said tearfully against her husband's chest in the later seclusion of her bedroom.

The wedding reception was held, naturally, in the great salon at Beechwood, a marvel of rosebuds and trailing ivy, candles and the flickering glow of the enormous log fire in the marble fireplace in which ten tall men could comfortably stand. There were rivers of sparkling, golden champagne and a wedding cake four tiers high of white icing and lovers' knots, white satin ribbon and silver lace and Mara Osborne danced with her husband James, her arms about his neck, her gossamer veil flung back for all to see the wicked sparkle in her amazing blue eyes and those who watched and won-dered how it would all end – in tears surely? – could not help but be amused at her complete and uncaring disregard for the look of icy disapproval on the face of her new mother-in-law.

'Will you dance with me, Elizabeth?' the brother of the bride asked the bridesmaid and those who overheard the words were quick to notice that already he had dropped the customary miss which should precede her name when she was addressed by a servant, which, after all, he still was. What was he doing here, anyway, they asked one another, since surely he had done all that was needed of him at the church? Give them an inch and they stole a mile, the damned working class, thinking themselves to be as good as those above them and was it any wonder? It had all started years ago when some of them had been given the vote and with it the right to take a hand in the running of the country and now the rest were at it, demanding to be enfranchised, including the women! This jumped-up broth of an Irishman would be wanting to include himself in all the social events of which, one supposed, his sister was now to be a part, and Johnny and Serena Osborne would need to be resolute to prevent it.

'I'm not supposed to be here, did you know?' Michael whispered in her ear as he guided her in a sedate waltz round the floor. His mouth was curved in a quite devilish smile.

'Really,' she said breathlessly, though of course she knew for had not she herself helped to draw up the guest list and oversee the writing of the invitations and there had not been one in his name.

'No, I slipped into the motor car with Mrs Osborne. She invited me, of course,' he added hastily, his eyes looking down at her with an expression of whimsical delight.

'My mother!' Her own eyes widened and her jaw dropped and he laughed out loud, turning more than a few heads in their direction, one of them Harry Woodall's.

'Jesus God, no! The old lady. The one they used to call Lacy.'

'Yes, so I believe.' Her manner had become a little prim as though she was suddenly aware, not only of the impropriety of their dancing so closely but of their dancing together at all.

'To be sure an' she's a fine one, so she is. Did you know she had a friend who was Irish?'

'No.' Would this man never cease to surprise her? He seemed to know things about her family of which they themselves were unaware.

'It's true. Her greatest friend was called Rosie O'Malley and could you find a more Irish name than that if you searched the length and breadth of the land? They were in business together, it seemed, this Rosie O'Malley and your grandmother, but sadly Rosie died young and your grand-

159

mother lost the dearest friend she had, she told me.'

'You seem to have a way of inviting confidences.'

'Well, aren't we Irish a silver-tongued race, Elizabeth, or so they say, with an endearing talent for coaxing others to tell us all their secrets. Because we like to reveal our own innermost thoughts and feelings we seem to have the knack of persuading others to be the same. Besides, old people love to talk about the past, hadn't you noticed? You should sit down with your grandmother and get her to tell you about herself and Rosie sometime. Sure an' she'd confound you with tales of what the pair of them got up to. They were both beautiful women, so they were, Elizabeth, but not as beautiful as you are. Jesus, but you're lovely. Like the wild roses I see growing in the hedge, but shy and quiet and not at all wild, as they are. But you could be, acushla, if you could just forget for a while that you are an Osborne of Beechwood Hall. I can't keep me eyes off you, so I can't, and if you don't stop looking up at me like that I'll be kissing you right here in front of your Daddy's fine friends.'

It was spoken without a pause to draw breath, the words about her grandmother and Rosie O'Malley, of whom Elizabeth had never heard, running directly into his passionate declaration. Her eyes were trapped by his, wide and beautiful and filled with an expression which should not have been there at all.

'Will you take a turn round the garden with me?' he asked simply. ''Tis hot as hell in here . . . I beg your pardon . . . Dear Mother, don't look at me like that. You're enough to maze the mind of any man with the sweetness of you . . . come outside . . . please . . .'

'Don't . . . please don't . . .'

'How can I not when you're here in me arms and the lovely smell of you is driving me quite . . .'

'I shall be forced to leave the floor if you continue, Mr O'Shaughnessy. Please, my mother is watching and everyone in the room is wondering why . . .'

'Why you're dancing with the Woodall groom, is that it?' and his merry Irish face hardened and the lovely light of mischief and something else besides left his eyes.

'Please don't start that again. It is nothing at all to do with who you are, or who I am.'

'Then what is it?'

'You make me . . .'

'What? Tell me what I make you do.'

'I cannot continue with this ridiculous conversation with the whole of the county staring at us and wondering what we are talking about . . .'

'Then come into the garden an' tell me there. You know, don't you, that there is something . . . ?'

'No, oh no, and if you persist in this foolishness I shall walk away and I don't want to create a scene on my brother's wedding day.'

'Then meet me somewhere. Ride out tomorrow to the spot where we . . . where we kissed one another. There, your face tells me the answer, my lovely rose . . .'

'Oh God . . . !'

'Yours or mine, Elizabeth? Catholic or Protestant?' His tone was ironic.

'Please . . .' Her voice was no more than an anguished whisper. Her body seemed determined to sway closer to his, closer than the eighteen inches which was proper. Her whole being strained towards him and her heart was bursting with the need to leave this public place, to slip out of the side door and, taking his hand, to run wildly, unhesitatingly to the summer house down by the lake, to slip inside and into his arms. To feel again the questing sweetness of his mouth on hers . . . and more . . . Dear God . . . much more . . .

He saw it in her eyes. The unfocused gaze of a woman whose body is empty and hollow with the need to be filled with love, the unconscious parting of her lips, the flush touching her high cheekbones, the press of her against him and he wanted to shout out his triumph, but abruptly, almost in between one unfinished note and another, as though at a signal from a hand of authority – that of Serena Osborne, had he but known it – the orchestra stopped playing and he felt her escape from his restraining hands.

'Thank you, Mr O'Shaughnessy,' she babbled and almost in a repeat of the night of Harry Woodall's coming-of-age party moved in a direct line to where Harry stood stiffly by the fireplace.

'It's awfully hot in here, Harry,' he heard her say, just the slightest hint of a tremble in her voice, 'and I am very thirsty. Will you take me for a glass of punch?' and smiling up at him, her lovely mouth tremulous, she put her hand in his and drew him, enchanted, towards the doorway which led to the small salon where refreshments were being served. It seemed to the assembled company to be a declaration which was lost on no one.

Serena sighed thankfully as Michael O'Shaughnessy, after kissing his sister and bowing in a most courtly fashion over old Mrs Osborne's frail hand, walked purposefully from the room and from her house.

9

Caitlin O'Shaughnessy glanced over her shoulder as she hurried across the stream of traffic which moved along London Road. She narrowly missed the shining bonnet of a rather splendid Humber motor car which was edging its way through the more indolent horse-drawn transport. The goggled driver who wore his cap back to front in a most rakish fashion was in danger of running into the back of an ancient Hackney coach but he still managed to stare appreciatively at the attractive young woman who had crossed his path before he roared off in the direction of Shaws Brow.

There was the constant scream and clangour of the maroon and yellow tramcars advertising Hudson's soap, Horniman's tea, Fry's chocolate and Birds' custard powder on their steep sides. They were double-decked, crammed with shop girls and bank clerks on their way to work, surging down the hill towards the landing stages at the Pier Head where they terminated. Enormous wagons lumbered amongst the more fleet vehicles, pulled by patient Clydesdales, head chains glinting in the early morning sunshine, their huge feet splayed for purchase on the frosted surface of the road, an aproned carter at their heads. There were brewers' drays, floats, bicycles, the drumming ripple of automobiles and amongst them moved pedestrians with the leisured self-confidence of those who were determined to treat the idiosyncrasy of the internal combustion engine with all the contempt it deserved.

It was twenty years since Liverpool had been at the peak of its power but shipping was still flourishing. Passenger liners and cargo ships were berthing on almost every tide. First class passenger traffic to North America was shared by the Cunard and White Star lines and even at this moment the great *Mauretania* was berthed at the Huskisson Dock, readying herself to sail to New York on the next tide.

Thousands of emigrants from Central Europe, Scandinavia and Ireland poured weekly into the city bound for America, Canada and Australia. Whilst they waited for a passage to their destination they were accommodated in large houses in the Great George Square district owned by the shipping companies. Their open-mouthed, wide-eyed presence about the station forecourt added colour and charm to the scene for many of them were dressed in their native costume. But Merseysiders were used to such sights in their cosmopolitan city where, linked in a kinship which was neither of blood, land, race nor colour, many of the travellers had remained, settled down, bred families, infiltrating their habits, their cultures, their thoughts and speech and religion into the life of the city. The average Liverpudlian thought himself to be boldly different, independent and self-reliant, merchant, clerk, seaman and dock labourer having a common unifying interest in the great bustling highway of the river.

Over the pervading, ever-present odour of the river and the sea to which it led, lay another smell which, so used to it were they, none of the city dwellers noticed. An exotic smell of spices, cheeses, fruits, raw timber and all the cargoes which passed through the endless sheds along the dockland. One seventh of all the ships in the world were driven along the river's intricate waterways. One third of all the goods Great Britain received and one quarter of all she sent away, passed through the great port of Liverpool.

Caitlin paused as she gained the pavement and glanced once more over her shoulder, smiling as she did so. Anyone seeing her would think she was an escaped felon on the run from the Borough gaol, the way she was acting, but it would be just her luck to run into one of her mother's friends and what would she say if she should be asked why she was entering the railway station so early in the morning, and on her own? To meet someone, perhaps? But who? The whole involved network of the O'Shaughnessy and Donovan family – her mother's relatives – lived in Liverpool so who would Caitlin know that would bring her here at this time of the day, or indeed at any time of the day, come to that?

Behind her was the Wellington Monument which depicted the grand old duke on his well-constructed horse pointing a finger into the sky as though warning the crowds about a time of doom to come. A Punch and Judy show drew a small audience at his feet, none of them caring, it seemed, about impending disaster, and a flower seller, laden down with what looked like wild violets, moved amongst them beseeching the gentlemen to buy a bunch for their sweethearts.

There were very few male heads which did not turn to look at Caitlin as she strode between the thirty-six Corinthian columns which supported the roof of the great building of the railway station, the single span of which was purported to be the largest in the world. She was tall and long-limbed, graceful and swift of foot. She had the dark hair and the blue eyes which were shared by all her family but where Mara and her sisters were white skinned, Caitlin was coloured bronze and rose and honey. A beautiful complexion with a scattering of freckles across her nose and cheekbones and if she had been brought up by a different family entirely to her own, she could not have been less like the rest of them. Where they were boisterous, volatile, gregarious, she was reserved, calm, unhurried, muted in their midst by her own self-possession. She was thoughtful and somewhat vague in her dealings with the household as though her mind was far away on some deeply private journey of its own A dreamer, her Mammy fondly called her, a dove in a nest of noisy cuckoos, with her nose always in books the titles and authors of which her Mammy had never even heard. Tolstoy? Yeats? Who were they, bejasus, but she was a good girl who never neglected her devotions and if she liked to be by herself and read her old books or write one of the endless letters she seemed to send off to those intellectual friends of hers from her convent days who was her Mammy to stop her? There was no harm in her having such an innocent hobby. She had grown into a tender-hearted, cool-headed young woman of whom any mother would have been proud and was highly pleasing to both her parents.

Today she was dressed in a tweed walking costume in a mixture of blues and greys faced with a vivid blue contrasting material about the hem of the ankle-length skirt and the cuffs and collar of the jacket. It was high-necked and snug and of a good quality. She wore black kid gloves and boots and a large black hat with a wide, turned up brim around which curled a dashing ostrich feather. Unlike Mara she did not concern herself with fashion or elegance but she managed to look well just the same.

The station forecourt was hectic. It was packed with motor taxis, horse-drawn hansom cabs, motor buses and private motor cars disgorging grand personages who were off, no doubt, on splendid journeys. A constant stream of travellers was moving to and fro between the great ships moored in the river and the trains from every part of the country which picked them up and spewed them out in their thousands each day. Liverpool was the gateway to the world and every man and woman in the station was intent upon passing through it, it seemed, and as soon as possible. A dozen different languages fell on Caitlin's ear as she pushed her way through the throng to the ticket office. The station was lit from above by a multitude of windows but the acrid smoke of decades had left its mark and very little light filtered through the grime. The same smoke swirled about thickly, shifting to reveal and then hide the huge hissing engines on the rails, enveloping the purposeful throng which went about its business with not a moment to spare.

Station porters called out to one another in the familiar adenoidal accent which had a lot of Dublin in it and a fair bit of Welsh since it was well known that Liverpool had been the 'capital' of North Wales since the first national Eisteddfod had been held there ten years ago. The porters trundled great and cumbersome trolleys of boxes, crates, trunks and expensive luggage to the danger of all those who stood in their way, followed by anxious passengers who glanced constantly at their watches, afraid of being left behind. Flags waved and whistles pierced the eye-watering, steam-drenched air and the stationmaster strode importantly about his business, which was to superintend the arrival and departure of a dozen trains an hour, cutting a dangerous swathe through the crowds.

The heady intoxication of the atmosphere, and her mission, quite went to Caitlin's head and she found she was grinning in a way which Mammy would not have approved of as she peered into the ticket office window.

'Manchester, please,' she said to the face behind the glass.

'First or third, Miss?'

'How much is first?' since, as a woman alone would she not excite less comment in a first class compartment? Not that she was afraid of anyone, male or female, who might try to interfere with Miss Caitlin O'Shaughnessy. She'd like to see anyone try, so she would, but this was her first trip to Manchester and though she had travelled by train before and was used to such things as door handles, window sashes and the purpose of the communication cord, she did not wish to appear at her journey's end in a flustered condition.

The bored face told her the cost of the ticket.

'I'll take a third, if you please,' she said firmly, still repressing the inclination to smile. She had no intention of throwing money away.

The journey was uneventful. She shared the carriage with an elderly working woman, decently dressed but shabby, who clutched a wicker basket to her and curtly refused an offer from a cheerful young man in a bowler hat worn at the back of his head to place it in the luggage rack.

'Righto, queen,' he said cheerfully. 'I just thought it'd be out o't way.'

'It's all right wheer it is an' if I wanted it up theer I'd a put it mesen.'

'Course you would, chuck,' and he winked at Caitlin. Aren't the elderly awkward, the wink said, making her an accomplice in the conspiracy of being young but she turned away sharply to stare from the window. She'd heard about men like him who struck up an acquaintance with a young woman alone, inviting her to a port and lemon, and who knew where that might lead, or so she had been brought up to believe. Don't speak to any strange gentleman no matter how polite, her Mammy had told her, for had she not heard the lurid tales of unconscious victims lured away to white slavery, though how anyone with an ounce of sense in their head could be taken in by such men was beyond Caitlin's understanding. Anyway, she was on serious business and the man wasn't born who could deter her from it!

It was a variegated landscape through which the train travelled. Great rocks that scattered themselves across the bare and barren slopes of the Lancashire landscape, jagged edges falling into craters which had been cut by man to extract what was beneath the ground. Scrubby trees, tough and dull, breaking suddenly into fallow farmland where sheep and cows grazed companionably together, and at the journey's beginning and end the train steamed and whistled through dark row upon row of narrow and scabby houses, palls of yellow-grey smoke, dismal streets seen below viaducts and from high, iron clad banks.

The clock struck eleven as she arrived at Victoria Station and giving the roguish young man a cold glance as he leaped to open the carriage door for her she stepped down in to the gloom and cavernous echoes of the platform. It was identical in its mad clangour, its busy commercial enthusiasm to Lime Street and she quickly found her way to the long sweep of Victoria Terrace where she hailed a motor cab with the confidence of a seasoned traveller. She gave the driver the address and settled back in the seat, no sign of her quivering excitement revealing itself in the smooth contours of her young face.

At last she was here, free from the cage her upbringing and culture had trapped her in and begorra she never meant to return to it. Never. Only the Holy Mother knew what it would do to Mammy and Daddy when they learned her purpose but she must stay true to her resolution no matter how it hurt them. She hated to do this to them, especially at this time. Mammy was still far from herself over what she saw as the wickedness of Mara's behaviour and she would be doubly grieved when Caitlin told her what she was to do. It saddened her that she was to be the one who was to heap fresh sorrow on to her mother's already burdened back but this was her life, and her belief and she must be allowed to travel down what she knew was the only road meant for her. For Caitlin O'Shaughnessy. There was no other course open to her. Singleness of mind and purpose, they had told her at the last meeting. Deeds not words, and that meant more than just sitting packed in rows with an enthusiastic group of women like herself and listening to others telling them how just was their cause. They knew it was just. She knew it was just and so here she was to offer her services to those who did more than sit on their behinds and talk about it.

The cab driver drew up at the address she had given him and before she had paid him or put a hand to the latch of the gate the door to the house opened enthusiastically and there was the one she had come to see and behind her was her daughter, young, beautiful, vigorous with life and purpose.

'Miss O'Shaughnessy?' she was asked. 'It is Miss Caitlin O'Shaughnessy, is it not?'

She drew in a deep breath. 'It is,' she said.

'Then come in, Caitlin O'Shaughnessy. I'm Emmeline Pankhurst and this is my daughter Christabel.'

'Sweet Mother of God, girl, what time d'you call this and where in the divil's name have you been? Your Mammy an' me have been out of our minds with worry all day. Your note said you'd be out until late but what sort of a thing is that for a decent girl to say and with the Mammy as she is at the moment. Jesus, Joseph and Mary, I'm surprised at you, so I am, and you usually so considerate. Now where've you been and with who, that's what I'd like to know ...'

'Let me get me breath, Daddy, an' then I'll tell you where I've been. Put the kettle on, Matty, please ...'

'Never mind "put the kettle on", Caitlin O'Shaughnessy, we'll have an explanation first, if you please,' for in Mick's heart and in that of the quiet woman by the fire who had once been his irrepressible, warm-hearted wife, was the awful dread that this one was to go the same way as the other. Mara's defection – for that was how Ellen, at least, saw it – had put grave doubts in their once complacent minds that they could trust their children to be doing what they said they were doing and what sort of state of affairs had it come to if every time one was missing from the table it gave rise to the dread Mammy suffered. Would you look at the heartache Mara had caused and at the bottom of it had been a man and surely, the way it looked at the moment, Caitlin was on the same slippery path to damnation. A note she had left, pinned to her pillow for Ellen to find and herself nearly going out of her mind already with what Mara had done to them. Since breakfast this morning when it had been discovered that Caitlin was not in her bed, she had been on the go, running to the window for a sight of her girl, backwards and forwards like a ball on a bit of elastic and himself sent for from work since nothing Grace or Amy, Bridget or Eileen could say would calm her.

'Now then, girl, let's have the truth of it,' he said sternly.

There was a deep and dreadful silence and at the glowing range Matty and Lucy slowed what they were doing since they had no intention of missing a word of this second melodrama to afflict the O'Shaughnessy household. Grace and Amy stood, arms akimbo, one on either side of their mother with Eileen protectively behind, their younger sister Bridget called home on some family crisis of her own leaving her children with their grandmother. Dermot was on the other side of the fire hidden behind a financial newspaper in a pretence of indifference, nevertheless he was all ears, and in two rows, one on either side of the table, was Maureen McGowan and her sister Teresa, Agnes Conroy, Ellen Maguire and Kate, Maeve, Siobahn and Ginny Feeney, Mick and Ellen's granddaughters. Beside them was Clare O'Shaughnessy, their aunt but the youngest of the lot. The grandsons, contemptuous of the carryings on of their elders and wondering what the fuss was all about, had taken themselves off with Callum, Donal and Eammon to the O'Shaughnessy boys' bedroom. These family gatherings were so familiar and so frequent and of no concern to them, they had agreed, so best leave the womenfolk to deal with it whilst they had a game of some intricate masculine nature. A series of bumps, a crash or two and the sound of a wild cry from above evinced little or no interest in those who waited with bated breath for Caitlin to speak.

'I've been to Manchester, Daddy.'

There was a collective indrawn gasp from them all. She might have said New York or Paris, so thunderstruck were they and by the fire Ellen bowed her head in humble prayer, or was it defeat?

'Manchester? Jesus God, what's in Manchester that you've to dash off there without a word to anyone and nearly kill the Mammy with the worry of it?'

A small silence, then, 'The Pankhursts, Daddy.'

'Mother of God, who are they?'

'Sure an' aren't they those lunatic females who are forever making a bloody nuisance of themselves demanding votes for women and God knows what else that occurs to them. They deserve to be locked up, the lot of them and I for one . . .'

Dermot's voice drawled sneeringly from behind his newspaper but before the words were out of his mouth his sister sprang across the hearthrug and tore it from his grasp. Her face was livid. Her aquamarine eyes, so like those of Mara and Michael, flashed dangerously and beneath their onslaught Dermot instinctively recoiled.

'Don't you dare say that, you spalpeen. They're not lunatic and how else can they make themselves heard only by being a bloody nuisance as you so lucidly put it. You think you're so grand with your piddling little job at the bank but the women I met today are more intelligent, have more judgement and discernment, more ability to think and plan with their shrewd female wit than you with your masculine arrogance could ever dream about...'

'That's enough, Caitlin.' Her mother's voice was harsh and meant to be heard in this kitchen where madness seemed suddenly to have taken over but Caitlin was not to be stopped. She was lifted a foot from the ground still, walking on air with what she had experienced today and she was not going to have it wrenched from her by anyone, even her mother. She was well aware that her mother was in a delicate frame of mind after what her own flighty and self-willed sister had done and she was sad for her, but because Mara had broken her Mammy's heart with her wilfulness it was no reason for Caitlin to give up what she had come to believe in so fiercely. She was nineteen and for the past twelve months she had read everything the library had on its shelves on the history of the movement and devoured the newspaper reports about the National Union of Women's Suffrage Societies, now called the Women's Social and Political Union. For fifty years women had been begging for equal voting rights with men, mostly by peaceful methods, but in the last few years that had changed to more violent means. They needed young women to keep the movement alive, Mrs Pankhurst had said, and Caitlin believed passionately that she must be one of them. Poor Mammy, one daughter disgracing the family in the oldest way known and now another to do the same, or so Mammy would believe, in this new and unladylike manner.

'Mrs Pankhurst is an educated woman and so are her daughters. I met women today who are going to change this country...'

172

'Don't talk daft, girl,' Grace said contemptuously, moving away from her mother to take her sister's arm but Caitlin turned on her, wrenching her arm away, a spirited kitten squaring up to the experienced battle-worn tabby. Grace was the eldest in the O'Shaughnessy family, the mother of six children herself, married for nearly fifteen years to a man who would clout her if she told him she wanted a say in the running of the country. Her job was to run the house and nothing else, he would tell her, as it was the job of all women and she had never heard anything as crazy as Caitlin's tirade in her life. And couldn't the girl see that all she was doing was worrying Mammy who had enough to contend with already, surely?

'It's not daft, Gracie, and no matter what anyone says I'm going to be a part of it.' Caitlin's breast heaved and her freckles stood out in her flushed and angry face as she glared round at anyone who would try to stop her. 'I've been going to a meeting or two ... oh yes ... when you thought I was ... elsewhere, but now 'tis out in the open, so it is, and I'm to become an active participant ...'

'What in God's name does that mean, child?' Mick could hardly get the words out of his appalled mouth and he moved to his wife's side, his hand on her shoulder to give her strength, or was it to gain it? No one, not even himself, could be sure.

'I'm going to a political meeting next week and when the cabinet minister who is to be on the platform starts to speak I am to ... get up and ask him if the government will grant votes for women. That's all, for now. Politely, with the other supporters I am to ask just the one question ...'

'Holy Mother of God ...' Ellen crossed herself and began to rock in her chair. 'What's to happen next, Dear Mother? Me own daughter to stand up and make a show of herself. A decently brought-up girl to shame herself and her family in front of men who will think her ...'

'There's nothing shameful in it, Mammy.' Caitlin ran to

173

her mother and knelt before her. 'They're all ladies, truly they are...' but Dermot could not forgive her scathing comments on his own male acumen.

'Not shameful, is it? Ladies, you say? What about those women at the meetings who get thrown out on to the street for being abusive, for spitting at the bobbies, tell me that? Nothing but prostitutes and drunkards, most of them, spouting foul language an' gettin' themselves arrested...'

'Holy Mother, bless us now and in the...'

'Burnin' decent people's homes...'

'You're a liar, Dermot O'Shaughnessy...'

'...breakin' windows an' doing untold damage, so they do...'

'That's enough, Dermot, that is enough. I'll not have another word said in front of these innocent children. Sure an' I don't know what's got into this family these last few months, so I don't.' Mick's voice, normally so quiet, so calm and moderate in this kitchen where outbursts of an explosive kind were common, silenced everyone in the room He rarely spoke above smiling moderation for though there was always someone raising their voice in a quarrel or a complaint, it was never serious, not like this.

'Take your children home, Gracie, and you too, Eileen and Amy. Go and collect the others, Maureen, there's a good girl, and you Dermot, go an' have a bevvy at The Bandy Duck, I want no arguments now. Mammy an' I will have words with Caitlin an'...'

'Let them stay, Mick, for I'll have no secrets in this house. Not from me own children. Sure an' Caitlin's been a good girl till now an' she will be again, won't you, darlin'? This ... this women's thing is nothin' to do with the likes of us an' won't she see it when she comes to her senses. Those sort of ... of women, the ones that go in for throwing stones at decent men are not right in the head, pet. They need a good man an' a few children and then to be sure wouldn't their time be taken up with what God put women on this earth for. Come an' give Mammy a kiss, darlin', an' then you an' me'll go to Mass an' ask the Holy Mother . . .'

Caitlin stood up slowly, her young face which had lost all its lively colour stiff and drawn. She loved her family dearly and this scene with her mother and father had been as bad, worse, than she had ever imagined but she couldn't give up. She couldn't allow her mother to think that she had only to whisk her off to Church for it all to be expunged. She really didn't know what she would do if they didn't accept it, if, like witl Mara, they cast her out of the family and turned their backs on her, but even if they did she knew she must go on. She was to help at the local branch of the WSPU, sitting at a desk and putting together the facts and figures of the abuse heaped on women in factories where sweated labour was common. Material for those who were to shout these facts at the political rallies and to the ministers who came to speak at them. She didn't know how she would manage when it was her turn to get to her feet and force the words from her dry throat.

'Will this Liberal government give women the vote?' was what she must ask, as women had been asking since 1906 when the Liberal party came to power. She had been brought up to be polite, to strangers at least, though in the bosom of her family nobody cared who said what to whom since they all knew no harm was intended. But she would not be in the bosom of her family and if threatening words and gestures were directed at her, as she knew they would be, could she still be polite, cool, unruffled, as Mrs Pankhurst had told her she must?

This was her first test.

'I'm sorry, Mammy, I can't come to Church just now but I'll go to Mass with you in the morning. And then I have to go up to the WSPU branch office in Duke Street to collect some handbills I have to give out at the Pier Head.'

'The . . the Pier Head?' Her father was horror-stricken.

'Yes. By the landing stage where the ferry boats come in.

There's sure to be a good crowd there . . .'

Mick found his voice again, full throated and as menacing as any of his family had ever seen him. 'Oh no you won't, my girl. No daughter of mine'll stand where all those rough men go down to the docks . . .'

'I'm sorry, Daddy, but I must.'

'We'll see about that, so we shall. You'll stay at home like the decent girl your Mammy an' me have brought you up to be and there'll be no gallivantin' about the city on business which has nothin' to do with us. D'you hear me, Caitlin, or must I send for Father Paul to have a word or two with you?'

Caitlin waited for her father to finish speaking, as polite with him as she had been with her mother. 'I'm afraid I must, Daddy,' then, smiling, nodding to her sisters, patting the head of her open-mouthed, wide-eyed niece Maureen, who was ten years old and ready to admire anything out of the ordinary, she crossed the room, opened the door, then closed it quietly behind her.

She had moved too quickly, they told her at Duke Street when she returned there the next afternoon, her blouse torn, the sleeve of her jacket hanging from its stitches, her hat which she had straightened with trembling hands missing its ostrich feather. There was mud on her skirt, lifted from the river's edge by an urchin who had not the slightest idea what she was talking about as he threw it at her. Why had she not merely given out the handbills, they asked her, putting one in any hand which would take it? That is all she had been asked to do, not speak to the crowd who had collected. It was inevitable that men would be drawn to a pretty girl like herself, that's why she had been given the job. The WSPU used every resource to hand, took advantage of anything which might further the cause and a fetching smile, a well-turned ankle were weapons which women had used since time began. So why should they not be used now in this much more serious endeavour if it brought results? But she must be careful. She must not incite them to take liberties, which they would, given half the chance.

Surprisingly, they had made no attempt to stop her, Mammy and Daddy, as she hesitated by the kitchen door that first morning. They had looked suddenly old and frail, as though defeat sat heavily on their bowed shoulders. She had turned to go, then turned again, trembling on the brink of giving it all up, for their sake. How could she do this to them, the two people who had given so much to her, but then how could she turn her back on her own ideals, her truth, the core of which these two had given her?

'Go on, child,' her mother said sadly. Her father would not look at her. 'Do what you must. We love you and believe in your judgement for you've been brought up to know right from wrong. We don't agree with it . . .'

'Mammy'

'No   don't . . just go and may the Mother of Jesus go with you.'

She had stood in the quiet patient presence of the great ships, the clustered, wrangling cranes perched on their high roofs above them, the long sheds ringing with the echoes of the men who laboured in them as the goods of the world poured into the port. Decent men who she was certain would listen to her, even if they did not agree with her. Men like her father and her brother-in-law, Terry McGowan, working men who would offer no woman an insult.

'They seemed interested,' she told the ladies of the WSPU, trying not to weep the tears of shame, of lost dignity, of injured pride and effrontery at the memory of those laughing faces, rough, good-natured on the whole, but turning to something else as she began to lecture them on their treatment of their own wives. Most of them had not got a vote themselves, being men without property, and they certainly could not see why women should have it and as for being told they were exploiting their own womenfolk by this chit

177

of a girl, pretty as she was, well, it was not at all to their liking. They had cat-called and jeered, saying, 'Listen 'ere, Mrs Woman, we don't need no silly cow ter tell us 'ow ter run our lives ...' which was the only phrase she could decently repeat to the sympathetic ladies of the WSPU. But when one man had shoved her in the back and another had done the same at the front, his big docker's hands closing over her breasts, the rest, excited by the plight of a young and vulnerable female, and encouraged by the indifference of the bobby who sauntered by, had wanted a feel as well, she had picked up her skirts, dropped her handbills and fled.

She was ashamed. There were women in prison at this moment who had suffered far worse than she, she told them. She would do better next time, she told them, imploring them to allow her to go out with her purple, green and white banner and her handbills on the next day. Dear Mother of God, hadn't one of their number, the sister of Mrs Pankhurst herself, Mrs Mary Clarke, been attacked last month, as she, Caitlin, had this morning and was so seriously injured she had died not a week since, becoming the campaign's first martyr. Caitlin had been no more than pawed and loathsome as it had been she would suffer it a dozen times a day if it meant only one of those uncouth labouring men would be made to think about her words.

'Come back in the morning, Caitlin, and we'll see,' they had promised her.

That same evening Ellen rocked by the fireside, her youngest daughter on her lap as Caitlin entered the kitchen. The child's head was tucked beneath her mother's chin and both pairs of eyes were unfocused as they stared into the glowing fire. It was nearly Christmas and the day was cold, not with the sharp cold of frost but bleak and damp and dreary, a raw wind whipping across the river and gripping the city with cruel, biting fingers. Not a day to linger anywhere, let alone the Pier Head, and though a cup of hot cocoa had been pushed into Caitlin's shaking hands by the ladies in Duke Street, she was chilled to the marrow as she let herself into her home.

Both her mother and Clare turned to watch her as she took off her jacket. She had pinned the sleeve back into place but the jagged edges on the shoulder still showed. Elsie Thompson, one of the younger members of the WSPU but seasoned in the battle they all fought now, had helped to sponge her skirt but she had still invited curious glances on the tram as she came up from town.

Her mother sat up slowly, lifting the child to the rug where she curled up beside the two purring tabbies who somehow always found their way there. Ellen's face was rosy with the heat, giving her an appearance of good health, but in her eyes and about her mouth were still lines of strain. They deepened as she surveyed her daughter.

'Holy Mother of God,' she whispered and her hand sketched a cross on her chest before it went to her mouth.

'It's all right, Mammy, I'm not hurt,' Caitlin cried gaily. 'Sure an' didn't I have a tumble as I was coming down the steps in Duke Street. Caught me sleeve, so I did, on the railings and wouldn't you know it there was a patch of mud waiting for me at the bottom.'

Her mother's eyes were wide and frightened. Her daughter was lying, of course. Hadn't she had the caring of her from the hour of her birth, as she had all her children, and didn't she know when one of them was not telling the truth? Or . . . at least . . . she had thought she did! Until this disaster with . . . with Mara, whose name must not be spoken, even inside her own head, she had thought that she knew all her children as well as she knew herself. Their joys and small sorrows, their childish hopes and dreams, their naughtiness and goodness, the latter the stronger, of course, all their winning ways, mischievous and without a bit of wickedness in them, or deceit, and would you look at the way one of them had turned out. And now this one was doing the same.

179

Denying her upbringing, her culture, her religion, telling lies to her own Mammy and getting up to God only knew what at these dreadful meetings she was bent on going to. She would not be stopped. Ellen had seen it in her face the night before, and this morning when she had left the house, and where, dear Blessed Virgin, would it finish up? Where would Caitlin finish up? In a prison cell being forcibly fed with a tube as Ellen had read they were, these   these women ... when they refused to eat. Her pretty, good-humoured, sensible daughter who, unlike Mara, had never gone against her Mammy and Daddy in her life. Until now. Quieter than the rest of them in her ways. Of course she had quarrelled with Mara. Who didn't since Mara had been enough to try the patience of a saint with her challenging waywardness, and now she was here, her Caitlin, looking as though she had been set on by ... Oh, Merciful Mother ... not that ... surely not that ...

Her face became the colour of wet cement and she put out a trembling hand, palm outwards as though to ward off an intruder and Caitlin saw it in her eyes and ran to her. She dropped to her knees and put her face in her mother's lap and the words she spoke were muffled. She knew exactly what was in her mother's mind.

'I'm not hurt, Mammy, really I'm not. I was only ... jostled a bit ...'

She looked up into her mother's face, her eyes wide with the truth of what she said and Ellen relaxed. She cupped her daughter's face in trembling hands and dropped a kiss on her forehead before folding her in her arms. Jostled a bit! Her lovely girl had been 'jostled a bit', but how could she stop her now? Lock her up for the rest of her days or until a suitable husband was found for her? And if one was, Caitlin would not accept it. In her own way she was as vigorous and obstinate as the rest of them. Irish, and with the Irish stubborn resolution in her to do what was needed to be done in the cause in which she believed. Hadn't it been that way for generations and wasn't this one just the same with the blood of the true men of the old country in her veins? She had always been relentless, even as a child, in her defence of the underdog, the wronged, fiercely standing up to anyone, no matter how much bigger than herself they were, if she believed they were taking unjust advantage of a weaker or smaller child. Ellen had seen her take a swing, her own small fist clenched, at the head of one of her cousins who had been teasing a kitten and she would argue, even with Father Paul, on some tenet of the faith which she thought repressive. Embarrassing it had been at times but then she herself was outspoken, though not with the parish priest!

'Will you not give it up, darlin'?' she asked her daughter now. 'Sure an' there are others to take up this cause you've found. Ladies who are educated and have influence, well connected in high places. I read only the other day about that big march they had up in London and the violence there was the worst they had ever seen. I'm so afraid for you, acushla. There were women sprawled in the mud so that decent men had to look away and over a hundred were arrested, so they were. "Black Friday" they're calling it.'

'I know, Mammy. I know all about it but it was because they had been promised a women's suffrage act and then the government told them that an election was to take place and women's votes would have to wait.'

'Nay, I don't understand it, darlin' . . .'

'When Mr Asquith's announcement was given out they were so disappointed . . . no, angry and frustrated they had no choice but to march on the House of Commons. There were hooligans standing in their way, tearing at their clothes and knocking them to the ground. "Teaching the women a lesson," they called it, Mammy, and it's not to be borne. That's what they're doing to us. To you and me and the rest of the women of this country and it is not to be borne. D'you know, when one woman complained to a policeman that he must not ... not hold her ... well, where he was holding her, d'you know what he said to her?'

Ellen shook her head numbly.

'He said, "I can hold you wherever I like today, my dear." That's what makes us as we are, Mammy. Elsie Thompson, a girl I met at the WSPU, said that Annie Kenny ... she's a leader in the cause ... told them that there was not one of them who would not have gone to their deaths at that moment if it would have helped the movement.'

Ellen crossed herself hurriedly, her face blanched.

'Holy Mother of God ...'

'She would have understood, Mammy ...'

'What! That gentle mother ...?' Ellen was appalled.

Caitlin stood up and shook herself in the manner of a dog which has been bested in a fight but is prepared to fling itself into the fray again.

'I'm sorry if it hurts you, Mammy, or frightens you, but I have to do it. And if I get the chance I'm away to London to march with the others, so I am!'

Terrified as she was for her lovely girl, Ellen was more proud of her at that moment than she had ever been of anything, or anyone, in her life.

10

Mara Osborne's daughter was born a month prematurely on the twenty-second of June 1911, giving her mother-in-law further cause for tight-lipped reproach. If the child had come, as was expected, at the end of July there might have been the faint ghost of a chance of convincing her friends that her first grandchild had been conceived within the marriage since a seven-month baby was not out of the ordinary, but who was going to believe it now, she asked grimly of her husband. Seven months. perhaps; six definitely not!

Fortunately the event was somewhat overshadowed by the coronation on that same hot summer day of 'good' King George, as he was to be known, at Westminster Abbey, and a great number of their friends, including the Woodalls, who were present at the ceremony were more concerned with the importance of that well-timed occasion than with the early arrival of Serena Osborne's first grandchild.

The Queen of the newly crowned King, once the fiancée of his deceased older brother, Edward, had the glorious name of Victoria Mary Augusta Louisa Olga Pauline Claudine Agnes, and again Serena was plunged into the deepest despair when her rebellious daughter-in-law who nobody, not even her husband, could control, decided to call her daughter Claudine!

'But my dear, if you feel you would like to name the child after our new Queen, and I agree it would be most appropriate, would not Mary suit?' which after all, she said privately to her husband, was a favourite for obvious reasons, of those brought up in the Catholic faith.

' 'Tis too plain, Mrs Osborne,' Mara replied sweetly from the depths of her silken pillows, sure, as she always was, of getting her own way.

'Then . . . Augusta, or Louisa, which are both very pretty.'

'Sure an' Claudine is pretty an' how many little girls will have such an unusual name?'

None, at least not in Serena Osborne's circle where Elizabeths and Helens and Sophies abounded. Even Daisy Brooke, Countess of Warwick, beloved of their late King, so rumour had it, and an acquaintance of Serena's, had been christened Christina Frances Evelyn, Daisy being no more than a pet name. Now, to the amusement and a good deal of somewhat cynical sympathy from her friends, Serena Osborne's first grandchild, born six months after her son's wedding, was to have the outlandish name of Claudine.

It had been a difficult six months for everyone except the one person who should have been expected to feel out of place in her new environment and with her new family. Mara, quite simply, felt – but for one thing – that she had died and gone to Heaven, though not even Heaven could be as splendid as her new life with James and she loved him with all her heart for giving it to her. Everything her Mammy had frowned on was quite taken for granted here at Beechwood and she sometimes felt a stirring – quickly subdued – of her less privileged upbringing and Catholic guilt when she imagined what her Mammy would say if she could see her now. She lay in her bed each morning and did not put a foot out of it until she felt like it. She sipped hot chocolate brought to her at her command whenever she had a fancy for it, carried to her in her bed by a smiling young housemaid. Her own tray piled with muffins and hot buttered toast, soft boiled eggs and fresh cut flowers and anything else she cared to ring for was brought to her as she curled like a pampered kitten amongst her satin pillows. She grew plump and rosy but she did not care for was she not to be the mother of the heir to Beechwood Hall and everything that entailed and entitled to take her ease? When she was ready her maid would pull back the curtains, pile high the already leaping fire and ask, respectfully, what Madam would care to put on from her extensive and rapidly growing wardrobe. Her days were spent at the milliners, the dressmakers, the glove makers, the boot makers, ordering whatever caught her eye. 'Put it on my account,' she would say as her 'man' staggered out to the carriage or the motor car beneath a mountain of parasols, hatboxes, boxes containing the most delicious and daring undergarments to enchant her young husband – who was to pay for them – and each item cost more than her Daddy earned in a month. She was enthralled with it and even the thought of what her Mammy would have to say if she knew of her daughter's extravagant and decadent life did not deter her. She was, at last, embosomed in the satisfying dream she had dreamed for as long as she could remember.

It was the hunting season when she and James returned from their honeymoon but even had she not been pregnant she would obviously have been unable to join those wild early morning rides which the rest of the family, with the exception of Serena, found so enjoyable since she had never been on a horse's back in her life and had no intention of starting now, she informed James firmly. Not for her the necessity of crawling from her warm bed and her lovely, fire-lit bedroom and flinging her pampered self into the clammy dawn of a winter morning. She would positively loathe the indignity of being heaved into the saddle by a groom, possibly her own brother if the meet was at Woodall, wearing unbecoming breeches and divided skirts, setting her mount at high fences in crowded fields as she had heard Elizabeth did, of falling a quite breathtaking distance from its tall back to the hard ground below. The Hunt Ball, yes, the hunt itself, no!

'But when the baby comes, darling?' her adoring husband asked wistfully, though his expression seemed to say, as he kissed her a lingering farewell, that it would be rather pleasant instead to remain with her in that dizzying rapture she swept him into whenever they were alone.

James Osborne could not get enough of his young wife, of her long white body and her pointed breasts which fell so eagerly into his greedy hands every night and morning. He was often to be seen by the servants sneaking up the back stairs of his own home to his wife's bedroom in the afternoon when he should have been in the office of the family shipping business learning the rudiments of ocean trading, or riding about the estate with his father and the land agent in his capacity as the son and heir to the farm land, the woodland, the shooting his father owned. One day they would all be his and it was his duty to see that the administration of them continued as it had done under generations of Osbornes before him.

But his young wife was still, in those early days of his marriage and indeed for as long as it would last, a magnet and an obsession to him. He might have been her lover and not her husband, the servants observed to one another, smiling knowingly, and was it any wonder she was already enormous with the child he had given her, quite obviously before the wedding ceremony. They had been prepared to patronise the upstart Irish nobody who had trapped their young master into marriage in the oldest way of all but they had not reckoned with the strong-willed, resourceful and ambitious young woman who would one day be their mistress. Though she had never, in their sense of the word, been waited on in her life she was certainly expecting it now, and just as promptly and efficiently as Mrs Serena Osborne, her high-handed manner told them.

From the moment she returned from her honeymoon in Rome, Mara had made it quite clear that nobody was going to put her in the place which they thought she should occupy. She had not been particularly impressed with the splendours of Rome or Florence, where her husband had taken her, though she did not actually say so, nor hotel life, nor sightseeing which she found not only tiring, but boring. Though she loved her husband and was enchanted with the 'small things' he showered on her in the way of delicate jewellery, lacy fans, sumptuous shawls and frilly parasols, she did find that twenty-four hours a day of male company was somewhat more than she could manage. She missed the feminine disposition of her mother and sisters, of her old friend Katy Murphy, to gossip and giggle, to share the intricacies of the latest hairstyles and the latest fashion and could not wait to get home to it, since in her mind was the certainty that now, as the respectably married Mrs James Osborne, Mammy could not fail to receive her back into the family's bosom. Despite her contempt for the bedroom she had been forced to share with Caitlin and Clare, the indignation she had felt at the constant upheaval brought about by the seething mass of nieces and nephews who invaded her mother's kitchen and her sure belief that she would one day move on to better things, she now found that she longed to go home and bask in the fascinated admiration and affection of her own people. Not for good, of course, since she was now to live at Beechwood, but she did miss the noisy chatter, the laughter, the easy-going, carefree life in the kitchen, the lilting Irish voices of her brothers and sisters, the banter and the wild and tempestuous quarrels which were all part of the colour and texture of her old life.

She could not wait to tell them of the wonders which had been hers, right from that first moment when she had been tucked luxuriously into the first class compartment of the London train at Lime Street railway station. Wouldn't the Mammy be thrilled to hear about His Holiness the Pope who Mara had actually looked at from her place amongst the crowds in St Peter's Square and she was longing to see their faces when she unwrapped the presents she had brought back for each and every one of them.

'I shall have to buy a new trunk to put them all in,' James had joked.

'Then buy one,' she had answered tartly, and he had.

'Mind that trunk,' were her first words as she was handed out of the Vauxhall motor car which had met them at the station on their return. 'You there ... what's your name?' to the footman who was about to unload it.

'Jackson, madam.' The man's face was quite expressionless as was that of Eaton, the Osborne butler, who was supervising the removal of Mr and Mrs James' luggage from the vehicle to their new suite of rooms.

'Well, Jackson, you'd best handle that trunk with proper care.'

'Indeed he will, madam,' Eaton intervened smoothly but

in his voice was the icy outrage of a servant who, employed by a family who knew about such things, had never in his life heard a servant addressed as 'You there!'

'There is glass and porcelain packed in it, so there is, an' I don't want it smashed to smithereens.'

'No indeed, madam.'

Her mother- and father-in-law were nowhere to be seen and Mara, who was well aware that they would never truly accept her as one of themselves and were quite likely to put on a front only when guests were present, was not surprised or in the least put out. She had what she wanted and would make sure that the life she was to live with James was a good one. She would do nothing to shame them, she had decided, realising that she had made a mistake – in their eyes at least – in greeting her family so emotionally on her wedding day. Bridget, Grace and the others had no part in her life here but she did not mean to stay away from Edge Lane just to please her mother-in-law. She was sure she could work out some pleasant routine which would allow her to have the best of both worlds. Bejasus, how could she manage to rear her baby when it came without Mammy's support and comforting advice and tomorrow, or the next day she meant to – oh, joy of joys – order the carriage, or even the motor car, and drive over to wheedle her way into her Mammy's heart again.

Elizabeth stood on the broad front step of the house waiting to greet James and her and Mara was surprised and somewhat pleased when her sister-in-law kissed her warmly on the cheek, smiling a welcome.

'Come into the drawing room. You must be cold after your journey and there's a good fire. Eaton shall bring up some tea and then I'll take you up to your rooms. I think you'll like what has been done to them while you were away.'

'Well, I should do, seeing I planned it and told that fellow how I wanted it doing.'

'I'm sure he has done exactly what you asked. It looks lovely and when you are rested I want you to tell me all about Rome and Florence and the other lovely places you and James visited. I have never been to Italy, only to France with mother and father a year or two ago so I'm longing to hear what you thought of it.'

Mara, as Elizabeth intended, was gratified by the knowledge that she, little Mara O'Shaughnessy from Edge Lane, had been somewhere the grand Miss Osborne had not and she was smiling warmly at the welcome her sister-in-law had given her as she followed her, and her own new personal maid, up the wide staircase to her own rooms.

These had been another bone of contention between her and her mother-in-law, in whose opinion the suite of rooms which were to be made ready for James and his new bride were perfectly adequate and needed none of the redecorating and refurbishing Mara seemed to find necessary. She herself had done them up as a bride twenty years ago, and she told James so coolly when she got him alone. They were pretty and extremely comfortable, luxurious even, and why spend the money which, on his eighteenth birthday, had come to him from her family? After all, as she was sure James would realise, what she herself had chosen was of the best quality...

Precisely, James cut in, rather tartly his mother was inclined to think, and when she asked him what he meant he told her politely that what had been allowed her as a young bride should be afforded his now, which was the decorating and furnishing of her own rooms to her own taste. Serena shuddered visibly, for what might that be, but James continued unperturbed. It was his money which was to be spent on them, he said courteously to his mother. The house would one day be his and so surely...

He had smiled and kissed her cheek and hurried away, presumably to see what the girl who was to be his wife was up to and who, with a warm glance from her exquisitely blue eyes, had Serena's son on a bit of thread tied to her little finger.

There was a master bedroom where Mara and James were to sleep for Mara had been brought up in a society where a man and his wife shared not only the same bedroom but the same bed and she wanted none of this – to her – strange custom of her husband slipping into her room from his own when he fancied a bit of love-making. What if she wanted it, she asked him indignantly, and himself not there to provide it? Was she to traipse about the corridors searching for him? Well, she didn't care what the upper classes got up to, she told him to his delight, he was to sleep with her, his wife, in the sumptuous and elegant comfort she meant to create for them in the rather austere rooms his mother had furnished to her taste, in the olden days, which is what they were to seventeen-year-old Mara Osborne. She herself would have a boudoir – Jesus, Joseph and Mary, she had always wanted a boudoir – which would be off the master bedroom, and her own private dressing room, where her maid would see to her mistress' hair, her wardrobe, her jewellery, her furs and shoes and all the indispensable functions a lady's maid apparently performed. And James would have his dressing room and in it his valet, and of course, their own modern bathroom.

There was to be white paint in the rooms, all of which were large and on the southeast corner of the house. Their enormous bed had a white panelled headboard and would be dressed with a white flounced valance and frilled and quilted satin counterpane. Beside the elegant fireplace was a silk-covered chaise longue on which Mara would recline during the day, two or three small velvet chairs, a dressing table beside the window to catch the light, with mirrors everywhere, all with glinting bevelled edges, one tilting on the dressing table and a free-standing, swivelling cheval so that she could see herself from her head to her toes. The room was light and pretty with no more than a touch of palest apricot and palest green, cluttered with all the feminine work tables and writing tables and draped embroidered shawls so dear to the heart of a woman. There were water colours on the wall, cut glass scent bottles and smelling salts, brushes and hand mirrors of silver and ivory, silk lined jewel cases and photograph frames of silver in which Mara intended to put her wedding photographs. The furniture was of the Sheraton style, simple and graceful, the curtains light and airy, allowing in the sunlight, and the wallpaper was a William Morris design in a dainty apple blossom pattern.

The bathroom was the talk of the servants' hall. There had been installed at Beechwood, naturally, a reliable circulatory hot water system, years ago, and there were three bathrooms in the house. They were functional with a claw footed, cast iron bath in each, a washbasin set in decorative wrought iron, a flush lavatory with a wooden seat and the rooms were covered from ceiling to floor, and the floor itself, in black and white tiles.

But Mara wanted something more than this, something different, something costly and grand and plushy, she told James. Wouldn't you think she would be satisfied with the greatly superior arrangement at Beechwood, the servants asked one another, but no, she must have marble and gilt, a carpet as thick as the clover-studded grass in the paddock, mirrors and exotic plants, enormous fleecy towels specially made in a deep shade of peach to match the carpet, and when they came back from their honeymoon, big as she was, it was rumoured, though how true it was none of the servants could verify, she and Mister James shared the enormous bath tub!

She and her new family dined together that first night, formally dressed, of course, the gentlemen, Teddy amongst them since he was fifteen now, in their immaculately tailored evening suits, the four ladies quite magnificent in their evening gowns. Serena was in black as it was less than a year since the death of her father. Elizabeth had chosen a straight tunic style dress in the very latest fashion, almost an Empire line, the waist high and bound with white satin ribbon beneath her breasts. It had a small train with a point at the back, short sleeves and was of white chiffon with appliquéd white satin trimming at the neck and sleeves. The folds of the skirt drifted in shimmering delicacy about her slim hips, not quite touching her white satin shoes. Her hair framed her calm face in a wide, shining, loosely upturned coil and was secured on the top of her head with intricately arranged mother of pearl combs.

But it was Mara, to the chagrin of her mother-in-law, who quite outshone them all, glorious in golden satin and net, narrow skirted with a low square décolletage bodice from which the softly rounded tops of her white breasts spilled quite outrageously, catching the eye of all the masculine company, even that of her father-in-law who was after all a man, and Teddy was seen to miss his mouth several times with his fork. The dress had a train ninety-one inches long – Mara had had her maid triumphantly measure it – which divided and swept back over her shoulders where it was fastened with invisible press-studs.

Inviting herself, since her daughter-in-law had somehow omitted to do so, was dainty little Mrs James Osborne the first, dressed in a gown of silver lace which Mara was positive must have been made for her forty years ago, with a wide crinoline which whispered against the carpet as she walked. She looked as beautiful now as she had done then though none of the table could vouch for it, of course. As the ladies were seated by the gentlemen the old lady caught Mara's eye and winked conspiratorially, just as though they shared some secret known to none of the others. Of course they had lived together for two months before the wedding and had got on famously, Elizabeth remembered, as Mara winked back at her.

'And how was Rome, Mara?' Serena asked politely, starting

the conversational ball rolling as was her duty as hostess.

'Grand, Mrs Osborne, thank you,' saying no more, not because she was shy or nervous but because she could honestly not think of anything she had to declare on the matter.

'Did you not think the Sistine Chapel quite breathtaking?'

'Did I, James?' Mara asked carelessly, turning to her husband, evidently not recalling it and Eaton could have sworn the mistress would choke on her soup.

They chatted in a desultory fashion during each course, being polite, treating Mara as though she was a guest and one to whom some degree of courtesy was owed. Mara did not appear to notice. She watched James carefully as he had instructed her so that she would be certain to use the correct utensil for each course, though by now she was pretty confident she could manage without him. The ladies left the gentlemen to their port, a daft idea in Mara's opinion since she really had nothing to say to these new female relatives of hers and would far rather have giggled in the deep sofa with James. Even Elizabeth, who was inclined to be friendly, was far too quiet for Mara's taste and the old lady would keep rambling on about *her* James and the friend she called Rosie and what the three of them had done in the old days, once even remarking that she was certain Lancer, whoever or whatever he might be, was lurking outside the window and would Jackson go out and tell him to be off. Evidently well used to the old lady's idiosyncrasies, the footman did so, or at least he left the room and none of the family appeared to be unduly concerned. They were a strange lot, the Osbornes, but she'd soon get the hang of them, she told herself cheerfully. In an hour or so she and James would be deep in the bliss of their new marriage bed and the delights they shared there and tomorrow she'd go and have a real talk with her own Mammy. She sighed in satisfaction as she took the dainty coffee cup and saucer her mother-in-law offered her.

She rang the front door bell of number 11 Edge Lane six times before anyone came to answer it. She had been surprised to find it locked since it never had been except at night when she had lived there. She had been just about to go round to the kitchen door, reluctant to do so for somehow that would have spoiled it since she had wanted to step down from her carriage – the motor car had been spoken for by Mrs Osborne – tell the coachman to wait, sweep up the path in her new sable coat, through the front door and into her Mammy's welcoming arms in one grand gesture. She had imagined herself summoning the coachman and the footman who had accompanied her to bring in the box and . . .

It was Matty who opened the door a crack and in a thin voice informed the grand Mrs Osborne that Mrs O'Shaughnessy was not in.

'Not in, don't be talking daft, girl, an' why did it take you so long to answer the door? See, get out of me way, keepin' me here on the doorstep like some pedlar.'

She put her hand on the door, ready to shove Matty irritably to one side, to give her a piece of her mind for her impertinence for did the woman not know how important Mara now was, but the maid stood her ground and it was beneath the dignity of Mrs James Osborne to wrestle with a servant beneath the interested gaze of the two who waited at the gate.

'Open the damned door, Matty,' she hissed, 'or you'll be feelin' the flat of me hand.'

'The mistress is not at home.' It was said woodenly, just as though the words had been learned by rote, repeated again and again until the somewhat simple woman had them by heart.

'Where is she then? An' where's Caitlin? Is she not at home either?' said in a deeply sarcastic tone. 'Jesus, Joseph and Mary, they can't both be out an' if they are I'd like to know where. At Church, is it? Well, then I'll wait.' She did, for a moment, for Matty to open the door to her but the woman simply stood there vacantly.

'Is the Mammy at Church, Matty, or is she not?'

'The mistress is not at home.'

'Sure an' if you say that once more, you half-witted simpleton, I'll box your ears until they ring. Now open the door an' let me in.'

She was about to push it open forcefully, sweeping aside the frozen-faced, blank-eyed maidservant, exasperated beyond measure, when it suddenly sprang wide open and in the doorway stood Ellen O'Shaughnessy, her Mammy.

But not her Mammy. This was not the rosy, smiling face, the loving smile, the welcoming, approving eyes, the bounteous, open-hearted mother who had loved her, scolded her, petted and cosseted her all her life. Not *her* Mammy who, though Mara knew she would be inordinately upset by her daughter's ... well ... wickedness, Mara supposed, would not be able to resist it when Mara asked her forgiveness and when she understood the splendid future which was in store for her daughter How could she not be glad that her girl had done so well for herself? Oh, she knew in her Mammy's eyes the marriage, indeed any marriage not blessed in Holy Mother Church, was no marriage at all and that by straying from their own firm Catholic faith Mara had sinned grievously, but she meant to put that right in the sight of God, the Church and Ellen, the last the most important. She would persuade James to come to Church and have a quiet ceremony of blessing, just her family and Father Paul. It would be like having two weddings, really. Of course there was the question of the child and its faith, which they had not yet discussed. Well, they hadn't had time, had they, not in all the sweeping excitement which had carried them along ever since that first dizzying ecstasy she and James had shared in Colton Wood. She was not awfully sure how the Osbornes would view their grandchildren being brought up in the true faith but she'd cross that bridge when she came to it. In the meanwhile she must get round this cold stranger who was barring her way and return her to the loving, reproving Mammy she had always known.

'Mammy . . .' she said tentatively, not awfully sure how to begin.

'There's no Mammy of yours in this house,' the stranger said.

Mara's heart plunged frighteningly. 'I don't know what you mean, Mammy.' Her voice rose childishly. 'Can I not come in? I've driven over to see you an' there's presents for everyone . . .' waving her hand in the direction of the two Osborne servants who stood, watching curiously, the trunk full of gifts between them.

'We want nothing from you, or yours. You are nothing to do with this family any more.'

'But Mammy, it's me, Mara. I've come to . . .'

'I don't care what you've come for, there's nothing here for you now. You sacrificed the love an' respect of your family when you lifted your shameless skirts for that heathen . . .'

Mara was appalled. 'Mammy . . . please . . .' Her voice rose even higher. 'Can we not talk inside?'

'I'll not have you in my house, you filthy slut . . .'

'*Mammy*!' Mara's wail of terror caused several passers-by to turn and stare and the men at the gate exchanged looks of indecision. She was the young master's wife, after all, and though those in the servants' hall had all waited for her to fall flat on her face, little upstart that she was, could they stand by and see her insulted, even by her own mother, especially in her condition? Master James would never forgive them if anything happened to cause her to miscarry. Should they not retrieve her and lead her gently back to the carriage and home, their expressions asked one another?

'Leave my house at once an' I'd be obliged if you'd not come back,' the woman with Ellen's face and voice said. 'You chose the path you took an' now you must walk on it.

Go home to your own folk for there's none of yours here.'

'Oh please, Mammy, don't say that. You're my folk, you know you are, an' I must come an' see you an' Daddy. This is my real home an' I couldn't bear it if I couldn't come an' visit you . . .'

'You should have thought of that when you lied to me and your Daddy. You said you were goin' to lectures an' talks an' we believed you. We trusted you, so we did, an' you betrayed us. You stabbed us in the heart but worse than that you turned your back on the teachings of the Church and this house when you fornicated with that . . .'

'Holy Mother of God . . . please don't . . .'

'How dare you speak of the Holy Mother, you wicked girl. I'll not have Her Blessed name on your filthy tongue. A slut ye are. A fornicating, lying slut who has forsaken her home, her family and her faith an' if the Blessed Mother can forgive you, I can't. Now get off my doorstep. I've just cleaned it.'

The last would have been comical had the situation not been so anguished.

'No . . . let me speak to you, Mammy. Please let me in. Let me explain . . .'

'What's to explain, girl? Sure it's as plain as the nose on your face what's been done to you. A month married, if you can call it that, an' four months gone with child by the look of you. What else is there to say?'

Mara was weeping brokenheartedly now and so was Matty who still hovered at her mistress' back. Further down the hallway Clare had her face in Lucy's starched apron, terrified to hiccoughing silence by the ferocious woman whose figure in the doorway blotted out the pale winter sunlight, and by the desolate sound that came from her sister.

There was a flurry of skirts and the sound of footsteps coming down the stairs and behind the cold and furious face of Ellen O'Shaughnessy, Caitlin's appeared. It was smiling in pleasure for though she and Mara had had their spats in the past there was a strong bond of family, sisterly affection between them. She had not approved of Mara's method of catching a husband, if that was what she had done, though Michael had told her in private that their sister genuinely loved James Osborne, even if the marriage was somewhat unorthodox, but it was all in the past now. There was the coming child to consider and there would be nothing more likely to heal the breach between mother and daughter than for Mara to put a grandchild in her mother's arms.

But what in Heaven's name was going on here? Mara weeping, her mother's face like a grey sheet of ice and Lucy and Matty wailing like banshees.

'Mara ... Mammy ... what's happening? Is Mara not to come in then?' she asked, though it was very evident that she was not. 'Mammy, you can't mean to turn her away, not now, not after all this time. See, Matty'll wet the tea and we'll have a wee talk by the fire ...'

'There'll be no wetting of tea, Caitlin, not for this one an' not in this house so get you back upstairs and attend to your own business. Go an' write a speech for the foolish women who believe in your eejit words an' who know nothing of the real world where families are shattered and broken by the ...' She bent her head for a moment in despair, Caitlin imagined, and both she and Mara moved compassionately towards her but she lifted her head and motioned them both away.

'Leave me be, Caitlin, an' you, get off my doorstep, madam. Go on, take yourself back to where you now belong.'

'Mammy, I never meant to ...'

'Mammy, will you not be lettin' her in, just for a minute?'

'Let her in, Mrs O'Shaughnessy,' Lucy wept, clutching the little girl to her. 'You're frightening the baby, so you are.'

Ellen turned on her, turned on them all, her eyes wild, her face now a bright, mottled puce except for the stark white line about her mouth. She had known Mara would come, of course she had, for her daughter, careless and warm-hearted herself, would think she had only to smile and hug her Mammy and all would be forgiven. Ellen had prepared herself for it. She would be cold, precise and positive. She would make her position known with the minimum of words and shut the door in the girl's face but she had not bargained for her child's pleading desolation nor for the fierce, painful longing in her own heart. This was Mara, her beautiful wayward girl, fruit of her womb, the delight and pride of her own ageing body, selfish, lazy, vain and often greedy but with a sweetness in her, a humour and strength which would make her into a fine woman when she had outgrown her girlish rebellion. But she had done a shameful, wicked thing, something Ellen could not countenance. Strong and enduring in her love, she was the same in her pitiless disapproval.

'Frightening the baby, is it? An' who's fault is that, I'd like to know? Not mine, no, not mine. It's this ... this one on me own doorstep who's to blame an' I'll not have her in me house again.' Realising that in her harrowing need to strike at Mara and at the same time to draw her into her own yearning embrace she was herself becoming hysterical, Ellen made a conscious effort to calm herself, pushing aside the comforting arm Caitlin would have put about her.

'Leave me be, girl, an' get back to them pamphlets you're so taken up with. Take the baby back to the kitchen, Lucy, an' you go with her, Matty. This is between me an' ... an' Mrs Osborne.' The last two words were spoken with quiet contempt.

'Now then,' she said, turning back to Mara as Caitlin, the two maids and the little girl trailed away into the kitchen. 'I've only this to say to you. You gave up all rights to be part of this family when you opened your legs for that boy. Sure an' he's as bad as yourself in this affair.' Her voice was calm now, and completely expressionless. Her face was blank and empty as though, in order to control the wilful feelings inside her which demanded that she draw her weeping girl into the home which had been hers for seventeen happy years, she must smother them. 'You've done bad things, girl. You've lied and cheated to get what you wanted. Not just your Daddy an' me but that boyo you've married. 'Tis the oldest trick in the world you've pulled, an' I despise you for it...'

'Please, Mammy, I'm sorry ... please let me come in...'

'... but the worse thing is your mockery of Holy Mother Church an' the way of life you've been brought up in. I pity you, my girl, an' I despise you. You're no child of mine...'

'Mammy, don't...'

'You'll burn in hell...'

'No...' Mara was clutching the door frame for support, shivering like an aspen tree in a wild wind. She could feel the nausea claw at her stomach and the bile rise to her mouth and she knew that in a moment the swirling mists in her head would blot out her last conscious thought, praise be to the Holy Mother for there was nothing she wanted more than to escape from this frightening woman who was masquerading as her dear Mammy. A cruel stranger who spoke with her mother's voice and used her mother's beloved face but who could not possibly be Ellen O'Shaughnessy.

'... so you can take your presents and yourself back to the life you chose when you let that boy have his way with you. Now, get off me doorstep.'

The door banged to with a crash which almost had it off its hinges and the two men at the gate jumped. Their young mistress leaned in anguish against the porch, tears streaming unchecked across her ashen face and on the other side of the door Ellen O'Shaughnessy clutched her arms about herself, bending over as though in agony. A strange sound came from between her bitten lips, like that of a wounded animal. Her hands were clenched into tight fists to stop them from straying towards the door handle and she cursed her mother's heart for not believing what her strong and absolute faith in the teachings of her religion told her was right

She heard the dragging footsteps of her girl on the porch step. She heard the gate click and a moment or two later the grate of horses' hooves on the road. It was only when the sound had died away to nothing that she began to weep as though her heart was broken, which it was.

They thought Mara would miscarry that night, even Serena afraid for the safety of the heir which, after all, grew in this girl's womb and must be considered.

'I can't manage without the Mammy, James,' Mara said, over and over again as though she was puzzled as to why he could not understand it. Did he not realise that, despite her love for himself and her resolute intention to be the greatest society hostess this corner of Lancashire had ever seen, she was still an O'Shaughnessy deep inside her, Irish and proud of it, bound by ties which could never be severed to her family, her culture, even her land over the water, and it was her mother who held the threads of them in her strong and loving hands. Mara had to be part of them, her real family, no matter what her new life dictated and she would be incomplete if she was not allowed to share that flowing abundance of love her mother directed at them all. It was what gave her solid ground beneath her feet, her own sense of being, and without her mother's love and approval, which she had been certain she could win back, she was no one. And like the child she still really was she could not wait to have everything as she wanted it to be. James must drive over to Edge Lane – this at two hours past midnight – and beg Mammy to reconsider. He must explain that in her condition Mara must not be denied her mother's attention, which she had had all her life and he was to impress on her that Mara could not, absolutely *could not* survive without it.

'Daddy'll persuade her, James, he always does. Talk to

him first,' and when James, no more than a boy himself, flung by his own male desire into this situation which with all the goodwill in the world he was not yet mature enough to manage with any degree of compassion, hesitated, she began to cry even more hysterically. Even worse, she flung her swollen body about the room, crashing into the furniture, threatening damage not only to herself and her child, *his* child, but to the contents of the pretty room which, only that morning, she had declared to be 'heaven'.

'Don't darling, please don't. Come to bed and let me put my arms about you,' hoping to distract her in the activity with which, up to now, she had been as enraptured as himself, but she had backed away from him as if he had suggested some disgusting perversion.

'Don't you touch me, James Osborne. Don't you come near me or by the faith I swear I'll stick these scissors into you.' Her hand had fallen upon the pearl-handled nail scissors which lay on her dressing table and she brandished them as she began to scream. ' 'Tis you an' your kisses which got me into this mess, so they did. If it hadn't been for you and your pretty speeches, sure me an' the Mammy would be as right as rain. You trapped me, so you did, an' now she won't have anything to do with me an' how am I to manage with a baby coming an' her not here to see me through it?'

'Mara darling, you will have the very best of care when the time comes, you know you will.' Misunderstanding completely the central cause of his wife's terror, James did his best to comfort her, following her warily as she thrashed about the room. Further along the corridor, and not caring for this kind of appalling behaviour in her house, though what else could one expect, really, Serena threw back the bedclothes of her own bed and rang the bell for her maid. She would have to go along the landing, she supposed, and put a stop to this nonsense before the whole household, servants and all, was brought from its bed. She could hear Johnny moving in the room which adjoined hers and lights were going on all over the house, she was sure.

A nerve-tingling wail and a shattering of what sounded like glass brought her to the realisation that she could not wait but would have to find and put on her dressing gown without the assistance of her maid. Footsteps padded by her door and when she opened it, Elizabeth, white-faced and trembling, stood just beyond it with Teddy and Eaton, looking strange in his own bulky plaid dressing gown, hovering at James and Mara's door.

'*I want my mother.*'

The word 'mother' should have warned them for didn't Mara always, just to annoy Serena, her mother-in-law was certain, refer to Ellen as Mammy, and on that last word the bedroom door was flung open and James, wild-eyed and grey-faced, stood there with the struggling, weeping figure of his wife in his arms.

'Thank God . . . thank God . . .' he babbled, looking directly at his mother who in all his young life he had never seen anything but self-possessed. He was not, of course, present when she had learned of his intention to marry the screaming, violent girl in his arms.

'The doctor, Eaton.'

'Yes madam.'

'Calm down, James.'

'Yes mother.'

'Pull yourself together, Mara.'

'You go to hell. I want my mother.'

'Help me, Elizabeth.'

'Yes mother.'

And for twenty minutes, until the doctor came to administer the dose which, repeated at intervals for the next few days, kept Mara Osborne in a state of limp placidity until acceptance came, Serena Osborne, in the tradition of the long line of aristocrats from which she came and which had deserted her only once in her life, protected her grandchild from its own mother.

She might not have been quite so determined had she known the child would be called CLAUDINE!

11

Harry Woodall watched Elizabeth Osborne as she trundled towards him the large ungainly perambulator in which lay her four-month-old niece, Claudine Osborne. It was a deep and sturdy vehicle, boat shaped, its solid wooden coachwork hung on leather straps attached to two large springs. The hood had jointed stays to keep it open and the grip on the handle was made of porcelain. Claudine was the fourth Osborne baby to be pushed about in it since Serena had seen no purpose in buying new for each of her children when the only time the perambulator was used was when Nanny took her charges for a turn about the grounds of Beechwood.

It had been a long and glorious summer this coronation year and each time the Osbornes gave a tennis party, held a picnic or a garden party where strawberries and cream were the order of the day, Serena was heard to remark to her friend, Lady Woodall, that surely this must be the last one since the weather must break soon. Day after day the sun flung its heat and golden rays on to the well watered lawns and massed flower beds which were the result of Serena's gardening activities. It was an activity in which a gentlewoman might take part without in any way being thought less of a lady, or even unfeminine. She did not actually touch the plant, of course. Wearing a gardening dress of beige resada, an eminently suitable colour and material, a wide-brimmed straw hat and a coloured apron she directed her team of gardeners in the planting and weeding, the mulching and hoeing and was considered knowledgeable and not at all strange in her hobby. Providing it did not interfere with her afternoon obligation which was the leaving of cards, paying calls and having calls paid on her, it was considered a fitting occupation for a lady such as herself.

But the custom of leaving cards and paying calls was the first duty of any lady, of course. Her cards were printed in copperplate, thick and about three inches by two in size. Lately Serena had given instruction for her telephone number to be added to them for though the instrument was rather inconveniently situated in the lobby between the smoking room and the gentlemen's downstairs lavatory, it was sometimes useful to use it for more informal social intercourse such as the giving or accepting of invitations. She had a card case made of ivory and on her hall table was a silver salver on which cards from callers would rest.

The giving and receiving of cards was an intricate commitment whose niceties must be observed. Serena, on meeting for the first time another lady at a dinner party or afternoon tea would not leave cards until further meetings had enabled her to be certain that the acquaintanceship would be desirable. Residents called on newcomers and not the other way round, the lady of the highest social standing taking the initiative. Any gentleman who left his card for a young lady and not her mother was considered ignorant and ill-bred and would not be received, and a gentleman caller never, *never* left his hat, gloves and walking stick on the hallstand lest he compromise his hostess' reputation, but would take them into the drawing room with him, laying them neatly on the floor beside his chair as he sat down for the designated fifteen minutes which polite society allowed.

Elizabeth was already well schooled in this upper class ritual. From the age of sixteen when she had left the schoolroom and put up her hair she had accompanied her mother when she called on her friends, sipping tea and nibbling on a biscuit, listening to such well-bred conversation as was considered suitable for her innocent, sixteen-year-old ears. She was competent in the small talk with which one lady engaged another. The absorbing question of the difficulties of obtaining decent servants, the fascinating challenge of the tight tube-like dresses which were fashionable and the awkwardness of walking when wearing one since they were so restricting one was forced to adopt a mincing gait or trip oneself up. The parties and balls that were planned for the coming winter, the charity work for the poor and needy who were always there, and the appalling behaviour of Mrs Pankhurst and her daughters who must surely be out of their minds to carry on the way they did were all discussed. Like the true ladies they were they could scarcely believe that others could demean themselves in such a way, and for what? Why should they need to vote after all, when their menfolk were perfectly capable of doing it for them and thereby take the strain on their own strong shoulders of the decision as to who should govern the country.

The ladies were deep in conversation on this bright autumn day, giving their whole attention to the engrossing subject of the glamorous Lady Cunard, born plain Maud Burke of a well-off San Francisco family, and the house she had rented in Cavendish Square in London which had a dining table of lapis-lazuli, or so they had heard. Pretentious, they all agreed and not one of the company would care to be invited to view it and if they were they would not accept. There was Serena Osborne and Lady Woodall, Lady Fenton, Sarah and Anne Hemingway, who were cousins of Johnny's, and languishing on the fringe of the well-bred group, Serena Osborne's daughter-in-law, Mrs James Osborne. No one spoke to her, nor even glanced in her direction and her boredom was very evident. She lolled, that was the only word Serena could bring to mind, like some hoyden schoolgirl, her eyes closed, her arms behind her head whilst the sun's rays, which every lady knew were anathema to the skin, poured on to her upturned face. She really was a trial and a tribulation to her mother-in-law with her complete lack of what Serena called finesse, and without the least pretence of good manners. One would think after almost a year of being James' wife and given the close and vigilant contact she had had with the Osbornes, the Woodalls and the other county friends who were Serena's guests that some of their breeding might have rubbed off on her but she was just as graceless, just as .. well, one could only call it common, as on the first day she had been forced upon them. She made no attempt at the courteous conversation ladies made with one another and one could only presume she had none. She seemed bored to distraction, letting it show quite disgracefully and Serena had a mind to speak to James about it since the girl took not the slightest notice of what anybody else had to say. If she had no interest in the social events to which as Serena's daughter-in-law she was naturally invited, then she should stay away.

There were shouts of laughter and cries of 'well done' and 'well played' from the direction of the tennis court where the Hemingway cousins, George, Amy and Alice, who had come over from Sefton Park with their mother, Sarah, were taking on James, Teddy and Tim Woodall in a frantic and unorthodox game of tennis which involved six players all taking turns to hit the ball in strict order. Had not Lady Cunard's strange decorative tastes taken up their complete attention Serena and Anne Woodall would have put a stop to it by now since it was somewhat boisterous and not at all the thing young ladies should get up to.

'Don't you want to join in, Harry?' Elizabeth called as she pushed the perambulator up the slope towards him. 'It sounds great fun whatever it is they are supposed to be playing. One of James' inventions, I'm sure. Honestly, would you think he was the father of this darling child?' swooping to peer beneath the hood into the baby carriage. 'He sounds like some schoolboy home for the vac.'

She adjusted something beneath the white, lace-lined hood, smiling and clucking at the baby and Harry studied the soft and quite breathtaking loveliness of her profile. Her head was on one side, her whole fond attention given to the child who was her niece, as his was given to her, and he sighed in unconscious bemusement since it seemed to him that she was the embodiment of pure motherhood of which all men dream, though the child she smiled at was not her own.

He cleared his voice. 'Shouldn't that infant be in the charge of the young woman hovering over by the trees?' he asked lazily, doing his best to sound light-hearted and concerned with nothing beyond the enjoyment of the shrieking tennis players. 'She looks awfully worried about something. I think she imagines you are going to take it out and play silly beggars with it.'

'Oh, that's the nanny mother has employed. She is one of those new Norland nurses that have become so fashionable and why mother has decided on her is a complete mystery. You know how Victorian she still is about such things. This one is completely different to the old nanny you and I had, Harry, and she is certainly very efficient. She has been trained, she tells me, almost as a nurse is trained, and between them she and the nurserymaid make it difficult to even take a peek at Claudine when she is in the nursery. And she is such a lovely child, so good-tempered, just like James. Look at her eyes, Harry, they're the most gorgeous shade of blue and green, so pale and pretty, like those of a kitten . . .'

'Dear Lord, Elizabeth, anyone would think the child was yours,' but it was said smilingly, with no intention to offend.

'I know, that's what mother says and Mara doesn't like . . .' She stopped speaking abruptly.

'What?' Harry, who had been lounging on one elbow on

a rug spread beneath the shade of a giant oak, sat up. There were hats and books and tennis racquets strewn about him, left there by the young people who were now bordering on the hysterical on the court. He pushed them aside and made room for Elizabeth to sit beside him. She darted a look at Nanny then into the perambulator as though considering whether it would be prudent to dare the woman's wrath by lifting the baby out but deciding regretfully against it, sat down.

'What is it Mara does not like?' Harry asked gently, reaching without thought for her hand and holding it in his own. She let him for it seemed the most natural place in the world for it to be. They were just below the terrace, the lawn sloping away from them in smooth, green folds down to the tennis court. There was a soft breeze bringing the smell of the velvet-headed roses from her mother's garden. About them was the tranquillity of an English country garden, beneath them was the strength of England's rich earth and above them the high, blue solitude of an English summer sky. What more could life give them, these children of the privileged ruling class of this great land, but they did not even consider their great good fortune as Harry's fingers, firm and sure about Elizabeth's told her that she was sheltered there in the palm of his hand. She was at peace. Home. Where she belonged. She could sense the calm strength of him, there for her to lean on, to cling to should she need it, his manner said, the warmth and the honesty in his eyes telling her quite plainly that she had but to say the word and it was hers for the taking.

She sighed contentedly. 'It's hard for her, Harry. She loves Claudine in a way you and I were never loved by our own mothers. I'm not implying that the affection was not there,' she added hastily, 'but with Mara and her baby the way of showing it is different, do you know what I mean?' She looked up at him in some confusion but he nodded, understanding as she had known he would. 'Naturally she knows she can't look after the baby herself because it wouldn't do, would it, and I don't really think she wants to. Not the messy parts, at any rate, but what she does need is to be able to have free access to the nursery whenever she wants it.'

'And can't she?' His thumb moved of its own wayward volition against the smooth flesh of her inner wrist and she felt a frisson of pleasure move through her. Harry really was sweet. He was gazing intently into her face, his own serious and concerned, for Mara, for the baby, or for her? She didn't know. She only knew it was delightful to have his whole attention, to have him listen to her in a way no one else did as though what she had to say was of the utmost importance.

'Oh no, Harry. You know that. Nanny wouldn't like it. One sees one's mother only once a day at tea-time, or perhaps twice if she comes into the nursery to say goodnight, and it interrupts Nanny's strict regime to have visitors calling at any time of the day or night they feel inclined to drop in. You know the routine as well as I do. The nursery suite has been done over to accommodate the baby and Nanny and the nurserymaids have their quarters there and they certainly don't want Mara interfering in what they do.'

It seemed not in the least unusual to either Harry or Elizabeth that three or four women were employed to look after one small infant who, perhaps before the year was out, would have a brother or sister to share with and no doubt more as the years passed. Nor that the suite of rooms in which they would all be installed should comprise of a day nursery, a night nursery, a playroom, later a schoolroom, bathroom and pantry, not to mention the bedrooms the nurserymaids occupied. Though they spent most of their time there, seeing to the needs of Miss Claudine Osborne, there would be a great deal of carrying up and down stairs from the kitchen by them for only simple meals would be prepared in the nursery pantry. The laundry for the maids and for the baby would be extensive and would be done by the laundry maids in the laundry at the back of Beechwood.

Children lived in a world occupied by themselves and their servants, both Harry and Elizabeth knew this and Mara must learn to accept it.

'It really isn't right that Mara should drift in there whenever she has a fancy to,' Elizabeth continued, 'and Nanny gets most upset when the order of the nursery is disorganised.'

'Do I detect your mother's words there, Elizabeth?' Harry's face was still serious, considering what she said carefully, but his lips twitched as he tried not to smile.

'Well ... yes, I suppose they are, but Mara has her own duties and mother is doing her best to ...'

'Fit her into her new life?'

'Yes, that's it exactly, Harry, and if Mara will keep interfering with the nursery and Nanny's duties, nobody will know where they are, will they?'

'No indeed,' his voice was grave, 'but tell me this, Miss Osborne, if that is the case how is it that you have your niece in that baby carriage when you have just gone to great lengths to explain Nanny's duties, one of which is, I'm sure, pushing the child about the lawn. Besides which, does your mama not think it slightly déclassé for her daughter to be seen trundling the thing about when there is a perfectly good Nanny to do the job. These things have a way of getting out of hand, you know.' His endearing, slightly lopsided grin told her exactly how silly it all was.

She began to smile, then to laugh out loud, lifting her face to the dense green foliage of the tree which was no more than three or four feet above their heads, the sun shining through it to dapple them in a moving tracery of light and shade. The arch of her throat was sweet and pure and Harry's hand tightened on hers. For a moment he was tempted to lift it to his lips and place a kiss in the centre of her palm but he knew this was not the time, nor the place, not with Serena Osborne and his own mother in plain view. Besides, she had been seventeen no more than six months and was surely too young to be considered yet for marriage which was, of course, what he intended. He knew he loved her now, had known from the day he had become twenty-one and had seen her, really seen her as a young woman. As Elizabeth Osborne, beautiful and desirable as any man could wish in his woman. Not James Osborne's young sister, not his sister Sophie's childhood friend but as herself, female, unknown and intriguing and ready, soon, to be loved. And he loved her. It had been as simple as that. His boyish, careless affection for what she had been was transformed, almost in that single moment when she had placed her hand in his where it fitted exactly, from the love a man has for a friend into that he feels for a woman. She was not quite a woman yet but when she was it would be he, Harry Woodall, who meant to have her. On her eighteenth birthday he would declare himself and that was next March. Six months. Perhaps by this time next year they would be married for despite her youth she was amazingly mature at times.

'You always manage to make me see things in their true light, Harry,' she was saying. 'Why should I not take my niece for a stroll in the park if I want to and why should not Mara be allowed to dandle her daughter on her lap for all to see? There is no shame in it.'

'We are all hidebound, Elizabeth. Our ... our class, if you like. Our parents were brought up in a certain way as theirs were before them and it takes a lot of courage and resolution to go against what we have been taught is correct. I doubt if they even question it. In fact I'm sure they see no reason to believe there could be another way to bring up one's children. But has it never struck you ... well, does it not seem ... odd, in view of Mara's attitude, that there is little or no show of affection between us? Our parents, I mean. I suppose they must be fond of us but why do they not say so ... or at least demonstrate it? Why should we be as we are? Why are we separated from each other by these rigid conventions? I am ... attached to my mother and father but . well, I hardly know them. When I have children I should like to feel they .. care for me and that, like Mara, if I took a fancy for it I could lift my child on to my lap and .. embrace it. Even join in at bathtime which seems to me could be a lot of fun. To hell with Nanny and her rules.'

He was smiling whimsically but there was a serious look in his eyes and about his good-humoured mouth as though to let her know he meant what he said. 'Rebellion, Elizabeth. I shall be a rebel father when the time comes, throwing out all the old conventions and bringing up my children to love me as I shall love them.'

She was staring at him in awed admiration, her poppy lips parted. Her eyes shone with delight and she lifted his hand which still held hers, to her cheek.

'Oh Harry, how marvellous and what lucky children to have you for their father. Will you really invade the nursery and dare Nanny's wrath?'

'With the right wife beside me, Elizabeth. One who thinks as I do'

She dropped her gaze then for there was something in his eyes which was strange, something she was not quite sure she wanted to recognise, not yet, so she avoided it, clinging to her girlhood and her innocence until she was ready, or was made to be ready by her mother, for the status of womanhood.

She sprang up, her body moving with fluid grace. She was simply dressed in a pale cream muslin afternoon dress. It was straight, fitting to her breasts and hips and just brushing the arch of her foot, with cream satin ribbon at the neckline and a broad satin sash three inches below her waist. She looked very young, younger even than her seventeen years. Her hair had been brushed until it gleamed and was plaited simply to hang down her back to her waist where it was tied with an enormous cream satin bow. She smelled of lavender. Her skin had the pale delicacy of porcelain, only her vivid green eyes the colour of emeralds, were exotic and vibrant in the girlish candour of her face.

'Thank you, Harry,' she whispered conspiratorially. 'You have given me courage to defy Nanny even further. Wish me luck.' Bending towards him for a brief moment, she winked before turning back to the baby carriage, manhandling it until it faced in the direction of the group of ladies. She gave him one last twinkling look over her shoulder then marched determinedly towards them. He saw her wave away the approaching figure of Nanny with an imperious hand.

'Thank you, Nanny. Mrs James and I can manage,' he heard her say as she continued regally across the lawn.

'I'm taking baby for a walk, Mara, if that's all right with you,' she said casually, giving to Mara the right which was hers of deciding what was to be done with her own child. Harry smiled before he lay back on the rug. He reached for one of the panama hats, placed it over his face and dwelled on the wonder of his heart which was filled with Elizabeth Osborne.

The conversation amongst the ladies stopped in mid-sentence at Elizabeth's words and Mara's eyes flew open. For a second or two the sunlight which had shone redly through her closed eyelids blinded her and she put up a hand to shade them.

'Will you not come with me?' Elizabeth continued. Her voice was quite neutral but there was a gleam of mischief in her eyes and Mara felt her heart which had stilled to a tedious half beat, quicken thankfully.

'You don't mind, do you, mother, if Mara and I take Claudine for a saunter down to the lake?' Elizabeth's voice was polite.

Claudine! Merciful Heavens, would she ever overcome the ignominy of having her first grandchild called by that outlandish name, Serena thought, for even now she was conscious of the careful glances which passed between her friends at the mention of it. It was so ... so ... theatrical and so absolutely typical of the girl who was her son's wife.

'But Nanny can do that, Elizabeth.' Serena's voice was as polite as her daughter's but there was an ice chip of displeasure in it. Mara had jumped up, as excited and eager as a child invited to a circus and Elizabeth was again made aware of the dreadful burden carried by this girl, scarcely older than herself, who was struggling to make a place for herself in this strange new environment of hers. She was a strong and wilful girl who would make it though, of that Elizabeth was certain, but every step of the way she had to fight not only her own upbringing, but Serena's. She wanted to conform for it was the only way she would be accepted but her rebellious, self-centred nature, her beliefs which had been instilled into her by Ellen made her fight her own self to achieve it and sometimes, as now, when her mother-in-law's friends discussed events and subjects about which she knew nothing, excluding her purposely, she lost the fight and became lifeless and colourless. At Elizabeth's words she was rejuvenated and her eyes snapped joyfully.

'Bejasus, I'd love it,' she said, forgetting in her relief that she had promised herself and James that she wouldn't say things like 'bejasus' and 'to be sure' and words of such an Irish nature.

'You push the perambulator and I'll walk beside you.'

With great enthusiasm Mara took the handle and, almost running, sent the baby carriage down the long slope towards the group of young conifers which stood at the bottom. Serena was seen to close her eyes in painful resignation.

There was a rustic seat beneath branches of the trees but Elizabeth moved beyond it.

'Let's go up to the lake and show Claudine the ducks,' she suggested.

'Aye, as far away from those old biddies as possible.'

'Well, if you say so, but my mother's hardly ...'

'She's as bad ... worse ... than the rest,' Mara said

heatedly, giving the baby carriage an angry shake. 'She doesn't want me to fit in even though she keeps saying she does. She enjoys seeing me on the edge of things making blunders with no one talking to me unless himself's there. She pretends to be helping me, so she does, but really she's glad when her friends snub me an' laugh at me behind me back when I say something Irish. How quaint, she says, as though I was some pet parrot just learning to talk but sure she'll never forgive me for stealin' her son.' Mara's brogue thickened as it always did under stress. She gave the carriage another savage shaking and Elizabeth put out a steadying hand.

'The baby has done no harm, Mara.' Her voice was mild. Immediately Mara was contrite. Turning to look back at the house to make sure that they were out of sight of the guests, she stopped and with a gesture of sheer joyful defiance, lifted her daughter out of the carriage. She tossed her into the air with all the careless disregard of a child playing with a doll, then cradled her to her breast, kissing the soft, round cheek with a passion of which Ellen would have approved. She did love her pretty little daughter and would have kept the child with her in her own boudoir, playing with her, nursing her, petting and spoiling her providing she could ring for Nanny to come and fetch the baby when she herself had had enough. She was in many ways Ellen's daughter but at the same time she thought it would be nice to be as Elizabeth was, a lady who conformed to the lady-like conventions and rules of her class, and the conflict it caused within her confused and upset her.

Putting the baby back in the carriage she sighed deeply, mutinously.

'Thanks for rescuing me, anyway. I sometimes think I'll be after going mad if I have to listen to your mother and the rest of 'em babblin' on about their servants and their children and the latest fashions . . .'

'I thought you liked clothes.'

'I do but somehow it's not the same when *they* talk about them.'

'That's because they are so much older than you are. Could you not become friends with some of the young married ladies? Amy and Alice are your age.'

'Sure an' the likes of them don't want to be friends with the likes of me, Elizabeth. They have their own circle and their own interests. I can't even go an' see my . . .' Her voice trailed away dispiritedly.

They had reached the lake by now and the ground was rough, making the progress of the baby carriage difficult. There was chickweed and comfrey and water violets clustered along the edge of the water and Elizabeth stopped to pick a violet, examining its delicate beauty carefully. This was not the first time she and her sister-in-law had skirted one another in awkward contemplation of the relationship which had been thrust upon them. They talked now and again in the stilted way of strangers who have been left together in the same room, polite and somewhat stiff, but both, for some reason, had made no further effort to nourish it. Now they were together again, alone, and would it end as it usually did with one or the other backing away?

'It's the Mammy . . . my mother. She won't see me, you know . . .'

'You mean she still won't allow you to visit her?'

'No, you see she's . . . we all are . . . Catholic and she believes I'm damned for marryin' your brother. That you're all damned, being Proddy, an' she wants no part of it, or me, now. And . . . well . . . I deceived her . . .'

'How?'

'When me an' James were . . . courting . . .' Mara bent her head and, surprising Elizabeth, giggled infectiously. The word was so foolishly inadequate to describe what she and James had got up to in his motor car and amongst the summer greenery in Colton Wood. Elizabeth, understanding her

217

amusement, began to blush then, catching Mara's twinkling glance, burst out laughing.

'Oh Mara, really, you should be ashamed, really you should but I can't help but laugh and I know I shouldn't.'

Elizabeth had a rough idea of what went on between a man and a woman in a physical sense for she was no stranger to the farmyard and, being of a practical nature, had worked out the mechanics of it for herself. She and Sophie had once peeped over the drystone wall into the paddock where George and Alfred and two of the stable boys had been putting her father's stallion to a mare. They had both been quite bewildered and somewhat afraid of the enormous 'thing' which had grown from the stallion's belly and by the raw, nervous excitement which had seemed to surround the men and animals. Several months later the mare had given birth to a delightful foal, another spectacle they had not been invited to view but, hidden in the hayloft had done so. They both had brothers, she and Sophie, and though strictly segregated by Nanny, had known from an early age of the difference between boys and girls and recently ... she must not think of that, really she must not ... he was ... he was this girl's brother ... stop it ... think of something else quickly...

'Well, I'm not ashamed, so there,' Mara was saying, tossing her head and laughing out loud, 'because it was lovely, what went on between me an' James, an' still does ... oh dear, I'm sorry...' and she covered her mouth with her hand, her eyes huge and apologetic in her grimacing face. 'I'm not supposed to speak of such things to a girl who's not married, am I? Damn it, it's hard to remember all the bloody rules ... there, I've done it again an' you'll be tellin' that fine Mammy of yours that not only does Mara Osborne enjoy making love to her husband and is not frightened of saying so but she knows a swear word or two into the bargain.'

Elizabeth was howling with laughter now, holding her hands to her midriff and after a moment's hesitation, for this was the grand Miss Osborne who was splitting her sides, Mara joined in. They leaned against one another in that absurd fashion unconfined laughter produces, begging one another not to go on for they couldn't stand it but each time either spoke they were off again until, at last, sinking down to their knees on the soft, thick grass beside the lake they managed, by taking deep breaths and not looking at one another, to let it peter out. Beyond a soft giggle or two they were silent then, a harmony that had been created by their laughter binding them in the beginning of a friendship. They lay back and gazed over the lake, watching the swans which glided on its surface, each bird leaving a V-shaped ripple in its wake, and the ducks which squabbled amongst themselves in the reeds.

'You were telling me about your mother,' Elizabeth said at last, diffidently, her manner implying that there was no gratuitous curiosity in the remark, just the sympathy of a female willing to share the problems of another, if it was needed, taking no offence, it said, if it was not.

Mara stirred. 'Yes.' Her voice was inexpressibly sad. 'She and Daddy were strict. Like yours, I shouldn't wonder. I went nowhere without someone to ... chaperone me, I suppose you'd call it.'

'Then how on earth...?'

'Oh that!' Mara laughed shortly, but it was not an amused laugh as before. 'I had a friend, Katy Murphy. Her Mammy an' mine went to the same church. We made up stories of Katy an' me going out together to the Academy, to lectures an' talks an' such so that I could get out.'

'And they believed you?' Elizabeth's voice was incredulous.

'Why shouldn't they?' Mara was indignant, then she sighed deeply. 'I'd not lied to them before, you see. At least nothing that mattered very much and I always confessed to Father Paul when I did. They trusted me and ... well, you know the rest but the worst thing for the Mammy is to know I shall burn in hell for eternity because ...'

'Mara!'

'Well, I will, Elizabeth. 'Tis true ...'

'Burn in hell! Why should you?' Elizabeth sat up violently and turned to Mara, on her face a mask of amazement that anyone could believe such nonsense. 'Even if there was such a place, which I'm sure there isn't ...'

'Elizabeth!' It was Mara's turn to be amazed and appalled. 'Of course there's a hell. My children will burn in it forever because of what I've done.'

'Fiddlesticks! What you did was not right, Mara. In fact I suppose you have been wicked in some way but it's all been made ... decent now. You and James are married and as for that innocent baby, how anyone can say that she had any part in anything bad ... well, they had better not let me hear them. It's absolute nonsense.'

Mara turned away, sighing even more deeply, for how could Elizabeth be expected to understand. On her face was an expression of sadness which sat strangely on her young, still girlish features. She would like to believe what Elizabeth was saying, really she would, but anyone in the Faith knew that Ellen was right and this girl wrong. Not that she would change what she had done, not if she was to burn in hell forever for she meant to fashion for herself and her children a place in this new world of hers. A safe place. A decent place where there would be acceptance and even respect. Besides, she was only seventeen years old, wasn't she, and death and what followed it was a long, long way off yet.

They walked round the lake, talking companionably, enjoyably, almost at ease with one another now, coming back up to the house by the long front drive and strolling round to the side entrance where the perambulator would be left for one of the footmen to lift inside. There were several gleaming motor cars parked on the wide stretch of gravel. A silver grey Vauxhall stood there, quite dazzling with its chrome lights and motor horn, the polished spokes of its wheels and the characteristic and graceful flutes along its bonnet. It belonged to the husband of Mrs Sarah Castle who had once been a Hemingway and it had brought him, herself, her son and two daughters to Beechwood for this afternoon's tennis party. There was Harry's bright red Austin Seven in which he, Tim and Hugh had squeezed themselves and beside it the most beautiful and gracious of all motor cars, the brand new Silver Ghost Rolls-Royce which Lady Woodall had persuaded Sir Charles to buy last spring after almost twelve months of persistent and female pleading which, as Sir Charles said peevishly, was the worst to resist. It was a splendid maroon with a black top, and polishing its bonnet with loving strokes was Michael O'Shaughnessy.

Mara shrieked in delight at the sight of him and several men who were working on Serena Osborne's two new circular flower beds in which she intended to plant hollyhocks, dahlias and other free blooming plants ready for next summer, turned to stare.

'Michael, darlin', there you are an' here's meself wonderin' when the divil I'd ever see the smiling face of any of you again,' she cried, reverting at once to the Irish brogue which was her heritage and which was so thick Elizabeth could barely make out what she said. Mara left the baby carriage and the baby within it to fend for itself and Elizabeth had no choice but to grab it to stop it from running back down the slight incline. She watched as, clasped in one another's arms, the brother and sister capered about the gravel drive in what she could only suppose was an Irish jig, uttering delighted cries on how grand it was to see one another, so it was, and how long it had been and how well the other looked.

'Sure an' aren't you the fine one in your lovely uniform an' begorra the hat suits you . . .'

'An' will you look at yourself, pet, in your pretty dress . . .'

'Can you really drive this owd thing . . . ?'

'Of course, an' one of these fine days sure an' won't I take you for a spin in it . . .' and it was only when the baby began to wail that Michael turned towards Elizabeth where she stood holding the handle of the baby carriage. Even then he did not look at her, and why should he, her strangely bereft heart asked, when his niece who he'd never set eyes on was waiting for his attention.

'This is me baby, Michael,' Mara said proudly, Elizabeth simply not existing at that moment. 'Sure an' I called her Claudine after the Queen.'

'Of course you did, acushla,' he answered tenderly, his arm about her waist, his nose under the hood of the baby carriage and Mara blossomed beneath his Irish approval. She'd known her family would like her daughter's name, of course she had, for were they not as exuberant and colourful as herself and though it was not strictly speaking Irish, it was as pretty as any name that came from the old country. Michael thought it was grand and so would the rest of them, when the eagerly awaited day came on which she would place her baby daughter in the warm and welcoming bosom of her family, her own family, where she belonged.

'Will I take her out, Michael?' she asked softly.

'To be sure for am I not her uncle an' longin' to give her a kiss?' which he did, cradling the baby against his uniformed chest.

At four months she had begun to smile at any face above hers and she was certainly ready to give her best to the lovely blue eyes which looked down into hers.

'Will you look at the colour of the eyes on her,' he said wonderingly.

'I know. A bit like Elizabeth's,' Mara replied dotingly and it was then he looked over the baby's head at Elizabeth Osborne.

They both felt it strike them, that sensation which was becoming increasingly familiar and increasingly terrifying. 'I won't be mesmerised by him this time,' she had told herself through gritted teeth as he and Mara had embraced. I will not let him touch my heart as he seems so easily able to do in some curious way. I will be myself, Elizabeth Osborne, daughter of the house of Osborne, born and bred a lady, cool, composed, polite but firm with inferiors, unimpressed by anything not taking place within my own society, distant, aloof and indifferent.

'So they are,' he said quietly, though his niece's eyes were more blue than green, handing the baby back to his sister. He stood in the sunshine, simply looking at her, the smiling curl at the corner of his mouth very evident, the vivid blue of his eyes which in the shaded corner of the house wall had turned to the colour of dark lavender dwelling on hers and telling her that though he smiled and was polite for Mara and the working men to see, he longed to be doing something else entirely. They both knew what that was, his narrowed expression told her.

'Mr O'Shaughnessy.' Her voice was breathless as her throat closed on his name, filled with air from her lungs which refused to go either up or down.

'Faith, Elizabeth, we'll have no formalities here,' Mara laughed. 'This is me big brother Michael, and your brother-in-law so there's no need to call him by his surname. 'Tis Michael to you, isn't it Michael?'

'That it is ... Elizabeth.'

'Michael then,' and her lips and tongue caressed his name for the first time, lingering on it as they stood, transfixed by one another until even Mara, the least sensitive of creatures, began to feel a trifle uneasy though she could not have said why.

' 'Tis a grand motor car, Michael. D'you take it with you when you go to see the Mammy?' she asked wistfully, easing the baby who immediately began to wail again back into the perambulator.

'No, oh no, acushla. 'Tis the bicycle still,' and even yet he could not drag his eyes away from the pale, strained face of

Elizabeth Osborne who, he was well aware, was deathly afraid of him and of her own feelings.

'You've ... seen her, Michael?' Mara tugged at his arm and this time he tore his gaze from Elizabeth, releasing her, and they both turned, thankfully, away from one another. He smiled at Mara.

'Yes pet, last Sunday.'

'Will she not ... does she ... mention me, Michael?'

He paused, gravely considering before he spoke. 'No, darlin'.'

She bent her head and he moved towards her, pulling her face down to his shoulder, his hand on her hair, and Elizabeth could not turn away in this private moment between brother and sister, though she felt she should. Such sadness should have no spectator, even one as sympathetic as herself.

'She knows about Claudine, doesn't she, Michael?' Mara's voice was poignant and Elizabeth was achingly aware that her sister-in-law, like herself, was really too young to be dealing with these adult emotions.

'She does, darlin', for I told her meself. But you'll have to be brave and patient, Mara. It'll take a while for her to accept . . .'

Mara lifted her head eagerly, teardrops spangling in her eyelashes. 'Will she accept it, Michael? Will she let me come home soon? I miss her and Daddy an' I want to show off me baby . . .' for, with the exception of Elizabeth, and James of course, nobody takes the slightest interest in her, her expression said. There were no lovely family get-togethers – forgetting her own resentment of the days she had been forced to share her life with her vast, sprawling family – no pleasing female gossip with an enormous pot of tea standing amongst them. No shrieks of laughter, no kisses, no hugs – except from James, of course – no teasing, no arguing, no abundance of the lively, loving, extravagantly hued stuff of life which was Ellen O'Shaughnessy's kitchen. She wouldn't go back to it for all the tea in China, she told herself, for she was to be a great lady one day, mistress of Beechwood, mother of the heir not yet born, giver of great parties and hostess to the cream of the society of Lancashire, but she would dearly like to go back home and boast about it now and again. What was the good of it if she couldn't share it with her family?

'Be patient, Mara. Sure an' I'll work on her when I see her next time. I'll tell her all about Claudine an' how she looks like Clare . . '

'Is the baby well?' she asked fondly, again forgetting the acrimony which had existed over the sharing of the bedroom.

'Fine darlin'. Startin' school next week, so she is.'

'Bejasus! School is it?'

'She's nearly five now, Mara, and the last baby . .'

'There's Claudine.'

'There is that, an' Bridget's in the family way again.'

He turned to Elizabeth, the expression on his face one of contrite amusement as though he was aware he should not mention something so tasteless as reproduction in front of the sheltered, ladylike presence of Miss Osborne of Beechwood Hall but she was no longer looking at him and when his gaze followed hers, his face hardened.

Coming across the grass towards them was his employer's oldest son. Tall, graceful, with the indolent arrogance of the privileged class into which he had been born. There was an air of good-humoured assurance about him as though he was quite certain of his welcome and he was smiling . . . at Elizabeth. Harry Woodall who would one day be Sir Harry Woodall. His eyes were warm and filled with that certain male intention which one man recognises instantly in another. There was love there, and desire, and a gentleman's attempt to keep the last hidden for was he not approaching a lady. Michael watched him come and inside him he could feel the churning rise of sudden jealous rage and savage frustration which held him fast in its bitter grip since it was very evident what was in Harry Woodall's heart for Elizabeth Osborne and what recourse had Michael O'Shaughnessy to that? She was smiling back at him, at the future Sir Harry Woodall, the look on her face the one of welcome Harry clearly had expected. It was more than welcome, it was of deliverance as though his coming had released her from some trap into which, unknowingly, unwillingly, she had been about to fall.

She held out both her hands to him and he took them.

'There you are,' she said, her smile brilliant.

'Here I am,' he answered. Without even glancing at Michael but with a polite nod to Mara who was, after all, Elizabeth's sister-in-law, he led her away with the ease of one who has the perfect right to do so.

At the last moment she turned to speak over her shoulder.

'I'll see you at dinner, Mara,' she said and though she tried hard not to do so her eyes met for a despairing moment those of Michael O'Shaughnessy's. In hers was confusion and in his was something neither wished to acknowledge.

12

The women were shoulder to shoulder on that bleak November day as they marched along Whitehall towards Parliament Square. They were all neatly dressed in sober colours for it would not do to appear frivolous or other than the resolute, serious-minded citizens they meant the country to know them as. Those who were obviously from the upper classes were more warmly clad, even more elegantly clad than the working women who stepped out beside them but what did that matter, what did class matter, when they were so firmly united in their resolve.

There were more than a hundred of them, their heads held high, their banners even higher. *Purple for dignity, white for purity and green for hope*, they proclaimed and the colours seemed to glow against the uniform greyness of the winter day.

The aim of the parade was to demonstrate the women's absolute purpose, their singleness of mind, their undiminished determination to continue their fight for equality, not just for themselves but for all women, and men, and they meant to make their case in the huge central lobby of the House of Commons on this, the first day of the new session of Parliament. But even before the long column of suffragettes had reached Parliament Square it was very apparent that even to gain its far side would require the greatest resolution.

'Here they come,' Elsie mouthed to Caitlin who strode out beside her. 'Lift the banners high, ladies, and let's show them what we're made of. Hold on to your hats.'

'Don't worry. Sure an' don't I have mine fastened under me chin with elastic. I only hope the spalpeens don't strangle me with it.'

They both tried to smile encouragement at one another as, strung out along the pavement the pack began to gather. To get from Whitehall to the Houses of Parliament the column of ladies must run the gauntlet of sneering, jibing, rubbish-throwing men and boys who were only too well aware that there was some 'fun' to be had here and though there were police constables already in evidence it was widely known they would not interfere.

There were many prominent ladies marching that day. There was Lady Constance Lytton, very frail still from her ordeal of the year before when she had been forcibly fed despite her weak heart. Striding out beside her were Emmeline Pethick Lawrence, Emmeline and Sylvia Pankhurst and

Mrs Cobden Sanderson who was the daughter of the great Richard Cobden, a reformer in his day in other fields. Just ahead of her Caitlin could see the wide-brimmed hat of Mrs Solomon whose husband had once been Prime Minister of the Cape and beyond her was Annie Kenney who, though she had not come from such exalted circles as many of her fellows was well known for her tireless work, her audacity and tenacious courage. Behind Elsie, her face inspired, holding the faith like a knight of old who went to do battle with the unbeliever, was Emily Wilding Davison who had been heard to remark recently that she would die if necessary for this crusade, this revolution on which they were all so firmly embarked.

Caitlin gritted her teeth and clamped her lips tightly over them as something caught her cheek a glancing blow. It was something soft and evil-smelling, just a small portion of the filthy substances with which all the ladies were pelted, and though it did not hurt her she felt an instinctive need to cry out. She held the pole of the banner firmly in her two strong hands with her handbag over one arm so she was unable to scrabble urgently at her cheek but it was hard to ignore the mess which slipped down on to her coat.

'Courage, Caitlin,' Elsie murmured. 'A bit of muck hurt no one, you should know that by now,' and Caitlin straightened her already straight back, lifted her head even higher and marched on. Elsie was right and none knew better than Caitlin O'Shaughnessy.

It had been on a day such as this one that she and Elsie had gone to Caitlin's first political meeting together here in London. They had been given their assignment at the little office in Clements Inn which was the London headquarters of the WSPU. It was from here that outright war had been declared in 1906 when it became clear that the Liberal Party which had just swept back into power with a huge majority did not intend to include votes for women amongst its big programme of social reforms. And it was from here that she and Elsie stepped out that day. Caitlin recalled that then, as now, the raw wind had found its way inside her warm coat, the one her mother had pressed and brushed for her the day before Caitlin took the train to London. When the time came to say goodbye Ellen had averted her face from Caitlin's kiss, letting her daughter know that she could not condone this thing Caitlin was about to do, nor her appalling behaviour in defying her parents' wishes. She was only just turned nineteen, no more than a girl, and she was going off with a woman not known to the family, and to London of all places. Nevertheless she would have no one say a daughter of hers was not well turned out, her bleak expression said as she thumped the flat iron over the good wool of Caitlin's best winter coat. She was off to do things, and say things, Ellen had been told, which she herself could scarcely bring herself to think about and Mick was like a man possessed at the thought of his lovely, well-brought-up girl going where he and her brothers could do nothing to protect her. They had read about them, as who had not, the suffragettes, horrified and terribly afraid, for how could they bear it if their daughter was damaged in some way and there were many ways of damaging a woman, God knows. Things that could be done to her which could not bear contemplating. They were quite mad, the wild creatures who fought for what could never happen and, in the opinion of most, deserved the treatment which was meted out to them for indecently exposing themselves time and time again to ridicule and abuse, but now Caitlin was to join their insane ranks, which was a different story altogether. How could they bear it? What kind of people was she to mix with and what radical, not to say non-Catholic notions might be filtered into her vulnerable mind? Impressionable, young girls were, gullible even, and God only knew how she would manage without her family to support her, protect her and keep away those swarming hordes of avaricious men who it was known preyed on young, unattached girls.

229

Ellen and Mick had pleaded, begged, forbidden, but it was all to no avail. Even Father Paul, when summoned, could not dissuade her. 'A woman's place is in her home, child,' the good father told her quietly, 'especially a young woman such as yourself. You have been sheltered from the evils of the world and brought up to believe in the chastity of women and the sanctity of marriage. Would you go against the teachings of the Church and your own parents?'

'Father, I shall do nothing to damage those beliefs nor shame my parents.' Caitlin's voice was patient but strong.

'But Mrs Pankhurst is inviting decent women to overthrow everything they were taught as children. Rise up, she is saying, rise up now, and surely you must know that such ideas cannot be right. The Blessed Mother herself...' but it did no good. She would go, she told him.

Her parents could do, or say nothing to change her mind. No threat or plea they made could deflect her from her purpose. They could disown her, of course, send her from her home and erase the sound of her name from the family circle as Ellen had done with Mara but it would crucify them to lose a second daughter, they had agonised in one another's arms in the privacy of their marital bed.

They had let her go.

On that first day, though she had felt an automatic and sudden need to cross herself and beg the Mother of Christ to protect her at this, her first meeting, she had stopped herself for what had that Sainted Mother to do with this? Instead Caitlin had taken her neatly folded banner from her handbag, holding it up for all those in the hall and on the platform to see, as she rose to her feet and asked the classic suffragette question of the Member of Parliament who was to speak.

'Will this Liberal government grant votes for women?' She knew, as Elsie knew, as all the women who had preceded her had known, that the gentleman would not answer, but though she had also been told that she could expect to be roughly handled she had not known in what way. Though she had thought about it and steeled herself to suffer it, when it happened she was not prepared for the ferocity, the sexual brutality with which she was manhandled from the hall. Both her hands were pinned behind her back leaving her breasts, though still thankfully protected by her blouse, exposed to any rough, lascivious male hand to fondle as she was dragged by. She and Elsie were thrown into the street, flung into the muck and horse droppings, deposited there only five minutes since and still steaming, by an enormous Clydesdale pulling a brewer's dray. As Elsie helped her to her feet, rounding on the circle of jeering men who came specifically to these meetings for this one purpose, Caitlin had known she could not do this. It was quite impossible. She was frightened and disgusted and humiliated and no woman should be asked to degrade herself as she was being degraded. She could not do this again, she told herself, but when Elsie began to harangue the rough men with a steely determination that said women could and would do what Caitlin knew was impossible, she faltered to Elsie's side and lifted her banner which, surprisingly, was still in her hand.

'Votes for women,' she quavered in a voice she did not recognise as her own.

They were arrested ten minutes later. They had been on the ground by then, she and Elsie, their arms wrapped protectively about their bodies, their faces turned from the men who were ready to abuse them in any way they could and only the Blessed Mother knew what would have happened had the police not arrived.

'Disturbing the peace,' the constables thundered as Caitlin and Elsie were hauled from beneath the feet of the foul-mouthed crowd. Even then the two women had struggled to protect their women's bodies since the burly clasp of the constables themselves was overtly sexual.

They spent the night in a cold, damp cell at Cannon Row

231

Police Station and the next day, refusing to pay the fine and be bound over to keep the peace for six months, she and Elsie were taken by Black Maria to Holloway Prison where Caitlin was to serve three weeks in the third division, and Elsie three months since this was not her first offence.

I can't do this, she said again to her recoiling, horrified mind as she was ordered to strip naked, with a dozen others, prostitutes, drunkards and vagrants, and climb into a flaking tin bath filled with grey scummed water in which it was obvious she and her group were not the first to immerse themselves, but she did.

I can't do this, she repeated, when she was given some odorous undergarments, a brown serge dress and a grey cap to wear, knowing they had been worn by dozens of others, but she did.

I can't do this, she told herself when she, now number 34, was pushed into a cell in which there was nothing but a plank bed resting on its side against the wall, a wooden stool and a slop bucket and where she was to spend 24 hours in each day for the next three weeks, but she did.

'No thank you,' she said, out loud this time, when they brought her a bowl of oatmeal, a piece of coarse brown bread and a mug of water, and when, after two days of politely refusing to eat she was taken from her cell, faint and dizzy, telling herself she absolutely could not do this, she finally knew that it was true.

The two wardresses took her arms, one on either side, their angry strength almost carrying her along the dark passage. Her feet dragged painfully as she did her best to keep up with them, did her best to lift her head in pride, did her best to keep her dignity. They were rough with her, careless of her pride and her dignity, and her person since these damned suffragettes were a bloody nuisance, making their work extremely provoking. It was not their fault that her weakened state made her barely able to stand up, let alone walk, and their rough, grim-faced handling of her said so.

The room to which they took her contained nothing but a plank bed, slightly lower than a table, and they forced her on to it, laying her on her back with little ceremony. Though she was too weak to resist them or indeed to make any show of defiance, they held her down, as though she might, one to each outflung arm, then waited, not speaking.

Two other burly women entered the room, their impassive faces giving the impression that this was a job they had performed many times and the sooner it was done with the better. Their 'guests' were sometimes obstreperous, those who knew the ropes, so to speak, and needed a firm hand and they were here to provide it. They were followed by two gentlemen who appeared to be in a great hurry, also irritated beyond measure by the vexed issue of the matter in hand. They wore ink-black suits and high wing collars, on their forbidding faces disapproval was mixed with their irritation, even anger. They had cold grey eyes which looked down at her as though she were no longer a human being but some inanimate and mindless species for which they had no particular care nor interest. No one spoke for several moments.

'Hold her steady,' one said, and they did, cruelly. The two already at her arms got a firmer grip on them, the third wardress at her head and the fourth at her feet. Hands restrained her, one on either side of her dirty grey cap, and her head and chin were forced back until they rested at an angle so impossible she felt her neck crack in agony. She stared up blindly into the face of the man, her body already abused, *raped* by what they were about to do to her even before they began. He looked down at her in a detached way, his face quite inscrutable and her drifting, confused mind wondered if he was a doctor and if so, did he study all those he treated in the same callous way. I must tell him not to do this. I must tell him I can't do it, really I can't, but she continued to stare up at him, wide-eyed, transfixed, her mind wandering, shadowy, her thoughts fragmented by her fear.

A cruel hand gripped her chin and she felt the touch of cold metal against her lips and her jumbled mind became ice clear as the clamp bit into her soft mouth. Sweet Mother ... help me ... give me the strength ... I can't do this ... I want my Mammy. Mammy, please ... and the steel gag was forced into her mouth. The man she could not see did something with it ... she felt his hands ... parting it wider and wider until her jaws were so far apart she felt her lips split at the corner. She began to panic, to struggle, but they held her in their inhuman embrace and there was no escape. On the furthest periphery of her vision she saw hands move to a jacket pocket and from it they produced a rubber tube ... Dear Mother ... please ... please ... and like some thin, flexible snake the hands began to run it, through the gag and down ... down into her throat. Her eyes ... why could she not close them ... why ... why ... watched it, several feet of it as it passed through the hands and along the gagging passage of her throat. The pain, as it tore her tender flesh snared her in agony and her throat closed on it. The hands produced a jug from somewhere, a jug of some liquid and above the smell of her own terror she caught a whiff of something rancid, something foul and even before it began to pour down the tube in great torrents her throat spasmed in horror. She was drowning, drowning in a thick viscous liquid and she really couldn't do it. But how was she to tell them? She struggled blindly, desperately and the hands that held her tightened their hold.

'Damn it, hold her head,' a voice roared and the first man leaned across her, lying bodily on her heaving, thrashing, terrified frame until every drop of the revolting mess had been emptied into her protesting body.

Satisfied that she had been 'fed', the man stood up, the second, unseen man removed the gag and the tube, the wardresses stepped away and on a swelling surge of nausea

234

Caitlin's outraged stomach threw back the liquid which had been poured into it. It went in all directions, like a fountain, or a volcano, coating the two men and one of the wardresses who had not been quick enough to get out of the way.

'Damn her and all like her,' one of the men said viciously. 'Fetch the other tube. We'll have to feed her nasally.'

I can't do this, her weak and outraged mind said, but she did. Every day, twice a day a rubber tube was inserted into one nostril. They were very thorough, very organised. One nostril one day, the other on the next and so on alternately. She could not stand the pain, she told herself as they tore into her throat and chest. The drums of her ears were bursting and her breast was on fire, and each time, when it was done, she was violently sick. She could not survive it, she knew she could not, but she did.

Those at the WSPU sent her home to her family to recover at the end of her twenty-one days and they all wept, her big, loving, appalled family, and her Mammy cradled her bruised, finely-drawn body in her comforting arms. Her Mammy for whom she had longed with the passionate need of a deprived child, rocking her to and fro, her tears falling in a great anguished tide on to Caitlin's unwashed hair, and Daddy threw himself about the kitchen, crazed and ready to kill those who had done this to his little girl. Michael had his cap and jacket on, asking his brothers who was ready to go with him up to London to find the perpetrators of this ... this crime against his sister's person and they all stood up and elbowed one another aside to be the first to volunteer. Sean, Dermot, Callum and even young Eammon who was only eight years old and not at all sure what had been done to their Caitlin, only that she had been in prison ... Holy Mother of God!

'There's nothing to be done, Daddy, nothing,' she had said at last, lifting herself wearily from the chair in which Ellen had held her, just as though she was six years old again. 'If we are all to get the vote we must fight for it. I have been ... slightly wounded, you might say, in this war but I'll recover.' She tried to smile reassuringly.

'Bugger the vote,' Mick roared, not really caring who got it, since he had one. 'I'll not have any child of mine abused like this an' that's an end to it. Look at you, skin and bloody bone with a hank of hair on top an' this bloody nonsense had got to stop, so it has. I forbid it, you hear me. You'll not go out of this house without my permission. Ellen, speak to her, tell her it's so.'

He turned away, his trembling hand to his face and his oldest son put his arm about his shoulders. Daddy was a quiet man, slow to anger and quick to make peace when tempers flared and the O'Shaughnessy ebullience overflowed. It was Mammy who ruled them, who saw they went to Mass, to school, told their beads and said their catechism and Daddy would sit in the chimney corner with his youngest daughter or one of his grandchildren drowsing in his lap, nodding and smiling and letting it all wash about him in pleasantly warm waves. But if he spoke, quite miraculously, everyone heard him and heeded what he said. Now he was like a man crazed and they were alarmed at the dangerously inflamed colour of his normally good-humoured face.

'Don't worry, Daddy,' Michael soothed him, though he himself would like nothing better than to take the balls of the men who had done this to his little sister and cut them off with a blunt and rusty knife. 'Sure an' she's safe now an' Mammy'll feed her up with her egg custards and beef broths an' have her as fat as butter within the week, so she will, won't you, Mammy?'

But Ellen didn't answer. She was watching her daughter with desolate eyes, eyes which could see the resolve etched into Caitlin's ravaged face. She was wafer thin, all hollows and bony ridges and on the childish, milk white skin of her neck, just where the collar of her blouse lay, were marks, some a pale yellow but others like smudges of charcoal. Her mother's heart raged at what had been done to her child for those were bruises on her neck and no doubt, when she got her upstairs and into the hot bath which Lucy and Matty were readying for her, there would be more on her body, but it was over, thank the Blessed Mother. Ellen would see to it that this was the end of it, one way or the other. Her girl was home. She had done her best, more than her best for the cause in which she had believed so fiercely and this time Ellen would find some way, even if they had to lock her up, to keep her at home.

Caitlin allowed herself two weeks in which time she was treated like an invalid, sleeping the clock round, waking only to refuse the creamy egg custards, the shin beef broth, the syllabub which her mother did her best to get her to eat. Somehow her stomach could not take the rich and nourishing food Mammy begged her to 'get down her', beginning to retch the moment anything thick and liquid was put beneath her nose. Bread and butter, a tasty piece of steaming fish and cups of hot, sweet tea. She craved solids, food she had to chew, and her strength, the reserves a healthy childhood had given her, began to return.

She walked on the Marine Parade beside the river, smelling the pungent smells of salt air, seasoned timber, coffee beans and spices. All the aromas which were associated with ships and cargoes, moving from the Lifeboat House and along beside the great, ocean-going liners. Past the observatory to the Salisbury Gate Tower. The companionship of the great liners soothed her, the long sheds into which, as a child, her Daddy had taken her, the echoing, cheerful noise of the dockers, singing, whistling as the goods of the world were stored there. The Huskisson Dock had the elegant shape of a Cunarder in its berth, its funnel brick red and black and beyond that the cream and black of a White Star. The scene was flourishing, bustling as passenger liners and cargo ships berthed or sailed on almost every tide and above her was the clackety-clack of the overhead train, the dockers' umbrella, as it was known locally, which ran from one end of the docks to the other. Her hand holding Clare's, the child's innocence and brightness and unquestioning acceptance of Caitlin as she had once been healed her more surely than the loving but ignorant sympathy of the rest of the family.

She had told them nothing of what had happened to her during her imprisonment for how could Mammy and Daddy survive it? How could they go on from day to day, living their lives when she returned to hers, as return she surely must, if they were aware of what was being done to her, what she was allowing to be done to her, what she was inviting to be done to her, which was what they would never understand.

'I go back to London tomorrow, Mammy,' she said quietly that night and the whole room froze into appalled silence. Even the two twined tabbies on the fireside rug seemed to become still for a breathless moment, their rich rumblings, the fire's crackle, the thump of Matty's flat iron on the table all dying away in horror.

'What . . . ?' The needle in Ellen's hand was poised over the shirt on to which she was sewing a button and Mick's newspaper drooped slowly down his body until it rested lifelessly on his comfortable paunch.

Everyone came to life at the same moment, even Matty thumping the table with undue ferocity. Ellen began to shake her head from side to side, the flesh of her face visibly slackening and sliding towards her chin, putty grey, but her eyes flashed with vivid, threatening life.

'Oh no, oh no madam,' she shrieked, 'never again. Over my dead body you go to that place again. Holy Mother of God, d'you think I want to see you lookin' as you did two weeks ago? Bruises on you from your neck to your knees . . . oh aye . . .' she turned ferociously to the open-mouthed assembly who had not been privy to the sight of her daughter's body as she had, her fury menacing those nearest to her as she stood up and advanced into their midst as though they themselves were at fault. 'Black and blue, so she was, an' in places that I'll not mention here an' who had the handlin' of her I'd like to know, but they'll not have the chance of it again.' She whirled to her appalled, speechless husband. 'Tell her, Mick. Tell her she'll not go again. I can't stand the thought of it. She's only a child . . . a child . . .' and throwing her apron over her face she began to weep into it. 'First one and then the other an' only the Holy Mother knows what I've suffered. What's to become of us, Dear Mother, what's to become of us?'

Clare, ready for bed in her long white nightdress, began to cry, huddling up against Lucy's skirts since her Mammy and Daddy were strangers to her in their madness. Wild-eyed and converging on their Caitlin as though they hated her and were about to do her a mischief. Her brothers were heaving about the place like maddened, frustrated, caged beasts and in the midst of it Caitlin remained, like a stone that stands erect from a river bed, isolated and steady. Water pours around it, savage and swift at times, even submerging it now and again but it does not shift and that was how Caitlin O'Shaughnessy was that night and on every other night when she left her home for what she knew was an impossible endeavour for her but which she did never-theless.

Three times she returned to them during that coronation year of 1911, broken in body, weakened and frail beyond mending, or so it seemed, and each time her roots, the closely meshed ranks of her family restored her so that she could fling herself back into battle once more.

There had been trouble in Liverpool that year as there had been trouble all over the country. Seamen's strikes and firemen's strikes, both asking for higher wages and overtime rates. They won, to their gratification, but the effect on other trades was electric. 'If them, why not us?' was the cry and August found 20,000 dockers in Southampton idle, and over twenty ocean-going liners held up because of it. Dissent had spread northwards, Liverpool and Manchester became involved and in Liverpool there had been savage rioting. Troops had been called in, firing their rifles and two men had been killed. Railway porters had struck to help the dockers and the Lord Mayor had made a proclamation warning the railway strikers that he would again have to call out the military and exercise his full powers under the Riot Act. Additional police had been brought in from Leeds and Birmingham to protect fifty tons of provisions which were being conveyed from Brunswick Dock station and on August 11th the Riot Act was again read out to the sullen crowd. A mass meeting of strikers on St George's Hall Plateau was dispersed by the police. Barricades were erected by a mob in Christian Street where again the military intervened and the Riot Act was read for the third time but by now the strike had escalated and the country found itself for the first time in the throes of a general railway strike. Industrial England was completely paralysed. Troops were used to overcome disorder and rioting and the parks of London became tented cities to accommodate them.

On August 19th the strike was finally settled and the month ended quietly but Ellen could see the toll it had taken on her husband. It seemed that the past two years had aged Mick O'Shaughnessy as though they had been twenty-two. First there had been Mara and the sorrow of her loss since as far as Ellen was concerned her daughter was dead to her and therefore to the rest of the family. She was well aware that had she weakened, discarded her own strong moral and religious principles the girl would have been welcomed back into Mick's loving, more lenient arms but it was against everything Ellen had been taught and she could not throw away that belief, even for her dear husband. And Caitlin. The constant worry of what the child got up to in London, was she in prison again, injured perhaps in the often violent confrontations which were reported in the newspapers between the suffragettes and the police who were called in to quell them? Hatchets and hammers some of the women had been seen to be carrying as they demolished the plate glass windows of Harrods and Selfridges. Cricket pitches and golf courses cut into with the words *Votes for women*, houses and churches set alight, stone throwing and worse and she knew Mick grieved silently, daily, hourly on his own masculine helplessness to protect his daughter, to stop her. She was sorry, she said, each time she limped home, but no, she must go on. They would win. They *would* win!

The summer of 1911 was the hottest for many years. The shade temperature in London was regularly over ninety degrees during the earlier part of August and on one day it reached ninety-seven. There was a long drought and the city of Liverpool sweltered in its fierceness. The strike did at least have one advantage in that Mick, with no dockers and no railway-men working, was laid off himself and though he fretted and fumed on how he was to support his family, roaming about the house and garden, getting under Ellen's feet and constantly agonising over what Caitlin was doing, he at least was able to rest in the worst heat of the day. He grew thinner and Ellen's once merry, carefree heart was as heavy and leaden as the oven-hot savagery of the sky.

But it was not hot on that November day three months later when Caitlin marched steadfastly through Parliament Square towards Westminster Hall. There was nothing unusual in this march. It was like dozens of others in which she had taken part. They were to hand in a resolution like the one which had been presented a year ago on 'Black Friday' but they did not really expect to reach even the door of the House of Commons for already the hooligans were pressing in. They were like madmen and she wondered, as she dodged a bamboo pole aimed at her head, why these men hated them so. Was it that they were frightened of the power women would have when they got the vote or was it the women themselves who threatened them? Were they

241

under the thumb of some mother, some wife and in this way alleviated their own feelings of inadequacy by subjecting other women, women who could not defend themselves and were unprotected by the police, to physical abuse?

They struck out wherever they could land a blow, but somehow, though she was accustomed – would she ever, ever become accustomed – to having her blouse torn and her hat ripped from her head, this was different. Three youths, leering and mad-eyed, had her by the arms and she became aware that she was being dragged away from her companions, beyond the great Abbey of Westminster where a dozen small battles were taking place towards a quiet back alley off Great Peter Street away from the throng of shouting people, most of them men hurrying to have their share of the fun.

She lost her footing and they hauled her along between them, laughing and excited at their luck in culling this prize for themselves, pulling her by her arms until she felt they would tear from their sockets. She could feel the heels of her boots scrape across cobbles. Her blouse had come out of her skirt and the white lace of her pretty chemise tore away beneath it, revealing the even whiter beauty of her flesh.

For a wild and fleeting moment it was as though she was back in another time and place, a time and place she had known three times now. Then there had been savage hands on her, cruel faces above hers as her body and her mind and her specifically female self was invaded and now it was happening to her again. Why? Why did men, males, the masculine gender wish to humiliate, hurt, grind down the female beneath the male boot? To break into and despoil a woman's body? Was it the one distinctive way he could demonstrate to her her own weakness, her own inability to defend not only her flesh but her instinct to build and nurture, whilst it was his to destroy?

She was screaming now, the high demented cry of an animal, a fox about to be torn to bloody shreds by the hounds and the sound bounced and echoed off the high dark walls of the cavern they had manhandled her into but there was no one to hear. There was tumult and commotion, screams and shouts, constables' whistles and pounding feet in the main area of battle, and one lone woman's fight for survival was not even noticed.

Even before they laid her on her back in a dirty corner one had his hand at the crisp cotton of her blouse, tearing at it feverishly in order to get a better view of what was beneath it. For a second she had one arm free as he held her with his other hand and she raked for his face but with an oath he forced it back above her head, twisting it cruelly to an unnatural angle and she felt something snap at her elbow. Her senses reeled beneath the onslaught of agony. Jesus Christ, her mind shrieked, would it never be resolved, this bitter war she fought for her sisters? She had thought she had given everything she had to give in the dreary cells of Holloway but it seemed she was now about to have violently taken from her that one precious right which belonged to all women. The right of her own body and the entitlement to give it, in love, to the man of her own choosing.

They were no more than fourteen or fifteen, the louts who had her, brawny youths who had never seen, let alone had a woman in their hands before and here was one Heaven-sent, so to speak, and moreover one which the constables, busy themselves in Parliament Square, neither cared about nor would be likely to punish any offence against.

''Old 'er bloody arms, Alfie,' a cockney voice gasped, 'an' let's 'ave 'er drawers off. Watch it now, strewth, she nearly 'ad me bloody balls wiv 'er feet,' but there was excitement in the way she struggled and the speaker's hands were already at his trousers. ''Urry up, Jack, for Gawd's sake . . . I can't wait . . .' another said hoarsely.

Should they strip her first, they were asking one another,

or afterwards when they had all 'had a go', fascinated by the way her naked breasts peaked into their greedy, grasping fingers. The dark shadow between her white thighs was revealed as her drawers were dragged down to her ankles, then tossed hastily to one side as they fought to be the one to part her wildly thrashing legs, and when the blows struck Jack's head and then landed across Alfie's back they both fell flat across Caitlin's heaving body like young felled trees. The third lad, his trousers round his knees, stared in stupefaction, first at his fallen comrades, then at the towering uniformed man who had struck the blows, and the evidence of his manhood and the proof that he 'couldn't wait' shrivelled away to nothing more than a walnut between his legs.

'Oh Jesus . . .' he shrieked, falling back, his hands to his private parts but it did no good as the giant hit him there with his stick and it was he who screamed then.

Caitlin was aware of nothing much after that. She slid in and out of a semi-conscious state, seeing only a man's face from which she recoiled violently, a voice, cultured, soothing, and strangely she was soothed. Dark walls and the heavy grey sky touching the rooftops, a khaki jacket about her shoulders, the material soft and smooth against her naked flesh. Her own scream as her injured arm brushed against something, the bells of an ambulance and a strong arm helping her up some extremely high steps.

'You're safe now. No one shall hurt you again,' the voice said, and she felt safe, even then, even after what had almost been done to her. The coat about her shoulders smelled of tobacco and a pleasant, aromatic cologne. The arm that steadied her was firm without being threatening and as others took her, trembling, from it she felt curiously bereft.

When she awoke she was in a clean and narrow bed in a clean and narrow room in which there were two dozen or so others like it. There were nurses and hushed voices, the smell of antiseptic masking something less pleasant and on a locker beside her bed was a vase of creamy white roses. They had been carefully arranged, she could see that, not just shoved in any old road as was the way of the busy nurse. No more than buds, glowing and pure and, in some way, healing.

She sighed and fell back into a sleep which was no longer torn with frightened dreams.

13

Ellen moved heavily about the bedroom in which Mara had once slept, re-folding the counterpane for the umpteenth time and replacing it on the bed in the corner. She tweaked at the curtains, peering out into the spring garden, admiring the daffodils and hyacinths which were clustered thickly down each side of the path and which she herself had planted. There was a vivid bed of blue crocus and another of yellow narcissus, both in immediate danger of being totally destroyed as several small O'Shaughnessys, McGowans and Conroys stampeded round the corner of the house and leaped wildly over them. The boys were brandishing sticks, cutting and thrusting in the manner of musketeers whilst the girls goodnaturedly screamed, as they had been ordered, pretending to be deathly afraid of their pursuers.

'When you get to the gate don't forget you've to surrender, Agnes, an' will you stop Mary from laughin' like that. Sure an' it doesn't look right if she's gigglin' all the time. An' what's Maeve supposed to be doin', jumpin' up an' down like that? Maeve, fall down like you were dead an' leave go of Ginny's hand!'

Really, girls were a trial at times, with no idea how to play a game properly. Callum lifted his sword, urging his troops towards the clustered group of the enemy who, when they reached the gate, refused to give in. Instead they walked off disdainfully, tossing their heads in the air, moving towards the front door and the more enjoyable pleasures of the kitchen where it was known Matty would be making fatty cakes.

'Bejasus, those daffs have come up grand,' Ellen remarked conversationally to the woman who lay in the bed, 'an' if them dratted children would keep off the crocus they'd last for weeks yet. Will I get you some to put on the dresser, darlin'? They'll take your mind off things a treat.'

'Holy Mother of God, 'tis not daffodils nor crocus I want the day but to be rid of this, Mammy. You'd think with the fifth things'd be easier but I swear this is worse than the first.' It was said weakly. The woman on the bed twisted her swollen body restlessly, trying to find a position which would give her some ease, take the strain off her aching back and legs, but whichever way she turned the pain nagged at her. Her hands plucked at her nightdress trying to smooth out its wrinkled state as though it was this which was causing her so much discomfort, then she lifted them listlessly to push back her sweat-streaked hair. It was a dark brown and she had the blue eyes of all the O'Shaughnessys with her mother's strong jawline and her father's slow, good-humoured smile, but she had nothing to smile about now, begorra, and she'd be glad when this lot was done with, so she would. And just let Joe Feeney try to get his thingy into her in the near future and she'd cut the bloody instrument off, begod. Five times in six years with Ginny not yet two years old and Church or no Church, this'd be the last.

'Never you mind, pet,' her mother was saying, 'it won't be long now. Sure an' haven't I sent for Mrs Flanagan an' if anyone can get things movin' again 'tis herself.'

'Jesus an' Mary, 'tis comin' again . . .' and Ellen's daughter began to heave and moan, straining back against the bedhead, sweat breaking out again on her sallow face and through the fabric of the fresh nightdress her mother had just put her in.

'Hang on to the towel, darlin',' Ellen said soothingly, showing none of the anxiety which was beginning to seep like acid through her veins. Bridget, the next girl in age to Caitlin though there were seven years between them, was strong and, having borne four children already, all girls, should have had this, a longed-for boy, surely, as easy as pulling a cork from a bottle, the four having made an easy passage for the fifth, so to speak, but Bridget had been in labour now for twenty-four hours and Ellen didn't like it, wishing with all her heart she'd sent for Mrs Flanagan hours ago instead of leaving it until this morning. One of the boys could have run through the dark night despite the wind and the lashing rain to fetch her and this little lot would have long been over. Mrs Flanagan had a way with a difficult or a long drawn-out labour – which exhausted the mother and was no good for the child – and Ellen could not forgive herself for putting her daughter through this unnecessary suffering when she was sure it would have ended satisfactorily hours ago under the expert guidance of the old midwife.

They were all downstairs. All the family crammed like sardines in a tin in the kitchen. Bridget's husband, summoned hurriedly yesterday when his wife had suddenly and ferociously gone into labour in Ellen's kitchen. Bridget's four girls, Mick and Michael, it being Sunday, Caitlin and young Clare and all Ellen's sons, roaming about from kitchen to parlour like restless prowling cats. Not that any of them could do any good but it was as though they sensed a crisis in the family and must be available should they be needed. Grace, Amy and Eileen had been here on and off during the past twenty-four hours with various children at their skirts, taking it in turns to sit with Bridget, taking it in turns to offer advice and recount memories of the thirteen pregnancies they had known between them. They had dozed, the three women, through the night, waking to brew tea and boil water when it had seemed at several stages that it might be needed and to encourage the labouring woman on the bed.

'Why don't you go to Mass, the lot of you?' their mother had begged, 'and ask Our Lady to intercede for Bridget. A little prayer wouldn't be wasted. I'd go meself but I might be needed.' Besides which she was very tired herself for though her daughters had cat-napped in the chair by the bedroom fire, Ellen had found she could not settle, not with Bridget labouring so long and so agonisingly and, brave girl that she was, doing her best not to yell her head off.

'Have a good shout, pet,' Ellen had exhorted her after one particularly harrowing spasm and Bridget had smiled weakly, swearing she would next time. The problem was she was becoming too exhausted to work at it, to do the hard 'labour' which the word implied, let alone shout, and prayed only that the Holy Mother would take pity on her and give her the strength to get the whole thing over and done with before much longer.

'Will I wet you some tea, darlin'?' her mother asked her now, returning from the window where, for the tenth time in as many minutes, she had gone to look for Mrs Flanagan. The boys were still leaping and shouting in that mindless way boys had, flinging themselves about with the enthusiasm and energy of their sex and age, engrossed in some eternal game which, now that the girls had gone, they could get on with in companionable, sensible male equanimity. Callum was the natural leader, despite being younger than his McGowan and Conroy cousins, and Ellen, even in her worried state, noted with half her mind that he was just the same as all her sons – and daughters too, come to that – wilfully determined on his own way and ready to fight anyone who got in it.

'No thanks, Mammy,' Bridget murmured in response to her mother's question. 'I'll have one the minute this is over.'

'Of course you will, acushla, an' it won't be long now.'

There was a tap at the door and when Ellen opened it she was surprised to see Michael's face staring at her out of the gloom on the landing. He had shared the family vigil ever since he had bowled up to the garden gate on his bicycle just after noon yesterday for his long weekend off. It was an indication of the worry he felt, along with the rest of them, that he had not stirred out of the house, foregoing his fortnightly Saturday night out on the town with Dennis Conron. Ellen knew it was her fault, that she should have kept her anxiety to herself and not allowed them all to see the unease which clenched at her heart but it was hard to be cheerful and reassuring when her girl was getting visibly weaker with every pang. Oh, she did wish Mrs Flanagan would get here and with her superior knowledge and good-natured common sense which had seen them all, herself included, through many a confinement, deliver this child safely.

'What is it, darlin'?' she whispered to her son.

'Will I be runnin' for the doctor, Mammy?' he said through the crack in the door which was all his mother would allow. In her opinion and those of her contemporaries who had gone, like her, through this ordeal more than a dozen times in their child-bearing years, men were not needed at this end of the procedure. They began it all, the spalpeens, eager and thoughtless, rampant bulls some of them, with their brains between their legs, but most were not encouraged in any way to be involved in the result of their Saturday night pleasures. So why should a doctor be needed, for God's sake? What was needed was a good midwife like Mrs Flanagan who, though she was not strictly speaking qualified in the profession, had that magical instinct with which some women are born to relieve their sisters of their burdens.

'Mrs Flanagan'll be here directly, son,' Ellen said, somewhat disapprovingly. 'She'll know what to do so don't you worry yourself. Go and wait with Joe' – Bridget's husband

– 'better yet, why don't you be takin' him to the Bandy Duck for a pint of Guinness?'

'On a Sunday, Mammy?' Michael smiled, knowing his mother's abhorrence of having a bevvy on the Lord's day.

'Well, 'tis a special occasion an' he needs takin' out of himself. He's worried about Bridget an' who wouldn't be . . .'

'Are you, Mammy?' Michael interrupted quickly.

'Well . . . 'tis been quite a time, son.' She glanced back into the bedroom where, for rather longer than Ellen would have liked, Bridget had been lying completely still, the slow rise and fall of her breast beneath the rumpled sheet the only movement in the bed.

'Let me run for the doctor, Mammy,' Michael pleaded and Ellen hesitated. Mrs Flanagan had been delivered a personal message by Dermot himself, and if anyone could be trusted to make sure she had it, it was him, but she was a long time coming and there was a look about Bridget, a look of . . . Holy Mother, pray for us now . . . well, she didn't like the look of her. Her flesh seemed to have fallen into the hollows of her face, and her eyes were set in deep, plum-tinted circles. Her skin was the colour of dough, dry and flaky with none of the healthy sweat of a woman in labour.

Ellen turned back to her son, her face twisted with her indecision. Michael continued quickly, 'Only when Mara was confined the Osbornes brought a doctor to her, so they say, and so I thought . . .'

He had said the wrong thing, of course, and he knew it at once for his mother's face closed up with a great snap and her eyes became cold and distrustful.

'We'll be needin' no doctor here, Michael O'Shaughnessy. Now send one of the women up. Not Lucy for isn't she as useless as a third foot but Matty'll do until Gracie or Eileen get back. I can't ask Caitlin with her unwed and that elbow of hers still gives her gyp. But I'd be glad if you'd run round yourself to hurry one of the girls an' ask Dermot to slip down to Mrs Flanagan's again, will you, pet. Tell her things are ... well, tell her to look sharp or the baby'll be here before she is.'

Ellen tried to smile at her own small joke but though her mouth moved in a grimace her eyes were anxious as they turned back to the woman on the bed.

Mrs Flanagan, Bridget's frantic mother and her three older sisters were there when Bridget's dead son was delivered on a great tide of blood which, no matter what trick Mrs Flanagan got up to, and she knew a few, could not be persuaded to stop. The foot of the bed was lifted on to two bricks brought up by Bridget's distraught husband and for an hour Mrs Flanagan worked on her patient, her own face waxen and rigid with weariness, her own body bathed in the sweat of her endeavours. Bridget lay in the bed, her figure which had been rounded with ripe fertility shrunken and beneath the counterpane, the motherly abundance of her drained away on her life's blood. Ellen had plaited her daughter's dark O'Shaughnessy hair to keep it out of her face as she laboured and the braids lay across her breast. Her closed eyes were no more than slits in their cavernous sockets and there was a pinched look about her nose.

The midwife rose at last from the bedside and drew Ellen compassionately to one side, passing a hand on which Bridget's blood was streaked through her own dishevelled hair.

'You'd best be sendin' for the doctor, pet. I can do no more. She won't stop bleedin', you see. She's in the hands of the Blessed Virgin,' sketching a cross on her chest. 'We can only pray and ... well ... I'm sorry, Ellen, but you'd best send for the good Father...'

Bridget died an hour later.

The Osbornes were at dinner when the front door bell pealed through the house. It had been a lovely day after a wild and windy night, the first really spring-like day of the new season. Johnny Osborne, his sons James and Teddy, along with his gamekeeper, had been walking the estate since dawn, shooting anything which might destroy the mating and brooding game. Stoat, weasel, polecat, jay, magpie, hawk and owl – if they could spot one – since the game birds they were rearing so assiduously for their own sport in the autumn must be protected from the predators who seemed to imagine the birds had been put there for them to prey on. The gentlemen were enthusiastic on the success of the day, telling one another what a simply splendid shoot it would be come August, and seated beside her husband Mara Osborne was quite noticeably glassy-eyed with boredom. She delicately spooned soup between her soft pink lips, her face quite blank and when, two or three minutes later, Eaton announced that there was a man to see her, it took her several moments to realise that he was talking to her.

'A man?' she asked vacantly. 'What man?'

'He says he is your brother, madam.' Eaton's whole demeanour spoke of his acute disapproval of this person who, as a servant himself, should have known better than to come calling at the front door of his master's home. His relationship to the young master's wife made not the slightest difference to Eaton. He was of the lower orders and as such should have knocked on the kitchen door.

'My brother?' Mara was visibly perplexed. 'What's my brother doing here, and which one is it, Eaton? Did he say?'

'Would it not be simpler to go to the drawing room and find out, Mara?' her mother-in-law suggested smoothly. 'No doubt it is some ... emergency at your ... at your ...' She was at a loss for a moment on what name to give the place where her daughter-in-law had once lived. 'Why don't you go along to the drawing room ...?'

Her words were interrupted by a violent crash as the door was flung open and in the doorway, his face wild and sweat-streaked, his blue eyes burning in it, was the chauffeur from Woodall Park, the very one who had driven Serena Osborne and her friend, Lady Woodall, into the city of Liverpool only the day before yesterday.

Johnny Osborne sprang to his feet, his face turning to a dangerous shade of outraged magenta and on his right his mother put out a hand to restrain him. He shook it off impatiently and the calm woodland green of his eyes became as vivid as an emerald.

'Goddammit man, am I to be forever plagued with these ill-mannered intrusions into my home by members of your family? Though I cannot object to your . . . calling on Mara since she is your sister I feel I have the right to demand that you do so in a more civilised manner. Can you not see my family and I are dining? Would it not have been more courteous of you to remain where you were put by my butler until Mara was brought to you? Is it too much to ask . . . ?'

But for all the notice Michael took of him Johnny Osborne might have been a bird in a cage twittering senselessly to anyone who would listen. He was calmer now and his eyes ran round the assembled company until they came to rest on Mara. He had a hand on the knob of each of the open double doors and for a second or two he stood there, reluctant, or so it seemed, now that he had found her, to move towards her. He looked at none of the others, not even at Elizabeth who sat frozen and white-faced, her soup spoon trembling slightly against her plate.

'Michael . . .'

Mara's voice was plaintive, begging him, please, not to tell her the dreadful news he was about to impart. It was dreadful, she knew that, since nothing else would bring him bursting into the Osborne dining room like this. She could see it in his tight-clenched face and the narrowing of his eyes as they looked sorrowfully at her.

'Please, Michael,' she said and her young husband stood

253

up behind her, putting his hands on her upper arms to steady her.

'You'd best come home, darlin',' her brother said at last, gently, sighing his regret to be the one to bring her such sadness.

'Oh sweet Mother ... not ... not the Mammy. Please say 'tis not the Mammy.' Mara swayed back against James and his arms went about her as she began to cry.

'No pet ... not Mammy. Come now, fetch the child an' we'll be goin' home. I've a motor cab at the door.'

'Tell me, Michael.'

'Not here, darlin'. Not in front of ...' and Michael O'Shaughnessy's contemptuous gaze ran over the Osborne family, moving from his sister's husband to her mother-in-law, to Teddy, Elizabeth, even her grandmother, Mrs James Osborne, who had once been kind to him, until they came to rest on the furiously enraged figure of Johnny Osborne.

' 'Tis sorry I am to be disturbin' your meal, Mr Osborne, and not to remain obediently in the place where I was put, but there's urgent family business needs seeing to an' I've not the time nor inclination to wait, you see. Me sister's needed at home so I'll be takin' her with me just now,' and he walked steadily across the room to Mara, cutting through the servants, through the silence and their astonishment as though they and it did not exist. He took her hands in his.

Without knowing why he did it since she was after all his wife, James let her go for a moment before he recovered himself. 'I'll come with you,' he said then.

'There's no need,' Michael answered without looking at him, putting his arms about Mara who began to go with him like a child.

'I'm afraid there is. If my wife is to be ... troubled then I wish to share it. And my daughter goes nowhere without my permission.'

At the head of the table Johnny Osborne sat down and beside him his mother again put out a hand, this time placing it over one of his. She seemed strangely moved by something and her eyes, which were still a clear and lovely silver-grey despite her great age, were luminous with tears.

Michael turned then, looking at James as though, for the first time, he recognised he was more to Mara than the man, boy really, who had once trifled with her and had, because of it, been forced to marry her. Michael had been prepared to hurry Mara with her child who would surely comfort his distraught mother, into the waiting cab and drive hell for leather back to Edge Lane. There had been no thought nor consideration in his mind for James since this had nothing to do with the Osbornes. This was an O'Shaughnessy tragedy. This was O'Shaughnessy heartbreak and would be kept within the family, shared with no one but close friends and Father Paul. Now it seemed he must give way to the rights of his sister's husband and the ignominy of it showed in the hardening of his face.

'Really . . . James, we can manage, me an' Mara . . .'

The girl in the circle of his arm suddenly surged forward throwing off his support and her own awful weakness. Her face was still white with dread but in her eyes was an expression which said she had had more than she could stand though she knew there was worse to come. Michael had driven over with news of such appalling proportions he was not even prepared to divulge it in front of people he considered to be strangers, and yet he and James were bristling up to one another like two schoolboys fighting over a handful of conkers and herself going mad with the need to know what it was all about.

She said so.

'Stop it, stop it, the pair of you. Jesus, Joseph and Mary . . .' failing to see her mother-in-law's recoil of disgust, though she wouldn't have cared if she had, '. . . will you get me home at once, James, an' if Michael says we're to take the baby then we will . . .'

'I really don't think it wise to take my granddaughter out

at this time of night, Mara. She's best left with Nanny in the nursery . . .'

Mara turned savagely on Serena. 'Don't you start an' all. Something . . . bad's happened at home an' the Mammy's sent for me . . .' which was how she had interpreted Michael's presence '. . . an' I'm to go at once an' where I go my child goes an' if James wants to come too then that's only right since he is my husband an' part of my family now.'

She turned abruptly, the soft, pearl grey folds of her georgette evening gown drifting about her. The gown was trimmed at the hem with the palest of pale grey chinchilla, rippling and very expensive but she kicked it impatiently aside as she strode towards the open door.

'Run upstairs and tell Nanny to get Claudine ready at once,' she called imperiously over her shoulder to Betty, the head parlourmaid, who was helping to serve. 'I'll be at the front door in ten minutes, tell her, so she'd best look sharp. Come along, James.'

James followed her swiftly. Michael stood awkwardly now behind the chair from which Mara had risen. His defiance had drained away, the sadness which he had brought with him into the dining room returning to his pale face. No one spoke to him and the servants exchanged glances for what should they do now? They could hardly carry on serving with him standing there and the master and mistress appeared to have been struck speechless by their daughter-in-law's high-handed ordering about of what were, after all, the mistress' servants.

All heads turned towards her as Mrs James Osborne the first struggled to get to her feet. The gentlemen rose as one, their common training bringing them from their chairs and her son leaped to help her from hers. He gave her his arm to assist her to wherever it was she wished to go but it seemed it was only round the table to face the young man who had so rudely interrupted their meal. She shook off her son's hand and placed her own on Michael's arm.

'Take me to the drawing room, young man,' she ordered him, 'and then you can tell me what it is that has brought you here.' She turned to the butler. 'Send in some coffee, Eaton. We'll drink it while we wait for Mara and James.'

James had never been to his wife's childhood home and though it was all he could do to cope with Mara's heart-broken weeping, the fretful cries of the baby who had not taken kindly to being whisked from her bed in the dark of the night, and the brooding silence of his brother-in-law, he felt a desire to stare curiously about him as they passed through the front door of the house in Edge Lane. Had he not known by now of the reason for Michael O'Shaugh-nessy's wild ride to Beechwood, disclosed sorrowfully by him once they had gained the privacy of the Osbornes' Renault motor car – the hired cab sent on its way by a disdainful footman since a member of the Osborne family would never travel in such a conveyance – James might have been forgiven in thinking that this was some family gathering which was no more melancholy than any other. There were people simply everywhere, of all ages and sexes. Crowding the hallway, going up and down the stairs, some even sitting on them, entering and leaving rooms which turned out to be the parlour and the dining room and at the end of the hall, the kitchen. There were gas lamps lit everywhere, smoky and flickering as the press of what he supposed to be family friends and relatives moved excitedly – it seemed to him – about the house and though voices were hushed there was an impression of outpouring in the air as though even in bereavement the ebullient Irish nature must break through. Bright-eyed children, dozens of them, were huddled together in corners, overlooked in the general confusion and hoping to stay that way, most of them eating something and there was indeed a delicious smell of cooking food drifting from the kitchen.

'Mara ... 'tis Mara, by all the Saints ...' they said, and the warm and sorrowing love swept along the hall from person to person as his wife, her daughter in her arms, was moved gently and fondly down its length, kissed and embraced by each and every one. All their faces were wet with tears now, all their eyes mournful but at the same time filled with curiosity and the absolute determination to be present when this girl was confronted by her Mammy.

'The Mammy an' himself are in the kitchen, pet ...'

'Will you look at the darlin' child ...'

'A sad loss, acushla, an' her so young ...'

'Such a lovely girl ...'

Not one spoke to, or glanced at James Osborne.

The kitchen was, if possible, even more closely jammed with people than the hallway. There were tall, black-browed young men, arms crossed over brawny chests or with their dangerous fists thrust deep in their trouser pockets, lounging against the whitewashed walls, ready, it appeared to James, to threaten anyone who dared distress further their grieving parents. Two maids, by the look of them, though it was hard to tell in this unusual social class to which he was not accustomed, worked feverishly at the kitchen range and half a dozen other women were everywhere at once with cups of tea and plates piled high with food. More children lolled against the shoulders of several seated adults and one was cradled in the lap of a priest.

Sitting quietly side by side on a wooden settle, hands clasped, their senses mercifully stunned by the enormity and suddenness of their loss were Ellen and Mick O'Shaughnessy. As James and Mara entered the room such a silence fell, even in the hallway through which they had just passed, a silence so complete it was possible to hear church bells pealing from far off in the distance.

No one spoke. The fire sputtered and the clock on the shelf ticked merrily. The baby, as though at a signal, began to grizzle and as she did so Ellen looked up at her daughter.

Their eyes met for the first time in fourteen months and everyone in the hushed room seemed to hold their breath.

It went on forever, the silence, and James felt his heart thud painfully in his chest. He knew how much Mara longed to return to the warmly beating heart of her family. She was trying hard to adapt her fiery, hot-tempered nature to the more restrained rhythm of the life she led as his wife, learning from his mother the day-to-day social pattern which must be hers if she was to succeed. She had style. She was young and flexible and willing. She was quick to learn and eager to please but she was also stubborn and wilful and it was hard for her. If she could just be allowed the sustaining encouragement of her own loving and volatile family, the means to escape to this house where her own mother was, she would more easily conform to his. James saw this with a surprising intuition and maturity, a sudden and clear insight into the mind of his young wife which would have astonished his own contemporaries. This moment was important to Mara. A sorrowful, even harrowing moment, but might not these two women, his wife and her grieving mother, gain something from it precious to both?

He felt Mara tremble at his side and her breathing was deep and quick as though she had been running then, with the sure instinct which he decided must come from her own experience of motherhood she moved through the press of people, looking at no one but her mother. Bending down to her she placed the fretful baby in Ellen's arms. Instantly, playing her part as though the Irish blood in her sensed exactly what was needed of her, Claudine stopped whimpering and settled herself comfortably against her grandmother's ample bosom. Mara sank slowly to her knees before her parents and with a graceful drooping of her head, a penitent gesture which was lovely to see, began to weep.

'Mara ... Mara darlin'.' It was Mick who spoke. He put out a hand to her, gently touching her wet cheek, smoothing away the tears with his thumb as he had a thousand times in the past, his own merry Irish face awash with the awkward, painful tears of a strong man weakened by grief. He wore a workman's collarless shirt, opened at the neck, and his trousers were held up by braces, in sharp contrast to the immaculate gentlemen Mara had become used to in the past year or so, but what did it matter? He was her Daddy, her expression said, and she loved him now more than she had ever done and her attitude told him so. His hair was greyer than she remembered and he seemed to her to have lost weight and when he stood up and raised her to her feet she went eagerly, thankfully into his arms. A sigh whispered about the room and handkerchiefs were held to streaming faces and to noses which suddenly needed an urgent blowing. The young men cleared their throats and the priest smiled.

But still Ellen sat like some wooden image, pale and tearless in the midst of so much overstrung emotion. Her arms, with the simple automatic reflex which was part of her nature, held the child tenderly but her eyes were fixed in a dreadful stare, those about the room thought, looking at but not seeing the loving embrace shared by her husband and her daughter. Her eyes seemed to stare right through them at pictures which gave her no joy nor comfort and beside her Father Paul set the child he was holding, Clare it was, on to her feet. He touched Ellen's arm but Ellen was lost in some world which no one here could share. It was as though she had withdrawn from them all, had gone to some place where they could not follow. To lose a child was an agony known only to the mother who bore it and how could they understand what was in her heart? Her head was cocked on one side, almost in a listening attitude, as though to a voice no one else could hear, a voice that spoke only to her mother's heart which had known so much pain and lost so much love. But here, in the sweet shape and feel and smell of the baby in her arms and in the presence of her daughter whom she had sworn was gone from them forever was surely love and to spare to fill the aching, empty space Bridget had left.

The child stirred in her arms. She was nine months old now, a lovely child with the vivid colouring of her Irish forebears. Round and rosy cheeks. Her dark hair swirled in a cap of dark curls about her head. Even her eyes were the lovely blue-green of her O'Shaughnessy heritage. She sat quietly for a moment, her gaze wide and serious, fascinated and not at all afraid of the crowd of strangers who were watching her so intently, then, as though feeling that something more was expected of her and delighted to have the opportunity to show off, she sat up and, leaning forward in Ellen's arms as though she was perfectly at home there, clapped her dimpled hands together and laughed. It was her party piece, just learned from her young nurserymaid and she was enchanted with it, with herself and with the effect it had on those who watched.

They all began to smile, all those sad faces. The young men stood away from the wall and uncrossed their truculent arms. The women exchanged those glances which seem to say, 'Would you just look at the little pet, and had not their Mara done well . . .' and Ellen O'Shaughnessy's eyes lost their stunned look as they rested on the upturned and rapturous face of her granddaughter. They softened and a little colour crept into her cheeks. They none of them missed the way her arms tightened about the child and they began to breathe more easily.

Still no one spoke until, at last, with a trace of the vigour familiar to them all and which they had thought to be lost to them forever, Ellen turned to her two maids who, like the rest, were waiting with beating hearts and bated breath to see what would happen next. Her voice was low but there was a touch of asperity in it.

'Pull that fire together, Matty, an' sweep the hearth, an' will you wet some fresh tea. Father Paul'll want another cup, won't you, Father, an' I'm sure Mr Osborne wouldn't say no.

See, Amy, take the baby. By the feel of her I'd be surprised if she didn't want her napkin changing.'

She rested her worn cheek for a second or two against the rosy one of the child, then put her in Amy's eager arms before turning to Mara.

'You'll be wanting to see your sister, God give her eternal rest.' She crossed herself reverently, then with a cry in which grief and gladness were mixed, dragged her daughter into her arms.

Michael leaned against the back of the privy, one leg bent, his foot resting against the recently whitewashed wall behind him. The garden was still and silent, unearthly in the silver wash from the threequarter moon which hung directly above his head. It touched the line of tall and slender poplars which stood in a row across the end of the long garden, their leafless outline like black lace against the moonlit sky. Down one side of each trunk the moon had trailed a silver finger and it bathed the stretch of grass in a glow as clear as the light of day. The two poles between which his mother's washing line hung, held up by the clothes prop, were plainly visible, the line a strand of silver white on which the clothespegs left there by Matty bobbed gently. The bushes and shrubs amongst which the children played in the daytime threw shadows, dense and mysterious.

The eerie beauty of it, the perfect stillness affected the lounging man to an even deeper sadness and he sighed deeply as he put a match to the cigarette which had hung limply from between his lips for the past two or three minutes. He took a long drag on it, drawing the smoke down into his lungs.

He could allow himself to think of her now. Now that he had done what he had to. Now that his mother and father were in their bed, perhaps not sleeping, nor even at rest as they needed to be, but comforted by the reunion with their daughter and granddaughter. Now that they had all gone, the Feeneys, the McGowans, the Conroys and Maguires there was time for him to reflect on the events of the evening.

It was very cold and he knew he should go inside and get to his bed but he could not give up, just for this brief moment, the lovely picture of Elizabeth Osborne which was etched like a cameo in his mind's eye, as she had looked just a short hour or two ago in the splendid gown ladies such as herself put on to dine. She had been afraid, he had known that, as she was always afraid of him and her fear had lent an added paleness to her creamy white skin. Her eyes had widened to an incredible beauty in her heart-shaped face and even in the midst of his own sorrow he had felt an overpowering need to go to her. To put a hand on her well-brushed hair and reassure her that she had no need of anxiety.

'Everything will be all right, my lovely girl,' he heard himself saying, though of course he had not spoken.

How lovely she was ... God save him, he could not get her out of his mind ... the dark, chestnut shining of her hair, the broad, tranquil brow beneath. The long tilt of her eyes, her lips, the colour of the wild poppies in the fields about Woodall. So quiet she was and yet he sensed in her a strong capacity for love. Elizabeth ...

He remained for five minutes in silent contemplation of the beautiful girl who could never be his, then, flicking his cigarette end into the drain at the side of the privy he turned and walked up the path towards the house.

14

Elizabeth was in the hall when they returned. She had been there on and off for the best part of five hours, roaming from her own room to the drawing room, then out into the wide, fire-lit hallway, unable to go to bed or even to settle to read a book.

'You might as well go up, darling. I'm sure we will all be told in the morning what melodrama has been played out in the bosom of Mara's family.' Her mother's voice was crisp and cutting and she yawned delicately behind her long-fingered hand to show how boring she thought the whole thing to be. You know how these Irish rustics are, her manner seemed to say. Everything is high drama and crisis and all over nothing at all. Disturbing decent people and creating turmoil where none is needed. A storm in a teacup in other words and she, Serena Osborne, believed it was really nothing to do with her, or her daughter, for that matter. If her son James felt the need to get out the motor car in the dead of night and dash across Liverpool dragging his baby daughter with him on what was probably a wild goose chase, then that was his affair and of no concern to them, for Heaven's sake.

She said so to her daughter.

'But Mara is his wife, mother, and surely entitled to his support.'

Both Johnny Osborne and his mother had retired for the night. Old Mrs Osborne had been escorted across the gardens to her own little house on the edge of the wood, her maid, an ancient crone by the name of Maggie who, it was

264

said, had been in her service for nearly fifty years on one side of her, her son on the other and a footman ahead to light the way. Mrs Osborne had been non-committal on the matter of the tête-à-tête she and the Woodall chauffeur had shared and was supremely indifferent to her daughter-in-law's outrage that it should have taken place in Serena's drawing room, saying only that the poor boy could hardly be left to stand in the hall like some tradesman, which was what he was, or worse, in Serena's opinion. She had known his grandfather, old Mrs Osborne said vaguely and a fine man he had been too. Irish, of course, well he would be, wouldn't he, and so naturally she felt concern for the family. Rambling, she had been, at least you could see Serena thought so, and she had intimated as much to her husband with a look which told him to take his mother home as soon as was decently possible.

'I'm aware of that, Elizabeth,' she said now, coolly, in answer to her own daughter's remark, 'and of course you are right but really, what could possibly justify flying off in the middle of the night like that and taking the child where surely it would be wiser she did not go. Heaven knows what sort of people . . .'

'Really, mother, anyone would think Mara came from some teeming, disease-ridden tenement instead of a perfectly decent, hardworking, God-fearing family, from all accounts. Heavens, Mr O'Shaughnessy works for father and so did his father before him. You heard Grandmother say so.'

'I'm afraid I don't care for your tone, Elizabeth, nor your manner. And may one ask where you came by such a store of information regarding the antecedents of Mara's family? From her, one supposes, and why she should feel the need to remind us all of her background I cannot imagine. One would think she would rather put it all behind her if she is to be successful in her new position in society. Not that she will be that entirely, I'm afraid. One does one's best but she is so . . . outspoken at times one finds it difficult to persuade one's friends to accept her.'

'She also does her best, mother, in a very difficult situation and I for one admire the way she has . . . adapted herself. I have become . . . well, I like her and she and James seem happy together.'

'Oh indeed, is that the way you see it, then? This happiness she and James share . . .' Her mother's voice was cold now and though it was fourteen months since Mara had become James' wife it was very evident that Serena Osborne had not and never would accept her into the close-knit society of which she herself was a part. Mara was tolerated and that was all. No matter how hard she worked at becoming the daughter-in-law Serena wanted and expected as her right, she would never fit in because Serena would not allow it.

'You are young and inexperienced, Elizabeth,' her mother went on, 'and it is not a suitable subject to discuss with an unmarried girl but I must ask you to believe me when I say that what James and his wife share is only a small part of marriage and when it . . . when it fades one must share some other interest, some other bond to take its place. You will know what I mean, I think. James is . . . has been . . . enraptured by Mara's . . . attractions which are quite splendid if a little . . . obvious, but when they and she become commonplace, believe me he will begin to look elsewhere. All men do, darling. It is a fact of life.'

'I don't believe it, mother.' Elizabeth's voice was flat and though she trembled inwardly since it was not often she defied her mother she was not going to allow Serena's icy disapproval to bear her down. 'I cannot believe that all men are . . . well . . . as frivolous and light-minded as you imply. I know nothing about . . . marriage . . .' meaning the physical relationship between a man and a woman since what other word was there but 'marriage' to describe such a thing '. . . but if James and Mara have committed themselves to one another . . .' Lord, how pompous that sounded but she knew of no other way to describe it '...then surely they must be ... in love, and why should that fade, as you put it?'

Serena tutted irritably, leaning forward to pour herself another cup of coffee. They were in the drawing room, she and her daughter, where they had gone when Johnny had led the frail elegance of Lacy Osborne away to her own house. The servants had retired at Serena's command, leaving the coffee to their mistress. The fire whispered in the grate, the flames throwing gold and amber shadows on the ceiling and walls and the smell of wood smoke drifted up the chimney. It was warm, calm with the tranquillity with which Serena liked to surround herself but there was an edge of strain in the air, a shiver of tension which, Elizabeth could see, did not please her mother.

'Really darling, I cannot imagine why we are having this ridiculous conversation. Heaven only knows what the ... well, shall we call him the common man does in the privacy of his marriage, perhaps because he marries for a different reason from the rest of us. For love, as they say, but as you and I both know we, and by that I mean the women in our society, marry where it is suitable. Where our parents think it will be the most beneficial for us. Like must marry like, Elizabeth, and though I wish with all my heart that James and his wife could be as successful in their marriage as your father and I, I cannot hold out much hope of it.'

'They say that grandmother and grandfather were in love, mother.'

'Ah ... well, that is another matter and one on which I would not care to comment.' Serena's face had become somewhat pinched and her eyes glanced disapprovingly in her daughter's direction before gliding away to the glowing flames of the fire.

'Why not, mother?'

'They were ... an unconventional couple,' by which Elizabeth knew that her mother had not cared for them. 'And

267

now I am going to bed and I suggest you do the same. Heaven knows when James and Mara will be home.'

The Renault drove smoothly up the drive, the gravel crunching beneath its tyres as the clock struck the hour past midnight. Elizabeth was at the front door with Eaton who, in his own words, could not settle unless he had locked the front door himself.

'Let me take the baby,' she said, reaching into the back of the motor car where Mara sat alone, the sleeping child folded in her arms. Mara was quiet and it was evident that she had been weeping but there was a composure about her which Elizabeth had never seen before. She sighed deeply as she stepped from the motor car and James was beside her at once, taking her hands in his, looking intently into her face.

'All right, darling?' he questioned softly, then putting his arms about her led her up the steps and into the house. 'Leave the motor there, Eaton. Don't disturb Gibson. He can move it in the morning.'

'Very good, sir. Will you be requiring anything else?'

'Yes please, Eaton. Coffee for me and I think Mrs Osborne would be glad of some hot chocolate, wouldn't you, my love?'

And that was what she was. His love. As Elizabeth followed them into the small drawing room where a fire had been built up by the efficient parlourmaid before she had gone to bed she knew quite without doubt that James loved Mara. Not just with the physical desire her mother had declared was all there was to her son and daughter-in-law's marriage, but with a growing strength and steadfastness, even a dependency which was returned by his wife. Their marriage was stormy at times. Elizabeth had heard them quarrel. Mara was high-handed and hot-tempered and James was stubborn. Their voices could be heard raised above what Serena considered the level good manners allowed on more than one occasion but more often than not this would be followed by a deep and eloquent silence which spoke of soft kisses, a delightful reconciliation in the privacy of their own room. Mara leaned on him now, thankfully it seemed to Elizabeth, as though he was the rock on which her life was grounded.

Nanny was sent for, her face set and disapproving since once again Mrs James had undermined her authority in the nursery by removing her daughter at such an inconvenient and unsuitable hour, despite her own strong protests. She took the baby from Elizabeth's arms, studying her charge with such fervour Claudine might have been returned from a journey to Timbuktu where, Nanny believed, the savages ate infants like her all the live long day.

'Will that be all, Miss Elizabeth?' addressing her cool question to the daughter of the house who, in her opinion and despite her youth and inexperience, had more sense than the child's mother.

'Thank you, Nanny,' and still Mara drooped frailly against James' comforting shoulder. Elizabeth waited, saying nothing, while James coaxed his wife to a sip of hot chocolate, kissing her cheek and her brow, holding her to him in a passion of sadness until, remembering that Elizabeth knew nothing, he looked up at her.

'It is Mara's sister,' he said quietly, and Mara's eyes filled with tears, 'and her ... her baby.'

'I'm so sorry. Are they ill?'

Mara turned her face into her husband's shoulder, clinging to him, but still there was that strange ... satisfaction? ... about her which Elizabeth did not understand.

'I'm afraid they are both ...' He seemed unable to go on.

'My sister died tonight, Elizabeth, God give her eternal rest, and the baby she was to have ...' Mara's voice was muffled. 'She started her pains yesterday at the Mammy's house but something was wrong and ... she and the baby ... a boy, Mammy said, died. Mammy took me upstairs to see her an' lovely it was she looked and the baby so sweet. She wasn't young, of course, Bridget. Nearly thirty, I'd say, an' hadn't the doctor like I had, not until the end an' it was too late by then. But she was me sister an' the whole family's that upset. Mammy an' I knelt an' said a prayer for her. Sure an' then we had a bit of a talk.'

Her voice was smug. She turned to look at Elizabeth and through the sad tears and Celtic need to dramatise which was part of her Irish nature, Elizabeth could sense the gratification in her. Why, she's pleased in some strange way that this has happened, she thought. Sorrowful naturally that one of her family has died but it has achieved something for Mara that she could not have achieved otherwise. It has returned her to her old home and she is glad about it. She and her mother are reconciled and she cannot help but be glad about it.

For a moment the image of her own mother drifted, cool and temperate – apart from the day on which this girl took her son from her – always in control of her own emotions. In fact Elizabeth could not say her mother had ever displayed any and she wondered as she watched Mara sigh and droop what it must be like to be so passionately devoted to one's mother as this girl so obviously was. How she must have suffered since she had married James. Even her religion which had been denied her, or which perhaps she herself had neglected for fourteen months was colourful and filled with mysterious rites which must satisfy the passionate nature of her. And yet she had not complained, at least not to the Osborne family. She had done what Serena had told her to do in the learning of her new role as best she could, trying hard to suppress what was really the essence of her own nature, the blithe Irish whimsy which had been in her and which was her.

'Mara, I'm so sorry,' Elizabeth said, her voice warm and soft. 'You and your family must be very sad.'

'Yes, the Mammy's heartbroken but ... well ...' She sat up and smiled a little at the memory. 'It was Claudine. I put her in Mammy's arms and she clapped her hands and laughed. You know how she does...'

'Oh yes.'

'...and Mammy couldn't resist her. And of course, if she accepted the baby she had to accept me as well...'

Clever Mara!

'An' so I'm to go tomorrow ... no, it's today, isn't it, James ... an' help her with the arrangements for the funeral. There'll be a Requiem Mass, of course. All the family will be there an' they'll be ... be buried together, Bridget and the baby...'

She began to weep again for really it was very sad. A double funeral. She had not known Bridget very well for she herself had been no more than a child when Bridget married Joe Feeney but they had been sisters after all.

'I'd like to come, if I may.' Elizabeth didn't know what made her say it unless it was that it seemed only right and proper. Mara was her sister-in-law, the wife of Elizabeth's brother and though there was nothing more certain than that Johnny and Serena Osborne would be horrified – James' expression told her that – and would no more consider attending Bridget's funeral than they would that of any common working person with whom they were not acquainted, surely, as a mark of respect, some member of Mara's family by marriage should be there besides James.

'Will you, Elizabeth?' Mara's face lit up with pleasure and she turned a look of glowing, growing affection on her sister-in-law. Despite her grief, or perhaps because of it, she looked very lovely in an unusually delicate way. She had changed hurriedly into the first gown which came to hand when the summons came to Edge Lane, a fine woollen day dress in a shade of blue which reflected the colour of her eyes. It was superbly fitted as all her outfits were these days, buttoned from throat to hem, the bottom dozen buttons undone to reveal a creamy lace underskirt, the lace repeated at the throat and wrists. She wore no hat and her hair was tumbled in shining disarray about her head. There were tears on her face and her eyes were dimmed with crying but her husband was gazing at her as if he adored every drooping curl and crystal teardrop she shed. She looked scarcely to be out of the schoolroom but for the magnificent curve of her breast, young and pathetically vulnerable but Elizabeth knew that beneath that frailty was a will and resolution which was strong and unbreakable. She would get what she wanted from life, would Mara Osborne, one way or another, but she would always try to be obliging, even charming, whilst she did it.

'I am to go to the funeral, mother,' Elizabeth repeated calmly. 'I believe someone should go from our family if only for Mara's sake.'

'I would prefer it if you didn't, Elizabeth,' the close-fibred tenacity which was carefully hidden from her family allowed to show for a moment. 'Really darling . . .' she laughed, a trill of merriment, 'you can imagine what it will be like. A jumble of Irish, Catholic hocus-pocus, prostrations of the soul and all that incantation and strange gestures they indulge in. I cannot see you, or James for that matter, being comfortable with it.'

'Comfort has nothing to do with it, mother, unless it is for Mara. She is family now and I think in the circumstances is entitled . . .'

'You will disobey me?'

'I hope I have no need of that.'

'I do not like it, Elizabeth.'

'I know that, mother. You have made it very plain but my conscience tells me . . .'

Serena cared nought for Elizabeth's conscience. 'I could stop you, Elizabeth. Forbid you to go.'

'I wish you wouldn't.'

Serena snapped shut the diary she was holding, the gesture symbolic of the closure of her mind to this suddenly contrary daughter of hers.

'Very well, but I am displeased with you, Elizabeth, and sad that you should override my wishes in this. It is as well we are to leave for London next week. Perhaps a season among the class of girls with whom you are used to mixing will remove these strange ideas you have about Mara's ... kind of people. They are not as we are. They do not think as we do and you will be as unacceptable to them as Mara is to . . well, you will know what I mean.'

'I do, mother and ... it makes me sad to hear you say so.' Dear God, was that *her* speaking, she had time to wonder, and it seemed her mother felt the same. She stood up and without another word to her daughter but letting her know just the same that she was severely offended, Serena left the room.

The soft and measured murmur of the five decades of the rosary sang like a much loved and comforting lullaby in Elizabeth's head. The clicking of the beads as they passed through dozens of fingers, old and young alike, was hypnotic, inducing a trance-like harmony, a beauty, profound and strangely mystical which they all shared and which for this one sacred moment she shared with them. It drew them together, even herself, into a completeness which in all her years of attending church with her own family she had never before experienced. Though the service, the Mass, she supposed it to be, was unfamiliar, it spread its wings of tranquillity over her, soothing, sorrowful but healing nevertheless and she was strongly aware of the benediction it must give to those who grieved the loss of the woman they loved.

Each decade represented some part of the life of the Holy Mother of God, Mara had explained to her the night before, fingering her own rosary before putting the smooth beads reverently into Elizabeth's hand. The first bead was the 'Our Father', she said, followed by the ten beads which were the

'Hail Marys' and the chain between was the 'Gloria'. Now, from more than a hundred throats the well known and much loved words which had comforted them from the time they could speak sighed musically, deep and solemn and blessed.

'Hail Holy.Queen . . .'

'Eternal Rest . . .'

'De Profundis . . .'

On and on until Elizabeth felt the grace and peace to which her family knew Bridget Feeney and her son would surely go, enter and settle in her own spirit and as she looked about her at the sorrowing but calm faces of Bridget Feeney's family standing about her coffin she knew a moment's envy for their unshakeable belief in what they knew was the true faith, and the composed acceptance it brought them.

She had known a frightening leap of gladness when, as James handed her and Mara from the motor car at the gate of the house in Edge Lane, Michael had been there to greet his sister and her husband. He had appeared taller than usual, the sombreness of his good Sunday black in which she had never before seen him accentuating the lean, flat planes of his face. The occasion had taken the incredible vividness from his eyes in which, up until this day, she had seen only the spirit of his Irish humour and the heat of his Irish anger. They were quite without expression as he took her hand for a moment, passing over her with no more than the civility one accords a guest in one's home. There was none of the warmth and tenderness she had seen there but had striven to avoid on the few occasions she had been alone in his company. In the stable-yard at Woodall; in Colton Wood and when she had danced in his arms at Harry's coming-of-age party. His eyes had spoken to her then of some communion between them, demanding nothing of her, at least not yet, but somehow warning her that she and Michael O'Shaughnessy shared . . . what? She did not know but his gaze had told her she must soon recognise it. He had kissed her, the only man as yet to do so, and even now her joyful flesh could remember how his mouth had tasted on hers. His hair, which he must have brushed furiously to smoothness earlier, was already unruly, falling across his sun-browned forehead in the way she remembered vividly it had done then.

'Miss Osborne,' he greeted her formally before turning to put an affectionate arm about Mara, leading her up the long, quiet, empty garden towards the front door leaving James and Elizabeth to follow as they pleased, not much use nor interest to him nor indeed to any of the family of which they were definitely not a part.

The house was peopled from wall to wall as it had been on the night of Bridget's death and each curious face was turned in the direction of the two strangers. Not Irish and definitely not Catholic, those who were both decided, and would you look at the fine clothes on the pair of them. They themselves were all in decent black, naturally, but not tricked up like these two who looked, in their opinion, as though they were off to a fancy dress affair. He must be poor Mara's husband, they whispered to one another, dressed in a frock coat, black waistcoat and a silk top hat which would have put the Lord Mayor of Liverpool himself to shame, had he been present. And the sister-in-law in her black silk and a hat which, though it was also black, was laden down with heavy, frivolous silk flowers, fashionable they supposed and undoubtedly expensive but not the sort of thing they liked at their funerals where plain and unassuming was more appropriate. Mind, that Mara was no better with a hat the shape and size of a cartwheel and a veil which was like mist over her becomingly pale and beautiful face. But then, even from being the smallest child, she'd liked to show off; to go one better than the rest of them and Mick had done nothing much to curb her.

Only one person spoke to Elizabeth. A girl a year or two older than Mara, obviously related but where Mara was white skinned this one had a rich honey and rose complexion which gave her a slightly foreign appearance. There was a scattering of freckles across her straight nose and her eyes were of the deepest blue. Her dark, richly curling hair was severely restrained in a smooth and heavy chignon at the nape of her neck which was long and graceful. She had a weary look about her, an expression which seemed curiously strained in a face so young. She was serious and controlled where Mara was, when allowed, outgoing and lively, but of course that was only to be expected today, but she spoke softly and kindly to Elizabeth, giving her a firm hand to shake, holding her other arm close to her side as though she was in pain.

'I'm Caitlin, Mara's sister,' she said simply. 'Thank you for coming.'

Elizabeth shared a carriage in the cortege with Mara, James and Michael O'Shaughnessy, her mind and heart still bemused by the muted solemnity of the ritual which had been observed about the coffin in the home from which Bridget and her baby son were to go to their final rest. Mara drooped sadly against James during the ride to St Mary's. They were engrossed in one another excluding the other two passengers and for the whole of the ten minutes it took the cortege to drive from Edge Lane to the church Michael did not speak a word to the girl beside him. Elizabeth could sense his arm next to hers just as though she, like Mara, leaned for comfort against some male support though there was a cool twelve inches between her and Michael.

Father Paul met the hearse at the splendid arched gateway of the church. It was April and in the meadow at the rear of the churchyard the trees were laden with blossom beginning to drift like fragrant snowflakes to lie like a carpet on the thickening grass. A venerable hawthorn, huge and graceful, hung heavy with flowers, casting its shade on the mother and father who had come to bury their daughter. Elizabeth, led by the quiet Caitlin, had held Ellen's startled hand for a second or two at the house, her compassionate young mouth trembling into a faint smile as she tried to convey her sympathy to the grieving woman. She had seen the momentary surprise and interest in the other woman's eyes, a look which said that though Ellen did not hold with her daughter's choice of a husband, nor his family who were not of the true faith, she was not displeased that one of them should choose to show respect for her girl who had died so tragically.

The priest led the coffin followed by Bridget's stunned husband and the long, wandering procession of mourners up the gravel path, into the church and, all of them curtseying and crossing themselves – except herself and James – to the altar. The coffin was placed before it and the congregation seated itself with much pushing and whispering into the pews behind those which held the O'Shaughnessy family. Elizabeth found herself seated between two astonished, dark-visaged men who, though they had evidently shaved for the occasion that morning, already had bearded shadows about their pugnacious jaws. They stood away from her, leaving her marooned on a tiny island of isolation, her difference to the rest of them obviously causing them and their dark-haired wives some alarm.

The Requiem Mass passed her by, no more than a drifting blur of colour, sound and fragrance. She knew several of the hymns and joined in valiantly, much to the amazement of those around her who had never before worshipped with a person who was not Catholic.

The reverent Father donned a beautifully embroidered purple cope and, taking the thurible, swung it to and fro, chanting softly as he moved round the magnificent coffin. No plain pine box for Michael and Ellen O'Shaughnessy's girl though her husband was no more than a dock labourer. The priest moved to the cross and the mourners joined him in some strange chanting then it was over and on a tide of weeping women and children Elizabeth was carried out into the sunlight. It dazzled her, blinded her and she would have wandered in the wrong direction had not a firm hand taken hers, leading her towards the gaping hole where his sister and tiny nephew were to rest.

At the last moment, as the full realisation of what she had lost finally shattered her stunned calm, Ellen began to moan and instantly they were all about her, her loving family, offering their arms, their brawny shoulders, their own grief and tears to mingle with hers. The strong hand which had gripped Elizabeth's so comfortingly, so surprisingly, had gone as Michael moved protectively towards his mother and father, to Mara huddled against her husband in the most fragile manner, indeed to any of his young brothers and sisters who might have need of him, and Elizabeth was left alone.

She did not return to the house in Edge Lane. He was there again beside her as the mourners drifted sadly away between the gravestones towards the gateway.

'Sir Charles lent me his motor car,' he said abruptly. 'I'll take you home.'

'No ... really, there's no need. I can take a cab.'

'That you'll not.' His voice was deep and quiet. 'The motor is at the house. I didn't use it for the funeral. My mother and father wanted the traditional ... well ... they are old-fashioned and wanted the grand horses and the black plumes. Sure an' you'll know what I mean. So we'll walk to the house and pick up the motor car. The fresh air will do you good after ...' He did not finish but she knew he meant after the ordeal they had both just suffered together. After death and burial the sight and smells of the budding spring would be good for them both, he was telling her. 'I'll take you back to Beechwood,' he continued. ''Tis certain Mara'll want to stay with the Mammy and Daddy and what Mara wants James provides. Isn't that so?' For the first time that day there was the ghost of a smile about his mouth.

'Your family?' she queried faintly. 'Will they not be waiting for you?'

'No, I told them I had to get back directly after the funeral, which is true, so they'll not expect me. I kissed the Mammy and she has the rest of them.'

'Of course.'

He did not touch her nor speak again on the walk from the church to his house. He appeared to be lost in his own thoughts and she did not interrupt them. There were cowslips in the grass verge at the side of the lane as they walked along Mount Vernon and as they came to Vernon Hall a pair of whitethroats chased each other through the bushes, singing their hearts out. The crab apple trees on the other side of the hedge were laden with pink blossom and crimson buds and the field in which they stood was yellow with buttercups. She breathed in deeply the fresh, young smell of the spring and felt a lift of her heart which somehow she knew he shared.

She climbed into Sir Charles Woodall's Vauxhall motor car which was parked in front of the O'Shaughnessy home and held on to her large hat as the vehicle roared away down the sunlit road which led towards Beechwood.

Why was she not surprised when he turned off the narrow lane into an even narrower one, she wondered? A lane deep in its hedges of may and hawthorne, its rutted surface jolting her against Michael's shoulder. Because it was inevitable, she answered herself. This feeling which came alive every time she and Michael met was like some budding flower which, without light or warmth, closes its petals and broods undisturbed in a quiet border. But let the sunlight touch it and the warm summer air and it lifted its head and bloomed. It had a colour and a fragrance which was enchantment, which was impossible to stand against and it appeared that not only could she not stand against it, she had no wish to. He ... the Woodall chauffeur ... let her not forget what he was ... had her senses so fast in a thrall of excited joy when she was with him that she lost all restraint, all sanity and reason, all the carefully nurtured beliefs and cultures of her childhood training and desired to do nothing but run heedlessly into his arms. Dear God, give her strength, this time, to ... to ...

He switched off the engine and turned to her at once. Deftly, as though it was not the first time he had done it, he removed the pins from her hat and took it off, throwing it carelessly somewhere to the back of the motor car. She let him. The stage Irishman he assumed at times was gone now. His eyes were alive. Not merry but alive with his ... what was it he was telling her he felt for her? Whatever it was she knew it was reflected in hers. He cupped her face in his hands and as if it was the most natural thing in the world for Michael O'Shaughnessy to do to Elizabeth Osborne, and so it seemed to her, he kissed her, then again, his lips soft and wondering.

'You have a kind heart, Elizabeth,' he said at last.

'Oh no ...' she answered breathlessly.

'Oh yes. No one else came.'

'James ...'

'Because of Mara only. You came without needing to. It gave the Mammy a moment's pleasure and I thank you for it.'

His lips continued to move in a leisurely fashion about hers. 'We should not ... do this ...' but her mouth opened beneath his, her breath warm and sweet.

'I dare say, but we will, won't we, Elizabeth? Unless, of course, you ask me to stop.'

'I don't think so ...' and her glowing, swaying demeanour said she was there, the woman he wanted; ready, should he demand it, to be taken.

He continued to kiss her in that slow, lingering way which told her there was all the time in the world now with no need to rush or hurry. Her mother thought her to be safely with her brother at the funeral of his wife's sister and nobody would be asking for Michael O'Shaughnessy on this day. She responded blindly, not caring at all what anybody should think or say or wonder at.

A last desperate cry from deep within her, from the part that was Serena Osborne's daughter, tried to make itself heard and for a moment she listened to it, a moment only, then her hands were deep in the tumble of his dark hair, pulling his head down to her throat which arched for his kisses.

'We'd better get you home.' His voice was hoarse with his longing.

She murmured her assent but her body was no longer controlled by sober, conventional Elizabeth Osborne but by the yielding female she had become in the embrace of Michael O'Shaughnessy.

'Sweetheart...' he murmured and continued to kiss her, his arms crushing her against him. He hurt her and she gloried in it. He placed her along the seat of the motor car where he could more easily savour the sweet flesh of her throat and chin and mouth, her body captured by his so that the trembling of their limbs blended and they became one entity. His fingers moved to her breast enquiringly and she welcomed them as they burned through the fine woollen fabric of her dress.

'Dear sweet Mother,' he whispered hoarsely. 'I cannot stop ... please, Elizabeth, stop me. The last thing I want is to ... distress you ...'

'I know ...' and her own voice was as out of control as his but still her lips clung and it was Michael O'Shaughnessy, his man's body heavy with his man's need who dragged himself away.

'Darlin' ... sweetheart ... Oh Jesus, I never meant it to go as far as ... Elizabeth, sit up, my lovely ... I must get you home ...' and he began to tidy her hair and her clothing with the tenderest of hands, doing his best to break the force which held them, to bring them back from the sensual world into which he had led her.

'It's all right, Michael...'

'I haven't ... hurt you, acushla ...?'

'No...' and she smiled now. He took her hand and turning it palm upwards, kissed it reverently, gallantly, and the gesture had in it all that he felt for her.

A bird began to sing. It sounded like a waterfall dropping through warm air, sweet and everlasting, but neither the man nor the woman heard it and if they had could it be any sweeter or more everlasting than the love which was growing between them?

15

It was the week after the funeral and Caitlin had been home for four months. She was a seasoned, war-weary, battle-scarred campaigner now, Elsie had told her kindly when she had called soon after Caitlin had returned from the London hospital in December, and until her arm which had been broken just above and below the elbow had healed they did not dare use her in anything which might become violent. The WSPU asked a lot of its members, she said, but Caitlin had done more than her share in the past year and must stay with her family until she was strong again.

'I've done no more than you or dozens of others,' Caitlin protested, 'and this...' indicating her arm which was strapped in a sling '...will be fine in a week or two.'

Ellen, who had reluctantly let in the woman who was, she was convinced, about to lure her daughter off again to the dangerous haunts and pursuits in which Caitlin had been so badly damaged, sniffed from outside the parlour door where she lurked, eavesdropping quite blatantly. Well, after the way they'd brought the poor child home wouldn't any mother worthy of the name be prepared to protect and save that child from further injury and she didn't trust these women in whom her daughter put such faith not to be up to some trick or other to get her back to London. She'd give the woman a cup of tea and one of her scones just come from the oven, for after all she was a guest in Ellen's home, but just let mention the words suffragette and London and Ellen'd be in there like a dose of salts and Miss Elsie Thompson would be over the doorstep before she could say knife. A week or two, indeed. She'd give Caitlin what for, talking like that and her with her poor arm strapped to her chest like a soldier returned from battle, but it seemed Miss Thompson was trying to persuade Caitlin not to go but to stay and Ellen relaxed enough to return to her kitchen and tell Matty to wet some fresh tea.

'That's as maybe, my dear,' Elsie continued, unaware of the protective mother who had just – fortunately – left the hallway and who, if she had heard her next words might not have been so sanguine, 'but there are ... there is the other ... wound you suffered. You are safe here at home and your mind is not subject to any kind of stress so you imagine you have overcome it but the next rally or march you attend might be as dangerous as the one where you were ... injured and ... well, it might be more than you could manage.'

'You mean I might run away.'

'Yes.' Elsie did not believe in mincing words.

'I was not ... raped, Elsie, merely ... fondled.' She shuddered at the word, at the memory of the horror of it and her face had a blanched look about it. It was eight weeks since and yet it was yesterday and Elsie was right, she could not erase it from her mind. And yes, she dreaded the very idea of putting herself in a situation where it might happen again but then she had dreaded every encounter she had faced in the last twelve or so months. She had told herself time and time again that she just could not do it, but she had, and she could do this but Elsie would not hear of it.

'I must be brutal, Caitlin, I can see, though I'm sorry about it for no one has been braver or more steadfast than you despite what has happened to you and I don't just mean your arm nor the men who ... well, I must speak up. You are of no use to us at the moment.' Her face softened and she put a gentle hand on Caitlin's. 'But you will be again soon and in the meanwhile you can still write and get about, can't you?'

Caitlin nodded. 'Then you shall come down to Duke Street and help us out there, like you did when you first joined us. There is a great deal of paperwork and though Miss Henshaw and Mrs Lilley are staunch supporters and very enthusiastic they are rather elderly and inclined to forgetfulness. You with your young, quick mind would be of enormous help to us whilst you are recuperating and then, when your arm is completely better and your memory of that day blurred, you shall come back to London with me, I promise.'

And so she was at her desk in the WSPU office when he came. The pale spring sunshine which fell through the long windows of the Regency house in Duke Street outlined her slender, black-gowned figure, shadowing her face and the man hesitated at the door, clearing his throat politely before he entered. Ellen had protested strongly, tearfully when Caitlin had declared that she was to take the tram down Brownlow Hill and along Hanover Street to the corner of Duke Street, saying it was too soon after her sister's death to even think of venturing out into the world again. After all she was in mourning and though she was well aware that in these modern times it was not thought of with the same solemnity as it had once been she did think Caitlin might wait a few more days before going to those dratted offices. Surely the suffragettes could get along without her in the circumstances, but the words had been somewhat half-hearted for with her new granddaughter in her arms and her ecstatic daughter on the opposite side of the kitchen fire, Ellen was quite taken out of herself for hadn't she and Mara so much to catch up on. Not that she wanted to hear about the Osbornes and their carryings on but there was plenty of family, *her* family news to impart and Caitlin had heard it after all.

Caitlin looked up as the man entered her small office, inclined to be nervous, he thought, wondering why until he noticed the awkward way she held her left arm to her side and he knew then that this was the one he had come to see.

'Good morning,' he said, ready to smile, leaning casually against the door frame. He was tall and strongly muscled, with the young and supple body of an athlete, vigorous and arresting and yet he must be over thirty, Caitlin thought. He had a strong face with a well-cut, well-defined mouth, slashed on each side with a vertical line which deepened when he smiled. There were lines across his forehead and another between his eyebrows, caused by frowning, she thought. He had a look about him which said he would suffer no fool lightly, indeed there was a certain commanding arrogance in the lift of his head but there was also sweetness and compassion in his expression as he studied her, too closely, she was inclined to believe. He looked smart, impeccably tailored and yet to Caitlin's eye there was an air of casualness about him. His trousers were whipcord, caramel-coloured, and his tweed jacket a mixture of brown and beige and there were leather gun pads on the shoulders. His cream shirt was beautifully laundered and his tie was a conservative brown. In his hand he held a tweed cap, looking for all the world as if he was off one of those sporting jaunts that only the rich and privileged enjoy. As though to confirm that he led an outdoor, fun-loving life his face was brown, darkened by the sun, and his hair a deep chestnut, short and carefully brushed. His eyes were thickly lashed and the palest grey she had ever seen, like water which has a sheen of ice on it.

'Yes?' she asked abruptly, disliking him on sight. He was far too handsome for his own good, and far too bold, she decided, and what was he doing here where no male foot ever trod?

'I see you are up and about,' he said winningly but there was something in his face which conveyed concern and another expression she could not recognise.

'Up and about? And what's that supposed to mean? And who are you, if I might ask, coming in here without so much as a by your leave? Did Mrs Lilley let you in? Really, she had no right to let anyone pass the door an' I shall tell her so.'

'Poor Mrs Lilley.' He grinned, revealing, as she knew he would, perfect white teeth and despite herself and her determination to be cool and haughty she felt an answering smile well up from somewhere inside her. She swiftly suppressed it, standing up to let him see that the encounter was at an end and if he had nothing better to do with his time then she had.

'Come and have tea with me at the Adelphi,' he said suddenly. Just like that, right out of the blue. Could you believe it, still grinning all over his silly face.

She gaped in astonishment. 'Are you mad? I don't even know you.'

'Yes, you do,' softly, serious now.

'I've never met you before in my life.'

'It was . . . in London,' he said gently in explanation and she was amazed that such cool, clear eyes could show so much warmth, even a strange tenderness.

'No . . .' she said and shook her head in denial but her voice was low and hesitant as she pushed the memory forcefully to the back of her mind. She would not be reminded, *she would not* and he had no right to come here and drag it from where she had buried it. She didn't want to speak to him . . . not to this man, for though she had not seen his

286

face at the time she knew now who he was.

'I'm sorry,' he said, 'really. I don't want to distress you, or offend you by ... well ...' He ran a lean hand through his thick hair, ruffling its well-brushed smoothness, his expression begging her to be neither distressed nor offended.

'I cannot say ... I remember ...' she mumbled but her heart had begun to thud erratically and for a devastating moment three faces, violent, greedy, mad with lust, flashed across her vision and she began to tremble.

'No, and do not wish to, I'm sure,' he said now, 'so we shall say no more about it except that I am glad you are ... recovered. Your arm is ... ?'

'It is mended now.' Her face had lost all its bright colour and she kept her eyes cast down. It was not that she felt shame since what had been done to her had not been of her choosing though there were many who would not have agreed. There were those who said that the suffragettes deserved everything they got and they got exactly what they asked for. Going about in the brazen way of harlots, could men be blamed for treating them as such and if they went a bit too far, well, it was bound to happen, wasn't it, for men had hot natures and these shameless women inflamed them.

No, what she felt was not shame, nor even embarrassment but a great sadness that she had been seen by this man in circumstances of brutish, obscene violence though why she should feel it mattered when she did not even know him was very curious. She was saddened that his eyes had seen her – an innocent and, yes, ignorant girl – in such a position. That her nakedness should have been exposed not, as she had sometimes dreamed, to the tender gaze of a lover but to three street louts, filled her with regret.

'I'm sorry,' and strangely she knew his sorrow was not for the outrage which she had suffered, though naturally it had incensed him, but for what was in her mind.

'Sure an' I'm better now,' but still she could not look up.

'I'm glad. You're young and strong, brave too, I realise that but ...' He had been about to say 'foolish' but some sudden tension in her, a narrowing of her vivid blue eyes as they instantly glared up at him, stopped him.

He straightened up, twirling his cap on his finger. 'I had quite a job finding you.' His voice was casual. 'I spent the whole of my leave trying to discover your name but those ... ladies ... pardon me but I was about to say "dragons"...' grinning audaciously '... at the Clements Inn branch of your movement are very tight-lipped. Finally I managed to wheedle it out of them that you lived in Liverpool. Very disapproving they were but when I explained that it was I who ... well ... they said I must call at the offices here in Duke Street and if you wished to ... thank me, though I need no thanks and would be horribly embarrassed if you tried, then my message, if I cared to leave it, would be passed on to you. But I had to rejoin my regiment in Ireland. There was some trouble with the third Home Rule Bill and the Volunteer Force which has been raised, but then I'm sure you know about that since your accent tells me you are from that part of the world. Anyway, I have only just returned so here I am and if you would do me the honour of ...'

'The roses ...' Her voice interrupted him.

'The ... ?'

'You sent the roses.'

'They seemed ... appropriate.' His glance held hers, serious again. His voice had warmed and deepened and inside her something was touched, stirring to life.

'I ... appreciated them.' She could think of nothing else to say, she who had talked for hours on end to those who, many of them, did not wish to listen.

'Then come and have tea, or coffee if you prefer, at the Adelphi.'

'I don't know you,' but she had begun to smile.

'If I tell you who I am, then will you come?'

'Holy Mother, aren't you the persistent one?'

'So I am, and you really do come from Ireland.' He seemed to be delighted with the fact.

'Born and bred in Liverpool, so I was.'

'Will you come then?' His eyes were bright with mischief and that other light she had seen in them earlier.

'I . . .' She laughed. 'Really, I don't know you.'

'Jack Templeton from Yorkshire. My people have a place near Wetherby so I'm a northerner like yourself which must weigh in my favour, surely?'

'Well . . .' She felt absurdly shy all of a sudden. 'My name is Caitlin O'Shaughnessy.'

'Caitlin . . .' and it seemed to rest pleasurably on his lips for his smile deepened.

'Yes.'

'Irish, as I said.'

'Oh yes,' and for some reason they both began to laugh.

She had never been in the Adelphi Hotel, she said in that forthright way he was to come to love so well and though she had heard about it and read of its magnificence in the newspapers nothing had prepared her for the wide, richly carpeted entrance and its great golden staircase, the flowers which flourished in vases on every table, the glittering chandelier which swayed in crystal droplets high in the ceiling. There was an enormous fireplace in which a log fire burned and before which ladies sat in deep armchairs, sipping tea and watching the rich, the famous and fashionable go by. There were porters everywhere surrounded by hatboxes, suitcases and vanity boxes ready to be lifted miraculously up to the bedroom floors by means of the new electric lifts.

The elegant rose-pink lounge to which Mr Templeton led her, holding her protectively by her uninjured arm, served tea or coffee or indeed anything its distinguished and wealthy guests cared to ask for, twenty-four hours a day, and the capped and aproned waitress assured the handsome gentleman, dimpling as Caitlin knew all young girls would in his charming presence, that she would see if Chef had some of his famous meringues left.

'You've been here before?' Caitlin asked and was not surprised when he said he had, no doubt in the company of a pretty woman.

'Tell me about yourself,' he demanded when they had each eaten two of the chef's meringues. 'I know you are one of that band of intrepid ladies who tell me they will have the vote...'

'If you are to make fun of my sisters, Mr Templeton, then I'd best be off,' she said tartly and rose at once but he stood up himself having been brought up to believe that a gentleman should never remain seated whilst a lady stood, and she was disconcerted. They looked so silly, both standing to attention beside the white-clothed table. The waitress was hurrying over, thinking they were about to leave before she had presented them with the bill and several ladies who were taking afternoon tea had turned to stare.

She caught his eye, her face stern and her jaw stiff but there was such good humour in his face, such an abundance of laughter in his eyes despite his attempt to be serious that she could not quell her own laughter which bubbled up inside her, and they both sat down, sharing that special sense of humour which can laugh at the ridiculous.

He took her hand and bowing his head in pretended remorse, begged her forgiveness. 'I meant no offence, believe me. I'm one of those foolish, or perhaps you would say enlightened fellows who actually believes in universal franchise though my mother would faint if she heard me say it.' Neither seemed to notice, or drew attention to it if they had, that he still held her hand. 'She thinks ... and these are her words, not mine,' he hastened to add, 'that Mrs Pankhurst and the other ladies, of which I suppose you are one, are not feminine at all but some sort of species which has evolved all by itself.'

'Many people do, Mr Templeton.'

He sat back in his chair, his grey eyes narrowed and smiling, the shine in them like the sun across the silvered waters of the river and she felt it move again, that tremor inside her. The curve of his long, well-shaped mouth as he smiled did something strange to her, just in the exact centre of her chest, and she found she could not tear her eyes away from his, even had she wanted to.

'Do you think you might call me Jack?' he asked gravely.

'I . . . might,' and her mouth twitched.

'And perhaps I could call you Caitlin?'

'Perhaps.'

There was a silence, deep with unspoken but shared emotion. Neither knew what to say, so astonished were they by their own feelings. They had met in circumstances of a bestial nature, she the victim, he the rescuer. She had given him no thought since, for in truth she had not known him, nor wanted to recall that day. He had been no more than gentle hands from which she would have recoiled, had she been in her right senses, because they were a man's hands. And then there had been the white roses. White for purity and in his compassion he had been telling her that despite the horror of her ordeal for which many would blame her and call her defiled because of it, she was still pure, still innocent, an innocent victim and, scarcely without knowing it, she had taken comfort from the gesture and begun to heal.

And he had been concerned for her. Why else should he come looking for her if not to satisfy himself that she was not irretrievably damaged, physically or emotionally. Her arm had been brutally broken but not her spirit, surely? That is what he had hoped and looking at her, shy again, her honey-coloured face tinted at the cheekbone with the rose pink of a young girl in her first encounter with . . . with what? . . . with the admiration a gentle man could show her, she was quite, quite enchanting. He was enchanted with her.

He was a regular soldier, he told her on that first day. An officer in a battalion of the Lancashire Fusiliers and if she was to ask him why he, as a Yorkshireman, had joined a Lancashire regiment then he could only say it was the Minden Yell which had decided him. Had she not heard of the Battle of Minden where six infantry battalions of the Lancashire Fusiliers had advanced against a French army which had outnumbered them by some ten thousand men. They had yelled, those six infantry battalions as they had charged the French, frightening them into submission, some said, but it had been stirring stuff to a lad of eighteen, he told her, so he had gone straight from his famous public school to Sandhurst. His father who owned land and bred horses had bought him a commission and during his four-teen years of soldiering he had seen some active service in South Africa and Egypt and had served in India and Ireland. He enjoyed it enormously, he told her. He was of a restless nature and the idea of travel and adventure had appealed to his young and foolish – he realised it now – sense of endeavour. To seek out danger in the enemy, to vanquish the foe, to make England's lands safe and to conquer the world for his Queen had been his schoolboy dream.

'Aah yes, she was still on the throne when I set forth to do battle, Caitlin, and I dare say you were not even born.'

'Good Heavens, Mr Templeton . . .'

'Jack.'

'. . . Jack, I am nineteen, you know,' bristling.

'Are you indeed, and I am thirty-two,' but grey eyes and blue both spoke, saying what did it matter. What did any-thing as unimportant as age or class matter now though why exactly they should have such thoughts was not awfully clear just yet.

He was the second son of his father and therefore had no expectations of the family business, he went on, and could do as he pleased, his unspoken words told her.

'The family business is . . .' Caitlin enquired politely.

'Oh, a bit of farming and the horses, of course,' he answered vaguely from which she deduced his father was a wealthy landowner, probably very much like Mr Osborne or Sir Charles Woodall.

He had two sisters, both married, like his brother, and a dozen nieces and nephews, a big family, close-knit and vastly inquisitive into his affairs, he added smilingly. 'They would like to see me settle down, as they are,' he said. His mother ran the village and the women in it somewhat like an army sergeant of his acquaintance, he told her smilingly, his eyes affectionate, making sure the people in her care ate what she considered good for them and changed their undergarments weekly. Her whole family, including his father, was completely under her thumb and she was the kindest woman he knew.

'She sounds just like my Mammy. In fact you seem to have exactly the same kind of family though there are a few more of us. Eight still at home and five . . .' she hesitated and her face grew sad '. . . no, four married.'

He could sense that something had troubled her but he did not question it, some instinct which had sharpened with his meeting of this woman telling him not to probe.

'Good God . .' was all he said, his boyhood training preventing him from saying more.

'And why is that?'

'Why is what?'

'Why do you say Good God?' He was to learn that Caitlin was not a woman who would let pass anything which surprised her or intrigued her. If she wanted to know she asked and expected you to do the same. Without being offensive, of course. But this was the first time she had challenged him in this way and he was nonplussed.

'Well, it is rather a large family.'

'And what is so unusual in that?' bristling again, and short of asking her if her father had ever heard of self-control, or her mother of birth control he could only smile and look

293

abashed. He would have to watch his tongue in future or be prepared to explain himself to this forthright young woman, he could see that. There would be a future, he already knew that. He had known from the moment he had first addressed her and he felt somewhat unsteady with the realisation. Her freshness and honesty took his breath away. Her penetrating gaze would allow no prevarication. She was dressed in floor-length black, a simple skirt of good quality wool and a long sleeved blouse of fine cotton over which her black coat fitted neatly to her knees. It was tied about the waist with a fringed sash of the same material and her black woollen beret was pulled well down over her hair to her eyebrows. It was a plain, even severe outfit, not at all fashionable, with no adornment whatsoever so why did she not look swamped by it, he wondered? Most women would but instead it enhanced her loveliness. Her skin was as warm as honey with rose at her cheekbones. Her mouth was full and the lips, soft and parted, were a flushed pink. Her eyes were blue, or were they green or somewhere in between, he could not decide, but they were as clear and steady as a child's and surrounded by long, softly drooping brown lashes. A sweet face and all set on a creamy neck which rose from its sombre wrappings, slim and delicate as a flower stalk. She looked fragile but he sensed there was a strength to her, and in her, a strength which showed in the firm jut to her small jaw and the resolute swoop of her dark eyebrows.

He never loved who loved not at first sight, he thought dazedly, and for him it had already begun.

'You are ... in mourning?' he asked softly, delicately, his eyes telling her he had no wish to pry.

She bowed her head for a moment and he had an insane desire to sweep her into his arms, to comfort, to take her sorrow from her in any way he could. To suffer it for her if she would only allow it.

'My sister died in childbirth last week,' she said simply,

then looked up at him and the expression on her face said she trusted him to make nothing more of it, not now, not here.

'I'm sorry.'

'I know you are,' and she did.

She told no one in the days that followed. They were used to her comings and goings by now. Her passionate concern for the WSPU was accepted by them and Ellen and Mick were only thankful she was not down in that terrible place where such dreadful things had happened to her. She had been safe here with them through February, in the wild month of March and that sad soft month of April in which Bridget had died. Caitlin came home each day to them when she had finished her business in Duke Street, smiling and content, it seemed, and with Bridget gone, even though Mara was returned to the bosom of her family they clung even more closely to this precious, damaged child of theirs.

He met her each day at the bottom of Duke Street, telling her sternly he would rather wait for her at the entrance to the WSPU offices, just as though he was certain some further dreadful thing might happen to her on the short walk along the once elegant little crescent of Regency houses.

'Mr Templeton . . .'

'Jack.'

'Jack, I have my reputation to think of, you know,' she laughed but there was light in her vivid eyes which asked when had Caitlin O'Shaughnessy ever given a fig for her reputation, at least not in the past eighteen months. When a woman suffers the indignities, the degredations, the publicity and high-toned outcry which follows those who called themselves suffragists she can hardly care for what people say about her. Nevertheless she was at home now and she did not wish it to reach her family's ears through the interested concern of Mrs Lilley or Miss Henshaw that the daughter of the house was being met by a gentleman on the very doorstep of the WSPU.

'Very well, Miss O'Shaughnessy, I shall wait for you where Duke Street meets Paradise Street and by the way, it's Captain Templeton,' raising his dark eyebrows in sardonic amusement.

It was his last day. Tomorrow he was to return to his regiment and the silence was heavy and dragging between them. They had walked along the Marine Parade as far as St Nicholas Churchyard where a troop of sandwichmen, their beat ended, were piling their placards against the brown stone of the old wall which surrounded it. It was already beginning to darken, the short spring day turning the sky to a lovely pink and gold over the river. Two dozen tramcars at the Pier Head terminus were all lit up and couples strolled arm in arm, just as though it was Sunday. The ferries were doing brisk business, darting like fireflies from the landing stage on their busy way to New Brighton and Seaforth. Though it was all bustle and cheerful noise Caitlin and Jack moved in a quiet and pensive hollowness in which only their anticipation of the parting to come had any meaning for them. Neither had spoken of it, of course, but both were aware that though this was the end of his leave, it was also the beginning. He would let her set the pace, his attitude towards her had told her, at least for now, but they both knew what was to come. Their hands brushed as they walked and for a moment his held hers and he turned to smile, as she did. They had slowed their steps as they reached the Pier Head and a newsvendor's cries shrilled above the sound of the clanking of the trams and the hooting shrieks of the ferry boats. There was the usual hurly burly of traffic, vehicles pulling up to and drawing away from the landing stage. He took her arm, ready to guide her towards the lighted tram terminus, both of them instantly aware of the vibrant electric shock which passed from him to her.

They noticed the sudden commotion at the same time. The tension of the crowds about them, a general surging of movement towards the entrance to the landing stage where the newsboy still shouted. Even above the roar of the traffic, on land and on the water, shrill cries could be heard and women were seen to raise handkerchiefs to their faces. Men stood, white-faced and stunned and one held a woman who had collapsed against him.

'He'll be all right, Margaret, he'll be all right,' he kept saying over and over again, her anguished head lolling against his shoulder testifying to her disbelief in his protestations.

'What is it? Jesus, Joseph and Mary, what's happened?' Caitlin began to move in the direction of the source of the tumult and the man beside her lifted his head with that air of command she had noticed in him at the office in Duke Street. It was as though whatever disaster had befallen, for surely one had to induce the stunned horror in so many people at once, he would quietly go about the best way of dealing with it.

'Wait here,' he told her but as he strode towards the crowd around the newsvendor she hurried after him. All about her she heard snatches of stricken conversation between men and women whose mouths could barely form the terrible words which jerked from them.

'... survivors picked up by the *Carpathia* ...'

'... White Star Liner from right here in Liverpool, dear sweet God ...'

'... message from the King and Queen ...'

'... mourning ...'

'... iceberg ...'

'... nothing but a few lifeboats and wreckage ...'

'... *Titanic* ... *Titanic* ... *Titanic* ...'

She had begun to weep, as every other woman was weeping and not a few men, even before Jack returned with the newspaper. He opened it, his face white and in an appalled whisper began to read out loud.

'... ill-fated vessel left Southampton last Wednesday bound for New York. Late on Sunday night she collided with an enormous iceberg and was badly holed and ripped along her side and within four hours foundered in water two miles in depth. There was onboard about 2340 souls. The first message from the *Carpathia* which had been summoned to her aid by wireless telegraphy and arrived at the scene of the disaster after the *Titanic* had taken her tragic plunge found only the lifeboats and wreckage. The lifeboats were occupied exclusively by women and children, no more than 705 of them, the rest having gone down with...'

'Don't ... oh please don't...'

She wept all the way home crouched against his shoulder in the motor car she had not even known he possessed, shedding the tears she had never shed for herself in all the months of her suffering, letting them go at last for the 1635 men, women and children who had perished on the splendid, the proud, the unsinkable ocean liner *Titanic*.

He held her protectively, fiercely to him as he led her up the daffodil-lined pathway to the front door and when Ellen opened it, white-faced and terrified, he gave Caitlin into her mother's keeping, and then tipping his hat politely, walked away leaving her daughter to explain his being there as she thought fit.

16

Bridget Feeney's was not the only funeral Elizabeth was to attend that year. Just as the London season was to close in July and the two families, Osbornes and Woodalls, were to return to their country estates, Sir Charles Woodall suffered a heart attack which killed him before his body hit the floor of the dining room.

The family and their guests had been about to be seated,

in fact the ladies already were, preparing to remove their gloves and open their napkins as was the correct thing to do when, like a poleaxed beast, Sir Charles went down behind Serena Osborne's chair, almost taking the footman with him.

It had been, in Serena's confident opinion, a most successful season. in view of the young gentlemen of good family and splendid pedigree, many of them wealthy, who had taken an interest in Elizabeth. She felt it was time to consider and strengthen the introductions she and her daughter had acquired at the many balls and parties they had attended and was ready to embark on a round of country visits now that the season was over, and of course, to entertain in her own home so that these potential marriage prospects might not slip through her fingers. Marriages which united great fortunes and estates and one good family with another must be carefully considered. She had great hopes, with her dear friend Lady Woodall, of Harry Woodall but it was only prudent to have alternatives in case the union she and Lady Woodall were working towards did not come about. Elizabeth had been ... well, the word she would use was difficult, or was it awkward ever since she had insisted on going to that awful funeral in April. Not quite so obliging, so docile as she had always been. She and Harry appeared to find a great deal of pleasure in one another's company, which was rather more than the mother of a marriageable daughter would normally allow, but since she and Lady Woodall were eager to see them make a match, she had permitted it. But Harry had not yet declared himself and Elizabeth seemed not to mind. She had been pensive and deep in thoughts which she did not disclose to her mother these last few weeks, sitting for hours in the tiny gardens in the centre of the square in which the house Johnny Osborne had rented for the season was situated, watching the children playing, smiling at their nannies, turning a deaf ear it appeared to Serena whenever she was called to dress for some occasion.

She was, after all, a marketable product though Serena would not have called her that in exactly those words. She must be kept in a cool, neat and unruffled state when she was on exhibition for eligible young gentlemen to view, young gentlemen preferably with a title. Early marriage was the ideal since it insured a longer breeding span filling the pedigreed nurseries with many children and the sooner Elizabeth was settled to it the better, in Serena's view.

They had done all the things a London season demanded. They had queued for hours in their carriage in the Mall with hundreds of other débutantes as they had awaited Elizabeth's turn to be presented to their Majesties. Daughters of the aristocracy, of the gentry, of army officers, of selected officials of state joining those born into the families of bankers, of merchants and persons engaged in commerce of all sorts. There were great changes in society which were not always for the better in Serena's opinion and the careful screening of ladies and their daughters which had taken place in the days of the old Queen, Queen Victoria that was, by the Lord Chamberlain's office for scandal and vulgarity had sadly been put aside.

On the day of her presentation, Elizabeth and Serena, with Johnny in black velvet court dress had moved slowly up the red carpeted staircase of Buckingham Palace. The bannisters were twined with red and white roses and lined with the magnificence of the Yeoman of the Guard. They had passed through the picture gallery and the three state drawing rooms until a roll of drums had announced the start of the proceedings as, led by the Lord Chamberlain, the Royal Family advanced through a ripple of curtseys to the dais. There were duchesses by the score, jewels and coronets, soft music and flowers and for two hours a file of young débutantes, each accompanied by an older woman, in Elizabeth's case Lady Anne Woodall, herself the daughter of a viscount, moved in stately procession to the presence of His Majesty.

Elizabeth had looked quite stunning, Serena thought proudly, taking credit for it, naturally, in her beautiful white satin court dress, her long veil and train. The three ostrich feathers which were obligatory and which on some looked quite ridiculous, gave Elizabeth, who was already tall, a regal grace which was matched only by Her Majesty Queen Mary herself. She curtseyed neatly and with great style and afterwards as she and Serena sat on the spindly gold chairs to watch the rest of the débutantes make their curtsey Serena knew that there was not one as elegant and mannered as her own daughter.

They went shopping for ballgowns at Monsieur Poiret's smart Parisian salon and to Marthe Câllot who, it was said, supplied the most delicious tea gowns, afternoon dresses, Ascot costumes and even exotic furs and for the next few weeks Elizabeth and her fellow debs were seen on every evening at all the establishments where it was fashionable to be seen, suitably chaperoned, naturally, where the young gentlemen might look them over. There were state balls and glittering parties, dances in ribbon-hung, flower-scented ballrooms. They went to grand houses, magnificently gilded and marbled, where the gardens were set out with striped marquees and fairy lights, where the tables groaned beneath lobster and quail, strawberries, ices, figs, nectarines and hot-house peaches and where Elizabeth was allowed just one glass of the champagne which ran, it seemed to her, from a tap which was never turned off.

There were smart 'affaires' at the Ritz where she danced to the famous Casano six-piece band, new dances with a strange rhythmic beat which were not at all like the waltzes to which Serena and Lady Woodall were accustomed. Sometimes they attended four or five such parties in one night, exhausting to them both, they agreed, but if Elizabeth was to be the discerning, gracious and worthy wife of Harry Woodall, hostess in his home and mother to his children she must do, and be seen to be doing all the right things at

301

the right time and if Harry who had remained behind at Woodall, came to hear of Elizabeth's popularity might it not be the inducement needed to get him on the move – seriously – in her direction. She was eighteen and this season would be her first and last, both Lady Woodall and Mrs Osborne hoped as they watched her ride along Rotten Row, a picture of grace and elegance on her well-bred hack. As they attended one lavish social engagement after another they agreed that her more confident if somewhat shy approach to the time-honoured observance of the privileged offering to the privileged their sons and daughters in the marriage mart was quite enchanting. They brushed shoulders with ladies and gentlemen as grand as themselves in Ascot's Royal Enclosure, the applications they themselves had sent in months ago seeking admission well received and granted. The naval and military tournaments at Olympia, dinner parties given by Lady This and the Duchess of That, ball after ball, luncheon parties, the meetings at Newmarket, the Chelsea flower show, the Derby run on Epsom Downs which they motored down to in Lady Woodall's Rolls-Royce motor car, driven by Lady Woodall's chauffeur, O'Shaughnessy, who had of course accompanied them to London. They went to the ballet and the opera and to receptions in all the best places in town where, in the same street, five or six such events were being held at the same time.

And, as it all came to a triumphal ending so did the life of Sir Charles Woodall and before the night was over the new baronet, Sir Harry Woodall, had motored down from his country seat to his London house in Mayfair to make the arrangements for his father to be taken back to Woodall for interment in the family burial plot.

Elizabeth and her mother travelled back to Lancashire with Lady Woodall and her daughter Sophie in the Rolls-Royce driven by Lady Woodall's chauffeur since it was felt that the presence of Lady Woodall's dearest friend, Serena Osborne, might give some comfort in the absence of other female relatives, to the stunned widow. Lady Woodall's sons returned home by train, accompanying the coffin which contained the body of their father.

The journey by car was spread out over two days. Following the Rolls was a second motor car, the Vauxhall belonging to Sir Charles Woodall and in which his son had sped on hearing of his father's death. In it were her ladyship's personal maid, Mrs Osborne's personal maid and the luggage needed overnight for the four ladies. Elizabeth and Sophie must maid themselves for one night, their mothers told them. The motor car was driven by a reliable man recommended by the garage where O'Shaughnessy took the Rolls-Royce for petrol, and by O'Shaughnessy himself.

Arrangements had been made by Sir Harry for his mother and sister and for Mrs Osborne and her daughter to stay in a small but exclusive hotel, one in which unaccompanied ladies might, with perfect propriety, accommodate themselves. It was on the outskirts of the pleasant country town of Market Harborough, roughly half-way between London and Lancashire, which he felt to be a long enough journey for his mother to suffer in her newly-widowed state. The hotel was set in well-proportioned gardens which were in turn surrounded by woods and fields ready to be harvested. Red brick glowing in the late afternoon sunshine, the rich fragrance of a rose garden and the smell of new cut grass. Deferential servants, comfort and reliable, familiar luxury for such a distinguished – and tragic – guest, her daughter and travelling companions. A suite of rooms, naturally, and three bedrooms, one for each of the older ladies with their daughters sharing the third and the understanding that suitable sleeping quarters would be found for the Woodall servants.

The ladies ate dinner in the privacy of their sitting room. They did not dress for the meal since Lady Woodall and her friend Mrs Osborne had agreed that in the circumstances the niceties might be disregarded for this one evening. They had bathed and changed from their motoring outfits, and, served by the unobtrusive and efficient waiter, helped by an equally self-effacing young housemaid, had eaten – as well as they could after such a shocking event – a splendid dinner.

'I shall retire early, I think,' Lady Woodall told her friend.

'You must be tired, my dear,' since it was not every day of the week one lost one's husband in such dreadful circumstances.

'I am, Serena. I do not really care for motoring,' Lady Woodall replied, leaving her daughter and Elizabeth to wonder if that was so why she had created such a furore over having her own motor car two years ago.

It was one of those still summer evenings which begs to be enjoyed, not from a drawing room window or even from an open doorway but in a flower filled garden, along a dusty, dusk filled country lane, in a field flowing with uncut wheat or hay, a stand of trees on which the late evening sun shines golden and shivering from leaf to leaf.

'Let's go for a walk, Sophie. It's too nice to go to bed.'

'It's nearly ten o'clock, Elizabeth, and will be dark soon.'

'Does it matter? It's warm outside.'

'But we are to be away by nine in the morning and I'm tired.'

'Oh do come, Sophie, please. It will be lovely walking in the garden.'

'Whatever for? You will be home tomorrow and can walk all you want to then. I'm going to bed.'

Sophie's woebegone face reminded Elizabeth that, despite the self-control which was bred into them in childhood, her friend had after all just lost her father and she was instantly contrite, fussing about Sophie until she was tucked up in bed.

'Sleep well, Sophie.'

'Thank you, Elizabeth. Good night.'

Elizabeth sighed and moved to the window. The journey

from London had been tedious, doleful even, for though she had heard her mother say a dozen times that Sir Charles and Lady Woodall had married not for love but for the benefit of their respective families which seemed so often to be the case in good society, Lady Woodall, with her husband's death, had fallen into the conventional role of grieving widowhood. She had averted her face from her friend's attempts to 'take her mind off things' and each endeavour by Serena to make a little conversation had been politely turned aside.

For the whole of the journey Elizabeth had had no choice but to study the back of Michael O'Shaughnessy's neck. It was a beautiful neck, as well she knew, falling into a reverie which cut off her mother's well-bred voice and the melancholy atmosphere of Lady Woodall's sorrow. Sophie had been as quiet and despondent as her mother, staring from the window with blank eyes and after a while Serena gave up and left Elizabeth in peace to continue her contemplation of Michael's neck.

It was the colour of warm amber, she decided, above the tight collar of his chauffeur's uniform. What she could see of his neatly trimmed hair lay in defiant feathery curls against his skin, fascinating her to the point where she felt an urgent need to slide back the dividing glass partition and smooth them into submission. His peaked chauffeur's cap was tilted ever so slightly to one side, almost jauntily, though Lady Woodall did not care for jauntiness and had told him on more than one occasion to straighten it. Elizabeth had seen him many times during the past couple of months when he had driven his mistress about London and had sat behind him when she and her mother had accompanied Lady Woodall to some lavish social function. She had felt his eyes on her and had been alarmingly pleased to be looking her best, at the same time telling herself that she was being foolish for what did it matter how Lady Woodall's chauffeur saw her? Despite the strange affinity which she acknowledged existed between them and the soft and surprising kisses they had shared on the day of his sister's funeral, which must, she now told herself, have been an act of madness on her part since he was nothing to her. Could be nothing to her. This was her life. These were her people and what the Woodall chauffeur said or did must not concern her.

Still she could not keep her eyes from continually turning towards him during that long drive, to his profile as he turned to study the traffic, horse-drawn and motor-driven which, until they got out on to the open country roads, flowed about the motor car. His eyelashes were incredibly long and curled upwards, almost touching his eyelids, and the curving corner of his wide, firm mouth seemed to smile, perhaps remembering the last time they had been alone together, she imagined absurdly. She watched his sure, bare hands on the driving wheel – another misdemeanour for Lady Woodall liked him to wear his chauffeur's leather gauntlets at all times. His hands were steady and brown, long-fingered, the nails clean and neatly trimmed. His cheek which was turned to her from time to time was flat and lean and the slant of his dark eyebrow was like the dashing wing of a bird in flight.

She had known all the time she was dithering about at the bedroom window where she was going, and why, and when she saw him, his cigarette glowing in the shadowed dusk beyond the lawn, his tall figure unfolding itself from where it leaned against the trunk of a gigantic elm tree she wondered why she deceived herself about this man. How many times in the past two years had she been alone with him? No more than twice and each time she had allowed ... *allowed*? ... him to kiss her. She had danced with him twice, been held in his arms in the presence of a hundred others, innocent ... *innocent*? ... and completely respectable under the gaze of her own family. He had made no demands on her with which she had not complied. He had said nothing to her to which she could take offence. He had been gentle, humorous, understanding her alarm, giving her none, really, only the truth which was obvious in the warm regard of his eyes and the softness of his kiss. They shared something, as he had said. Something which, when the opportunity arose, drew them to one another in a way she had known with no other man, even Harry. This man touched something inside her, brought something to life which had previously lain dormant and though it terrified her, even now as she moved quietly down the long sloping lawn towards him, she gloried in it. She could feel the familiar turbulence begin, just below her breasts, rising to fill her throat so that she could scarcely breathe let alone speak and when he held out his hands to her she was glad just to cling to them, saying nothing.

'I prayed to the Blessed Mother to bring you to me,' he said simply. His voice was soft, even reverent. 'I've been here an hour, hoping, but when I saw you coming towards me, begod, didn't I think you were a ghost. Sweet Jesus, it's beautiful you are. I can think of no one but you ... these months in London, watching you, no more than a sacrificial lamb being taken here and there for those bloody gents in your society to look over ... sure an' it was more than I could stand sometimes ... Sweet Mary, it's babbling I am ... it's just that ...'

She looked up into his face. It was working with some strong emotion which longed to break out, to lash out, even at her who was, she realised now, no more than the pawn in a game of marriage and had no voice, no choice but to be obedient to her parents in the playing of it. And it was eating him up.

'Elizabeth ... I'm going mad, so I am ...'

'Oh Michael, please ...' The soft line of her compassionate young mouth moved in distress and without hesitation he drew her into his arms, folding her so neatly against his own body it was as though each line and curve, each muscle and bone and fibre, made and formed in their mothers' wombs had been specially designed to fit, like this, to one another. Her face pressed into the curve of his throat just below his strong, knotted jawline. Her lips parted against his brown skin. Her arms went round him, crossing over one another at his back, holding him to her fiercely, dangerously. She crushed her body so close to his he could feel the soft firm swell of her breasts beneath the fine cotton of her summer blouse. He wore only his chauffeur's trousers and a clean shirt into which he had changed at the thought, the hope, that he might see her, and their separate flesh had little between it but the thin fabric of their lightweight clothing.

He drew her deeper into the stand of the trees which lay in the darkening peace about the garden. The sky was rapidly losing its summer light. Towards the west, as the sun had vanished below the horizon the green and yellow shades its going had left changed to brown and orange, then, in an arc above the brown, to rose pink and above that again to plum purple. The twilight was going fast now, the sky fading as the glorious colours were lost in the rising shadow of the earth and the silver mistress of the night took the place of the golden master of the day. A full moon was rising large and gleaming above the trees which hid Michael and Elizabeth.

They were both trembling. He held her away from him for a moment, her arms still resting about his waist as though she could not bear to lose hold of him. He looked into her grave face and her eyes were frightened, not of him, he knew that now, but of this fierce emotion, this strong and undeniable emotion which had them in its grip. Strong, yes, but sweet, warm, beautiful in its strength.

'You know what has happened,' he said helplessly, his voice breaking for a moment. He lifted his hands and as though freeing her, looked away from her, up into the shifting moon-silvered leaves, his face filled with a strange fury, his eyes a pale and transparent blue in the soft, shadowed moonlight.

'Yes.'

'Goddammit, Elizabeth ... Goddammit...' His voice rose angrily but he had nothing else to say, it seemed, for what could he say to this lovely daughter of a landed gentleman who, it was very certain, was not for him. Chauffeur to another landed gentleman, was Michael O'Shaughnessy, since he was now in Sir Harry Woodall's employ and, as a man, and as the man who loved this girl, it was very apparent to him where Sir Harry's affections lay so what hope had he, what future had he to offer her when faced with the violent storm which would erupt should he lay claim to her. Mara had married this girl's brother and it had only *just* been allowed. Only just reluctantly accepted by the society which had bred James, but then Mara was a female with no other function in life but to stay at home and keep her husband's house, breed his children and take a very minor part in his masculine life. She had no responsibilities. They rested on her husband's shoulders. He could still do what he had been brought up to do, even if his wife was, as they would see it, a bog Irish colleen from the working-class suburbs of Liverpool. James Osborne had no need to make his way in the world, a world in which, under different circumstances, Mara might have proved a drag on his chances of success. A clever girl, even if she came from an inferior class, could always heave herself up to her husband's level, but Holy Mother, it could never work the other way round. A man like himself could never be more than what he was. He had no education to speak of, no training in anything but the rudiments of motor car maintenance. He was intelligent and capable of hard work, practical and sharp-witted, but he had not that hard-headed shrewdness, that clear-headed subtlety that would lead him into some profession, like their Dermot for instance, and which might provide a bright future for himself and his as yet unborn family. He was too easy-going, too good-humoured, light-hearted if you like, to do what Dermot did, to *get on*. He was content as he was, moving through life at a pace which suited him. He felt he had achieved a step up in life when he had been trained to become the Woodall chauffeur and he could honestly think of nothing he would rather do. A feckless Irishman, drifting contentedly through the days like a will o' the wisp, he supposed people would say of him, and up to now he hadn't given a tuppenny toss.

'Michael, oh hush ... hush...' He had not realised he had been groaning, almost weeping if he were truthful, out loud into the night. He felt her hands on his face and her kisses on his chin and cheeks and when he crushed her passionately against him, hot against his mouth.

'Dear sweet Christ, I love you, Elizabeth ... I love you so much...'

'Michael...'

They sank to their knees on a bed of soft wood anemones, their arms still hungrily about one another and for several minutes each mouth searched out and found the lovely taste of the other, of flesh warm to tongue and lips, as they breathed in the perfume of firm young skin, caressed the texture of flesh which was flushed and alive and waiting, listened to heartbeat and pulsebeat and the growing rhythm of need which moved from body to body. Hands and lips on the silken arch of a dark eyebrow, the fluttering moistness of an eyelid, the curve of an arching throat, the inner tenderness of an ear, a soft earlobe. Her hands were in his hair, guiding him and his warm, ardent lips to the satin of her cheeks and chin and to the sweetness beneath it. His breath was quick and heavy and when the brown owl hooted, causing a small commotion of birds settling to sleep in a yew tree, neither heard it.

With the eagerness of the lover he longed to be his hands went to the buttons of her high-necked blouse and she made no protest. Sighing, she lay back as one by one, more slowly

310

now as he recognised what was truly, at last, about to be his, he undid them, exposing as carefully as a man unveiling a treasured and rare jewel, her snow-white, rosy-peaked breasts which no man but himself, he knew, had seen. His hand pushed aside the cotton of her blouse and the lacy, ribbon-tied wisp of her chemise, pulling them both out of her skirt, then slowly, so slowly he realised that this moment was as precious to him as anything he had ever known for it would come but this once, this first time, he slipped both garments from her and her breasts strained forward to feel the touch of his hands. But still he did not touch them. His fingers traced the rich satin of her shoulders and upper arms, trailing sensuously to every part of her upper body. He bent his head to run his tongue where his fingers had been and she began to moan and gasp, raising herself unconsciously into the position a woman assumes to receive a man and at last he put an enquiring finger to one engorged rosy nipple.

'Michael . . . please, Michael . . .' and as her breath rasped out his name both his hands reached out and cupped her eager flesh, one hand to each breast and they fitted exactly into his palm. His breathing was laboured now and he could feel the heat and turbulence of his own masculinity strain within its confinement but still he lingered, marvelling at her compelling, flaunting beauty.

'Sit up,' he whispered, watching when, as she did so, her breasts fell forward, heavy with their own weight in his hands. He reached up and released the ribbons of her hair and she was cloaked in it, drowned in its darkness stark against the whiteness, the rose-flushed whiteness of her body. He bent his head, taking each nipple in turn between his warm, moist lips, filled with an urgency now, as she was. Gasping and bemused and totally his, he knew it, and by all that was Holy, he was ready to oblige. Her hands lifted to pull his head down to her, to her taut, thrusting breasts, to anything he cared to take. She helped him remove his shirt,

311

her hands trembling, murmuring his name, her own breathing as harsh as his own, pressing her half-naked body up against his brown chest, whimpering in her throat as the coarse black curls which were scattered there brushed against her straining nipples.

'Michael ... Michael ... Michael ...' she said over and over again, beginning to swing her head from side to side, the great cape of her silky hair flowing like dark water across first one breast then the other. Her hands were plucking at his shoulders, creeping across his back as he laid her down again, beginning to scratch, pulling at his belt. Her teeth bit at his neck and chin and her hips lifted as she urged him to do something, whatever it was, to ease this hot and curling pain which was ready to explode in her belly.

He had pulled up her skirt to her waist and was wrestling with the ribbons at the waist of her drawers, knowing she was as close to orgasm as he was himself, when it happened and though he did his best to ignore it since this was what they both wanted, or so his eager male body told him, he was savagely aware that she had become completely still. His heart loved her so. Her sweetness, her compassion, her goodness for she was good, Elizabeth Osborne. She, of them all, had been the only one to befriend Mara. She, of them all, had shown kindness to his mother in her grief. A dutiful daughter, obedient to her heritage, true and loyal to those she loved. And she loved him. Oh yes, she loved him with all the strength of her brave heart but she was no longer offering her body to him as she had done moments ago. He had stripped her half naked. With his knowing ways he had brought her virgin sensuality to life and he was about to – what was the word – deflower her, take her maidenhead, make her his own in the only true and complete way a man can own a woman but she was not going to allow it, not now.

'What is it?' he whispered, ready to be rough as all men

are when they believe they are to be denied what they thought to be theirs.

She did not answer but her averted face spoke for her and though he loved her, his masculinity, his maleness wanted, needed to do something to hurt her.

'What is it?' he repeated, and his tone was angry.

'I must get back,' she said coolly, not looking at him.

'Why ... for God's sake ... Why ...?' He was a man. He had not yet regained control of himself and he hated her for what she was doing, or preventing him from doing.

'Please let me go,' and he did, with a fierceness he could not moderate.

'I'm sorry.' Her voice was barely audible for how could she explain the unexplainable to him. She was Elizabeth Osborne, unique and unrepeatable and how would she be when her female body had been pierced by his and her female need had been assuaged and the hot mindless passion she was in was done with. How would she feel about the man who, saying he loved her, had taken what seemed a hasty and indecent advantage of her momentary weakness. She was afraid and dazed, her breathing still laboured as he pulled her roughly to a sitting position and then turning from her, bent his head to his arms which he clasped about his knees. Slowly his mind was beginning to take over his maddened and unreasonable body which still wanted to do nothing but have Elizabeth Osborne beneath it. He breathed deeply, hungrily as though he could not get enough air into his lungs and his shoulders trembled as if with great weariness.

Slowly he raised his head and his eyes were again deep and soft with his love. He said nothing, just reached out and from somewhere retrieved her pretty chemise and somehow tied her into it, the ribbons still far beyond his shaking fingers. They longed, as they fumbled with the fastenings to mould and caress, to smooth and fondle, to hold the rosy flushed beauty which brushed against the back of his hands

313

as he did his best to put her back to the way she had been half an hour since. Her blouse was next, the sleeves awkward because she was, the buttons impossible, then he sat away from her again, his brown body sweated and almost invisible in the warm summer gloom.

'I'm sorry, Elizabeth,' he said at last. 'I should not have ... not to you. I love you, you see. That's why. Because I love you.'

She did not speak, just sat there trembling and shivering, her hair falling over her bent head and shoulders, her face hidden, and when he turned to put a gentle hand on her shoulder she flinched away.

The expression on his face was appalled. 'Don't ... aah don't, sweetheart. Don't turn against me. Jesus, Joseph and Mary ...' His voice was anguished. 'I'm a man, not a bloody statue, but I've never forced a girl yet and I wouldn't ... especially you ...' He stood up violently and put out a hand to help her up and this time she took it. She stood quietly before him as he shrugged into his shirt, still not meeting his eyes.

'Elizabeth, look at me. Look into my face or by God I think I'll go mad. I love you. Holy Mother of God, you're the heart of me. Everything that makes life sweet is in you an' that's why ... I'm sorry. You're the loveliest ... Jesus, I thought you wanted to go on ... and so did I, but not like this, don't let us be like this. God help me, please try to understand.'

'I do, Michael.' Her voice was quiet. With fingers which still shook she did up the buttons of her blouse, tucking it neatly into the waistband of her skirt. She found her ribbon and with one swift movement had her hair up in a deftly tied knot.

'I had better get back to the hotel,' she said, politely he thought, as though he was some passing acquaintance.

'Mother of God, tell me what you're thinking.' His voice was harsh and urgent. She was not doing any of the things

314

he had expected her to do, that was what was troubling him. She was calm now where he had expected her to be tearful and clinging, ready to accept the comfort of his arms and his sure love. She said she understood why he had made love to her with such joyful eagerness but she had said it in such a matter of fact voice he thought he would really rather have had the hysterics.

'You asked me if I understood,' it was as though she had read his mind, 'and I said I did. What else can I tell you?'

'But . . .'

'Please Michael, I must go. Sophie will miss me.' Polite again!

His sudden grip on her arms was dangerous. He felt the pain of her rejection overwhelming his love and his caution, his endeavour to be gentle with her.

'Don't do this, Elizabeth. Listen to me when I say I love you. I've had . . . women, you must know that, but before God, by all I hold most dear, I didn't love them. I love you. I love you more than . . . Sweet Mary Mother of God, I love you. If I didn't I would have persuaded you to go on without the slightest compunction and you know I could have done it, don't you?' He was desperate to have her believe him.

'I know, Michael, but now I must go.'

'Damnation . . .' It was like trying to catch mist in his bare hand. She really couldn't see why he was so violently angry. He was unsteady with it, needing her to turn to him, to tell him that everything was all right between them, that she . . . yes, that was it . . . she had not once told him . . . said the words . . . in all the sweet and blinding passion which had seized them, she had not said that she loved him.

'Elizabeth, don't leave like this . . .'

'I must . . . *I must* . . . please let me go . . .'

'When we get back then? Say you'll meet me somewhere . . .'

'Please Michael, let go of my arm.'

And when he did she turned and began to run wildly in

the direction of the hotel leaving him with the feeling that some dreadful mistake had just been made and one that he would regret for as long as he lived.

Apart from the drive back to Beechwood she did not see him again until the day they buried his old employer. Sir Charles Woodall's funeral was vastly different to that of Bridget Feeney and her son. It was dignified and splendid, showing none of the outpouring of emotion which had been so abundant and so right from the hearts of the O'Shaughnessy family. A solid and impressive mass of black-suited gentlemen, cold and contained, ladies in mourning veils, correct in every detail. A procession of Woodall relatives and Woodall tenants, Woodall employees and Woodall friends moving in strict order of rank to and from the ancient churchyard where Sir Charles was laid to rest amongst centuries of Woodalls with all the pomp and ceremony of the titled gentleman he was. No one shed a tear, except perhaps a kitchenmaid or two, for Sir Charles had been a good master.

Michael O'Shaughnessy wore the same black working man's suit, waistcoat and black bowler hat that he had worn for his sister's funeral in April. He stood at the back of the church with the rest of the household servants. Elizabeth's eye met his as she walked with her arm through Teddy's behind Mara and James who followed her mother and father but the expression on his face was grave and gave no sign that he was acquainted with her rather better than he should have been. He smiled at Mara who, in the early stages of her second pregnancy, clung to her young husband's arm.

From the corner of her eye as Elizabeth passed from the church into the bright summer sunshine which seemed so out of place on a day such as this, she saw him take the arm of the pretty, tearful parlourmaid beside him. She felt the incredible sensation hit her right between her breasts, a hot and burning sensation which was as unexpected as it was unfamiliar. Her family were grouped about the widowed figure of Lady Woodall and Teddy hesitated for a moment, holding her back. He was only a boy still and not at all sure of his part in these painful proceedings except, as a gentleman, he knew he was expected to give his support to any lady who might need his arm, as his sister appeared to do now. Her fingers were digging quite painfully into his flesh and when he turned to peer down into her face he was bewildered by the expression he saw there. She was looking back to the porch where the servants from Woodall Park were coming slowly from the sorrowing dimness into the benevolent relief of the sunshine. The rest of the mourners had already drifted away towards their motor cars but the chauffeur, what was his name? the one who was the brother of Mara, was just emerging, bending his tall frame to avoid cracking his head on the low porch. There was a very pretty girl, a parlourmaid, Teddy thought her to be, clinging to his arm. She was smiling tearfully, shyly into the chauffeur's solicitous face, glad of his comfort on this sad occasion, it seemed.

Elizabeth's fingers were like a vice on his arm, then, roughly, with an urgency which amazed him she began to pull him, almost at a run, down the church path to where their mother and father stood.

'Hurry up, Teddy,' she muttered through clenched teeth, her voice tart.

'Why?' he asked, bewildered. 'What's the rush?'

'Mother and father are waiting for us, that is why, you stupid fool,' was the astonishing answer. Her cheeks were poppy red and her eyes glittered in what he could have sworn had he not known her better was fierce and bitter anger. But what had she to be angry about, her bemused brother asked himself and only Elizabeth, and perhaps the chauffeur, could have told him the answer, and that was hidden away in the slashing memory of what had happened in a little wood on the outskirts of Market Harborough.

317

17

'I'm off to see the Mammy, Elizabeth. I shall take Claudine with me but to tell the truth I don't want to drag along that damned nanny your mother insists on sending with me wherever I go just as though I can't be trusted to look after my own baby. And you should see the poor woman in Mammy's kitchen. She looks for all the world as though she's been set down in a foreign country, not understanding a blessed word of the language the natives are speaking an' as for their customs, God almighty, you'd think for sure she was in the land of the Hottentots. We can't have a nice cosy chat, me an' the Mammy, for haven't I the feeling she's repeating everything we say to your sainted mother. So if I tell her you're to come with me she might not make such a fuss.' Mara hesitated, smiling ruefully. 'On the other hand if she hears you're to visit the home of the dreadful O'Shaughnessy family she'll more than likely have the vapours and forbid you to go. Tell you what,' she leaned forward, a wicked grin on her face, 'why don't we just skip out of the side door and tell Gibson to get out the motor car and drive us over to Edge Lane? He'd do it for you. Your father isn't using it because I heard him an' James talking about riding over to Woodall to discuss with Harry something about himself taking over as master of the fox hunt.'

Mara twitched aside the curtains in her sister-in-law's bedroom, looking out over the white-rimed gardens of Beechwood. There had been a heavy hoar frost during the night and each tree and shrub, each blade of grass and stone path was glazed and sparkling in the pale winter sunshine. But its ethereal beauty was given no more than a cursory glance. Mara turned away and on her face was an expression which had become increasingly familiar in the past two years and Elizabeth smiled inwardly, waiting. When Mara looked like that she wanted something. Her smile was bright and artlessly beguiling since she was not quite clever enough to keep her scheming hidden so it was obvious to Elizabeth that whatever it was she had in mind it was planned right down to the minutest detail but at the same time she did not want Elizabeth to know it. It must appear to be a spontaneous thought which had just popped into Mara's charming head.

And she could be very charming when she wanted something even if she was somewhat transparent in the way she went about it. Her husband, still as much in love with her as he had been on their wedding day, much to his mother's chagrin, found her irresistible and could deny her nothing. He was overwhelmed, not only by her charming ways, which could be very sweet and even sensuous when they were directed at him, but by the passion which she was still able to arouse in him. In the warm privacy of their rooms her wanton display of sexuality made him and kept him her willing slave still and it was a wondrous thing to him how she knew, a decently brought-up Catholic girl as she was, the many ways to tease and tantalise a man as she did himself.

'Don't touch me, James,' she would order haughtily when his fingers stroked up her thigh and attempted to invade the soft, moist centre of her womanhood, 'I am reading,' but her half-closed eyes told him it was only a game she played. He would smile and move away, his intention well displayed for her admiring gaze since they were both naked. He would drape himself with apparent unconcern against the fireplace, even light a cigar but her casually widening legs, the tantalising lift of her full breasts, the gleam in her eye, the careless but saucy way she lay back to allow him a further glimpse of the rosy pink core of her drove him to madness. It went on for hours sometimes. She would pose, still as a statue, pretending to be astride a horse, on a low backed chair or on the hearthrug with the fire glowing on her, legs sprawled, one hand behind her head, her breasts, young and firm and pointed, on magnificent display. She wore garters, lacy and definitely not ladylike, and nothing else, gold chains about her waist and wrists and ankles, or long strands of knotted pearls, and nothing else. Even his top hat, and nothing else, binding him to her with silken bonds of love and her amazing sexuality. Her imagination was endless and incredibly inventive and they often wondered, laughing together in the secret way of lovers, on where it came from. After all she was a well-brought-up and sheltered girl, reared in the true faith and how had she learned the art of pleasing a man as she did her husband, she asked him coquettishly, but what the devil did he care, he answered her; he was just bloody glad it was himself who was enjoying it, reaching for her again.

'Do you know what I was thinking, Elizabeth?' she continued now, moving awkwardly away from the window and across the bedroom to lower herself into the armless velvet chair which stood beside Elizabeth's glowing fire. Elizabeth was sitting before her dressing table whilst her maid, Minty, put the last pin in the shining arrangement of curls at the back of her young mistress' head. With a final deft flick of the hairbrush the maid stood back to smile into the mirror, waiting for Miss Elizabeth's approval, then, at Elizabeth's smiling nod, left the room.

Elizabeth turned to Mara. 'No, what were you thinking?' smiling affectionately at her sister-in-law. Mara always used that same cajoling tone when she was going to put forward a perfectly plausible reason why she should do or have something of which she thought you might disapprove.

'I was thinking, last Sunday it was, you remember, when your mother had gone over to Woodall in the Renault to say goodbye to Lady Woodall. Your father and James had taken James' new Austin for a spin and I wanted to slip up to Edge Lane to ask Mammy about something. Well ... it's a bit embarrassing, me being in the family way again an' your mother is ... well after all, my Mammy's had eighteen and ...'

'Eighteen!' Elizabeth's mouth dropped open in amazement.

'Oh yes, didn't you know?' Mara seemed quite unconcerned, just as though there was nothing unusual in bearing so many children. 'Mind, only thirteen of us lived. Anyway, as I was saying ... now what was I saying, oh yes, I was wanting to be off up to Edge Lane an' not a divil of a motor car to take me. Short of ordering a taxi-cab ...' which, naturally, was out of the question for a lady such as herself '... there was no way I could get there. Besides, it would have been very inconvenient, so I was thinking, why couldn't you and I have one of our own? Motor car, I mean. There are lots of ladies ...' and she was certainly one of those now '... who drive one an' I'm sure that you and me ...' meaning of course not Elizabeth at all, but Mara Osborne '... would soon get the hang of it. Michael could teach us when he gets back from Scotland. Oh, I know it will be a while before I could even get behind the steering wheel ...' indicating the bulk of her eight months of pregnancy '. . but when I can just think how wonderful it would be to dash off to town or home to see the family without having to beg permission from your father or your mother. Well you know what I mean.'

Elizabeth did know what Mara meant and she sympathised with her but the assumption that James, not to mention her mother and father who would be horrified, would allow his wife to drive herself and presumably her two children, his two children, dashing about the countryside just as though she was anybody, was preposterous. He was indulgent to a ridiculous point with his young wife, being hardly more

321

than a boy himself, but he had been brought up on how a lady, one of his class, should behave. A motor car, certainly, but chauffeur driven. Chaperoned, in other words, protected, and not flying about unaccompanied as the so-called new woman was apparently able to do.

'You can certainly ask him, Mara, but really, I can't see him permitting it. He would think it improper, you know how he is.' And you know how the rules of our society are, her manner said. 'Not that I don't think it's a splendid idea. I do. It would be lovely to go wherever we wanted, whenever we felt the need, but I don't hold out much hope. Mother wouldn't even allow me to have a bicycle. She thought them bold and unladylike, not to mention downright dangerous. Of course the freedom it might have given me was without doubt the prime reason for forbidding it. It is only recently that she has allowed me to ride without a groom. When we were children, Sophie Woodall and I were permitted to wander on the estate alone. I suppose because we were only children but as soon as a girl reaches a certain age and is . . . marriageable and therefore valuable, she is treated as though she were an imbecile child who must never be left alone, nor allowed a thought of her own.' It was said somewhat bitterly and Mara looked at her sharply but she was too concerned with her own needs to trouble herself with Elizabeth's odd manner.

'Yes, I know all about that, Elizabeth, but I shan't give up just the same. Anyway, will you come with me this afternoon? Sure an' it will do you good to get out of this 'owd house for an hour. You hardly ever seem to go anywhere since Sir Charles died and the Woodalls went into mourning though why that should affect you, I'm sure I don't know. Holy Mother, you've a face on you like a wet weekend and I'm sick to death of seeing you mope about the place so put on your bonnet and come an' see the Mammy. She was asking after you only the other day. She's a soft spot for you, did you know that, ever since you came to Bridget's funeral an'

322

she'd be as pleased as a dog with two tails if you were to drop in and have a cup of tea with her.'

It was nearly nine months since Mara's sister had died and in that time everything that Mara had hoped for had been realised. The ice, once chipped away from about Ellen O'Shaughnessy's unforgiving heart, had never returned and though the sadness of Bridget's death would always be there the renewal of her relationship with her wayward girl and the acquaintance of her new and captivating granddaughter had done much to ease her pain. It was almost like the old days, Mick said fondly, as the swirling colour and music of his wife's kitchen was brought back to life with his daughters laughing and talking nineteen to the dozen, children shouting and grizzling and chasing each other about their mothers' skirts, the kettle on the hob forever singing and his Ellen chiding and hugging them all at one and the same time. Bridget's four little girls had taken up almost permanent residence at their grandparents' house, poor motherless mites, but who minded? Only the absence and often harrowing return of Caitlin from the secret life she led in London took the almost perfect shine from the renewed content with which he and Ellen began and ended each day.

Mara spent almost as much time at Edge Lane as she did at Beechwood now, monopolising Serena's carriage or the motor car, sweeping off down the gravelled drive and away towards Liverpool without so much as a by your leave and if James didn't put a stop to his wife's high-handed attitude to what was after all Serena's carriage and his father's Renault, she would. She said so firmly to her son. She would have thought a woman in her condition would have been content to stay at home where she belonged instead of junketing about the place like any working class person. She gave such offence to Mara that her daughter-in-law felt bound to remark that not only was the Old Queen dead but her son as well. After all this was 1912 and it was perfectly

323

proper for pregnant women, yes pregnant she had said and pregnant she meant, to go about in society.

'Not in mine,' Serena answered her cuttingly, distastefully, wondering for the thousandth time since James had brought this little upstart into her home, how she was to bear it.

It really was amazing, even Mara herself thought so, how satisfying she found it to be among her own people again. She could remember so clearly her own desperate yearning to be somebody, to marry a gentleman and live in a splendid house, to have servants and a carriage and lovely clothes, but most of all to get away from the noisy, uninhibited, garrulous, what she saw as *common* members of her quite ordinary family. She wanted to be a lady. To have a lady's exclusive and personal use of some luxurious room where, unless she invited them, no one could intrude on her privacy. In her naivety she had not realised that that was exactly the opposite of what her loquacious nature needed. The non-stop gossiping, voluble and running on like a merry stream through what would otherwise have been the dryness of her life, was food and drink to her. Talk the hind leg off a donkey, they did, her mother and sisters, and how despairingly she had missed it in the polite atmosphere of Beechwood Hall. She and Elizabeth had become friends, spending time in one another's sitting rooms, discussing fashion, sharing many a joke as they learned to relax with one another. She had discovered that her sister-in-law had a quiet sense of humour not instantly apparent, a liking for a sly dig at authority in the shape of Serena Osborne, and could be trusted. She was always willing, even eager it seemed to Mara, to listen to the reminiscences of Mara's – and her brothers' and sisters' – childhood which was particularly gratifying, allowing Mara to talk for hours on end about Clare and Eammon, Dermot and Caitlin and Michael. They shared a love for Mara's baby daughter of whom she was inordinately proud but when all was said and done she was not really one of them. Irish. An O'Shaughnessy with the gift to talk, to laugh and weep and all at the same time.

'Come on, Elizabeth,' she coaxed now. 'Bejasus, let's go an' have us a good laugh at the Mammy's.'

Elizabeth had not seen Michael O'Shaughnessy for five months. She had, she admitted to herself, stayed at home going nowhere without her mother in all that time simply because she was afraid of what she might do without Serena's protection. She would have laughed out loud six months ago at the very idea of hiding behind her mother's elegant skirts but she readily accepted that there were none better to protect her from the madness which she and Michael had shared. A wild fired madness running through her veins which would undeniably have led to disaster, had it not been for her own fear, for once tasted how could they give it up? It was not that she was ashamed, Dear God, no ... She believed that he spoke the truth when he said he loved her but what difference did that make to the heart-breaking situation which had arisen from a few innocent, deliciously forbidden kisses. How did she feel about him? She was afraid to face the question and even more the answer. To probe the aching hurt their separation had caused her, was causing her, since never a day went by when she did not spend hours brooding on that half an hour of rapturous joy, of wonder, of ... what? What was she to call it? She was eighteen. What did she know of life, of love, of passion flowing from male to female, from woman to man, from lover to lover? She only knew that she longed for a sight of him, for the sound of his whimsical Irish brogue, exaggerated she knew because it amused him to caricature his own Irishness. She dwelled for hours on the shape of his curling mouth, the flyaway tilt of his dark eyebrows, the long sweep of his gold-tipped eyelashes, the untidy tumble of his thick hair, his hands reaching out to her, smoothing her face, her throat, her ...

There she stopped, again not because of shame but because of the exquisite feeling which, whenever she remembered it, began to uncoil itself in the pit of her stomach and the pain which it left when she forced it to die. She was so afraid, so terribly afraid. Afraid of herself and of him and there was nowhere to hide for she knew that when he returned with Lady Woodall from Scotland he would come for her. Nothing would stop him and the only wonder was that he had been so patient and had left her alone for so long. He would have her. He had said so in the frantic note which had been thrust into her hand by a curious gardener's lad who had waylaid her a month ago as she walked in the walled confines of the denuded rose garden. She had it now in her pocket. She had smoothed it out a hundred times, crumpled it again despairingly, wept over it, kissed it and folded it tenderly to fit into a protected place against her heart. 'I love you,' it said simply, 'and nothing will stop me from claiming you. We will be together. Elizabeth, you must believe me. I am trying to be practical,' his words told her, 'to work out some way we can be married but you must be patient with me,' and through it all his love was like a gleaming thread sewing the words together into a lovely chain to bind her to him.

But the longing to see again, just once, the mother who had borne him, the sisters and brothers in whose veins ran his blood, the house in which he had been a boy, a youth, a young and carefree man was too much for her and within the hour she and Mara and Claudine were chugging through Childwall and along Score Lane, turning left into Edge Lane behind the stiff and disapproving back of Gibson, the Osborne chauffeur. He had not been informed by the master that the motor car would be required this afternoon, he had said, and he was just cleaning it so if Miss Elizabeth . . .

'Glory be to God, can you not clean the thing tomorrow?' Mrs James Osborne had cut in from behind the master's daughter, turning up her Irish nose as if she was the bloody Queen of Sheba and for two pins, had Miss Elizabeth not been there, he would have told Mrs High and Mighty

Osborne that without his master's command he could not get out the motor car, no, not for anybody.

They were welcomed ecstatically, Mara swept into half a dozen pairs of arms as though she had not been seen for six months instead of the day before yesterday. The baby, eighteen months old now and as blithe and sweet-tempered as the rest of them, was passed from hand to hand, kissed and hugged, petted and dandled in a way Elizabeth knew her mother would have abhorred, bearing it all with the equanimity which seemed to be bred in this lovely family.

'Sure an' aren't you the fine ones,' Mara's admiring sisters declared, studying without envy the high fashion of Elizabeth's outfit. She wore an ankle-length fitted coat and a hat with a turned-down brim just like a mushroom, in the exact same shade of violet blue. The coat was trimmed with pale grey fur at the cuffs and with it she had a stole of the same fur which wound round her throat twice, the tails of it almost brushing the floor.

Mara, her bulk hidden beneath a cape lined with Russian sable, was equally approved of and wondered at, not least the way in which she flung the garment carelessly in the direction of the kitchen chair where the cat often curled itself, its cost and beauty of no consequence, it seemed.

'Come an' sit yourself by the fire, Miss Osborne . . .'

'Elizabeth, please.'

'Matty, wet the tea for Miss Osborne an' pull the fire together and will you be having a piece of me fruit cake? 'Twas made but an hour since an' will keep up your strength until you get home. See, fetch the footstool for Miss Osborne, Lucy, an' will you shift Finbar from the rug, Amy, for isn't the spalpeen keeping the warmth from Miss Osborne's . . .'

'I shall be offended if you don't call me Elizabeth, Mrs O'Shaughnessy, really I will,' wanting to put her arms about this bustling, kind little woman and tell her how much she loved her son. Pour out her fear, her confusion and pain and the anger which pierced her heart at feeling it. It was overwhelming her, taking the ground which had always been safe and stable from beneath her feet and if she could only confide in someone, tell them that she was being torn in two most cruelly; ask someone what she should do, it might help to clear her mind. But it could not be this woman who was only just coming to terms with her own sorrows. She wouldn't understand. Not that some woman loved her son as Elizabeth did, but that it should be Elizabeth who loved him. It had undermined the very foundation of her family when Mara married Elizabeth's brother and the horror, yes, horror it would be to Ellen O'Shaughnessy to discover her beloved boy wanted to marry another member of the gentry would surely destroy her. A good Irish Catholic girl of the same class as herself she would want for her son, for all her sons, so that they might continue in the decent and proper way of life she and her forebears, Mick and his forebears had begun fifty-odd years ago. It was unnatural for their kind to mix, to mate, to merge their blood with the class above them – or below – and it would be uselessly cruel of Elizabeth to even speak of it.

In the time it took her to be seated in the best chair in the warmest corner of the kitchen these thoughts hammered through Elizabeth's brain, spikes being driven in with a remorseless strength which made her head ache.

'And what's the word on Caitlin, Mammy?' she heard Mara ask, and there was pain in the anguished sigh with which Ellen answered, shaking her head sadly.

'Ach, she's still away down in that Godforsaken place and only the Blessed Virgin herself knows what the child suffers. She's been arrested again. I saw her name with me own eyes in the newspaper,' crossing herself fearfully, the very idea of the frail and beautiful girl in the hands of those beasts once more almost more than she could bear. 'She'll not listen to her Daddy an' me an' the things you read in the newspapers, sure they make my blood run cold an' no doubt Caitlin will be amongst those who are involved, chalking things on pavements, smashing windows, cutting words in golf greens, bowling greens an' even paintings in public galleries. Did you read where they're setting fire to empty houses, bejasus, decent folks' homes an' Mother of God, me own child striking the match. An' her only just twenty. Living away from home an' with no one to protect her against them heathens...'

'She'll be all right, Mammy,' Mara soothed, sorry she had asked now, longing to have her mother's concern centred on her, who was soon to give birth to her second child, but Ellen was not to be stopped.

'... an' where she'll find a decent Catholic lad to marry her is beyond me. Those who know her won't want a girl who's been ... well ... been in prison, no matter what for, an' who's been gadding about in foreign parts with no daddy or brother...'

'London's not foreign parts, Mammy.' Mara was becoming exasperated.

'... an' she should be wed now, at her age, with a child or two, like yourself...'

Seizing her chance Mara sat down heavily, one hand beneath the burden in her belly, the other to the small of her back.

'If you've a cushion, Mammy, I'd be glad of it, so I would. Me back's been giving me gyp just now...'

Instantly contrite, and diverted as Mara intended, Ellen was at her daughter's side, waving an imperious hand to Matty to run for a cushion from the parlour.

Gradually, as the voices flowed round her, a remark or two being directed in a kindly manner at herself; as the laughter echoed about the high ceiling where Mick O'Shaughnessy's shirts aired beside his daughters' under-drawers, the bodices and freshly ironed petticoats; as a smiling child crawled into her lap and fell asleep, trusting

329

implicitly this strange person since it had never had cause to do otherwise, Elizabeth felt the strength and serenity of this united and loving family enter into her and when it was time to go, Mara and Ellen and her daughters were astonished to find their well-bred visitor had fallen asleep too.

'God rest her, will you look at the loveliness of her,' Ellen whispered, 'an' her with Finbar in the lap of her smart frock,' and when Elizabeth woke it was to rosy smiling faces and a fond pat from Ellen who could not resist the temptation to soothe any stray child – into which category Elizabeth apparently fell – who might need it.

'Come again soon, Miss Osborne, pet,' Ellen exhorted, then turned to embrace her daughter, 'and you, darlin', look after that wee girleen up there . . .' just as though her granddaughter was off to the poorhouse instead of the cosy, sheltered comfort of the Osborne nursery.

'I will, Mammy.'

'May the Holy Mother of God bless you an' keep you, darlin', an' mind them steps an' see . . .' to the Osborne's affronted chauffeur '. . . don't you be driving that dreadful machine so fast, mind . . .'

James Osborne and Hugh Woodall had wandered off on some business of their own and the two remaining men moved round the restive animal with all the anxiety of two concerned nannies studying a fretful child. Several grooms hung about with the same expression of solicitude, the weight of the worry they felt showing in their tendency to sigh and bite their lips. One even chewed his fingernails. A third man who crouched beneath the horse's belly, his hand gentle on its quivering fetlock, rose suddenly and with an air of one delivering the news of the relief of Mafeking, declared that the hunter was 'in fine fettle now, sir, and can jump with the bloody best, though none'd be better than 'im'.

The relief was enormous. Stable lads smiled and wiped

their brows, moving away to continue tasks which had been interrupted as the head groom inspected Sir Harry's Monarch. One or two began to whistle cheerfully as the hunter was tenderly led away to his stable with a great deal of fond chaffing from those who looked after him.

'Thank God for that,' Sir Harry breathed, reaching into his pocket for his cigarettes. He did not, as might have been expected of a gentleman of his wealth and position, carry them in a gold cigarette case but in the simple packet in which they were sold. He offered the packet to Johnny Osborne who refused, then taking one himself lit it and inhaled deeply. 'If he'd been permanently lame I would have had to put him down but Jackson is a bloody marvel with the bloodstock. I don't know what I'd do without him. Monarch was damned expensive, I don't need to tell you that, sir, but apart from any financial consideration I'm fond of the beast.'

'I can see that, my boy. He's proved himself on the hunting field more than once. But then if you don't mind my saying so you're a damned fine horseman which brings me to this matter of stepping into your father's shoes as Master of Foxhounds. You know it is a tradition of the Sutton Meet, provincial as it is, to have a member of the Woodall family as its master and I'm also aware that you did not expect to take up the position so soon. Your father's sudden death grieved us all, Harry, but we must carry on with our duties to the living and traditions must be upheld. The hunting season is well under way and as yet no one has taken over the mastership of the Sutton Meet.'

There were dogs in the yard, dozing in small squares of sunshine or sniffing in corners at any of the scents which took their canine fancy, retrievers, spaniels, terriers, not to mention the twenty couple of hounds which could be heard baying in lunatic fashion in the kennels. The two men, and several of the animals bounding hopefully about their legs, crossed the cobbled stable-yard, turning the corner towards a new building which had been put up to house the four motor cars which the Woodall family now owned. There was a certain rank odour about the place they had left behind, familiar to both men since their childhood, of horses and dogs. There were grooms and tangles of harness and all the paraphernalia of the stable but here, as they moved into what was the twentieth century, was the smell of petrol, sun warmed leather and the wax with which the Woodall chauffeur polished the shining motor cars. He was not there now having driven Lady Woodall up to Scotland to visit an old friend of hers but the boy who had been employed to assist him, a young apprentice mechanic, was diligently and lovingly attending to the already mirror-like surface of the splendid Vauxhall which had belonged to Sir Charles Woodall.

''Mornin' sir, mornin' Sir Harry,' he said respectfully, touching his cap before turning his tender consideration to Sir Harry's nippy little sports car. Hugh's runabout, brand new and a great novelty to him, was nowhere in sight, its amazing qualities no doubt being displayed at this very moment on the frost coated lanes about the estate to his once playmate, James Osborne.

Harry moved slowly across the yard, opening the gate for Johnny to pass through, then both men, dressed in their riding breeches and boots, the casual but expensively cut tweed jackets they wore for a morning's canter, strolled down the rough paddock at the back of Woodall Park.

It was almost Christmas and the sharp frost of the night before had lain a white, crisp carpet across the grass which was melting as the sun touched it. Round the edge of the paddock there were still thick white patches of it, squares where the hedges laid their shadows and in long pointing fingers beneath the bare trees. The dogs bounded joyfully ahead, the spaniels' ears lifting comically like birds' wings as they raced over the rough ground. A pheasant broke cover at the dogs' approach, tracing an erratic flight towards the trees. The beauty of the morning silenced the two men, a silence neither wished to break.

Harry blew a thin stream of smoke into the still air then threw his cigarette end into a clump of half-frozen bindweed, treading it carefully into the dormant ground. As he moved his lean muscled frame had the indolent arrogance, the patrician grace which seemed to be inbred in the male of his class but there was nothing haughty nor imperious in his manner. His face had a friendly warmth in it, there was a certain pleasant humour about the turn of his mouth, an agreeable amiability in his clear brown eyes. He was very handsome though his features were somewhat irregular and there was an engaging cheerfulness in his expression which drew both men and women to him. He looked older than his years, no doubt because of the sudden death of his father and the thrusting on to his young shoulders of the burden and responsibility of the title and the estate which went with it and which he took very seriously. From being a carefree young gentleman who, though trained in the care of his ancient inheritance, had done his share of all the things young gentlemen are entitled to, he had become Sir Harry Woodall, baronet, holder of the trust centuries of Woodalls had handed down. A trust which entailed the taking and nurturing of the land, the people – *his* people – and the respected name of his forebears. A mighty encumbrance for a young gentleman who had expected at least another ten years of freedom from his charge since Sir Charles had been no more than fifty-six years old when he was struck down.

'I'll take it up, of course, sir,' Harry said quietly, speaking of the hunt, 'and all the other duties my father left me. There is a lot to be learned but I have my steward Jethro Peach to help me I shall take my place on the bench at Quarter Sessions and continue, as my father did, as well as I am able, to sit in Petty Sessions here at Woodall. There are poaching offences and some tenants are not above the falsifying of weights and measures, you will know what I mean,

sir, and I shall see to the affairs of my tenants. Good God ...'
he smiled boyishly and it lit up his face, 'I do sound a
pompous ass, don't I? I'm sorry, sir, I don't mean to and I
can assure you that I have other things on my mind beside
the estate.'

He delved into the pocket of his jacket again and bringing
out the battered packet, took out and lit another cigarette.
He was evidently under some strain, running his hand
through the tumble of his light brown hair, clearing his
throat and studying with great interest the glowing end of
his cigarette.

'I hope you have, my dear fellow,' his companion said
mildly. 'You're only a young man yet, despite your ... sudden responsibilities, but I can only hope that should you
feel the need you will come to me for help or any advice I
might be able to give you. Our families have always been
close and my wife and I have been particularly fond of you.
You know that, I hope.' He humphed-humphed a time or
two in the embarrassment a gentleman feels who has been
brought up in the tradition of never showing his feelings
whatever the occasion.

Harry turned, pleased and smiling towards the older man
and Johnny wondered at the diffidence this young man
seemed to feel. Good God, surely he knew he was the most
eligible young bachelor in South Lancashire with his title,
his great estate, the wealth which was now his, and a more
agreeable young man one could not hope to meet. He was
not clever in the sense of academic achievement. He had
been expensively educated at one of the foremost public
schools in England but he had been trained for nothing
except the care of his land and those who lived on it. He
had applied himself diligently in order to understand the
complex structure of the family holdings and was taking to
it well since he had a nature well suited to his position in
life. He was intelligent and had great charm in a quiet sort
of way and could be depended on always to be a gentleman

334

in the true sense of the word. Johnny could not think more of him if he had been a member of his own family and he had said so to Serena only the other day. They had both sighed, thinking of their daughter.

'There is something, sir, if I may.'

'Of course, my boy. You have only to ask.'

'I wish it was as simple as that, sir, indeed I do. It has been in my mind for quite a while now but ... it was not the right time when ...' He pushed one hand deep into his jacket pocket and put a booted foot on the lower rung of the five-barred gate which led from one paddock to another. A jay, startled by the sound of men's voices, swooped up from a tangle on the edge of the wood, winging off for cover with its typical sore-throated scream. Harry watched it go, then turned suddenly.

'It's Elizabeth, sir,' he said quickly as though he must get her name out before her father laughed him to scorn but Johnny Osborne had begun to smile, his green eyes dancing, as hers did.

'I hoped it might be, lad,' he grinned now. 'Go on.'

'I love her, sir.' No more than that. A simple statement. The truth of it glowing from eyes that were steady and without guile or conceit. It was as though nothing more need be said for that was what Harry Woodall was. The man who loved Elizabeth Osborne. Youthful and with not much experience of women really bar the usual shenanigans gentlemen of his class got up to with maidservants and shop girls, but his honesty shone from him and he was ready to lay his honest soul at the feet of this man's daughter, his staunch expression said.

'She is a lovely girl, Harry,' her father said softly, 'but may I ask what you mean to do about it?'

'Why, marry her, sir, of course, that is if she will have me,' Harry said, surprised at the question, 'and with your permission, naturally.'

Johnny Osborne shook his head as though in some

astonishment, not at Harry's request but that there should be any doubt about his own immediate granting of it.

'Harry, my wife and myself, your mother and your father, God bless him, have hoped for this since you and Elizabeth were no more than children.'

'Really, sir?'

'Good God, man, can you not see what a wonderful match it will be. I don't just mean for our families, yours and mine, but for you and Elizabeth. You are ... she has, there has been a special fondness between you, we have spoken of it often, the four of us, but we were determined not to be seen to be pushing you towards one another. My dear chap, I couldn't be more delighted and Elizabeth's mother will be ... well, after the ... Forgive me, I don't wish to appear ill-mannered but when James married ...'

He threw back his shoulders, his expression saying it was not something that a gentleman should discuss with another, not even one who was to become a member of the family, but he had been sorely tried by it as Harry would understand.

He lifted both hands, gripping Harry's right one between them, pumping it up and down joyfully.

'But Elizabeth, sir?' Harry questioned, for Mr Osborne seemed to be taking it for granted that the girl Harry wanted felt the same way about him.

'Why don't you get over to Beechwood and ask her, my boy?' Elizabeth's father said.

18

It was later the same day and in her drawing room Serena Osborne was studying the letter which had just been delivered by the fifth post. She scrutinised its contents with such care she did not appear to notice that her daughter who had just entered the room was dressed in her outdoor outfit.

'Darling, there you are,' she said gaily. 'I've just had this note from Anne ... Lady Woodall. She and Sophie are to come home tomorrow. As it is Christmas in two weeks' time she feels she must be home for the sake of the boys though of course there will be no festivities whilst she is still in mourning. Despite that I'm sure she will consent to a small dinner party here, en famille, naturally. Perhaps on Christmas Eve, if only to give the boys and Sophie a small break. They will celebrate – if that is the right word in the circumstances – just the five of them at home. A sad Christmas, I'm afraid, but with the hunt on Boxing Day which I suppose the boys will attend it should not be too dreadful for them.'

She looked up and smiled pleasantly at Elizabeth and for the first time took in her daughter's attire. Her expression became puzzled.

'Are you going out somewhere, dear?'

'I've just come in, mother.'

Serena's face hardened instantly. 'Oh, and where may I ask have you been? You said nothing at luncheon about going anywhere.' Her eyes narrowed with a gleam which told her daughter she was not at all pleased. Elizabeth, as a girl of only eighteen did not have the right to dash about willy-nilly without her mother's consent and certainly not unaccompanied.

'I ... Mara and I took Claudine out in the motor car.'

'I see, and who gave you permission to take the motor car and to give orders to a servant without my knowledge? I assume Gibson drove you, and am I also to assume your father said you might go?'

'I'm sorry, mother, I understood that the motor car was not being used. Father and James had gone over to Woodall and ... well ... Mara and I...' The words tapered off somewhat hesitantly as a look of sudden understanding drew her mother's face into lines of crimped disapproval.

'Are you trying to tell me that she ... that you and Mara have been to visit her family?' Serena's voice was icy. 'That without my consent or knowledge you called on ... on persons with whom our family are not acquainted? Really, Elizabeth, I thought better of you, a girl brought up as you have been. If Mara feels the need to visit her family then I suppose that is something about which I can do nothing though I do object to my granddaughter being exposed to such an environment. But I will not have you going with her, do you understand?'

'Mother, what harm can there be in visiting the relatives by marriage of my own brother?'

'That is enough, if you please. You know very well what my feelings are on that matter, Elizabeth. And this is not the first time you have defied me. You insisted on going to the funeral of a member of the family ...'

'Mara's sister, mother.'

'I do not care who it was, Elizabeth. I will not have my daughter consorting ...'

'Consorting! Really, mother, they are perfectly respectable people and I can see no harm in accompanying Mara now and again when she visits them.'

'Can you not, Elizabeth? You can see no difference between their family and ours, is that what you are saying? Merciful Heavens, girl, think what you are about. If you insist on calling on Mara's mother, it will not be long before she imagines she can call on Mara and even on you. She and Mara's sisters ... how many does she have, is it five or six? ... Heaven forbid ... will be over here for afternoon tea whenever the fancy takes them ...'

'Don't be silly, mother.'

'I will not have it, Elizabeth, nor will I tolerate this wilful manner you seem to think appropriate. They are not our sort, Elizabeth, and I will not have any member of my family associating with them except where it absolutely cannot be avoided,' and Serena could not imagine such an occasion. There was a pained expression on her face as her mind defended itself against pictures of her well-bred son and the common woman he had married. 'Now, I advise you to go and change. Your father came home some time ago and is bathing. He and I have something to discuss before dinner so I suggest you spend the time considering what I have just said,' but despite her mother's cold anger Elizabeth had the strange feeling that Serena was hugging something to her which pleased her enormously.

As Minty brushed her hair, long, smooth strokes which scarcely moved Elizabeth's head, she stared sightlessly at the reflection of the girl in the mirror. Herself. Elizabeth Osborne. The well-brought-up daughter of a prominent and respected family. A girl who had been taught to believe, and *had* believed in the tradition of respect and obedience to the conventions of her class. Of duty to one's heritage, to one's family. A girl versed in good manners, trained to do and say the right things at the right time. How to behave in the drawing rooms of her mother's friends. A girl who would be a fit wife for a gentleman brought up in the same customs and usage as herself. Elizabeth Osborne, a girl who was in love with an Irish chauffeur who, in her mother's opinion, came from a family fit for nothing.

And she did love him, this afternoon had finally shown her that. In the slightly wary but warmly disposed atmosphere of the kitchen where Michael O'Shaughnessy had grown up; in the intimate heart of the laughing, loving, quarrelling tempest of family life into which she had been carelessly admitted, she had accepted into her bewildered mind what her heart had known for a long time: her love for the son of Ellen O'Shaughnessy. Curiously, though she had never before entered a working class kitchen, apart from the day of Bridget's funeral, she had felt at home there, so completely at home she had fallen asleep with one of its children upon her lap. The sisters of Mara had smiled and been indulgent of what had seemed to her a dreadful lack of manners on her part and Michael's mother had kissed her soundly and called her 'pet', apparently seeing no difference between her and the dozen other children who ran riot about the kitchen.

But it would not do, of course. Not any of it.

Her own pale face stared back at her from the mirror, her eyes, usually so brightly green, subdued to a dull glimmer, all the brilliance drained out of them. What was she to do, her mind asked mutely? The excursion to Mara's old home had had a sweetness which had soothed for a while. It had covered with a soft blanket of peace her own troubled and dangerous thoughts which had hummed first with hope, then with despair, ever since she had received Michael's note. Perhaps . . . perhaps it could happen, her heart had whispered eagerly but at the same time her well-trained and obedient mind had scoffed contemptuously at the very idea. She and Michael were of different worlds. Her world did not overlap with his in the slightest degree except in the way servant and mistress merged as one did the bidding of the other. She could not make it any different and neither could Michael and when he came home tomorrow she must somehow, though God knows how she would manage it, get to him and tell him so before he came storming over to Beechwood to confront her father. Dear God, the very thought of it terrified her, made her want to run and hide from the chaos of loving him but where, where could she hide herself? She didn't want to love him. She didn't want the turmoil, the anguish their love would bring, not just to her but to their families. Her mind conjured with the day Michael, his father and brothers had driven to the house to meet head on the conflict caused by James' seduction of an O'Shaughnessy daughter, as they believed it to be, and was it to happen again with herself as the main player? Her father would kill Michael, she was convinced, or Michael would be arrested for trespass, or breaking and entering or whatever charge her father could dredge up to put him in gaol for as long as possible.

Her mind was in shreds and despair settled on her as Minty buttoned and hooked her into the dinner gown she and Serena had chosen while they were in London, a gown of diaphanous ivory chiffon scattered with tiny seed pearls. It was shaped like a tube, cut low and draped cleverly beneath her breasts and was held there with ivory ribbon. Minty had twined the same ribbon in her dark hair but when she offered her young mistress her jewellery box asking which piece Miss Elizabeth would like to wear, Elizabeth shook her head. With a last smile at Minty she went down to dinner.

She could hear laughter coming from beyond the drawing room door as she approached it. Her father's distinct and apparently cheerful boom over the tinkling notes of her mother's. It seemed Serena's earlier ill humour had evaporated, she remembered thinking as the footman opened the door for her. She stood for a moment in the doorway and though she was not aware of it her sadness gave her the lovely fragile delicacy of a lily, unadorned as a flower is unadorned.

'Elizabeth my dear, how splendid you look,' her mother cried, amazingly, and coming across the drawing room to meet her, with his hands held out to take hers was Harry. Her heart, which had begun to thump anxiously, ready for disapproval, for coolness, difficulties, perhaps even the sharp side of her mother's tongue again, leaped with gladness and when her hands rose and met Harry's, their fingers entwined and clung. Her eyes became alive, vividly green and almost she went on tiptoe to put a kiss on Harry's cheek. In his eyes was the tremor of desire she had seen there before and had not recognised and there was something else which seemed to tell her that tonight, or if not tonight then very soon, he would set to rest the desperation which haunted her.

341

A great and soothing peace fell over her for here, surely, was the hiding place she sought.

They laughed a lot at dinner, she remembered, her mother and father in the best of humours, so much so she saw Mara exchange bewildered glances with her husband since she had never seen her mother- and father-in-law so merry. They discussed Christmas and the proposed dinner party on Christmas Eve, the Boxing Day hunt and the possibility of some shooting. James asked after Monarch, Harry's hunter, and the conversation rippled about the dinner table as sweetly as a clear, unsullied stream. This, this was what her mother meant by like meeting like, by like mixing with like, and her tranquil glance as it caught Elizabeth's told her so. The food was excellent and the wine splendid, her father beseeching everyone, even the ladies, to take another glass, and another until Mara showed the most amazing and giddy inclination to laugh as she did at home and even to tell an Irish joke which was quickly suppressed. She knew by now Serena Osborne's abomination of anything she termed 'vulgar' which included almost everything from the cradle to the grave.

But tonight they were all perfectly at ease with one another. They were with their own kind. They understood instinctively one another's habits and relationships, and were deeply uninterested in people outside their own small world. They always, always knew each other's friends since they were their friends as well and even their cousins and nephews were often shared since they were frequently related by marriage. They knew who was a bore at parties, which gentleman was drinking too much or gambling too heavily and which lady was losing her looks or her reputation. Who had been débutante of the year and how many marriage proposals she had received. They used words like 'delightful', 'intelligent', 'amusing', 'civilised', 'charming', and 'witty' and Elizabeth knew Mara had the greatest difficulty in applying any of them to members of her own family and when James was seen to whisper in her ear Elizabeth was not surprised when the pair of them rose, saying they would retire early, implying that Mara's fecund state made it necessary.

The two gentlemen who were left sat only for fifteen minutes over their port and cigars and when they returned to the ladies in the drawing room Elizabeth was prepared for her mother's suggestion that she show Harry the magnificent new specimen of camellia which had been introduced recently to the conservatory.

They did not speak at first. The conservatory was hushed and the living things in it seemed to display serenity and peace. It had once been an orangery, large and ornate, built on to the south facing wall of the house. The orange plants, the original reason for its existence, were reduced to a very minor role now, placed in tubs lining the glass walls as rarer, more exotic plants became the fashion. Designed to create an illusion of a far-off tropical paradise it was filled with a dozen species of palms, with hanging baskets spilling waterfalls of fragrant verbena, with orchids, magnolias, and bougainvillaea covered with flowers of scarlet, cerise and deep pink. There were coloured singing birds in cages, white wickerwork chairs deep in bright cushions, small tables and delicate statuary all grouped together or standing in solitary splendour and all arranged with the unfailing good taste of Serena Osborne.

The smell was warm and sweet and Elizabeth felt the need to hold her breath as a humid oppression took hold of her.

'Is it very cold outside, Harry, d'you think?' she asked. She had never cared for her mother's 'winter garden' and would have much rather shared this important moment with Harry in some other place. She was perfectly certain it was to be important, of course. Her mother knew Harry had not the slightest interest in camellias, nor indeed in any subject of a botanical nature. This was just the time-honoured way of leaving herself and Harry alone for some purpose and what other could it be but a proposal of marriage? Had it been warm, a warm summer's evening, they would have been invited to walk in the rose garden or some other equally appropriate place.

'It was when I drove over. There was another thick frost forming. Look at the clear sky. You can see every star and there will be a moon up before long just above the lake. Good hunting weather,' he added inconsequentially. He was vividly aware of the lovely girl who walked slowly ahead of him picking her way among her mother's plants. She shimmered in her floating gown moving on silent slippered feet in the subdued glow of the electric light Serena had had installed. She turned to him, suddenly smiling with such an intensity of what seemed to him a great and joyous release, he moved forward to take her hand expectantly.

'What is it?' he asked, almost whispering.

'Let's put on our coats and boots and walk down to the lake,' she said eagerly.

'It will be very cold,' he nearly added 'my darling'. She seemed so ... so ... damnit, he didn't know how to describe her. She appeared to be ... delighted about something. Was that it? As pleased to see him, to be with him as though they had been apart for a long time. Eager, thankful that they were together. Dear God, but she put a shine on his life, a warm, shining enchantment which he could hardly contain. He must have her soon, as soon as it could be arranged and hang the gossip an early wedding might cause.

'It doesn't matter. Oh please, Harry, go and retrieve your coat from wherever Eaton has hidden it and wait for me here. I won't be more than five minutes.'

The cold made them gasp and conscious of her submissive availability to him tonight he put an arm about her shoulders, hugging her to him as they walked briskly down the steps from the conservatory, along the path which ran beside the house and round to the wide lawns at the front. There was a series of mysterious sloping inclines leading away into the frosted distance, the reflection of the millions of stars and the splendour of the rising moon turning the dark-coated green of the lawn to the magic of luminous silver. The grass snapped beneath their booted feet as they stepped on to it and though the icy chill struck at their faces their young blood coursed beneath their civilised coverings of cashmere and mohair, of expensive fur and well-cut leather.

The moon cut a path of gunmetal across the water, reaching the reed-spiked edge of the far side of the lake and together, his arm still about her shoulders, they stopped to absorb into their country bred hearts the bewitchment of the scene. The trees were as fragile as lace etched against the silver black of the night and for a moment neither wanted to speak. Then, gently, he turned her to him.

'You know what I am about to say, don't you Elizabeth?' His manner and voice were grave, solemn almost, making her aware that this was a moment of great consequence to him, perhaps the single most important moment of his life and he wanted her to know it. He was a gentleman. She, if it was her wish, was to be his lady. Good-humoured and cheerful as it was his nature to be he would have her know he was not light-minded.

'I think so, Harry.' She was just as serious, knowing how much it meant to him.

'They . . . our parents have this quaint custom of sending us off together, pretending they have not the slightest notion of what we are about but, naturally, I have spoken to your father and he has given me permission to . . .'

'Oh Harry, I do love you,' she burst out spontaneously, meaning it truly and for a moment he was taken aback. The light in his eyes which had shone with a stern and steadfast intent blazed into smiling joy, into love and the laughter which simmered never far below the exterior of Harry Woodall.

'Elizabeth,' he groaned in exasperation, 'I'm supposed to

say that first, then ask you to marry me . . .'

'Well, ask me then, and when you have done so and I have said yes perhaps you would like to kiss me?'

'Oh God, I might have known it would go like this. I wanted to do it properly, as you deserve, my darling.' At last he had said it and it tasted so sweet on his enchanted tongue, he said it again. 'My darling, my darling . . . dear God, but that is what you are, my darling . . . my darling . . . please say you will marry me. Will you? Be serious if only for a moment . . .'

'Yes Harry, I will.'

'Dear God, have you any idea how much I love you?'

'Show me, Harry.'

He lowered his head and his mouth was placed reverently upon hers. For an agonised moment she thought she was going to refuse him as other lips and other arms awakened her memory to a scalding clarity, then Harry's voice murmured her name and she knew it would be all right. She was safe now and always would be with Harry. Dear Harry. Harry whom she had loved since she was a child. Gentle Harry, filled with loving kindness, a laughing joy which was growing to ardour as her lips – taught by others – opened like a thirsty flower beneath his.

'Show me, Harry,' she said again, her body pressing itself delightfully against his, 'love me, Harry, please love me . . .'

'Dear God, I do . . . I will . . .' and if his bewitched senses had time to wonder at the magical response of the inexperienced and virgin girl he was to marry it was lost in the mists of his love and the demands of his masculine loins which, naturally, must wait, as a gentleman's masculine loins were prepared to do, for his marriage to his lady. On his wedding night he would take her, pure and untouched by any man's hand, to his bed and there in the church-blessed sanctity of marriage he would . . . he would . . .

It took all his strength and resolution as a gentleman and the future husband of this lovely and amazingly loving girl who had not the faintest conception of what – physically – she was doing to him, to put her unsteadily from him, to take her by the hand and lead her away from this magical place where, by God, he might forget his upbringing and the traditions he had absorbed from birth and do something which could seriously offend her.

When they entered the drawing room fifteen minutes later they were both flushed. Johnny Osborne rose to his feet questioningly and Serena held her breath, waiting. Harry still held Elizabeth's hand.

'We ... Elizabeth and I have something to tell you.' He was very boyish, endearingly so in his triumph.

'Indeed, my boy?' Johnny did his best to appear casual.

'Yes sir. Elizabeth has consented to be my wife so with your permission we would like to announce our engagement on Christmas Eve.' He grinned, his eyes dark and glowing with loving pride, his happiness so overwhelming him not for a moment did he wonder why the hand of his bride-to-be had become suddenly as cold and rigid as the frozen reeds about the lake they had just left.

Michael O'Shaughnessy was hurrying as he ran the chamois leather over the shining surface of the bonnet of her Lady-ship's Rolls-Royce. As soon as he had put the final polish on the motor car he would drive it into the garage, settle it down for the night as once he had done with Sir Charles Woodall's fine bloodstock, and then, until tomorrow morning when Lady Woodall might need him, he would be free. He, with Lady Woodall, her daughter and their personal maids, had returned to Woodall Park no more than an hour ago but he was in a fever to be away, to finish all his duties and ride over to Beechwood where his love lay, where his heart lay.

For the past five months his mind had done nothing but consider how it could be done, going over plan after plan in which he might persuade Elizabeth Osborne to slip away from her family's protection and meet him somewhere to discuss their future. He had ridden over there a dozen or more times on the motor cycle which had replaced his bicycle and had even managed to pass a note with sixpence to go with it, into the hand of a gardener's lad with instructions to give it to no one but Miss Elizabeth. He had idled about in the gateway, not exactly plucking up his courage to go boldly up the drive to ask for her since he was not afraid to do that, but afraid that if he did she would be the one to suffer for his actions. She loved him, he had no doubt about that. He had held her in his arms, taken most of her clothing from her body which had been as eager as his and he knew when a woman was ready to be loved. And Elizabeth, unless she loved, would not have allowed what he had been ready to do to her. She had sighed and stretched herself languorously for his eyes to see and his hands to caress and by God, with all his heart he wished he had taken her, persuaded her, loved her when he'd had the bloody chance. If he had she could not have drawn back as she had done then, and had continued to do these last months. If he had she might have quickened with his child . Oh sweet Mary . . . and they would have been glad to have him as her husband, a husband for the damaged goods he had turned her into and which no other man, at least of their class, would want. But like the gentleman he was, he thought sourly, he had allowed her to pull away from him because he loved her, covering her body with the reverence of the true lover.

Aye, he was her true lover and he meant to have her this time if he could just get her to slip away into the winter night and into his arms. Marry her, he would, and to hell with the lot of them. She'd damn well do as she was told . . . Holy Mother but he loved her, ached to be with her, just to see her sweet, troubled face, but before the end of this year of 1912 which was no more than three weeks away she'd be Mrs Michael O'Shaughnessy, begod! His mother would help them, he was sure of it, for hadn't she taken to Elizabeth as far back as Bridget's funeral, God give her eternal rest, saying she was the good-hearted girl to come to see the final putting to rest of a woman she didn't even know. Give them a room somewhere in the tall house in Edge Lane until he himself could find a cosy place in which to shelter his love. He'd get the sack, to be sure, from the Woodall household for didn't the bloody gentry hang together and if the Osbornes took fright at the thought of an Irish mick for their son-in-law, as they had an Irish colleen for a daughter-in-law, then it wouldn't be long before the Woodalls were doing them a favour by replacing himself with someone else as their chauffeur. But that wouldn't matter. He and Elizabeth could go anywhere they wanted in this big country where chauffeurs could command a decent place and a decent wage with motor cars swelling in numbers all the live long day. No, she'd want for nothing, his lovely girl, for wouldn't he work his fingers to the bone to get it for her. He meant to see her tonight, somehow, and tell her his plans for them and perhaps before Christmas was over they'd be man and wife. With an air of no more than casual interest he had found out from Mara – who had been only too eager to boast about the lovely rooms at Beechwood Hall – the layout of the first floor and where, in conjunction to her own, Elizabeth's rooms lay. Mara, bright as she was, had not seen beyond his random questions, neither could she resist babbling on to the Mammy about how many bedrooms there were, how many bathrooms, suites – whatever they were – the length and height of the luxuriously carpeted hallways and staircases, until he felt he could have found his way blindfold from the French windows of the drawing room where he meant to force an entry, to the room where Elizabeth slept.

The idea of it thrilled him. To enter her room while she was asleep. To move across the soft carpet and stand beside her bed. To look down on her sleeping face, her hair loose and spread in a sensual tumble on the pillow. He smiled at the thought, his strong mouth curving in a wry twist at the romantic notion that he might wake her with a kiss, a soft kiss at first so as not to alarm her, his hands on her shoulders lifting her up into his arms. She would wear only a fine nightdress of some thin, clinging stuff and when she realised who it was she would drift into that lovely posture of aban-donment, slipping the nightdress . . . Jesus, Joseph and Mary . . . he must stop this . . . *stop it*, he told himself sternly, at the same time finding it hard not to smile at the sweetness of his dream. His thoughts were leading him where he was not sure he wanted to go. Well, he wanted to go there, of course he did, but he was not some bloody seducer with no idea in his mind but how to get into Elizabeth Osborne's bed. His intentions were absolutely honourable. He needed, at the moment, to do no more than talk to her. To have the chance which had been denied him for all these months of telling her . . . no, asking her . . . He must make no demands but rely on her love for him and her recognition of his love for her so that they might discuss what they were to do about it. They were young and healthy and surely they could make a life together. As he had been telling himself for the past five months, there were opportunities for men like himself, go-ahead sort of chaps who knew what the future held in the new mechanical age of the motor car. He was a man who knew about machines. In the two years since he had become the Woodall chauffeur he had taught himself to understand the engine, to take it apart and put it together again and the experience and knowledge he had gained would ensure he would always have employment. He would give her a good home. His Elizabeth.

'What were it like up in Scotland?' a voice asked him, breaking into his thoughts and he looked up sharply for he had thought himself to be alone. It was the young apprentice mechanic who had been taken on to help him with the maintenance of the Woodall motor cars and who would one day be a chauffeur himself. No more than fourteen, the lad was looking at him with avid curiosity just as though Michael had been up to the far wastes of the Arctic. 'Do they speak t'same language as us then?'

Michael laughed. 'Not really, Billy,' remembering the tortured sounds he had barely understood and which had passed for conversation in the highlands of Scotland. The only language he had recognised had been that levelled at him by more than one pretty housemaid at the castle of the Scottish laird with whom Lady Woodall had stayed and who was related to her in some way. They had made it quite plain what they had in mind with the attractive young Sassenach in his smart black chauffeur's uniform and dashing peaked cap. The shape of his well-turned leg had been very clear in his knee-length black polished boots and when he donned his gauntlets and goggles they had been more than a little impressed. They had never seen a chauffeur, they had managed to convey to him, and only one or two motor cars since their master did not care for the 'demented' things.

Oh aye, that language had been easy enough to fathom out and he had been sorely tempted since he was but flesh and blood, after all. In fact one pert little thing with jiggling breasts and a behind to match had persuaded him to put his hand up the leg of her bloomers and then to take them off completely. His fingers had explored the sweet, dark moistness at the core of her and, of course, one thing had led to another but she had borne him no grudge when he had kissed her goodbye at the back of the stables.

'What do they speak, then?' Billy wanted to know.

'Well, 'tis supposed to be English but not a bloody word of it could I be understanding.' He stood back to admire the satin shine on the motor car in which his own face was mirrored. 'Sure an' they say the Irish have a brogue you could cut with a knife but them up there take a bit of beating. Now then, me laddo, if you'll step out of me way I'll put this beauty away an' then I'll be off.'

'Where you off to then, Mr O'Shaughnessy?' To Billy the smartly outfitted chauffeur who drove not only the splendid Rolls-Royce but the Renault which had belonged to the old Sir Charles Woodall, was something of a god-like figure. A man who knew motor cars better than anyone in Liverpool, it was said, and who was to train Billy in the maintenance and driving of them. His respectful admiration was unbounded.

'Never you mind where I'm to be off to but if we don't get up to the kitchen soon we'll get no tea an' that's a fact. Mrs Barney doesn't take kindly to latecomers so just hold them garage doors open while I get the motor in. Did you clean Sir Harry's Austin like I told you?' he continued as he climbed into the magnificence of the Rolls. He started the engine which ran as smoothly as a purring cat.

'No, I didn't, Mr O'Shaughnessy, on account of it not being there,' the boy answered, holding back the door of the garage which had been built to hold at least half a dozen vehicles.

'Where is it then?' Michael asked as he drove the Rolls carefully into its allotted space to the left of the Renault. 'Is it round the front of the house? You know I like them all to be cleaned every day.'

'Sir Harry went off in it just after you came back, Mr O'Shaughnessy, so I never got the chance to do what you said. I cleaned both of 'em yesterday though an' did the . . .'

'Well run round to the front of the house, there's a good lad, an' see if it's come back. You an' me can give it a decent going-over in the morning but for now just a touch with the . . .'

'It's not there, Mr O'Shaughnessy. I know particular on account of Sir Harry goin' over to Beechwood with the ring. They was all sayin' in the kitchen he were only waitin' for 'er Ladyship to get back so he could 'ave it off 'er. It were 'is grandmother's or summat . . .'

'Steady on, lad, sure an' you lost me five minutes ago.

What ring? What in hell's name are you rattlin' on about?' but already there was a faint warning tremor beginning to ripple deep inside him. Nothing he could describe easily, or even place or give a logical reason for but it was there nevertheless. He had closed the door of the motor car very, very carefully and now he did the same with the garage door before turning, just as carefully, towards Billy.

'What's been goin' on while me back was turned, Billy?'

'Nay, it only 'appened yesterday, Mr O'Shaughnessy. Well, last night, Mrs Blythe said, though it wasn't official like, an' even 'er Ladyship didn't know 'til you brought 'er 'ome just now. Mrs Blythe said we wasn't to speak of it to no one. Mind you, it were Sir Harry what told us this morning. We was all havin' us breakfast. Well, you could have knocked 'er over wiv a fevver, Cook said, 'im coming into the kitchen so early but he felt he 'ad to tell us, he said, seein' as 'ow we was 'is people an' she'd be our mistress one day. That's what he said. They was all there, the family. Master Tim an' Master Hugh with a bloody big bottle of champagne an' all, an' it were only six o'clock in t' mornin' an' there we all was, drinkin' champagne.'

'Billy ... Billy, will you let up for a minute, for God's sake. I can't make top nor tail of this bloody story. Start at the beginning...'

Sweet Mary, Holy Mother of God ... don't ... please don't let it be what I think ... not her ... not my ... and all the while the boy's voice droned on, not very impressed, it seemed to say, with what had happened, except for the champagne and the immensely bizarre sight of his employer and master up as early as he himself was.

'Who...?' Michael's voice was no more than the sound a throat makes when it is being gripped by two strong hands and Billy turned in surprise.

'What?' he said.

'Who ... is ... it?'

'Who's what?'

'Jesus Christ...' The violence of the approaching pain was barely held in check and the boy reared back, alarmed by what he saw in Mr O'Shaughnessy's eyes. Michael struggled to control himself. To ask the question and hear the answer which he knew was about to crucify him.

'You ... are ... saying ... Sir Harry ... is ... to ... be ... married? Is that ... what you are ... saying, Billy?' His lips barely moved over his tightly clenched teeth.

'Aye, Mr O'Shaughnessy. Isn't that what I just told you?'

'Who to, Billy?' and really, he could not bear the answer and when it came, as he knew it would, the menace in him was so visible and so lethal young Billy cowered away from him. Mr O'Shaughnessy looked like he was going to hit him, really he did, though what he had said to arouse such rage he couldn't imagine. He'd only told him about the excitement of Sir Harry and the young miss from Beechwood who the master was going to marry and why that should turn the good-humoured chauffeur into a bloody madman was beyond Billy's placid imagining. And would you look at him now, stumbling off towards the paddock as though the devil himself was after him or summat.

Billy watched him go, his mouth hanging open in amazement.

19

'You must go home for Christmas, Caitlin, or I shan't be responsible for the consequences. Look at you. Your bones will break through your skin before the week's end if you don't get some rest and some decent food inside you, child. Even soldiers are entitled to take leave now and again and it's time you did the same. How many times have you been arrested in the last six months? You can't remember! Well, I can and if you won't go home of your own volition then we must send you. Your mother will be upset enough when she sees you and if you wait any longer I doubt she'll even recognise you, that's if you have the strength to get on the train. Have you looked in the mirror lately?'

The speaker peered anxiously into the face of the thin, hollow-cheeked girl who sat at the desk, her pen flying swiftly across a sheet of paper, her eyes narrowed in the dim light of the December day as she busied herself with some report on the suffrage cause to which, her attitude said, she was dedicated with her whole heart, mind and obviously suffering body. She had no time to spend in idle conversation let alone holidays and Elsie Thompson tutted irritably as she leaned across and deftly snatched the pen from Caitlin's hand.

Caitlin sighed and leaned back resignedly in her chair but she did look up and Elsie knew she had her attention.

'Go home, Caitlin. Just for Christmas, and take that young man with you.' She smiled gently as Caitlin flushed a bright and rosy pink, the colour giving her, momentarily, the look of the fresh young girl and the loveliness which had once been hers, then it faded away and her eyes snapped in her pallid face.

'And which young man is that?' She lifted her head indignantly but Elsie continued to smile, refusing to be intimidated.

'You know very well who I mean. That handsome soldier who meets you on the corner from time to time though what he sees in a scarecrow like you is beyond me.'

'Elsie!'

'Oh yes, scarecrow I said and scarecrow I mean, Caitlin O'Shaughnessy, and if he's anything about him which he must have or you'd not be interested in him, then what I want to know is why he doesn't send you off home himself? That arm of yours pains you still, doesn't it? and if you allow those wardresses to bully you as I know from experience they do, then it's never going to be any better and if your handsome soldier hasn't the gumption to make you take a rest from ...'

'He is not my handsome soldier ...'

'Oh, then who does he belong to, tell me that?'

'He is only a friend ...'

'Then if he is a friend he should be able to tell you that you are doing yourself and the cause no good by driving yourself as you are doing. How many meetings were you thrown out of last week? Three? Yes, I thought so, and no doubt manhandled by a dozen upright citizens whilst they were about it and I shouldn't be surprised if you didn't carry a bruise or two where it doesn't show.'

'Well ...' Caitlin shrugged dismissively.

Elsie sat down in the chair on the opposite side of the desk, quiet for a moment as she gathered her thoughts about her. She studied the girl who was fighting so desperately, as they all were, to gain victory for the women of the country and not for the first time she wondered if the desperation, one might almost call it an obsession, which had manifested itself in Caitlin was altogether to do with their fight for equality. Of course she wanted just that as they all did, but somehow in these last six months there had been something else in the girl. Something almost ... well, guilty, remorseful if you like, a sense that Caitlin was battling not only male prejudice but something inside herself which was wounding her dreadfully, and could it have anything to do with the smart and very evidently aristocratic officer with whom Elsie had seen her on several occasions. A gentleman, and in the sense of the class barrier Caitlin was not a lady. An officer in some smart regiment, no doubt, who was dallying, was that the word, with a woman in a station of life beneath his own and fair game because of it.

And yet Caitlin was not the kind of girl whose head could be turned by a bit of flattery and attention from a man in uniform, indeed from any man, and neither was she the kind of girl that sort of man gave attention to. Not now. Six months ago she had been soft and pretty, slender and honey-skinned with roses at her cheek, bright eyes and glossy hair enough to turn any man's head. When she had recovered from her injury and been returned from her family's care she had been a girl with whom any man would have been only too pleased to trifle but now she was gaunt and brittle, drawn out into a fine and slender thread which could, if she was not careful, be snapped into two drifting and broken pieces.

So, with this in mind, how did the good-looking officer fit into her life? Not as some fanciful, light as thistledown adventure with which two attractive young people passed the time, that was for sure, but a solid and unyielding emotion, at least on his part, which would not disintegrate at the first sign of trouble since it was not her pretty face which had attracted him, that was obvious

'We have all been frustrated lately, Caitlin,' she began slowly, feeling for the right words, and Caitlin knew it was true Suffragettes of many schools and parties had come together since Black Friday and had evolved a Conciliation Bill intended to combine them as one party. For a time they had thought it was to be considered by the government but like previous bills it had been what the politicians liked to call 'shelved'. Lloyd George and Ramsay MacDonald were both strong believers in women's suffrage but they were unwilling to give it in a form which would only have enfranchised single women with property. Women in that category were for the most part elderly and conservative so neither of the politicians was prepared to give the vote to them. There had been further bills but the government had refused them. The Democratic Reform Bill the previous July was drafted to include only men and so Christabel Pankhurst had made the decision to adopt a yet more violent policy.

'I myself have seen you stuffing a paraffin-soaked lighted

rag in a pillar box,' Elsie continued, 'and helping to set fires in empty buildings and we were together when the orchid houses at Kew Gardens were destroyed.'

Damage had been extensive. Telephone wires had been cut and hundreds of false fire alarms given in order to create as much chaos as possible. All over the country women had been committing what were known as 'offences' and they were becoming too serious for the authorities to tolerate. 'It is going to get worse, not better, if we get no results, you know that, don't you Caitlin, and only the strong will survive it. Do you know what I am saying to you, my dear?'

'Yes.' Caitlin's voice was bleak.

'So will you go home and recuperate for a few weeks? Let us see if this Franchise Reform Bill which is to reach its next stages in the House in January comes to anything. The WSPU is to suspend militancy anyway until then so go and pack your bags and take the next train to Liverpool.'

He had got leave for Christmas. The 2nd Battalion of the Lancashire Fusiliers in which he was a captain was stationed in Ireland and on his way home to Yorkshire he was to stay over in London for a few days, he had said in his letter. He had stopped asking her to marry him in October. She had not seen him since then but he was waiting for her on the corner by Lyons Corner House when she left Clements Inn. He was still in his uniform and her heart, that tricky and uncontrollable organ no matter how she tried to subdue it, leaped in gladness at the sight of him. She wanted to run, to pick up her skirts and ignoring the amazed stares of the pavement crowds, run with giddy love into his arms which had held her on only two occasions. She could feel them yet, strong and ardent, eager and yet strangely tender as they had shared those two enchanted embraces. She wanted him now. She longed with every particle of her weakened, female body to let him take her to some tranquil refuge, to soothe and comfort her, to smooth away the terror and the pain, the brutalising indignities which were almost daily heaped upon her, to heal her with the simple beauty of the act of love. She had not experienced it with any man but with him it would be beautiful, of that she had no doubt. And she needed it. She needed it, and him, so much so her heart was wrenched with it and the only mending of it was in his arms and she wanted to tell him so. To tell him simply to love her as he wanted to, as she wanted him to, but she could not. Not yet. Not now, perhaps not ever.

He had come back to Liverpool in June, two months after they had parted on the day of the sinking of the *Titanic*. Nothing was said, not in words. He had taken her for tea again at the Adelphi and across the water on a ferry boat to New Brighton. He drove her in his motor car to the sands at Bootle, where they had walked along the bank of the estuary, the sun-dappled waters sliding along beside them, stopping to watch as a great ocean-going liner steamed up the river from the sea towards its berth. The south swinging curve of the coast hid the city of Liverpool and there was nothing to be seen but the villas of the wealthy sitting comfortably amongst the sand dunes and across the water the great sky-snipping lattice of the New Brighton Tower. Further on Waterloo and Seaforth shone pleasantly in the warm summer sunshine and from the base of the tower the pier swam delicately out into the water, girdled on both sides by white sea-promenades stretching away up the coast to Egremont.

There were sailing ships still, darting among the steam-laden, iron-clad dignity of the great liners and merchant vessels. A busy river, swaggering and splendid, a thriving, thronging highway dancing with eager craft, tall frigate and fussy tug-boat moving side by side in perfect harmony, as the man and woman were. The air from the sea was fresh and unpolluted and they were content in those first days of being together again to be silent, to smile or talk a little, to sit in amazingly companionable ease and do little else but draw in from each other that sense of knowing, of learning, of being together. She would not, could not spend more than an hour or so each day with him, she explained, since her Mammy would have a blue fit if she even knew of his existence. On that day in April when he had taken her home and put her weeping into her mother's arms, her mother had accepted her explanation that he was a gentleman connected with the WSPU which was only a small white lie really since it was he who had . . . well, he would know what she meant. She herself was home only on some business for the movement and must spend a part of each day at their headquarters in Duke Street and it was sheer coincidence – or the greatest of good fortune – that he had found her in Liverpool at all.

No, she was sorry, but she could not tell her parents about him – since she might not see him again anyway, her heart sinking at the appalling prospect – though she did not voice this last. Mammy and Daddy would be seriously distressed if they knew about him. She hoped he understood, and he did, since by then he knew a little about her. She was from a respectable working class family of the Catholic faith and though she was singular in being allowed – if that was the word – to work for the suffrage movement as she did, it was understood by her, by them and now by him, that she was not a girl with whom young men trifled.

He did not touch her, not even to hold her hand until they parted. For the second time.

'Will you walk with me on the Parade before I motor to Wetherby? I must visit my parents before I return again to Ireland but if I can arrange it I will return to my regiment via Liverpool. If I do, will you meet me here next weekend?'

They stood by the open door of the motor car with nothing to say now and those walking by, seeing them together, the strained and tight-lipped look of parting on both their faces, might have been forgiven in thinking he was off to fight a long and dangerous war in foreign parts from which he might not return.

'Will you meet me here next Saturday?' he asked urgently.

'Yes,' was all she said, and not caring in the least about the stares of those who passed them, he drew her gently to him, tucking her head beneath his chin and holding her there. She sank against him, coming home. It was the embrace of friends with nothing of sexuality in it but when he released her and stepped back to look into her face there was a radiance there which had in it all he wanted to know.

She was there a week later, just where he had left her but this time it was she who was going away. Back to London on the three-thirty train from Lime Street railway station.

'But you can't go, not today. I sail on the tide tomorrow and I thought . . .' He ran his hand through hair already unruly with the speed at which he had raced across the Pennines in his motor car. He really didn't know what he had thought, or hoped, for that matter. Perhaps that she could make some excuse to escape from her family that evening. That they might dine together though he had realised that he was being overly optimistic to expect that but it might be possible to take her out for the afternoon in his motor car. A run somewhere into the surrounding countryside. To Huyton or Childwall or along the coast to Hale Park. They could take tea in one of the old inns which still existed here and there, walk in country meadows through the burgeoning wildflowers, talk and make plans to write, for further meetings when he had leave and now, all there was was this. This hurried parting in which he sensed that already the sweet beginning they had forged in the past few months was strangely altered. She was tense, pale of skin and her eyes were inclined to avoid his. She fiddled with her bag and within the space of two minutes glanced three times at her watch.

'Do you really have to go today?' he asked grimly.

'I should have gone yesterday but I had promised you I would be here.'

'But why, for Christ's sake? Surely the movement won't

disintegrate if you delay your departure for twenty-four hours?' His disappointment made him careless with his words. 'You could take the same train tomorrow, Caitlin, please. I had so looked forward to ... to being with you and ... well ... I shall be away myself tomorrow. Wait until then, please.' He reached for her fidgeting hand and bent his head to look into her face. She was still in deepest black wearing what looked like the twin to the unflattering woollen beret in which he had found her in April but she looked beautiful beneath it, her honey-coloured skin warm with rose and bronze, tremulous with cast down fluttering lashes which hid the expression in her eyes.

'What is it, Caitlin?' he asked gently, holding firmly to her hand which she was trying to pull away. He wanted to put his arms about her as he had done a week ago but some instinct warned him against it. He knew with absolute certainty that she had felt as he had, that this sweet emotion which had come to them so swiftly, so gently, so strongly was as sure in her as it was in him but she was telling him now, without words, but in the strange way she was acting that it had not existed and they must part as though they were no more than casual acquaintances. What had happened to her to change her from the tranquil, sweet young girl with whom he had fallen in love at first glance, into this nervous stranger who twitched away from him with distressing force.

'Has something happened at home? Is it your family?'

'I don't know what you mean, Jack. It's simply that I've a job to do, as you have and ...'

'I know that.' He tried to speak patiently but fear was stirring up an urgency in him he could not control. He had done his family duty for a week, riding about the estate with his father and elder brother, dining with friends, sitting through several afternoons of calls with his mother, attending several parties in his honour and dancing with innumerable pretty girls, with one of whom his Mama, and hers, hoped he might settle down and all the time he had chafed to get back to this one. This warm, lively, bright-eyed and lovely young woman whose mind was perfectly attuned to his as no other had been and whose body he desired as he had desired no other.

'I'm sorry, Jack, but I really must go. I have packing still to do and I'm meeting one of our women at two. I just have time to catch the tram...'

'Damn the bloody tram...' and saw her flinch away for a moment from his violence. 'I'm sorry, really, I have no right to ... but...' He made a great effort to control himself. He must not lose her now through his own snarling anger. 'If it comes to that I can run you home, or even to London. I can catch a boat from there.' His face lit up at the idea. Having her beside him for hours as they motored through the summer afternoon and the lengthening twilight. Stopping perhaps in some small country inn ... but she was appalled at the idea, he could see it in her face and he quickly stepped away from her, realising that she had caught the drift of his thoughts which seemed to have a will of their own. He had not meant ... he must make her understand that he had not meant...

'No, really, there is no need...' she said, and he could contain himself no longer.

'Why are you being so confoundedly polite, Caitlin? What has happened between us, and you know something has ... recently ... it cannot just be shrugged off...'

'Nothing has happened between us, Jack. Nothing. We ... you were kind to me ... brave ... in London and last week. The time in April when I was ... recovering ... you were ... it was very pleasant...'

'Pleasant! Goddammit, woman, stop babbling like some well-brought-up schoolgirl and say exactly what you mean. Tell me what is in your mind and not what you think good manners demand.'

'There is nothing to tell.'

363

'Damnation, I deserve better than this, Caitlin. You knew ... and agreed last week ... and the time before ... I saw it in your face. You let me think we were to spend a few hours together before I returned to my regiment so let's drop this pretence. Tell me why you are doing this, if you please. I am not a man to ...'

'All right! All right ...' She turned away, staring out at the river which was bleak and murky today. There were low hanging clouds like grey blankets put out to dry on a washing line, filled with rain which would soon fall. Seagulls screamed and dived for the rubbish tipped from a passing freighter and the hoot of the New Brighton ferry boat scattered those which had settled on the water. She spoke to them, to the river and not to him.

'I have work to do and I cannot be distracted from it. A ... colleague called the day after you left and I was ... reminded. Not that I need reminding of what I believe in. Sure an' it's the tune I've marched to ever since I first heard of the ... of what the women, *our* women were willing to suffer to achieve what they believe in, what I believe in. Women can be so many things now, Jack. They can be a mayor, a nurse, a mother, a doctor or teacher or factory hand and yet they are not considered intelligent enough to vote for the government of their choice. A man can be a proprietor of white slaves or a drunkard but he is considered fit to voice his opinion in how the country is run. Do you not think that unfair?'

She turned to him, her face passionately vivid.

'Of course I do, have I not said so, but that is not the argument here, Caitlin ...'

'It is, Jack, oh yes it is. If I am ... diverted from what I have set out to do, then that is one less woman who can fight for the others.'

'I wouldn't stop you, Caitlin.'

'Oh yes you would, Jack,' and her face softened, smooth and warm with her love for him, her eyes filled and brimming with it and for a hushed moment, as he read in them what she finally allowed him to see they drew close to one another. She was ready to step into his protecting arms, to sigh with thanks as she felt them close enduringly about her, then her face closed up like a flower from which the sun moves on and she backed hastily away from the dangerous proximity of what she most wanted.

'Christ, Caitlin, don't do this. I won't let you go . . .'

'You must . . .'

'No, if you go now I shall find you in London. I'll not let you go . . .'

'Please . . . please, Jack, don't make it any harder than . . .'

'I shall make it so bloody hard you'll not have a minute's peace. Do you think I give a damn about your cause? It's you, what it has done to you . . . and will do. Stay with me, Caitlin . . . marry me . . .'

He stopped then, the words still whispering on his lips, the truth of what he was asking of her, begging of her, demanding of her glowing in his pale, ice grey eyes, making them like velvet. He watched as her face was transformed from harsh denial to a blazing glory of joy, then with a cry of pure agony she whirled away from him and began to run along the parade towards the Pier Head.

His letters started to arrive a week later, addressed to her at Clements Inn and in each one he begged her to marry him. He would do nothing to curtail her activities in the WSPU, he told her. She could continue her life just as it was now, going to rallies, meetings, speaking to women's groups as she had begun to do. She was a seasoned campaigner now who proudly wore 'the Holloway Brooch' and what she had endured and won and could describe to others made her a valuable publicist. It crucified him to think of what was being done to her, but he was proud of her and her courage, and as her husband he would be proud to let others see it too. Marry him, he beseeched her, over and over again, take his name, be his wife as well as a suffragette, be his love, his treasure, let him take care of her, provide her with a comfortable home in London from which to carry on her work, to return to when she needed to recover from her frequent imprisonment.

She answered him. She told him of the small moments of her days and weeks, of the loveliness of Green Park that summer and the walks she took there. Of the weather and the new hat she had bought, of how she missed him and remembered the sands at Bootle. She embroidered the sometimes comical events of the meeting where she had heckled a prominent Cabinet Minister and of Mrs Pankhurst's remark that 'a smashed pane of glass is a most valuable argument in modern politics' and of the many 'welcome home' dinners she attended for women released from gaol. She did not tell him how many were for herself but he knew, of course, since the sudden ceasing of her letters told him where she was. She did not tell him of her own ordeals, the heart palpitating in fear, the noises in her head, the coldness of her spine, the pain of the straps which were used to hold her down, the terror of the men's hands on her jaw, the bite of the steel gag, the bleeding agony of cut gums and lips, the panting and heaving and vomiting afterwards.

He came home in October and for several minutes held her in his arms while she wept. He weakened her frail and abused body further with his love and clouded her mind to the clear-cut issue of what her life was about and for that first hour she let him. She clung to him like a child, like the breakable, defenceless female she was and had she not shared a room with another member of the WSPU would have taken him back there and allowed him to love her, to heal the sharp and corrosive wounds her mind bore.

'Marry me, for God's sake marry me before they kill you,' he implored her, holding her with the strength and tenderness of the true lover but she sent him away brutally since it was the only way she could carry the burden of his loss.

He did not ask her again. He did not write again except to tell her he would be in London in December. She must do what she would with it, his bald words told her, and here he was, tall and stern. As she drew nearer and he finally recognised her, he was appalled at what she had become.

'Sweet Christ,' was all he said as she swayed in the light breeze which blew on the corner where he stood waiting for her, catching her in his arms as she would have fallen. 'Dear sweet Christ...'

He took her to an hotel and she made no protest.

'My wife and I would like a decent room for a couple of nights,' he said to the receptionist with the courtesy and arrogance of his class which could see no reason why such a thing would not be immediately available. 'Have my luggage sent up, will you? My wife's seems to have gone astray but I am assured it will arrive shortly. When it does I'd be obliged if you would keep it down here for a while. The crossing from Ireland was very trying and my wife is exhausted so arrange for us not to be disturbed, will you? Just a tray, I think, with clear soup and a little fish, perhaps chicken, whatever the chef can manage at this awkward hour, oh, and a bottle of claret.'

He was a gentleman, there was no doubt about that, an officer of the King's army and his wife certainly did look as though she had suffered in the crossing of the Irish Sea so with the efficiency, tact and courtesy with which such persons are served, Jack Templeton and his 'wife' were installed in a comfortable suite of rooms, fires glowing in the bedroom and drawing room, hot water in the gleaming bathroom, the lavender-scented sheets of the double bed turned down by the cheerful maid, the curtains drawn against the deepening winter's night.

He undressed her, removing every stitch of her clothing until she was naked, his own face whitening at the bruises on her wafer-thin body, black as ink on her tiny breasts and turning yellow and green on the insides of her arms.

'Jesus God . . .' and tears stood in the icy cold grey of his eyes as she allowed him to see, at last, what had been done to her. 'Oh Jesus God . . .'

He had put his own soft silk shirt to warm before the fire and, unable to bear her frailty a moment longer, he slipped it over her head before laying her, unresisting, between the sheets of the bed. He fed her soup and a spoonful of delicately-grilled turbot, a sip of claret and, without speaking except for the sort of soothing, encouraging sounds one makes to a tired child, tucked the soft blanket about her chin and turned off the light.

She awoke once, startled to find herself curled against the naked chest of a man but his voice called her 'darling' and 'sweetheart', his hands were comforting and warm, his arms strong and protecting and, knowing she was safe, she slipped back into a deep and dreamless sleep which lasted for another ten hours.

He was still beside her as she stretched and yawned and turned towards him and this time, when he pulled her into his arms she stayed there. There was only the soft splutter of the fire and the rustle of silk as the shirt fell to the floor beside the bed.

20

Mara's second child was born at the beginning of January, an event which might have been overshadowed by the excitement and splendour of Elizabeth and Harry's engagement had not the child been a boy. A male heir for the house of Osborne and therefore cause for great celebration even if his mother had, in Serena's opinion, been delivered of the child in an embarrassingly speedy and effortless manner. It came, she supposed, from being of peasant stock and the frequency with which their class produced children which surely could only be called vulgar. Eighteen, the girl's mother had borne. *Eighteen*, Mara had told her, proud of the fact, apparently, as though it was something worth boasting about and one could only blame the husband, surely? Her own, being a gentleman, had imposed himself upon her only on rare occasions after she had given him two sons and a daughter which was only right and decent, and one could only hope that James would practise the same code of honourable behaviour in the future. Two children in two years, perhaps a third later, another son, or even a fourth in due time was really enough for any man to wish for and if James was the gentleman he was brought up to be he would see to it, easing his own masculine needs in the discreet way gentlemen had always done.

One heard, of course, about what was known as 'birth control' advocated by a certain Marie Stopes but the less a lady knew about that the better. It was rumoured that since the start of the new century the birth rate had fallen quite considerably which must prove that some depraved women were availing themselves of this indecent practice. Serena mourned the passing of the old values at the same time giving thanks for her own position in life and the code of conduct which would ensure that Elizabeth, when she became Lady Woodall, would continue in the well-bred behaviour in which Serena had schooled her.

'What shall you call him?' she asked her daughter-in-law anxiously, quizzing the folded, pink-skinned infant Mara held on the crook of her arm. He was no more than an hour old and reluctantly, since once she had been told that her grandson was a fine healthy child she had no more interest in him, or his mother, Serena had done her duty and gone, with Johnny, to take a look at him. She had refused a 'hold' of him politely, the moist sucking baby lips, the screwed up angry face, the waving plump hands of her grandson not quite to her taste, besides which, might he not do some dreadful thing on, or to her immaculate afternoon gown? She could see the Irish blood in him, she distastefully told her husband later. In the thatch of dark hair, still damp from his mother's womb, and the shape of his chin which was definitely pugnacious. The colour of his eyes was too early to tell though Mara swore they would be the blue green of her own.

'Christian.' Mara's answer was prompt and decisive, making it plain to her mother-in-law that she would brook no argument. That she, and presumably James, had given this some thought and that the matter was not one on which she meant to quibble. Her jaw, remarkably like that of her new son, was set in that stubborn, even wilful line her mother-in-law and her doting husband knew well.

'I would have thought James more suitable, Mara,' Serena observed, taking a step back from 'Christian'. 'It is a family name after all. There has been a James Osborne in almost every generation.' Except for her own husband who was unaccountably christened Sean by Serena's capricious and in her opinion quite dotty mother-in-law, but who had, at the earliest opportunity, called himself Johnny.

'I like Christian and so does James, don't you James? And sure isn't it a king's name, just like Claudine is a queen's.'

'I know of no king called Christian,' Serena answered icily.

'Well, he's not king yet but he will be.'

'Oh, and who is that, pray?'

'Won't he be King Edward the Eighth one day? Our own king's eldest son, so he is. Edward Albert Christian George Andrew Patrick David,' she rattled off, just as she had learned it, parrot fashion. 'An' if it's good enough for the King and Queen of England then it's good enough for me an' James. Christian Patrick Osborne, so he is.' She looked down in satisfaction at the child who sucked indignantly on thin air and on the other side of Mrs Osborne's bed the nurse hovered, murmuring that 'mother' should really be preparing herself to ... well ... baby was ... should be put to ... would be hungry, at which Serena hurried away, her mind shying from pictures of that plump baby mouth fastened greedily on Mara's equally plump nipple. Dear Heavens, how was she to tell her friends of this latest gaffe of Mara's? Claudine had been bad enough but now the honourable name of Osborne was to be burdened again with some outlandish, theatrical name which quite obviously appealed to the dramatic in her son's dreadful wife.

But it was for an entirely different reason than the one she had given to her mother-in-law that Mara had chosen the name of Christian.

'Will you not let me take Claudine Mary to Mass with me, pet?' her mother had asked Mara on the last half a dozen occasions when Mara had called at Edge Lane. 'I know you can't come with me now,' a twisting spasm of pain in her rosy face, since it was all she could do to live with the horror of knowing that her fallen daughter would never achieve the Catholic heaven which the rest of the family would finally rest in. She was lapsed, a backslider, a member of the true faith no longer since her marriage to James Osborne and it took all her mother's strength and overflowing love to overlook her daughter's sins. Even now she prayed nightly on her knees that Mara would be allowed to return to the fold somehow, perhaps bringing James with her, though she held out little hope of that. But the baby, her own little granddaughter, surely could enter the Church, be baptised – despite the ceremony she had gone through at the Osbornes' Anglican place of worship – in the true faith. Mara led that husband of hers about by his nose, a bad thing in Ellen's opinion, but which, if gone about in the right way, might at least redeem the souls of the innocent children of such an unholy alliance. But on this Mara was hesitant, stubborn even, her mother would have said.

'I can't, Mammy,' picking at the folds of her gown which

371

stretched across her round, taut stomach.

'Don't say that, darlin'. Sure an' James wouldn't be any the wiser if I was to take her with me to see Father Paul.'

'I can't Mammy, really. Don't ask me. The Osbornes would kill me if I took their grandchild into the Church let alone to see Father Paul.'

'And what's wrong with that, girl? You're a ... well, you were Catholic an' surely there can be no wrong in just letting the Father put a drop of Holy water on the child's head. What harm would it do?'

'They wouldn't like it, Mammy ...'

'An' how d'you think I feel, child, knowing me own daughter and granddaughter'll suffer in purgatory ... ?'

'Please Mammy .. don't ...'

Ellen made a great effort to control the fear and fury which sometimes pulled at her until she didn't know which way to turn. It was more than she could bear some nights when she lay in her bed beside her peacefully snoring husband who, now that she and Mara were reconciled, was as content as a cat in a basket. But that was just like a man. A good man, sure, and a practising Catholic but without the imagination and forward-looking eye of herself. It was the immortal soul of her child, and her child's children that Ellen cared about and was afraid for and if she could just draw Mara's baby daughter into the loving fold of the Church it would ease the worry somewhat.

'I'm sorry, darlin'. I don't want to upset you, not now ...' for who knew what adversity she might cause her heavily pregnant daughter if she frightened her with tales of a heretic hereafter. The thought could not be borne, particularly with Bridget scarcely cold in her grave. 'It's just that I'd be the happiest woman alive if this little pet and the one to come were Christians.'

And so here he was. One at least who could be called Christian which almost soothed Mara's troubled heart and

372

perhaps in a year or two, before that Nanny upstairs had her daughter too deeply ingrained with the Protestant faith, she would defy her husband and her husband's family and guide her children into the true faith with which the O'Shaughnessys were blessed. So Mara comforted herself somewhat confusedly and in the months following Christian's birth, as he grew plump and handsome, looking exactly like his father, alleviating Serena's first fears about his appearance; brown hair and deep brown eyes flecked, as James' were, with gold, and without a scrap of the Irish O'Shaughnessys in him that Serena could detect, Mara's anxieties subsided and she found it easier to close her ears to her mother's persistent exhortations. Her children thrived, despite their non-Catholic upbringing and for the first time since her marriage she was supremely, completely content.

The change began on the day of her son's christening. A ceremony of dedication rather than naming and which was often delayed until a child was five or six months old by which time the name, or names had long been settled. Family names perhaps, passed down from generation to generation. Names of a favourite uncle or aunt who might be inclined to make a bequest to their namesake in their will. It was altogether a serious and long drawn-out decision and Serena did her best to delay it, perhaps until after her daughter's wedding, she suggested, hoping, Mara was quite aware, that she could persuade her obdurate daughter-in-law to change her mind about her grandson's name. For days and weeks it went on. The suitability of James, or Edward, or even George if she really insisted on a royal name but Mara was adamant. She and James, but mostly Mara herself, Serena complained to her husband in private, had decided on Christian Patrick. Besides which, though Serena knew nothing of it, naturally, in those first few weeks Ellen O'Shaughnessy was becoming quite obsessed with taking the child into the Catholic faith and the sooner the

Anglican christening was over and done with the sooner Mara's Mammy would let up on it.

The christening ceremony was known as the 'shortening'. The day began with the baby being carefully washed by Nanny in glycerin-softened water and thoroughly powdered in the violet talc she favoured. He was wrapped in warm undergarments, the February day being cold and treacherous and not at all fit for the christening of so young a baby in Nanny's opinion. Master Christian was a strong, even lusty child but even so, agreeing with the *real* Mrs Osborne, the end of May or even June would have been more appropriate. A layer of petticoats followed, abundantly lace-trimmed, and next it was the turn of the actual christening gown itself. Mr Osborne, Mr James Osborne, the baby's great-grandfather had first worn it over eighty years ago and it was made of white silk, slightly yellowed, and delicate lace. It had a very full, long skirt, over three times the length of Master Christian and the six other Osborne infants who had worn it. The bodice and hem were intricately embroidered and in the insertions of the panels were tiny embroidered frills. A wide horizontal band at the bottom of the skirt served as a foundation for yet another embroidered flounce. A christening cap, embroidered and frilled to match the dress, was tied firmly under Master Christian's chin with satin ribbons. Blue, of course, as he was a boy, an old superstition but one which had moved through the generations until its purpose, to keep away witches, had been lost in the mists of time.

It was a very smart occasion, of course, with the ladies of the family, even old Mrs Osborne who was now a great-grandmother, elegantly and expensively dressed in outfits which had not been purchased in Liverpool. Mara was in blue, a vivid greeny-blue silk with a jacket bodice and a calf-length open tunic overskirt covering a narrow hobble skirt which was very fashionable and considered extremely daring. It was close fitting and simple, nipping in her waist and emphasising her lovely maternal bosom. The dress had

374

a high collar at the back and with it she wore an enormously wide-brimmed hat from which a long ostrich feather curled. Her eyes, under the shadow of its brim, were the exact shade of the dress, shimmering when the light caught them, just like the gleaming fabric. Her boots of a soft blue kid had high heels, and in them she was an inch or so taller than her immaculately tailored husband to whose arm she clung.

Old Mrs Osborne had chosen an outfit in her favourite dove grey with a dash of white at the neck and on her large hat. She looked frail and crumpled beneath its huge brim, somewhat confused, one or two guests noticed, escorted by her youngest grandson, Teddy, who at sixteen was now taller than his brother. Exceedingly handsome, everyone agreed, in the customary morning coat, single-breasted waistcoat, striped trousers and silk top hat.

Serena Osborne, erect, head held high for one must show pride in oneself in even the deepest adversity, which surely could be said of her with a daughter-in-law such as she had. Soft lilac and white she had chosen in the smoothest and lightest of wools with a high-necked blouse and a wide hat trimmed with white feathers. She looked a picture of restrained elegance and good taste but it was to her daughter that the accolade of true beauty was awarded and surely the credit for it must go to the personable young man to whom she had just become engaged. They positively could not bear to be apart, or so it seemed, their hands meeting and clinging whenever it was decently possible, their eyes smiling deeply as their glances met, their identical expressions seeming to speak to one another, saying all the things lovers say when they think themselves to be unobserved. Of course Serena Osborne and Anne Woodall made it their business to see that the newly-engaged couple were never alone together and that their devotion to one another was kept within the bounds of decency, but the girl positively glowed whenever her eyes met those of her

375

bridegroom-to-be. She was dressed in a warm cream, a gleaming *poult de soir* which was fitted in simple lines to her lovely figure. There was a touch of cream lace at her wrists and her hat was wide and decorated with cream tulle roses, full blown and quite exquisite. She wore no jewellery except the magnificent Woodall diamond, said to have been in the family for three hundred years and worn as a betrothal ring by all the Woodall brides.

The ceremony progressed smoothly, Master Christian ready to smile at every face which presented itself to him, as good-humoured as his father, though Nanny insisted tartly that it was merely wind. She and Etty, the first nurserymaid, who held the fetching Miss Claudine Osborne, wore their best Sunday dresses with broderie anglaise aprons, collars and caps and around them clustered the three godparents, two male and one female, cousins of James' from Serena's side of the family, and it was whilst they were at the font that it was noticed that Mrs James Osborne had a strange, one could almost say ferocious expression on her face, which until then had worn a sweetly smiling expression. She turned away as Nanny passed the boy over to the godmother, saying something to her husband which no one could catch and he appeared to be soothing her as one would a restive child.

The tables in the wide salon at Beechwood were set with magnificent lace cloths, damask napkins and massed with arrangements of white flowers, exotic camellias from the hothouses, snowdrops and lily of the valley from Serena's garden and cut only thirty minutes before the guests arrived. The christening breakfast to accommodate the hundred or so guests, since this was after all in honour of the heir to the Osborne estate, was absolutely splendid. Dishes of lobster carefully cut up, tiny pies with flaky pastry, pigeon, veal and ham, capon and tongue, fresh salmon, cold game, salads, small pastries, compôte of fruit, blancmanges and jellies, fruit tarts and ice creams and, of course, champagne to toast

Master Christian Patrick Osborne. And in the centre of the table in pride of place was the extravagantly white-iced christening cake.

There was a good deal of arranging and re-arranging of the elegant and languid guests, the family and by now fretful babies as the hired photographer marked the occasion with the taking of the family photograph. Mother seated with the newly christened infant on her lap, his long tucked robe spread out across her own vivid skirt, with father standing behind, his hand upon her shoulder. Included next was Miss Claudine who pulled her father's hair, laughed when she should have been serious and was chided soundly by Nanny who said that really, it was time they were back in the nursery. The whole family, smiling and stiff with the elder Mrs James Osborne not at all sure she wished to be photographed without her husband and who, for some reason, would insist upon calling young Mrs Osborne Rosie.

Master Christian had received a wealth of gifts. Silver mugs engraved with his initials. Patterned porcelain, silver spoons and pushers inscribed with nursery rhyme motifs, all exquisite and vastly expensive. Coral rattles and teething rings which would be put away by Nanny as too good to be played with. They were admired by the indolent, lounging gentlemen and the cool, well-bred ladies and then there was a general drifting towards carriages and motor cars by those who had long journeys to make.

'You can take the children up to the nursery now, Nanny,' Serena ordered calmly, turning back to continue her conversation with Lady Eleanor Fenton whose own daughter Penelope, with Sophie Woodall, would be bridesmaid to Elizabeth. There was no question in her mind or Nanny's that she was the one to tell her servants what she wished done in her home or that she would be obeyed and when Mara's voice rose above hers she stiffened in amazed affront.

'No, not yet, Nanny. I'll take Christian an' sure Elizabeth will take Claudine for a wee while, won't you, Elizabeth?

Sure an' 'tis a shame for them to be missing their own party so away with you to the kitchen Nanny, an' get yourself a cup of tea and take Etty with you for won't the pair of you be glad of it after hanging about all this time.'

Nanny stood open-mouthed whilst Mara scooped her son from her arms, then her eyes turned to Serena, her mistress, her expression said, waiting for further orders since surely this extraordinary behaviour would not go unchallenged. Hanging about indeed, and with Etty who was no more than a nurserymaid and not a person Nanny would 'hang about' with. Elizabeth, hesitating only for a moment or two, took Claudine from Etty and she and Harry began to move towards the window seat in the wide bay which overlooked the sloping lawns to the lake.

'Perhaps she would like some fruit, Harry,' the silent company which surrounded Serena heard her daughter say. 'Put a spoonful in a dish, will you? Strawberries, I think, with a little sugar and cream.' Harry moved to do as he was bid, aware, as they were all suddenly aware, that something unparalleled was about to happen.

Mara, smiling indolently at her husband and taking his hand, cradled her son in her free arm, carelessly, the company were inclined to think, in fact in the exact way she did everything, you could see the thought in Serena's ice chipped expression.

'Well, sure an' there'll be no fruit for you, me lad,' looking down at her son, 'but you can come with your Mammy and Daddy, so you can, while they have a sip of champagne together. Fetch me a glass, will you darlin',' to James, 'and you and I will drink to the newest Osborne. To the next in line, I suppose you'd say,' and completely unaware, or so she would have the assembled guests think, of anything unusual in her behaviour, she strolled after Elizabeth and sat down beside her. Her smile was charming. She swept the company with it, her children on show for all to see and admire, her manner unconcerned, young Mrs Osborne

378

in her husband's home, her home, where she might do and say whatever she pleased providing it was not unkind or ill-mannered. She turned to beam at her sister-in-law, sighing with pleasure.

Serena's face jerked and her husband who stood beside her put a restraining hand on her arm. We have guests, it warned, and with a great effort she controlled herself.

'Oh dear,' she said calmly, 'do you think this wise, darlings?' addressing her daughter and daughter-in-law together for her guests must, for appearances sake, be made to think that Elizabeth was as much at fault as Mara in this since who would believe that the well-bred Elizabeth Osborne could do anything seriously wrong. Two naive and inexperienced young women who, when they were told of it, would be quick to take the advice and be guided by an older and wiser one. 'The children must both be awfully tired, the sweet things,' she went on, 'and would be far better off in the nursery, don't you think?'

'No, I don't, Mrs Osborne,' Mara answered calmly, 'and if they're tired the pair of them can have a nap right here. Many's the time I've been cuddled in my Mammy's lap and gone to sleep an' to be sure it's done me no harm. A bit of a treat for them instead of being shut up in that old nursery.'

Serena's expression was frigid but her pedigreed control could not be faulted. There were murmurs, discreet and perplexed as those further away asked their neighbours what was happening. Several ladies of Serena's age were grim-visaged and ready, if it had been permissible, which of course it was not, to stand up next to her and give this impudent and upstart minx a sharp lesson in good manners. Keep the children downstairs, indeed, when everyone knew that the best and only place for them was in the nursery or the schoolroom, in charge of Nanny or a governess, spending time with their parents only at a specified period of the day. Naturally the Osborne children must be present today, particularly the boy for it was his own christening, but to

379

keep them here in adult company was not only ill-bred but not at all good for them. Sentimentality towards one's offspring only led to a lack of discipline and the problems which were only too prevalent in the inferior classes. Witness the children's mother!

Serena turned smilingly to her son. 'If you and I might have a word in private, James . . .'

'Come now, Mrs Osborne, 'tis only for half an hour or so then they can go back to Nanny. A wee party for them,' and lifting up her wide-eyed son Mara gave him a resounding kiss on his rosy cheek, dandling him like some bog-Irish peasant, Serena moaned later to her husband, on her silken lap, indifferent to any . . . er . . . mishap which might occur, was certain to occur if he was not taken, and soon, to the nursery.

'Mara darling, perhaps mother is right. They are awfully small to be at a grown-up affair like this,' James faltered, thunderstruck and bedevilled between his mother and his wilful wife.

'Like this? Begorra, 'tis the child's christening party, so it is, an' shouldn't himself be present at it? And we couldn't let him stay without Claudine staying too, could we? Would you look at her eating that fruit just like a little lady. Good as gold she is, Jesus bless her, and happy as a skylark on her Aunty Elizabeth's knee.'

She was deliberately exaggerating her Irishness, Elizabeth knew, just as Michael had done, caricaturing the brogue which she had almost eliminated from her speech. Throwing it in the faces of her mother-in-law and her mother-in-law's well-bred friends and the astonishing thing to Elizabeth was why? Why now? It was as if she was returned to her mother's homely kitchen with her own family about her, those who kept their children close to them, petted them, nursed them, fed them, often from their own plates. Who kissed them soundly a hundred times a day since they were always handy. Who picked them up the minute they cried and, if it was not convenient, had at their beck and call a dozen loving relatives to do it for them. She remembered the day of Bridget's funeral. There had been scores of children, from toddlers to sixteen-year-olds, part of the grieving family just as they would be part of any occasion which affected it, joyful, painful, despairing, exciting. And Mara was telling them so. She was simply being Mara. For over two years, ever since she had come to live in this house, she had merely been a shadowed copy of Serena and Elizabeth. Stiff and unsure of herself, prickly and ready to bristle at anything she did not understand in an effort to hide her ignorance. Her own warm, irrational, impetuous, quick-tempered nature had been severely battened down as she had aped the cool, well-bred upper class English women of her husband's family. She had been eager, desperate to conform, to take her place in their society. Except in their bedroom with her young husband, Mara O'Shaughnessy had ceased to exist as Mara Osborne had struggled to emerge. She was as beautiful as they – more so – as expensively and fashionably dressed as they – more so again – but beneath that smooth exterior, that strict curb she put on her own volatile nature she was still Ellen O'Shaughnessy's wayward, rebellious girl and the struggle to keep her prisoner, to allow no one but James and occasionally Elizabeth to see the real Mara had become too much for her.

And the sight of her son, *her* son being carelessly handed without so much as a word to her on how she might feel, to a Proddy set of godparents had opened the prison gates with a grand flourish to allow Mara O'Shaughnessy to escape to the outside world. They had been creaking for some time now, those gates, since it had seemed to Mara, as her second pregnancy had progressed, that no matter what she did or said, no matter how perfect her behaviour she would never fit in, never be accepted as one of them. The birth of her son, making her position strong and unbreakable in the

381

Osborne family, had brought her rebellion that much closer and today it had erupted. God's Holy Nightshirt, they could take her or leave her, her manner said as she smilingly sipped her champagne. She was sick and tired of being someone she was not and if they refused to have anything to do with her, which would surely be the case now except when they were forced to it on family occasions, then to the divil with the lot of them. She was tired of struggling to erase her Irish brogue, so she was, and would speak just as she always had. She was Irish and proud of it.

'Come on, James,' she called to her husband. 'Come an' nurse your son. Sure an' a fine boy he is an' one to make any father proud, aren't you, darlin'?' and the guests were treated to a mortified Serena Osborne forced to back down from this ill-mannered confrontation with her own, formerly biddable young daughter-in-law. It would not be forgotten nor forgiven, Serena's expression told them, and it was certain that if they had been en famille there would definitely have been more said on the subject.

Mara unconcernedly dipped ripe strawberries into her glass of champagne, delicately biting into each one with relish. Her son of whom, to tell the truth, she had become bored now that she had made her grand revolt had been passed to her husband who held him unhappily. He loved his wife, adored her, he would have admitted, and was secretly thrilled with her defiance of his mother since it was her strong will and audacity which had attracted her to him in the first place. If they had been alone he would have made love to her with the fierce passion she aroused in him but he was really not at all happy with the now irritable baby on his lap, from whom was coming a growing and quite appalling aroma, and the knowledge that his formidable mother, so used to having her own way, was about to make life most uncomfortable for him.

Mara O'Shaughnessy had revealed herself at last, as she really was and intended to be from now on. She had defied her mother-in-law's authority over her, thrown down the challenge and been victorious and so, with an imperious nod of her head to a hovering footman, she sent for Nanny and Etty, declaring that it was time for the children to be put down for their sleep.

'I'll be up to see them in a wee while, so I will,' telling the tight-lipped, scarlet-faced guardian of her children, her mother-in-law, and indeed any of the guests who cared to take note that Mrs James Osborne would have the ordering from now on, not only of her own life but of her children. She would do as she damn well pleased and if it pleased her to go to the nursery at any time of the day or night she chose, then she would.

'Sure an' it's been a grand day, so it has?' she remarked smilingly to her sister-in-law. She sipped her champagne, her hand in the crook of her husband's arm and her brilliant gaze met every one of those who dared to cross her.

They were to be married in June, Sir Harry Woodall and Elizabeth Osborne, for no matter how they tried to persuade her Serena Osborne would not, absolutely would not agree to a spring wedding, particularly after the fiasco of her grandson's christening which, if she lived to be a hundred, Serena would never forget. She had thought that the worst moment of her untroubled life had been the one when she was told that her eldest son, the heir, had eloped to Gretna Green with an Irish girl but since the christening she had come to the full knowledge that that had been merely the start of it. There had been nothing but trouble since. Far from ostracising Mara from polite society, her display as the lively, insolent but always amusing girl she really was seemed to have entertained those there, even won their arrogant admiration. To Serena's chagrin Mara was slowly and amazingly beginning to be accepted, if not by all of Serena's friends, at least by their daughters, young married ladies of her own age and their husbands who were inclined to applaud her different and somewhat defiant behaviour. This was 1913, after all, and women were fighting to escape the mould in which society had set them for centuries. The suffragist movement with which Mara's own sister, she had told them, was involved, had been extremely militant recently and though of course Mara and her newly-made young married friends did not advocate the burning down of schools and even of the Royal Mail they could not help but be elated, in strict contrast to their own mothers, by the rebellious nature of these perhaps foolish but certainly brave young women. Many of them were of their own class, doing and saying things they themselves had never dared to say.

Except Mara Osborne!

It was not, naturally, that Mara wished to be a suffragette, as her sister was, and indeed neither did any of her new friends but it seemed Mara's delightful defiance of the 'old ways', the very fact that she should know anything about them, coming from a different society as she did, was a symbol of what they saw as a new freedom. She was so very original in her ways and ideas. Vastly entertaining with the strange and whimsical sense of humour which must be Irish, they supposed. At first, because of her background, they had been wary of her but since the birth of her son, which, rightly, gave her a protected and special place in the Osborne hierarchy and consequently their society, she had been much more relaxed. Indeed 'good fun', they would have said, and very beautiful and they really could not understand why they had not seen it before. She was gaining a reputation for being one of the most dashing and expensively dressed ladies in Liverpool, seen in many homes from which, unless accompanied by her mother-in-law, she had previously been excluded and where her fresh and flippant wit and growing confidence in her own power to use it, made her a welcome guest. Privately they might have admitted that she was still somewhat – what was the word – earthy perhaps, but still decidedly amusing.

She and James had begun to gather around them a circle of what Serena distastefully called 'the smart set', young people of good family, married and unmarried, who went about together, to the race meetings at Aintree and Doncaster and Goodwood, to the theatre, to balls and to parties where there was little or no chaperonage. There was much flirting, driving about in fast motor cars, a love of pleasure and self-indulgence which Serena found not at all to her liking and she was not inclined to allow her daughter, the future Lady Elizabeth Woodall, to be a part of it. The husbands in this smart new set did nothing but drink and gamble, she had heard, and amuse themselves in a way she did not care to think about and as for the ladies, it was rumoured that one, whose husband owned race horses, had become involved with one of the jockeys who rode them!

Mara was no longer the compliant young girl she had been at the start of her marriage, anxious to please, earnestly doing her best to emulate Serena's perfect and well-bred manners. She was careless now and all too obviously no longer impressed by Serena's standards of ladylike behaviour, going her own shiftless way and taking Serena's son with her. She was even talking of learning to drive and not only that but demanding her own motor car, for Heaven's sake, and had persuaded James to take her to Manchester to the North of England Motor Show. She meant, she had informed the dinner table airily, to have one of the very latest Morris Oxfords she had seen in the exhibition hall for her very own.

And as for the children, she had them out at any time she fancied, no matter how inconvenient to Nanny who was muttering of giving in her notice since she was not used to such behaviour in one of her mothers and how was she able to maintain any sort of routine in which children, good children that is, thrived. There was nothing more certain,

Serena had told her daughter-in-law, than that her children would grow up to be hooligans.

Serena deplored it all, saying that society, in the proper sense of the word, seemed to be coming to an end and that she was thankful that her only daughter was to be married and would then be her husband's responsibility and no longer hers and Johnny's. Not that Elizabeth was allowed to go about with Mara and James, Alice and John Hammond and the rest of the 'fast set' her son and daughter-in-law consorted with, and was scarcely ever alone, even with her fiancé, since it was the custom for young ladies about to be married to be even more closely guarded. And Elizabeth herself seemed content to stay within the environs of her home, not even caring to indulge in her favourite pastime of riding unless she was accompanied by Teddy or her father. She stayed in her own rooms or walked in the garden with Serena, taking an interest in her mother's horticultural activities. Her behaviour was exemplary and one could only wish that Mara could follow her example, Serena complained to her husband, and stay at home with her children. She was leading James badly astray in this company they kept and she trembled for the future of the Osbornes.

Mara had been beautiful on her wedding day. It had been a vibrant beauty, alive and brilliant. Her eyes had glowed in triumph and glory. Her cheeks had been flushed and not at all pale and maidenly with that strange innocence which all brides appear to have. She had been in a state of thrilled excitement, brimming over with a sensuality which James Osborne had awakened in her. Already carrying her first child, though her pregnancy had not then altered her figure, she had seemed to bloom, almost to explode in her lovely young womanhood.

Elizabeth Osborne, on the other hand, was as pale and submissive as those who came to see her married would wish a lady of their class to be. Tranquil and graceful as the pure white fronds of magnolia and mock orange blossom in her bouquet, they all agreed. Her gown was of silk appliquéd with misty lace with a garniture of seed pearls at the high neckline, the wrist and hem. She wore a simple Juliet cap, again encrusted with seed pearls, on her dark and shining hair which was rolled up around it leaving her long and slender neck vulnerably exposed and she was shrouded from head to foot in the exquisite nun-like mist of her veil. She looked ethereal, unreal in her luminous beauty as she floated down the aisle on her father's arm. Her face was composed behind the mystery of her veil, and her lips formed in a small smile as she looked up into her bridegroom's face. It was noticed that after she had passed her bouquet to Sophie Woodall her right hand had crept out from beneath her long veil, altering its smooth line, somewhat to her mother's annoyance, and had reached for Harry Woodall's. His had clasped it reassuringly, ardently even, and there were a few teared eyes amongst the maid-servants at the back of the church since it was obvious the young couple were very much in love.

How perfect they were, the handsome, aristocratic bride-groom and his glorious bride, it was whispered as they moved together towards the church porch. Hand in hand, it was noticed, and not at all in the usual manner of bride and groom. It was customary for the new wife to do no more than place her hand on her new husband's arm but it was evident that Sir Harry and Lady Woodall were not to be conventional. Even their kiss at the altar had been warmer than those who watched were accustomed to see-ing. Lady Woodall's white satin-shod feet moved gracefully across the white rose petals which were scattered at the porch and to the delight of the vast crowd of the Woodall and Osborne servants and tenants who had been unable to get into the crowded church, she again lifted her face for her husband's warm, quite lingering kiss. Sir Harry's emo-tion was very evident. His bride, now that the ceremony was done with, was quite magnificent, becoming rosy and

387

flushed, gazing up at her new husband with her eyes alight with gladness, or so it seemed to them. There was a pealing of bells and as the newly married couple climbed into the carriage lined with white silk and pulled by four beautifully matched white horses, those who had seen her pale and virginal tranquillity at the altar remarked on the change in her. One would almost have thought she was relieved to have it over and done with.

There was a striped marquee on the lawn at Beechwood. The June day was blue and golden and the gardens, supervised for weeks by Serena Osborne who had threatened to fire every single one of her gardeners if they were not perfect, were perfect. There were servants by the score, silver trays of champagne and a bridal cake weighing over two hundred pounds, all white frosted and cast about with white rosebuds and white satin ribbon. It was noticed as Elizabeth and Harry, Sir Harry and Lady Woodall now, cut it, that Johnny Osborne wiped a fond and fatherly tear from his eye and Sir Harry, kissing his sister, as pretty as she was ever to look except on her own wedding day, whispered that she would be next.

The young Mrs Osborne was quite radiant, strolling about the lawn and chatting to her new friends, a glass of champagne in her hand – the Veuve Cliquot laid down by Johnny Osborne nine years ago for just this occasion – her hand in her husband's and about their feet darted their pretty two-year-old daughter, Claudine. An adorable child with her mother's good looks but completely out of hand, of course, since her mother had shooed away the only person who could control her, her nanny.

'Don't be silly, Nanny,' the guests heard her say, 'she can come to no harm with her own mother and father, can she? And I forbid you to hover like that, just as though I couldn't look after my own child. Take Christian back to the nursery for he's a bit young for all this, so he is, but Claudine will stay at the party with her Mammy, won't you, pet? Will you look at her, James, picking those flowers for her Grandmammy . . . what? They're your mother's prize zinnias? Well, she'll not begrudge her granddaughter a posy, now will she?'

Elizabeth and Harry moved among their guests during that lovely, sun-filled afternoon shaking hands and kissing cheeks, the bride's veil thrown back to reveal the serene happiness on her face. The sloping lawn which undulated down to the lake was crowded with elegant ladies, their parasols shading their white skins from the warm and harmful rays of the sun, with gentlemen who stood bareheaded, their silk top hats tucked beneath their arms. Many sought the welcome shade of the trees which were clustered here and there about the wide gardens, some even strolling as far as the edge of the woodland which surrounded the Osborne estate. The lake swam in a haze of midges and the comfrey and willowherb which edged it were reflected in the flat, placid water. The lovely, honey-coloured house, the home of the Osbornes these sixty or so years, seemed to shimmer in the heat.

Several of the guests who lounged, champagne glasses in their hands, beneath the stalwart chestnut trees were startled to come across the uniformed figure of the Woodall chauffeur – known by many of Lady Woodall's friends since he had driven them about the town with her ladyship – lurking, they could think of no other word, amongst the trees. He had, they supposed, driven Lady Woodall to the church and back to Beechwood so what was he doing here and why was he not celebrating with the other servants, those who could be spared from their normal duties? The sending of the daughter of the house into the ancestral home of her new husband was an important event and one to be rejoiced at, not only by the family but by their servants as well. The man looked very strange and really, should they report him to Johnny Osborne, for the fellow must surely be drunk. He appeared to be unaware of their presence, watching with fiercely staring eyes the progress of the bride and groom as they began to move back towards the house where they would change for their honeymoon journey.

'What the devil are you doing here, my man?' Sir Roger Fenton ventured to ask him. 'Should you not be in the servants' hall where you belong?'

The man turned and it was then those who watched remembered that he was the brother of Serena and Johnny Osborne's daughter-in-law and really, they could only sympathise with Serena on being related, if only by marriage, to this wild-eyed, tight-jawed chap.

'You're right, sir,' he answered civilly enough. 'To be sure that's where I do belong an' I'll be getting back to it.' And without another word, not even of apology, he turned on his heel and left.

For the first five minutes he did no more than gaze at her naked body, the body he himself had divested of its fine wrappings before laying it out on the bed. He did not touch her. His eyes moved across the silken smoothness of her white skin and lingered on the round firmness of her rosy peaked breasts, the perfect mound of her pudenda shrouded in silken hair as dark as that on her head, the length and grace of her legs, the satin of her thighs which he parted as a man will who is to reveal the treasure for which he has searched all his life.

'You are so beautiful,' he whispered, kneeling over her, his own naked body as beautiful as hers. He was lean, with wide shoulders and narrow hips, the scattering of coarse blond hair on his chest running down his flat stomach to his swollen manhood. The lights were soft in the sweet-smelling bedroom of the suite he had reserved for the one night they were to be in London, and they cast their rosy glow over the bodies of the man and woman on the bed. 'I've waited so long ... loved you ... Elizabeth ...' and with the emotion the sight of her body visibly aroused in him no longer in his control he entered her body, almost painlessly, letting his love flood into her, overwhelming her with the strength of it. He groaned and trembled and Elizabeth lay quite still, not at all sure what to expect next. Harry lay along the length of her, his body still nailed to hers and was there something else he wished to do? But nothing further happened and she allowed herself to relax. She had found it ... not unpleasant. She loved Harry, of course she did, and wanted nothing more than to be a good wife to him, to give him pleasure and friendship, love and companionship for the rest of their lives. She had no detailed knowledge of the mating between a man and a woman and if this was all it entailed, then she would give it gladly.

The next time, in the early light of the new day, he had made love to her more slowly, smoothing her body with his strong, horseman's hands, curling his fingers about her breasts, taking her nipples in turn into his mouth and for an exquisite moment she was returned to that dark summer night beneath the trees when ... when ... but this was Harry, her husband, who was lingering over the hollows and curves of her hip and stomach and the white skin of her inner thighs, turning her this way and that to study every inch of her. He kissed her instep and her toes, moving up her body to the back of her knees and it was then she began to feel that small stab of warm excitement, that stirring of joy which grew in the pit of her belly, just as she had when ... when ... He saw her arch her back and throw back her head and instantly he plunged himself into her, driving away the tiny, barely lit flame he had kindled before it had time to flare into the fire she had been certain was to consume her. Next time ... next time ...

'I love you, dear God but I love you,' he said, joyfully, cradling her to him in a passion of gladness that she should have experienced so soon the rapture he could give her and she loved him too dearly to tell him that it had slipped away before she had had time to grasp it.

They spent a month wandering hand in hand in the sun-drenched glory of Italy, lying in fields ablaze with poppies, on golden deserted beaches where he kissed her to within a shadow of arching, languorous love. They swam in lazy turquoise seas and idled the days and nights away in a passion of lovemaking which seemed to dazzle him, defeat him, smite him to the core with its intensity. When he entered her he became another man. The sweet-natured, humorous man she had always known abandoned himself in groaning trembling orgasm and if she was not so affected, did it matter when it was her joy to make him so happy. She learned to accept it, to receive his love with a grace and gratitude which turned her from girl to woman, blooming in his love as a well-tended flower will bloom.

He took her to Venice and to Rome, to Florence and to Capri, showering her not only with exquisite and costly presents but with the depth and breadth of his endlessly adoring love. His head rested on her breast each night as he slept and if, as she cradled him thankfully to her, another face than his smiled whimsically at her in the dark, she had only to waken her husband and his passion for her to send it drifting like a ghost into the formless shadows of the past.

21

The day following the wedding of Elizabeth Osborne and Harry Woodall was Derby Day at Epsom and the general opinion amongst those who knew about such things was that the King's horse, Anmer, stood a good chance of winning. The horses milled about behind the starting line, thirty-three highly strung thoroughbreds, the purple and scarlet of the royal colours standing out brilliantly amongst the rest as the riders waited for the white flag to go down.

It was the most gruelling race in the British flat season and the crowds were packed tight about the bookmakers' placards. There was music from the band near the grandstand and the brassy strains of the roundabouts on the heath. There were row upon row of motor buses, motor cabs, and the motor cars in which the highest classes of British society had travelled to the race.

Tipsters whispered into any ear which was prepared to listen, of the winner which was known only to themselves. Evangelists shouted of Jesus and His second coming and the bookies shouted the odds. The smell of steaming food wafted from little booths. There were some eating caviar and sipping champagne and others munching on their home-made sandwiches and quaffing their ale. The black-faced minstrels strummed their banjos and over it all the blue sky stretched heavenwards, marking no difference between king and commoner though naturally they were separated as was proper to their station.

'They're off,' thousands of voices roared as the horses flung themselves forward, the pounding of their hooves on the turf thrilling thousands of ears.

The King's horse was well back in the field.

The deep swelling roar rose from the crowds on both sides of the course at Tattenham Corner, growing in volume as the front horse cleared the bend but suddenly, for some reason the sound changed, though in what way those who had not such a clear view could not say. The noise became shrill and filled with horror and the voices of women predominated. There were screams and hoarse urgent shouts of alarm.

'Jesus Christ, it's a woman . . .'

'. . . on the course . . .'

'Oh my God . . .'

'What in hell's name is she about?'

'   the bloody fool . . .'

The King's horse was racing faster than a train and was just as lethal when it hit her and those nearest swore they heard the breaking of her bones. The horse went down, pinning the jockey in his cheerful colours beneath it and beside him the woman lay on her back, her arms outstretched as though in crucifixion.

Above the heads of the crowd another placard was raised high and on it was written a dramatic message.

'VOTES FOR WOMEN', it read.

In March, three months before Emily Davison died beneath the hooves of the King's horse for the freedom of others, becoming the movement's first intentional martyr, the Prisoner's Temporary Discharge for Ill-health Bill was hurried through Parliament, but it was never after that first time called anything but the Cat and Mouse Act. Let out on licence from prison when their hunger strikes brought them to a point of dangerous weakness, the women, if they could be located, were re-arrested the moment they had recuperated sufficiently to be put through the ordeal all over again. In those first months Emmeline Pankhurst was released nine times after hunger and thirst strikes only to be imprisoned once more after each brief respite.

But she was not the only one to suffer it and in late August, Captain Jack Templeton almost carried the thin, waif-like woman he loved across the forecourt in front of Lime Street Railway station.

'Could we not go to a hotel, Jack?' she was saying as he lifted her carefully into the back of a taxi-cab. 'You know how hard you tried to get me into the Adelphi last year. Well, I'll willingly go now . . .'

'I know you mean to make me laugh, Caitlin, and thereby weaken my resolve but you are not succeeding. I asked you three months ago to go home to your mother and recover your strength but you would not do so, and so this time I am making certain that you do.'

'I was perfectly well looked after by Mrs Willis and that housemaid you insisted on installing in the kitchen. Two women to wait on one. They cosseted me as though I was a chronic invalid. Every night when I got back there was an enormous meal ready, enough to feed my whole family, so there was. Fires half-way up the chimney and hot baths run for me every minute of the live-long day. Begorra, I was treated better than the King himself and when you were away the three of us rattled about in that great house like three ollies in a jar.'

'It was not a great house, just a modest villa and what in hell's name are ollies?'

'Oh, I forgot you're not from working-class stock like meself, bejasus. Do you mean to tell me you've never played ollies, and you a northerner?' Though her voice was weak her eyes shone with bright humour.

'Never, I'm sure of it, so tell me what it is and then be quiet and save your strength. I dare say you'll need it where we're going an' sure won't you be doin' enough talkin' to suit the whole Irish lot of you.'

'Ollies are marbles, and stop making fun of my brogue.'

'I believe I have heard of marbles and I love your brogue. Now, lean on me, my darling, and let us gird our loins for the battle to come.'

'Yes,' she sighed against his shoulder, the thought of the battle to come dissipating what small store of strength she had conserved for this journey. The last term of imprisonment had almost finished her, she was well aware, and though once she would have gone on playing their game of cat and mouse; would have died gladly to further their cause, as Emily had died, not now. Oh no, not now. She had known it would happen, of course she had. That was why she had fought him at the beginning. She had known he would weaken her fervour; divert her spirit and her resolve away from the suffrage movement with his love, dazzle her eyes and bemuse her heart so that nothing else mattered but him. It had happened, but it had taken nine long months before she had finally admitted it. They had broken her body with their torture but never her resolution. It had taken Jack Templeton's love to do that.

'Let me do the talking,' he said as the taxi-cab stopped outside the house and she almost smiled. Let him do the talking! Glory be to God, he'd be lucky if he managed to get in even one small word ... edgewise!

She had sent a telegram and they were expecting her. Mammy was half-way down the path before the cab driver had stopped, her arms wide and ready to envelop her beloved, wayward, difficult, courageous girl. Caitlin had been home a time or two in the last nine months, to eat her mother's ample meals – when she could – and repair the damage done by the authorities to her body and spirit. In the closely familiar shelter of her irrepressible family she had sat slightly apart, nursing herself, healing herself as she listened to their ceaseless, good-humoured laughter and talk, letting the wholesome innocence of them – for that was what they were, innocent – wash over her. She gained her strength from this source of her being, from this home, these people and what they gave her enabled her to return restored, if only partially, to fight again.

Now, here was her mother, the heart of it all, ready to draw her into the warmth of the well spring, her face already wet with her easy tears, tears of joy shed for the return of the wanderer.

'Darlin' ... oh darlin'...' and for a few speechless seconds they just stood, arms locked about one another, pinned together in an ecstasy of love. Caitlin leaned into her mother's strong embrace, her eyes tight-closed as her own tears began to flow and her weakness, her body's frailty was held upright only by a savage resolve of strength on her part.

They were all there then, streaming behind her mother in a maddened crowd of excitement and delight, each determined to have their Caitlin in an exuberant hug, to give a loving kiss anywhere it might fall. Her three older sisters and umpteen of their children, several boys of various ages and a pretty little girl of about six or seven, Jack thought, who must be the youngest, Clare. Ellen had released Caitlin now to Gracie and Amy and Eileen. Her hand was to her mouth as she watched them and in her weeping eyes was the full horror of the flimsy human being she had just held in her arms. She had felt the brittle, ready-to-snap bones of her, the stick-like feel of her arms and shoulder blades and her mother's heart was aghast. Would you look at her, her expression said, ready to fall down like a bit of matchwood if she hadn't been held up by their Sean's strong, sixteen-year-old arms. As delicate as eggshells, she was, and her skin the colour of skimmed milk, and as Jack watched quietly from his position on the edge of the family circle he could see the firming resolve in her face, the expression which said Caitlin O'Shaughnessy had made her last trip to London and his own heart was thankful.

'Daddy's at work, darlin', and Dermot, and of course Michael couldn't get away but Sean here played wag from his job to be at home when you came, didn't you, pet? He's errand boy for Hemingways now and Donal starts next month an' as for these two,' indicating Eammon and Clare, 'well, shouldn't they be at school an' all but ... well, 'tis a great marvel to have you home, thanks be to the Holy Mother an' I couldn't say no. Now then, Eammon, leave Caitlin be. Can't you see the darlin's dying to sit herself down after her long journey so run in an' tell Lucy to wet the tea. Oh, you're there, Lucy, and Matty. Well, say hello to Caitlin ... no, don't jump on her like that, Clare ...' for Glory be to God, they'd have her over, the spalpeens, and her as insubstantial as a bubble with her face paling even more if that were possible at the vigorous energy of her welcome.

Caitlin turned to him then, her hand still held by Clare's,

looking for support from her only source of it for the past year and Jack moved forward. She held out her free hand, her face, or so it seemed, gaining colour as he took it and all about her her family became quiet, staring curiously, or in bewilderment, or with animosity at this stranger – who was he, anyway? – who was holding on to their Caitlin with a familiarity they did not care for. They had seen him come through the gate with her, holding her arm in support, but they had supposed him to be the cab driver, which was daft really when you noticed the way he was dressed and now here he was, smiling and taking Caitlin's hand as though he had every right to do so.

Caitlin turned back to her mother and Jack could feel her tremble. She was ready to collapse and it was his intention to have her somewhere in this house and tucked up in a bed within half an hour no matter what was said. He did not want her to be tormented by her mother's anguish or rage or recrimination if that was what Mrs O'Shaughnessy had in mind, though it seemed to him that the only emotion the mother of Caitlin O'Shaughnessy felt was a deep and despairing concern for her child. Caitlin must sleep, rest, do nothing but sit, perhaps in a bit of sunshine, eat her mother's nourishing food, sleep again and have nothing but tranquillity about her until she was strong enough to discuss her life, past and future with her parents.

But until then he would talk for her. He would say all that needed to be said before he returned to his regiment.

'This is . . .' Caitlin was saying, leaning against him and he held her close and about them her family began to eye him coldly.

'Jack Templeton, Mrs O'Shaughnessy, but don't you think that before any introductions or explanations are made it might be a good idea to get Caitlin to bed. As you can see she is not at all well . . .'

'Oh Jack, I'm perfectly . . .'

'No you are not, Caitlin, and I know your mother will

agree with me, won't you, Mrs O'Shaughnessy, that our first concern is for you. You can do all your talking when you have had a rest. Now I am sure your family,' smiling round courteously at the open mouthed faces, 'will forgive you if you go straight to bed.'

Ellen O'Shaughnessy's resentment of this smooth-talking gentleman – for that was what he was, a real gentleman – evaporated as she saw the sense of his words. Sweet Mother, the child looked half dead and what her Daddy would say when he saw her couldn't bear thinking about. She could go in her own bedroom where only Clare slept now and it had better be soon, as the stranger said, or by the look of her she'd crumple like a bit of fragile lace into a heap on the garden path.

He let the women take her though there was nothing more he wanted than to be the one to put her in the modest lawn nightdress she still insisted on wearing, lay her tenderly between the clean, sweet-smelling sheets he was sure Ellen O'Shaughnessy would have on all her beds and hold her against him until she fell into the deep, exhausted, healing sleep she needed so desperately. But he must do this thing in the proper way. Caitlin must not be dishonoured in front of her family. One thing at a time and the first was her need for rest.

The oldest boy, Sean, had Mrs O'Shaughnessy called him? led him awkwardly through the front door and into the hall, hesitating as to whether this gentleman should be put in the parlour at the front of the house, or taken into the kitchen.

'The kitchen will do, lad,' he said kindly and he was ushered in there followed by a silent group of awed children ranging from Sean, who at sixteen was no longer a child, right down to a little boy he had heard one of the others call Finbar in a hoarse whisper when the child had fingered his own splendid portmanteau.

They stood about him wondering what he would do next

just as though he was a species from another planet and might perform some interesting trick, their eyes wide, some of them the same lovely blue as Caitlin's.

'May I sit down?' he asked and Sean nodded and taking the comfortable armchair beside the fire Jack sank into it. Immediately the children all scrambled to squeeze in about the table, sitting shoulder to shoulder on the two benches, hands on chins in silent and fascinated appraisal of him.

One of the women, Caitlin's sister, hurried into the room a moment or two later, demanding hot water and a clean towel and ordering one of the maids who stared at him in exactly the same bewitched way as the children to make up a pot of tea, a lightly boiled egg and a slice of toast.

'Best butter, mind, and thin. Cut up fine an' take off the crusts.'

When this was done and placed daintily on a tray which the woman whisked briskly away the maid resumed her unblinking scrutiny of him, the second one sidling up beside her.

'Perhaps you could tell me your names?' he said at last to the row of children, anything to break the silence, but no one was willing to be the first to take the plunge.

'Well ... er ... Sean, is it?'

Sean nodded.

'How do you like your job? At Hemingways, your mother said. Is that not a shipping firm?'

'Aye,' and the boy nodded again.

'An errand boy? That must be ...'

'I'm to be put up soon, so I am.'

'Are you really? To what?'

'In the warehouse, with Daddy.'

'Aah, and ... er ... your father is ... what does he do ...?'

'In the warehouse,' young Sean answered scornfully for hadn't he just said so.

'Of course, forgive me,' and Jack could feel the sweat

400

begin to form on his upper lip. The room was like a furnace. There was a delicious smell of bread baking and on the stove something bubbled enticingly in a pot. He still wore his overcoat since no one had thought, or cared, to relieve him of it. Standing up he took it off, looking to the maids to take it from him. For a moment one of them hesitated not at all sure Mrs O'Shaughnessy would care to have this stranger's overcoat hanging on her hallstand, then she took it, stroking without thinking the fine quality of the wool from which it was fashioned.

At last they came back, the four women, and immediately he stood up politely. Ellen was crying and one of her daughters had her arm about her. They were all deep in distress and he thought he knew the reason why.

'Holy Mother of God . . .' Ellen was moaning and without acknowledging his presence she sank down into the chair on the opposite side of the fire and put her face in her hands whilst her daughter continued to pat her shoulders. They were all in some state of shock and the children had transferred their attention from him to their mothers and grandmother.

'What is it, Mammy?' Sean asked, his boy's voice anxious. He was not a child and he was not a man and he felt awkward with these women's emotions. 'Is our Caitlin not well then?'

'No, she's not, darlin',' his mother answered, her voice muffled in her hands. 'Oh Mary Mother of God . . .' and again her voice broke.

'What is it, Mammy?'

'Don't ask me, son, for sure I can't bring myself to speak of it.'

'Well, I bloody well can an' if I had me way I'd flay the lot of 'em alive, the bastards. I'm sorry, Mammy, but sure I can't keep it in me. What those monsters have done to her is more than anyone can understand. Her poor back and those bruises on her . . .'

'Amy, that's enough.' Ellen's voice was high and angry. 'You'll not shame your sister...'

'Tis them that should be ashamed, Mammy, for what they've done to her. Sure an' it's obvious that ... well ... that they've handled her ... indecently. And her poor mouth. She'll lose those teeth if she's not careful. Sure an' it's enough to make any woman want to join this movement of hers for the more of us is in it the quicker it would give women the right to fight the way she's been treated. I've a good mind to go down to Duke Street and offer me services, that I have. Oh, Jesus, what will the Daddy say when he sees her ... and Michael and Dermot. God almighty...' and Amy turned away, putting her face to the wall in anguish.

'Tis done now, child,' for when would Ellen's family, whatever their age, be anything but children to her, 'and there's nought we can do for her but make her well again, but I'll tell you this and I swear it on the Cross that killed the Son of Our Lady, it's over my dead body she goes again. She's staying at home, so she is an' when she's herself again she can work in the office of those damned suffragette women if she must, but she's not going into prison again, ever. Holy Mother, she's not twenty-one yet and if I have to stop her by refusing permission...'

Suddenly she stopped speaking, lifting her head to look at Jack who still stood, correctly since there were ladies on their feet, beside his chair. He waited for her to say something but she seemed surprised to still find him there in the midst of her family's crisis and her eyes, wet with her distraught tears, became shuttered.

'Mrs O'Shaughnessy,' he said softly.

'What ... who...?' and slowly she rose to her feet. She smoothed her apron which was stained with the water with which she had sponged down her daughter's abused body. Her confusion deepened as he bowed gallantly. None of the men she knew acted in such a strange way unless it was that husband of Mara's. And who was he? What had he to do with their Caitlin? And didn't she know him? Had she not seen him before somewhere?

'Jack Templeton, Mrs O'Shaughnessy,' he said. 'I brought Caitlin home to you.'

'Yes . . . ?'

'May I ask how she is?'

'Asleep now.'

'She will need a good deal of that in the next few days. She is very . . . frail.' He said it with such tenderness, with such an abundance of love that Ellen O'Shaughnessy's face softened, but only for a moment.

'An' what the divil is it to do with you, Mr . . .'

'Templeton.' Jack's voice was infinitely patient.

'Aye, I heard you the first time but what I want to know is who you are an' what you're doing fetching my daughter in here the way you did. Faith, an' if her Daddy or her other brothers had been here there'd have been a few questions asked before now, I can tell you. Not that Sean here,' turning to the boy with a fond look, 'couldn't have defended her with his life but he's young yet and . . .' Suddenly aware that she was digressing she bristled up to Jack like a small, full-breasted pigeon, her cheeks aflame with indignation at his insolence in still being here in her kitchen. 'So I'll have the truth of it, if you please, Mr Templeton an' if I find you've been . . . well, that my daughter has been . . . compromised in any way . . .'

'Mrs O'Shaughnessy, your daughter is the most honourable and honoured woman in my life. I hold her in the greatest respect and if I could spare her a moment's pain or worry I would do it. But she won't allow it. She is generous, loyal and brave and the dearest woman in the world to me and I am proud . . .' he paused. 'Will you not sit down, Mrs O'Shaughnessy, for I fear you are to have a great shock.'

'Jesus, Joseph and Mary . . .' Ellen crossed herself feverishly and her daughters clustered protectively about her but

403

Jack moved across the space which divided them and took her hands in his. He smiled gravely as he spoke.

'Caitlin and I are married, Mrs O'Shaughnessy. She became my wife six months ago. Now will you sit down and let me tell you all about it?'

An appalled silence followed his words. They might all have turned to pillars of salt, like Lot's wife, so still did every one of them become, even the restless Finbar who surely could not have understood what had been said. The hands of the two maids froze on teapot and kettle and all the paraphernalia of the endless teamaking which went on in this house, only their heads moving as they turned to stare, slack-jawed, at this well-mannered, even agreeable gentleman who had just announced that he and Miss Caitlin were man and wife. God's Holy Nightshirt, their incredulous expressions said, what could happen next in this house which, during the past few years or so seemed to have had one drama after another piled on to its groaning back? First Miss Mara running off with that gentry chap and defying the ideals of this upright household and the edicts of the Catholic Church to which they all belonged, and then poor Miss Bridget, or Mrs Feeney as she had become, dying in childbirth and taking her baby with her, and now this. Where would it all end, they appeared to ask one another as they exchanged glances.

It seemed the same thought was in the mind of Ellen O'Shaughnessy as, pulling her hands savagely from Jack's she staggered back into her daughters' arms, teetering there as though she would faint. Every scrap of colour had drained from her already strained face and in it her eyes were blank and uncomprehending, surrounded by great pools of liver-toned skin. Her mouth fell open, closed, fell open again and she swallowed painfully. No one spoke.

Jack cleared his throat. 'I'm sorry, Mrs O'Shaughnessy. I know this is a dreadful shock to you. I really don't know what to say to make it any easier. There is nothing, I suppose, except to repeat how sorry I am that you have learned of it in such a way. We would naturally have told you as soon as we could but Caitlin was involved ... she has been imprisoned many times ... you will have heard of the Cat and Mouse Act? Yes ... well, I was in Ireland ... I am a soldier and the time never seemed to come when we were both able to ... well ...' He became brisk then, not meaning to be unkind but they were still standing about as though he had told them they were all to go to the gallows within the hour and he wanted one of them, preferably Caitlin's mother, to say something, anything in response to his stumbling words. 'I wished to be with her when she broke the news, you see, but she ...' He sighed and his gaze wandered off somewhere above Ellen's shoulder as though he saw something he would rather forget, 'she only came out of Holloway yesterday ... two weeks they kept her this time and .. you have seen the result. I am to return to my regiment tomorrow and I could not leave her ... again ... for strangers to care for her, so I brought her home.'

Still no one spoke but deep in Ellen's throat a sound began. A deep sound, soft and terrible and on the bench where she sat between her cousin Mary and her brother Eammon, Clare O'Shaughnessy's face crumpled in bewilderment. She began to cry, the sound mingling with that made by her mother, a high-pitched keening which filled the warm and homely room as though the devil himself had been let loose there. Jack's face paled.

'Mrs O'Shaughnessy, I beg you not to be ...'

'Oh sweet Mother of God ...'

'Please, madam, don't take on so. I know we should have waited and done this in the correct way. Spoken to your husband and married as Caitlin deserves but she needed looking after .. '

'Are you saying she was not looked after in her own home?' Amy Conroy left her mother's side and hurled herself at Jack and he stepped back smartly, ready to grasp her hands which seemed in imminent danger of reaching for his eyes.

'Indeed I am not, Mrs ... er ... I merely meant that whilst she was in London she had no proper home and I provided it.'

'So that you could take her there whenever you had a fancy to ...'

Jack's eyes narrowed dangerously and a mask of anger stiffened his normally good-humoured face. His lips moved in what could only be called a snarl and it looked as though he might be tempted to give Amy a thick ear, or so young Sean thought as he dived round the table in defence of his sister, but Jack, trembling slightly, drew himself into a fist of tight control and his voice was icily polite.

'You dishonour your sister, madam, and my wife and I demand that you retract that insult. To her and to me ...'

'You're nothing but a swine who preys on defenceless young girls.' Amy was weeping helplessly and the other two were doing their best to calm her, and her mother, at the same time longing to give him a piece of their mind, he could see. He looked about him despairingly for what else could he do, or say? They were not listening to him. They seemed not to hear anything beyond the fact that he and Caitlin had lived together in the same house and their marriage appeared to be of no importance to them. It was as if it had not even happened. The mother had lost her senses, standing poleaxed in the midst of her daughters. The children were crying, or stupefied and the boy was ready to knock him down if he said another word. Only the two maids appeared to be in their right minds as they watched the drama avidly.

He tried once more. 'Mrs O'Shaughnessy, will you not sit down and for Caitlin's sake listen to what I have to ...'

'Get out of my house.' Her voice was like the sound chalk makes scraping down a blackboard. 'An' get out now before me husband comes home or I swear he'll kill you. For your sake I'm telling you to go now.'

'I'll do no such thing, madam, or if I do my wife goes with me.'

She gasped as though he had landed a blow to her stomach, which was how she felt. 'No . . .' she moaned. 'She stays here with her family.'

'I am her family, Mrs O'Shaughnessy.' His voice was softer now, compassion for the suffering woman who could still not bring herself to believe what was unchangeable making him gentle with her. 'She and I were married in church last April . . .'

'She's bin home since and said nothing . . .'

'I could not force her to tell you, Mrs O'Shaughnessy, and I'm sure I don't know why she didn't,' though after seeing her family and the fierce closeness of its Catholic boundaries, he was beginning to realise why Caitlin had not done so. 'As I said, I am a soldier and away from home . . .'

'Have you told your mother, Mr Templeton?'

'No.'

'And why not?'

'When Caitlin is well I intend taking her home to my family. I explained to you that neither of us has been . . .'

'Are you Catholic?'

'No.'

'But you are a gentleman.'

'I hope I am, Mrs O'Shaughnessy, but I really don't know what that has to . . .'

'Do you not?'

'No, I don't and if we could just sit down and talk this over before Caitlin wakes up I would be obliged. I don't want her to be upset by . . .'

'You don't want her to be upset! Faith, I'm her mother . . .'

'And I am her husband. My first loyalty, my concern is only for her. You can all go to hell for all I care but my wife is not to be troubled with this. She is all I care about. Is that

407

clear? I love your daughter, Mrs O'Shaughnessy, and she loves me. We are man and wife in the eyes of the law and of God...'

'Oh no, not in the eyes of God...'

'In the eyes of God, madam. I don't care whose God and I will not allow Caitlin to be made to feel guilty. I will not have her victimised or harassed in any way and if you cannot give me your solemn pledge that you will do none of these things then I shall take her away and find a quiet place to leave her to recover.'

'You cannot...'

'I can, Mrs O'Shaughnessy, and I will. If you send me away now I can guarantee when my wife wakes up and finds me gone she will follow me. Ill as she is she will get up from her bed and...'

'Oh, Jesus and all His Angels ... don't ... please...'

'I apologise if this upsets you but it must be said. She loves me. She is my wife. She is honest and the most courageous woman I know. She loves you and her family but she will not stay with you if I tell her to leave and I will unless I have your promise that you will look after her and keep her safe for me until I return. Believe me, Mrs O'Shaughnessy, if you want to keep your daughter you must accept me as her husband since that is what I am.'

Ellen O'Shaughnessy bent her head, defeated.

22

The smart little Morris Oxford motor car which Mara had finally badgered her husband into buying for her was delivered to the garages at the back of Beechwood Hall in early May. Already it promised to be a fine summer and the warm spring sunlight gleamed on the glossy paintwork and polished chrome of the splendid two-seater reflecting the flushed face of its owner in its shining surface. It had a forest green body with wheels and leather upholstery to match. There were headlamps on either side of the bonnet near the windscreen and two more directly in between the front wheels. The handbrake was placed for convenience just outside the driver's door and behind that rested the spare tyre. There was a small window at the back so that the driver could see behind when the hood was up. A De Luxe model, naturally, with electric lighting, for nothing but the best would do for Mrs James Osborne.

A Bullnose Oxford, Mara explained proudly to Elizabeth when her sister-in-law came to call, and the two women moved round the automobile where it was parked in the yard since nothing would suit Mara but that every person in the household and every visitor must be shown, and admire, her new and novel toy. There were several ladies in the society in which Mara now moved who drove motor cars, certainly, after all this was 1914 and indeed there had been a Ladies' Handicap Race at Saltburn where a Mrs Wikey had come second. So why should not Mara who was considered quite a pace-setter do the same? Not that she had any wish to race, of course, but she had every intention of driving over to Edge Lane before the week was out, she confidently assured Elizabeth, and could see no reason why she should not motor down to London for the season, driving herself and anyone who cared to sit beside her. This last was not, naturally, said in her husband's hearing.

The annual migration of the upper classes to the capital city had already begun with the first large ball taking place in fashionable Mayfair on the first of May and with the return of their Majesties from Paris at the end of April the London season was now well under way. Mara had dozens of new outfits to wear – and meant to buy dozens more – made to fit every conceivable occasion from breakfast until past midnight and was eager to show them off to London society. The house in Belgravia which Johnny Osborne had rented was ready for them and Mara could not wait to begin the delights of what would be her first season, and the impression one would make arriving in one's own dazzling two-seater roadster would be a splendid start to the proceedings.

'Don't you think the colour's just grand?' she beseeched her sister-in-law breathlessly.

'Indeed I do and it is very appropriate.'

'Why? What d'you mean?'

'I was under the impression the Irish considered green to be their colour.'

'You're right, so you are. I hadn't thought of it.' Mara smiled delightedly. 'The Irish green, begorra, an' me choosing it without even thinking of it. That's a good omen, so it is, an' with a bit of owd shamrock to fasten to that round thing on the front of the ... the ...'

She turned to her husband who was on his knees examining the brightly painted spokes of the rear wheel. 'What d'you call it, James ...'

'The bonnet.' Without looking up James answered his wife and not for the first time Elizabeth wondered at the ... well, she could only call it telepathy which existed between James and Mara which meant that each appeared to know what was in the other's mind without the need to voice it. She supposed it came to all couples who lived together and who were bonded by a strong love, putting them in tune with one another's thoughts and feelings and even in the most mundane of conversations each was aware of what the other was thinking. It had happened to herself and Harry, but it had happened long before they were married, she remembered. Perhaps because they had been brought up in the same circumstances and with the same beliefs but Mara and James had been raised in completely different cultures and despite forecasts to the opposite had made a happy marriage.

'That's it, the bonnet, though why they should call it a bonnet is a mystery, sure it is. It looks nothing like a bonnet, but anyway, don't you think it's grand an' will you look at the windscreen. See, it can be raised to protect you from the wind and the hood goes up and down like the one on Christian's baby carriage.' She pressed the bright chrome horn, smiling at the sound which came from it since she meant to use it constantly to warn pedestrians, cyclists and other motorists to get out of the way of the hazardous Mara Osborne.

'Listen, darlin',' turning to face Elizabeth, her blue-green eyes snapping with excitement, 'why don't we learn to drive together, then you could borrow Harry's Austin while he takes the Vauxhall. Do say you will. Think of the fun we could have driving about together . . .'

'What, in two motor cars?' amused as always by Mara's lack of reticence and her belief that her enthusiasm should be shared by all and sundry.

Mara looked crestfallen for a moment, then refusing to be dismayed by Elizabeth's logic climbed nonchalantly into the motor car, placing herself behind the steering wheel and clutching at it as though she meant to be off down the drive this very moment. Elizabeth fully expected her to say 'brmm, brmm' just as her baby son did when his father sat him on his knee behind the steering wheel of his own little roadster. She honked the horn again, looking so like her fifteen-month-old Christian that Elizabeth laughed out loud.

'Don't fiddle with anything, Mara,' James implored his wife anxiously as she began to explore the many mysterious knobs and dials and levers on the vehicle's dashboard.

'Be careful, Mrs James,' Gibson, the Osbornes' chauffeur beseeched, since the splendid little machine was to be in his care and already he considered it his baby in the growing family of automobiles he maintained. There was Mr Osborne's Renault and Mr James' Austin and now this little beauty and really it was going to break his heart, he knew it already, to see a woman driving it.

'I wouldn't have to fiddle if one of you would get up here and show me what it all means,' Mara answered tartly, looking from one worried male face to the other. There were several grooms loitering admiringly at the gate which led into the stable-yard since young Mrs James was always worth seeing when she made up her mind to cut a dash which it seemed she was about to do at any moment.

'How do I start it?' she demanded to know, peering at the dashboard with furrowed brow and the stable lads nudged one another excitedly.

'Now then, Mrs James, don't you think you'd best get down an' let me put her away in't garage. Soon enough to be learnin' to drive when I've had a chance to look her over.' Gibson's voice had more than a hint of patronage in it and those who watched saw Mrs James' face take on that expression of mutiny they all knew so well.

'Don't talk daft, man. Sure an' it's as easy as kissin' the blarney stone so I'd be obliged if you'd get up here an' show me what to do.' Mara spoke with the mixture of Irish brogue and the cultured tone of privilege she had picked up in the three and a half years she had lived at Beechwood and which so charmed her new friends. She turned the steering wheel imperiously and was delighted when the two front wheels of the motor car turned with it, crunching on the gravel.

'Mrs James ... please ...'

'Now darling ...'

'Come on, Elizabeth, climb aboard and Gibson shall give us our first lesson.'

'Mara, you can't be serious.' Elizabeth, fascinated as she always was by her sister-in-law's confidence and enthusiasm, stepped back, shaking her head but she was laughing and there was an excited spark of interest in her own vivid green eyes. It would be fun to drive a motor car and with her mother no longer in control of her, indeed with no one to tell her what she must or must not do since Harry treated her as an intelligent adult who had the capacity to decide for herself how she was to spend her days, it would be a pleasant and very sophisticated means of getting about. She would have no need to wait for Harry to find time to take her into Liverpool or on an outing to wherever she had a fancy to go since with her own motor car, which she knew quite positively Harry would not deny her, she could go about independently, and whenever she liked.

'O'Shaughnessy will take you when mother isn't using him,' Harry had said but she had made excuses, saying she had no wish to interfere with the older Lady Woodall's arrangements. She could not tell him the real reason, of course. She could never tell him the real reason.

'I am serious. Holy Mother, if you don't get in, you and Gibson, then I'm off on me own.'

'You can't start it without cranking the startin' handle, madam,' Gibson told her severely. 'The engine won't fire else.'

'Well crank the thing then! Mother of God, have I to do everything meself.'

Gibson drove, of course, steering the smart little runabout down the long winding drive with Mara and Elizabeth crammed in beside him, both ladies hanging on to their smoothly arranged hair as the wind played havoc with their maids' handiwork. Of course, they would wear the proper hats and veils when the time came but they had not been prepared for this spontaneous adventure and both were bareheaded.

'Let me steer it, Gibson,' Mrs James commanded on the third circuit of the house. There were faces at every window, housemaids and footmen who had been told of the unprecedented excitement which was taking place outside. That young Mrs James was up to her usual shenanigans and with the absence of Eaton whose day off it was, they were

413

delighted with the chance to lighten their own drab day.

'What is it, Jennings?' Mrs Serena Osborne asked her maid. 'That is the third time that automobile has passed beneath my window. Who can it be? One of the boys, d'you think? Go and tell them to stop it at once. How can I rest with that dreadful noise going on.'

'It's Mrs James, madam,' her maid said from the window, 'going round and round.'

'Going round and round?'

'Yes madam, in her motor car.'

Serena shuddered. Dear Heaven, was she never to have any peace from that awful, awful girl? If it was not one escapade it was another and really, it was more than she could bear sometimes. It had been bad enough during that first year when her son's wife had been like some lovely, but quite hopelessly gauche spectre at every gathering Serena and her friends had shared, making one social gaffe after another but at least she had been quiet about it and biddable in her effort to please. Now she was a constant irritation and thorn in the side of her mother-in-law as she moved noisily about the place, voicing her dreadful Irish opinions, speaking in her awful Irish brogue and doing things Serena could hardly bear to contemplate. Driving a motor car now, if you please, and no doubt planning to cavort about the county for all to see and sneer at.

'Miss Elizabeth's with her,' Jennings said, somewhat slyly, Serena thought, well aware that her daughter was no longer under her control.

'Come away from that window at once. If you have nothing to do then perhaps you could see to the cleaning of my gloves ready for the season.'

'They are already done, madam.'

'Then do them again.'

'Yes madam.' With a last sighing look at the motor car in which Gibson, Miss Elizabeth – Lady Woodall now, of course

414

– and young Mrs James were perched like three birds on a fence, the maid moved reluctantly to her mistress' glove drawer.

'You can get down now, Gibson,' Mara commanded airily. 'I think I've got the hang of it. You sit beside me, Elizabeth . . .'

'Mrs James, please, you cannot possibly mean to drive it yourself?'

'Why not? I've watched you. In fact we both have, haven't we, Elizabeth, an' there doesn't seem a lot to it.'

'Please sir . . .' appealing to his master who, though not by a great deal, was more level headed than this wilful girl he had married. 'Mrs James hasn't a grasp o' steering yet, never mind t'gears. They're very . . . complex, sir, an' then there's the handbrake lever an' t'foot brake . . .'

'I agree Mara. Please get down at once. Until Gibson can find time to teach you I must insist that you don't touch the motor again.'

'Rubbish! I want to learn to drive an' so does Elizabeth, don't you, Elizabeth?'

'Well, I must say I find the idea quite thrilling.' Elizabeth held the door on the passenger side with one hand, smoothing back her hair with the other. The attractive little car had awakened a great exhilaration in her. Her eyes were bright and her cheeks had a flush of rose in them. She leaned over the side and breathed on the already highly polished chrome of the headlamp, rubbing it with the sleeve of her fine lawn dress, then turned back to Mara. She took a deep breath and her smile widened, telling Mara all she needed to know.

'There you are, James. We both want to learn.' Mara lifted her chin defiantly and the grim expression on Gibson's face which declared he would like nothing better than to tan her behind for her, aye, an' Miss Elizabeth's as well, became even grimmer. Spoiled rotten, Mrs James was, by this pleasant-faced, good-natured, softhearted boy who was her husband, and Miss Elizabeth egging her on in a way no lady should.

'We really would, James,' she was saying now, smiling in that way she had. Just like her mother she was, sometimes, though naturally Mrs Osborne would never want to take part in such an unladylike pastime. 'Gibson could teach us together, couldn't you, Gibson? I know you're busy with your duties but perhaps an hour or two each day...?'

'No, my lady, I'm sorry, but...'

Mara flounced down from the high seat of the Morris, her face quite unconcerned. She smoothed back her ruffled hair, pushing a wilful curl carelessly behind her ear. 'Never mind then, Gibson. We'll not be troubling you, not at all. Me brother'll teach the both of us on his day off which I believe is next Sunday so you can get back to whatever it is you do in the owd garage,' reducing Gibson's specialised mechanical training to nothing more than that of an oddjob boy. 'Come along, Elizabeth, get down,' she ordered and when Elizabeth did as she was told, fumbling with the door handle for longer than was necessary, she put her hand through her sister-in-law's rigid arm and drew her towards the side door of the house, beckoning her husband to follow. 'Give it a good wash an' polish, Gibson,' she added over her shoulder, 'for if we're to be off out in it on Sunday I want it to look its best. Glory be, won't Michael have a surprise, Elizabeth? Now come and have a cup of tea and then we'll go an' see the children. You should see the boy, walking all over the place he is and Claudine...'

The words Mara spoke were heard like the faint sounds of birds twittering in the trees at dusk as they settled for sleep. Muted and soft and barely audible above the roaring in Elizabeth's ears which threatened to deafen her, or send her running like a terrified child to the only safety she knew which was without doubt that of her husband's arms. Michael O'Shaughnessy did that to her, had done that to her for the past eleven months and even before that, she fully admitted. Oh God, why could she not hear his name, see his tall, light-footed figure striding across the stable-yard when she ventured there with Harry? Why could she not even think of him in the security and calm of the bedroom she and her husband shared, without being whirled about as though she was caught in some vast and emotional vortex? She had imagined that when she and Harry were married; when she belonged to him in that final and irrevocable way a woman belongs to a man; when her flesh had joined his in that sweet and fundamental joining from which there was no way back; when her virginal innocence had been taken from her by another man, Michael O'Shaughnessy and the unique hold he had on her would be shattered forever. She could not belong to one man, her mind had reasoned, and still think of another. She loved Harry and the truth of that was steadfast in her but the needs Michael had aroused in her, the . . . dear God, could she call it love, this thing which still turned her heart in her breast and fired the pit of her belly in her longing for what he had almost given her? Could she?

And why had Michael not gone when she had married Harry? Why had he not left Woodall Park and found himself another job? She had expected him to. She had expected, hoped, never to see him again but the remembrance of that July evening last year when she and Harry had stepped down from the railway carriage in Liverpool on their return from their honeymoon and found Michael there, ready to take their luggage, was still as clear as though it was yesterday. Smiling he was and touching his cap and wishing her good evening; calling her m'lady, which, strangely, Harry did not seem to think unusual considering she was Michael's sister-in-law The back of the brown neck, the familiar curling lift of his hair beneath his peaked cap, his firm, long-fingered grip on the steering wheel had caught her breath agonisingly and made her speechless and it had taken all her strength and her husband's concerned arms to get her out of the Vauxhall and up the wide staircase at Woodall to her new bedroom.

'Breeding, d'you think?' Lady Woodall had whispered to her daughter, her eyes gleaming hopefully, though surely it was a bit soon.

If only she and Harry could live elsewhere, Elizabeth had agonised on that first night in her new home, which of course they couldn't. If only Michael would leave, or Harry fire him, which of course he wouldn't since Michael had done nothing to warrant it. If only ... if only ... if only ...

She knew she clung to Harry more than she should have done in the weeks that followed, though Harry was patently delighted with her devotion and her surprising inclination to tempt him into their bed on every possible occasion.

'I love you, Harry, I love you, I love you. Come upstairs and make love to me,' she would whisper in his ear. Make me yours again and again. Put your mark on me, dominate me, subjugate my body with yours, she was really saying to him, make me forget him, bring me to a sobbing, clutching, binding climax of love in your arms, make me pregnant, and several weeks later she realised, in a sobbing wave of thankfulness, that he had.

Their son was born in March, exactly nine months after their wedding day, somewhat to Serena's dismay since it seemed inappropriate to be so fertile, so early in marriage. He was Charles James Woodall, a proper name in Serena's opinion, a son for the house of Woodall and Elizabeth whispered it to herself as she held the lustily yelling, angry scrap of humanity against her breast for the first time. He would be her protector against the hunter Michael O'Shaughnessy, she told herself thankfully. He had not yet been bathed, the birth smell of blood still on him and she knew that the midwife who hovered beside the bed thought her exceedingly strange as she breathed in the solid substance of him, her child; as she kissed the still damp whorls of brown hair on his tiny skull and took in her own the starfish hand which waved its fury against his mother's bent head.

Surely now, her mind beseeched, she would be safe from Michael O'Shaughnessy? She had a husband and a child and the man who still moved on the periphery of her life would no longer have the power to move her as he had done for so long. It had been many months since she had visited the stable since being pregnant she could no longer ride but she was also reluctant, she well knew, to let him see her carrying another man's child. She had won, slowly and painfully, some measure of peace in her husband's home and her child's nursery but now, dear God, now she had committed herself not only to seeing him in the distance and having him dwell on the edge of every conscious thought in her head, but also to being in his company, hearing him speak, seeing him smile, touching his hand, perhaps, having him touch her as he taught Mara and herself to drive.

'I don't think I care to learn to drive after all,' she told her husband the following Sunday morning. 'I have enough to do with Charles and really, do I need a motor car when I have you to drive me about?'

'Just as you like, my darling, but Mara will be very disappointed.'

'It will make no difference to Mara whether I learn to drive or not, Harry. You know Mara. If she has made up her mind to do something she will go ahead and do it no matter what anyone else does or says.'

'I suppose you are right, sweetheart. In the meanwhile if you are not to go with Mara why don't we go back to bed and continue what we were doing, and so delightfully too, I might add.'

They were taking their breakfast together in the privacy of their own sitting room, the sun lying in a golden stream across the peach velvet carpet Elizabeth herself had chosen. Harry sat back in his chair sighing his supreme content. His eyes were still warm and sensuously narrowed in contemplation of his lovely wife and the lovemaking they had recently enjoyed. In a little while they would both go to the nursery to see their baby son, to hold him and pet him, to kiss and comfort him should he need it, even to bathe him if Harry could persuade Nanny to allow it since he had meant what he said to his wife regarding the upbringing of his children. Charles was not to be pushed into the background of his parents' life, as he and his brothers and sister had been, but was to be included, with any brothers and sisters he might have, in its loving heart.

He was smiling when the knock came to the door and when he heard it he moaned in dramatic laughter.

'And there was I imagining I was to take you back to bed and repeat that delightful experience you and I have just shared. Tell whoever it is that your husband has a fever and must have complete bed rest .. '

Elizabeth was still laughing as she opened the door. It was Mara.

'Jesus, Joseph and Mary! Are you not dressed yet?' she said, walking boldly into the sitting room, smiling broadly, ready to wink at Harry, sharing the intimacy of Harry's bathrobe and Elizabeth's own negligee of quite indecent transparency. 'Faith, an' there's meself so excited I couldn't sleep a wink. Michael's already been over to Beechwood to fetch the Morris and me in it and he's sitting out on the drive at this very minute waiting for us. Thanks, Harry, I'll have a cup of coffee while I wait for Elizabeth. Elizabeth, faith an' begorra, what ails you, girl? Get your clothes on and stop hanging about with your mouth open. Ten minutes, no more, mind. Put your tweed walking skirt on, Michael says, for it'll be cold in the motor, oh, and a veil for your hat.'

She smiled in excited anticipation, a child about to be off on a much longed-for treat, her eyes brilliant in her rosy face. She wore the new motoring outfit she had bought during the week in readiness for this splendid day. A holland dustcoat and what Mara considered a sensible hat which was far from suitable though very fetching despite the substantial veil which draped from it, and in her hand was a pair of goggles over which she was ready to laugh with her good-natured brother-in-law.

Elizabeth felt the carpet beneath her feet shift a little and her body was instantly moist with perspiration. She felt cold and queasy at the same time and her voice trembled as she spoke.

'Oh no, I cannot manage it, Mara, not today. I'm sorry but Harry and I haven't been to see Charles yet and then I have to ... I have to ...' She turned desperately to Harry who was trying on Mara's goggles and not looking at his wife at all so he missed the agitated appeal on her face. And it was doubtful that if he had seen it he would have understood.

'Harry ...' she went on despairingly. 'Harry and I have to ...'

He turned to her then, his expression somewhat bemused, no help at all to her, she could see and somehow she must think of a logical excuse, one which Mara would accept as to why she could not sit beside Mara's brother on this day or any other.

'We have to ... what was it, Harry ...?' and as she swayed towards him he closed one eye on the suggestion of a wink, endearingly, infuriatingly, since he thought she was referring to his suggestion that they should return to bed.

'Well my darling, whatever it was,' grinning, 'I'm sure it can wait until later and so can Charlie, for once. Mara has a prior claim on you so go and get dressed. I shall manage somehow without you. I shall look at the estate accounts until you get back ...'

'Harry, let me help you then.' Her cry was desperate and both Harry and Mara looked at her in astonishment.

'With the accounts, Elizabeth?' He was clearly puzzled and she knew she must go no further or his mind which until now had put its own interpretation on her reluctance to leave him might begin to probe more deeply and wonder. Neither he nor Mara must have the slightest suspicion that the reason for it might be Mara's brother.

She laughed, her voice still somewhat inclined to shrillness. 'Of course, how silly of me. I promised myself, and Mara, that I would learn to drive and so I shall,' and in the shortest time possible, her panic-stricken mind told her. One lesson, this one and then no matter what anybody said to the contrary she would declare herself ready to drive her own motor car, or perhaps Harry's little Austin. Just this once she would sit next to Michael O'Shaughnessy and only because, without creating a fuss, she could not avoid it. She would listen earnestly to what he said with the care of the most ardent student, then she would walk away from him and never come into his orbit again. It would be difficult, she was well aware, but it could be done if she was careful. She had no need to go near the garage or the yard where the motor cars were parked and cleaned and she could order the vehicle, when she could drive it, to be brought to the front of the house from where she could drive it away. It could be done, she told herself feverishly as she pulled on the sensible tweed skirt she had been advised to wear. Her blouse was neat and modest and the hat she chose was one she had bought and never worn. It was a velvet toque, high and unbecoming with her mass of hair pushed severely up beneath it. It had a hard line and she had thought it smart when she had tried it on at the milliners but now she knew it made her seem older than she was. All to the good, she told herself as she and Mara moved out of the side door of Woodall and into the sunshine where Michael waited.

He had his back to her. He was running a chamois leather over the already gleaming bonnet of the Morris, breathing on the surface and then buffing it to an even greater shine. Without knowing how she knew she was instantly aware that he was as afraid as she was and that his apparent preoccupation with the machine was merely to give the appearance of calm unconcern. Hers and Mara's boots crunched on the raked gravel and she saw him tense at the sound and when he turned the brilliance of his blue-green eyes and the expression she saw there struck her a blow in the chest which almost had her reeling. She could feel the shock of it spin round and round as it reached her head and she knew a moment's desperate need to put a hand on Mara's arm to steady herself. Her footsteps quickened as she was drawn towards him by a force she could not control, fascinated by the brown smoothness of his freshly shaved face, with the taut vigour and supple grace of his tall body. Her heart began to knock frantically and her mouth was so dry she could barely answer his polite greeting.

'Good morning, m'lady,' he said impersonally, though the tension which stretched at once to breaking point between them would have been obvious to anyone less self-absorbed than his sister. They looked at one another across the barrier of her marriage to Sir Harry Woodall and the birth of her son and they were both immediately aware that it was just the same. That nothing had changed. He was older. His young frame had filled out and he was a man now, broad-shouldered, deep-chested. His face had matured, the expression on it harder, harsher, less whimsical than once it had been and it was because of her, her instincts told her. He still loved her. He made no attempt to disguise it and he knew she loved him, and though the knowledge that another man had taken what was rightfully his and had implanted his seed in her was bitter in him, souring a certain sweetness that had been his, it made no difference. He could not now be first – and had he been first he would also have been last, his expression told her – but one day she would be his, in some way, make no mistake. Did she understand, did she? and her eyes told him that she did. She'd fight him. She would defend herself and her marriage, the son who was the result of it, but she understood the strength and endurance of what she and this man shared.

It took no more than ten seconds, less, this silent

exchange between them but it seemed an eternity. Mara spoke, her words dropping into the vacuum into which they had fallen, shattering its dreadful silence.

'Holy Mother, if you're to call your own sister-in-law by her title, Michael then we might as well turn round and go inside. She's Elizabeth to you, so she is, aren't you, darlin'?' squeezing Elizabeth's arm. 'Now then, who's to be first at the wheel, meself or Elizabeth?' and without waiting for a reply she climbed confidently into the automobile and placed herself behind the steering wheel.

Just for a second they looked deeply, honestly into one another's eyes, acknowledging what was there for had it not always been so between them, then he smiled at her, with her, though he spoke to Mara.

'And shouldn't I have known it'd be yourself, Mara O'Shaughnessy. Now move over an' make room for ... Elizabeth,' Elizabeth, oh my Elizabeth, 'and I'll do the driving, at least for the first five minutes, that's if yourself's no objection to it.'

It was so easy and it was Harry himself who made it that way. What could be more sensible than the Woodall chauffeur giving his wife a further lesson or two, he asked her, in the technique of driving a motor car? The more practice she had the more competent a driver she would become and who better to develop her skills than O'Shaughnessy? So O'Shaughnessy went with Sir Harry and Lady Woodall to the motor show held at Olympia in London and helped her ladyship to pick the motor car of her choice. A Bullnose Morris, like Mara's, and offered then and there to sit beside her until she was accustomed to it. Sir Harry was of the opinion that his wife would benefit from it. After all, though she had shared the tuition Mara had received it would surely only be wise to have O'Shaughnessy's undivided attention without Mara's careless flippancy to distract her, a suggestion made by O'Shaughnessy but one with which Harry

424

entirely agreed. She was very precious to him, after all, and he would feel much happier if he knew she was gaining experience with the best possible teacher. No, he would not be distracted by the choice of Elizabeth's colour for her motor car. A serene pearl grey which, he supposed, she was telling him suited her nature and the manner in which she intended to drive, for the bright red spokes on the motor car's wheels revealed the dash of the rebel in her, or so her husband told her in the ardent, lamp-lit intimacy of their bed.

'But I can drive Mara's motor car, Harry,' she said breathlessly, still fighting Michael O'Shaughnessy's irresistible compulsion for her. 'I don't need another lesson, really I don't. You should see me rattling up the drive and I have even learned the complexities of double de-clutching. Now that I have my own vehicle I'm sure I shall be able to master it immediately and there will be no need to bother the chauffeur –' *the chauffeur* – 'any further.' The words, spoken with the chilling impersonality with which their class addressed their servants, almost stuck in her throat but Harry was absorbed with the full perfection of her breasts and the sweet taste of her nipples in his mouth and did not hear her falter. 'And if you think I need an hour or so to get used to the controls then I will practise on the drive with you beside me, darling. Oh, please say you will, please.'

'Let's not talk about motor cars at this precise moment, my love. I have things on my mind other than double de-clutching so why don't you . . .'

'Harry, listen to me. The motor will be here tomorrow and I must get this settled, really I must.'

'Get what settled?' smoothing the still slightly rounded satin skin of her white stomach and the delicious mound of the silky hair at its base.

'The motor car.'

Harry sat up. He was becoming increasingly impatient with his wife's obsession with the damn motor car and the

425

matter of her learning to drive the thing. He loved her so much he wanted her to have exactly what she desired from life, just as she had given him everything he wanted from life. If he had been of that turn of mind he would have been inclined to go down on his knees each night and give thanks to God that she had chosen to love Harry Woodall. She was his heart, his soul, the very sum and substance of what he believed in most. She had fitted into his life with the perfect ease of their shared upbringing. She had brought a richness to his days and an enchantment to his nights but he did wish she would choose some other time to talk about this matter of O'Shaughnessy and the motor car.

'My darling girl, you shall drive your abominable machine wherever and whenever you like, within reason of course, since I could not bear to part with you for more than an hour at the most,' smiling, kissing the white shoulder she presented to him, 'but I would feel happier if you would allow O'Shaughnessy to sit beside you until you are accustomed to the feel of the new motor car. Humour me, my darling. You are very precious to me and O'Shaughnessy is a very experienced driver. Now then, lie back and turn into the light so that I can see . . .'

They drove through the splendid wrought-iron gates of Woodall Park, returning Tommy Perk's salute as he ran from the lodge to open them. She was at the wheel, her feet dealing smartly with brake pedal, clutch and accelerator. They did not speak as she turned right towards Tibbs Head. The automobile ran smoothly across the same railway line that Michael had skimmed over on his bicycle so long ago and when he ordered her to turn left she did so without question since he was the instructor. They passed Rainhill Cottage and on down the grass edged track towards Colton Wood. There was a gate which he got down to open, indicating the direction he wished her to take which told them both what they already knew, that she really needed no further driving lessons. She guided the vehicle into the sheltered peace of a smooth clearing at the edge of the wood.

She sighed as she switched off the engine, a sigh of resignation, it seemed. A sigh which said that what had happened, what was to happen, was inevitable. They sat for several minutes, their shoulders almost touching, the sounds of the unseen creatures of the trees and the undergrowth which had ceased at their approach beginning to stir again. The leaves lifted in a haze of pale green smoke as the breeze moved them on the branches, new and lively, and on the far side of the wood in the Woodall paddock a mare whinnied for her foal. Sunshine slipped easily through the network of new summer growth on the trees, touching the sliding waters of the stream to their right, the one in which James Osborne had first seen Mara O'Shaughnessy. A great bed of yellow iris glowed as bright as the sun itself beside it.

It was as though they dare not look at one another so great was the magnetism which had drawn them together again. What might a glance generate if they were to chance it? they seemed to be asking one another in the deep silence. He fumbled in his pocket and brought out a packet of cigarettes, offering it to her. Though she did not smoke she took one, watching in a fascinated, dream-like state as his hands went about the business of withdrawing the cigarettes, the striking of the match, cupping it for a moment in the palms of his hands before putting it to her cigarette which she had placed between her lips. She bent her head to it and when she looked up to blow out the smoke his eyes were on her. They were narrowed and in them was an expression of waiting. The match burned his fingers and with a muffled oath he shook it out without lighting his own cigarette and tossed it into the damp grass beside the car.

'Elizabeth.' His voice was harsh. 'Now that I have you here to listen to what I must say, I don't know what it is. I've had the words in me head for months, so I have, all very neat and just right to tell you what is in me an' now they're all gone. Sure an' whoever heard of an Irishman with nothing to say?' He tried valiantly to lighten his voice but there was heartbreak in it.

She clung to her self-control, drawing on her cigarette, meaning to be calm, to be dispassionate for she knew she must tell him to leave Woodall Park, and her. To get out of her life, to make one of his own. To find a new job, a new place, a new love ... oh Dear God ... That was why she was here, wasn't it? Wasn't it? The cigarette smoke caught in her throat and she began to cough and with a deft movement he took it between his fingers and threw it after the match.

'But what is there to say now,' he went on vaguely, 'that would make any difference? I was hoping you would change your mind about the driving and not come, but Mother of God, hoping has nothing at all to do with wanting, d'you see? I can't seem to see beyond you but I must. We have to come to some ... some end, some conclusion. Don't you see, Elizabeth, if things don't ... finish they go on and on, never ending ... hurting forever. Beginnings need endings an' somehow I have to get you out of my way for I can't go on unless I do. I have to find out what I mean to you but I think I know since you'd not come out with me ... rashly, would you?'

'No.' Her voice was low and clear as she spoke for the first time. 'But I think it would be best if I turned the motor round and went home. I have a husband and child waiting for me there.'

'Dear Christ ... d'you know how that ... crucifies me ... but you're right. Even so I'm not going to let you,' and turning he pulled her roughly into his arms.

'Michael ...'

'Tell me to stop, then.' His eyes were an inch from hers, narrowed slivers of fierce blue in his sun-darkened face.

'Michael ... Michael, I love my husband.'

'Do you so, like this ... like this ...?' and his mouth

came down hard on hers with the hot, sweet passion which instantly lit the fire in her she remembered so vividly. Their lips clung and could not part and he pulled her closer to him. With one hand he held her at the back of her neck, his fingers moving in a desperate caress and when the other moved to the buttons of her lightweight shirt she could hardly wait to feel it against her naked, willing flesh. Her breasts lifted joyfully as her body responded to his touch, then suddenly she was awkward, sharp, bitter even for it seemed this man was about to force on her a situation she really had no wish to resist and she hated him for it.

'Don't ' Her hands went to his, pushing them away. 'Don't make me '

'Make you, Elizabeth?' His breath was ragged, his voice rough 'You want me as much as I want you and what else have we, you and I? What else can we have but this, Lady Woodall. This is like one of them grand books the ladies read, so it is. Only it's usually the footman . . .'

'Michael, stop it, stop it ' Her face was suddenly, surprisingly, wet with tears as she began to weep harshly. 'Can't you see that it won't do, none of it ..'

'Why did you come then?'

'I had no choice '

'No choice, is it? Your your husband forced you, is that it? Jesus, Joseph and Mary, he must be blind, out of his bloody mind to let you out of his sight. I wouldn't if you were mine '

'He trusts me.' She could not stop her desolate weeping for she felt as though her heart, her very flesh was being clawed in sheer physical anguish. Harry, her shield and protector, had sent her out defenceless and vulnerable and now she, and him, were threatened, their marriage, the future peace of their child, their life as a family was threatened unless she could get herself away from this danger Harry's concern for her safety had placed her in. She had known it would be like this, of course she had and yet she had still come, irresistibly drawn here by this man who had fascinated her for nearly five years and it was up to her, not Michael, who had nothing to lose but his job, to get herself out of it.

'Don't ... my lovely girl, don't cry,' he said, his voice shaking. 'Oh my darling, I can't think straight ... what in hell's name am I to do ...?'

'Go away, Michael ... please ...' and she turned her back on him, repudiating him, hurting him badly, she knew. She hunched herself up against the door and her shoulders shook.

'For good, you mean?' he asked her harshly.

'Yes.'

'I can't do that, Elizabeth. I can't get away from you. I told you, I must get rid of it, this ... what I have for you, but faith, I don't know how ...' His breath shuddered in his throat. His brow was furrowed as though the bewilderment of finding Michael O'Shaughnessy in such a state was beyond his comprehension. 'Sure an' if I knew how to do it, don't you think I would? This is not just an ... adventure, Elizabeth, you know that, don't you?'

'Yes.' Her voice was muffled but she sat up and turned to him, ready to believe from the calmness of his voice that he was going to let her go. Not physically since she knew he was not holding her here against her will, but emotionally. That he was willing to let her escape from his heart, that he was prepared to give back to her what he had taken in that first moment in the stable-yard at Woodall Park. Her peace of mind!

'Shall we say goodbye then, darlin'?' His face was harrowed by the pain, and yes, the fury of it.

'I think we must,' and hers was the same.

'Well then, kiss me for the ... last time.'

'I think it would be best if I didn't.' The tears fell, washing across her face and dripping in a torrent to the crisp cotton of her shirt. Her face was contorted and she moaned softly in the depth of her, an animal moan of sheer pain.

'What a bloody waste,' he said, tormented by her grief, and his own. 'What a sheer bloody waste.'

'No ... never ...' and without meaning to she put her hand tenderly on his cheek. He turned his mouth into it, his lips warm and parted in her palm, lingering there before moving, dreamlike, to the pulse in her wrist. They each meant to do no more than retain the feel, the touch; to carry the memory of whatever it was that had always drawn them together, to take it away with them to cherish when the days apart, the months and years apart became drab, or wearisome, but it was too late. Really, had it not always been too late as, with a soft cry of love, she fell against him and his arms rose to take her.

23

They all went to Cottingham in July, the Osbornes and the Woodalls. It was speech day at the school where James and Harry, Hugh and Tim Woodall had been educated and where seventeen-year-old Teddy Osborne was in his last year but one.

It was very hot, a Saturday, and the headmaster's lawn was clustered thickly with parents, friends, boys old and present. There were flowers everywhere, not just in the massed flower beds but on the ladies' wide-brimmed hats. The Officers Training Corps, sponsored by the War Office and joined voluntarily by almost every boy in the school except those who were not physically up to it, had marched hither and yon, showing off their smart paces and somewhat ill-fitting uniforms to their admiring families. Teddy, as his house's senior NCO had paraded his 'men', dismissed them and had joined the family party. He was handsome and boyish and very conscious of his own appearance amongst the sea of straw boaters and striped blazers, amongst the silk hats and sunshine, the gowns of muslin and chiffon and lace, the parasols and white kid boots, and the strawberries which were the ritual of every speech day.

The London season had been a busy one but very gay, filled with parties and balls, visits to Covent Garden to see the Imperial Ballet and Opera Company. *Boris Godunov, Le Coq d'Or* and the magnificence of *Legende de Joseph* with the new and riveting star, Leonide Massine. There were visits to the theatre to see *The Passing Show*, the outstanding success of the year; *The Dangerous Age*, modern and very daring; Oscar Wilde's *An Ideal Husband*; Shaw's *Pygmalion*, which Serena had said from the first would not be suitable since the word 'bloody' was actually displayed for all to see in the advertisement outside the theatre.

They had motored to Ascot, gaining admission to the hallowed Royal Enclosure, a luncheon hamper made up by Fortnum and Mason in the boot of the older Lady Woodall's Rolls. It had been cold on the first day of the meeting and the ladies wore their furs, sable and mink and chinchilla looking somewhat strange over their light and summery dresses. They drove to Epsom Downs for the splendid spectacle of the Derby, a record crowd of nearly four hundred thousand accompanying them. The traffic jams were horrendous, with motor omnibuses jostling for position amongst the Rolls-Royces, the Mercedes and Daimlers, the irritation of it somewhat mitigated for Serena by the honour of standing almost shoulder to shoulder with the frock coated figure of the King and his Queen who wore an ermine mantle. Johnny had placed a bet, only small since Serena did not approve of heavy gambling, and had won at twenty to one on the outsider Durbar the Second.

Then there was the Henley Regatta, the banks of the river jammed with punts and small bobbing boats in the lee of gaily decorated houseboats. Again there were flower-bedecked hats and smart boaters, blazers and parasols, the water sparkling like wine in the sunshine, laughter over strawberries and cream. The naval and military show at Olympia, the Hendon Aviation meeting, the Chelsea Flower Show and the Court Ball at Buckingham Palace where there were two thousand guests, amongst them Mr and Mrs Johnny Osborne, their son James and his dashing Irish wife who was heard to declare at frequent intervals that the Mammy would never believe this, never in a million years. Accompanying them were Lady Anne Woodall, with her son and daughter-in-law, the vibrantly beautiful Elizabeth who had once been an Osborne herself.

There was only one flaw to mar the otherwise magnificent splendour of the 1914 London season, the sense of eternal well-being which polished the golden days; the rich and endless contentment those who enjoyed it felt they were perfectly entitled to, and that was the silly – Serena was sure of it – talk of war, for Heaven's sake. It was said, by whom she was not awfully sure, that the Germans were determined on it. The financial market showed it, a stockbroker friend of Johnny's told him, adding that Germany had been amassing gold for months and that the gold reserve in the Reichsbank was at a record level. Germany had collected almost every debt that was owing to her from other countries, leaving her debts to them outstanding and the reasons for that were obvious.

Serena was not awfully sure she understood since it was not obvious to her and when, on June 28 the Archduke Francis Ferdinand, heir apparent to the crown of Austria and Hungary was murdered by some unknown Serb in the Bosnian capital of Sarajevo, the furore it caused was a mystery to her. Why should it concern them, she asked Johnny? She was getting ready to go to the theatre at the time, trying to decide whether her pearls or her rubies looked best on the dark wine-red gown she was to wear and Johnny's somewhat vague explanation that the Archduke's murder would be an excuse for the Austrians to attack the Serbs, with Germany's approval, was of no great interest to her. Her main concern was that the Court Ball, due to be held on the 29th, was, because of the crisis, to be postponed until July. So inconvenient when one had made arrangements to find they were all to be changed.

The season drew to a close. Everyone was whistling or singing 'Hello, hello, who's your lady friend?' Everyone except the Woodall chauffeur, that is, as he supervised the loading of the Woodall ladies' heavy boxes and trunks on to the wagon which would deliver them to the railway station from where they would travel by train to Liverpool. The three ladies would motor home, staying overnight at the small and exclusive hotel in Market Harborough used by the family whenever they undertook the long and wearying journey from London to Lancashire. Three smaller suitcases containing what the ladies would need for an overnight stay were packed into the capacious boot of the gleaming Rolls-Royce which awaited them at the front of the elegant town house in Kensington which Lady Woodall rented for the season.

Lady Woodall's daughter Sophie, almost twenty now, had just completed her second season and it was rumoured in the servants' hall that, having been paraded in the marriage market once again she had been – in their parlance – 'spoken for' by a young man of impeccable breeding and enough wealth to make him acceptable to the Woodall family; the second son of a baronet who would, unfortunately, not have a title but who, nevertheless, was perfectly suitable for Miss Sophie Woodall. A wedding next spring, they were saying, their lives, and hers, to dependably run on as they had always done. The assassination at Sarajevo meant little to them, or indeed to many of the working class, a remote event which, if it was to affect their country, would not be dealt with by the likes of them. All this talk of growing conflict, of a predestined disaster was so much claptrap and would all be smoothed over, after all the Kaiser was some sort of relative to their own King George, wasn't he?

Their two ladyships and Miss Woodall stepped into the Rolls-Royce at precisely eleven o'clock that morning. The older Lady Woodall nodded pleasantly to the chauffeur who held the door open for her, as did Miss Woodall but an observer might have noticed that Lady Elizabeth appeared to avert her head, hurrying so quickly into the back of the motor she almost missed her footing.

'Careful, m'lady,' the chauffeur murmured politely, putting out a sun-browned hand to steady her but she chose to ignore it, indeed seemed to flinch away from it though it was noticed by no one but himself. His face was without expression, granite-like in its rigidity but about his mouth a white line appeared as he closed the door behind her.

The traffic was heavy as they edged out of the secluded square in which the house was situated. The wide avenue they entered was crammed with horse-drawn carriages, wagons, motor omnibuses, their passengers on the open top deck sweltering in the late July heat. It had been a glorious summer, or so those who did not have to work in it said, the hot sun pouring its golden blessing down from a high blue sky, day after perfect day. It was time they got out of London, the older Lady Woodall remarked, for it had become far too sultry for her taste. It would be very pleasant to return to the cool country breezes which blew from the river and across the new farmland to Woodall Park; to get away from all this, indicating the darting figures of errand boys and postmen, of bowler hatted businessmen, white coated delivery men on grocers' carts, all mingling in what looked like a mad confusion in the dust-laden heat. There were horse-drawn trams and horse-drawn hackney cabs which had survived into this new fourteen-year-old century, for though it was said that there were 132,000 motor cars

435

on the roads they were owned by the small minority of the wealthy and privileged.

It was almost five o'clock when the Rolls reached the hotel, gliding up the neatly gravelled driveway which was shaded by the blessed relief of century-old oak trees, pulling to a smooth stop at the wide front door. There was a small flurry of efficient welcome for the three ladies who would, naturally, take the three best rooms in the hotel but no, Lady Woodall thought a private sitting room would not be necessary, didn't Elizabeth and Sophie agree? The last time they had stayed here she had been recently widowed and had not wished to offer herself to the public's curious gaze but tonight she thought it would be rather pleasant to dine in the hotel's dining room. It was very exclusive, of course, and since it was becoming increasingly fashionable to dine out, in fact it was considered very sophisticated to do so and having come straight from the London season where such things were accepted, were even commonplace, she and her daughter and daughter-in-law would like to dine at about eight o'clock.

The food was excellent and the service superb though it was noticed that young Lady Woodall was inclined to pick at the dishes put before her. She sipped her wine with an air of distraction and when spoken to jumped quite visibly.

'Are you not well, my dear?' her mother-in-law asked her.

'I am rather tired. I think I will have an early night. I am longing to be away early in the morning. It is almost six weeks since I saw Charles, you know, and Harry, of course.' She made an effort to smile and into Lady Woodall's mind slipped the pleasing thought that perhaps there was to be another child in the nursery before the year was out.

Elizabeth lay in the dark, her eyes wide open, so widely stretched apart she felt she would never get them to close again. Sleep was impossible as it had been except for the sudden and total snatches of insensibility into which she had now and then fallen ever since the day in Colton Wood when Michael had made love to her with a savage passion, a luminous joy, an enchantment she had not known existed. Even now, seven weeks later, she still felt the hot longing for him stir in the pit of her belly and her nipples immediately hardened. Her breath quickened as the memory of that warm afternoon drenched her wretched body. She had known nothing like it, nothing, not in all the months she had been wife to Harry Woodall. Michael had possessed her, burned her with a pure sensuality, drowned her in physical pleasure until at the end of an hour she had been limp, bruised and exhausted. Her body had been submissive to his, satiated, with nothing left for her husband.

He had looked at her then, turning her naked body this way and that on the soft woodland carpet, studying the way the sunlight fell on her white skin, turning it to gold and amber, raising her arms above her head, sighing over the lift of her proud breasts and the fine line of her graceful neck and back. She herself had outlined with a questing delicate finger the hard muscles of his shoulders and chest, the fine scattering of black hair which ran down his flat stomach, the smiling tilt of his strong mouth until he lifted her again on to his flaunting manhood, both of them experiencing again an explosion of male and female joy which was more than that of the body, or even of the heart. It was the identity of two spirits merging into one.

Now she turned her face violently into her pillow, afraid that she might be unable to stifle the moan of sheer need which trembled in her chest and throat. She was hot and damp with sweat. Her fine nightgown was plastered to her body and abruptly she sat up and pulled it over her head, tossing it to the floor.

Michael, Michael, Michael. Her heart and pulse beat in a two-part rhythm, thudding in her chest and temple and at her wrists and she felt she wanted to drum her heels on the bed in frustrated anger. What was the matter with her, for God's sake? She had made her decision in that long anguished night seven weeks ago when she lay in the dark next to her peacefully sleeping husband. Harry had made love to her with a sweetness, a tenderness, a gentleness which Michael O'Shaughnessy had not shown several hours earlier and the experience had been a bitter one. No matter what Michael had done to her, no matter how he tried to convince her to the contrary, she knew she loved Harry. But why did Harry's lovemaking not match the opened flood gate of glory which had swept her away with Michael, and why, oh dear sweet Jesus, why did she still long for her mother-in-law's chauffeur with a passion which was making her ill? She had lost weight. She could barely force herself to eat and if she did not pick herself up and get on with her life soon someone, Harry for one, would begin to notice.

Michael had tried to see her, to corner her in the stable-yard, to follow her when she went out in her motor car, even to send her a dangerous note – again – by the hand of a young gardener's lad but not once since that day had she been alone with him. He had terrified her with the determination of his onslaught and she was desperately afraid by the look on his face today as he handed her into the Rolls that he would not stand it much longer. He would do something insane, try to speak to her when others were present or even in the mad savagery of his pain and need, speak to Harry, tell him he loved his wife and that he believed she loved him. He was ready to do anything, say anything in his despair. He had been triumphant on that day in Colton Wood, making her his again and again, bringing her to orgasm again and again until her brain was dizzy and she had been mad with delight and ready to promise him anything if only he would not leave her.

And afterwards, as she allowed him to button her into her clothes, smooth back her tangle of hair and even laughingly tie the ribbon which held it she had known in her stony heart that this was the first and last time she would ever make love with Michael O'Shaughnessy. She had let him drive her back since she did not trust herself to control the long trembling of her body, listening to his jubilant hopes for their next meeting.

'Sweetheart, we must make our plans for the future. You must see that now. I love you and by God, you've proved you love me. Not that I didn't know it before but now ... now you're mine, really mine and soon ...'

His voice had been a song, a lilting Irish melody of love and hope and sweetness but she had closed her ears to it and run from the motor car the moment he pulled up in the yard as though the devil himself was cajoling her.

She heard a clock strike somewhere but could not count how many times. She turned her head on the pillow to try to hear the sound better and against the moon-dappled light of the open window there was the shadow of a man. Her heart leaped in her breast, a leap of initial fear, then gladness, followed by despair. She could see no more than his head and shoulders as he hauled himself over the window sill but even in the silvered dark she knew who it was, and really, could she pretend surprise? Had she really believed that at the first opportunity which presented itself to him he would not come to her, had she, and the answer almost made her laugh.

He was not aware that she was awake and she could sense his stealth and wariness. He listened for perhaps thirty seconds before he began to cross the room towards her.

She startled him when she spoke.

'It makes no difference what you say or what you do. I cannot leave Harry, nor do I want to.' Her voice was cold, falling into the warm darkness like a sliver of ice.

After a moment's hesitation he continued to move towards her. She could smell him. Tobacco and the familiar clean tang of the soap he used, nothing more since he was not a man to employ cologne or the scented shaving soap of a gentleman. He could see her now, her dark hair spread in wild disorder on the white, lace-trimmed pillow informing him as nothing else could of her state of mind and restless lack of sleep. He was acutely aware of the depth of her eyes, the outline of her mouth and her naked arms and shoulders above the tumbled sheet. As though she had not spoken he put out a hand and touched her cheek, a fleeting caress which moved, featherlike, along her jawline, down the pure column of her throat to her shoulder and though her heart was in agony she savagely knocked it away.

'Don't touch me again, not ever again. Once I was weak and allowed it, but not again.' She sat up, holding the sheet about her naked body and hitched away from him, leaning defensively against the bedhead and at once he swayed away from her, holding his hands up slightly as though to let her know he meant her no harm.

'I didn't realise that you had allowed it, Elizabeth.' His voice was cold and quiet. 'Faith, an' there was me believing it was something we both wanted. Are you saying I forced you?' but still he did not see the unsparing, pitiless resolution in her. He had only to talk to her as he had not been allowed for seven weeks, convince her of the rightness of what they must do, would do, and she would be as she had been then. She could see the conviction of it in his shadowed face.

'No ... no, of course not but I'm telling you it will not happen again and I would be obliged if you would leave my room the same way you came in and at once. I do not know why you think you have the right to come here ... no, I take that back, after what happened the last time we were together I suppose you do have some cause to imagine you would be welcome but you are not. That was a mistake and one I do not intend to repeat. Please leave me now.'

'You're talking rubbish, so you are. There can be no going back. You and me are bound now by what we did ...'

'Because we made love, you mean?'

'Yes ... oh yes, my darlin' girl ...' and he leaned towards

her yearningly, his face softened, his strong mouth curving in tender remembrance.

'I have made love to my husband dozens of times since, Michael O'Shaughnessy. Surely that gives him more right to me than you.'

If she had spat in his face he could not have been more shocked. She could see the gathering violence in him and for a moment was terribly afraid she had gone too far but she must not weaken now. She must not allow his agony and rage to divert her from the decision she had made no matter what fury his pain might unleash in him. It was as if she was his wife and had admitted adultery to him, so great was his bewilderment at the damage she was doing.

She saw his eyes close, a purely instinctive reflex to try to keep out the images her words had evoked and he groaned harshly.

'You bitch   shut your mouth, you bitch . . .' He rocked back on his heels, almost falling and without thought she put out a steadying hand, then withdrew it lest he see it as a sign of weakening but he had bent his head for a moment and did not see the gesture.

'Did you think that because you and I had . . . lain together Harry and I would stop being husband and wife?' she pressed on. Her voice was high and she even managed a laugh, watching with raw and bleeding nerves as he recoiled again. She had the feeling she was beating an already mortally wounded animal but she must make him believe that she loved Harry. And if she had any feelings for Michael O'Shaughnessy they were of a purely carnal sort. She was crucifying him, and herself, but *this must end*. She was Harry's wife. She had a child, Harry's child. She loved Harry and her son and there was nothing, ever, for Elizabeth Osborne and Michael O'Shaughnessy. If she could hurt him enough, convince him absolutely and without question, stop this vacillating she had engaged in for the past few years, let him go, then surely he would. Go and leave her in peace with Harry, find peace himself?

'I cannot bear to think about it,' he was muttering in a broken voice, 'so I turned me mind away. Holy Mother of God, the thought of you doing with him what we did is more than I can stand.'

She was gripped with an overwhelming need for haste, a desperate need to get this over before they were both destroyed by the pain.

'I am his wife. I have a life with him and our son. What else did you expect? You and I . . . I really don't know what came over me, after all, you are only my . . .'

His head shot up and even in the shadowed darkness she could see the malevolence in his eyes. His hands gripped her shoulders cruelly and he began to shake her. Her head lolled dizzyingly. Her hair moved in a swirling cloud about it, falling across her face and breasts which were revealed as the sheet fell away but his eyes were narrowed slits, too suffused with his rage to see her wild beauty.

'Your husband's bloody chauffeur, is that it?'

'Yes . . . something like that.'

'. . . who you amused yourself with. By God, I ought to wring your fine, ladylike neck for you, so I should . . .'

'Take your hands off me.'

'Sure an' you were glad enough to have them on you in Colton Woods. "Do it again, Michael," you begged me . . .'

'I was out of my mind. Now, let go of me or I shall ring that bell and call for the porter to . . .'

He let go of her suddenly with one hand, the other holding her steady as he struck her across the face. He was mindless in his male horror of what she was saying to him. What she was doing to him and his love for her, ready to break and smash her female body, the body he had loved and which, she had told him, he shared with Harry Woodall, her husband. He'd known that, of course he had, somewhere deep inside him where he did not allow himself to look but now she had dragged it out, forced him to see it and thrown what he had given her into the muck and slime and then stamped on it with contempt.

'You had better go,' she whispered, her hand to the imprint of his on her cheek.

'You're right, madam.' The menace in him was visible and deadly and he rose to his feet, backing away from her as though she was a cobra about to strike, or perhaps afraid of the damage he might inflict on her if he stayed. His bitter loathing of her froze her where she lay. Her breath caught in her chest. Her eyes were aching, desolate, tearless as they watched him stumble to the window but she managed one last flick of the whip with which she had flayed him.

'It might be best if you found another job,' she said carefully. 'My husband will give you a decent reference. You are a very good chauffeur and mechanic.'

'Holy Mother in Heaven,' he whispered, 'where did I get the idea you had a heart? You're your mother's daughter, aren't you? Exactly the same as all the rest of them. Nothing to do with your time but find amusement with a bit of rough. Discover if a common working man is the same inside his trousers as the gentlemen you're used to. Jesus . . . I thought you loved me. Sweet Christ, the most menial, uneducated lass in the land knows more about love than any lady of your class. I've loved you for years. Ever since I first saw you . . . no more than a schoolgirl . . . I've had no one but you in me eyes, or me heart, or here . . . deep in me guts . . .' striking his belly, 'but I shouldn't have wasted me time. You're not worth it though I must say you were the best . . .' here he used a word she had not heard before but whose meaning was very obvious '. . . I've ever had in me life. Sir Harry must be congratulated on his choice of woman, though bejasus her morals aren't much to speak of. So I'll have that reference when I get back to Woodall an' in case he doesn't appreciate what you've got there between your legs, m'lady, I'll give him one in return. In fact I've a mind to sample his goods once more before I take meself off. It'll be a long time before I find a woman who's as generous with her ... favours as you are, Lady Woodall.'

He drifted quite casually away from the window, with all the time in the world, it seemed, coming towards her with the graceful, cat-like tread she knew so well, a predator with its prey cornered and ready for the taking and she backed further against the headboard, clinging desperately to the sweat-soaked sheet, holding it to her naked body as though it would shield her from his attack. He was smiling lazily now, all signs of the distraught and wounded man gone and in its place was the insolent confidence of the male aggressor, one who is certain of his own worth and his own strength.

Deep inside her an explosion of excitement spread up from her belly and down her thighs and she knew she was ready to throw off the sheet, ready like any wanton to expose her naked body for the pleasure of this man whose words should have humiliated her, flayed her, and had not.

'Don't . ' she whispered, 'aah, don't ' for how could she stop him? How, when she did not want to?

'Don't, madam .. don't, you're saying?' he mocked her. 'Sure an' isn't that the very thing you've been wanting from me ever since you turned those pure and innocent eyes in my direction four years ago. Even then you lusted, Lady Woodall, an' even now you're ready to open those fine, well-bred legs of yours to me '

God help her it was true!

'And who am I to turn away from what's so delightfully offered me ...' and he pulled away the sheet and took hold of her ankles with so savage a grip she felt the skin of them scrape raw. He dragged her down in the bed, laying her flat for his own pleasure and already she had begun to moan and reach for him. He laughed triumphantly In a moment he had divested himself of the uniform which was a symbol of his servitude to this woman's husband, an equal to her now in his nakedness, then he was upon her, tearing into her with none of the sweet love, the strong and tender passion he had shown in the past. She clung to him as the only steady thing in a world filled with pain and glory, joy and a growing terror.

He did not kiss her, nor speak. When he had done he rose from her sweat-soaked body, dressed himself, then turned a last contemptuous look on her sprawled limbs.

'Don't bother to get up and see me out. Sure an' I wouldn't want to embarrass you.' He grinned mockingly, touching his finger jauntily to his tumbled hair then with a last insolent salute he climbed over the window sill and vanished from her sight.

She lay for an hour without moving, her body riveted to the bed, her eyes still on the window through which he had gone. A marble statue of unmoving, maimed beauty, her hair across her face, her limbs flung about, her eyes unblinking, hypnotised and made senseless by the pain which washed over and over her in fluent waves. She hurt so badly she was afraid to move in case it intensified but slowly, as the early summer dawn began to lighten the sky in the east, her female body moved itself into a sitting position and she began to rock. Stiffly she wrapped her arms about herself, whimpering and rocking and longing for the relief of tears but none would come. She was alone, without Michael, her mind would keep telling her, the lesser hurt of her abused body scarcely noticed. She had not realised before, when he had been *there*, that the knowledge of his presence though she had not seen him, the blanket of his love though they had been apart had been a sweet and comforting shelter in her life.

Now he was gone. She had sent him away and she was inconsolable. She must go somewhere and hide. Hide until she was healed. Get back to her own lair, her own shelter and lick her wounds, rest and recover from this dreadful emptiness, fill it ... with what? And take up ... what? She was drowning in the pain of it but worst of all was not her agony, but the agony she had inflicted on Michael. She had degraded him and he had returned it and what had shone clean and bright between them was tarnished because it was the only way to cut him loose from her.

She rocked back and forth, her eyes hot and dry but when, later, they came, respectfully, to tell Lady Woodall that it was time to rise, that breakfast was served and the motor car was waiting at the front of the hotel, she was composed and ready, ready with a sorry tale of how she had bumped into the bathroom door and hit her cheek against its frame.

They did not look at one another as she stepped into the Rolls. She even managed to make light small talk with Sophie and her mother-in-law on the journey home, averting her head from the back of Lady Woodall's chauffeur and when they drew up to the wide front door of Woodall Park she alighted and moved up the steps into her husband's arms with the shuddering thankfulness of a warrior returning from a battle which had only just been won.

'Would you believe it,' Harry said at dinner that night as he accepted a glass of wine from Wilson, 'O'Shaughnessy's given in his notice. He had no sooner put the motor away when he came into the estate office and said he was leaving. After all these years. Well, you can be sure I asked him why and where he was going, but he wouldn't, or couldn't say. Is it a question of money, I asked. He's a damned fine chauffeur and mechanic and I told him so but he only smiled and said he'd been told that quite recently. I shall be sorry to lose him. I told him that as well but he would not budge, nor would he accept a rise, he said. He'd like to go by the end of the week, he said, or sooner, if it could be arranged.'

Elizabeth lifted her fork to her mouth and placed a morsel of something in it. She had no idea what it was since it tasted of nothing she could recognise. Sawdust, perhaps, but then she had never eaten sawdust so how could she tell? Her mother-in-law sat, her mouth open in what she realised later was a most unladylike manner, spluttering in astonishment since O'Shaughnessy had said nothing to her and how was she to manage without a chauffeur? She had dozens of engagements in the next few weeks after being in London for so long and this was most inconvenient, and thoughtless of O'Shaughnessy and what on earth could be in his mind, had Harry any idea?

'Well,' Harry was thoughtful as he sipped his wine. 'I have an idea he may be going into the army.'

Elizabeth's hand jerked and the fork she held clattered against the plate. She did not speak, though, and no one appeared to notice since they were all, servants included, staring in bewilderment at her husband.

'Why on earth should he do that?' and the servants seemed to press closer since they were agog to hear about this unprecedented behaviour of O'Shaughnessy's.

Harry sighed and then looked up, first at his mother, then his brothers who, with himself, might be the most affected by it, his sister, and finally his beloved wife from whose white face enormous eyes stared at him. She would know of course what he meant, since she, unlike many ladies, read the newspapers. She was afraid for him. That is why she looked as she did.

'There will be a war, I'm afraid, though not, I hasten to add, of long standing,' since he did not wish to alarm them. 'The Germans are determined on it and . '

'War? Oh Dear God, no . His wife's voice was high and desolate and at once he stood up and moved round the table to her. Kneeling down, to his mother's embarrassment since she really did deplore this habit Harry had developed of demonstrating his affection for his wife in public, he put his arms about her and drew her tenderly to him.

'Darling, you must not upset yourself, really you must not . . .'

'Not war! Dear God, not war .. ' Her voice was muffled against his shoulder and he looked up at those about the table, his face perplexed. He was quite bewildered by this show of emotion on Elizabeth's part for though he knew she loved him he had not thought to see her so distraught when, as yet, war had not even been declared. It would not be long, those in high places knew, though he was aware that the average English family had no inkling of the danger. It was the last weekend in July and the headlines in the newspapers had screamed only this morning that 'Europe is Drifting to Disaster' and declaring that the country was 'On the Brink of War'. Had she not seen them, he wondered? Russia had ordered full mobilisation and here in Britain military personnel on leave had been recalled to their units. Even at Lords a cricket match had been halted when all reservists had to leave abruptly. Britain had pledged herself to support little Belgium whom the Germans threatened and unless intervention could be managed diplomatically, war was inevitable.

Elizabeth was weeping unrestrainedly now. Even the senior Lady Woodall was affected by her distress, standing up majestically to move to her daughter-in-law to pat her shoulder in sympathy. A young wife did not want to be parted from her husband so soon after marriage, she could well understand that, though it was not absolutely certain that Harry would go. But still, she should not carry on like this, particularly in front of the servants. It was really not the thing and the best course her son could take would be to lead her upstairs and do his best to get her pregnant again before he himself went off to fight the Germans which was what he had implied he was to do. Another child would take Elizabeth's mind off the parting.

On August 3rd the Belgian king telegraphed from Brussels to his fellow monarch King George V for assistance in this, his country's most desperate hour, but by then it was too late. Germany had declared war on Russia and the German army was poised to march on France and the quickest route to victory was through Belgium. On the night of

August 4th, having received no reply to her ultimatum that the German invasion troops be recalled from Belgium, Britain went to war with Germany.

When they heard the news the British people spilled into the streets of London and other major cities, a huge throng of men in straw boaters and women in flowery summer dresses and hats, good-natured and beside themselves with excited, optimistic patriotism. If the Germans wanted war, then by God they'd got it and those few men who were already in uniform found that their countrymen wanted nothing more than to queue up and shake their hand. Union Jacks waved and a huge mass of people moved up the Mall to the gates of Buckingham Palace. They were delighted when the King and Queen appeared to wave from the balcony, their subjects cheering the outbreak of war as though they were all to be off on a grand holiday. They were to go to war in a mood of great confidence and excitement and what a glorious affair it would be.

Up and down the main thoroughfares of towns all over the country bands marched, rousing the citizens, particularly the men, since a great many of them were needed to fight for their country, and in Liverpool it was the same as in hundreds of villages, towns and cities. There was a queue of men over two miles long in the Haymarket, eagerly pushing its way towards the recruiting office to take the King's shilling. The 3rd Battalion of the Lancashire Fusiliers recruited two O'Shaughnessys on that first day though it was not known that they were brothers since they did not take the oath together.

The rush was such that it took over a week to push through all the thousands who pressed there, for the worry to the would-be volunteer was that the war might be won before he got to it. It had happened so quickly, the common man told his neighbour. A week or two back it had been no more than a storm cloud on the European horizon and now it was a full blown hurricane and if it came so quickly might it not go the same way? Best be sure and enlist at once.

Harry Woodall was doing his best to fulfil his mother's hopes in those last few days before the war got into its stride. He had no idea what he was to do as yet in his country's defence though naturally whatever was required of him he would carry out but in the meanwhile – and not because his mother, privately, thought it expedient – he made love to his young wife with a desperate and loving passion which, had she been her normal self, she might have found alarming. It was as though he was unconsciously dedicated to the creating of life, the enduring constancy of the future and its generations which, though he would not have dreamed of saying so to Elizabeth, was suddenly so unsure. Men would die and sons would be born and the vital flame that was Harry Osborne would never be extinguished. His thoughts did not run in that precise way, of course, but what was the joining of his flesh with that of Elizabeth's if not that of life itself, of living?

She held him to her, her deep, almost maternal love enfolding him, her body receiving his time and time again, willingly and without shrinking though her heart and spirit were crushed with grieving for Michael O'Shaughnessy. Though Harry told her in an effort to take the white-edged pain from her face, which naturally he thought was on his account, that he would probably . well, most certainly be expected to fight for his country, as all decent, full-blooded Englishmen would, it would not be for long and, smiling whimsically, he would take great care of himself and she was not to worry.

She did not hear his words or if she did they made no impact on her since she was still deep in shock and later, when Harry had gone, she was to wonder at her own cruel insensibility. Why had her desolation over Michael blinded her to the equally frightening possibility of Harry leaving her, as Michael had done, and never returning?

And how was she to tell him she was pregnant again when she did not know if the child she carried was his or that of the man who had once been his chauffeur?

24

On an evening in August, along with Elsie Thompson and other members of the movement, Caitlin Templeton attended a women's meeting in London convened to show the women of the nation 'What War Would Mean'. Mrs Fawcett of the National Union of Women's Suffrage Societies was the main speaker. She told them, the hundreds of the rebellious and militant WSPU who were among them, that she was to offer the facilities of these societies, theirs included, if they agreed, to the embattled nation in its time of trial. They were veterans of violence and arson, weaned on prison and force-feeding but if for the time being they were prepared to turn their backs on it, support their men and the war effort, their sentences would be remitted since His Majesty was confident they would commit no further crimes of disorder.

'Well, that's that then,' Elsie said to Caitlin, 'at least until the war ends. Emmeline and Christabel are to join the recruiting drive and exhort the young men of the country to rise up and fight the "German Peril" but I don't know if that is quite my line.'

'What will you do then?'

They had walked from the hall where the meeting had been held along streets which still seethed with crowds whose mood of contagious excitement had not abated since the declaration of war. It seemed that everywhere you went young men were flocking in the direction of recruiting centres to join up and if they had not yet done so were being coaxed, or shamed into it by music hall stars such as Phyllis Dare with her sentimental and patriotic songs.

Nobody quite knew what was happening in the week following August 4th with every person one met rushing around in circles or wandering about in a daze, certain that one should be doing something but not awfully sure what it was. They only knew that what they were about to embark on was something of a patriotic crusade. The young men were affected by a feeling almost of exaltation and the young women could not help but feel left out of it, they complained. The young men, stepping out with their rifles – though they had not yet been given a uniform – some of them going each day to the training ground from their homes until they were called, found it splendid to have perfect strangers regarding them with admiration, young ladies smiling and bus drivers wishing them luck and refusing to take money for their fare.

Lord Kitchener, now Secretary of War, was to lead them into victory, an idol, the 'rock of the Empire' they called him as he made an appeal for 100,000 volunteers to increase the strength of the Regular Army. He had them, and more, before the month was out.

'Oh, we don't want to lose you but we think you ought to go,' sang Phyllis Dare, and go they did to the tented camps which were already being set up to accommodate them.

'Will you look at them already,' Elsie said to Caitlin as a long, uneven column of men, some in cloth caps, others in bowlers or straw hats, marched mostly out of step behind the straight-backed, khaki-clad figure of a sergeant. Their heads were high and they winked saucily, proudly, at any young lady whose eye they caught as they made their way to the railway station. Behind them marched an assortment of children and young girls. The whole scene had an air of ebullience and joie de vivre about it as though the lot of them were off on a grand outing.

'What will you do, Elsie?' Caitlin persisted as they walked along the leafy road which led in the direction of the small villa where Caitlin and Jack Templeton had lived since their marriage eighteen months earlier. Built in the last century slightly out of the city, it was within easy reach of the factory or the office of the lower middle class gentleman for whom it had been built. It was detached, separated from its neighbour by a dense screen of foliage. Compact in design, most of the ground floor rooms communicated with each other, with the kitchen and pantry built into a self-contained wing. There were sash windows at the front, with French doors opening out at the back to a long walled garden. The floors were of polished wood but Caitlin and Jack had covered them in a haphazard, casual fashion with dozens of cheap, gaily coloured rugs. The ceilings were high and finished with ornate central roses and moulded plaster cornices. It had been gloomy and darkly painted when Jack rented it as a refuge for Caitlin during her militant days but a 'painter chappie' had slapped some cream paint on the walls and ceilings and with light curtains and a few pieces of worn but comfortable furniture, not many for even then it was as though they both knew it would not be for long, Caitlin had settled into it whilst she waited for Jack to come home to her It was not grand nor imposing: it had an abundance of flowering plants in copper bowls, a couple of cats in the fire-warmed kitchen, for what was a home without a cat or two, Caitlin said, perhaps remembering the kitchen at Edge Lane, a cabinet filled with a wafer-thin dinner and tea service – a wedding present from Elsie – a picture or two which they had liked, of no value whatsoever but pleasing to the eye, and the deep and luxurious comfort of their huge double bed. But a home, nevertheless, to where Caitlin had dragged her bruised and abused body when it had needed mending. To the ministration of the tight-lipped, gentle-handed woman Jack had found in Wetherby to look after her Mrs Willis had known Master Jack since he was 'nobbut a lad', having been parlourmaid to Mrs Templeton before her marriage and though she thought 'nowt a pound' to London she had been glad of a steady, live-in job now that her own old man had been taken.

She was at the door to meet the two women, telling them tartly, just as though it was her carpet and her house and they were merely children in it, to 'wipe them feet', bustling off to stir up Aggy and fetch them a pot of tea, dying to know what 'the lass' would be up to now that war had come. Master Jack would no doubt be in the thick of it and what was this slip of a wife to do whilst he was at it, she wondered. Not sit at home on her behind twiddling her thumbs, she'd be bound.

'I'm going to join the VADs, Caitlin,' Elsie told her as they sipped Mrs Willis' expertly brewed tea and nibbled one of her scones from the batch she had just knocked up that afternoon for the lass's return. 'I don't think anyone has the least notion of what's going to happen, you know. I have a reporter friend who has just come back from Germany and he tells me they have been preparing for this for years. Determined on it, he says, and they are so well set up compared to us that this talk of it being over by Christmas is all balderdash. It's going to be a long do, Caitlin, and that means . . . well, I don't wish to upset you with Jack likely to be amongst the first to go over to France with the BEF, but it means . . . casualties, and nurses will be needed. And not just nurses. Drivers and all the things men do. Mrs Fawcett was right. We can be of some use to our country, now,' said somewhat bitterly, 'but I can't see myself manning Red Cross posts and mounting campaigns to encourage young men to go and kill other young men. So I shall do the opposite and try to help mend those . . .'

'In France?'

'I should imagine so, when I'm trained.'

'Where will you go to train?' Caitlin's voice was strained and her expression was one of anxiety in which a curious resolve was mixed. Her scone lay half eaten on her plate.

'One of the London hospitals, I suppose.'

'Then I shall come with you.' As she said the words the anxiety slipped away as though a great decision had been made for which she was thankful. She straightened her slender back and her gaze as she looked at Elsie was steadfast.

Elsie appeared surprised. She put her cup carefully in her saucer before speaking. 'But you're a married woman, Caitlin. I'm not sure they'll allow it.'

'Then sure I'll not tell them. If Jack's in France and I have a chance to be near him, then faith I mean to try.'

'They won't take you under twenty-one.'

' 'Tis my birthday next week.'

Elsie looked troubled. 'I don't know, Caitlin. Are you sure it's the right thing to do? The fighting will be spread over a large area, one supposes, and the hospital bases will be nowhere near the battles.'

'How d'you know all this, Elsie?'

'I don't, Caitlin, I'm only guessing but if they're going to fight the Germans then they'll do it well away from where the wounded are. Or should I say the wounded will be taken to a place of safety and that is where the nurses will be so I doubt you'll see much, if anything, of Jack. But I suppose it will be no worse than what we've gone through these last few years. By God, we could teach those generals a thing or two about fighting, couldn't we, Caitlin?'

The first thing that struck Caitlin as she walked up the long, sun-warmed path of 11, Edge Lane was the strange air of quiet which lay over the house. There were no children at play and the front door which ordinarily would have been standing open to allow free passage for the constant stream of people who crossed Ellen's threshold was closed tight shut.

She put her key in the lock and entered the hallway. She

had not let them know she was coming home but still, by now she would have expected some welcome, some lively face peering from the kitchen, some glad greeting even if it was only from Lucy or Matty. Were they all gone to Mass, perhaps? It was not Sunday.

'Mammy,' she called anxiously. She put down her suitcase and moved apprehensively up the hall towards the kitchen door.

'Mammy,' she said again and there they were, her Mammy and Daddy, sitting one on either side of the fire as she had seen them do a hundred hundred times throughout her lifetime and on Daddy's knee was Clare and all three wore the expression she had seen on so many faces in the past few days.

Clare, being a child and not quite understanding why there was such a to-do but sad because her Mammy and Daddy were, jumped down from her Daddy's lap, her face instantly turning to smiles and ran to Caitlin, flinging her arms about her and pressing her face into Caitlin's waist.

'They've both gone to be soldiers, Caitlin,' she said importantly, then turned up her bright face, gratified to be the one to break the news. 'Michael, an' Sean, an' Callum says he's to be off as soon as he can because he doesn't see why Sean should go an' not him, begorra. Dermot says they can't spare him from the bank but Uncle Dennis, Uncle Thomas and Uncle Terry,' naming her older sisters' husbands who, though they were really her brothers-in-law she had always called 'uncle', 'have all gone down to .. where is it, Daddy?' turning to her father and when he did not answer, 'to go for soldiers too. Uncle Dennis says to be sure an' isn't he sick of being a dockie an' a bit of excitement would be just the...'

'That's enough, Clare.' Mick stood up and seemed to shake himself. He laid a hand briefly on his wife's bowed head then turned to Caitlin, holding out his arms to her and she moved thankfully into them, taking her young sister with her so that for a moment it was a coming home, the safe return she was always afforded.

'Darlin', we didn't know you were to come home, but sure 'tis grand to see you, grand. Look Mammy, it's Caitlin.'

At last Ellen lifted her bowed head and in her eyes was the bereft and bewildered look which was being repeated in women's eyes up and down the length of the land. They were not excited by it all, as their menfolk were. They were not filled with a surging, exploding fervour of patriotism, though naturally they would do their duty and send their husbands, their sons and sweethearts off to war without, if possible, shedding a tear, at least for them to see. They were proud of them, of course they were and it was only right that they should be clamouring to get at the Germans. There was a savage and natural indignation against them for had they not all heard by now of the atrocities done in Belgium, but Caitlin could see it in Ellen's face that, Sweet Mary, it was hard for a mother to part with her sons.

'Oh darlin',' was all she said and when Caitlin ran to her, kneeling to embrace her, she could feel a quality of frailness about her mother which she had never known before. Even when Mara married James and Bridget died, when she herself had been broken on the cause of suffragism and then done as Mara had done and married an Anglican Englishman, Ellen had recovered from the blows struck her, rising above it with her staunch and unextinguished spirit still alive.

But these were her sons. The beloved ones, her jewels, and what was to happen to them without their Mammy to watch out for them? Michael and Sean already gone and Callum, at fourteen, clamouring to follow them and if he wasn't watched, being a big strong lad, likely to do so. And she had three more. Dermot, who was sensible, thanks be to the Blessed Virgin, said he would not go but what of the others if this thing dragged on? It couldn't bear thinking about.

'They've gone, Caitlin,' she wept brokenly. 'Off to Aigburth this morning. A thousand men, they say, marching off to Sefton Park and some to assemble at the Transport Depot on Tranway Road. Gracie's Terry and Eileen's Dennis have been told to go to Knowsley Park, Lord Derby's estate. He's going to form the "Pals Brigade" of the King's Liverpool Regiment so as to keep all them who are mates with their own. Dennis was made up with it, so he was, an' Eileen doin' her best not to cry. Silly bugger he is . . .' the last word sitting strangely on her lips since Ellen didn't hold with swearing, 'wearing his badge already, the one Lord Derby gave out. The Eagle and Child he said it was called though already them as are wearin' it are callin' it the Constipated Duck. He thought it was funny an' there was his poor wife left to look after three bairns and I wouldn't be surprised to see another on the way before long. An' then Michael an' Sean this morning. Orders came an' they had to go, they said. Telegrams they got, the pair o' them . . . what was it, Mick, that they were to be in?'

'The 3rd Battalion the Lancashire Fusiliers.'

'That's it, the 3rd . . .'

'Jack's gone with the 3rd Lancashire Fusiliers, Mammy.'

Ellen, for the first time, looked fully into her daughter's face and in her own was a puzzled expression. Then, her eyes coming to sorrowing life, she dragged her daughter back into her arms.

'Ach, so he is, an' there's me with only me own troubles on me mind an' you with a husband to worry about. An' sure we're not the only ones, pet, for everywhere you look they're marching away to God knows where an' leaving broken hearts behind them, so they are.'

'Now, Mammy, you must be brave an' not let yourself get upset . . .'

Ellen turned on her husband with a spark of her old spirit in her. 'Not get upset, is it, Mick O'Shaughnessy, with two of me sons an' me daughters' husbands going off with rifles in their hands to kill other men and ... and be shot at themselves.' Her hand sketched a hasty cross on her breast. 'And wouldn't I be a poor mother if I wasn't to have a bit of a cry about it ...'

'Of course you would, darlin', an' you know I didn't mean that but ...' Mick didn't know how to go on for didn't he feel like having a good cry himself? They had all been at it only an hour since, Gracie, Amy and Eileen, come to see their brothers away before they hurried home to watch their three husbands do the same. It seemed their whole life had been turned upside down and himself not able to do a bloody thing about it.

'Will I wet the tea, Mrs O'Shaughnessy?' a tear-filled voice from the scullery asked for was not normality made up of such things and Matty was shrewdly aware that they must get back to it or they would go under. In a minute, just as though the everyday question had cleared the air somehow, she and Lucy were bustling about with teacups and sugar basins and Mick was at the fire with the poker.

Caitlin took off her coat and sat down in the chair opposite her mother and Clare leaned against her knee. The cats stretched and purred on the rug and Michael stirred his tea and but for the sighing and the strange and alarming quiet, the kitchen was as it usually was, even if only in appearance.

'Where is Jack, then?' Michael said at last.

'His last letter came from Ireland but sure an' he's bound to be back in England before long. He'll be among ... the first to go.'

'Aah darlin', now you're not to worry,' Ellen said to her daughter, her face creased with compassion, the very words for which she had rounded on her husband spilling from her lips, but the instinct was to comfort, to say something, anything to take that harrowed look from the sufferer. She didn't know her daughter's husband very well since they lived, Caitlin and Jack, such a strange and disconnected life, hardly together for more than a week at a time and then

459

only seldom. They had come to Liverpool on the day before Christmas last year, sleeping – and the less she dwelled on that the better – in the room Caitlin had once shared with her sisters, though even yet Ellen could not accustom herself to the fact that the personable and polite gentleman who had, presumably, shared her daughter's bed, was her daughter's husband. A nice enough chap who obviously worshipped the ground her Caitlin walked on and who was forever up and down getting her this and that and begging her to have a rest and not to stir herself. He'd helped with the dishes and the setting of the table, just as though he'd done it all his life, smiling good-naturedly and playing a game of chess with young Eammon. You couldn't help but like him though it had been awkward on Christmas Day when the question of Mass had come up.

'I'll come with you,' he'd said cheerfully, unaware of Ellen's horrified glance at Caitlin. 'That is if there is no law that says I may not.'

'Er ... no ...'

'Then Caitlin and I will walk there. She tells me it is not far and the walk will do her good, won't it, my darling.'

My darling! He'd called her that, to everyone's amazement but his wife's, during the whole of the two days he and Caitlin were at Edge Lane, but why they should be amazed had not occurred to the loving family who were as free with their 'darlin's' and their 'pets' as only the Irish can be. But though he'd done his best to fit in, he was a gentleman, with gentlemen's ways and his constant bobbing up and down whenever Grace or Amy or indeed any female over the age of ten rose from her chair was very unnerving. Opening doors for every woman in sight, he was, and with the house filled to bursting with O'Shaughnessys and Maguires, with Feeneys and McGowans and Conroys, he was at it all day long.

'What will you do, pet, now that the suffragettes are to disband ... oh aye, sure an' I read the report of it in the newspapers the day. You'll be comin' home with Jack away?' Mick asked her hopefully.

'Well . . . that's what I wanted to talk to you about, Daddy. Will you not sit down?'

Mara could hear her Daddy's voice as she put her key in the lock and she turned to Elizabeth, her face slackening in fear.

'Holy Mother, what now?' she begged to know and as though to protect what was growing within her she put her hand on her rounded belly.

The two young women were both unnaturally pale with a strained expression on their faces which was identical. It was a hot day, as the summer had been hot and they wore light and pretty ankle-length dresses of crisp muslin, Mara's the palest blue and Elizabeth's of her favourite ivory. They were simple with elbow-length sleeves and a dropped waist around which a wide satin sash was wound. Their hats were enormous with the brim turned up at the front, framing both lovely young faces, and decorated with osprey feathers. They were elegantly and expensively dressed for both had wealthy husbands, looking just what they were, two ladies of the upper class paying a call on others of the same society, though of course this house and the people within it did not fit into that category at all.

At the gate was Johnny Osborne's Renault with Gibson triumphantly standing beside it for Mrs James Osborne was once more with child and her husband had threatened her that if she drove her own Morris before the child was born he would sell the motor and she would never have another.

In Elizabeth's arms was Charles Woodall, five months old and already as handsome and sweet-tempered as his father and running in ahead of the two ladies were Claudine and Christian Osborne.

At the sound of their grandfather's raised voice the children stopped and turned back apprehensively to their mother. They were used to loud voices at Granny's house – as opposed to Grandmama's – for in what other way did any of them ever converse with one another, but this was not at all like that and even they, young as they were, could tell the difference.

'Jesus God, will you listen to him,' Mara whispered, and clutching Elizabeth's arm to draw her with her, ventured up the hallway and into the violent storm of the kitchen. For a moment they were not noticed. The little girl huddled against her mother's skirts and the boy's face lost its puce determination to be first in the kitchen as he stared open-mouthed, as they all did, at Mick O'Shaughnessy.

'. . enough to have me sons taken from us an' sent God knows where to be shot at . .'

Ellen moaned feebly by the fire.

' . . without you takin' yourself off as well, Caitlin O'Shaughnessy. Sure an' I've stood by all this time an' seen things done to you that no father should have to see, aye, an' ashamed of meself for allowing it, I was, but I'll not have it any longer, d'you hear? Your poor Mammy's nearly in her grave with the lot of you an' can stand no more so you'll stay here and mind her until that fine husband of yours comes home, so you will. Soft I've been, soft in the head an' me own heart broken up with it but no more, d'you hear, no more '

Mick shook his head like some maddened beast plagued by flies, turning this way and that to avoid the nipping, biting, hurting pain of it and yet even as he spoke there was a growing uncertainty in him, a crumpling of his bold Irish spirit which knew, really, that he was beaten. That though he was doing his best to hold her, this courageous, great-hearted daughter of his, he might as well try to catch water in his closed fist. She was twenty-one next week, besides which, she was no longer his to hold. She was Mrs Jack Templeton now, a married woman answerable to no one but her husband. As she had just told him.

The group at the kitchen door fidgeted nervously and waited, afraid to say anything which might madden further the sorely tried father's heart of Mick O'Shaughnessy, but Ellen, catching sight of Mara, threw her apron over her head and wept even more brokenly.

'What is it ... Mammy, Daddy?' Mara beseeched, a small girl again flung into an adult world with which she was not awfully sure she could cope. 'What's ... Caitlin done?'

'I'm to go nursing, that's all,' Caitlin answered her calmly. 'I'm to train at a London hospital ...'

'Aye, an' then where to, tell me that?' Mick's voice was bitter.

'I don't know, Daddy, but I want to go to France, if they'll let me. That's where nurses will be needed.'

Ellen rocked in her chair, her anguish too deep for words.

'Well ...' Mara was plainly at a loss and behind her Elizabeth stood quietly. She didn't know herself how she had got here or for what reason. She knew what brought her, of course, and her own weakness appalled her. Harry scarcely out of the house and here she was with Mara, driven by the compulsion of her love to this house, drawn like a magnet to the source of the deepest pain she had ever experienced, ready, it seemed, to go on suffering it into infinity. Would she never let go ... would she ...? She had come, ostensibly to help Mara with the children since her sister-in-law had been insistent that she must have them with her whilst she broke her awful news, but of course it was more than a wish to help Mara which had compelled her to come. Where was he? Where had they sent Michael? In what part of the country was he training? Was he already in France? Where had he gone, where? Those were the questions which raced round and round in her head and, as it seemed from some painfully casual questioning on Elizabeth's part that Mara didn't know, where else to find out but from his own family?

She could still hear his voice and see his face as he

had tipped that last jaunty, uncaring salute in her direction ... Dear God ... was it only four weeks ago? She had told him to get out of her life and he had but could she have known at the time that this was to happen, this disaster, and if she had would she have done what she did then? If it had been in her power to see what was to happen in Europe would she have sent him off so cruelly? Watched him go to be a soldier, to fight, to fall, perhaps, on the battlefield, injured, or even die. She had pictured him moving to another part of the country, finding work, the work for which he was trained, making a new life, lost to her for good but safe, whole, alive, not flung across the channel in a uniform of khaki with a gun in his hand. Now he was gone with her bitter words corroding him, souring him and the gaping wound his going had left would never be healed. She did not know what she could do, or even what she wanted to do for if they told her where he was, what difference would it make? She only knew she felt an instinctive, almost animal need to be here, where he had been such a short time ago, perhaps to hear a word from his mother that he had been smiling, calm, not cheerful exactly, for how could the man she had crucified with her words, be that, but surviving, enduring.

'I'll be as safe as houses, so I will,' Caitlin was saying. 'Even if I go to France, sure they're not likely to put the hospitals in the direct line of fire, now are they? They'll not be wanting the wounded ...'

Again Ellen moaned and rocked.

'... to be where there's danger. Now come on, Mammy, stop crying an' see who's here, will you? Sure an' it's Claudine and Christian come to see their Granny an' will you look at the pair of them. Grown six inches since I saw them. Come here, darlin's and give your Auntie Caitlin a kiss. You remember me, don't you?' laughing as the little girl peeped curiously from the safety of her mother's pale blue skirts. 'An' don't tell me you're shy for if you are you'll be the first O'Shaughnessy to be stricken by it.'

She stood up and taking her father's hand led him to the chair she had just vacated. 'Sit down, Daddy,' she said tenderly, dropping a long, slow kiss on his forehead, then turning she put her arms about her sister.

'Mara, 'tis bonny you look an' that James of yours has been at it again, I see,' indicating Mara's splendidly burgeoning figure, ready to smile if only someone else would.

Mara lost her woebegone look and glanced down complacently at her own stomach. She smiled and patted it. 'Sure an' he's a wild one that husband of mine and what I want to know is when yours is going to get started?'

Caitlin began to laugh, hugging Mara closer to her 'Trust you to say such a thing, Mara O'Shaughnessy. Never the delicate flower an' never one to curb your tongue. An' as for me an' Jack, begorra we'll be starting a family when we're ready.' She glanced at her mother, then away again hastily as Ellen began to emerge questioningly from beneath her apron. Caitlin was well aware that her mother would be puzzled by her own curious words. A child came when it was good and ready to come and the teaching of a certain Dr Marie Stopes would be anathema to Ellen. 'And where is James, by the way?' she hurried on. 'Off to shoot some bird or other or is it fox hunting the day? I never can remember ' but at her words Mara's face crumpled and she began to wail

'Oh Sweet Mary ' Ellen wailed with her and so did Claudine and Christian at the sight of their Mammy and their Mammy's Mammy in tears.

'What is it, Mara, for pity's sake?' Ellen stood up and so did Mick, this new drama fetching them from their chairs and to their daughter's support at once since surely, in her delicate condition, she needed it.

Mara wept piteously, her head on her Daddy's shoulder, the meaning and text of her words lost on a hiccoughing mumble. Ellen turned fearfully to Elizabeth, her face haunted, and it was left to the woman who loved Ellen O'Shaughnessy's son to tell them.

'It's James . . .' she began, a catch in her voice. She wished she could weep as copiously and without restraint as Mara was doing but her upbringing forbade it.

'Holy God . . .' Ellen's face whitened even further and she crossed herself reverently for surely something must have happened to the grand husband of her daughter just when he was about to be a father again. She had a momentary picture of Mara in black, her two, perhaps three fatherless children about her, but then Elizabeth spoke again. Mrs O'Shaughnessy should know by now that whatever happened, when it happened to Mara, it was always worse, more harrowing, more dramatic and therefore caused more suffering. Never to one to do things by halves, was Mara.

'He . . . went this morning to Bury to the barracks of the . . .'

'Jesus God . . . and so did Michael and Sean. Oh Mara, pet, your two brothers and your husband in one day . . .' and for one dreadful moment Elizabeth thought she would faint or scream or weep, or even laugh hysterically. He had gone only this morning. An hour or two earlier and she might have been here to wish him God speed and what a phenomenon that would have been. Dear Lord, the irony of it. If it were not so tragic it might have been laughable. She really didn't think she could bear much more . . .

The child was heavy and restless in her arms and without thought, for what was more natural, Ellen took him from her, dandling the future Sir Charles Woodall on her motherly hip, jiggling him casually for was that not what one did with a fractious baby, whatever his class!

Elizabeth moved away and stared out sightlessly into the dusty garden. She felt a hand on her arm and turning sharply looked into the compassionate eyes of Mara's sister, feeling strangely heartened by the expression she saw in the vivid blue eyes, which, though they were not exactly the same shade, were so like those of her brother.

'There's ... more?' she asked. Understanding was in Caitlin's expression and a kind of affection for were they not all as one now, the women of this land, they asked?

'My husband.'

'Aah...'

'And tomorrow my other brother, Teddy ... only seventeen ... and my husband's two brothers. All the men I love gone in two days,' and the one she loved the most had gone from this house.

25

The first boy, for he was no more, to be brought into the ward that day cried softly and monotonously for his mother. Caitlin clenched her jaw the better to withstand it, trembling, though she did her best not to, or at least to keep it from Sister who would, quite simply, not allow it.

She had been at the hospital for three months now, living in the nurses' home, her room, one of a dozen or more, no bigger than a cell. She wore a uniform of mauve check in a hardwearing cotton, a great trial to many of the VADs, some of them ladies who had never dressed in anything coarser than silk in their lives, but to Caitlin it was a vast improvement on the prison garb with which she was harshly acquainted. It had a high starched collar fastened with a collar stud and a voluminous apron which covered her from neck to ankle. Thick black stockings and flat-heeled black shoes with what looked like a vast cotton shovel on her head, attached beneath the shining knot of her hair at the back of her head with tapes.

She had passed the first month in a confusion of sounds

and sights and smells which at first had horrified, terrified her. Pain, the pain to which she herself was no stranger was more than she could stand, she told herself, as once she had told herself in prison but now, as then, she had steadied herself, given herself to it and to those who suffered it in the only way she knew: totally. Red-shaded lamps at night, endless stone passageways in which at first she had lost herself continually, Sister's voice, impatient, sharp, gentle and supportive, the moans of wounded men, the silence of the dying, sterilisers and sink rooms, stenches so appalling she could not breathe, vomit and blood and the sweet smile of a lad from Cumberland who had no arms, no legs and no comprehension that they were gone.

From the clanging of the handbell which shook her savagely from exhausted sleep in the morning until the moment she fumbled her way into her cot at night she was bombarded with it and she knew quite conclusively that she couldn't bear it. But she did. She learned, in that first month, to use a thermometer, to make beds, wash moaning, helpless men and give enemas. To steel herself against vacant staring eyes and senseless incoherent mutterings, to hold mutilated stumps for bandaging, to shave men and feed them, to clear away the emission from their bladders and bowels. And worst of all, how to make as decent as possible the broken bodies of the dead, washing and bandaging their dreadful wounds for the last time. Bedpans and their reeking burdens, backache, the breathcatching, eye-watering smell of Lysol and all the time she was never free of her terrible fear for Jack, searching the casualty list in *The Times* with heart-stopping terror, searching the post for his letters, and then there was not only Jack. Her two brothers were in France and her four brothers-in-law, and Elizabeth's husband, and though she scarcely knew either him or her they were in a tenuous way connected with her family.

All through September and October the Roll of Honour grew longer as the newspapers reported heavy casualties;

at Le Cateau, during the retreat from the bloody battle of Mons and in the battle of the Marne.

Jack, as she had told her father he would be, had been amongst the British Expeditionary Force which was ferried across the channel between August 9th and 24th, 160,000 professional soldiers who had undergone long and thorough training and had battle experience in South Africa, India and Egypt. A small army by German standards, indeed the Kaiser had called them a 'contemptible little army' but they had fought with commendable courage at Mons, at Marne and Ypres and had been virtually destroyed to be replaced by the hundreds of thousands of Kitchener's Army.

The first battle of Ypres in October was fought in conditions dominated by mud and wintry cold, continuous fighting which brought the wounded flooding into the wards in great stinking waves. As Caitlin and the other VADs unwrapped blood-caked bandages, the smell of the thick yellow pus which erupted from the soldiers' suppurating wounds filled the wards, the corridors, the hospital. They came in such great numbers that despite her inexperience Caitlin found herself working alongside fully qualified nurses, poking and scraping wounds for bits of broken bone then binding the gaping holes as best she could. Bed after bed was filled with desperately ill and wounded men, men calling out in their delirium for Mary or Lil or Elsie, for mother or ma or mam, or lying in achingly quiet silence, eyes unfocused, faces the colour and texture of the underside of a mushroom. Pathetic faces, despairing faces, bewildered faces, faces hidden in filthy bandages which when unwound proved to be no face at all. And all the time she looked for those she knew.

And still they came as autumn drew on, convoy after convoy of exhausted, frightened and damaged men, going not only to the London hospitals but to hospitals all over the country. Head wounds, stomach wounds, amputations, tetanus and gangrene, handed over to young women like Caitlin who were totally unprepared for them. A baptism of blood and fire which some of them did not survive.

At the end of November the pace slackened a little as the crisis at Ypres ended. The intense cold at the front, as the civilians had now begun to call it, brought large scale activities to an end. Since the start of the war in August 90,000 men had been lost, most of them young officers and long-serving regular soldiers.

Caitlin had not heard from Jack for three weeks and her step was heavy as she paced the platform at Liverpool Street station with a dozen other VADs, awaiting the train carrying the latest casualties from France. They usually arrived at night, the hospital trains, gliding silently and smoothly alongside the platforms to avoid the harsh bumping and the distress it would cause their passengers. There was a long line of ambulances beside the platform, stretcher bearers and volunteers, many ladies of high rank, ready to give their somewhat inexpert but very devoted services to those who might need them.

On a platform further across from the one on which Caitlin and the others waited there was a troop train about to steam on its way from the deep, cathedral-like cavern of the station, filled with cheering, cap-waving soldiers going to the front, burning to reach the front. They were straight from their barracks and makeshift training camps, volunteer soldiers with shining cap badges and shining boots, immaculate puttees and all hung about with pouches and ammunition belts and haversacks and as the train prepared to pull out a military band played 'God Save the King'. There were women with rigid faces, resolute in their determination not to cry. Mothers beseeching Willy or Fred to 'be careful', just as though they were boys again setting out for their first day at school, which, to many of them, was how it seemed and how they remembered that day not so many years ago. There were wives and sweethearts clasped fiercely, unashamedly in strong but excited arms, being exhorted to 'cheer up and give us a kiss' since they wouldn't be long gone and there was no need for tears. Every day this scene was being enacted, almost by the hour since an average of twelve ships left Dover in a twenty-four hour period, as they streamed from every part of the country, Britain's best, all dying to get there and when they did, managing it, some of them, within days. Naturally none of these knew this. Mothers and fathers gave their sons gloriously and if they did not return had not their beloved died in the noblest of causes?

Further down the train a chorus of 'Hold your hand out, you naughty boy' was doing its best to drown out the national anthem and Caitlin prayed that the troop train and those who had come to see it off would be gone before the arrival of the convoy. She was tired, exhausted to the brittle bones of her and at the end of the week when she had three days off she meant to crawl into her bed in the house in Queen's Square and sleep and sleep until it was time to return to duty. She knew she should really travel up to Liverpool to see Mammy and Daddy. This might be her last chance for months but it was a chance she did not want to take. She just did not feel, not yet, that she could face the anguish of her mother and father and listen to their constant, heartbreaking fear for their sons. Ellen wrote to say that she had joined a group at Church which was involved in bandage rolling and she had knitted dozens of pairs of khaki socks which included two pairs for each of her sons and her sons-in-law so that they would all have a decent pair to change into when their feet were wet. She was sure Caitlin remembered how easily Sean took cold if he wore wet socks and she and Mrs Murphy had decided to make that their war effort. And had Caitlin heard that Liam O'Shaughnessy, Auntie Maggie's boy, Caitlin's cousin, had been wounded at Ypres, God save him, and would she look out for him at the hospital and tell him to get better soon and that his Mammy was praying for him.

No, she could not bear it and what if Jack should write,

or even come home on a 72-hour pass which some of the soldiers were now getting? Suppose he came to the little house in Kensington, or to the hospital to look for her and found her gone? She had not seen him since last July when he had sailed for Ireland since even when he returned he had gone immediately to France with the BEF. She had only his letters, the outpourings of his heart, of his love and longing for her. They were filled with nothing else. He never spoke of the war, of today, of what he did now, but of memories of yesterday, a string of bright jewels which he longed to place about her neck and of the future to come when those jewels would multiply and their real marriage together would begin. He wrote of the days by the river when they had first met and the remembered sights and sounds and the sharp aroma of the River Mersey along whose banks they had walked. Of the skylark which had poured out its ecstasy in liquid notes, so high in the sky it had been no more than a dot hanging there, and the delicate loveliness of the meadow daisies in which they had walked beyond Blundell Sands.

He did not speak of sump-pits and duck-boards and the mud which was so deep and viscous it sucked the very boots from your feet, nor of the rats which were so enormous, so ferocious they cared not what you did to try and kill them as they ate the very food in your hand. And he certainly did not tell her of the nightmare of Mons, the barbed wire on which hung crucified and rotting bodies, the whining of the constant shells, the grey wall of German soldiers coming shoulder to shoulder towards the British lines, the tangle of writhing bodies when the stutter of the machine guns fell silent. The louse eggs which hatched on men and officers alike, the flooded trenches and the soldier who had drowned in a shell hole of sucking green slime.

The troop train thankfully had left and so had the weeping women when the ambulance train drew smoothly up to the platform and from the moment it arrived the VADs were kept agonisingly busy under the command of Sister Andrews who was in charge of them, sorting and grading the casualties with no time, it seemed, for the finer instincts of compassion or sorrow, or even of horror, into their different groups for ferrying by the fleet of ambulances to the hospitals of their destination. They were not men, nor young fallen warriors but merely dirty wrapped khaki bundles labelled 'Head', 'Stomach', 'Amputation', 'Burns' and it was her job to sort them out and despatch them to their proper place.

There was silence, or moaning, a scream or two as a stretcher was jerked. Some whistled or spoke cheerfully to the nurses since at least their wound, though not mortal, had been bad enough to get them home. Twenty or so could walk. They wore bandages thirty-six hours old about their heads and they shuffled along the platform, each man with his hand on the shoulder of the man in front of him, the first led by a doctor, a terrible line of blinded men who she was to take into her care.

It was as though her brooding thoughts about him only minutes earlier had made him materialise out of the hissing, drifting steam of the engine which had drawn the hospital train from Dover. He simply stood there, gaunt and filthy, his peaked officer's cap set at a strangely jaunty angle on his head, his uniform still coated with the mud of the trenches. His Sam Browne belt was dulled, as was the once superbly polished leather of his boots and his jacket buttons were tarnished. He carried his greatcoat across one shoulder and on the other was a knapsack.

The stretcher bearers dodged round him, cursing him quietly as he stood there not appearing to know what to do next. It was as though he was coming from some nightmare and the reality of waking confused him.

One of the passing casualties was no more than a distorted hump beneath the blankets which covered him. A wooden wedge was held fiercely between his teeth and his eyes flashed round frantically implying such agony it was unbearable to look at him, let alone touch him, and yet Captain Jack Templeton did, putting a delicately gentle hand for a moment on what he took to be the bundle's shoulder. It was at that moment his wife called his name.

He looked up slowly, still yet in his private nightmare, sharing it with these damaged men he knew so well and it was only when she began to move, at first slowly then more quickly until she was running towards him did he see her. The expression on his face was so despairing that, when she reached him she stopped abruptly, making no effort to touch him, but stood an arm's length from him, afraid to even put out a hand to this stranger. Afraid not of him but for him.

'Caitlin?' he said unbelievingly.

'Jack . . .' Her voice was thick with tears.

'Caitlin .. oh Caitlin.. ' and his own broke raggedly. His greatcoat slipped from his shoulder and his knapsack followed it. Released, his arms rose and frantically, desperately he clutched her to him, tucking her so close beneath his chin and against his body she could feel the brass buckles of the shoulder straps of his Sam Browne cut into her breasts. He bent his head to hers and crossed his arms savagely behind her back and she felt him tremble as though he could scarcely manage whatever thoughts were in his head.

'Templeton, may I ask who this .. this person you are embracing happens to be and may I also remind you that you have men in your care who need you now.'

Still Jack stood, paralysed and deaf, his hold on her all he had of sanity and Sister Andrews, no stranger to the horrors men had seen and which came back with them from the trenches, waited for a second or two before speaking, more gently this time.

'I must insist, Captain, that you let go of my nurse. She is needed by far more urgent cases than you.'

* * *

He took her straight to bed, the lovely clean ivory lines of her, the fresh lemon scented smell of her, the soft whole feel of her woman's body beginning the process of healing him, if only temporarily, of what ailed all of those who had been in battle for three months. He did not say so, even to her then, but nothing had prepared him, professional soldier that he was, for what was taking place in the trenches of today's war. Cavalry charges and sweeping manoeuvres across great open spaces were what he knew and the mile upon mile of holes in the ground in which and from which he and his men, most of them gone now, had fought, was still raw in his mind. He was a soldier and he would recover and go on to fight other battles but for now and as soon as possible he had told her urgently in the taxi which took them from the hospital to Queen's Square, all he needed – desperately – was to sink his body into hers. Sister Andrews had given her permission to take her three days now instead of at the end of the week and they had gone, wordlessly, still clinging to one another for were they not both damaged somewhat, to the blessed peace of their home.

They scarcely moved out of the bedroom. Mrs Willis left them alone, depositing overflowing trays of nourishing food outside their door, herself alarmed by the staring, dirty scarecrow who had come home to them. The sooner this damned war was over the better, if he was anything to go by, and in the meanwhile and for as long as she could she'd see to it that he got at least three decent meals a day. The lass would see to the rest. Seventy-two hours, Mrs Templeton had whispered to her as the Captain staggered up the stairs towards the bedroom, both women united in their determination that he would go back looking a sight better than when he came.

Whilst he slept Caitlin filled the room with great bronze-headed chrysanthemums and kept a fire burning and lamps lit against the dark November weather and when he awoke she was there closing the door on Mrs Willis and the rest of the world, taking him wordlessly into her arms. He made love to her again and again, just as Harry Woodall had done to his own wife, as though the male instinct to put his mark on his woman, perhaps to fertilise, to make life, though he knew she was not yet ready for it, had been honed sharper by the acts of death he had seen in the last three months. The room was warm, with the curtains drawn and in it she moved about naked since she knew it pleased him, cleansed him to see her undamaged white body, to watch her brush her long hair, cream her hands and apply the French perfume he had got for her from somewhere, all the soft female things which women do to please their men. The softly curved, pink-tipped lift of her breasts, the turn of her narrow waist, the flow of her hips and long slender legs, the movement of her hands, sadly red and chapped now but graceful as she touched his body and soothed his shifting nerves to peace. They were at peace, both of them, finally, their love renewing them, their mingling sighing breath no longer jagged and spiky with tension.

'Do you have any idea how much I love you?' he asked her.

'Yes, my darling, I do.'

'I can make it if I have you to come home to.'

'I'm here, Jack.'

'It will be later rather than sooner, you know that, don't you? They said by Christmas but that, of course, is nonsense. They're slaughtering us in our thousands, Caitlin.'

'I know, darling.'

'Or crippling or maiming us.'

'Yes.'

'It's a bloody cock-up ... sheer hell ...'

'Hold on to me, Jack.'

'And we're letting them do it. Boys from school, most of them, longing to fight for Justice and Freedom, a glorious thing indeed. Going into battle with their swords held aloft

476

and being slaughtered for a few inches of ground nobody really wants.'

'I know,' for had not she herself seen what it was doing to hundreds and hundreds of young men and such a monster could not be appeased in three short months. They had talked about it briefly in this precious space of time they had, and of the possibility that she might be sent to France but he had not tried to stop her though she knew it devastated him to think of her in danger. She was a woman and it is the natural instinct of the male to protect his woman but she was first a person, a human being with the same rights he had, a partner in his life and her decisions were as important as his own He had chosen to do what he did and she must be allowed the same freedom.

'When it is over'

'I know, my beloved, I know,' and like all lovers they fell to dreaming about what they would do when 'it was over'

The telegram came a week later and for a brief crucifying moment before she opened it, she died. It lay in her hand where the porter had unwillingly put it, his eyes not quite meeting hers, his sympathy very apparent and quite simply she could not open it Whilst it remained sealed Jack was still alive For as long as she cared to leave it sealed, then Jack lived

'You must open it, Templeton,' Sister Andrews said gently.

'I know, Sister,' but she could not.

'Would you would you like me to do it?'

'No thank you. If I may I'll go to my room.' It would be not better, but more dignified if she suffered it alone. She had shared Jack's life and she had been given his love. She could not share his death, if that was what the envelope contained, with anyone.

'Come back when you're ready, Templeton,' telling her it did no good to brood. There was a war on and the living, if that was the name which could be applied to the damaged wrecks who lay along the wards, needed her more than the dead.

The telegram was from her father. Her brother Sean had been killed in action. For several moments she wanted to laugh and sing and shout out loud her gladness, to lift her face to Heaven and give thanks to the Blessed Virgin who, in her infinite mercy, had taken not her beloved Jack without whom she really did not think she could go on, but her younger brother. It was only Sean who was dead. Not Jack, not Jack. Mother of Jesus, thank you ... thank you ... but deep inside her the memories of her childhood rose up and in them was Sean, four years her junior but strong and ready to fight anyone who looked sideways at his sisters. A cheerful, wilful, engaging young scamp but with a steadfast core in him which could be relied on to defend his family, his best pal at school, his country, and now he was dead. Not yet eighteen years old and he was dead. He would not be needing his Mammy's warmly knitted khaki socks now.

She began to weep desolately.

She was given twenty-four hours, spending most of them on cold platforms and colder trains, huddled with soldiers of all ranks going in different directions.

Her mother still held the Army Form B101 in her hand, the letter of formal sympathy from the officer in charge of records, a major who said it was his painful duty to inform her that a report had been received from the War Office notifying him of the death of Private Sean O'Shaughnessy which had occurred on November 13th. Cause of death; killed in action, it said and the woman who was his mother and the man who was his father could not seem to get to grips with their devastation. Not Sean. Not Sean. Dear Holy Mother, he was only seventeen and should not have been there in the first place, not at his age. A baby, a boy who had his life yet to live. He had lied about his age to get in and now they had killed him.

'Mammy, it's me, Caitlin,' she said to the silently grieving woman who rocked slowly by the fire, still in the dress she had put on yesterday morning. Father Paul was there and Gracie, her tears slipping silently down her chalk-white face as she went about the eternal business of wetting the tea. In the scullery Lucy sobbed and Matty scolded her sharply and could be heard telling her to pull herself together since it did Mr and Mrs O'Shaughnessy no good to have her snivelling about the place. Gracie, thinking no doubt of her own husband who was already in the trenches and Rory, her eldest and at sixteen ready to do what Sean, God rest his soul, had done, could barely speak as she put her sorrowing arms about her sister. Crouched lifelessly at the table Mick stared into a corner with blank, unfocused eyes.

'Daddy, it's me,' Caitlin said softly, sitting down beside him on the bench and putting her arm about his suddenly frail shoulders. Daddy had always been strong, a comfort and protector, the shield which had guarded Caitlin throughout her childhood, the support to which she clung as she grew. Now, she realised, he was an old man, each blow his children, wittingly and unwittingly had struck him, weakening him. Mara, Bridget, herself, Michael and now the death of his beloved son Sean had drained his strength and would it ever be restored to him? Would he, or her Mammy ever be the same again?

'Where's Clare?' She directed the question at Gracie for both Ellen and Mick, deep in shock, could not be reached, it seemed.

'Amy took her. She and Eileen were here. Matty ran round for us when ... the telegram came. Sure the Mammy was screaming ... so we thought it best. Faith, I never want to hear the like again.'

She wiped away the sad tears with the corner of her apron and watched as Father Paul took her mother's lifeless hands in his. He encountered the piece of paper Ellen clutched and gently, murmuring soothingly, he tried to take it from her but as though it was the last link she had with her dead son she turned on him, violently struggling to retain it.

'No ... 'tis mine, 'tis mine. Father. 'Tis all I have until they send me back his body.'

Mick bent his head until his chin rested on his chest and Caitlin brushed his sparse hair back from his forehead as he groaned, then, beckoning to Gracie to take her place she got up and went to her mother.

The priest sat back wearily. He had lost count of the number of times he had had to perform this sad duty in the last three months. The 'Liverpool Pals', men who had enlisted in one body wishing to fight shoulder to shoulder with their mates, battalions of them, were serving together and dying together and Father Paul found he was comforting mothers, sweethearts, wives, who lived next door to one another and who had lost their loved ones on the same day.

'Mammy, look at me,' Caitlin said steadily. 'See, 'tis Caitlin. Will you not give me a kiss? Sure an' I've come from London to be with you so will you not put your arms about me. We're all grieving for Sean, darlin' '

'Caitlin . . ?' Ellen seemed puzzled and her eyes, set in plum-coloured circles in her grey face, stared in bewilderment. 'Caitlin .. ?'

'Yes, Mammy.'

'Oh Caitlin .. 'tis Sean, darlin'   Sean .. '

'I know, Mammy.'

'They sent me this ...' She stared down at the crumpled paper, then as Caitlin tried to take it from her, pulled it sharply away from her, clutching it fiercely in her old hand. Her face became truculent.

'No, you can't have it, Caitlin. Not yet.'

'Why Mammy? You'll not be needing it.'

'Oh yes ...' and a cunning look shifted into her eyes. 'They'll not give me my boy unless I show them this, you see, so I mustn't lose it. In a minute I'll put it away safe but I'll just hold on to it for now.'

Sweet Mother! Caitlin fell back on her heels, her face appalled. It was as though the formal letter notifying Ellen of her son's death was some sort of receipt without which she could not claim her son's body. She believed, in her innocence, as perhaps thousands of women up and down the country believed, that their dead sons and husbands would arrive home, neatly washed and packaged, as dead loved ones were, in a coffin. That Sean, dressed appropriately in the khaki uniform in which his mother had last seen him, would be just as he was then. Pale and tranquil in death, of course, and savaging her mother's heart with a pain she really could not bear, but which she must, ready for the grand funeral it would comfort Ellen to give him. Flowers and black horses with black plumes. Decent mourning for them all as they paid their last respects to the boy who had been taken so tragically, and so young, from the bosom of his family. Requiem Mass and choirs singing and a burial in the graveyard where dozens of O'Shaughnessys already lay. Amongst his own where Ellen could go each week and put flowers on his grave as she did for Bridget and the baby.

So, naturally she needed the 'receipt' to receive him, didn't she?

Caitlin bowed her head, her sorrow, her anger, her pain nearly choking her as she prepared the words to tell her mother that her son would never return to her. Not in any form, since the many ways a soldier could die in the trenches of France would not be a sight on which a mother would care to look. If he could be found. If there was enough of him left to be found he would be buried in an army cemetery sewn in hessian sacking. Ellen was holding on to her reason in the belief that, as was only right, her Sean would have the funeral to which any of her family were entitled and somehow Caitlin, since no one else understood, must tell her the truth.

26

Mara was delivered of twin girls in January, much to her
mother-in-law's dissatisfaction since she had hoped for
another son. Was it not just like Mara to produce, not a son
but two girls and surely she did it to spite Serena which
seemed to be her purpose in life, or so Serena thought.

'Heavens, the nursery will be filled to overflowing if Mara
does not put a curb on this . . . this productivity. Four children in as many years which I suppose, when one considers
the number her mother is said to have borne, is quite moderate. But no doubt, with James to be home soon for surely
he must be due some leave, we may expect a further
addition to their family within nine or ten months.'

'Mother!'

'Elizabeth, you know I'm right and with no wish to appear
ill bred you will surely agree with me that she is very . . .
fruitful.'

Elizabeth sighed as she replaced the delicate bone china
coffee cup in its saucer, then put them both on the small
coffee table at her side. She had been up to see Mara and
her amazingly beautiful children, marvelling on how easily
and how well her sister-in-law seemed to achieve perfection.
Her own son at birth had been as wrinkled and droll as a
pink monkey, pulling faces at his father, or so Harry had
insisted, though she herself had thought him quite enchanting. But Mara's twins were like two exquisite dolls with dark
curls in whorls upon their neatly shaped heads, rosy round
cheeks and perfect rosebud mouths. Identical even to the
colour of their eyes which were a vivid blue-green.

'The colour will no doubt change,' Serena had murmured

disdainfully, 'it always does,' but Mara would have nothing said about them, kissing and fondling them with all the enthusiasm of a child with two new and very novel toys.

'Sure an' will you look at them, the darlin's, an' just wait until their Daddy sees them?' whereupon Serena left in a great huff, the reference to her son as *daddy*, deeply offending her, much to Mara and Elizabeth's amusement.

The day was bitter with that icy east wind which cuts across the Pennine range straight from the plains of Siberia. Flurries of snow pellets had rattled against the motor's windows as Edwards, Lady Anne Woodall's new chauffeur, a man of thirty-five or so who was not fit for the army because of his bad chest, drove Elizabeth to Beechwood.

She drew closer to the fire, wishing her mother would ring for Betty to put some more coal on the wisping embers. 'I am to have my second child soon, mother,' she said coolly. 'Does that not make me .. fruitful?'

'Well, with Charles not yet a year old you and Harry have been rather precipitate but ...'

'It is not considered so indecent where your own daughter is concerned, is that what you are saying?'

'No, that is not what I am saying, Elizabeth, and I would be obliged if you would not put words into my mouth. Your husband is a baronet and naturally wanted a son to carry on the line. You have given him one and now, with perhaps a daughter to come, particularly in the circumstances...'

'What circumstances are those, mother?'

'Well, with the war looking as though it might go on for some time '

'And Harry might be killed.'

'Elizabeth! You are not to say such dreadful things. You must not even contemplate it. In your condition it can only be morbid and dangerous.'

'But it is true, mother, you know it is, and not just Harry . '

'Please, I beg of you, don't say another word or I swear

I shall have to ask you to leave. We must not dwell on such awful possibilities but think only of how brave and proud our sons are to be serving their country and if they should be asked to make the supreme sacrifice as ... as some are doing then we, their mothers and wives, will only feel honoured to have given them to such a great cause. Death in battle is chivalrous and ...'

'Does your friend Dorothy Malcolm think so, mother?' Elizabeth's voice was calm and her face expressionless. 'She lost a son and a brother, I believe, at Ypres.'

'You must not take that tone, darling, really you must not. Dorothy Malcolm ... well, one can only be sorry for her but I am sure she is comforted by the knowledge that Julian died for his country and will ...'

'I should not be so philosophical if it were my son.'

'Don't be silly, Elizabeth. Charles is ...'

'A baby still, I know that, but I feel the same way about Harry. I could not bear it if ... if he did not come home to me.' Just as I could not bear it if Michael O'Shaughnessy, whose child I might now be carrying, should die in this madness which seems to have engulfed our world. All the young men, the dashing, carefree young men who had marched off to the 'front', that exciting, somewhat mysterious but very desirable arena which each and every one of them could not wait to reach. The romance of it, the mystery and uncertainty of it, the glowing enthusiasm and lofty idealism of it, and so they had set off on a glorious enterprise ready to endure any hardship they were asked to endure to achieve it. In a fever they had been, cheering and whistling – she had seen them herself marching through the streets of Liverpool – to get there before it ended and now, many of those who had gone six months ago would never come back. Julian Malcolm she remembered as a shy, palely handsome young man who had gone to school with James. And Sean O'Shaughnessy, Michael's younger brother at seventeen had been killed at Ypres. Instantaneous death, the letter from his Commanding Officer had said. He suffered no pain but his mother did, for Elizabeth had seen her suffering it. She had gone, after a decent interval, with Mara to convey her condolences to the jubilantly Irish mother of the dead boy, jubilant no longer, alas, but an empty shell, dry-eyed and hollow-cheeked, not at all sure she believed her son was dead since no one had shown her his body. Elizabeth had meant to do no more than sit for a moment with Michael O'Shaughnessy's mother but instead found herself with her strong, compassionate arms about the anguish and despair of her, saying nothing but just giving her own grief since the boy was the same flesh as the man she loved.

When would it end? All the evidence, or so her father, who had high ranking friends in army circles, told her, seemed to indicate that an Allied victory would take place in 1915. Britain, France and Russia were all capable of it with sound men in charge, so Johnny Osborne's friend said, and the early victory Germany had counted on had been halted at the Marne. Both sides had dug in and a complex line of trenches stretched from the North Sea to the Swiss frontier. Behind those lines were the intensive training camps at Etaples and Rouen where conditions were arduous and the discipline severe though Harry had described Etaples to her in his letters as a very beautiful place, particularly on a fine morning for it overlooked the river mouth with the picturesque woods of Le Touquet and Paris-Plage on the opposite bank.

It was of these things he wrote, and of her and their son and the child to come and she knew little of his life in the lines. Mara's letters from James were the same, she had told Elizabeth, talking of nothing but when he would be home and Teddy seemed possessed by the urgency of getting back to his horse High Jinks and the possibility of getting leave before the hunting season ended. He had not done so and neither had James nor Harry and now James had two more daughters and what were they to be called, Serena wanted to know, dreading a repeat of Claudine and Christian.

'Mairin and Ailis,' Mara told her smugly, a child on either arm.

'Mairin and . . .' Serena repeated, not even sure she could pronounce such outlandish and, one presumed, Irish names, her expression telling Mara exactly what she thought but she did not even bother to argue for as she said brokenly to her husband later, what was the point of it? The girl had been a part of the family, a thorn in its side to be precise, for over four years now and there was nothing to be done about it. Gaelic names, Mara had explained, not caring in the least that these were the English daughters of an English gentleman. They required good English names, aristocratic names, ladies' names but that meant nothing to Mara as she hurtled about the Lancashire countryside in that obnoxious motor car of hers, visiting her fast friends again, now that her shape had been restored to her after the birth of her twins. She wore the latest fashion of straight, short dresses in the brightest of colours and not at all suitable for a matron of her years – twenty! – and status, and what they got up to Heaven alone knew It seemed so improper with her husband fighting for his life and his country in the trenches but when Serena remonstrated with her Mara said that James had told her 'not to brood' and though she missed him dreadfully and longed to show him his two new daughters, she intended to do as he suggested.

Elizabeth's second son was born on a dark March night six weeks later. She had been to see Ellen O'Shaughnessy that day. Ever since the death of Michael's brother and her visit to his grieving mother she had found herself drawn to the house in Edge Lane and had been made welcome. She would not, naturally, admit even to herself that it was in the throbbing hope that some word might be spoken of Michael. That his mother might let slip some word of where he was, or how he was; if he and the battalion of the Lancashire Fusiliers in which he served had been in action, had been heard from; perhaps there would be a letter of which a word or two might be read out to her.

But it seemed Ellen was absorbed with her dead soldier son, rather than the one who still lived and fought in France and made no reference to Michael. The first searing agony of the loss of Sean had dulled to the constant drumming pain a deep wound leaves, manageable now that it was bandaged and out of sight and the life and day to day dramas of the O'Shaughnessy family were drawn out once more against the warmth and solid comfort it was Ellen's duty and joy to give them. She had other children who needed her, she explained sadly to Elizabeth, and she had her faith, of course, which said that she was not to give herself up to the self-destruction an absence of hope would lead her to. Sean was in heaven now, for an innocent boy such as he would surely have gone straight there the moment the bullet hit him. Oppression and despair were a sin and her own immortal soul would be re-united with his, and that of her Bridget, of course, one day and could she look them both in the face on that memorable day and tell them she had neglected her duty on their behalf?

'And your child, Elizabeth. Sure an' it'll be any day now, by the looks of you,' she continued, smiling at the enormous bulge of Elizabeth's stomach. 'You'd have been better to stay close to home the day, pet, with that lot to see to.'

'Yes, my mother-in-law would agree with you but . . . I just felt like . . . coming to see you. I hope you don't mind . . .'

'Mind! Faith an' 'tis a pleasure to have you here, you know that. Mara was over this morning in that infernal machine she drives, wanting to take me to the Pier Head for a spin, whatever that is, but when I said no, bejasus, could she stay for an hour or so to chat to her Mammy? Oh no, she was off to the railway station, begod, to serve cups of tea to the soldiers and why wasn't she at home minding the babies is what I want to know. I must do me bit for the war effort,

Mammy, she says. And hasn't this family done enough for the war effort, I asked her. What with my poor Sean gone, God rest his sweet soul an' Michael over there suffering only the Blessed Virgin herself knows . . .'

Elizabeth's heart gave a great plunge and seemed to swell in the space left to it by the child. She distinctly felt the unborn baby move, a sudden, unexpected movement since she had felt none for over a week now, a sure sign that her time was near, Mara had said knowledgeably. Dear Lord, oh dear Lord, give me the strength to appear unmoved, to remain calm and no more than politely interested in this woman's son, but despite her resolve she could tell that the expression on her face must have altered for Ellen put out an anxious hand to her.

'What is it, child, a pain?'

'No, no . . .' she managed to gasp. She smiled, a grimace really, to reassure Ellen that she was perfectly all right and that she must, must go on about her son but Ellen was full of contrition.

'Sure an' there's me babbling on about Michael when you've a man of your own in the very same predicament.' She turned to Matty, calling over her shoulder to the girl to fetch a cup of tea for Lady Woodall, the incongruity of herself and a baronet's wife taking tea together beside her homely fire of no consequence.

'Please, Mrs O'Shaughnessy, I'm perfectly well though a cup of tea would be lovely, but please, do go on about . . . Michael.'

Michael . . . Michael . . . Michael. She had said his name out loud to someone else, to other than the four walls of her bedroom when she was alone and it tasted as sweet as honey on her lips.

Ellen, the mother, the vessel in which her children had been cherished and loved before their birth, could not resist talking about one of them.

'Aach, not a lot to say, has young Michael. He's in the

trenches, he tells us, but it's very quiet. Not a lot doing, he says, for which the Holy Mother be praised,' sketching a hasty cross on her breast. 'Letters and food parcels and plenty of pairs of my socks he'd be glad of because his feet get awful wet. He says they have boards to walk on but the mud's a bit of a problem. He knows how I worry about wet feet so I do, the lad of him.' Her eyes were warm and soft for her son and she failed entirely to see the exact same expression in the eyes of her guest and would not have recognised it if she had for what had Lady Elizabeth Woodall to do with Ellen O'Shaughnessy's soldier son?

'And   is he to be home soon, do you think?' Elizabeth's voice was as neutral as she could manage it.

'Well, your guess is as good as mine, darlin', for who can tell in these troubled times what's to happen next. Billy Murphy was given seventy-two hours but he couldn't get home, he told his Mammy, because the way things are with the railways he'd no sooner be home than he'd have to be off again. Mary Murphy was in tears over it when I saw her at Mass yesterday an' her praying for a sight of him, like we all are, but I suppose we've no choice but to put up with it. An' then there's Gracie's man, and Amy's and Eileen's. None have seen their children for nearly six months an' them growing wild with no man to control them. Rory, that's Gracie's eldest, has been brought back twice from the recruiting centre, him being no more than sixteen, but he'll slip through, you mark my words, an' my Caitlin talks of nothing else. I was only hearing this morning about that German submarine that sank the *Princess Victoria* only eighteen miles from the Mersey an' her nothing at all to do with the war Just a pleasure cruiser, she was, but innocent folk went to their death.' Her seamed face was unutterably sad and she sighed deeply. 'All the sons, Holy Mother, all the dear sons   '

She fell into a deep and unhappy silence, sipping her tea and staring into the fire, the sympathetic presence of Lady

489

Woodall causing no strain on her as a hostess. She had grown so fond of this lovely girl, this sister-in-law of her own daughter. A kind girl, filled with a natural compassion and understanding unusual in one so young. She seemed to have an awareness of what others suffered and though nothing was actually said the very fact of her being there gave a curious comfort. She had a serenity, a calmness of manner which soothed, an air of cool good breeding which nevertheless hid a heart of gold and also, Ellen was convinced, some inner, well-controlled turbulence which was puzzling since she seemed so settled in her life as the wife of Sir Harry Woodall and the mother of nearly two of his children.

But a lady, in the true sense of the word, with a warmth which she seemed eager to share with a woman like herself, who was not of the same class.

They were both startled out of their own private reveries by a knock at the front door and when Lucy, at Ellen's irritated request, went to see who it was, Elizabeth was taken aback by the warmth of the greeting Ellen gave the pretty young girl who entered the kitchen behind the maid. A small girl, fresh and dainty with the pale pink bloom of a hedge rose. She was creamy skinned and dark haired with the startling blue-green eyes which seemed to shine from most of the O'Shaughnessy faces. She wore red, a warm scarlet coat of good cloth and a woollen beret to match. She sparkled and glowed with youth and energy, making Elizabeth feel slow, bovine and enormous with the weight of her child. She looked no more than sixteen.

'Mary Kate, darlin', 'tis yourself.' Ellen smiled, drawing the girl into her arms, 'An' me not expecting you until tomorrow. Faith, 'tis lovely to see you, so it is, an' how's the Mammy an' Daddy?' Without waiting for an answer she guided the girl towards the chair she herself had just vacated. 'Now take off your coat an' sit yourself down by the fire for it's a cold day an' Matty'll pour you a drop of tea . . .'

490

She stopped, her hands to her cheeks, then spun like a plump round top back to Elizabeth who, due to her size, had been unable to get up out of the nest of cushions Ellen had placed to support her back.

'Will you look at me forgetting me manners an' here's Elizabeth ... you've heard me speak of Elizabeth, haven't you, Mary Kate? Mara's husband's sister herself, married to Sir Harry Woodall where Michael used to work, an' this is me niece, Elizabeth. Mary Kate O'Shaughnessy.'

'Miss O'Shaughnessy.' Elizabeth nodded courteously and the girl bobbed her head, ready to bob a curtsey as well in such grand company, shy and lovely and completely overcome by the presence of this great lady of whom she had heard so much from her Auntie Ellen.

'And what's the word about Willy, then?' Ellen begged to know. 'Has his arm healed?' turning to Elizabeth in explanation, 'Mary Kate's brother was wounded in October,' then back to Mary Kate, 'an' what about Peter? Has the Mammy heard from him? She has ... oh thank the Holy Mother, for to be sure she was worried out of her mind when last I saw her. An' how's yourself, pet? Pretty as a picture, sure you are, isn't she, Elizabeth? But then the O'Shaughnessys always had the bonny looks...' preening, and all the while she talked the girl did not speak except to answer her aunt's questions but sipped her tea and glanced shyly at Elizabeth just as though she was in the company of Her Majesty the Queen.

Elizabeth could feel her own head begin to droop, smiling to herself at her own maternal inclination in these last weeks of pregnancy to nod off at the most unlikely and inappropriate moments. Really, it was most embarrassing and Serena had taken her to task about it, saying if she was tired she should keep to her room. The soft, babbling murmur of Ellen's voice washed over her like a flow of warm, soothing water. Very pleasant ... so pleasant ... and it seemed not at all out of place, nor even considered ill-mannered in this warm and homely kitchen where children and animals slept as and where they pleased.

It was the sound of Michael's name which brought her sharply, painfully, from her comfortably dreaming state. Her head snapped up and her heart began to knock heavily and though she had not yet got the drift of what Ellen and her niece were saying, something seemed to warn her that she was about to be seriously wounded by it.

'. . came this morning, Auntie Ellen, so I told the Mammy I'd come right over an' let you read it. Glad you'd be to have the news that himself's in the pink and due for some leave in April, so he is.'

'Oh, thank the Holy Mother an' all Her Angels, an' aren't you the blessed child to be thinking of me. Sure an' you don't know what this means to me, darlin'? See, give it here .. that is...'

Elizabeth watched in a still uncomprehending horror as Ellen, just for a moment, hung politely back from the proffered letter since it was, apparently, addressed to this lovely young girl, then, as Mary Kate smiled and shook her head, almost snatched it from her.

'If you're sure, darlin',' after all Michael wrote it to you an' with you an' himself to be married.'

'No, really, Auntie Ellen, it's all right. There's . well, I took a couple of pages out for they were   well, a bit private . .' She hung her head prettily and blushed.

Elizabeth moaned soundlessly deep in her throat, both her hands clutching the swell of the child within her She had turned the colour of wet clay, she knew she had for she could distinctly feel the warm, life-giving blood drain away from her head, going God knows where for her whole body felt as though it was immersed in icy water. Right at the core of her something stabbed sharply, the pain stitching itself into the small of her back.

'Jesus, Joseph and Mary!' Ellen leapt from her chair and the letter Michael O'Shaughnessy had written to the girl he was to marry drifted lightly to the floor, just at Elizabeth's feet. She wanted to reach forward and snatch it up from where it lay and read what Michael had said to . . to . . though what was the use since the girl ... Oh God, she could not stand it . . had taken out the 'private bit' and so even if she could have read it ... been allowed to by the girl he was to marry, she would have been denied the sweet words Michael O'Shaughnessy had written. What message of love had he addressed to this girl who was to be his wife and whose love for him, now that it had been revealed, shone from the clear blue-green of her O'Shaughnessy eyes.

She could not manage the pain, the dragged-down, reeling agony of it, of knowing that while he had been vowing his love for her, for Elizabeth Woodall, whilst he had been pursuing her, seducing her, impregnating her, he had every intention of marrying the decent Irish Catholic girl his mother, and presumably himself, had wanted for him, his own cousin, who he had been courting in a most proper manner, for how else would they allow it, ever since she was of marriageable age.

As easy as kissing the blarney stone, they said. Tongues as smooth as silk, they said and it was true of Michael O'Shaughnessy. He had been lightly amusing himself with her, and no doubt an assortment of parlourmaids and shop girls. How would it be with a lady, he must have idly asked himself? What was beneath the ladylike, well-bred exterior of the daughter of the gentry, he must have wondered, eyeing her as she turned her innocent and inexperienced gaze upon him, and by God, he had found out. He loved her, he had said and she had believed him. He had said he would marry her and she had believed him. He had spun a cobweb of lies which she had taken for the truth until one day, nine months ago, she had let him make love to her which was all he had wanted of her in the first place since here was his betrothed, his wife to be, innocent and lovely as a woodland violet. This ... this child, since she was no more, had been chosen and nurtured, protected and cherished, her virgin body guarded for her husband and that husband was to be Michael O'Shaughnessy.

'Dear God . . .' she gasped, her eyes staring and tearless, her voice rasping. She bent over, her head almost on her knees and her whole body was on fire with the anguish. She couldn't look up at the two concerned faces which bent over her for if she did she might strike out at the younger one, ready to damage it, to take away its young beauty, to mar the perfection of the smooth skin, to tear at the clear eyes and the . . .

'Dear Sweet Mary, is it the child, d'you think?' Ellen asked as though Mary Kate would know such a thing, turning this way and that in her agitation. She was well aware that her niece was an innocent girl and should be got away from the trauma of childbirth, which would be known to her soon enough when she married Ellen's son, but Lady Woodall was a person of some importance and must be attended to at once. Got home to her own bed and her own doctor which she was sure to have, to the place where she could give birth in the proper manner befitting her station.

'Mary Kate, darlin', run out to the chauffeur, there's a good girl, an' ask him to come in at once. Tell him . . . tell him that . . . no, never mind, I'll tell him. Lucy, Matty,' as Mary Kate dashed excitedly from the kitchen and down the hallway in the direction of the front door, 'help me with her coat and . . .' What else? You could see the indecision on her fire-warmed face. What else could she do to ease the sudden and obvious agony of her guest who, it appeared, was about to give birth on Ellen O'Shaughnessy's fireside rug.

'Please Mrs O'Shaughnessy, help me up.' Elizabeth's voice was harsh and her fingers dug painfully into Ellen's arm.

'Oh Mother of God, should you be on your feet, pet?'

'I must get home . . . I must get home . . .' The words were forced through gritted teeth. And away from you and

494

this house and that girl out there who is to know, to share, to have given to her all the joy and all the passion, the sweetness I myself once knew and which is now like the taste of ashes on my tongue. It is not her fault but I hate her just the same and if I am not got away I shall surely do her harm.

The thought hammered like a spike into her head. She must get home. To the safety and darkness of the room she had shared with Harry, to the safety of the lair to which all badly wounded animals return and in which they do their best to recover the strength which is draining from their wounds with their life's blood, as hers was.

'Will I put you into Michael's bed, acushla?' Michael's bed! Dear Lord, into Michael's bed . how could she bear it? 'Sure an' I'd be glad to have the looking after you, so I would,' the voice of Michael's mother told her, 'until you feel after moving. Just a rest for an hour or two perhaps...'

'*No* .' The word was almost a scream and Ellen reared back in alarm as Elizabeth lifted her face to her Ellen had never seen such agony, no, not in all her years of helping at the births of the many infants she had watched come into the world. Gracie with her six, and the round dozen of her other daughters' Only when Mara's children were born had Ellen been excluded but in almost twenty years she had never once glimpsed the suffering which was buried deep in the eyes of the girl before her Surely ... surely . all women knew the pangs of childbirth, a physical pain which could not be avoided but this woman was in . . was in hell . . Ellen could see it in her eyes. She recognised it since she had known it herself when her boy was killed. But why . . what was it that . . . ?

Almost she knew. It was on the very edge of her perception, the reason why Lady Woodall had . had ... but then Lady Woodall grasped her arm and the fragile awareness fled away.

'Please, please Mrs O'Shaughnessy, get me into the motor

495

... please ...' Elizabeth, who was on her feet now, turned awkwardly, still bent in the position of a creature severely wounded. The front door crashed on its hinges and Edwards hurried up the hall and into the kitchen, his face white since it was his job to take care of her Ladyship and if anything happened to her or the child she was carrying he would have a hard time explaining to Sir Harry what his wife was doing so far from home, so near her time.

'Edwards ... please ... as quickly as you can ... get me home ...'

She had a son, a second son for the house of Woodall and though the nurse who had been hastily called to attend the birth and look after her when the doctor's job was completed tried to put the boy in her arms, begging her to have a peep at the handsome little chappie, she refused to do so.

'I'm too tired now, nurse. Later, when I have rested.'

She lay in the dark and watched the firelight dance on the white ceiling, swirling and spiralling in pink and amber shadows. The raw pain which had nothing to do with the child who had, two hours since, torn his way out of her, ate bitterly into her soul and she hated. *Hated.* She hated Michael O'Shaughnessy with the same depth and passion with which she had once loved him and because of it she was afraid to look at the boy who might be his son.

The room was warm and comfortable, luxurious even. She was alone. She had insisted the nurse leave her and the child was in the nursery and, she supposed, at the breast of the woman hired to care for his no doubt healthy infant appetite. Her own breasts ached with the binding which had been knotted about them to stop the flow of milk. She could hear the nurse moving quietly about her own dressing room next door where a small bed had hastily been erected so that she might hear her ladyship should she call, and all she could feel was hatred, hatred and jealousy, bitter and vile in her mouth. She turned into her pillow and wept silently.

It was Mara who brought him into her the next morning and later Elizabeth was to smile about it for who else but her sister-in-law would have the sheer gall to stride into the Woodall nursery and calmly pick her own nephew, for that was what he was, from his cradle beneath the furious and icy disapproval of his nanny.

'Will you look at the spalpeen. As handsome as the day and strong as a little bull. Sure an' doesn't he have the look of...'

Oh God, Oh Dear God ... Elizabeth's mind could get no further than that desperate plea to the Almighty, if indeed He existed, as she waited whilst Mara considered who the boy favoured. Her thoughts were babbling and frantic as they skittered from one limp reason to another regarding the child's strange resemblance to ... to ... what was Mara going to say ... and not only that but how was she herself to feel, how would she love him if he was Michael O'Shaughnessy's son?

'It's James, that's who it is, begorra, and my twins. He has the Osborne nose, can you not see it but his hair's as dark as the night and ... now what colour are his eyes, darlin' for the wee divil won't open them for his Auntie Mara.'

She turned to Elizabeth, smiling, 'Well ...'

'Well what?' Elizabeth said weakly, her own eyes resting on the dark head in the crook of Mara's arm.

'What colour are his eyes?'

'I ... I must confess I have not seen them.'

'Not seen them? How could any woman with a son only hours old not have seen her blessed child's eyes? Bejasus, the first thing a mother does is examine his fingers and toes and sturdy limbs, you should know that. She admires the curve of his new-born cheek, so she does, and decides the exact shade of his new-born hair. And as for his eyes ...'

Well, she knew the old harpy, meaning her mother-in-law, had advised her that Mairin and Ailis' beautiful eyes would change but sure they hadn't done so yet. They were still

497

the shade of aquamarine which was their O'Shaughnessy heritage. Now she held Master Woodall, Elizabeth and Harry's son in her arms and was he to have the brown eyes of his father or the green of his mother?

'They were closed when . . .' Elizabeth began to lift herself in the bed, her eyes on her son's dark hair which, now that he had been bathed, drifted in soft curls about his head. Her arms trembled and shifted restlessly on the neatly folded-back sheet which the nurse had arranged across her and her breathing quickened.

'Can you . . . see them?' she asked hesitantly, then more crisply, 'has he opened them?' for really Mara was taking an unreasonable length of time studying the boy's face. Her hands began to flutter and twist.

'No, the wee thing won't lift those dark lashes for me. Sure an' they're like a girl's, so long and curling and just at the end they're tipped with gold.'

Tipped with gold!

'Let me see.' She was ready to snatch him from Mara's arms now, pushing back the bedcovers and almost on her feet, bringing nurse running from the corner where she had been lurking, afraid that Lady Woodall might do something foolish and her to stay in her bed no less than two weeks.

'M'lady, don't you put your foot out of bed, if you please. I'm sure Mrs Osborne will hand the child to you,' since Mrs Osborne had taken it upon herself to bring him from the nursery which should surely have been her job. And as for Lady Woodall, well, only last night she hadn't wanted even a peek at him, she thought acidly. These high class, finely bred ladies were often like that, not knowing their own minds for two minutes together.

'Here sweetheart, go to your Mammy then,' and for the first time Elizabeth looked down into the face of her son as he settled comfortably into the crook of her arm. He yawned and turned his face towards her breast as though he knew this was the place for him. His mouth searched against the fine silk of her nightgown for the friendly nipple he had become so happily acquainted with, and accustomed to, and without thinking, doing what she had not done for Charles, nor even considered, she feverishly unwrapped the binding from about her breasts and before the appalled nurse could utter more than a gasp, put her son to her breast. His mouth seized on it and instantly the bond was forged between Elizabeth Woodall and Michael O'Shaughnessy's son.

Oh yes, she knew it at once. Without seeing the colour of his eyes, and did it matter anyway? She knew unshakeably, with that infallible animal instinct which is inherent in the female when she holds her new child, that this child's father was Michael O'Shaughnessy. There was nothing obvious of the O'Shaughnessys in him for her own hair was dark. He could have been anybody's child but it was in the line of his brow, in the way his closed eyes were set in this delicate skull, in the shape of his winging eyebrows which the mother recognised as those belonging to the man she loved. Here was Michael O'Shaughnessy's son. His fingers, plump and pink with health, curled about her own as his father's had curled about her heart and always would. He was beautiful. He was hers and Michael's and the tipped golden eyelashes confirmed it. She loved him and she loved his father whatever might happen in the future, to Michael or to herself.

'Elizabeth, d'you think you should?' Mara laughed for though she seldom nursed her own children since she had no intention of spoiling her superb figure, nor of curtailing her social activities, it did her working-class Irish heart good to see her sister-in-law do something which would horrify her upper class mother-in-law.

'Why not, he's mine, isn't he?' and even nurse was quite amazed at the fierce way in which Lady Woodall seemed to be guarding her son.

27

The Gallipoli Campaign began in April. The Dardanelles Strait was strategically of the utmost importance to the Allies since it was the only naval route from the Mediterranean to the Black Sea and the site chosen for the attack, the Gallipoli Peninsula, was obvious, at least to those who knew about such things. The success of the undertaking depended upon efficient planning and ruthless aggression and in the event neither was forthcoming and its failure led to the almost casual beginning of a great and ultimately tragic enterprise, one in which the thousands of young men from Britain, Australia, New Zealand and France who stormed the beaches of the peninsula went to their deaths.

It was a major amphibious operation which involved such wonders as aircraft, landing ships, submarines and radio communications. It was to be a glorious adventure, those who were to take part in it told one another, an adventure which would open up the Dardanelles to the British Fleet and what could be wrong with that, they asked?

Lieutenant James Osborne came home on leave in March, arriving in his dashing little Austin Ten motor car which, whilst he was in France, he garaged at the home of a friend in London. The gravel of the drive sprayed up about its wheels as he drew up with a flourish before the wide front steps of Beechwood and before he had barely turned off the engine his wife was in his arms. Only a few days' leave, he said, since he had been transferred from his battalion in France to one going overseas within the next week or two and Mara, to her mother-in-law's disgust, could not keep her hands off him.

'Kissing and . . hugging and all for the servants and her own innocent children to see,' Serena told Elizabeth when she visited her daughter and her new grandson who had been born two days before. And Serena herself, who was after all James' mother, when all was said and done, was barely allowed to embrace him before Mara had him up the stairs and the bedroom door shut behind them.

'You will know what I mean, I'm sure, darling,' Serena drawled, loosening the tails of the magnificent fox stole she wore about her shoulders, and Elizabeth did for Mara had told her only last week when she had heard James was to be home. In that carelessly impudent way she had, her eyes sparkling gleefully in anticipation! It seemed that James had said that she must take a good look at the floor since she'd be seeing nothing but the ceiling whilst he was home

'Really, what the servants thought I can only imagine,' Serena continued, not awfully sure she liked the way her own daughter was smiling. 'Your father was quite disgusted since he wanted to sit down with James and have one of those long talks gentlemen seem to like. About the war, of course, and what is going on in France And naturally he would have liked to know if James had seen anything of Teddy, or Harry and the Woodall boys. Not a sign of any of them in all this time Seven months without the faintest notion of how things are with them, except through their letters which, as well you know, say absolutely nothing. And now, when we have a chance to obtain first-hand knowledge from James, Mara selfishly whisks him off to   well . . we won't dwell on that, will we for we can guess,' Serena shrugged in disgust, 'and he was not allowed even a glimpse of the twins despite the fact that he has not yet seen them Pardon dear? The? oh of course, the new boy .. your son

yes, very pretty, darling . ' surveying from a safe distance the sleeping form of her latest grandchild, of whom she had so many now, in the nest of his crib and who nurse seemed to think she should scrutinise. 'Mmm, and who does

501

he look like? Not Harry with all that dark hair, and his eyes, what colour are they ... hazel, you think, charming ... now then, what are you to call him?'

'I had thought Alexander, that is if Harry agrees.'

'Alexander ... charming ... now where was I?'

'I will hold the baby, if you please, nurse,' Elizabeth interrupted, and to Serena's bewilderment her daughter nursed her new son the whole time her mother was there, barely looking up from her absorbed study of his sleeping face, and really, as she said to her husband later, one could only despair for Mara's strange and outlandish ways seemed to be rubbing off on their daughter.

James stayed for three days, quieter than anyone remembered him, and thinner, wanting nothing more, it appeared, than to sit and hold his wife's hand with his children about him, perhaps one on his lap, to walk with her in the gardens pushing the baby carriage containing Mairin and Ailis, if you please, with Claudine and Christian positively shrieking about him, and what was to happen next in this strange world into which they had been suddenly flung, his mother pleaded to know. Eager each of the three nights to be alone with his wife, impregnating her again, Serena was certain, and he himself only twenty-two years old. The father of four children at the age of twenty-two and she shuddered to think of how many he would have by the time he was thirty. It was all that girl's fault, of course, bringing her working-class, Irish and Catholic traditions into this house which had known only gentlemen's ways ever since the first James Osborne had bought it and now would you look at it, filled from top to bottom with screaming, out-of-hand children whom their mother did nothing to control and moreover, interfered with Nanny when she attempted it.

The first British landings at the southern tip of the Gallipoli Peninsula began on April 25th and when the campaign was over left behind were 46,000 Allied dead, most of them

British soldiers. They were killed by bad leadership, lamentable tactics, poor food, scorching heat, heavy casualties and dysentery.

But how they fought, those gallant young men, amongst them a brigade composed entirely of battalions of the Lancashire Fusiliers and the legends of their bravery were many and great. Six Victoria Crosses before breakfast was how the newspapers reported their performance on that fatal day. Cutters were used to transfer them from the cruiser HM *Euryalas*, towed by picket boats as far as the shallow waters of the beach where the cutters were cast off. As the leading boats touched the beach, the Turkish army opened fire, slicing into the soldiers as they tumbled and floundered in the water.

Of those who died a great many drowned, simply dragged down by the weight of their seventy-pound packs.

'Thous't given us a bloody job here,' one man, seven times wounded, said to his officer who was Lieutenant James Osborne as they struggled together to reach the beach which was later named 'Lancashire Landing', and where Lieutenant Osborne was to die that day.

Mara screamed in genuine agony when the telegram came, then fell senseless to the drawing room carpet. The piece of paper and the buff envelope which had contained it drifted down beside her.

They had been just about to have coffee after dining, in fact Betty was still leaning over the small table she was placing by Mrs Osborne's knee and when the wounded animal cries of her mistress' daughter-in-law rent the warm peace of the drawing room, she was afraid to move in case she might further shatter the paralysed composure of Mr and Mrs Osborne and set them to moaning as Mrs James was now doing.

Johnny and Serena Osborne made no attempt to pick up the telegram. They knew what it contained, after all, so there seemed no point in reading it. The pain would be crippling

503

enough without seeing its cause actually in writing. Later, when they could manage it, they would look at the words which were breaking their hearts, if not their English, upper class spirit, but for now, best keep a hold on their dignity and bearing. Leave the histrionics to their son's wife, or his widow, as she now was. They had risen when the telegram was put into Mara's hand and now they both stood absolutely still, their well-bred faces like marble, their cultural upbringing quelling their need to moan as Mara was moaning.

Nobody moved. Eaton studied young Mrs James' crumpled figure where it lay beside the sofa and in the thirty seconds before Serena Osborne remembered who they were, he felt that he had relived Mr James' young life, most of which he had known. The placid, even-tempered child, the growing, amiable schoolboy, the well-mannered youth who had conformed entirely to his class and upbringing. Who had done exactly what his ancestry demanded of him with one exception and she lay, her senses beginning painfully to return, on her mother-in-law's pedigreed carpet. An engaging young man who had followed the course life had set out for him at birth and now, it appeared, he was dead.

Betty, *her* upbringing showing, began to weep for surely someone should be helping poor Mrs James but Mr and Mrs Osborne appeared to be struck dumb and fixed in the fearful posture they had assumed as they came to their feet when Eaton had brought in the telegram. Poor Mrs James was beginning to stir now and in a moment, if Betty knew her, which they all did, would be screaming her head off again and really, they could not leave her there as she was

Serena Osborne moved then. Her composure was complete. Her face was set in ghastly lines of self-control, her eyes deep and dreadful in the ash of her face. She moved stiffly to her husband and took his flaccid arm.

'See to Mrs James, will you, Betty.' Her voice was hollow but it had a strength in it which told Betty and Eaton and even her stunned and severely weakened husband that they would manage this dreadful thing in the correct and proper manner of their class even if their daughter-in-law did not.

Betty would not forget that night in a hurry, she told the other servants, and for weeks afterwards she regaled them with tales of the high powered, wellnigh uncontrollable hysteria of her young mistress who could not, would not accept that her husband was dead. If it had not been for the combined efforts of Miss Elizabeth, Lady Woodall, who had herself only recently been confined and who was hastily sent for, and Betty herself, there was no doubt Mrs James would have burst into the nursery and wept all over the huddled and certainly terrified figures of her four children. She wanted them with her, she screamed, for they were all she had left of James and not only that she wanted her Mammy and Daddy and Elizabeth was to drive over to Edge Lane and fetch them at once. Or better still, Nanny was to dress Miss Claudine and Master Christian, Miss Mairin and Miss Ailis and have them put in her motor car and she would go at once to her Mammy's house for there was nothing here for her now. She would move back to Edge Lane, she wept, her very grief as dramatic and impressive as only Mara could display it.

Not that her suffering wasn't genuine, Betty was certain of that, for when this Irish girl, who was really no better than Betty herself, had come to Beechwood as a bride, no matter what any of them might have thought of her she had brought love with her. Master James had adored her, they had all known that, and she had felt the same way about him, despite her flibberty-gibbet ways.

A lovely young man, Betty wept as she ran down to the kitchen for fresh tea, and now he was gone and Eaton was hard pressed to persuade the young maids who were inclined to bury their faces in their starched aprons and weep too, that they must get to their beds. Mrs Castle, the housekeeper and the cook, Mrs Pritchard, who was blubbering over memories of the 'gingerbread men' she had used to make for Master James, would sit by the housekeeper's fireside for a while longer just in case they were needed, they said, and fortified by a tot of Mr Osborne's finest Scotch whisky, they mourned the passing of the Osborne son.

Mara slept at last, her head on Elizabeth's shoulder, the crumpled dinner gown of gold satin and lace she still wore riding up about her shapely legs. She had wept furiously, piteously, bitterly, brokenheartedly, declaring like a child who cannot believe that it is being punished when it has done nothing to merit it, that she could not live without James, and what was to become of her and her fatherless children? It was not fair, it was not just, she had cried, tearing at her hair in a most terrifying way. She alternated between a deep, despairing grief and a savage rage that she should be the one to suffer it and Elizabeth was sorely tempted to do as she asked and bring Ellen O'Shaughnessy to her stricken daughter. Only the thought of her own mother restrained her since she was aware that Serena would never, never forgive her for bringing one of the Irish into her home. In her own grief she was in pain too and at this moment should surely be considered as much as Mara?

Slipping her arm from beneath Mara's neck, she eased herself from the bed which, six weeks ago, Mara had shared for the last time with her young husband. She stood at the side of the bed and looked at her sister-in-law and in the shaded glow of the lamp which was still lit Mara had the appearance of a broken doll which has been tossed aside by a careless child. Beside the bed the exhausted Betty snored gently, her cap askew and her apron stained with tea for Mara had been violent at times.

With Mara quiet now Elizabeth began her own inward grieving, which was of the deepest sort, for her brother. She could not believe he was dead, not James. It seemed but a moment since that day when he and Teddy and herself had ridden over to Woodall to see Harry's new hunter. He and

Hugh had gone off on some schoolboy escapade of a sexual nature, their youthful faces agog with the excitement of it. They had been vigorous, their young hot blood pumping through them at this, their first, or possibly second encounter with what was really the most enjoyable pastime in the world, their eagerness to get away had seemed to imply, and now it was all finished. James; an endearing, light-hearted boy who had gone to war with a jaunty angle to his officer's cap and who had come home six weeks ago with a man's face beneath it. What had he seen in Flanders, in the trenches where the sound of shellfire was so fierce they said it could be heard in the county of Kent? From where an increasingly alarming number of casualties came. From where, it was rumoured, they were bringing their boys home in trainloads, limbless and blinded, mutilated and emasculated, some with their nerves in such tatters they would never be the same again. What had happened there to the carelessly good-humoured young man who had been her brother and who had come home so quietly last month and then gone away to die? They had seen the casualty lists, those at home, and heard of this one or that, friends, sons of friends who would never see English skies again but somehow it had not quite touched home, not quite touched the family of which she was a part. Not until now. She had thought the worst that could happen to them had happened on this day, but this day could happen again and again, for there was still Harry, Teddy, Tim and Hugh. They were still in the line of fire. And so was Michael O'Shaughnessy.

She moved away from the bed where Mara lay in troubled sleep and crossed to the window, resting her cheek against the cold window pane, looking out at the dark and familiar silhouette of the garden where she had spent her childhood, where she and James and Teddy, when they could escape Nanny, had romped and played the daredevil games thought up by her brothers. She had known little affection from her parents but she and James and Teddy, perhaps because of it, had been close and fiercely loyal to one another. They had not been overly demonstrative for that sort of thing was frowned on in their society but they had known a great fondness for one another. She could really not imagine Beechwood without James in it, calling for his chestnut mare or burning down the drive in the fast little sports car he had come to love. Where was he? In which bit of unmarked ground did he lie in this far-off Gallipoli to which he had been sent, and had he had friends about him when he was put in it? She was not awfully certain even of where it was or what British soldiers were doing there but whatever the reason it seemed he had been vulnerable to shell and shot and all the other devilish devices which were bound and determined to kill those she loved. Harry, Teddy ... and Michael.

Aah, Michael. She could see his smile now, a smile that had enchanted her and broken her heart at one and the same time. Michael who was lost to her as surely as if it had been he who had died on April 25th as well as James. She loved him, of course she did, and would never stop for he was entrenched deep in her heart, the roots of him nourished, cherished, by the love she bore him and though he was to marry his Irish cousin on his first leave, so Mara had told her, what difference did that make to the way she, Elizabeth Woodall, felt about him? For twenty-four hours after the birth of her son, until that son had been placed in her arms, she had hated him because of what she had thought of as his infidelity but she had come to see that Michael had no obligation to be true to her. She was Harry's wife and she had told him so and told him to go away and so he had gone and if he had found a woman to comfort him, could Elizabeth Woodall complain of it? She had nothing to offer him. They had nothing to offer each other. Harry would be home when this bitter war was over, he would, *he would*, and she could not allow herself to think otherwise and when he did she must make a life for them and for their sons since

Michael O'Shaughnessy's boy would be known as Alexander Woodall and no one, not even his true father, would know that Harry Woodall had not bred him.

Only she, and perhaps one other, would ever see Michael in the boy, in the certain way he held his head and the way he frowned, that ferocious dip to his eyebrows which Michael had, and the gold which tipped his long dark lashes. Only one other and that was Ellen O'Shaughnessy for surely a mother would recognise the son she loves, the son to whom she gave birth, in that son's son.

Elizabeth remained for several days at Beechwood, Alexander with her. Her presence seemed to give some comfort to her grieving sister-in-law and it was certain that Mara would get none from Serena. Whilst Johnny Osborne rode his broad acres, sadly surveying the inheritance which would never belong to his older son, Serena remained closeted behind the door of her own suite of rooms, seeing only close friends who came to pay their respects to the bereaved parents. On the one or two occasions Elizabeth saw her, bearing up, of course, for what else would Serena do, she was in the deepest black of mourning and, Elizabeth thought, would be until the end of her days.

Mara spent most of her days with her mother, taking her babies with her, accompanied by a young nursemaid since she refused to allow Nanny to go with her, saying she was miserable enough without the disapproving presence of the 'old harridan' to make things worse.

It was from one of these visits several weeks later that she drove straight from Edge Lane to Woodall Park, depositing her family in Elizabeth's nursery before coming into Elizabeth's sitting room.

She dropped her bombshell without the slightest idea of the havoc it was about to cause.

'Michael came home this morning, Elizabeth. From France. Two weeks' leave and the wedding's to be on Saturday. You did know he was to be married, didn't you? Yes, well, the Mammy asked me specially if you'd come, so she did, though it'll not be the grand affair the first son of the family would normally have, not with Sean . and James .. so recently ` she sighed deeply, 'you know what I mean, but she'd like you to be there.'

She sighed again, her heart heavy and aching in her breast, drifting across Elizabeth's sitting room like some palely pretty, sombrely dressed ghost, her vigorous spirit quenched by the burden of the grief she carried. It was only a month since James had died on that blood-soaked beach and the loss of her young husband was almost more than she could bear. She wore the deepest black and to Serena's gratification and astonishment was, though it sounded strange to say it, even to herself, the perfect model of widowhood. Mara had seemed to be flighty, light-minded, those were the words Serena would have used, and was not a girl to feel deeply the loss of anyone, even her own husband, but her true sorrow and the depth of it had surprised her mother-in-law and in some way softened her attitude towards Mara. Like so many of his comrades James had been buried almost where he fell and though the parson at the Anglican Church where the Osbornes worshipped had spoken his name, along with other local young men who had given their lives in the service of their country, it had not been the same as a decent, honourable funeral. They were all in the full black of mourning, naturally, and if Serena had anything to say about it, which she undoubtedly would, they would stay in it for a full year and a day, as had been proper in her's, and her mother's time, even if today's modern women thought that to be going too far. James had died, as so many of his contemporaries were dying, the most gallant death in the noblest of causes, a sacrifice which it was a privilege to have made, by him and by his grieving family. Victory over death. What a balm that thought was to Serena and all the other bereaved mothers and James was enshrined forever in her heart, as he was in Mara's, she was gratified to see.

Though it was the end of May the day was cold and Elizabeth had instructed the maid to heap up the fire with coal. The glow from the flames leaped delicately across the pale amber silk of her sitting room walls and turned the glossy white paintwork to apricot. The long tawny curtains of velvet at the windows were partially drawn to conceal the fine drizzle which drifted in relentless swathes across the parkland of Woodall. Mara's hair was still starred with it for she had driven herself over from Edge Lane, neglecting in her casual disregard for everything but her own heavy heart to put on her hat and what protection there was in the confines of her Morris had been allotted to the shivering nursemaid and the children in her care. Mara had tossed her driving coat carelessly on to the velvet-backed nursing chair which stood beside the window and she leaned against its back as she stared between the curtains at the dismal scene beyond the misted glass. Her eyes were bleak, not at all interested in Elizabeth's answer, nor in the wedding itself which would be an ordinary affair, in Church, of course, but with none of the splendour or even the joy with which her own had been blessed. Most weddings today were like that. Simple and hasty for the soldier bridegroom was most likely off to war the next day and wanted only to get his bride into bed whilst he was still capable of being a man, a lover, since he might be dead, or worse, by the week's end.

Elizabeth felt her mind slip a shade away from reality and towards the strange sensation that this was happening, not to her, but to the calm woman, whoever she was, who sat with the newspapers still on her lap and which she had been studying when Mara was announced. This woman would know anguish and the most searing pain shortly but at this moment all there was ... was nothing! A great empty nothing which would be filled, when the insensibility wore off, with something, but which, at the moment, did not hurt at all. When Mara had gone and she was alone she would lose her control and be left winded and gasping like a woman in labour and the end result could only be agony.

'Elizabeth?' Mara's voice was sharp and she had turned to stare, her face somewhat bewildered so that Elizabeth knew that despite her calm and seemingly normal behaviour, she must have appeared strange in some way to her sister-in-law.

'Begorra, you look as though you'd seen a ghost, so you do.' Mara moved towards her, the black silk of her mourning gown whispering about her fine-boned ankles.

'No, I'm quite all right, really, it's just the ... sadness of it all.'

'Sadness? A wedding?'

'No, of course not, but those who are unable to be here...' already the numbness was beginning to wear off and she had started to gabble, to gabble anything which might distract Mara from noticing her own increasingly odd behaviour. She couldn't stand it. Although she knew it was to happen she couldn't stand it. She wished she could die of it, she really did, but of course no one dies of hopeless love, nor of despair. One only lives on in the most dreadful pain, hoping, surely, that one day it would come to an end. Ever since Alexander's birth she had been waiting for the news that Michael and his pretty little cousin ... what was her name ... she couldn't remember as the haze began to fill her mind like smoke in which she was losing herself. Ellen had presented her future daughter-in-law on that day with all the pride of a woman who is well pleased with the suitable wife for her beloved son and on Saturday ... oh Dear Lord ... I cannot ...

'Are you to come, then?'

'What ... ?'

'Elizabeth, will you listen to what I'm saying an' stop looking about the room as though you hadn't the faintest notion of where you are, begod.'

Elizabeth turned her head with a great effort in the direc-

512

tion of her sister-in-law. 'I'm sorry, Mara, you must thank
your mother for me but I really don't think .. well, not
whilst we are still mourning .. James. It is most kind of
her, but...'

'Well, I'm to be there, so I am, and I'm mourning just as
much as you.'

'Of course you are.' Oh please ... please let me stay in
this place of mists for a little while longer. Just until Mara
has gone. Let me remain in this state of stunned shock, this
half-feeling for a little while longer. When I am alone I can
release it, the pain and the loss, the waste, and let the hurt
of it wash from me, explode from me in any way it must.
I can lock the door and release the heartbreak and the
desperation where no one can see it.

'...but you are . the sister of the bridegroom.. '
she went on unsteadily, hoping Mara would put down her
trembling voice to her grief for James, 'and it is only natural
that you should want to see your brother married. She is
your cousin, is she not?'

'Yes, Mary Kate.'

That was it, Mary Kate, Michael's bride .. Mary Kate.

'So give my good wishes to ...' Could she say it? Could
she speak his name ... and hers, without crumpling from
her chair, crying out her savagery at the ordeal she could
barely handle. She must.

And she did. She drank tea and discussed children's ail-
ments, the chances of Harry getting some leave, what Mara
was to wear at the wedding for of course it must be black,
the possibility of a fine day for the ceremony. When she
herself was to resume driving, possibly the Austin Seven
two-seater which Harry had left in the garage behind the
stables. She held Mara's hand and comforted her when Mara
wept for James which she did at least half a dozen times a
day seeing no need to hide her pain as her mother-in-law,
and even Elizabeth did. Whenever she felt the need she
wept and Elizabeth wished she could do the same. She held

herself in tight, fierce clenched control until her teeth ached in her head and even her hair seemed to be in pain. Mara drifted from the chair to the window, then to the fireside, then repeated the circle, unable to keep her own pain-burdened body still, her voice stumbling over and over on her husband's name. James ... James ... James ...

And then she was gone.

Elizabeth could not stay in the house. Alexander was due to be fed but she could not stay in the house despite the heaviness of her milk-filled breasts. She could not bear to stay in the house and though she knew that soon her mother-in-law and her sister-in-law would be dressing for dinner and would be expecting her in the drawing room, that within the hour the dinner gong would sound calling her to the meal which she and Lady Woodall and Sophie shared at the enormous dining table, she flung herself down the back stairs to the cupboard which was close to the side entrance. No one saw her go. Selecting some stout boots ... whose? ... probably Harry's when he was a boy, and a warm, hooded cloak, she crept out through the side door and into the spindrift of the early evening rain.

She walked blindly away from the house, not knowing, nor caring where she was going. What did it matter? What did anything matter but the need to escape from her own thoughts which were crowded, painful with images of a virginal white dress, a virginal sixteen-year-old shrouded in a misty veil. Of a man in uniform, of church bells and white rose petals, of the laughter and tears of a wedding day, of smiles and a shy rosy face lifting for a kiss. Of that virginal white dress being taken from that sixteen-year-old body and ... her heart could not stand to go on but her mind did not care about that as it remorselessly painted picture after picture of the pretty bride Michael was to take for his wife on Saturday, and of Michael himself, blue eyes vivid in his brown face, dark hair tumbling endearingly above them as he took her virginity from her.

514

She had not seen him for almost a year and yet he was as vibrant and alive in her mind, in her heart where she kept him cherished, as though it had been but that morning. She imagined, stumbling through the endlessly dripping trees as the rain fell in a mist from a sullen sky, as it drifted in a great moving curtain across the pasture where the horses usually cropped, that she could feel his presence where once he had exercised Harry's hunter, and hear his cheerful whistle as he curried the splendid animal's coat to gleaming ebony.

She stumbled on, her bare head bent to avoid the steady rain for she did not think to protect it with the hood, her hands plunged deep in her pockets. The cape was shorter than her skirt and the hem of it was soon heavy and dragging with moisture but still she went on. The rain dripped from her hair across her forehead and caught on her eyelashes and she blinked to clear them and to clear the pictures of Michael O'Shaughnessy which her mind's eye had created to weaken her. He was there beside her, walking in step with her, his stride longer than hers and she moved more quickly to keep up with him. He waited for her at the gate in the hedge, smiling his impudent smile, his eyebrows raised enquiringly as though to ask where she had been. He was leaning against a tree trunk, a cigarette between his lips, the smoke making him narrow his eyes, the rain dripping on to his bare head and plastering his hair to his skull. He was everywhere, her love, everywhere she turned. She could even smell the cigarette and hear the hiss as he threw it, still burning, into the wet undergrowth.

Michael! Not Michael . . . a soldier in a khaki greatcoat . . . not Michael . . . this did not . . . this was merely a figment . . .

Michael! Why was she not surprised, why had she never been surprised to find him standing just where her imagination had put him? It seemed natural that her own tortuous thoughts had made him materialise into this world of shadows in which she floundered, brought him here to tell her that the love Elizabeth Woodall and Michael O'Shaughnessy shared could not be flung aside, of no use nor worth to either of them. That it must be recognised for what it was, precious, treasured, prized by them both, that it must be voiced on this last day. *This last day*.

He stood away from the tree and walked towards her. She had stopped in the middle of the clearing and the rain fell unimpeded directly on to her bare head and across her face. Her skin glistened like white marble and her lips, just as pale, parted as her tongue licked the moisture from them.

He spoke first, his voice sighing and somehow thankful. 'I had to see you before the ... I prayed that you would come. Called you and here you are,' as though it was no surprise to him.

'Yes, I must have heard you, somehow ...'

'You know about the ...' He could not say the word to her.

'Yes, Mara told me.'

'I'm sorry, my darling.'

His darling! Dear God, she was still that.

Her voice was thick with tears. 'What is there to be sorry about? You have chosen a bride and on Saturday she is to be your wife.' Someone must say it.

'Does it hurt you, Elizabeth, as much as your marriage hurt me?'

'How can you ask?'

'Then that is why I'm sorry. Last time we were together . '

'Please . . don't .. '

'I must. The last time all I wanted was to have you suffer as you made me suffer but that was then and now I cannot bear to see you in pain. But .. a man must marry, or so they say, especially now when . ' The inference was not lost on her. When a man could die the next day, or the next,

· 516

and how else could he live on if not in the child he might leave behind. It was the male instinct to perpetuate itself, after all.

'Do you love her?' The eternal question a woman asks a man when she has lost him to another.

The silence which followed was filled with the sound of rain dripping from leaf to leaf, pattering to the ground where it sucked its way into the lush vegetation. She died a little as she waited for his answer.

'Yes,' he said at last, 'as you love Harry Woodall. I have known her all my life, as you have known him. She's of my ... class, sure an' I never thought to hear meself say that but you'll know what I mean. She's ... acceptable to my family, part of my family, if you like, and she ...'

'Loves you?'

'Aye ...' and he sighed deeply, sadly, for what he could not give to Mary Kate. Nothing left, it seemed, but affection and the kind of life to which she was accustomed. Nothing left for it had all been given to the woman who stood before him. Her luminous face told him he had given her the answer she needed.

Their eyes clung, sending messages of some urgency, the silent, invisible cord which had bound them together for five years as tight, tightening even further, drawing them across the clearing until they were face to face.

'Oh God, Elizabeth ...' he groaned, his face drawn into harsh lines of pain and for a moment she was distracted from her need to be in his arms by the expression which was stamped there. He was altered from that young and smiling man she had once known. There was a maturity, a sense of having grown up, gone on, of experiencing something which only he and perhaps those he fought beside had known. Eyes which stared, unfocused, at a shadow she could not see. A fine-drawn vulnerability in his body which made her want to draw him into her arms, not with passion but to provide the comfort and reassurance she gave to her son when he had taken a tumble. There was a thinning of his mouth and a fast beating pulse in his temple and an inclination, she thought, to keep a sharp eye out for whatever might be hidden over the horizon.

They did not speak again. What was there to say which had not been said? He lifted his arms and held them out to her and she moved into them blindly, thankfully. His lips searched for hers and she gave them to him. Her arms crossed at his back, holding his body to hers, as his did, and the rain fell and mingled with the joyless tears they both shed.

Harry came home in July with the exact same look about him that Michael had had. He had been gone ten months and he was to be home for ten days, his last letter had told her. It took him two days to get to the harbour at Boulogne, across the channel to Folkestone and from there to Liverpool. And he must allow the same for the journey back. Six days and nights left in which he would be held in the arms of his beloved wife, when he would walk in the park and woods of Woodall with his toddling son and meet for the first time the boy Elizabeth had given birth to in March. The joy of reunion for which he had longed, for which Elizabeth had longed, was almost more than they could bear. So poignant was the moment that for several minutes they stood locked in one another's arms before the smiling servants until Harry's mother and sister almost tore him out of her arms in their longing to hold him. The experience for them all was overwhelming and none of them could speak, so thick with tears were their throats.

They patted him and cleared their throats and the elder Lady Woodall wiped her eyes on a scrap of lace, the unusual circumstances, for surely these were unusual times, justifying the loss of self-control which had been ingrained in her from childhood. She had three sons at the front. Serena Osborne had had two, but one was already gone and could

Anne Woodall be blamed for being somewhat less disciplined than was normal?

It was as though they were entertaining a polite guest in their home, a gentleman who was never anything less than courteous and attentive, smiling a bright and cheerful smile which never quite reached his eyes, saying all the correct and dutiful things which were expected of him and listening with well-bred interest to whatever they might wish to say to him

He had bathed and changed at once, his mother's barely hidden disapproval at the state of his uniform and his boots, Elizabeth noticed, causing him a certain amount of strain.

'Heavens, Harry, what on earth have you been doing to get yourself into such a state?' she had asked her son fondly. 'You must give your uniform to Wilson at once to be cleaned, and your boots, then we shall have a sherry in the drawing room whilst you tell us all about your adventures in France'

She meant to be gay and cheerful, to keep from her son her unease at the hollows in his drawn face, the deep and weary circles about his eyes, but Elizabeth saw him wince.

'Come on up, sweetheart,' she said gently, taking his arm and leading him towards the wide, curved staircase. At its foot Nanny stood with Alexander in her arms, his face sleeping and rosy, set in the frill of his white bonnet, and struggling in the arms of the nursemaid, Flora, was Charles who, having been told that 'Father', who was a soldier, was to come home, demanded to have a look at him.

'The children   ' Harry murmured dutifully

'Later   ' and he went with her thankfully She was all he wanted He didn't want his mother who, it appeared, though she smiled her well-bred smile, was on the brink of amazing tears He did not want Sophie who was dying to tell him of the Red Cross meetings she was attending and her intention, if she could persuade her mother, of going to train, as a VAD in a hospital for officers near Warrington.

Just until she married her young fiancé, of course, who was, naturally, at the front. Though Harry was ashamed of it, at that moment he was not even concerned with his sons.

He loathed the war. He had served nearly three hundred days of discomfort, of dullness, of strain and fear, of dirt and death and disease and the constant need to pretend that he didn't mind at all being shelled and shot at. He was a junior officer with barely a month's training when he had been shipped to France where he had been expected to take charge of men in the dreadful ways of war, in battles which seemed incomprehensible to him. He had shared the dirty and dangerous lives of his troops, mounting raids, cutting the enemy's barbed wire and replacing their own, leading attacks in which men had fallen on either side of him whilst he had survived unscathed.

Now he wanted, craved, only the sensations his wife could give him. He wanted delicacy and softness, luxury, his wife's eyes soft and sleepy, then warm with sensuality, her low laugh, the sunlight in her dark hair, lacy feminine things, silk stockings and dainty underwear, white skin, curving and erotic, satin smooth breasts heavy in his hands, clean silken sheets and the smell of the lavender in which they were stored and his wife's body ready and willing, eager as she had always been, and was, spread upon them just as he remembered, with all the wise and knowing perceptions of love a woman can bring to the man who loves her.

But the two worlds, the world of the soldier and the one in which those at home lived were too far apart and the gap was unbridgeable. No matter how Elizabeth Woodall loved the man who had come back to her in Harry Woodall's body, no matter what she gave of herself to him in her attempt to bring him peace and comfort and love, he had been home no more than forty-eight hours when it became obvious to her, who knew every nuance of his character and mood, that he was restless, even somewhat irritable.

hey took their sons for long walks in the park and Harry
d his best to play with Charles but she could see that it
as a great relief to him when Nanny came to take them
ck to the nursery. He had admired the handsome and
creasingly vigorous charm of the new baby, remarking
at he resembled the Osborne family more than his own.
e was happy with the name Alexander, as he had told her in
s letters, though there had never been one in the Woodall
mily. He had tossed him in the air and, as he had dreamed
 doing in the dugout which was his 'home' whilst the war
sted, nursed him on his awkward lap, but not for long.
   'I'm sorry, darling,' he apologised to his wife, pushing his
nd through his hair, his thin face strained with the effort
 'enjoying' himself in this much loved environment which
d been his home since birth. 'I can't seem to ... well,
u must find me extremely dull ... I can't explain it. I
apped at Petch this morning when he took me around
e estate and tried to tell me how he has managed it while
was away. The poor chap thought he was doing his duty
d so he was but ... well, he asked when I was going back
d what it was like out there. Had I seen any action, that
rt of thing and, well, to tell the truth it got on my nerves.
 you like it out there, he asked, just as though I was there
luntarily.'
   'Don't worry, sweetheart, I'm sure Petch ...'
   'I don't give a damn about Petch.'
   'No, of course not, and why should you ...'
   'For God's sake, Elizabeth, don't be so bloody understand-
g. I was infernally rude to the man and you are saying it
esn't matter.'
   'No darling, I'm not saying that but Petch knows that you
e ...'
   'What?' Harry's eyes narrowed and he tapped a cigarette
rvously against the packet, then lit it, dragging the smoke
eply into his lungs.
   'That you are under a strain ...'

521

'What does he know about it? What do any of you know about it?'

'Well, nothing, I admit, but perhaps if you told me . . .'

He turned his back on her and strode to the window of their bedroom, staring out broodingly to the wide lawn where Nanny and Flora were taking a decorous turn about the gardens with the baby carriage. Charles staggered ahead of them, his clear child's voice floating up through the blue and gold summer air and Flora ran after him, gathering him up into her arms where he squealed with laughter. Elizabeth was bringing up their children to be less restrained than he and his brothers and sister had been and he was glad but it did nothing to soften the hard and bitter stone which lay in his chest. Only his wife's white flesh, her sweet breath and soft lips, her loving hands and the utter submersion of his body in hers released him from the unreality of the days he was spending in his own home. It was all make-believe this world, and though it would break his heart to leave her, to subject himself and her to the harrowing parting to come, he could not wait to get back. He knew what he was going to this time, of course, and dreaded the thought of it but it must be done. It had sapped his strength of mind, being with his family, muddled the certainty of what he and thousands upon thousands like him were doing. He had felt like a stranger in his own home and the sooner it was done with the better. The turmoil of emotion was almost more than he could cope with and even Elizabeth, who had always known him better than anyone, did not understand. The real world was in France.

They parted by the stretch of woodland known as Crow Nest, presumably because of the large number of crows which nested there each year. Edwards was to pick him up on the drive which ran past the trees to the gates and take him to Lime Street station but he had wanted to leave her without his mother and Sophie being present. He had already said his goodbyes to them. He needed to remember his wife, until the next time he should see her, he told himself quickly, standing quietly on her own in the simple white dress he loved her in, his home and hers behind her, their sons safely sheltered there. This is where they started their lives, he and Elizabeth, and against this background she must remain in his memory until he came back to her. He loved her so desperately and was afraid of leaving her now that the time had come. She was the refuge to which he would return, his safeguard against the fears which haunted them all in the line, the defence standing between him and the horrors which, until he had gone to war, had never troubled the secure and careless mind of Harry Woodall.

'I'm sorry, I'm sorry, my darling,' he whispered into her hair, his khaki-clad arms crushing her to him: 'I love you more than life. You are my life, you see. As long as I know you will be here . . .'

'I'm here, Harry. I will always be here.'

'Will you be here, just here beneath the trees when I . . .'

'Yes, my love, in this exact spot.' She smiled serenely up at him, then cupping his face with her hands placed the long sweet line of her mouth against his, parting his lips with her own. She wanted to say all the things women who love say to the loved one who is leaving: 'Take care', 'Be careful', 'Don't take unnecessary risks', but she knew it made no difference. She had no idea, none of them had at home, what Harry and hundreds of thousands like him did 'over here' but she knew now, from Harry's manner, that it was of a savage nature for what else could have changed her endearing, sweet-natured, good-humoured husband into the harrowed, grim-faced man who had come home to her.

He turned to look at her as the motor passed through the gates where Tommy Perks lifted his hand in a respectful salute, and her white dress shimmered beneath the deep shade of the oak tree. She raised one hand and he was not to know that it was at exactly the same place that Michael

O'Shaughnessy had said goodbye to her in the eddying rain eight weeks before.

28

On July 1st 1916, a fine sunny morning, those who lived were to remember, the great offensive involving five French divisions and eighteen British, the 'big push' for which they had all waited, began.

At dusk the night before Captain Jack Templeton of the 2nd Battalion Lancashire Fusiliers had ridden towards the British trenches to have a look at the route by which his men were to advance if the attack went as planned the following morning. On the left side of his cap he wore the primrose-yellow hackle awarded to the regiment in 1901 for extreme valour at Spion Kop and in recognition of two centuries of service. Jack had fought at Spion Kop on January 24th 1900 and had lost many friends among the 32 officers and 290 men killed that day and it was in his heart that fine evening that he might be about to do so again the next morning. Or perhaps it was his turn. The odds against him surviving after almost eighteen years of service were heavily stacked against him.

It was a peaceful evening. The British guns were firing but there was no answer from the Germans as thousands upon thousands of men on an eighteen-mile front prepared themselves for battle. Many were already in the trenches and he nodded pleasantly to a group who crouched against the seven-foot parapet of earth and sandbags which protected them from the enemy's small arms fire.

'Evenin', sir. Looks to be a nice day for it,' one said and Jack smiled and nodded again. The noise from the bombardment made speech almost impossible but, according to his superiors, it would destroy and pulverise the enemy in his trenches and tomorrow the Tommies would be able to stroll across no-man's-land at a steady pace with, as one particularly optimistic staff officer put it, 'rifles at the port'.

There were men on the march, and some, who were reserves and further back in the lines, listened to a concert by the band of the Leeds Pals. Rare ones for brass bands were Yorkshire lads and though they were many miles from home, apprehensive about what was to happen to them at daybreak, they listened with evident enjoyment.

Men sang softly as they tramped, particularly those of the Welsh Regiments, mostly hymns for it seemed appropriate as their muffled marching whispered through the falling darkness. There was a feeling of optimism. Morale and hopes were high for at last they were to get to grips with the Boche and defeat him, they told one another. Massing to go over the top, they were intensely excited and confident for this was to be the breakthrough to end the stalemate of the past eighteen months and the war.

Jack's thoughts turned, as they always did, to Caitlin, knowing she would be waiting, as all those behind the lines were, for what tomorrow would bring. She had been in France for almost a year now, meeting Jack whenever they could get a few hours, two days, a night, their joy in one another heightened to almost unbearable proportions by the knowledge that each time could possibly, was probably, the last time they would ever see one another. They walked hand in hand along empty sands and through sand dunes festooned with barbed wire, talking, looking at one another, touching, storing up in terrified minds the memories which might be all they would have in the years to come since Caitlin was in the same danger, if not to quite the same degree, as Jack.

Once they had gone to Paris. She had been nursing at Number 22 General Camp Hospital situated between the villages of Dannes and Camiers then. It lay behind the sand dunes of the coast just under the slopes of the low hills near the railway line that served the half a dozen hospitals which had been built there and which took the gassed, the burned, the blinded before they were labelled and shipped home like so many badly wrapped parcels to whoever was to take charge of the agony she herself had done her best to ease. She tended the choking, the crippled, the emasculated, the shell-shocked men who were sent back from the line and she waited for him, for her husband, for his letters.

Sometimes it was too much for him.

'They go on for miles, you know,' he had burst out one night when they had managed to snatch three precious hours together at an inn on the outskirts of Etaples, his voice coming from the dark just as though he could not hold it in for a moment longer, surprising even himself. 'They were only lines at first, no taller than a man and at the first rain they fell in, burying the very men they were meant to protect. I saw a man buried alive one day, did you know that?'

'No, darling.' She had drawn his head to her breast and cradled him with all the loving intensity of a protective mother and he had huddled into it as though he were indeed a child.

'Not a pretty sight, Caitlin, especially when the barbed wire held him firmly and prevented us from getting to him. Now they build them more stoutly with sandbags and wooden sides. Quite home from home it is, with dugouts for the officers to sit in with their telephones and camp-beds and bottles of French wine. You daren't move, of course, or a German sniper will have your head off your shoulders before you can say *Guten tag*. They panic, you know, the young soldiers and one of them only has to scream and in a minute half the platoon is in a frenzy. You can't blame them, of course. Fear is the most potent killer and they are only boys, most of them. I swear if it wasn't for some of the old lot, those who went over with me, they'd all be raving

526

lunatics. Then there are the grenades and trench mortars, the shrapnel, the incendiaries and the gas. And the gas blinds them, or fills their lungs ... or both ... Well, you've seen them, haven't you, Caitlin ... Oh Jesus...'

She had held him close, this fine, strong woman of his who had had her share of torment, letting him babble on in the dark, letting him reach a catharsis as he told her of constant water and mud, of trench foot and trench mouth and trench fever. Of fleas and rats and a stench so appalling every man in the line regularly vomited what little decent sustenance he was allowed, and she let him tell her these things though of course she already knew. She let him talk as he had done for the past year, allowing him to drain from himself the grim terrors which infected them all and which gave him the strength to go on, a strength others as weary and sick of it all as he, did not have.

Jack had been for eighteen savage months in the trenches, a seasoned warrior, honed and blooded at Ypres, at Mons and the Marne, an old hand at turning away from bloated, half-buried corpses and the obscenity of the crucifixions which took place regularly on the barbed wire. Caitlin's own brother, seventeen-year-old Sean, had died that way, killed not by the enemy's bullet which had shattered his leg but by a compassionate sniper from his own battalion when Sean had been out there in no-man's-land for seventeen agonising hours, one for each year of his young life. His mother didn't know that, of course, and never would but Jack had found out and told Michael who was a sergeant in the platoon commanded by a friend of Jack's.

They had wept together, Caitlin and Jack's brother-in-law, for the little brother who couldn't wait to 'get in on it', then they had put it behind them, as they all did, those who were in France and moved on to the next grisly encounter. To dwell on it led to madness. They had all learned that and there were already enough nerve-shattered men staggering the thin line between reason and sanity.

Now, on the night before the first Somme offensive, though he was not a religious man, Jack said a small, almost apologetic prayer to Someone to keep his wife safe.

On the following day 21,000 of these same young men died and another 40,000 were wounded. It was a day like no other in British military history, a shattering defeat, a major watershed as many of the new army battalions were annihilated and the bald realisation came that the way ahead would be long and hard and that the war would only be won at the cost of continuous and staggering losses.

But they did not know it then, those young men who waited on that most beautiful day of the war for their platoon officer, Lieutenant Hugh Woodall, to blow his whistle, to lead the way up the ladder with a revolver in one hand and a cigarette in the other.

'Come on boys,' he shouted, just as though he was on the playing fields of the famous public school he had attended only five years before and where he had learned to be a soldier.

He had gone no more than a yard or two when a yellow mass of lyddite shrapnel burst around and above him, and both he and those men whom he had encouraged to go over the top and advance with him were shattered into pieces, gone as if they had not existed. Blood, bone, muscle and tissue erupted into the cloudlessly blue sky before it rained down on those who followed and who continued to advance at a slow walk. Other men, stricken before they barely got over the top, were heaped about their feet, men who were beyond their help but who they did their utmost to avoid, as they did those who crawled about to escape the madness, some of them doing their best to hold in their own blood with weakening fingers.

Subaltern Teddy Osborne, his face haggard with pain, both his legs soaked in his own blood, could not climb over the monstrous hill of dead and wounded men so he simply lay down with them. A hail of fire from rifle, machine gun, high explosives and shell raked his position, causing those who were already dead to jump and those who were not to scream. They were still coming on, those who had left the trench after his platoon, falling to the left and right of him, on top of him, some of them, so that he feared he would be buried alive. He wanted to vomit and was convinced he was going to lose consciousness. Digging his nails into the bit of earth beneath him he fought the nausea. He must not faint, he must not or he would be left for dead but the blood poured from his shattered legs and the last thing he saw before he slipped away into darkness was the large and very evidently badly wounded soldier who fell across him, blotting out the endless arch of the perfect blue sky.

First Lieutenant Tim Woodall continued to go forward, until he became aware that there were very few in the line of attack capable of going on with him. Diving for a flat, shallow hole made by British guns he lay for several minutes in the company of a private and a sergeant as the hell which had been let loose only five minutes since waged above their heads.

'What are we to do, sir?' the sergeant asked.

'Bloody suicidal to go on, if you ask me,' said the private.

'Nobody did, soldier, so shut yer bloody gob.'

'Yes ser'nt.'

'Our orders are to go on, ser'nt,' Tim Woodall said calmly.

'Righto, sir.'

They stood up, the three young men, then fell back again, their bodies riddled with bullets. They did not feel them, of course, only their impact, though none of the three were dead. There was no pain, nor fear, for the chemistry of their bodies anaesthetised them so that they could lie together in what seemed a quite companionable fellowship as the battle savaged those who were still on their feet. They made no sound as they died, the sergeant and the private, but First Lieutenant Woodall was still alive as darkness fell and the first rat came to sit on his chest. He began to scream then. It was his twenty-first birthday within the week but he did not see it, of course.

The first intimation of what had happened began for Elizabeth with an urgent tapping on her bedroom door and, when she had fumbled her way from the deep sleep she was in, the voice of Wilson saying there was a telephone call for her.

'Who is it, Wilson?' her body beginning to shake with the palpitations of her heart, a condition suffered by all those who were awakened in the dead of night, or indeed at any time, by an unexpected knock at the door for did they not all live in fear of the telegram boy, the policeman with messages of death.

'It's Mrs Osborne, m'lady.' Elizabeth's heart beat like a drum in her breast and ears as she ran, her bare feet scarcely touching the carpet of the stairs. What time was it . . . ? twenty-five past two in the morning, and what else could it be but the events which were taking place in France. They had all heard, naturally, of the 'big push'. The Somme offensive, it was called, though most of those who spoke of it were not awfully sure where the Somme actually was or even what it meant. But this was going to be it, her own father had told her enthusiastically, having been informed presumably by those military friends of his in high places. One concentrated effort, one big battle and it would all be over and involved in that last fight were Harry and Hugh, Tim and . . . and Teddy. And Michael, her heart whispered frantically.

And which out of those would most concern Serena Osborne?

'Mother?' She could not control the quiver in her voice.

'Elizabeth . . . darling, it's . . . Teddy . . .'

Oh God, Teddy . . . her little brother, not him, not him as well as James . . .

'Mother . . . ?'

'Wounded, they sa¸ ...'

'Where ...?'

'I'm not awfully sure, darling. A friend of your father's telephoned from the War Office ... so kind of him to let us know ... the casualty lists make no mention ...'

'Mother, what kind ... of wound?'

'Again ... I ... we don't know. He has been taken, they say, to a hospital in London. We are to go at once ...'

'Mother?'

'At once ...'

'I'll come with you ... if I may. Teddy is ... I would be glad to ...'

'Of course, darling ...' Her mother's voice lost that rather high, extremely controlled tone which spoke of a restraint so rigid it was tearing her to pieces trying to keep a grip on it. She had managed it, obedient to the code of her class which said she must, when her eldest son was taken, but now the one she had left had been wounded, seriously, the voice at the other end of the wire had said. So how was she to do it again? How was she to hold on to that iron willpower which said she must not show weakness? It was proving very difficult.

'The children will be all right with Nanny?' Serena knew how ... well ... unusual her daughter was in their upbringing, somewhat like Mara in that she took an active part in their day-to-day routine, going to the nursery, having them out to play about her feet and even – worst of all – actually feeding the infant at her own breast. When Elizabeth had come over to be with them on the day they had heard of James' death, Serena had discovered her nursing Alexander by the fireside of her own room and had taken her to task over it. She was blatantly exposing her bosom to the gaze of her maid who, one could see, did not know quite where to look. A very different girl now, was Elizabeth, from the one who had gone as a bride to Woodall Park three years ago.

'Yes mother, Nanny is very capable and so is Flora. I have complete trust in them both to ... and Lady Woodall and Sophie are here, of course.'

'There has been no word of ... Harry.'

'No.'

'Nor Tim and Hugh ... ?'

'No.'

'We must pray ...'

'Yes mother, I do.'

'Of course.'

Already Elizabeth's mind was moving into a more ordered rhythm dealing with arrangements and instructions for the caring of her children whilst she journeyed with her mother and father to London. With the packing of what she would need, what would she need for her stay ... how long would she stay? The necessity to be organised kept at bay, for the moment, the picture of Teddy ... dear, young Teddy ... bleeding, mangled, perhaps blinded ... oh no, not that ...

Her mother interrupted her disjointed thoughts, snatching her back from her contemplation of clean underwear, a change of clothing, stout boots – why? – a reminder to tell Nanny not to forget Charles' nightlight, as if the good woman would ... perhaps Mara would come over ... Alexander's teething fever ... and the new little one ... a daughter born in March and not yet weaned.

'We're to motor down, your father says. The trains are so unreliable ... an hour, Elizabeth. Can you be ready in an hour?'

'Yes, mother.'

It was almost full daylight, the long summer day breaking just after four o'clock, when the Renault, driven by Gibson, drew away from the gates of Beechwood. The low sun sparkled on the raindrops which had collected in the hedgerows and not yet dried from last night's brief shower. The fields were thick and yellow with uncut hay and wheat, alternating with those of bright green studded with daisies

532

in which cattle grazed. The road stretched out before them and Gibson went at it as though he was S. F. Edge the racing driver himself, but neither Johnny nor Serena Osborne objected. He had left the kitchen in a turmoil of tears and lamentations as the news of the young master's affliction had reached the servants, most of them young housemaids and kitchenmaids for the men had all marched off to fight the Hun alongside Master James and Master Teddy. Mrs Pritchard could not bear it, she said brokenheartedly, really she couldn't, if they were to lose that young imp, what with Master James gone an' all well, it just could not bear thinking about and now, Gibson thought, would you look at them in the back seat, the master and mistress sitting side by side, bolt upright, their faces like death masks as they waited to find out the condition of their only son. Miss Elizabeth, on the small folding seat facing them, her back to himself, did her best to make some conversation, anything to fill the awful silence but he could tell she hadn't the heart for it herself.

Elizabeth stared off at the far distance, her thoughts in a fever of dread. There had been growing rumours of the enormity of the casualties which were flooding back across the channel from the fighting in France. FORWARD IN THE WEST. FIERCE BATTLES ON THE SOMME had been the headlines in the newspapers and the elation at home when the reports of the first battle arrived was overwhelming. Those who had men at the front rejoiced for this must mean they would be home soon. At the same time they could not help but worry, but surely this must mean the end of it 'over there'.

It had taken some days before casualty lists could be compiled and though, at first, early reports had suggested casualties had not been heavy, a strange dread had begun to filter into the hearts of the families who guessed that their boys were in the battle which was taking place. A feeling of disaster to come, a premonition that things were not going quite right.

The Osbornes saw the first ambulances when they reached the Midlands. The roads were lined with people watching in appalled silence as the slow crawl, just come from the railway station, went by them, the bright red of the cross on their sides glaring in the full summer sun. These were 'our boys' in there and they couldn't believe it. This was the first time they had come into contact with the actual result of war, except for the partings with their loved ones and they couldn't believe their eyes. What were they doing so far north and if they were being brought up here from as far away as London, how many of them were there, for God's sake? Women were weeping in a most distressed manner, but children as children will, ran alongside the convoy, hoping for a glimpse of something grisly.

They reached Number 3 General Hospital which was on Wandsworth Common late in the afternoon and even as Gibson inched his way along the road which led up to its entrance Elizabeth could feel the awful sweat of dread begin to seep through her underclothes, sticking them to her body, a dread of what they were to see inside, certainly, but more than that, much more, for she had never known such pandemonium in her life.

Everywhere, simply everywhere she looked were ambulances, all of them open at the back and packed about them were people, not sightseers in the prurient sense, but what seemed to be ordinary, decent men and women searching and hoping not to find their especial loved one. There were lines of the vehicles waiting for their turn to get into the hospital courtyard where the entrance was situated. They were parked wherever there was a space and from them stretcher bearers were lifting stretchers and on each one was a bundle, a khaki-clad, unidentifiable bundle with rough dressings clapped to its wounds, filth-encrusted bandages caked with the mud of France, the blood of the soldier who bore them, and all the other substances which had been picked up, first in the field of battle and then on the long journey he had endured. There were orderlies, drivers, stretcher bearers and harassed nurses directing them all. A quick scrutiny of the label which had been attached at the casualty clearing station, most of them red, meaning therefore serious, informing those who were to receive them of the approximate nature of the injury sustained.

'I can't get no closer, sir,' Gibson told his master, his own face white and sweated with horror. 'I don't want to get in the way of ...'

'No ... no, of course not, Gibson.' Johnny Osborne's voice came from some hollow place to which this appalling sight had flung him but turning courteously to his rigid wife he asked her, just as though they were to alight before the house of a friend, if she would mind walking the short distance to the entrance of the hospital.

'Not at all, my dear,' but her own stunned shock was apparent in the way her hand trembled on her husband's as he helped her down into the road and the haunted look in her eyes which tried desperately not to see what lay about them. There were flies for it was hot and when one alighted, straight from some soldier's wound, on to her cheek, she recoiled in horror.

'Elizabeth ...'

'Thank you, father,' and like three marionettes they jerked their way through the agony, the filth, the sickening stench of soiled clothing, the moans and retching, the rustle of breathing, the gurgling, screaming, writhing sea of men. Elizabeth tried hard not to stare at them, at the terrible things which seemed, however sharply she turned away, to meet her eyes, but there was no escaping them. White bone glinting obscenely in the sunshine as it tore through gaping flesh, blood, scarlet and seeping through pads which had worked loose in the mad mêlée of the journey, heads swathed in grey bandages from which ... Dear God, what was it that crawled ...?

She could feel her head begin to spin and her stomach

heaved, hot and filled with bile and amongst the moans which the suffering masses expelled into the hot and stinking air she could distinctly hear her own.

It took three hours but they found him. The wounded had the name, rank and details of their injuries attached to them and the coloured label which denoted the seriousness of those injuries, the possibility of haemorrhage or convulsions or any other condition which might need immediate emergency treatment, and even in the chaotic conditions which prevailed some semblance of order had been retained. Did Mr Osborne know the nature of his son's wounds? No, then he must see how difficult it would be to find him. Was Mr Osborne aware that casualties had come in from the fields of battle at the rate of 12,000 an hour on the first day and they were backing up from here to the Somme and though she, a passing VAD, would like to help him surely he could see that it was wellnigh impossible... No, she had not heard of Brigadier General ... yes, she was aware that he ... a telephone call to the Brigadier ... really, she had no time and the telephone could not be tied up ... yes, Mr Osborne might search if he cared to and did not get in the way of ... those were all 'Heads' over there ... 'Eyes' had gone to Fulham Eye Hospital...

They found him lying quietly on the floor of the corridor, side by side with dozens of others who were in the same sad condition as himself. A narrow passage had been left for hurrying nurses, VADs, orderlies and stretcher bearers but every foot of space on either side of it was taken up by wounded men. There were filthy soldiers sitting and standing, those who were capable of it, sharing a cigarette, a quiet word, soothing their comrades who cried for their mothers, or screamed for an ending to their agony but Teddy Osborne didn't scream nor indeed make the slightest sound. He was deep in blessed shock, a flat grey ghost as insubstantial as a wisp of smoke or a bit of ash which will disintegrate at the first touch. His face was streaked with mud, days old,

536

and his hair was plastered lifelessly to his skull. He was tranquil, dying it seemed, and glad to do so for at nineteen life without one's legs is no life at all.

Sitting at his head, his back against the wall, his knees drawn up to his chin, his own uniform caked with blood – his or Teddy's? – a rough and filthy bandage slapped haphazardly about his shoulder, was Michael O'Shaughnessy. He had a hand on Teddy's shoulder and it patted and soothed and comforted though Teddy was not aware of it.

When Elizabeth bent down to them his head rose and his eyes met hers and in them was a reflection of all the horror he and her brother had shared since July 1st 1916. He showed no surprise.

'I looked after him for you,' was all he said.

29

Michael O'Shaughnessy was suffering from a shrapnel wound in his right shoulder which of course meant that he could not use his right arm, neither to fire a rifle, draw his bayonet, dig a trench, salute an officer nor indeed do any of the things required of a soldier, but his left arm was sound and it had no trouble wrapping itself about Lady Elizabeth Woodall when the time came.

Johnny Osborne, with the help of his Brigadier General acquaintance, had his son transferred within the hour to a hospital for officers in Richmond. A private ambulance, naturally, a private nurse and an elderly doctor who had rooms in Harley Street and was unfit for duty in the army but who was to monitor Teddy Osborne's condition on the journey

Elizabeth moved through the next few hours with that

strange feeling she had known several times in her life before. A feeling of being outside of herself, of not really being herself but some other woman watching with compassion and a great feeling of sorrow the confusion and shocked state of Elizabeth Woodall and the bewildered suffering of those about her.

That first moment, those first desperate fumblings with words and emotions too great to be put into words, would never be forgotten and for years afterwards, when in the minds of the generals and politicians it was all over, if not in the minds of those who had suffered it, vivid memories of that day would always remain, ice-clear and sharp-edged, down Elizabeth's years.

Her mother, her face cut like marble, hollows about her temple and her cheeks, her eyes deep and cavernous, kept her mouth tight clenched to keep in the moans and whimpers she desperately wished to utter but which she could not allow to escape. She was a lady of breeding, one who had been brought up to hide, indeed not to have feelings which could weaken, even wound, particularly when one was in the company of the lower orders for one must set a good example. Her back was as straight as a ruler, unbending, unbreakable it seemed, as was her spirit, but her eyes were dreadful to see as they looked down at the pitiable bundle of dirty rags which was all that was left of the bright-haired, engaging boy she had watched go off to do his bit.

Elizabeth's father, now that he had been given some task which did not allow for brooding, a task which put to work his talent for command, for giving orders – also bred in him by his life as an owner of land which must, naturally, be managed – lost his dazed look of incomprehension. Before Elizabeth's eyes he became brisk, forceful, using that energetic enterprise which those who are of the ruling class must have to rule. His son would not be left to lie amongst the ... well, he would not, of course, use the word 'riff-raff' to describe these brave and devastated men, but it would be far more suitable for the boy to be amongst his . . . own kind.'

'I cannot be held responsible for your son's condition if you move him again,' the frantic doctor informed them, when he could be persuaded to 'get to' the desperately wounded young officer.

'He cannot surely be in a worse condition than he is now in,' the young officer's father said.

'He could be dead, sir. I must be blunt. He is not far off that state now,' turning compassionately for a moment to the mother of the wounded boy who had seemed, though no sound had come from her, to moan.

'Nevertheless I have sent my man to bring an ambulance, at my own expense naturally, and the necessary medical people to look after my son until he reaches the hospital in Richmond.'

All along the corridor, in rooms which led off them, in every nook and cranny which could be used, soldiers were being relieved of the rough dressings which had, many of them, been applied thirty-six hours earlier, and fresh bandages administered to their dreadful wounds, perhaps only temporarily until they could be got to a doctor. There was not time, it appeared, for the blessing of anaesthetics and the cries and groans of the soldiers were terrible to hear. Terrible sights and terrible sounds as the bandages were removed for what was beneath was not for the squeamish. Torn and mutilated limbs, bloodsoaked stretchers on which lay suspiciously quiet men, yellow pus on the walls and on the floors where the nurses' feet slipped in it. The air was thick with the reek of it and it seemed to Elizabeth's appalled senses to be everywhere, oozing from uncovered flesh and transferring itself without favour to every man and woman who dealt with the suffering soldiers. There were buckets everywhere overflowing with reeking dressings and the overlying, eye-stinging smell of Lysol. Orders were shouted to 'lift that one' and 'fetch that one', 'take that one up to the ward', and a moment of controlled emergency when a grey-faced boy began to convulse and in the midst of it all Lady Elizabeth Woodall stood with her back to the wall against which Michael O'Shaughnessy was still propped and next to her her mother watched her son dying, surely, before her tortured eyes.

It was done with, at last, and without exchanging a word with the man who had, in his own hoarse words, 'looked after her brother for her', Elizabeth followed her mother and father and the stretcher containing what was left of Teddy along the nightmare corridor. As she reached the door which led out into the heaving courtyard she turned and over the mass of suffering humanity which had been brought back from the front, she and Michael exchanged glances and the message they had for one another was understood.

It was three days before she saw him again. Her mother and father and herself had put up at an hotel in Richmond so that they might be near Teddy until it was known whether he was to live or die. He had been infected, as he lay in the muck and mud of the churned up battlefield, with what was known as gas gangrene. In that mud was manure put down by careful French farmers before the horror descended upon their farms, and many other substances which entered the open wounds of those who fell. The bullet wounds had not been in themselves of a serious nature, but both of Teddy Osborne's legs had simply become a mass of putrid muscle rotting with the gas. The wounds had ballooned up and the only way to give Teddy Osborne a chance of life had been to amputate. It had been done roughly and quickly in the field hospital.

But a new and relatively successful treatment had begun quite recently to reduce the high degree of sepsis and gas gangrene. Hypochlorous acid ¼% solution was the result of experiments carried out earlier in the war and though it was not the complete answer, in the case of Lieutenant

Osborne it appeared to be working. Drainage tubes were attached to a large syringe which was injected into the tube every three hours to irrigate the wounds of his stumps, an agonising procedure, but three days later the son of Serena and Johnny Osborne still lived. Whether he was pleased by the fact was another matter.

'I think I might go home now, mother,' Elizabeth said. 'It seems Teddy is . . .'

'Don't say it, Elizabeth, for pity's sake, say nothing more,' and what was left of Serena's spirit lifted her head and straightened her back. 'It's best not to . . . tempt fate, darling, do you not agree?' reaching for her daughter's hand and Elizabeth was made aware, if she had not already discovered it in the last three days, that beneath the calm, unruffled composure her mother showed to the rest of the world she was suffering quite dreadfully and her superstitious need to propitiate fate confirmed it. They had both been exposed to sights which neither, in their sheltered lives, had been expected to see. They had been subjected in the last few days to harrowing pain and grief though of course the full horror of it was all carefully wrapped away and hidden from those who visited the private and sanitary hospital in which Teddy now lay. But they had seen it. They had seen what war can do to young men. And they had both survived it and, Elizabeth hoped, had a better understanding, not only of the war but of each other.

She leaned forward and spontaneously kissed her mother's cheek, the first time she had ever done so when not obliged to it in the formal way of greeting or farewell.

'Will Gibson take you, my dear? He can return here on the following day. Your father and I really have no need of the motor at the moment.'

'No mother, thank you. If he could take me to London I'll travel by train.'

'Are you sure, Elizabeth? You know how they are at the moment with the movement of troops.'

'No, really. I'll telephone Mara when I get to London and she will meet me at Liverpool.'

Number 3 General Hospital on Wandsworth Common was calmer than on the last occasion Elizabeth had been there though there was still a certain amount of movement of ambulances and stretchers. The corridor where Teddy and Michael and hundreds of other soldiers had lain was empty of all but nurses and orderlies and one or two 'walking wounded' moving carefully against the wall. It was cool now and smelled of disinfectant and beneath a window on a polished table someone had placed a bright bowl of marigolds.

A nurse directed her to where she might obtain the information she needed, then rustled away on more urgent business.

She was told to wait. It was not visiting time. Was she a relative? A clock ticked and a porter began to whistle quietly as he pushed an empty trolley out into the sunshine beyond the door.

The ward was jammed with beds, scarcely room between to allow more than the passage of a nurse or doctor but the men in it were sitting up, even walking about with no sign of the desperate injuries Elizabeth had seen here three days ago. This was a ward where men smoked a cigarette and read books or newspapers and talked to one another with none of the dreadful faces and despairing eyes she had seen then. These men would recover. Their wounds would heal and they would be well again, well enough to return ... Dear God ... to the fight.

He was in the end bed. His arm was strapped to his chest with a clean white bandage and he lay in a clean white bed. He was next to a window and he stared out on to the far reaches of the common, his face unutterably sad, she could see, even from where she hesitated at the door. He had not seen her.

'Thank you, Sister,' she said to the hovering nurse. 'I can

542

see my ... friend.' The nurse moved away, back to the bed in the corner where a screen had been put up to shield a man having a wound dressed but Elizabeth sensed her interest. A lady, a real lady who was not his wife, visiting an enlisted man, one of the ranks and what was the story behind that, she was wondering. Strange things were happening in this mad world the war had flung them into and the class barriers appeared to be tumbling down about their ears, swept away on the tide of change.

Elizabeth was dressed in the same sensible outfit she had thrown on four nights ago. Her skirt was of navy blue flannel, flared and short, just reaching the tops of her highheeled buttoned kid boots. A simple cream silk shirt and over it a knitted three-quarter cashmere coat of paler blue with a fringed tie belt. She wore no hat because she had simply forgotten to put one on in the dash from Liverpool to London. Her hair was brushed to the back of her head, tied with a wide ribbon then left to tumble down her back, not dressed in any way her maid Minty would have approved of, with strands escaping to wisp about her neck and ears.

He had still not seen her, absorbed, it seemed, in his own tortuous thoughts but as she walked slowly up the ward the men fell silent. Two nurses in handkerchief caps and bibbed aprons who were bending over a dressing trolley straightened up to stare, watching her go by but by now all her attention was on Michael and she scarcely noticed them.

He looked thinner and the warm amber of his face had gone completely leaving him fine-etched and pale. His hair, newly washed, fell in a thick tumble about his forehead and he had recently been shaved. The sunlight which streamed across his bed touched his one hand and it was restless, plucking at the bedclothes, smoothing them. A blue dressing gown lay at the foot of the bed and the sight of it reassured her. He must be able to get out of bed and walk, she remembered thinking incoherently as, suddenly aware of the quiet, he turned and looked directly at her.

His eyes blazed their message of joy, a brilliant lighting up of love and welcome and his left hand, frail somehow and vulnerable, rose and was about to reach out for hers before he remembered. He replaced it slowly and carefully on the bedcover and she wanted to run to him, to pick it up and cradle it to her face and lips with her own two strong hands. So many things she wanted to do, but of course she couldn't.

She reached the bed in a series of drifting, dream-like steps, aware of the eyes which still watched them, of the whispers which hissed from bed to bed and it was not until she heard the nurse's brisk voice enquiring whether Private Wilks required a chin strap to support his open mouth, the sound of metal against metal as the dressing trolley was moved and a rise in the hum of the conversation which had ceased when she entered the room, did she dare to speak.

'Michael.' Speak! What was there to say to this man at this particular moment beyond his name? She loved him and if they had been alone she would have done her best to get him into her arms, to have her arms about his weakened, hurt body. Her eyes were unfocused with the love she bore him flowing from her to him. They were soft, warm and inexpressibly lovely and her smile, that of lover greeting lover, cherished him, enfolded him in the knowledge that nothing had changed between them nor ever would.

She watched as the strain ran from him, emptied from him in a tired, weary torrent and when he was emptied, was replaced with the strength and sweetness of their love. He smiled, a smile of great relief as she began to heal his body, and whatever it was that ailed his mind.

'My love,' he said, softly for no one else to hear, the tenderness in his voice almost toppling her resolve to be steadfast.

'I came as soon as I could.'

'Your brother?'

'Is still alive. I am on my way home. My children...'

544

'To be sure.'

'I couldn't leave you ... go home without ...'

'I know.' The hand which still shifted on the bedclothes lifted helplessly and, uncaring of the man in the opposite bed who still watched them furtively from behind his newspaper, she covered it with her own and it became still then, peaceful at last.

'Tell me about Teddy.'

'Sure an' there's nothing to tell, so. He was wounded. I brought him in, so I did,' and the whimsical Irish curve to his mouth was returned for a moment.

'Please ... tell me ...'

'There was nothing ...'

'I know there was.'

'You don't want to hear, my darling, not really.'

'Please ...'

He studied her face with that careful, minutely searching scrutiny that lovers have for one another. Not an eyelash missed, not a fraction of an inch of white skin overlooked, every line and curve dwelled on with a passion of love and a concern which could not be concealed. In her eyes was the steady, clear sighted depth of a woman not easily alarmed now by life's confusions and even nightmares. A strong woman who had known bereavement and loss and the pain of both and she would not easily be put off nor be weakened by what he had to tell her.

He sighed and looked out for a moment towards the peace of the common where children played and dogs scampered and the blue and gold of the summer day lay over this corner of London. He turned and lifted his hand before he spoke, tenderly and smilingly tucking a drifting tendril of her hair behind her ear, then recaptured her hand for he needed something to cling to as he told her of her brother.

'He was hit in the first wave of men who went over, I'd say. I was in the same battalion as him, the 3rd Lancs but he wasn't aware of it. I used to watch him sometimes when he didn't know . . . on parade . . . he was a bit like you, did you realise. to look at, I mean. Aye, he had a way of lifting his head so . . . when I could I'd watch him.' He shook his head in wonder. 'Jesus, I loved you . . . so much . . . even to watch your brother was . . .' He sighed deeply 'Anyway, my platoon followed his. I was hit by shrapnel within minutes . . . no, no, sweetheart, 'tis only a bit of an old wound . . . not like . .' His hand gripped hers fiercely and his eyes burned into hers, savage and filled with longing and she wanted to place her mouth on his then and there. Her eyes told him so but he must go on. He did, reluctantly.

'I found a funk-hole . . . a shell hole . . . filled with men, dozens of them, with no room for more. Dead a lot of them so I . . . I heaved them out, poor sods, to make room and found him there .. underneath. It went on all day, hour after hour . . . men falling in on us, but I kept them off him. It was as though it was .. part of you, d'you see, Elizabeth? Your flesh. My arm . . . it was useless but I was conscious and the wound was where I could get at it. We have a dressing in our kit so I had put that on to keep it clean .. that's when . . . Holy Mother, Elizabeth, you don't want to hear this.'

'Please, my darling. '

'God love us . . .'

'Please .. '

'Well . . . when it was dark I carried him in . . .' Said so casually. Carried him in. With one arm. ' .. and got him to the casualty clearing station but there were so many of them. They lay on stretchers and when they ran out of stretchers, on the bare ground. The guns were still going and the night was . . . on fire with them. I waited for him . . . tried to keep him warm. The doctors were overrun, you see, and when . . . one finally got a look at him .. his legs . . . the gangrene had got him .. we'd been .. fifteen hours. You know the rest, Elizabeth. They cut off his legs. Jesus, I'm sorry, I couldn't let him go on his own. They were herding us like bloody cattle on to the ambulance trains and then to the hospital ships. I fought to stay with him ... they wanted me to go with the walking wounded but ... I ...'

'You brought him home.'

'Aye.'

'I will never ...'

'What, my love?'

'Love anyone as I love you.'

'I know that now. You know I feel the same?'

'Yes.'

'I'm to come up north ... to convalesce. Will you ... meet me?'

'Oh yes.'

She had been home a week when his letter came, barely readable for it was written by a right-handed man who was forced to use his left. He was in a hospital near Prescot and was waiting for her.

He was to remain in the hospital for three weeks, surrounded by the strong and protective abundance of his O'Shaughnessy family. His mother who could not bear to have her hands off him and who did her weeping in the dead of night so as not to distress him. His young wife who hardly knew him as a man, only as a teasing cousin and so continued to treat him as such and was not at all disconcerted, it seemed, to have him be the same with her. He was strong, the doctor told them, despite his two years in the trenches and he had his well-fed, well-nourished childhood to thank for the robust constitution which had healed him so quickly. Another couple of weeks at home with his pretty young wife and he would be as good as new and ready to be returned to the trenches, though he did not voice this last.

Through the bonny month of August he and Elizabeth Woodall met on every possible occasion. There was no holding back this time and though Elizabeth was fully aware that after he left the hospital Michael slept each night of that last two weeks in his wife's bed, she gave everything of herself that he needed.

The Battle of the Somme continued and by the end of July an advance of about two miles had been made, the struggle for the churned, blood-stained mud continuing into August. Elizabeth had a hurried note from Harry to say he was well and in Richmond First Lieutenant Teddy Osborne continued to hang on to the thread of life which somehow defeats even the most stubborn will to die. Serena and Johnny stayed with him.

The casualty lists grew and in them was the name of Woodall, printed twice, for the sons of Lady Anne Woodall who had died within minutes of each other on July 1. Lady Woodall, taking her daughter with her for comfort, had gone to her family in Scotland no longer able to face the sympathy of her friends nor indeed to remain in the house in which memories of growing boys were too much for her to bear.

'I don't know where the bejasus Michael gets to on that old motorbike of his, so I don't,' Mara said to Elizabeth on one of her restless visits to Woodall Park, her five children crammed into the back of her Morris motor car with their nursemaid. James Osborne had left the last of his young seed implanted in his wife's womb on what had proved to be his last leave. Another girl born in January and called for reasons known only to Mara by the name of Rose. 'Sure an' he's never at home and the Mammy giving him a piece of her mind for neglecting poor Mary Kate. An' him with that arm of his only just out of the sling.'

'Does he tell no one where he is going?' Elizabeth asked carefully, the baby, weaned abruptly when Elizabeth had gone to London to find her brother, kicking rapturously on her knee. Damaris Woodall, conceived on Harry's first leave in 1915 eight weeks after Michael O'Shaughnessy had married his Mary Kate, and almost four months old now. As like Harry as any female child can resemble the man who fathers her and still remain female. Fair curls and brown eyes with the Woodall sweetness of smile and sunny nature and, after Alexander who was the joy of Elizabeth's heart, a delight to her mother

'No, off for a run out to see undamaged fields and farms, says he Oh, an' why is that, says the Mammy for Mary Kate never speaks up I've seen enough devastation to last me a lifetime, says himself, and that shuts the Mammy up, I can tell you. Mind, you can't blame the spalpeen for wantin' to get away from Mammy an' Mary Kate an' Gracie. Sure an' they're forever fussing about him an' asking if he's warm enough, in *this* weather, an' would he like a drop of tea or a bite of cake. God love him, he'll be glad to get back over there at this rate.'

'Has he had word?'

'No, the doctor said a wee while yet but it won't be long.'

'I'm sorry'

'Aach, an' isn't he the lucky one when you think of...'

'I know, darling, I know.'

There was no end to the love they had for one another in that enchanted timeless time they had together as summer ran down towards autumn. They had found an old inn deep in the Delamere Forest, far from the road where the motor cars dashed past. Bumping over barely defined tracks on Michael's motor cycle, her arms clasped tightly about his waist, their combined hilarity disturbing nothing but woodcock, grouse and rabbit. They had never laughed together, never known the merriment, the sheer joy of smiling in happiness with nothing in their lives, it seemed, but the everlasting belief that it could go on forever They idled in forest glades, the energy of the sun soaked up by the canopy of leaves above their heads so that it was cool as they lay in each others' arms on the mossy bed beneath. There were butterflies and the call of the birds, the rustle of the breeze in the sturdy rhododendron which grew freely beneath oak and beech and yew.

'*Under bracken lies gold, Under gorse lies silver, Under heather lies lead*,' Michael chanted and when she had asked him what it meant he told her it did not refer to the metals mentioned in the rhyme but to the richness of the soil where those plants grow.

'How do you know?'

'Did you ever hear of an Irishman who was not concerned with the land? It's something my old Granddaddy used to say to me when I was a wee boy. He came over in the famine, or was it his father? Anyway, we have a love of the land, so we do and one day, when all this is over, sure an' I'd like to own a bit of land again, like the O'Shaughnessys once did.'

'My darling . . .' and her heart was overwhelmed with the need to make this moment precious which, surely, might not come again, this magical time which was just theirs. They would pull up in the front yard of the inn, greeted by the sympathetic and not overly moralistic landlady who had been young and in love herself more than once, or so her manner implied. They would spend an ecstatic hour or two, or even three if it could be managed, in the herb-scented bed she provided them with, dreaming and whispering as lovers do, of the future which they were both well aware they would not spend together. From the window there was nothing to see but trees and wood anemones, the sky arching over them and the sounds of the peaceful lives of the creatures who sheltered there but by Christ, he hadn't come here to gaze out of the bloody window, he told her passionately.

'This is not wrong, Elizabeth. You do believe that, don't you?' he'd said to her on their first visit there.

'With all my heart,' winding her arms about his neck as he locked the door behind them.

He had undone the buttons of her blouse with his clumsy left hand as she stood quietly, knowing he needed to do it himself. He concentrated sharply on them, and on the beauty of her breasts as they were revealed, heavier now for she had borne three children and nursed two, and though it stabbed his half-healed shoulder, he lifted both hands to them, cupping each breast, rolling each nipple between gentle fingers, caressing slowly, carefully, surely, not wishing to neglect any of the sweet sensations his hands and heart created, for himself and for her. He knelt to draw down her skirt and underclothes, then leaned back to search out and study every line of her, turning her round and round, putting his face against her flesh to smell the musky aroma of her female body, pressing his lips against her back, her buttocks, the dark, mysterious bush between her thighs and the smooth satin skin which surrounded it. He was enchanted with her and when she demanded to do the same to him, removing his tie and then, piece by piece, the rest of his clothing until he too stood naked it was as if this was the first time for both of them, not only with each other, but ever.

His lips found her nipple and it hardened in his mouth and when he laid her on the soft, deep bed his hand ran down her stomach and his fingers searched until they found the hot, sweet moisture at the very depth of her woman's body. They were overwhelmed by the exquisitely sensual and yet glorious truth of their love. It was sharp and almost unbearable in its intensity and yet it had a goodness, a warmth, a strength which came from the long years of turmoil and the furnace in which it had been fired, making it unbreakable.

Later they walked a little way into the forest, stopping in a breathlessly quiet glade. The sunlight which glimmered and danced through the leaves above them lit her hair and his to a dark burnished chestnut. They were somewhat alike as they stood for a moment before moving on, handclasped beneath the canopy's spread, tall, loose-limbed, graceful and dark. Two young and splendid animals well suited to one another and when he asked the question she was not surprised. She had been expecting it every day since he had come back to her.

'The boy, Elizabeth?' and her heart moved gently, painlessly since she would not lie. He was a man who was to go back to the devastation of war and if she could give him something to take with him, some bright remembrance of their love to comfort him, please him in the dark days ahead, could she deny him? She who loved him more than life.

'Yes . . . ?'

'Is he mine?'

'Yes, my darling.'

She heard him sigh in deep pleasure and when he turned her to him she was bathed in the radiance of his love. There were tears on her cheeks and he wiped them away with his thumb before he kissed her.

'Thank you,' he said simply.

'Michael's gone,' Mara said gloomily to Elizabeth on a day of blustery rain and high scudding clouds which looked more like November than August. 'The doctor said today and off he went. The Mammy's in tears, an' Mary Kate, an' sure wasn't I glad to come home, so I was, though Beechwood's not much better. Begod, Elizabeth, when's this damned war to be over, will you tell me that for I'll go mad, so I will if it's not soon. Sean and James dead, and the Woodall boys. Poor Teddy . . . well . . . nineteen years old and himself with no . . .'

'Mara . . for God's sake shut up!'

Mara turned in amazement to her sister-in-law, her own unhappy thoughts scuttling from her mind at the absolutely awful expression on Elizabeth's face. Elizabeth who, no matter what the provocation never, *never* lost control of the well-bred composure she had been brought up to maintain. Elizabeth who had never been less than good-humoured, beautifully mannered, tranquil and undisturbed and who was now ready to tear out her hair in a storm of weeping.

'Holy Mother of God, Elizabeth, I'm sorry. I never meant to ...'

'Shut up ... shut up!'

'Godalmighty, I didn't mean to say that about Teddy, really I didn't ...' quite frightened really because she had never seen anyone, even amongst the O'Shaughnessys who were noted for their emotional displays, carry on as her sister-in-law was doing.

Mara had gone, taking her children and her remorse with her and in the window seat looking out over the windswept gardens of Woodall Park, Elizabeth grieved for Mara's brother.

His letters began to arrive the next day.

30

'There is a woman to see you, m'lady. I told her you were not receiving callers but she asked me to give you this and begged you to see her.'

Despite the war and the changes it had brought, not only in the lives of almost every family in the land but in the classes which divided it, Wilson, like Eaton at Beechwood, still believed in the old ways and he certainly knew the difference between a woman and a lady and the person who sat in the hall where he had put her was definitely not the latter no matter how she was dressed.

Elizabeth raised her head from the newspaper she was studying and Wilson was struck and not for the first time by the thought that whereas grief in some ladies took away any pretension to looks they might have had, in his young mistress it only seemed to enhance them. She could only be twenty-one or two and yet she had the mature and quite exquisite beauty of an older woman. Fine drawn, he would have said, her sorrow chiselling her features and moulding her white flesh to such lovely lines it was impossible to describe her. Her eyes were still that vivid green she had inherited from her father, clear and intelligent but her mouth was soft and tremulous with youth. Poor lovely girl, the old man thought, deep in her sadness and yet she was still unfailingly considerate to those in the area of Woodall Park, the tenants and servants who had lost sons and husbands on the Western Front, just as though nothing like that had happened to her. The two young men of the house vanished into thin air, at least Master Hugh had, though Master Tim's body had been found and buried with the thousands of his comrades who had fallen with him that day. And her own brother withering away in his room at Beechwood, refusing to come out or do any of the things his distraught parents tried to persuade him to do. Mr Osborne had fitted out a small pony trap to allow the boy to get about the estate at least but it was said he would have none of it and it was rumoured, though how true it was he couldn't say, that Mr Osborne kept all firearms under lock and key, so frightened were they that Master Teddy might ... well ... the lad was in a poor way so one could only draw one's own conclusions as to the reasons for that.

And then there was Sir Harry himself. Still out there with not a scratch on him but only the Good Lord knew how long that would last. The battle of Delville Wood where Sir Harry had fought alongside Highlanders and the South African Infantry Brigade had been devastating and of the 121 officers and 3,032 men who had fought their way into the wood, only 29 officers and 751 men had survived. One of those officers had been Sir Harry Woodall. The battle, never dormant, had erupted again on a great scale on September 25th and then once more on November 13th and it was said General Sir Douglas Haig had been desperate to achieve a breakthrough. Casualties were increasing with every minute and in the cities and towns and villages of Great Britain more and more homes were receiving those brief and dreaded telegrams. 'It is my painful duty to inform you . . .' they read, tearing the heart and spirit out of countless thousands of men and women who waited at home.

In September tanks were used for the first time but of the thirty-one which crossed the German lines, nine broke down and five ended up like beetles on their backs. Nevertheless their appearance on the field lifted the spirits of the British infantry soldier but the Somme offensive was effectively brought to a standstill in November when the heavy rains made any further progress impossible.

That had been five months ago and there was to be another big push soon, it was said. Wilson waited impassively for his mistress' answer.

'Who is she, Wilson?'

'A Mrs Templeton, m'lady.'

Elizabeth frowned and put down the newspaper. 'I don't think I know a Mrs Templeton, Wilson. What is that she has given you?'

'A note, m'lady,' bowing slightly as he presented the silver salver to the young mistress. Elizabeth took it curiously, unfolding it with suddenly trembling fingers though she could not have said why they trembled. It had only four words written on it. 'I was Caitlin O'Shaughnessy.'

If anything, though Wilson did not know how it could be possible, her Ladyship turned even whiter, every last vestige of colour draining away from her face. She was wearing grey, a fine gabardine suit with a military look about it, the skirt six inches from the ground and rather full, the jacket belted with large, hip-level patch pockets. Under it she wore a crisp white shirt, pleated and tucked like that of a gentleman's evening shirt. Her hair which, unlike many others, she had refused to cut short, was brushed smoothly back from her face and arranged in a low, simple knot at the back of her head. She had on black patent laced boots with a high heel.

'M'lady, are you unwell?'

Elizabeth took a deep breath as she clung tenaciously to her whirling senses. She dug her nails viciously into the palms of her hands, so deeply they left four bright red crescents there for several hours. The inside of her head was filled with the most appalling images, the worst, of course, was that Caitlin had come to tell her that Michael, like Sean and James, like Hugh and Tim, was dead. But why should Caitlin feel the need to inform Lady Elizabeth Woodall that her brother had fallen on the field of battle? That Lieutenant Michael O'Shaughnessy, commissioned in the field because of his actions under fire and the bravery he had shown in rescuing a young officer on the first day of the Somme offensive, had been killed. Elizabeth had seen Mara only yesterday when the bright two-seater Austin Ten sports car her sister-in-law had exchanged recently for the Bullnose Morris, had whipped up to the front door of Woodall, throwing gravel two feet into the air with the force and dash of its speed. Reckless was Mara these days, hurtling about the countryside in the pursuit of pleasure, in the pursuit of a relief from the boredom, the utter boredom with which her day was filled. There was nothing to look forward to, she moaned, with James dead and her parents-in-law so taken up with their wounded son they had no time for parties or dances, or even with a guest or two for dinner.

No, Mara mentioned neither Michael, nor her brother Dermot who, in January of this year, when compulsory conscription had begun, had also gone to the front. Dermot had been one of those who had turned a blind eye to the posters which had appeared on the streets of Liverpool and indeed on the streets of every town and village of the country.

IS YOUR BEST BOY WEARING KHAKI? IF NOT DON'T YOU THINK HE SHOULD BE? IF HE DOES NOT THINK THAT YOU AND YOUR COUNTRY

ARE WORTH FIGHTING FOR, DO YOU THINK HE IS WORTHY OF YOU?

DON'T PITY THE GIRL WHO IS ALONE. HER YOUNG MAN IS PROBABLY A SOLDIER FIGHTING FOR HER AND HER COUNTRY – AND FOR YOU.

Women all through the land had been under a great deal of moral pressure to send their men to fight and though many women had been appalled by it, there were many more who had been hysterically militant in their efforts to aid the recruitment of men for the army.

The Order of the White Feather had been one such group and so dreadful had been their behaviour a story had been circulated about them in which a man fresh from receiving the Victoria Cross from the King at Buckingham Palace, and out of uniform, was handed a white feather!

So, Dermot had gone at last, leaving the bank to manage somehow without him and his Mammy was devastated by his leaving. One son dead, two in the trenches and their Callum, at seventeen, doing his best to join them. Even Michael's promotion to the officer class had done nothing to salve the wounds Ellen had suffered, and still suffered every day in her agony over her sons' welfare. What did she care if her eldest son was Lieutenant Michael O'Shaughnessy, indistinguishable in his smart uniform from Sir Harry Woodall whose chauffeur he had once been. She wanted him home, and Dermot, where she could watch over them, love them and scold them, bully their wives and bring up their children, when they had them, and generally lead her family in the way they should go as she had always done.

Michael's wife, Mary Kate, had given birth to a daughter, praise be to the Holy Mother, a fine and bonny child, at the beginning of May, nine months since his convalescent leave last year so he had been fit enough in some ways, it seemed, the darlin' boy. Cliona, Mary Kate had named her, Irish, of course, and a name given, so it was said, to a fairy princess and there was her Daddy far away and never a sight of her had the boyo had which was a cryin' shame, so it was. But now he was an officer he should be able to manage a bit more leave, Caitlin had told them, and though it wasn't fair at all, it seemed an officer was somewhat more privileged than an ordinary soldier.

Elizabeth stood up as Caitlin was bowed into the room by the butler who shut the door quietly behind him. She smiled in genuine pleasure and holding out her hand moved towards her visitor.

'Caitlin, this is a lovely surprise. Mara told me you were home. That you had a daughter now and that your mother was . . .'

'Pleased as punch would be the right description since it means I have to stay at home, m'lady.' Caitlin smiled whimsically, looking so like Michael Elizabeth felt her heart move painfully.

'Really, but please Caitlin, you must call me Elizabeth, as your mother does. We are almost related, after all. Mara is my sister-in-law and . well . . . I am very fond of your mother. Come and sit down and I'll ring for tea.'

'No, please I won't take up any more of your time than I need.'

'Nonsense. You will have a cup of tea, I insist. Let me take your coat and come and sit here by the window. I was just reading the . . the casualty list in *The Times* when Wilson said . . . I'll put it away for really I can't bear all those photographs of the wounded men and . . and the ones they find on the battlefield and print in an attempt to identify Can you imagine the feelings of their relatives, seeing the faces of their . . their husbands or sons . '

'I know. I'm sorry, Elizabeth, about your brothers .'

'Please . . . say nothing. It is so difficult . . we have all lost . . .'

'Yes.'

There was a deep sad silence as both young women contemplated the devastation which had swathed through Caitlin's family with the loss of her younger brother, and the action which, all in one day last year, had killed two sons of the Woodall family and rendered their mother senseless with grief. Subaltern Hugh Woodall, 2nd Battalion the Lancashire Fusiliers, missing, believed killed in action. First Lieutenant Timothy Woodall, 2nd Battalion the Lancashire Fusiliers, killed in action. Lieutenant Edward Osborne, 3rd Battalion the Lancashire Fusiliers, wounded in action. Two fine young men dead on the threshold of what would undoubtedly have been splendid lives, both gone, like James, into the bloodsoaked earth of France, Teddy maimed for life and how would the parents of all three ever recover from it, if they ever recovered from it. Elizabeth would not care to hazard a guess.

Harry had come home on compassionate leave when his brothers were killed, his face like granite, his eyes bleak and staring and not even the sight of his new daughter, his and Elizabeth's third child, could melt the ice-cold calm of his isolation. Three days and three nights of politeness, of a deathless courtesy which had only faltered as he bade her farewell. It was as though he dare show no emotion, reveal nothing of what was inside him lest he get out of control and him not able to put it all together again. If it should leak out, even the minutest drop, might that drop not become a trickle, a stream, a raging torrent which would render him empty and useless. He and Teddy were the only ones left. The only sons out of five young men who had gone to war with the innocent and cheerful gallantry of young unblooded warriors and the harshness of it was almost more than his damaged mind and undamaged body could accommodate.

'Oh sweet God, Elizabeth . . .' he had groaned desolately into her shoulder as, for the second time, they had stood beneath the oak tree in those last few moments, then he had straightened up and marched away without a backward glance to where the motor car waited.

'Your husband is . . . well?' Elizabeth managed to say. Caitlin had just come from London, so Mara had told her

559

carelessly before Christmas, in that flippant manner she had adopted since James had died. Yes, pregnant she had been after all this time, begorra, and what could be more inconvenient than giving birth in a casualty clearing station behind the lines in France, which, it seemed, had almost happened. Trust Caitlin, who was a beggar for getting into trouble – Elizabeth remembered her suffragette days surely – but she had come home in the nick of time to give birth to her daughter. She was staying with the Mammy for a few days and what she would do with her days now was anybody's guess.

'Yes ... thank you,' or was when I last heard from him, Caitlin's eyes told Elizabeth. He could be dead by now, of course, as could Sir Harry Woodall.

'And you, you are here to visit your mother?'

'Yes.' Caitlin smiled. 'She asks me to remind you that she has seen nothing of you for months now. The kettle's on whenever you have a minute, she says.'

'That is most kind of her and I will certainly do my best to ... to visit her,' but of course she wouldn't for how could Elizabeth Woodall sit in the same room with Mary Kate O'Shaughnessy and her child, Michael's child? She could not.

Elizabeth and Caitlin chatted politely for ten minutes or so. Caitlin accepted a second cup of tea and a wafer-thin biscuit, asked after the baby ... Damaris, what a pretty name, and the progress of Master Charles and Master Alexander. Elizabeth knew, of course, that her brother had ... yes, a girl born at the beginning of this month, wondering slightly at the extreme pallor of her hostess' face, wondering if she might have said something to upset her though she could think of nothing. So many babies and so many young fathers who had not seen them ... and ... God forbid, perhaps never would, her own included.

Elizabeth, her heart thumping badly out of control, somewhere in the region of her throat, she thought, where it had leaped at the mention of Caitlin's brother, fought to keep calm since she must not appear in any way out of the ordinary. She must nod pleasantly and smile when required and listen courteously to whatever it was Caitlin was to ask of her Her mother's training and example got her through.

'And you are to go back to London to await the return of your husband?' she questioned, raising her eyebrows delicately, not wishing to pry, naturally. Caitlin had been a VAD since the beginning of the war, Mara had told her, when the suffragettes had 'closed down' – Mara's words – for the duration. Almost three years of caring for the bodies of men broken in battle, suffering the shelling and the ... well, whatever it was the soldiers suffered out there since not one of those who had come home seemed inclined to talk about it.

'That's what I've come to talk to you about, Lady Wo ... Elizabeth.'

'Really?' Elizabeth put her cup carefully into the saucer before turning back to her guest. 'What have I to do with it.'

'When my child was born in January I remained in London in the hope that I might get into one of the hospitals there. I have a good .. woman to look after her and it would have been no problem to return to nursing. I was aware that I couldn't go back to France to be near my husband but I thought ' She paused and her mouth worked painfully. 'They wouldn't hear of it despite the experience I had gained in field hospitals and casualty clearing stations. I had a child. I was the mother of a baby whose father was in the trenches and I had a duty well, you will understand. So I came to you, and this house.'

'I beg your pardon.'

I must nurse, you see. I must do something . after what I have seen what they, the men, have had done to them, especially since the Somme offensive. I can't just sit at home and be nothing but a mother. Please . ' She put an urgent

561

hand on Elizabeth's arm, 'I mean no disrespect. Faith, you're no doubt a wonderful mother,' she smiled, 'as all mothers are. Mammy makes a career out of it but I can't just see myself doing nothing else until Jack comes home.' The words were defiant since she *must* believe that Jack would come home.

'But what has this to do with me and this house?'

'It belongs to your husband?'

'Yes.'

'Would he have any objection to you turning it into a hospital?'

'Dear Lord . . .'

'With me in charge. I'm a good nurse and I know where I can find others. The War Office would provide doctors and the necessary medical staff and supplies. They're desperate for hospitals, Elizabeth, and big houses like this one are ideal for the nursing of convalescent . . .'

'I know. I have already been approached.'

'And you refused?'

'My mother-in-law . . . well, she was mistress here and it was up to her to make the decision, after all it had been her home for nearly thirty years, but now, with two of her sons dead . . .'

How could she say that so casually, she thought, even as she said it. Hugh, dear likable Hugh, steadfast and somewhat solid but brave when it was needed. James' partner in so many schoolboy escapades. And Tim who had died a week before his twenty-first birthday knowing nothing but the merest taste of the lively fun and excitement young people had known before the war, the carefree joy to which they are surely entitled. A boy, like all the other boys who were gone.

How could she refuse?

She cleared her throat and blinked rapidly while Caitlin looked away politely, calmly, giving Elizabeth a moment to recover.

'My mother-in-law is not ... well. She is with relatives in Scotland so the house is my responsibility now. But I would have to write to my husband ...'

Her voice tapered away for several seconds as she studied the self-contained face of Michael O'Shaughnessy's sister. She had his colouring, the O'Shaughnessy colouring and his firm jawline, softened by her femininity but the strong family resemblance moved her deeply.

'Tell me about it,' she said softly. Tell me about Michael O'Shaughnessy and Harry Woodall and all the young men who are fighting. Tell me what it is they do. Tell me about their war for they will not. Only you know and I feel I must. I have lived a life of pampered, sheltered luxury. I have been afraid so often. Afraid to move away from the life, the customs, the rules of my own class but mostly I have been afraid of the man who is your brother. I have lost him because of it but I cannot go through my days hiding from what is not of my world. I have seen the suffering at the hospital in London. I have seen the half-dead man ... boy ... who came back to my parents and watched his desolation slowly killing him but perhaps if I knew what my husband suffers I should not be so helpless, as I am helpless with Teddy, when Harry comes home to me.

'Believe me you don't want to know, Elizabeth. It is not ... pleasant.'

'You know.'

'Yes, but I have not seen it, only the result of it.'

'How do you know of it then?'

'From my ... husband.'

'Tell me what he told you.'

Caitlin sighed, her gaze wandering beyond the open window to the somewhat less than perfect garden of Woodall Park. All the young men had gone and Ernest, the old gardener brought out of retirement, had his work cut out with only a fourteen-year-old lad to help him.

'It's the sheer bloody brutality,' she began, quite coldly,

563

quite dispassionately, which made the telling worse. 'The inhumanity, the slaughter of a whole generation but that is not the half of it. They are human beings who have not been recognised as such ... and brave for they go back again and again, most of them, even though they know what it is they are going to. They are cold and wet to the skin, with mud and clay dragging them down and . I have heard them weep, Elizabeth, not from their wounds or the pain they suffer but just to be dry for an hour, just to be warm for a moment. The stress is so great. They are dying in ditches and holes and in meadows and lanes and their blood makes the poppies grow, did you know that? They are mown down like wheat in a field when the harvester comes. The machine guns are levelled and they fall back into the trenches before they have gone a step, back on to their comrades who have yet to suffer the same fate, and they are aware of it. They fall back and the Germans counter attack, then we attack them and the Germans fall back but the officers, your husband and mine, keep urging them on, for that is their duty...'

Dear Christ . . that is why Harry looked as he did, flinging men again and again into . .

'They lose their friends and some of them go mad in the shell holes. Quite deranged with what is known as "commotional shell shock" which are the waves of a shell explosion. Even the rats which keep them company scream in terror, my husband tells me. And they are only boys, so many of them, crying like babies. They become children again and like children they just cannot cope with it. They have a song ...

      If you want the old battalions
      I know where they are
      If you want the old battalions
      I saw them, I saw them
      Hanging on the old barbed wire ...'

Her voice broke in agony but she went on as if now she had begun she must let it all spill out of her, at least as much of it as this woman who sat before her could manage. 'The shells land in the trenches. Earth and mangled bodies...'

'Please...' Elizabeth's anguished cry tried to stop her now but Caitlin seemed not to hear.

'The gunfire never stops. The walking wounded, those who are still rational, come struggling in with luggage labels tied to their tunics, day and night for days on end. They cannot hear what you say to them they are so stunned with it and there are those who never come back, of course. There are so many unburied corpses the stench is unbearable. They lie in shell holes and dugouts and gun pits and it is impossible to put them decently in the ground. They live with fear and death...'

She stopped abruptly and put a trembling hand over her eyes. 'That is what your husband is suffering, Elizabeth, and mine and that is no more than a fraction of it. Do you want to hear more?'

'No ... I'm sorry...' Elizabeth's voice was no more than a whisper. She put a hand out to the one which lay on Caitlin's lap and held it tightly. Her face was wet with tears she had not known she had shed but she was calmer now and so was her voice when she spoke.

'You shall have your hospital, Caitlin. Tell me what you need and how to go about getting it. Put your baby in the nursery with mine but...'

'Yes?'

'There is a condition.'

'Which is?'

'That I help you. That you teach me to help you.'

It didn't take long. By the end of June all the main rooms and most of the bedrooms had been cleared and the fine old furniture which, most of it, had been part of the Woodall inheritance for generation after generation, was stored carefully in attics and cellars. All supervised by its young mistress who held it in trust for her husband, for his son and his son's son. One day it would be brought out and lovingly dusted and polished and set back in its rightful place but until then where it had once stood were beds waiting to be filled by damaged men Elizabeth Woodall and Caitlin Templeton would do their best to repair.

The conversion of Woodall Park into a Red Cross Auxiliary Hospital was completed by the end of August and as Elizabeth said ruefully to Caitlin, her mother would despair if she saw her daughter's hands. She had learned how to blacklead a grate, though she hoped she would never be called upon to actually do one, given a hand in the scrubbing of what seemed to be miles of corridors and bedroom floors, with a disinfectant so strong you could not speak nor scarcely breathe within ten feet of it.

They were at full stretch almost at once. The new offensive of the third Battle of Ypres, commonly known as Passchendaele had begun on July 1st, providing Woodall Park Auxiliary Hospital with more casualties than it could possibly cope with, but it did, receiving men who had been shot, wounded by shrapnel, gas bacillus cases, amputees and men who had been gassed by chlorine and could barely breathe.

The rain began in France that week, turning the trenches and dugouts, the shell holes and gun pits of the Western Front into a quagmire, four feet of mud and water through which infantrymen, including those of the 3rd Battalion the Lancashire Fusiliers must wade, must fight and live, must sleep and eat and die and the advancing British army, if advance it could through craters and mud, came under remorseless raking fire.

It continued to rain, ceaselessly, and men sank up to their thighs in mud, yelling for their comrades to drag them clear for though they were prepared to suffer the dangers of rifle fire and shell fire, to be sucked slowly into the grip of the foul slime was surely the stuff of which nightmares are made. Two weeks later it was still raining and soldiers who had stood, some of them for six days and six nights, holding a flooded strategic front line trench were brought out with their feet three times their normal size and with no feeling in them whatsoever.

'You can stick a bloody bayonet in them for all I care,' said one soldier, 'in fact I wish you bloody would then I could go home to my old woman.' Trench foot, it was called, but it was not until the swelling began to go down that the intolerable, the indescribable agony attacked and the whimsical soldier got his wish to be with his old woman when they amputated both his feet. Some of his comrades lost not only their feet but their legs as well.

The morale of the British army began to deteriorate. There were mutterings of 'murder' and 'wholesale slaughter' and breaking point was often very near as men and horses and tanks floundered – and sank – in a sea of choking, foetid mud. By the end of September 900 yards had been gained by the Allies. A costly success since it had taken ten weeks to achieve what General Haig had calculated would take two days but still he pressed on and the casualties continued to pour once more across the Channel.

The last stage of the third Battle of Ypres was the muddiest, bloodiest combat ever known in history, a correspondent was later to write. The countryside in and about Passchendaele was battered, beaten and torn apart by a torrent of shells and explosives and on to it all fell the incessant rain. On to the ruined pill boxes, dead men, broken rifles, discarded equipment, desolation and misery. Grey, low leaden clouds, a grey landscape dissected by the ruined Menin Road which led through what had once been Chateau Wood.

At the end of October the Germans began the use of mustard gas.

Major Sir Harry Woodall, MC, decorated and promoted

in the field for his bravery under fire was moving along his forward trench when the shelling began. This was a 'good' trench, thick and deep and though at the moment the duck-board did little to keep his men's feet dry there were plenty of dugouts where a soldier might rest and good communication trenches.

Major Woodall stopped to speak to his sergeant who stood on a fire platform, wiping ineffectually at the rain which dripped persistently inside the collar of his greatcoat from the brim of his helmet and the sergeant smiled wryly. It was a habit none of them could get out of, despite the fact that they were wet right down to their underwear and the rain which trickled down their necks made not the slightest difference to their condition.

'Them lot over there should've issued us with umbrellas instead o' bloody rifles, sir,' he said in an attempt at humour. He and the Major had been together for over three years now and he was not awfully sure he liked the look about his officer's eyes. Gaunt his face was, with nothing left of the cheerful optimism the Major had brought with him in 1914. The strain and exhaustion had all of them at breaking point. It was nothing to do with fear for they all felt that and the Major, like most of them, had overcome it. It was the very fact of overcoming it day after day after day that made men crack.

The Major, when the first shell dropped no more than a foot from him, turned swiftly, instinctively away from it but the shell did not burst. There was a small popping sound, like a quiet cork coming out of the bottle, then nothing. There were more, all small and landing along the line of the trench but they appeared to be duds!

The sergeant stepped down from the fire platform to get a better look, rubbing at his ankle where a sensation of burning had suddenly begun and a man along the trench began to cough and retch.

'Gas,' the Major shouted, calm and steady, and in a

oment or two all the men had donned their respirators
r they were well drilled.

The attack lasted for eight hours, the gas shells churning
to and around the trenches and at the end of that time
e men in the respirators could barely breathe.

By nightfall every officer and man was either dead or
hospital. The offensive ended on November 2nd. The
sualties, with those on the Somme the year before, had
ped out a generation of young British manhood.

31

ey were decorating the Christmas tree in the parlour as
approached the house. He could see them as he opened
e gate. The curtains had not been drawn and the light fell
ross the dark garden, touching the grass and the shrub-
ry his grandmother had planted nearly sixty years ago
th a filament of gold.

The fire-lit, lamp-lit room seemed, as it usually was, to be
ll of people. The Christmas tree against the far wall was
tall its peak touched the high ceiling and Donal, big as
was and teetering on a step ladder, was having a great
al of trouble in placing the fairy which had perched there
ery Christmas for as long as the soldier at the gate could
member. Eammon was holding the ladder steady, leaning
s weight against it, his young face turned up to his brother
d it was obvious that he was directing the operation in
e way he thought it should go and it was also obvious
om the expression on his face that Donal was letting him
ow exactly what he thought about his instructions.

Clare bobbed up from where she had apparently been
mmaging through the box of Christmas decorations,

themselves as old as the fairy, and held up a golden ba
admiring the way the flames from the fire danced on i
surface, then she placed it, tongue protruding in deep co
centration, on a low branch of the tree. She stood back
admire it, then vanished again from the soldier's vision.

There were several other children. Was that Eileen's Fi
bar? Almost as tall as the step ladder and Bridget's Kate
how old would she be now? God's Holy Nightgown
fourteen and almost a young woman, so she was. There w
Dennis and Flynn, both McGowans and crowned with the
father's bright red hair ... God rest his brave soul ... ar
standing with his back to the fire, his pipe in his mouth, h
thumbs in his braces was Mick O'Shaughnessy himself. I
took the pipe from his mouth and said something
Eammon, prodding the air with it and Eammon stood ba
to allow Donal to descend the ladder.

There was a shift of light and colour, of orange and go
on the walls and ceiling as the flames flickered from wh
he knew would be a great roaring fire. He could see so
halos of amber against the walls where the lamps stood, tI
scarlet of Clare's dress and the silvery glitter of tinsel,
strand of which she had wrapped about her neck. She ar
Kate had begun to dance now, arms about one another
a parody of one of the new ragtime two-steps which ha
become so popular since the war began. He could hear tI
faint strain of the gramophone through the closed window
Heads bobbed and children moved about the room, excite
hands lifted, stretching to put baubles, tinsel, candle holde
on any branch they could reach. The door into the h
stood open and through it his little mother came bouncin
and even from the gate where he watched the soldier w
aware of the fiery red poppies in her cheeks and the wispi
of her grey hair about her face which he knew came fro
her exertions in the kitchen. Her sleeves were rolled u
and her bare forearms would certainly have a fine film
flour still clinging to them. Her apron was snowy and in h

and she held a plate of something, no doubt straight from ʌe oven, and as if in confirmation those in the room, her ⹃usband amongst them, clustered about her. She kissed one ℩nd then another, offering her rosy lips last to her husband. ⹃here was a great deal of laughter and when the soldier ⹃rew near he could see his parents standing beneath a ⹃unch of mistletoe.

Hᴇ felt like crying. He could not help it. It was just as he ⹃emembered it. Just as he remembered the last twenty or ⹃o Christmases he himself had spent in this house. He could ⹃ot swear that he could recall the earliest ones of his child⹃ood and since the war began this was the first one he had ⹃pent at home but it seemed to him that those he had known ⹃ame rushing back, crystallising into this one moment in ⹃hich he watched those he loved – unseen – in their joy. ⹃verflowing with love and a strong loyalty to one another, ⹃ith laughter and squabbles, with all the sweetness his ℩mily had shared ever since he could remember.

For a moment it was as if those who had gone would ⹃ome crowding in behind his mother demanding a mince ⹃ie for he knew that was what Mammy had just baked. From ⹃hristmas Eve until the end of Boxing Day, batch after batch ⹃ould come from the oven in a seemingly endless supply ℩nd surely Sean, or Terry, both gone on the wire, Rory, ⹃racie's boy, wounded in Ypres, wounds from which he ℩ad died, Callum and Amy's James, just eighteen the pair of ⹃em and already in the line, would be there in a second ⹃r two, the room packed with them from wall to wall as it ⹃as on every family occasion, happy or sad. All the dear ℩ces. All the dear faces that were gone . . .

It was as though she sensed him there though he had ⹃ld no one he was coming. There had been no time. Those ⹃ho were to have a week's leave between the third Battle ⹃f Ypres and the start of what they knew would come in the ℩arly weeks of 1918, had simply made for the nearest trans⹃ort to get them home. Precious days could be wasted on the journey besides which a soldier could be walking up to his own front door before the telegram which he had sent to say he was coming arrived.

He saw his mother lift her head and turn it cautiously like an animal which scents an intruder. She put out her hand to the rowdy horseplay which was taking place over the last mince pie and Donal and Eammon froze, looking at her in mystification. His father spoke, then turned to stare at the window as his wife was doing but with a shriek which could be heard at the Pier Head, Donal said later, and seriously disturbed the smaller children, she threw the plate she was holding to wherever it cared to fall, turned, vanished, and within five seconds had wrenched open the front door. The light streamed out, a tunnel of warmth and safety along which he was drawn straight into her arms.

'Michael, 'tis Michael, thanks be to the Holy Mother, 'tis Michael,' she screamed into his ear, her arms about him so tightly he could not speak. His kit-bag dropped to the ground and he clasped her to him in a passion of love and thankfulness, his cheek resting on her hair.

They were all at it then, shrieking their delight into the night sky, arms pulling him into their loving embrace, voices urging him to tell them how long he'd got and had he seen any Germans and his Mammy was seriously discommoded when she found she had to give him up. Curtains were twitched at several windows up and down the street and a mother or two, those whose boys had not come home for Christmas and some who never would, shed a quiet tear for Ellen O'Shaughnessy's happiness.

There was a sudden hush then. In the light from the open doorway a young woman stood, no more than eighteen or nineteen years old, small and pretty as a wood violet, her eyes like stars in her shy face. In her arms was a baby, true O'Shaughnessy since she gazed about her in evident enjoyment of the hullabaloo, well used, it seemed, to the lively exhilaration, the ever-present capacity to laugh or cry without the least need for apology in this family of which she was a part. Its youngest, newest member in fact.

They fell back then, even Mammy, for she knew this woman and this child must come before her.

'Michael . . .'

'Mary Kate . .' but his eyes were on the infant in her arms. The merry-faced, black-haired, blue-eyed child who was his daughter.

' 'Tis your wee girl, Michael,' his mother said unnecessarily, her pride so visible the child might have been all her doing.

'Cliona . .' and then, almost as an afterthought though not one of them noticed since it was the first time he had seen his daughter, 'and Mary Kate.'

Stepping forward he swept them both into his arms, burying his face in the sweet curve of the child's neck. His mother burst out crying again and it took five minutes at least to get the whole damn lot of them back inside the house with the children doing cartwheels on the grass, Mick told Gracie later, wiping away a tear from his own eye.

You must let Mara an' Caitlin know, darlin',' his mother said to him the next day. 'Sure an' they'll be dyin' to see you, an' Caitlin'll want news of the front,' just as though Michael was privy to the battle plans of the generals themselves. 'You've not seen Jack, I suppose?'

'No, Mammy.' He sat before the kitchen fire, not saying a lot, his Mammy was inclined to think, perfectly happy to do nothing but hold the child in his arms whenever he could. Last night he and Mary Kate had shared the room in which he had slept since they were married. As Ellen had done when she wed Mick nearly thirty years ago, Michael's wife had come to live in Edge Lane. When the time came she would be mistress of this house as the wife of the eldest son but until then she played the role Ellen had played in her young days. She bustled about the kitchen in the way

573

Lucy had done before she went to work in a factory making
munitions for the war, she and Matty, in effect, Ellen's maids,
working to her orders. Mary Kate saw nothing unusual in it
since she had been brought up exactly as Ellen had, knowing
her place, her function in her husband's and in her new
family's life. Mary Kate would have other children, hopefully
one in nine months' time, and, as they had always done,
they would fit in together like the pieces of a jigsaw, one
piece interlocking perfectly with another. With Michael, Cal
lum and Dermot ... Holy Mother keep them safe ... in
France and all the girls married but Clare, there was room
and to spare. Mary Kate and Cliona had what had been the
girls' room with Clare in the small attic dormer next to
Matty's in which Dermot had slept an' sure didn't they all
rattle about like ollies in a bucket.

'He's in the same battalion as you, isn't he, pet? I thought
Caitlin mentioned the Lancashire Fusiliers.'

'Right so, Mammy, but in a different platoon.' Michael
gazed intently into his daughter's face and she gazed back
at him curiously, then reached to pull at his nose. Their
eyes studied one another, exactly the same shade of blue-
green, with long, amazingly gold-tipped lashes and as
Michael leaned to kiss the pink satin of her rounded cheek
she grinned amiably. Ellen watched in satisfaction, her heart
soft and pleased, pleased with the evident affinity which had
sprung up between father and daughter, then she turned to
Mary Kate, ready to draw her daughter-in-law forward for
her husband's attention since surely she was entitled to it
but the girl was peeling sprouts for Christmas dinner in
what appeared to be perfect equanimity and who was Ellen
to interfere. Perhaps last night had been sufficient ... well
... she didn't want to dwell on that but she still could not
dispel the small seed of unease which had settled next to
her own thankfully beating heart. She was a silly old woman,
of course she was, but Michael did seem more taken up
with the child than with his own wife.

'Caitlin will want to hear the news from France, Michael, what with Jack being there an' all, you know she will. Besides, will she not be longing for a look at her own brother? Why don't you ask Doctor Clancy at number nineteen if you can use his telephone? He'll not mind, God love him, and Caitlin has her own instrument in that grand office of hers. Nothing at all to do with the house so you'd not be disturbing himself, though he wouldn't mind, what with you bein' his chauffeur all those years and an officer now, just like him. What? Yes, doing better at last, thank God and the Blessed Virgin, though he's not himself just yet, is he, Daddy, or so Caitlin says. Wicked, wicked so it is, what those Germans are doin' to our boys . . .' sketching a hasty cross to keep them from doing it to hers. 'But there, talking about Caitlin and Mara I was. An' you'll be wanting to see that lovely wee girl of Caitlin's as well as Mara's lot. Fine ones they are, so. Mind, Caitlin's girl's not a bit of O'Shaughnessy in her, poor wee mite, though I dare say she'll grow into a beauty like her Mammy. Eyes as grey as that cat,' pointing her mixing spoon at the tabby at Michael's feet, 'but her hair's dark with big fat curls, just like that sweet morsel on your knee. Her grandmammy's darlin', aren't you, pet?' dropping a kiss on Cliona's head and the baby directed a sunny smile in her direction. Michael held his daughter against him, carefully resting his cheek on her dark hair and she plopped her thumb in her mouth and settled companionably in the crook of her father's arm.

'She'll likely be busy, Mammy, it bein' Christmas Day. They'll be putting on special festive things . . . oh, I don't know . . . making something extra for them poor buggers who . . .'

'Michael!'

'Sorry Mammy, but you can't help but feel sorry for them and that lad of Osborne's. I wonder how he's doing, have you heard?'

'Aach, poor wee boyo, an' him so young to be shut up in

575

that room of his, so they say, an' never wantin' to come out again.'

'Perhaps it would have been better if he'd been left where he was in that shell hole...' Michael muttered, more to himself than her. His mother's face was unutterably sad and her mixing spoon was still for a moment, then, in a paroxysm of beating which said she'd have no misery on this lovely, unexpectedly special day, on this day which was the birth day of the Holy Mother's Blessed Son, she directed Mary Kate, Matty and Clare in the laying of the table in the dining room. She'd have it right today of all days. Only eight for dinner, not forgetting Matty for the woman was one of the family after all, but then the rest of them, Gracie's, Eileen's and Amy's families, and Mara and the children would be round directly after for whatever was going. High tea and high jinks, she'd be bound, presents and a sing-song under the tree perhaps, Christmas crackers an' a drop of the hard stuff for the two Michaels and though they could not help but be sad for those who were gone, some of them forever, sure an' wouldn't they all meet in that lovely Heaven her religion promised her and in the meanwhile they must thank the Holy Mother for what they had. They'd gone to Mass that morning, of course, all of them including the baby and Ellen might pop down again later to ask for the hundredth hundredth time for protection for her sons and all the other mothers' sons and to light a candle each for Sean and James Osborne, for Rory and Terry. But while the turkey was basted for the last time would Michael just slip to Doctor Clancy's and telephone his sister to let her know he was home. Mara was coming anyway so no need at all to telephone Beechwood, tell Doctor Clancy, just as though Michael was still five years old and must be given detailed instructions before he could be trusted to run an errand.

She had gone down to remind Caitlin that they were to have a special Christmas tea party at four o'clock with the children, just for an hour. Charlie and Alex would be all right, with Nanny and Flora's help and the two babies, Damaris and Lucy, might just make it through even if it was so near their bedtime. It was Harry they would have to watch and she wanted to warn Caitlin though why she felt she should when Caitlin was a trained nurse she didn't know. It had already been an exciting day for them all, hectic in the nursery by the look on Nanny's face and whether Harry was up to it must be considered, but a nursery tea, a few little presents beneath the tree, the familiar childhood routine he had known might just be managed.

He had kept pretty much to their room since he had come home, afraid at first to let the children see his face in case it frightened them but, as children do, after the first stare or two they had accepted father, of whom they had heard, naturally, back into their sheltered lives. The curiosity of having father at home was apparently more of a novelty than his actual face and though he had turned out to be somewhat quieter than they had expected, him being a soldier after all, they had accepted that too. He had told them gravely that he would play with them when he was better so that was all right. They knew that soldiers got wounded. They had seen them, at a distance, in the garden of their own home so with the trust of the very young who have no reason to do otherwise, they accepted.

Caitlin's room was empty and as Elizabeth turned to leave, prepared to go along to the wards to look for her, the telephone rang. She sighed and cursed under her breath. She was in a hurry to get back to Harry who had just had his burns bathed and would be, in Mrs Willis' jargon, 'all of a dither' with it. For an hour or so his nerves would be in tatters since the burn on his right leg, just above the knee, was still infected, a nasty mess of erupting matter and he would need the comfort of her hand in his, her arms about him, her kisses, her presence, the comfort she gave him like a mother with a sick child. But the telephone might be important and she could hardly ignore its jangling demand.

She picked it up and his voice hit her like a body blow from a heavy fist. It rendered her sightless and deaf and without even the strength to take the breath which she needed simply to go on living. From somewhere inside her a wave of reeling emotion rushed over her as the spirit of Michael O'Shaughnessy which had remained at the edge of her life for the past eighteen months touched and re-kindled her dormant heart. It burst at once into a frantic, ferocious joyful fire of love, blazing and consuming her with longings she had buried when he left her.

'Caitlin...? Is that you?' His voice was quizzical, warm with affection for his sister and Elizabeth clung to the instrument as if it was the only thing which kept her from falling to the floor. The loud and hurtful knocking of her heart and the sound of it in her ears made it difficult for her to hear what he said but she could sense the laughter in his voice as though he thought he had taken away his sister's power of speech.

'It's me, darlin', Michael. I've got a few days' leave and hasn't the Mammy been at me to telephone and get you to come over to Edge Lane, if you can. I'm at Doctor Clancy's and ... Caitlin ... are you there, pet...?'

His voice died away and she could see him as she knew he was now, his air of authority gained in three years at the front, eighteen months of those in command. She could see his dark curling hair in the nape of his neck, the dark tilt of his eyebrows, the set of his firm chin, the laughing blue-green of his eyes, the long, gold-tipped eyelashes, a hundred tiny, wonderful details which, as she stood there, tremulous with love, trembling with shock, the receiver clamped to her ear, had each and every one the power to bring her to her knees.

'Caitlin...?' His voice had become hesitant and she knew he knew who it was on the other end of the line, at least with his heart.

'Who is that? It is Caitlin ... Mrs Templeton ... ?'

'Michael.' It was barely a whisper but he heard it over the miles of telephone wire which separated them and in the singing, joyful, fearful recesses of his heart.

'Jesus God ...' she heard him say, then his voice became no more than a faint mumble as he evidently spoke to someone nearby. It went on for perhaps thirty seconds but it seemed an hour, a day, a week as she waited, died a thousand deaths until his voice, his beloved voice came back to her.

'It was ... Doctor Clancy ... oh Sweet Jesus ... Elizabeth, darling ... I can't believe it ... to hear you. Say it again ...'

'Michael.'

'I never hoped ...'

'Where are you?'

'At home.'

'For how long?' terrified that someone, Caitlin, would come into the room and snatch him from her.

'A week.'

'Oh God, only a week?'

'Where ... for Christ's sake where ... ?' his voice harsh and ready to break.

'I don't know.'

'Do you still drive?' his thought processes beginning to function before hers.

'Yes.'

'The inn, tomorrow at three.'

'Michael, it's Boxing Day.'

'Damn it to hell ... the next day then?'

'Yes .. oh yes ...'

'Get Caitlin, for the love of God ... while I can still speak coherently ...'

'I love you, Michael.'

'Still ... ?'

'Yes.'

'I love you, Elizabeth.'

* * *

579

The landlady was not surprised to see them, she told them amiably, knowing by now, of course, that neither of them was free and should not be here at all, but showing them up to their room just the same. Christmas only just over an' all but it was nothing to do with her, was it? This terrible war did things to people and made them do things they'd never have dreamed of before. Life was short and him bound to be a soldier though he was in civvies today and you'd to take what you could before life or death finished you off, was her opinion for what it was worth. Lovely young couple though. Shame...

They stood for perhaps five minutes, leaning in to one another like two young trees which have been battered by storms, clinging to the only support which could sustain them. He turned her face up to his, cupping it carefully with hands which trembled slightly. His mouth came down on hers, so gently it was scarcely more than a breath, lingering to taste the sweetness and texture and delicate odour of hers. It moved to her cheeks, her jawline, and to each eye then he wrapped her in his arms again, blind and rapturously happy for this moment which had been allowed them.

'Sweet Christ, I've longed for this.'

'I know, I know, my darling.' Her own blaze of joy was almost more than she could bear. She had been prepared for this buffeting surge of emotion but the strength of its reality weakened her and she clung to him, to his enduring capacity to bear her woman's frailty.

'I didn't mean to see you ... to try ... my family are ...'

'Don't, my love ...' Her voice was barely audible as she burrowed deeper against his chest.

'But when I heard your voice ...'

'I know ... Dear God ... I know. I cannot say ... how much I love you.'

'There's no need, there's no need between us,' he groaned painfully, 'and yet I must hear it ... and say it. You are all of my world ... all I need ...'

580

'Yes...'

'This is all I need, for now ... to hold you and yet I know when you go it will tear me apart...'

'What are we to do?' The pain in her voice was dreadful.

'Nothing ... there is nothing except this.'

They made love and afterwards, breathless, lost, bemused by the perfection of it, they smiled at one another in wonder, sitting up in the sweet-scented, herb-scented bed to study and imprint on the memory the curve of a graceful neck, the turn of a strong muscled shoulder, the loveliness of a pink-tipped breast, a long shapely leg. When would this happen again? Would it happen again? How could they know, and so they must possess again and again, be greedy, taking all they could, giving all that was needed.

'Hold me again,' she whispered, her eyes telling him her desolate thoughts which were mirrored in his and they clung desperately together, terrified of the coming parting. She knew she should go now. She knew she should have gone half an hour ago for Harry would be anxious. He could not understand, he had said, why she must drive over, today of all days, to visit her grandmother since the old lady would never know whether Elizabeth had been or not which was precisely why Elizabeth had chosen her as an excuse, an alibi. She could not declare she was to visit her mother or Mara because later, if it came up and it was discovered she had been nowhere near them, how could she explain it? Her grandmother's confusion was well known and it would cause no comment if Elizabeth said she had been there and old Mrs Osborne said she had not.

'It is Christmas, darling,' she had said gently, 'and I really feel it would be nice if I popped over for an hour or two,' feeling no remorse nor guilt for was it not Michael ... Michael ... she was going to see.

But she could not make the same excuse again. This would be the only time they could meet here and because of it she was reluctant to leave him. This, this communion of her body with Michael's might not come again and how was she to bear it? He would go back to France, to the war which had torn her family apart, and his, and the probability was that he would remain there, with Sean and Rory, with Tim and Hugh, and with James who had fallen at Gallipoli and all the other fine young men who had simply vanished into the bloodstained earth over which they had fought.

'Nothing can touch us, my darling,' he said, his voice suddenly calm. 'We are indestructible, you and I. What we have cannot be destroyed, you know that now, don't you?' and he was telling her as he read her thoughts with the perception which had always existed between them that should he die their love would not. 'Don't despair, my dearest love. I'll always be here with you.'

Their love was strong, steady, the love of a mature man and woman. The tempestuous, tense, frightening love of the girl and the young man had been tempered with trust, honesty, patience, dedication. Romantic love, the dazzling emotions which assail the young, had merged into the understanding and experience of true lovers who could endure. They would endure, together or apart.

She felt the knowledge fill her heart and mind, soothing her, calming her fears and she was at peace and when they rose to dress she was able to stand at the window with him, her back to him, his arms about her and, perhaps for the last time, look out with him at the stark winter beauty of the forest.

'There is one thing.' His voice was low as he spoke into the tumbled mass of her hair.

'Yes?'

'The boy.'

'Yes?'

'I ... would like to see him.'

'I know. If I could, I would.'

'Perhaps ... a walk in the direction of Colton Wood. Both of them to arouse no ...'

582

'It's too far for them to walk, Michael. They are so young and I cannot take the car out again.' Her voice was anguished. She knew this was the last gift she could give him. This was his son whom he had never known and a man could not be denied one look at his son, a picture to take with him as he went into battle.

'Well, in that bit of woodland at the back of Woodside Farm?'

'Hollin Wood?'

'Yes.'

'It is so close to the house.'

'Please ... Elizabeth ... I would dearly love to see him before ...' His dark face pleaded and his eyes narrowed, the lashes about them tipped with the same gold as those of his son, his expression that of his son when he desperately wanted something for which he would not beg. How could she refuse? She knew he meant to do no more than look at his boy. He would make no trouble, no demands, hurt her, for their love was too precious to him to gamble with. It meant more to him than anything in the world, even his own son. He was a man now, a complete man who knew his responsibilities to others, as she did. It was this which made the union between them so absolute. It was this which made them so uniquely strong.

'I'll try, my darling.'

He sighed thankfully, then turned her into his arms for their last kiss.

They were charmed, her two young sons, when mother suggested a stroll after lunch in the garden. They went out often with Nanny and Flora, romping and playing the games boys of their age love so much but to go for a walk with this lovely mother of theirs who was such fun but who recently had not been to the nursery as often as once she had done, made them feel very important indeed.

'It is rather cold, m'lady,' Nanny said doubtfully, herself

583

surprised at her mistress' suggestion, but who was she to argue?

They took the path which led from the side of the house, the two small boys, warmly wrapped in woollen leggings, bright woollen jumpers and hats, dashing and darting ahead of her, excited beyond measure by this unexpected outing. They were ready to go along the safe walks they always went with Nanny and Flora. Down the slope of the lawn, across the park to the lake's edge where they usually fed the ducks, keeping of course to the paths where the perambulators containing the babies, Damaris and Lucy, could easily go.

'This way, Charlie,' their mother called and they both turned in surprise, then delight as she indicated that they were to go off the well-trodden path and actually venture into the wood.

'In the wood, mother?' Charlie questioned, hardly able to believe his ears.

'Why not, darling? Let's have a little adventure.'

'A 'venture?'

'Yes, just the three of us. I'm sure two big boys like you would love to go exploring.'

They were not awfully sure what exploring was but if mother seemed willing and unafraid then so were they. Alex, bolder than his brother, had already left the path, his sturdy legs carrying him into the thick and somewhat soggy layers of last year's leaves which covered the ground. It was milder now than it had been before Christmas and the ground was not hard. The woodland floor was open to the skies, the branches of the trees bare of leaves except for the conifers, their bark a lovely autumnal red, their needles bluish green.

'Look mother, Christmas trees.' Alex stood in the clearing, his earnest young face staring up at the branches.

'Yes, darling.'

'Bigger 'n ours.'

'They are, darling.'

The boys roamed on, pouncing on cones and needles and broad, wet leaves with all the joy and enthusiasm of two young explorers discovering gold. Her heartbeat was fast and filled with delight. They were so beautiful, her sons, and soon, soon, she would be with the father of one of them. Her eyes darted as swiftly as they did, moving from tree to tree from behind any of which he might suddenly appear.

He was walking towards them slowly on the same rough woodland path just as though he was a farm worker, a woodsman, a tenant of Woodall who had every right to be here and she blessed his consideration for at the sight of him the boys were not in the least alarmed.

'Good afternoon, m'lady,' his eyes going first of all to her, then to Charlie who must of course be acknowledged. 'Good afternoon to you, lad,' nodding pleasantly and at last, at last he found his son, her son, theirs, 'and good afternoon to you . .'

He stopped then and she could see he was making a tremendous effort to control his emotion, to be natural, to be no more than a passer-by speaking politely to chance-met strangers but his eyes were bright with unshed tears and his broad-shouldered frame was trembling quite visibly.

Both boys had stopped to stare with the unabashed curiosity of children. Alex held a pine cone in his hand and Michael, not knowing how else to approach the boy, squatted down on his haunches before him.

'What have you there, boyo?'

Not accustomed to being called 'boyo', particularly by a man he had never met before, the child was not sure how to respond.

'Is it a pine cone, then?'

'Yes.'

'Sure an' you can tell whether 'tis going to rain with one of those fine things, so you can.'

585

'Really?' and the boy inched up to the father and gazed into the face which, now that they were together, could be seen to be so like his own.

'Indeed, if it's tight closed it's to rain, you see, and if it's open then the day will be fine, so it will.'

'I've got one, too,' Charlie said, demanding his share of attention as children will and Michael, with a great effort, turned from his son to Harry Woodall's.

'So you have. Now keep them with you and when someone says, "Sure now, is it to rain tomorrow?" you'll be able to tell them. Now isn't that a wonder?'

Both children, enchanted to be the possessor of such a magical gift, leaned confidentially against his knee and his arm; at last, he could hold his son, he could touch and hold his son, their son, born of their love. The child made no protest when the stranger hugged him for a brief moment, a brief moment which only one of them was aware might never come again.

'You have fine sons, m'lady,' he said and his eyes were dazzled with love, looking at her over their son's head.

'I think so.'

'Their father will be very proud of them.'

'Yes.'

He knew it was over then. The boys were fidgeting to be on, to find more of these marvellous things which would amaze and impress Nanny and Flora, Damaris and Lucy with their power.

He let them go. He let his son go, watching him run 'ike the wind, like a young free animal which knows no fear only love and when Michael turned to Elizabeth they were both weeping.

'Thank you,' he said simply.

'You are to go soon?'

'Tomorrow.'

'I will always love you.'

'I will always love you.'

'Goodbye.'
'Goodbye, my heart.'
'We *will* meet again.'
'Yes.'

32

Caitlin paused for a moment listening to the strains of the gramophone in one of the wards as it plaintively sighed that 'Smoke Clouds Set Me Yearning'. It vied for attention with an orderly who was wheeling a trolley ahead of her whistling the more cheerful 'If You Were the Only Girl in the World'.

These were only two of the songs which had caught the popular imagination of the millions of young people drawn up in the weary round of work and killing, pain and suffering, toil and endurance, meetings and partings which seemed as though they would never end. 'Pack up Your Troubles in Your Old Kit-Bag', and 'It's a Long Way to Tipperary' were two more and they exactly matched the mood of those to whom the excitement and the heroics had long turned sour. It was March 1918 and the war had gone on far too long and, by the look of it, was far from over as word came that another German attack was expected.

'Mornin' Sister,' a cheerful voice said as a man in a wheelchair, his legs hidden beneath a blanket, made his way along the passage where Lady Anne Woodall had once arranged her social engagements and chatted to her friends on the telephone. It was still there on a small table by the window but another line had been installed in the room where Sir

Charles Woodall had once seen to estate matters and which was now Caitlin's.

'Good morning to you, Corporal, an' how's yourself the day?'

'Fine, Sister, or at least I will be when I've had me dressings done.'

'Aach, a brave wee man like yourself'll not bother about a little thing like dressings, an' Sister Nolan's the fine one with the bandages.'

'Now then, Sister, none of yer Irish blarney with me.' He grinned impishly, his rugged northcountryman's face good-natured despite what had been done to him. 'Now i tha was to say tha'd do them for me I'd feel a sight better.'

'Get on with you. Sure an' isn't it yourself who's been kissing the blarney stone so don't let me hear you've been giving Sister Nolan a hard time of it.'

She was smiling as she entered her office, the smile which was reserved for them all, the smile of comfort, of hope, o promise of a relief from their pain. The smile that told them that it would be all right, really it would, and that, should i turn out not to be, then she was here to help them throug it. That she was theirs, available whenever they needed he and that with her to guide them they would not flounder The moment that she had closed the door behind her i slipped from her face like a flimsy mask leaving it weary and strained.

'Aye, an' who were that tryin' to get thi' to come an' hol his hand then? Just as if tha'd not got enough to see to wi'ou tekkin on every Tom, Dick an' Harry what comes throug them front doors. See, sit thissen down and get that insid you. I saw thi' coming along the hall from t' kitchen doo so I asked Cook to put thi' up a nice boiled egg, some toas an' a brew so I'll have no backchat and thi've to get ever bit down, mind.'

The woman who spoke had been standing somewhat t the side of the shadowed room, hiding, Caitlin knew, fron herself, making sure that the door was closed with her on this side of it before speaking. She had placed the tray on Caitlin's desk and as she advanced into the centre of the room the expression of determination to have her own way was plain on her face.

Caitlin sighed but with an air of resignation moved round the desk and sat down. Mrs Willis, come with her from London to 'keep an eye on her for Master Jack' had caught her fair and square and would put up with no nonsense. She would stand over her just as though Caitlin was a child, making sure she ate every morsel, dipping the toast soldiers into the runny egg yolk and popping them herself into Caitlin's own mouth if needs be.

'Sip tha' tea, lass. I made it good and strong.'

'I can see that, Mrs Willis. Sure an' it will rot me insides by the colour of it.'

'Never you mind, it'll lift tha' up a treat.'

'Really!'

'Aye, an' when tha's finished tha' can get up to that room o' thine an' have a nice lie down. I 'appen to know tha' was up four times in t' night to that there young chap what's got the gas in his chest an' why them young women on t' ward couldn't give him oxygen wi'out callin' on thee is a mystery to me.'

'What were you doing up yourself then? Spying on me, I'll be bound, so that you can write to Jack and tell him his wife's not keeping her promise to take it easy...'

'Ha, that's a laugh! You, take it easy! If it wasn't for me tha'd be on tha' feet twenty-four hours a day, letting them poor beggars kill you alongside themselves.'

It was a well-worn road, this conversation which went on almost daily between Caitlin Templeton and Edie Willis and though Caitlin swore that it made no difference what Mrs Willis said or did, she would do as she pleased, they were both aware that the older woman kept the younger within the bounds, if only just, of what her body and mind could support. Caitlin ran the hospital, from the ordering of the supplies to the supervision of its nursing staff and of the wounded as they arrived, first to be fumigated and bathed before they were put to bed. There was the administrative work, the endless laundry to oversee, the cooking not only for the wounded and sick men but for those who looked after them, all to be arranged and put into order by 'Sister' Caitlin Templeton.

But besides this Caitlin did as much real nursing as she was able since it was for this that she had begged Elizabeth Woodall to give up her home. She needed to be amongst these suffering men, each one of whom could be Jack. She needed to give herself to them for it was only in that way did she feel she shared what her beloved husband suffered in this everlasting, unendurable war.

'Will tha' go to tha' bed then?' Mrs Willis stood over her threateningly.

'I am supposed to be on duty, Mrs Willis.'

'I know that, my lass, an' if anyone asks for thi' I promise to fetch thi'.'

Caitlin smiled and at once the weary strain was gone from her and the freckle-faced, rose and amber beauty which had once been hers returned. Her blue eyes lit up and she shook her head.

'Sure an' you're worse than the Mammy, so you are, but ... well, I'd like to go up to the nursery first, then I promise I'll have an hour on the bed.'

'Good lass,' and with that Edie Willis picked up the tray and bustled efficiently from the room. She could trust this young woman to keep her word. She had found that out in the four, or was it five, years she had now been with her. It was Edie's war effort to look after Mrs Templeton which didn't seem much, but when you thought of all them lads Mrs Templeton looked after, well, you could see what an important part Edie Willis played in this war.

Caitlin sat for five minutes, looking out of the window on

to the wide, rolling lawn which surrounded this beautiful house. The office was to the side but from where Caitlin was she could see massed banks of rhododendron bushes, not yet in flower but glossy leaved and heavy with buds. There were huge old trees under which generations of Woodall children had played and spread beneath them the new-born glory of daffodils, wild and growing wherever they pleased. There was a narrow stone pathway leading from the back of the house to the front and, as she watched, Sir Harry and Lady Elizabeth Woodall walked slowly along it moving in the direction of the sweeping lawn, the deer park and the lake which lay beyond. They would have been to the stables to see what were left of the beautiful horses which had once crowded there, long since gone into the mud of Flanders. There was only an old mare and a fat pony on which Charles and Alexander were led round the paddock, a sad reminder of the bloodstock the Woodall family had once owned.

Sir Harry's arm was threaded through that of his wife and he leaned against her somewhat, still favouring his right leg which had been horribly burned by the mustard gas. As Caitlin watched them turn the corner of the house she faced the awful truth that she would see Harry Woodall dead if she could arrange it for Jack to take his place. That in one dreadful sense she hated Elizabeth because she had her husband home with her, and for good, whilst Jack still struggled to live in the horror of the trenches. Though Harry was not the same man who had marched away three-and-a-half years ago, and never would be again, he was here, alive, safe in the love of his wife and Caitlin wished with all her heart that Jack could come home to her, even in the same pitiable condition as Harry Woodall. Where was he? Where was Jack? Was he alive, dead, wounded, asleep, fighting, being shot at, shelled, buried in mud, suffering, afraid ... where ... Dear Sweet God, all these years of living and not knowing, of hoping, believing that at this precise moment

he was alive because his last letter, received yesterday, said
that he was but it had been written two weeks ago and since
then he could have been killed in any one of the numerous
and fiendish ways war kills a man, so many men, fine young
men ... and women too. Poor Elsie Thompson, her comrade in so many other kinds of battles, dead on the Somme
in the ambulance filled with wounded men she had been
driving to the base hospital. Dear Elsie and other young
women had given their lives, many of whom had been suffragettes like herself. It seemed so long ago, those days of
the WSPU and the campaign. Would they finally get what
they had fought for when this war was over, since surely
they deserved it? By God, they had proved their worth,
so they had. They had been considered worthy of being
slaughtered as men were. Would they now be considered
worthy of voting as men did?

There was a great deal of noise coming from the nursery
and when Caitlin opened the door it seemed to her that
there were certainly more than the four children who lived
there in the room. And should it fail to surprise her to see
Mara's five leaping around like dervishes, for did they not
create havoc wherever they went? Mara would allow no one,
not even their Nanny, to check what she described as their
'high spirits' and of course, with Serena Osborne possessed
by the needs of her younger – and indeed only son – had
they not become as wild and uninhibited in their behaviour
as their O'Shaughnessy cousins. They were all inherently
sweet-natured, a trait they had inherited from their father,
but any child will take advantage of lack of supervision and
Mara's children were no exception.

And where was Mara, Caitlin asked herself irritably, as
Miss Claudine Mary Osborne flung a cushion at her Woodall
cousin, Charlie. Nanny and Flora had enough to contend
with in the care of Charlie and Alex, Damaris and her own
little Lucy, who at fourteen months of age was as fast on her
tottering legs as any of them.

'Master Christian, will you calm down and lower your voice. Little gentlemen do not shout. And will you please retrieve that cushion at once, Miss Claudine. No, I will not pick it up for you and I do not care if Nanny and Etty do it at home. You are not at home now. In this nursery children do as they are told ... Master Alex, please ...' since naturally, even a good child will copy one who is being naughty, 'put down that paint pot and take that paint brush away from your sister's face ... Flora, for pity's sake, get hold of Miss Lucy, she is about to lose her napkin. Sit down, Miss Mairin and stay where you are put ... no, Miss Ailis, when I say no I mean it ... Oh, Mrs Templeton, there you are. I do apologise but when the nursery is so crowded ... well, with only two of us it is rather difficult. Mrs Osborne had to go ...'

'I quite understand, Nanny ...' and Caitlin really did. It was too bad of Mara to leave all five of her children in the Woodall nursery, going off God alone knew where on one of her frequent and unexplained jaunts in her bright red two-seater sports car. Serving tea and cigarettes to soldiers at the railway station just coming on leave or returning to France, she said, but on the few occasions Caitlin had been in the vicinity there had been no sign of her sister. She did not always leave her children here, of course, but no doubt when she did her Nanny and the nurserymaid who helped her would be sitting by the nursery fire with their feet up for it would not occur to the dashing and irresponsible young Mrs Osborne that the Woodall Nanny would be hard pressed to care for nine children, particularly when five of them were hers.

Lucy, on spying her mother, hurtled on her plump and unsteady legs towards her, flinging herself against Caitlin's apron and smiling her gap-toothed smile in bright rapture. She had Jack's eyes, a pale velvet grey, and Caitlin's dark and curly hair which Nanny had brushed into a fat ebony sausage from her forehead to the back of her head, gleaming with that sheen only children's hair has. Caitlin's heart turned over with love for her. She picked her up and the offending napkin, wet and sagging, slipped from the child to the floor. Sitting down at the nursery table she cradled her daughter to her. The other children gathered round for Auntie Caitlin told the most wonderful stories and might she not be about to do so now?

'Sit,' she said and they did so, pushing and jostling one another just as she remembered she and her brothers and sisters had once done in the kitchen at Edge Lane. They waited expectantly and she looked round at the bright faces of the children of the men who had gone to war nearly four years ago, only one of whom so far had come back.

Claudine, the eldest, nearly seven years old and so like her mother it was quite startling to see. A beauty already and a little madam, too, her grandmother O'Shaughnessy said fondly. Christian who had been demanding since he was three years old to be called Paddy for was he not an Irishman like his grandfather and uncles? Five years old with no memory of the man who had sired him, dead these three years. Mairin and Ailis, three years old, identical and always spoken of in the same breath as though they were the same person which it seemed sometimes, uncannily, they were. And Rose, Rosie Osborne, named thus by her mother for reasons best known to herself since the only Rose the Osbornes had ever heard of was grandmother Osborne's long dead friend. Rosie, born after the death of her father and eleven months after her twin sisters, a beautiful, green-eyed child who looked like no one unless it was her Aunt Elizabeth. Two years old and a bit, and more Irish in her ways than the lot of them put together.

The Woodall boys, Charles and Alexander, at four and three years old no match for their Osborne cousins, but already the conflict showed, particularly between Charlie and Christian. Even now Charlie was doing his four-year-old best to push the sturdy Christian off the bench and the two red faces testified to their silent struggle.

'Stop it, boys,' their Auntie Caitlin said and they did. They knew the voice of real authority when they heard it.

And Damaris. Harry Woodall's sweet-tempered daughter with her mother's strength and beauty and her own baby charm. She was two years old next month and she and Caitlin's own Lucy were already inseparable for they had been together now for almost a year.

But the cuckoo in this nest of boisterous, healthy, self-willed young fledglings was undoubtedly Alexander Woodall. Whenever Caitlin looked at him, serious, frowning and yet with a merry turn of humour which often surprised himself, she had a feeling she had known him before though she could not have explained exactly what she meant by that. He was dark like his mother, with clear hazel eyes and the most glorious gold-tipped lashes you ever did see and in Caitlin's private opinion was the apple of his mother's eye.

They were so beautiful, the children of the soldiers. The lost generation of young men, one of whom was hers and when, Dear Sweet Mother, when would the father of her child be returned to her? He had been home on leave just after the new year. For a week. Gaunt and exhausted so that for the first twenty-four hours he had done nothing but sleep, waking only to mumble an apology before dropping again into the pit where peace was. They had made love later with the fierce hunger of the starving who are never sure where their next meal is coming from. Rocking and weeping in his arms, distressing herself and him with the passion of her fear, she had known a great sense of premonition, of warning, and although she had buried it deep within her breaking heart it had caused her to neglect the precautions she normally would take to prevent pregnancy which she had neglected only once before. It was as though she must make life, if she could, balance somehow the loss, if it should come, of the man who had loved her for nearly seven years. She was certain she was pregnant again and she hugged the sweetness of it to her, just as she hugged her daughter. Holy Mary, Mother of God, pray for us now and ... keep him safe ... keep him safe. Keep them all safe, those who are left. Michael whose own baby daughter was almost a year old and who surely, on his last leave at Christmas, had made his Mary Kate pregnant again. Dear God, it was as though she was obsessed with these bright flowers which must grow to replace those that had been cut down.

'Once upon a time...' she began and nine faces turned in bright expectation towards her. Nanny and Flora heaved a sigh of relief.

Elizabeth led Harry down the lawn and across the deer park towards the lake, taking care not to step out too briskly though she longed to do so on this fine English spring morning. Well, almost spring though the air still had a nip in it, as Ernest the gardener had just reminded them.

'You want to keep well wrapped up, m'lady. Powerful contrary this time of the year can be. Now watch your step sir ... beg pardon, Major ... them steps are slippery with that bit of rain we had.'

'Thank you, Ernest...' and the gardener's lad at Ernest's elbow gazed in awe at this hero who had returned from France.

Fallow deer were grazing beneath the trees at the edge of the woodland and they raised their heads nervously at the sound of Elizabeth's and Harry's voices. The white spots on their coats stood out in the shadows and the bucks, ready to cast their antlers in the next month or two, pawed the ground restlessly.

The air tasted like wine, sweet and pure and it was drawn into Harry's damaged lungs as easily as it had once been, years ago when he had run as swiftly as the deer, round this very lake, his brothers at his heels. His wife's hand was

596

warm in his and within him he felt again the stirring of the tiny bud of hope which had lain furled and dormant, so deep he had not known of its existence until recently. The tiny fragrant bud which was almost ready to bloom. He had made love to her last night. He had made love to *her* last night, not at all like those other undignified moments when she had done her loving best to arouse his body and had failed so disastrously. Not her fault, of course, and not his that his manhood had been so shattered he had given up hope that it would ever be mended but her patience, her love, her strength had been there, every minute of every day and night since they had shipped him home, and last night he had made love to her!

'I love you,' he said, turning to smile at her, lifting her hand to his lips, delightfully aware that she was looking at him as a woman looks at a man. He grinned then, almost boyishly

'I know you do, my darling,' and she smiled back, one eyebrow raised delicately, provocatively, flirtatiously, he would have said, remembering the previous night.

He threw back his head in sheer enjoyment. 'I want to run, just like we did on the night I first realised I loved you, do you remember?'

'I certainly remember running several times down this very slope but perhaps we had better postpone that until . '

'It was on the day I was twenty-one and you had been dancing with . . I can't even remember who it was now, one of the estate workers, I think . . no, now I recall who it was O'Shaughnessy . remember?'

'Really ' She kept her voice steady but her interest was suddenly attracted to the blazing trumpet of a daffodil at her feet and she leaned to touch it.

'Aah, what times they were then, Elizabeth.' His voice saddened momentarily and the burn marks on his face which were beginning to fade, stood out quite vividly, then his smile returned. 'But we must not look back. We must look ...'

'To the future, Harry.'

'Indeed yes. The children and what they will achieve.'

'Yes.'

'We are very fortunate, my love.'

'Yes ... and perhaps ...'

'What is it, Elizabeth?'

'Perhaps we might consider another ... now that we ...'

He grinned wickedly and the engaging young man he had been almost four years ago returned. He was not quite twenty-nine years old but the horror of trench warfare and the mustard gas attack he had only just survived had taken their toll. His face was ravaged by the marks the burning gas had left. Though he and his men had worn respirators, after several hours these had become ineffective and the gas he had inhaled had entered his lungs so that for a long while he had been drowning in the infected fluid which filled them. He had been blinded, his eyelids inflamed and gummed together with matter and for several appalling weeks it had not been known whether he would see again. The gas, invisible and lethal, had eaten its way through his uniform and he had suffered agonising water blisters, all of which had turned to putrid matter in the long dragging haul through the waist-deep morass of mud to the casualty clearing station. From there, over a period of several agonising days, he went first to the goal of all the suffering men, to Blighty, and then to his own home at Woodall where there were doctors and nurses and his devoted wife to care for him.

'Race you down to the lake,' he said to her now and it took all her carefully controlled, well-hidden determination to deter him. Was he getting better? Was he recovering? He was damaged and frail still, subject to setbacks where a loud and unexpected sound could reduce him to the state where he needed desperately to crawl beneath the nearest table but it seemed he was beginning to raise his head and look about him with interest. He could spend more than an hour with the children now, instead of the bare five minutes he had managed three months ago.

And last night he had made love to her. Gently, carefully, afraid that his weakened strength might not carry him through. His orgasm had been rapturous and if hers had not quite matched his he was not aware of it. She loved him as she had always done, as she always would, as her beloved friend. He was the man with whom, when she was no more than a girl, she had chosen to spend her life, but who had never captured and held her heart as Michael had. She loved him. He was the best man she knew, steadfast, kind, funny and loving, but the man to whom she belonged, heart, soul, mind, muscle and fibre, and always would, still fought in France. Michael ... would he come home, would he, and if he did, what was to happen? Of course she knew the answer. Elizabeth Osborne and Michael O'Shaughnessy had commitments which could not be set aside but then neither could their love and he was still there, deep and safe and treasured in her heart. Where he would always be.

She took her husband's hand and Michael O'Shaughnessy's spirit took her and led her into calm waters.

The gleaming red roadster snarled its ferocious way through Knotty Ash and on towards Prescot, its mad passage causing heads to turn and stare, then stare again when they saw the driver was a woman. A beautiful young woman with a mass of dark tumbling hair which she made no attempt to restrain as the wind whipped it from beneath the dashing red beret she wore. She was laughing and her brilliant blue-green eyes were turned again and again from the road to the handsome officer who sat beside her.

'Hey, steady on, darling, or you'll have us in the damned ditch, the speed you're going,' he said.

'Not me, boyo. Sure an' I've been driving for years and

I've not had an accident yet. I like speed,' and to prove it she pressed her foot harder on the accelerator and the motor car flung itself forward at an even greater velocity.

'Why don't you let me drive, my pet? You did drink rather a lot of champagne at lunchtime,' but the handsome young officer did not seem unduly nervous, in fact his laughter was as wild as hers.

'Fiddlesticks. Just because I've a drop took doesn't mean I can't drive the motor car, Barney, and you can take your hand off me knee, so you can, or I won't be responsible for the consequences.'

'Then tell me where we are going?'

'Not until you've taken your hand off me knee.'

'You know you don't mean that, darling.'

'Don't I so?'

'Spoilsport.'

'Spoilsport, is it? What a lot you know.'

'I do know you're very beautiful and all I want is to finish my leave with ... well, you know what I want, my lovely Mara. Would you send a soldier back down the line in the bloody awful state I'm in especially as this might be the last time? We have a name for girls like you, we gentlemen, and it refers to a part of our anatomy which does not like to be teased, particularly as it might not be functioning for much longer.'

The car slammed to a violent stop as Mara put her foot on the brake and she and the officer almost shot over the windscreen. Traffic which was following was forced to swerve wildly and had the motor directly behind not been travelling at a much slower pace it would have run into the back of them. There were curses and a great shaking of fists but Mara took not the slightest notice.

'You can get out right here, Barney Hayward, so you can, and I'd be obliged if you'd not bother to telephone me again. I'll not be spoken to as though I was a . well, 'tis a lady I am an' I'll be treated as one, so.'

'Mara...' The officer was agonised in his remorse. He wouldn't insult her for the world, he said. Of course she was a lady and surely she knew she meant the world to him. It was just that she drove him mad with her loveliness, she really did, and he didn't know what he was saying and after the other night when she had allowed him to ... Dear God, it was a memory he would take back to France with him, a cherished memory that ...

It was a game they both loved to play. The young officer and Mara Osborne, for was that not what life was? A game. To get as much fun out of it as was available, as much laughter and champagne, to dance and make love, to seek out sensations which were new and thrilling which told them they were alive. There was a bloody war on, after all, and you had to have something to make you forget the stark terror, the appalling discomfort, the never-ending danger, the boredom, the sheer bloody boredom of life as it was now.

'Say you forgive me and then ... well, if you do, let's go on to whatever it is you have in mind and make the next few hours the most memorable either of us have ever known. What d'you say, my lovely Irish colleen?'

'You won't be impudent again?' her eyes two inches from his, laughing and wild.

'Impudent! Me? I wouldn't dare.'

'Sure an' you already are, you rogue. What's that hand doing back on me knee? May the Saints look down an' save me from a divil such as yourself,' but she made no attempt to stop it when it crept beneath the short skirt which had ridden up her silk clad legs. She allowed it to reach the lace at the edge of her silk French knickers before slapping it away, still laughing.

His pale brown eyes grinned knowingly into hers and, as the chemistry of his male body told him that not only was he ready but so was she, they became darker. A deep warm brown she remembered so well from years ago ... when

601

was it ... so long ... so long, then one of them winked in that bold way Captain Barney Hayward had and the hazed memory vanished.

Mara laughed. She re-started the engine and pressed her foot on the accelerator. Tipping back her head and to the tune of 'What a Friend We Have in Jesus', she and the captain beside her bellowed the song soldiers were singing in every trench in France.

'When this poxy war is over, no more soldiering for me ...'

33

It was several minutes before the two women became aware of the growing tumult of noise. Though it started quietly enough, first with a hooter or two, the faint melody of bells, then a factory whistle, it increased gradually until there was nothing else to be heard but a great conflict of sound. It seemed as though the whole city had gone mad. It could only be compared to the noise of an uproarious, rowdy party at which those who had been invited had lost complete control of themselves, perhaps drunk more than they should and simply erupted into a delirium of goodwill. Ships' sirens tore at the air, rending it apart like flimsy fabric, flinging their joyous message across wet-slicked rooftops so that in her kitchen in Edge Lane, Ellen O'Shaughnessy turned to stare in amazement at her elderly maid.

'What in God's Holy Name was that?' she asked nervously, then crossed herself since surely it was needed. Times were uneasy. A body never knew from one day to another what disaster might strike and was one about to bludgeon her now?

'Holy Mother of God!' Matty echoed and it was then the maroon exploded, away to the west where the river lay, but loud enough to make both women jump violently.

There was a drumming of footsteps on the stairs and Ellen's daughter-in-law burst into the room. She was wide-eyed and pale-faced and to her breast she clutched her child with the frantic desperation of one who knows marauders are at the gate but is prepared to defend it to the death. The child cried lustily, struggling to escape its mother's alarming, vice-like grip but her hold did not lessen. She crept fearfully across the flagged kitchen to huddle with the others against the chimney corner and each one of them, even the baby, babbled their dread, making no sense at all.

They had been preparing the vegetables, Ellen and Matty, in readiness for the family's midday dinner. They would all be home in an hour or so and on this drearily wet day Ellen could think of nothing more nourishing than a good pan of stew for wouldn't each one of them be as cold as charity when they came in, God love 'em. Best braising steak, for though food had become increasingly scarce as the war progressed Matty had come home from the butcher this morning with what was a real treat for them all. With plenty of spuds, carrots, onions and a dash of mixed herbs thrown in it would make a lovely change from the meat which had been their portion recently, meat Ellen, in better times, would not have given to the cats. The meal would be cooked to perfection, of course, as only Ellen knew how and guaranteed to put strength into growing bones, solid fibre into growing muscle with good solid flesh on top of that. She might even chuck in a dumpling or two, for himself was very partial to a dumpling. A good lining to their stomachs was what was needed on a day like this, and the lot of them restored and sent back to school and himself to the warehouse with their bellies as full as Ellen could safely stuff them.

The noise continued, getting nearer, it seemed to Ellen,

and she pushed the young woman and her child protectively behind her for though it didn't seem all that threatening for it had a glad air about it, she meant to see no harm came to her son's wife and daughter. Whilst he was away Mary Kate and Cliona were in her care and would she ever forgive herself if anything happened to either of them?

'What is it, Mrs O'Shaughnessy?' the maid faltered, holding before her the small knife with which she had been scraping the carrots, ready to defend herself and those she loved with it despite the weapon's inadequacy.

'The divil if I know, but whatever it is it's making an unholy row about it, so it is.'

'Have the ... the Germans come, d'you think?'

'Don't be daft, Matty, an' stop making that silly noise, Mary Kate. Sure an' you're only upsetting the baby.'

'The Germans...'

'Are in the trenches in France where they belong.' Ellen tutted irritably and though she was still somewhat wary about it she risked a step or two away from the chimney corner, closely followed by Mary Kate, the howling child and the maidservant, so close that when she stopped they all bumped into her.

'Whist, will you stop your noise, girl, an' give Cliona a biscuit. I can't hear meself think.'

Her words were interrupted by another violent sound this time made by the crashing of the front door as someone opened it with such force it hit the passage wall, cracking and resounding through the house like a volley of pistol shots.

'Holy Virgin Mother, protect us now and in the hour of our need,' Mary Kate began to jabber, crossing herself and her child, ready to fall to her knees for surely it was the Germans and everyone had read of what they had done to women and children in Belgium.

'Be quiet, girl,' Ellen quavered, but she grabbed the heavy brass poker which stood before the kitchen range. She'd

604

rain anyone who threatened her family, German, English, Irish or Hottentot, it made no difference to her. Just let whoever it was come through that kitchen door and Bejasus he'd be sorry he'd chosen this house to invade.

The hullabaloo came in with the intruder and over the whistles and hooters could be heard the voices of people cheering, shouting, singing and someone was whistling 'Tipperary'. She had never heard the like before and as she picked her way dazedly towards the door into the hallway, there was Mick, her husband and behind him the hallway was full of ... people? ... children ... her next door neighbour, Mrs Donovan, weeping she was, an' would you look at himself. His overcoat not buttoned, nor his jacket and waistcoat beneath, and where was his hat? The old fool ... on a cold day like this to be out without his hat. But ... but it was only just gone eleven o'clock and what was he doing home at eleven o'clock? And the children ... Eammon and Clare ... and Finbar, his face split into an enormous grin. Bejasus, she was ready to faint, so she was ...

'Oh, darlin' ...' Mick said, clearly under the spell of some enormous emotion which he could not control for the tears fell freely from his eyes and poured across his seamed face. They dripped on to his crisp white shirt and his wife felt her blood freeze with fear. Not again, please Holy Mother ... not again ...

'What ... ?' She held out her hands placatingly, ready to ward off the awful news he was about to tell her for surely it must be awful to have her husband weeping like a child. And yet he was smiling, smiling through the tears and his arms were wide and joyous, ready to receive her, to receive them all, the whole world, into his jubilant embrace.

'Ellen, darlin' ... 'tis over ... 'tis over ... the war ...'

'Over ... ?'

'Yes, darlin'. They signed the armistice at eleven o'clock an' the news was given out ... sure an' didn't I come straight home ... but the whole city's at a standstill ... the tram driver just got off the tram and the conductor ... right in the middle of Dale Street an' I had to walk. Jesus, Joseph an' Mary, the crowds ... dancin' they are, factory girls in their overalls and shawls ... bobbies ... soldiers blowing horns and beating tin trays ... decent women capering about like children...'

'Mick...' She swayed towards him and behind her Mary Kate and Matty began to scream with joy and the baby, even more terrified, strained away from her hysterical mother, hiccoughing and not at all sure where to look for comfort in this mad world. She was accustomed to the O'Shaughnessy ebullience in all its varied forms but this was something more. This was shrill and feverish, hectic with some emotion which was too much for her and she wailed loudly into her mother's shoulder.

They were all at it. Eammon and Clare were doing a fair imitation of a foxtrot round and round the table. Finbar, not knowing what else to do to show his jubilation, was performing handstands against the kitchen wall and out in the passage and beyond in the wet and dismal garden, a dozen children did cartwheels, some of them not awfully sure why unless it was because they had been let out of school and told not to come back today. Mrs Donovan and Matty fell into one another's arms and wept loudly for though it was a day they had awaited for years now, Mrs Donovan's Ernie, a fine boy the same age as young Michael O'Shaughnessy, would never come back.

Mick and Ellen stood clasped in one another's arms in a small circle of quiet. Ellen laid her cheek on her husband's broad chest and he rested his on her greying hair. His tears fell and so did hers and though their hearts were filled with the thankful peace of knowing that at last, at last they could go to sleep at night and wake up in the morning without the dreadful fear of that telegram informing them that another of their sons was no more, what of those who had already been lost to them? They were glad, of course they were, that there would be no more killing but how could they not help but think of Sean and Rory, of their daughter Gracie's husband, Terry, of Mara's husband, James, and the rest? For four years they had lived with it and slept with it, wept over it and died a little as their children went into danger, so Dear Sweet Mary, could they be blamed for thinking, even at this joyful moment, of those they would not see again?

Mick put her gently away from him, his big hands resting on her shoulders, and smiled down at her. The look they exchanged was both solemn and joyful.

'They'll be home now, pet. Michael and Callum and Dermot an' all the rest of the fine sons of this country so we'll dry our tears and smile for them, when they do.'

'You're right, acushla, so you are, but what a lot to be done before then. Them beds need airing so I'd best get a move on.' Stretching up she kissed him soundly on his wet cheek, then, happy to be about something in the service of her family, she bustled away to check the contents of her airing cupboard just as though they were all to appear on her doorstep within the hour.

Mary Kate jiggled her crying baby and her blue-green eyes were like stars.

'Hush darlin', hush baby, don't cry for isn't your Daddy to be home soon.'

'Will I be helping you make the beds, Mammy?' Clare had relinquished her brother to the arms of her cousin Teresa McGowan whose Daddy would never, sadly, come back from the war, but three of Clare's brothers would and if Mammy was to set about the task of preparing for their return Clare was eager to give her a hand. She had been only seven, a mere child she told herself, when Sean and Michael, and later, Dermot and Callum had gone off in their fine new uniforms with real guns over their shoulders but she clearly remembered the sadness of it all. Sean, God give him eternal peace, was among the glorious dead now, though Clare was not awfully sure why it was glorious to be dead. She was aware that Sean would have gone at once to the lovely Catholic Heaven her Mammy and Father Paul had told her about, his soul cleansed of all mortal sin but on the quiet, though she wouldn't dare breathe a word of it to Mammy, she herself would rather be a tiny bit sinful and alive!

'To be sure you can, pet, though it'll be a day or two before they'll be home. 'Tis a long way from France and with all those soldiers on the move the trains are bound to be packed. Then there's the boat over the water . . .' Ellen's voice was rapturous as she cleared a way through the packed hall, elbowing cheerfully aside children who were still crackling with excitement. There was no doubt in Ellen's mind that from eleven o'clock this morning, an hour ago now, the trenches in France would have been steadily emptying. That the boys would be shouldering their kit-bags and shaking hands with their mates before hailing some convenient transport which would bring them all safely back to their wives and mothers where they belonged. With this lovely thought in her mind she began to hum a little tune as she and Clare hurried up the stairs.

'We'll do Callum's bed first, darlin',' his mother said. 'We'll have to get that scamp Eammon up here to move some of his things. Will you look at the state of the place,' flinging her arm in a dramatic circle to indicate the aching tidiness of the room which she herself had 'bottomed' only that morning. She tweaked the bedspread on Eammon's bed and pulled the curtains into a more becoming line before giving her attention to the bed in which Callum was, thanks be to God and the Blessed Virgin, to sleep safe at night. She flung back the bedspread then, clapping her hand to her mouth, ran back to the head of the stairs.

'Teresa . . .'

'She's not here, Gran.'

'Who's that then?'

' 'Tis Siobahn, Gran.'

608

'God love you, pet, run to Matty and tell her to put the kettle on. I want plenty of hot water ... and see, look for the hot water bottles, will you, darlin'. They're in the cupboard under the stairs, so. And ask Mary Kate to give the stew a stir...'

'Yes Gran.'

'There's a good girl.'

Her daughter, who had followed her on to the landing, trailed her back into the bedroom, doing her best to keep up with her mother's triumphant headlong dash.

'Will I have to give up my room, Mammy?' she queried anxiously.

'Aah darlin', did you not want to lose it then? No, well I can understand that, so I can, but then where will Dermot sleep? Sure an' he's a grown man and a soldier come home from the war and won't he want to sleep in his own bed again, darlin'?'

'But where will I sleep, Mammy?'

'Well, we'll have to give it some thought, acushla, but don't fret, we'll find somewhere ...'

'I don't want to go in with Matty, Mammy.'

'No, of course you don't, pet, but to be sure won't you be pleased to have your brothers home again, all of them, and t'would only be a Christian thing to let Dermot have his room again when...'

'Couldn't Dermot go in with Eammon and Callum? There's three beds in there. Sean's bed ...'

Ellen stood up violently, her face suddenly ravaged with pain and Clare was pushed unceremoniously to one side.

'Let's have no more of this, child. Fetch me the single sheets from the airing cupboard an' we'll make up Callum's bed.'

'I don't want our Dermot to have my room, so,' Clare protested, her face taking on that mutinous expression which was a familiar one to her mother. They were all the same, her children. Self-willed, stubborn, liking their own way so should she be surprised that this one came from the same mould as her older brothers and sisters? All her children had spirit and a lively inclination to be opinionated on many subjects such as when they should get out of their beds in the morning, whether they should attend Mass or Holy Communion, or even the Confessional. Should they not be allowed to go where they pleased and with whom, have the right to wear the latest – and quite shocking – shorter skirts showing not only the ankle bone but an inch above. What was the world coming to, she asked herself distractedly, and now here was the child, her eyes brilliant in her flushed face, ready to do battle with her own Mammy over who was to sleep where in Ellen's own house. Of course, Dermot could go in with Eammon and Callum but somehow she just couldn't bear the idea of anyone, not even one of her own sons, sleeping in the bed which had once been Sean's. She could see him now, his lovely, laughing face, all clean and scrubbed, his hair wet and curling over his forehead from the 'good wash' his Mammy insisted on at bedtime, his imp's eyes doing their best to stay open as he drowsed on the pillow

'Aach Mammy, I'm too old to be kissed,' he would grumble as she went from bed to bed, tucking her boys in, enfolding them in her safe, loving embrace, but holding his face up just the same. In this very bed, and now he was gone and really she didn't know how she was to bear it. Especially now that they were all to be back soon and himself not with them.

'Now listen to me, lady . . .' she began, her sore heart shortening her patience but from downstairs the commotion became even greater, a swelling of ecstatic jubilation which rose up the stairs, vying with the pealing of bells, the sirens and hooters and from the street outside, the shouts, the singing and, Holy Mother, was that the Boys Brigade Band coming round the corner from Jubilee Drive? The whole world was going mad with joy and as if to confirm it a shrill voice called up the stairs, begging Mammy to come down for Gracie and Amy and Eileen were here.

'Daddy's got the whiskey out an' says we're all to have a tot, so we are...'

'Does he indeed?' and instantly she was diverted, the image of each and every one of her family, grandchildren included, as drunk as Paddy McGinty's goat, winging her out of the bedroom and down the stairs, Clare hard on her heels since she'd never tasted whiskey.

They danced and they sang, round and round the kitchen table, down the hall and out into the long front garden. The rain had stopped and a watery sun had streaked the oyster grey of the November sky. The trees were bare and skeletal, still dripping their burden of rain which had fallen that day but those who cavorted in the O'Shaughnessy garden, along its path and beyond the yew hedge into the street were too happy to care. It was over. The war was over and their boys were to come home. Men and women were embracing, weeping unashamedly, whilst others waved the Union Jack, sang 'For He's a Jolly Good Fellow', though to whom they were referring was not awfully clear, and 'Tipperary'. Lorries and horse-drawn drays crammed the roadway, one or two horses shying nervously at the jubilant, singing, whistling, cheering crowds and Clare O'Shaughnessy thought she would never forget this day if she lived to be a hundred. She had never in her young life seen such emotion, and her family could carry on with the best when the occasion demanded it. It was grand, it really was, and she supposed, after all, she'd best let their Dermot have his room back. He deserved it, he really did. All these rejoicing people could not be wrong. They were heroes, those who were to come home and she'd be a poor sort of thing if she couldn't let her own hero brother sleep in his own bed.

Several miles away at Woodall Park, the ancestral home of Sir Harry and Lady Elizabeth Woodall, two women clasped

611

one another in a fierce embrace, the strong emotional experiences which they had shared during the last two years fastening them, rock-like, into a silence which could not be broken with words. They did not weep for they were beyond the relief of tears but merely stood, drowning in the thankfulness, the wonder, the outpouring of gladness and yet at the same time, the sadness which was to become the common emotion of the whole nation.

The end had come at last. The day had come they and thousands upon thousands of British men and women had yearned and hoped for through the long war years and yet, now it was here, neither thought it was an occasion for wild celebration.

They were both aware, as most were not, that the suffering and dying would go on. Men right here in the hospital would continue to die of their wounds and those who did not die would very likely never recover. There were men who would continue to cough up their lungs, stumble about on one leg, or none at all, or with a white stick to guide them. There were men who would, for years, dive for cover beneath a table at any loud noise and there were others who would be unable to cope with it and would die later, by their own hand.

It was very quiet. The 'boys' here were not making a great song and dance, as the rest of the country was. There were no whistles or songs or cheering in the wards, just a shrug or two and a collective sigh as they remembered the familiar figure of a comrade who had not come back with them, and never would. He had gone in the muddy trenches, his old tin hat at a jaunty angle, the drab of his khaki stained and filthy. They remembered him tramping through squelching mud and the thick dust of passing traffic, on the tilting, unsteady duck-boards, a fag end in his mouth around which a wry grin formed. They saw him with his heavy pack and his rifle, swearing and exhausted but going forward just the same. It was said that the King was making a speech about it up in London and that 'Land of Hope and Glory' was being played at every street corner. That folk were going wild with it. That even in the rain which was coming down in stair rods they were wearing Union Jack flags stuck in their hat-bands but then those were the ones who had never been 'down the line' as they had.

'Let's have a cup of tea,' Elizabeth said to Caitlin, when at last they drew away from one another and Caitlin smiled.

'Why do we always turn to a cup of tea at times of great sorrow or happiness? Sure an' you can be certain the Mammy will have one in her hand at this very minute.'

'Of course she will. Can you just imagine how many women up and down the land are putting the kettle on at this moment.'

'I'll ask Mrs Willis to fetch us a pot . . .' but as Caitlin spoke there was a sharp rap at the door and without waiting for a reply it was opened by the plain, no-nonsense woman with eyes as kind as the summer skies, though she would have been horrified if anyone had said so in her hearing.

'I thought tha' might like a brew,' she said shortly, putting the tray down on the desk with a crash which implied she was seriously out of sorts.

'Thank you, Mrs Willis.' Caitlin stood up, her well-starched apron rustling in an efficient sort of way and before Mrs Willis could escape her she put her arms about her, holding her stiff, resistant figure in the warm embrace she had just given Elizabeth. Elizabeth watched, her own eyes bright with warm, unshed tears. Mrs Willis did not respond for a moment or two since she was not one for 'fuss' but then she relaxed and awkwardly patted Caitlin's shoulder whilst she allowed herself to be warmly hugged.

Caitlin let her go and their eyes searched one another's for several seconds, understanding flowing between them.

'He'll be home now, Mrs Willis,' she said softly, her eyes luminous, their vivid colour somewhere between the corn-flower blue and emerald green all her family shared.

'Aye lass, that he will, an' he'll need a deal of looking after, I'll be bound.'

'We can do that, you and I, Mrs Willis, when we've got him home for good.'

'An' when'll that be, d'you reckon?'

'I don't know. I wish I did, but they'll all be coming back soon, those who are . . .'

'Aye lass.' Mrs Willis patted Caitlin's hand comfortingly. Who knew better than Mrs Templeton what devastation and suffering their boys had undergone? Had she not shared it with them in the casualty clearing stations and field hospitals in which she had served behind the line? And she had nursed the wounded and seriously ill men from the battles of Passchendaele, Cambrai, Arras and the Marne and what was to be known as the Battle of Picardy, or the second battle of the Somme, doing her stalwart best to put them to rights. Twenty-four hours a day, if Edie Willis had let her, working herself to a shadow, miscarrying the child she had conceived on her husband's last leave at Woodall but there, it was all over and what was Caitlin Templeton to do now, Mrs Willis asked herself. Stay at home and be a housewife and mother? Not her! The very idea made her laugh since Mrs Templeton, for as long as Edie Willis could remember, had worked and suffered to put to rights whatever she considered to be wrong. A suffragette before the war, in and out of prison and Edie herself had seen the gap at the back of her mouth where the steel gag had sheared off a tooth on one of the many occasions she had been forcibly fed.

But that fight was over an' all. In recognition of the great service performed by the millions of men who had gone to the front, universal suffrage had been granted to all men over the age of twenty-one and in June of this year old Lloyd George had finally given the vote to women, or at least to some of them. Those over thirty who were householders or were the wives of householders, a compromise measure which had benefited neither Edie who was not a householder, nor Caitlin Templeton who was only just twenty-five. Still, it had been won and this woman had nearly been killed in achieving it. Her clear eyes and steady gaze were as dear to Edie Willis as if Mrs Templeton had been her own daughter, if she'd had one, which she hadn't, nor a son neither, but she wouldn't have dreamed of telling her so, not in words anyway.

'I'll get on then,' she remarked tartly. 'There's still things to be done, armistice or no armistice.' She turned on her heel and marched away, somewhat in the manner of a sergeant major who is sure his troops are up to no good behind his back.

Elizabeth rose and moving lightly across the room put her arms again round Caitlin, hugged her briefly, smiled and without speaking left the room.

Caitlin sat down slowly, the meaning of it beginning, at last, to find its way into her weary, battle-scarred heart. It was over. It was finally done with. There would be no more desperate partings, exquisite but harrowed meetings, no more letters which broke her heart because each one might be the last communication she would ever have with her beloved husband. No more horror nor fear nor grief, nightmares from which Jack, and she, awoke screaming and if they should continue to suffer them, they would suffer them together, she and Jack. Nightmares in which blinded men, gassed men, men who were legless, limbless, emasculated, who followed her through the mud and stench and rotting putrefaction of the endless battlefields of France. It was over. All those hundreds upon hundreds of anguished faces she had seen on hundreds and hundreds of stretchers, the broken, mutilated bodies she had nursed or prepared for burial or shipped back to Blighty with their pathetic labels tied to them reading 'Head', 'Stomach', 'Chest', as though they were so many packages.

She had become a woman during the past four years. Grown up, moved on from the intensely idealistic young girl she had once been. She was experienced and capable with no vestige of illusion left of the holiness of her mission. She was mentally and physically drained but she and Jack would renew one another and bring up their children to be free-thinking, brave-hearted and clear-headed in a world where war and violence, which had been seen on a scale which could not be imagined, would not happen again.

It was over and Jack was coming home. It was over. She put her face in her hands and wept.

At Beechwood Hall, the home of the Osborne family, a young man sat quietly in a chair beside the window overlooking a stretch of somewhat neglected lawn. It was winter now and the grass had stopped growing but it was evident that it had been left uncut for many weeks as the summer ended. There was a terrace directly beneath his window leading down in a series of wide mossy steps to the long slope of the grass on which once upon a time half a dozen gardeners would have worked. At the bottom of the slope was a small lake, its edges choked with chickweed and comfrey and overall was a slight but unmistakable air of sad neglect.

A man, evidently come from a side door of the house, walked slowly across the winter lawn, an elderly retriever padding at his heels. They both walked stiff legged, the man's shoulders slumped, his back bent, the animal's head down. When the man stopped so did the dog, standing patiently at the man's heel until he was ready to move on again. The man turned and stared up at the window of the bedroom. His face was quite without expression but there was an aura of such misery about him it was possible to sense it even from a distance. He seemed to be sunk in his own despair but after a moment or two he moved on. When he came to the edge of the lake he stopped again, standing for perhaps five minutes, the dog beside him, before drift-

g, aimless and without direction, towards a bare stand of
es.

The young man did not move. His chin was sunk deep
his chest and but for its slow rise and fall and the pulse
ich beat in his temple he might have been cut from stone.
 had light brown hair, thick and flourishing, which curled
orously at his neck. His flesh was pale, colourless, though
was firm with youth. His brooding eyes stared from deep
ckets, a dulled chocolate brown surrounded by long, dark
hes and his mouth was hard, without humour or warmth.
ere was a quality of hopelessness about him, of emptiness,
 unhearing, unseeing, uncaring numbness which was
illing in one so young and yet it was possible to see
him some faint remnant of an attractive, perhaps very
od-humoured youth.

The door opened quietly, somewhat hesitantly, as though
 woman who entered was not sure of her welcome. Ser-
a Osborne was in her late forties now and had once been
autiful. She still was in a faded, sadly passive way, her
nner vague and indecisive, her eyes, strangely, with a
t of nervousness in them. She was starkly dressed in an
tfit which had been fashionable two years ago, an after-
on gown of black taffeta with a double line of buttons
ning down the skirt to meet a double ruching of silk. The
dice had magyar sleeves finished with the same ruching.
he smiled in the general direction of her son though
 did not actually look at him, moving quietly across the
ep carpet with the hushed reverence of one entering a
eral parlour, an expression on her face to match. Her
ds were tightly clasped in front of her just as though
y were clinging together for support.

Teddy darling,' she said tentatively. There was no answer
 she moved round the chair in which he sat until she
s standing in his direct line of vision.

Teddy.' She made a great deal of effort to keep her voice
t though it was difficult, or so her manner seemed to

say, when the person to whom she spoke continued to sta[re] at the bodice of her dress as though she was not there [at] all. In fact just as though he still gazed out of the windo[w]. His eyes had not changed their focus nor his face [its] expression of hazardous ill-humour.

'There is news, Teddy.' Her voice had a slight quiver [in] it. There would be no joy in the telling of it, nor in [the] receiving, that was obvious. There was still no answer.

'It's over, darling,' she went on and for some reas[on] known only to herself and perhaps to the man in the cha[ir] she took a small step backwards, just beyond his reach. 'T[he] war, Teddy, it's over. The armistice was signed at elev[en] o'clock.'

She had his attention now. Slowly he raised his head a[nd] looked into her eyes and the expression in his was appalling. Now that the light struck his face fully it was possible to s[ee] the ravaging of his youth, the deep etching which pain ha[d] left, the twisting of his mouth which had been made f[or] laughter. It was wide, strong, curling up at the corners a[nd] yet drawn into a frozen expression of bitter, savage, hati[ng] rage.

But, 'Is it really, mother?' was all he said, the quiet co[m]posure of the words contrasting harshly with the expressi[on] in his eyes.

'Yes, darling. The news just came through ten minut[es] ago.'

'Indeed.' His voice was polite, expressionless, witho[ut] interest. He was waiting only for her to move, his mann[er] said, so that he could continue his silent gazing at the stret[ch] of garden which had been his sole occupation for the pa[st] two years. What did it matter to him whether the war [in] France was ended, or indeed if it went on into eterni[ty]. What did anything matter to him any more? War or pea[ce] it made no difference to his life since he had none. He w[as] already dead, killed on the first day of the battle of t[he] Somme in July 1916, and entombed in a pit so deep a[nd]

618

ack his young and fertile mind could not comprehend it
it simply switched itself off. If he allowed his imagination
ll rein it would drag him headlong into the depths and
ver his body which still lived no matter how he tried to
ll it. So he did not think. He simply sat for what else can
man do who has no legs?

'Well, I will leave you, then,' his mother said. 'Your father
feeling unwell.'

'Really.'

'Can I ask your man to bring you anything?'

'There is nothing I want.' That he can give me.

'Very well, darling. I'll look in later.'

'Thank you, mother.'

It was not until she had gone, the faint aroma of her
rfume lingering after her, that he began the slow and
onised weeping.

ross the Channel in France, although Cease Fire had been
unded, one or two snipers, wishing to boast that they had
ed the last bullet in the war, kept on popping away for
veral minutes. Just a bit of bravado, really, and no harm
ne except to one of Ellen O'Shaughnessy's sons who fell
ck dead into the trench from which, jubilantly, he had
st climbed.

34

ara Osborne was twenty-three years old when what was
be called the Great War ended, a widow and the mother
five children. She was also very beautiful. Her russet-
eaked hair had life and warmth in its dark depths, it was
ck and springing about her well-shaped head for like

many of her fashionable contemporaries she had had it c
short in what was known as a bob. On most the style la
flat and smooth, following the shape of the head, but o
Mara it leaped up in a riot of shining curls, an exotic, flan
boyant, chrysanthemum bloom, spilling over her forehea
and about her ears in a positive explosion of movemer
When she shook her head her hair swirled and bounce
with a life all its own, making those gentlemen who admire
her, and there were many, want to plunge their hands int
it, to bury their ardent faces in it and from there to procee
with any game she allowed them to play.

And didn't she have the most incredible eyes, those wh
were under her spell agreed, of a shade somewher
between green and blue, with a wicked sparkle and glint
them which spoke of her intense love of life and all th
bounty it had been good enough to heap on her. Aqu
marine, one of her lovers had called them, helpless an
hypnotised, but she had merely tossed her flower-like hea
and laughed, a gesture she made when she was not abs
lutely certain of the meaning of some word or remark mac
to her. For though she was bright and quick witted, sh
had never read a book in her twenty-three years and he
education had been sketchy due to her own complete lac
of attention to the nuns who had taught her.

One of her admirers was in her bed when the uproa
began.

'Jesus, Joseph and Mary, what's that?' she asked, as h
mother was to do some minutes later in her own kitche
the news taking somewhat longer to reach those in Live
pool than in London. She sat up abruptly, her lovely, ros
nippled breasts falling forward in the most delightful wa
or so the man beside her thought.

'Christ, what does it matter?' he answered thickly, reac
ing from behind her, holding the weight of her breasts
the palms of his cupped hands. He rolled the tight pir
nipples between his thumb and forefinger, then sat up hin

self, placing his legs one on either side of her, leaning her back against his chest. He bent his head, burying his face in the curve of her neck and shoulder, biting the flesh, then licking the marks his teeth had left. He pulled her more closely to his chest, pushing his penis between the cleft of her buttocks, ready to continue the erotic games they had indulged in for the past six hours, in fact ever since they had stumbled, laughing and befuddled, from the taxi which had brought them from the Café Royal.

Around the bed, scattered on the luxurious carpet, hanging tipsily from chairs and tables and even from the exquisite chandelier in the ceiling were articles of clothing, those they had flung from nervous, excited fingers as they had greedily undressed one another at four o'clock in the morning. His uniform, that of a Major in the Queen's Own Cameron Highlanders, lay in half a dozen different places about the luxurious bedroom, breeches in a khaki puddle by the door since he had been relieved of those first, followed by underwear, boots and socks. He remembered wondering dazedly how Mara had achieved the almost impossible task of removing his breeches whilst he still wore his knee-length boots, but she had, followed by his uniform trench coat, his jacket, belt, straps, tie, shirt and lastly his officer's peaked cap.

They had been to the Alhambra to see George Robey and Violet Lorraine in *The Bing Boys*, followed by dinner in the restaurant of the Carlton Hotel from where they had gone on to the Café Royal. The Grizzly Bear, the Temptation Rag, the Castle Walk; all the very latest dances had been performed by what seemed like hundreds of frenzied young officers and their female companions, their intention simply to have a bloody good time, to suck from what might only be a few days left of life every last morsel and drop of juice it contained; to wallow in any excitement or decadence they could lay their hands on; to indulge their young, still unbroken bodies in any way they could, while they could.

621

Swaying and stamping and bending in a mindless orbiting revolution, a vortex of deep throbbing music from America they called jazz, of champagne cocktails and Russian caviar, of endless cigarettes which had turned the expensively furnished and decorated room into a shadowy, mist obscured fantasy where men searched for dreams to blot out their nightmares and women did their best to make them come true. They were home from the front, young gentlemen, all of them, wealthy and pedigreed for who else could afford the rare and expensive commodities, among them the women, which were on sale to them in London.

Mara had worn a sheath of emerald green satin with very evidently nothing beneath it, indecently clinging, or so her mother would have thought, lovingly following every curve and crevice of her magnificent body, revealing the saucy peaks of her nipples, the slender sweep of her waist, the twin spheres of her perfect buttocks, the narrow niche between them. On each of her velvet-skinned arms had jangled a dozen gold bracelets, and a rope of gold beads like tiny, irregularly shaped nuggets swung wildly about her neck and down to her knees. She had shimmered in the pearl grey cigarette smoke, swaying gracefully, tantalisingly dangerously close to her partner, her eyes narrowed and barely focused, stopping to laugh through the candlelight at Second Lieutenant Dickie Ainsworth, Subaltern Rupert Harding, Captain Gil Fleming, all of whom she knew, and a lot more besides. The blare of the music, the tinkle of champagne glasses, the huge excitement of living on the edge of disaster, blowing kisses and waving to acquaintances, knowing exactly, despite the champagne she had drunk, in what way her behaviour was affecting the man who was her escort. But this was the stuff of life to her. A game she loved to play. A grown-up game that male and female indulged in and which suited her so well since she knew deep in her Irish, Catholic heart that, like her mother, she would love only one man in her life, and he was dead.

622

Like bright jewels glowing against the drab of khaki her own expensively outrageous clothing lay scattered. The gleaming pool of green satin which was her dress, one high-heeled shoe in the exact same shade flung on the dressing table, the other, from which the man beside her had drunk French champagne, hanging from its heel on the bedpost. Delicate wisps of emerald green silk stockings which she had had specially made to match her gowns, and a drift of lace which might, or might not have been an undergarment of sorts. Dozens of gold bracelets, circles of light in the glow from the lamps which were still on, caught on several fragile ornaments where they had been thrown as though at a hoop-la stall on a fairground.

She still wore the rope of gold beads. The man lifted it and began to twine it about his own neck, binding himself and Mara together until her head was forced back into his shoulder and her body was lying flat against his own, her back pressed tight to his lean stomach. His hands kneaded her breasts, his fingers pinched her rosy nipples, his eyes watched them peak and harden and he grinned. Only two days ago his had been amongst one of the battle-worn units which had been withdrawn from the Battle of Meuse-Argonne to be replaced by an eager, fresh army whose intention was to cut the Metz-Sedan Railway and by so doing to frustrate the movement of German troops. He was thirty-two years old and had fought – against all odds – for four years in the trenches and this, this woman, or any other like her, and what they did together was what he needed – like a drug – when he was on leave. Whole, clean, healthy flesh: white, womanly curves and hollows: the lusty smells of sex and expensive French perfume, scraps of lace and delicate flimsy things, a woman's laugh, throaty with desire: mem-, ories to take back down the line.

But she was not responding as she usually did. Her attention was captured by the increasing volume of noise which was floating up to the hotel window, a cacophony of hooters and whistles, shouts and rattles like those one heard at a football game, Major Sir Miles Hamilton was inclined to think.

'Mara, lie still and kindly allow me to continue . . .'

'But what the divil's going on outside? I never heard such a din in my . . .'

'Does it matter, really, does it matter when we are having such a delightful time together? I have a fancy for a game of captivity using this magnificent rope of gold, what say you, my darling? And do you know what would make it all the more . . . piquant, do you? Some of that marvellous stuff Andy Mason had with him at that last party of his. Do you remember? A snort of that and you and I could play . . .'

'Miles, will you untie me at once before you strangle the pair of us?'

'What a lovely way to die though, darling. Bound to the most beautiful creature in London, both of us naked as two babes . . .'

'Miles, you spalpeen, I'm warning you, if you don't let me go . . .'

'Yes my pet, what will you do?'

She twisted round somehow and looked up into his pale silvery-blue eyes and not for the first time wondered what was going on behind their mild and smiling regard. Though there was no outward sign of it she could sense the cat-like tension in him. A stillness which she had seen in the young tom which used to hang about her mother's kitchen door when their own fireside tabby was in the vicinity, or when it stalked an unsuspecting sparrow pecking at the sparse grass. A dangerous menace which had no concern in it for the intended victim. She had seen it in the faces of many of the young warriors who came from the front where they had been taught to kill, to overcome the enemy at any cost. They knew nothing else, many of them coming as they did straight from the schoolroom, and could they be blamed for bringing that same destructive element back from

rance? And it added a spice, an erotic flavour of danger to
heir lovemaking which lifted them both to such an explosion of multiple orgasms it was as though they were
bout to die. Major Sir Miles Hamilton and others like him
were dangerous young animals concerned only with two
hings, killing and lovemaking, and somehow Mara thought
he two often overlapped. It was the most exciting experi-
nce she had ever known.

Twisting further until her body lay flat on his she began
o kiss his open mouth, still tied to him about the neck, her
own mouth wide and greedy. She moved her sinuous body
n an urgent and growing rhythm, thrusting her pelvis deep
gainst his rigid penis. Raising her hips she took him inside
er. Swiftly he tossed off the golden necklace and she sat
p, straddling him and as the bells of victory rang out, so
id their own shout of triumph.

When they emerged from the hotel suite which Mrs Mara
Osborne always reserved when she was in town, wan and
both somewhat frail-looking, the peace was several hours
ld, but never mind, a bottle of bubbly would soon put
hem back on course for the fun they intended to have, they
old one another as they headed in the direction of the
earest party. There would be one, naturally, in someone's
lat, or in one of the elegant houses owned by many of their
mutual friends in Mayfair or Kensington.

'I'll have to go home and see the Mammy and Daddy
omorrow, so I will,' Mara promised Miles as they staggered
nto the taxi he had hailed. 'They'll be expecting me now
hat the war's over and my brothers will be back. There'll
e a big celebration. Why don't you come with me? You
ould put up at the Adelphi. The O'Shaughnessys give the
est parties you're ever likely to encounter, boyo.'

'Really darling? How . . . lovely, but I think I'll stay here
f it's all the same to you. And I wish you would. Jesus, Mara,
he whole city will be alive with festivities to celebrate the
nd of the war and you're contemplating dashing off to . . .

where is it ... Christ, Liverpool ... !'

Mara's 'Irishness' was absolutely delightful and Miles loved it but he was not at all sure he cared to sample it en masse, so to speak. He was well aware of her background as all the boys were, and in these days, did it really matter? She was the widow of one of them, after all, frequently seen in London in all the fashionable places since the death of her husband, James, who had gone to school with Miles younger brother.

'Oh, I shan't stay long, to be sure. Now that the war's over I might be bringing the children back to London with me, God love 'em. Sure an' I miss them something awful when I'm away but I was always afraid that they might get bombed in one of those dreadful air attacks an' if that happened the Mammy'd never forgive me.'

Miles wondered on the strange contradictions of this quite fascinating woman who, only half an hour since, had played his game with such abandonment and brought them both to a thundering climax, and yet was now talking as if she was still a child who must bow to the will of a parent. Her 'Mammy', whom she frequently mentioned, seemed to play a large part in her life which was curious considering how she spent much of it!

'I might take a house,' she mused, squeezing his arm with excitement as they sat back in the taxi, 'an' then I could stay up here more or less for good. I could bring Nanny and a governess for the girls. I suppose Christian'll have to go to school soon. The Osborne boys always do and he'll be six in January.'

'Really.' Miles stifled a yawn behind his gloved hand making a mental note to determine when Mara Osborne' children – how many were there, he had quite forgotten – were to be in town and to avoid her when they were. He was not even slightly interested in anything of a domestic nature. Mara was a delightful companion, so lovely, so wicked, so daring, independent, carefree and abandoned

626

but the thought of her as a mother, with a brood of young Osbornes about her, was quite appalling.

The press of people along Piccadilly was absolutely impenetrable and after honking his horn for several impatient moments the driver turned to them, informing them that there was no way he could get through this bloody lot! Beginning to catch the fervour of excitement and joy which was affecting the ordinary people of whom, after all, she was one, though she was not about to admit it to the aristocratic young man accompanying her, Mara stepped down from the taxi and was immediately surrounded by dozens of exultant Tommies who all, they said, wanted to kiss her. There were thousands of people, brewers' drays, buses, lorries, private motor cars, rattles, whistles, officers exchanging caps with enlisted men, well-dressed women in expensive furs arm in arm with bus conductors and policemen. She and Miles were carried along amongst them and from somewhere ahead a band was playing.

'Come on,' a voice shouted, 'the King's going to speak,' and right there in front of Buckingham Palace, as the band struck up 'God Save the King' Mara Osborne felt the boyish but loving spirit of her dead husband move into her wilful Irish heart and she wept for him. As women up and down the land were weeping for husbands and sweethearts and sons who would never come home to them. It was as though finally, this day they had all yearned for had shown them once and for all what telegrams and letters from commanding officers had never been able to do. They were gone. They would never be back as those who still lived would now be back. They had never seen their dead bodies nor stood beside their freshly filled-in graves, but now they knew, and they wept.

The woman on the bed made some slight murmuring sound, no more than a whimpering sigh in which a word or two only could be deciphered but those in the bedroom

627

instantly turned towards her and her daughter Elizabeth knelt beside her bed.

'Mother, I'm here, darling. What is it?' but Serena Osborne did not hear or if she did, did not acknowledge her presence.

'Mother, it's me, Elizabeth . . .'

Still no response. Serena Osborne continued to lie neatly on her back like a well-packaged parcel beneath the firmly tucked in sheets which the nurse seemed to think necessary. Her breath caught at her throat again before it rustled down into her lungs where it settled for what seemed an eternity before being expelled noisily, painfully on its return journey. Each one must surely be her last, those who stood about the bed believed, but in shuddering uneven spasms she continued to live. Her parted lips were dry and cracked, like the sands of the desert on which no water falls, deep fissures broken open by the furnace of her illness and Elizabeth moistened them gently with a damp cloth which she took from the table beside the bed.

The dying woman was beyond such consideration. Her chest continued to rise and fall but she had taken on that look of dusty pallor, of empty scooped-out greyness which heralds the onset of death.

A pretty ormolu clock on the mantelpiece erupted suddenly into a tinkling song as it sounded the hour and both the doctor and nurse who were in attendance automatically checked the time by their own watches, the doctor's a superb half-hunter on a chain across his well-upholstered stomach, the nurse's a neat fob on her rigid bosom.

The doctor cleared his throat and put his hand lightly on the shoulder of the woman who knelt beside the bed.

'Will you not take a rest, m'lady? Nurse will call you at need. We do not want another patient, now do we? I do not mean to presume but you have scarcely closed your eyes in a week and with your father's death yesterday . . .'

'I am quite all right, Doctor Carruthers.'

'No, you are not, Lady Woodall. You are exhausted and with this dreadful pandemic making such inroads up and down the country, indeed around the world, the low state you find yourself in can only put you at greater risk. You have been beside your parents all this time. No one could have been more devoted but I beg of you, go and sleep for an hour or two.'

'I slept last night, Doctor.'

'Half an hour, no more, and I am worried about you. You do not look yourself at all, m'lady, and I would be failing in my duty if I did not tell you so. And I must also tell you that if you do not come out of this sick room your husband threatens to come and carry you out.'

Elizabeth turned sharply, almost overbalancing. The expression on her face showed her utter consternation. Her voice was low, a whisper in the hushed room and it was absolute in its conviction.

'You must not allow it, Doctor Carruthers. You must not allow my husband to come into this room. You are aware of the state of his lungs since he inhaled the mustard gas and I am surprised that you have not refused his admission, not only to this room but to this house. There is grave illness here, as you must surely know, and besides the danger to himself there are children in the nursery at Woodall Park. Not only my own but those of my sister-in-law. How could Harry be so foolish?'

'He is concerned about your . . .'

'And not about his children?'

'You know how he is, m'lady.' They all knew how he was, the poor fellow, his lungs not the only part of him to be damaged in the trenches in which he had fought so valiantly for over three years. He was wounded in ways that did not show on the outside of his good-humoured, sweet-natured self. An inclination to be nervous with people he did not know well coupled with a stubborn resistance to going beyond the perimeter of his own walled estate. The doctor

629

had seen him jump a foot in the air at the slam of a do
and when his wife was out of his sight for longer th
five minutes he would smile engagingly and make sor
courteous excuse with the charm which was an intrins
part of him before going off to search for her. Oh yes, th
were all well aware of how Harry Woodall was, includi
his lovely wife.

'I realise that he is ... that he is somewhat vulneral
and is inclined to ... to worry when I am away from hi
but he must not come here again. Has he been in conta
with anyone in the house, the servants? You know ho
virulent this thing is. You said yourself that it is spread
direct contact. You must impress upon him...'

'He is most anxious about you, m'lady, and...'

'Please doctor, send him away, make him go home. T
him how dangerous it would be if one of the children
well, you will know how to word it.' Tell him he is putti
his children at risk. That he could carry it back to the
Make no mention of his danger, she was telling him, for
all costs Sir Harry Woodall must be protected from the fr
state of his own injured mind.

The woman on the bed opened her eyes, opaque slits
the deathly caricature of her face. She moaned faintly ar
incredibly, her hand fluttered beneath the bedclothes, doi
its best to escape them. Elizabeth, who was still looki
fiercely at the doctor, turned again swiftly. She freed h
mother's paper-thin hand and held it to her cheek.

'What is it, darling? Can we get you something?'

The mask on the pillow twitched in the parody of a smi
a skull with grinning teeth too large for the ghastly fa
Serena Osborne's mouth made a great effort to steady its
and her eyes were knowing in recognition of her daught
Her voice, when she finally managed to speak, was surpr
ingly strong.

'You ... were ... right, Elizabeth,' it said.

'Right, mother? In what way?'

'About Dotty Malcolm.'

Elizabeth leaned closer, her face sad and bewildered
nce her mother must still be wandering in that tortuous
aze of memories which had held her for the past three
ays. Ever since the influenza which was killing people, not
 their hundreds, not in their thousands but in millions
ound the world, had struck her down. Johnny Osborne,
izabeth's father, on the very day that the Armistice was
reed, a week ago now, had been the first to succumb to
e deadly virus which had come to be known simply as
panish 'flu since the first report of its ravages had seemed
 come from Barcelona. Twelve hundred had died in one
ay, it was said, and even more in Paris as its insidious
orror had crept over the boundaries of the great city
wards the English channel, helped, no doubt, by the great
ass of soldiers who were on their way home.

But, those in the know said, there was no need for con-
rn in Britain for the murderous microbes, should they
rive on these shores, would mingle with dust and would
 blown away by the prevailing westerly winds and what
e wind could not manage, the rain would. The dratted
ings would be drowned, one presumed, and so the great
itish public had breathed more easily. The disease had
en compared to the Black Death of the Middle Ages which
as ludicrous really in these days of modern medicine and
e new drugs which, thanks to the war, had been evolved,
d when the first victims began to fall prey to headaches
d body pains, sore throats, dry and red, catarrh and dread-
l chesty coughs, they were taken by complete surprise. In
e United States of America a system for staggering work
g hours was devised to avoid overcrowding. Cinemas,
eatres, dance halls and libraries were closed but from
ew England to Texas people died like flies, including the
octors and nurses who had pledged to save their lives or
 least ease their passing.

In Great Britain a man could leave his home in the best

of health and collapse before he got to work, right in th
street where the beleaguered ambulance service did its be:
to pick him up and transport him to the overcrowded hosp
tal, but the germs were vicious and death often occurre
within hours of the onset of the infection. Cemeteries ha
been established on Salisbury Plain to accommodate th
Australian troops who were billeted there and who die
there, their fellow soldiers making their coffins and diggin
their graves. Newcastle, Wigan, Manchester, London, whol
cities had come to a virtual stop as coal miners, train driver
firemen, policemen and telephone operators succumbed t
the illness.

And now it was the turn of Serena Osborne.

'Do you want to see Dorothy Malcolm, mother?' Elizabe
asked her softly, her mind dwelling briefly on her mother
friend who early in the war had lost her only son, Julia
and her younger brother.

'No...' Her voice was no more than a thread of sound
'Do ... you ... remember ... you said ... if ... you .
were ... her ... you ... would ... not ... be ... prou
... to ... lose... a ... son ... but ... angry...?' A chol
ing gasp between each word.

'Don't talk, darling ... rest,' for surely her mother mu:
be rambling and losing her strength over nothing.

'I said ... an honour ... to ... give ... son ... in .
great cause...'

'Mother, it is all over now.'

'You ... right ... I ... wrong ... a ... son .
precious...'

'Let me put my arms about you, mother ... res
darling...'

'*I was wrong*, Elizabeth...' Serena's voice strengthene
amazingly and so did her hand in Elizabeth's, gripping
fiercely. The spots of middle age which Serena had don
her best to avoid with creams and lotions stood out on he
skin and for a brief moment Elizabeth considered that he

632

other would not have to suffer the trials and afflictions of
ld age which she had dreaded. When a woman has been
eautiful as her mother had it was doubly hard to relinquish
outh, even the illusion of it.

Serena's eyes opened wide for the last time. 'I was ...
rong, Elizabeth. It ... was ... not ... an honour ... to
ave ... my sons ... killed and maimed ... not at all. My
oor boy ... my poor Teddy...'

They were the final words Serena Osborne spoke as she
ied in her daughter's arms.

he double funeral of Serena and Johnny Osborne took
lace in the family burial plot of the parish church of Croton.
 was attended by more than two hundred people, many
f whom could not get into the tiny, twelfth-century church.
lose friends and family of the dead couple, dignitaries of
e city of Liverpool, the wealthy and influential of Lanca-
hire, Cheshire and Yorkshire, and from the south where
erena Osborne had been a girl. A double funeral for a
ouble tragedy in a family which had known more than its
hare of loss.

Husband and wife were carried together in a gleaming,
orse-drawn hearse pulled by six coal-black horses since
er daughter knew Serena would prefer it to the motor
hicle she had never quite accustomed herself to. The lane
om the estate gates was bordered by a silent strand of
state workers and farm labourers, tenant farmers who had
orked the Beechwood land all their lives, those who had
een too old to offer their services at the front. Their wives
ood respectfully beside them in their decent black and
ere and there were men, younger, who rested on crutches
r saluted from wheelchairs.

The church was so full it was impossible to move or to
e one's neighbour for though Serena had been somewhat
mote, inclined to leave the women of the village and the
ed cottages to their own devices, unlike many ladies of the

manor house, Mr Osborne had been good-humoured an
generous and there were many in the crowd who had ber
efited from his kindness. Rents overdue had not bee
pressed and he was not averse to lending his prize bu
from the home farm in the service of their cows. There wa
many a sturdy animal grazing in the lush meadow of a tenar
farm which was there by the courtesy of the squire, as som
of them had liked to call him.

The day was cold and hard with a white frost paintin
every surface and laying a crisp carpet beneath the feet c
the mourners. Though it was not yet December it had turne
to the kind of weather one expects in mid-January. The sk
had an infusion of deep pink in it, shading to lavender wher
it met the hard earth and the frozen sun was a pale golde
ball just above the black-laced skeletons of the trees. Eac
sombre-clad member of the funeral procession wa
wreathed in a fine mist from their own breath and many c
the gentlemen stamped their feet as unobtrusively as pos
ible as they gathered about the grave.

The women of the family looked quite magnificent i
their black for though it was a sad day the intense cold ha
put a sparkle in their eyes and a flush of pink at each chee
Serena's daughter-in-law, the widow of her son, was i
ground-length black furs, her exquisite face doing its be
to look pale and sorrowing beneath the incredibly dashin
black fur hat she wore and which looked decidedly Russia
to the somewhat disapproving, upper class, older society c
Lancashire. Should one look so splendid when one va
mourning a member of one's family, they were inclined
ask one another, watching the widow as she carelessl
allowed the sable about her high-heeled boots to trail acro:
the frozen ground. Of course it was well known that Mar
and Serena Osborne had hated the sight of one anothe
Mara being, in Serena's opinion, no more than an Iris
trollop from the back streets of Liverpool who had snare
Serena's son in the oldest and most common way know

woman. Her five children were clustered about her for here she came from every member of the family, from the eldest to the youngest, mourned its dead together, and of course she was well aware of the sadly dramatic picture they all made as they grieved the passing of the matriarch and patriarch of the family.

Elizabeth, Lady Woodall, who had not brought her children, wore a black wool coat with a deep fur hem and a high mandarin collar which framed her face. Her cloche hat was pulled low over her ears and forehead, hiding her hair and from beneath it her vivid green eyes looked out beyond the wide grave to something only she could see. Happier times, perhaps, when Harry Woodall, his brothers Tim and Hugh, James Osborne and his brother Teddy, had raced their ponies as boys across the fields which surrounded the graveyard. Five careless youths of whom only two remained. Her husband stood to attention beside her, his face composed, but his eyes were bleak and subject to a strange inclination to dart about as though he was expecting an attack of some sort and must keep a sharp look-out. A lovely man, Sir Harry Woodall, with not a mean bone in his body but not what he had been four years ago, but then were any of them?

Old Mrs Osborne leaned heavily on the arm of a woman, obviously a servant by the cut of her clothes and the shapeless and unfashionable style of her bonnet, a woman almost as old as Mrs Osborne herself. Dear Lord, Lacy Osborne, who used to be Lacy Hemingway, the dead man's mother and so old one tended to forget she was still alive. Surely well into her eighties but still with a spritely look about her even if she did resemble a bit of fragile, crumpled old lace. Deep, silvery grey eyes, she had, which did not shed a tear for the passing of her only son though she seemed very moved when her great-granddaughter, Mara Osborne's youngest and called Rose, was, at the end of the service, lifted up for a kiss.

'Rose...' old Mrs Osborne quavered. 'Look at Ros[
Maggie,' she demanded of the old servant. 'Look at tho[
green eyes ... it's Rosie...' the colour of the child's ey[
surely not unusual since the man they had just buried h[
had eyes the very same shade, as did Elizabeth, his daught[
and the child's aunt.

'Aye my lass, 'tis thy great-granddaughter ...'

'No, it's Rosie...'

The child, born after her father died, was no more th[
three years old but she was dressed all in black, a miniatu[
of her mother in a beautifully made wool coat trimmed,[
were her three sisters' in expensive fur, with a tiny [
bonnet and a muff. They looked enchanting but really, w[
it the place or the occasion to bring children? But then th[
was Mara Osborne for you and would you look at them, f[
Heaven's sake, now that their mother had moved away fro[
the grave, racing about between the headstones as thou[
they had just been let out of school, the excitable Irish[
them very evident. The boy, heir to the Osborne estate no[
was like a young colt, unsteady and quite giddy with t[
lack of restraint his mother, and presumably his Nan[
allowed him. He was tall, about five years old, handson[
like his mother, but wild and unmanageable, it appeare[
with no one caring what he did until the officer who sto[
with Mara Osborne's sister, Mrs Jack Templeton, caught hi[
by the arm and in a minute had him standing as quietly a[
respectfully as he himself was. No one knew the officer, th[
decided amongst themselves, feeling that they should f[
he was obviously a gentleman with that air of good breedi[
which was instantly recognisable, at least by them. A ma[
in the Lancashire Fusiliers, with that certain weary, drain[
look all the men seemed to bring back from the front.

Elizabeth Woodall was discreetly supervising the placi[
of the smartly dressed mourners into the many splend[
motor cars which lined the road outside the churchyard a[
those who watched and waited politely for their turn we[

ell aware that this should have been the duty of her husband who was still, it appeared, guarding his back.

Sir Roger and Lady Fenton were there with their daughter enelope, herself a young widow, and who had once played dizzy game of tennis with Elizabeth's brothers, aeons ago. ady Anne Woodall, Elizabeth's mother-in-law and an old iend of Serena Osborne's, come down from Scotland here she now lived since the death of her husband and vo sons. Mrs Sophie Lawrence, Miss Sophie Woodall that as, and her husband who had been wounded at Cambrai nd invalided home to England. Hammonds and Hemingays, Ponsonbys and Robertsons and Taylors, many of them elated to the Osbornes by marriage.

Mara was deep in conversation with an attractive, blackoated gentleman who, it was felt by those who watched, as making her laugh far too loudly. Should she be laughing all, they whispered to one another, on a day such as this? /hat an example to set her children and no wonder they ere as unruly as a basket of kittens.

They were vastly intrigued, those who had come to bury ohnny and Serena Osborne, by the arrival of a youth who as obviously of the working classes and who, without so uch as raising his cap in the direction of the bereaved ady Woodall, flung the bicycle he was riding against a headtone and leaped from grave to grave until he reached Mara Osborne. He spoke to her rapidly in a thick Irish brogue, ose nearest to her said, so thick they none of them could peat what it was he said to her but whatever it was, it was nough to elicit a shriek from James Osborne's Irish widow hich could surely be heard in the land over the water om which she came. Her sister and the officer, the sister's usband it had been discovered and who now held her arm, urried across to Mrs Osborne and after what appeared to e a most dramatic discussion in which Lady Elizabeth /oodall was involved, the three of them were ushered into e splendid silver grey Vauxhall Prince Henry motor car and were driven away at speed by the gentleman who had only five minutes since, been making Mara Osborne laugh out loud.

She was not laughing now.

35

Elizabeth leaned her back against the side of the window frame, drawing her bent knees up to her chin and clasping her arms about them. She was crouched on the padded window seat of the big bay which dominated the recently restored comfort and splendour of the drawing room, the room which, until last week, had been ward three, surgical of the hospital at Woodall Park which she and Caitlin had helped to run. It still held in its oak timbered panelling and floor and the rich plaster of its ceiling the lingering smell of Lysol and carbolic soap. And could she hear on the thin December wind which whispered down the wide chimney the agonised echo of Second Lieutenant Archie Windom's screams, nineteen years old and an officer in a Leeds battalion, who had twice a day been forced to suffer the torment of having the ghastly wounds in his stomach dressed.

It seemed impossible somehow that in this lovely room hushed and tranquil now with no sound in it except for the quiet hiss and splutter of the logs burning in the fireplace so much suffering had been witnessed and yet for almost two years virtually every spare room in the ancient house had been as crammed with beds as this one had been, each containing some maimed, mutilated, pain-racked young man the war had chewed up and spat out like a pulped seed.

There was beauty and peace here now. The plain, lately

leaned, thick piled carpet in a deep shade of apricot, thirty feet square, was surrounded by yards of polished oak flooring. Deep chairs and sofas in the palest green velvet had been brought from the attics where they had been lovingly stored in their wrappings of sturdy linen. Low tables, waxed and burnished to a mirror-like gloss, were scattered with books, newspapers and half a dozen vases of freshly picked chrysanthemums of every shade from creamy white to the deepest bronze. There were lamps, ready to be lit as the day faded, not by an army of parlourmaids as in the days before the war but by the simple flicking of a switch. Electricity had been installed in 1912, to the great alarm of the servants, one of whom had been heard to remark wonderingly that he'd 'never seen 'owt like it in all my born days. Tha' pressed a teat on t' wall an' a bluddy light come on in bottle on t' ceiling!'

On the wide stone hearth was an enormous copper tub, scoured and polished until it reflected the loveliness of the room in its bright surface, filled to its brim with applewood logs cut from the trees which stood in the park about the house. In the fireback the wood burned fragrantly, the flames licking up and around the crackling logs and next to the tub were firedogs, as old and venerable as the house itself. There were low stools and fat pouffes all in various shades of green where weary feet might be rested or lively children be persuaded to sit and read a book.

Though the room was restful now there was an air of waiting about it as though, in the last few days, it had quickly become accustomed to laughter and movement, to the sound of children's voices and perhaps a dog or two. This had always been a family house and generations of Woodalls had sprawled here since the house was first built.

As though to confirm it a golden retriever which had been gazing into the flames of the fire, its muzzle resting on its paws, heaved itself to its feet and padded across to the window, flopping down beside Elizabeth, unable to bear

639

the distance between them for a moment longer. Its tai
moved lazily, greeting her. Its eyelids drooped a time o
two then it sighed into a contended doze.

At the mullioned windows, three in all, one on either sid
of the fireplace and the third the bay in which Elizabeth
sat, were floor-length silk curtains in a rich shade of crean
patterned in the same deep apricot as the carpet. Elizabeth
pushed one aside and stared pensively down the long slop
of the gardens towards the lake, sighing as deeply as th
dog.

As she watched, a small figure emerged from the stan
of trees which lay to the left of the house. He was alone bu
for a dog, not a splendid pedigreed animal like the one a
her feet but a rough-haired mongrel somewhere betweei
brown and black in colour and it was apparent as he an
the boy drew closer that he had a decidedly roguish ai
about him. His legs were short and so was his tail and a
of them moved in a blur as he darted, his nose to the groun
from tree to tree, from one clump of growing matter t
another, barely able to keep up with the wonderful assor
ment of smells he encountered. In thirty seconds Elizabeth
saw him lift his short leg and contemptuously water th
ground half a dozen times.

She smiled, the smile lighting her smooth face as thoug
a candle had been lit behind her eyes. They narrowed an
gleamed to a vivid green and her face was transforme
from the somewhat elusive beauty reminiscent of her dea
mother to a delightfully flushed loveliness which was quit
irresistible. Her skin, so pale only a moment ago, becam
warm, her mouth curled upwards at each corner and eve
her hair seemed to come to life, a curl or two escaping fron
the neat chignon at the back of her neck as she lifted he
head in laughter. She watched the boy, Alexander, her son
come on towards the house, his head bent in deep reveri
the dog frisking about his feet. The trees behind him wer
stark, charcoal grey skeletons against the washed out blu

of the sky, and the pale lemon sunlight threw long shadows across the grass.

Alexander Woodall was almost four years old and should not have been out alone. He was tall for his age, a sturdy boy with chocolate-coloured hair which ran in a riot of curls about his head. His eyes were a deep, clear hazel, not brown nor green but both shades speckled together, surrounded by the long, gold-tipped lashes which, as her husband said to her ruefully, would not have gone amiss on a girl. Not in the boy's hearing, naturally, for he was teased enough about them as it was by his brother and cousin and Harry Woodall was not a man to hurt anyone, let alone his younger son. A beautiful boy, dark and amber-skinned as a gypsy with none of the golden English looks of his brother and sister.

And where were his brother and sister, and the abundance of cousins, Mara's children, who had all set out with Nanny and Flora, the nurserymaid, an hour ago for an expedition to Colton Wood? A squabbling, straggling line of warmly dressed children from seven-year-old Claudine, Mara's eldest, right down to Caitlin's daughter, Lucy Templeton, who would have her second birthday in January. Flora had pushed the old baby carriage – how many babies had been transported about the garden in it? – ready to take on board any toddler who fell by the wayside which would probably be Damaris who was almost three, and Lucy herself. So why was Alex on his own with only the scruffy mongrel for company, the one found in the stable yard several months ago? It had been an endearing scrap of lively, enquiring eyes and a tail that threatened to wag its owner off its own feet and 'Gawd knew where it had come from', Mr Jackson had said. Alexander had adored it from the first moment the rough tongue had given his face a thorough cleaning, begging to be allowed to keep it. They had all sparred over it, of course, especially Christian and Charlie, who had both declared they would make it their own, feed

641

it, groom it, train it to guard the house and grounds but at the end of a week it had been Alex, anxious and frowning, who still went to Cook each morning for scraps to feed the growing puppy, and brushed the rough coat and cleaned out the corner where it slept. It had been given grand names by Christian and Charlie, Caesar and Prince and Major but, knowing exactly where its future lay it had answered only to Scruff, the name Alex called it by.

The child turned and called to the dog, his face breaking into a clear and luminous smile of love and instantly Elizabeth could see the man who was his father shine from him. The man who was at this moment mourning the death of his young wife.

A pang of sadness hit her, right between her breasts, and she gasped with the pain of it. The dog at her feet raised its head, then sat up and placed its muzzle in her lap.

'Dear God, but it's hard, Tawny,' she said out loud, and the dog cocked her head as Elizabeth spoke her name. She had not been born when the man who was in her mistress' mind had last been seen in these parts, Christmas 1917 it had been, since she was only seven months old, but with the understanding sympathy of a much older dog, she hitched herself a little closer to Elizabeth's stroking hand.

'What is he feeling, d'you think, girl?' but the dog had no answer. In Elizabeth's mind was the clear remembrance of the sadness and yet the joy of that day three weeks ago when they had buried her mother and father. A deep sadness for she had loved her good-humoured father and, despite their differences, had held her mother in a kind of resigned affection.

But the joy had come from the incredible and sudden sound of his name, the name she had carried sweetly, sorrowfully in her heart for more than eight years. The name of Michael O'Shaughnessy. They had sent his younger brother, Eammon, to fetch Mara and Caitlin for it seemed Michael's young wife had perished with hundreds of others in Liverool of the Spanish 'flu and as if that was not enough for Ellen and old Mick O'Shaughnessy to be bludgeoned with, news had been brought by young Michael, home compassionately from France, that his brother Dermot, the O'Shaughnessy's second son, had been killed on the day, at the very hour the war had come to an end.

'Michael's with the Mammy and Daddy now but you're to come at once,' Elizabeth had heard the distressed boy say as he put out strong young arms to take hold of his half-fainting sister, her cry still echoing in the trees from which, at the sound, a flock of crows had risen. Then Caitlin had been there, and Jack her husband, himself just back from France, for the soldiers were beginning to come home now. The children had begun to wail because their mother was, and Harry ... Dear God ... Harry ... please don't let Harry be troubled, not now, not at this dreadful confused moment, and it *had* been confused as the mourners had waited politely for this further O'Shaughnessy drama to unfold itself and be resolved and for themselves to be placed in one of the long line of motor cars which awaited them and carried them away to more comfortable quarters.

Poor, poor Ellen, how was she to stand it, Elizabeth could remember thinking in the muddle of explaining to Harry and at the same time giving her attention to those relatives and friends of her parents who expected to return to Beech-wood where sherry and sympathy would be exchanged. Poor Ellen, to have lost a son in the irony, and agony, of the last moment of the war, and with that contemptuous lack of feeling the fates seemed to heap on those who looked the other way for an unwary second or two. Thank God for Jack, had been her fervent prayer, as Caitlin's husband had ushered his wife and Mara into the waiting motor car which sped off towards Liverpool.

She was about to open the window and enquire of her approaching son the whereabouts of the others and why he was alone, when the drawing room door was flung open.

Mara and Caitlin entered the room, Mara first, of course with that careless disregard for the niceties of polite society which said she did not think it necessary for Wilson to announce her. She was Lady Woodall's sister-in-law, for Heaven's sake, family, and where she came from family treated one another's homes as though they were their own.

'So there you are,' Mara declared, airily waving away the disapproving figure of Elizabeth's butler who still hovered at her back, trying his best to do his duty despite the wilful ways of young Mrs Osborne. You could tell a lady by her attitude to servants, his attitude said, as he shut the door quietly behind his mistress' visitors.

Mara advanced into the room, flinging her furs and her dashing Russian hat on to the sofa, reaching into her handbag for her cigarettes even before she sat down. Her older sister, Caitlin, followed more slowly, moving across the vast expanse of carpet until she stood in front of Elizabeth. The faces of the two women were for a moment hidden from the third and the glance they exchanged was warm and affectionate, strong with the unity which had grown between them during the last years of the war. Caitlin placed a hand on Elizabeth's shoulder then bent to kiss her cheek before moving away with no word spoken, perfect understanding between them.

Elizabeth sat up and put her feet to the floor. She turned her head for a second, watching as her son and his dog took the side path round to the stables and the companionship of Mr Jackson, with whom he had a curious bond; Mr Jackson who had once been head groom at Woodall but was now with only two beasts in the stable, barely more than handyman.

She stood up and moved briskly to the bell beside the fireplace giving the impression of a woman just awakened from a dreaming state who suddenly realises that she has duties to perform as a hostess.

'We'll have tea, I think,' she murmured, 'before the tribe

eturns. There'll be little hope of conversation once they descend on us. Off to Colton Wood with Nanny and Flora, so they told me, but knowing Nanny she won't keep them out long in this weather. Despite the sunshine it's very cold. And how is your mother?' turning to Mara. 'I have promised myself I will call on her as soon as . . .'

As soon as what? she questioned even as she spoke the words. Her mind sought desperately to give a legitimate reason why she had not already been to visit Ellen but it could not. They did not know one another very well, she and Ellen, but she had been in the O'Shaughnessy home in the past; she and Mara were related by marriage and though she was well aware that Ellen and herself were from two completely different social classes, the fact should not and did not, as far as that was concerned, make any difference to Elizabeth. Only she knew the reason why she had stayed away and she could not explain it to Mara.

'Sure an' I don't know what's to stop you, so I don't. The Mammy would love to see you and if you and Caitlin were to come over more often . . .' The words Mara spoke petered away slowly. Her voice was petulant and both Elizabeth and Caitlin knew why, and how the sentence would have been completed. *If you and Caitlin were to come over more often then I could get back to where I belong.* 'You have your motor and could drive over whenever you pleased,' she went on, her voice growing stronger as she warmed to her theme. 'Oh, I know Harry doesn't like to be left on his own for long but glory be, an hour wouldn't be missed. And you know how the Mammy likes you. Ever since the day you came to Bridget's funeral she's had a soft spot for you, Elizabeth, and as you've both suffered a recent bereavement it would be a comfort to the both of you, so it would. An' a bit of company for her the day. Something to take her mind off her troubles.'

She smiled winningly at Elizabeth but it was really not her mother's grief that was in her mind, nor Elizabeth's ability to soften it. It was her own dire need to return to London before Miles Hamilton forgot her. Who knew what diversion he might have found, or had offered to him in her absence? He was devastatingly good-looking beside being one of the most eligible bachelors in London. She had known him for more than a year now, meeting him on one of the lightning leaves he seemed able to contrive, due no doubt to his family connections. Seventy-two hours they had shared in the frantic searching after pleasure, self gratification and indulgence, sensation, any sensation which would blot out the memories of the war left behind in France. They were two of a kind, she and Miles, she had decided, concerned only with living life to the full, greedy for the bodily enjoyments they gave to one another, for luxury, for diversion – of any sort – and if Mara was no available Miles would simply find it elsewhere. Three weeks now she had been in Liverpool and if she didn't return herself soon to his attention and his bed, she would find someone else in it when she did. He was the second son of a second son of a great and aristocratic family and, had it not been for the war, would have continued to be no more than that but his older brother had died at Ypres and his uncle, the present Earl, had lost both his sons at the battle of the Somme. Miles Hamilton was the sole heir to the earldom!

And Miles Hamilton was hot for Mara Osborne and Mara Osborne meant to keep it that way. Duchess of . . . where was it? . . . Bejasus, she could never remember but what did it matter if she, little Mara O'Shaughnessy from Edge Lane, could stick a title in front of her name? Of course, Miles would not care for her children, she was well aware of that but, like all unpleasant problems to which she had no immediate answer that would be put away to a dim corner of her mind until she was forced to face it by which time some remedy would be sure to emerge. She would think about it later. Keep the children well out of his sight and

646

thoughts until she had him well and truly snared. In the meanwhile the children could stay here in Elizabeth's nursery.

In her usual self-absorbed, self-willed, self-centred way she gave no thought to Elizabeth and Harry in whose home she meant to leave them, nor to the children themselves. They were happy in their child's world, secure, protected, loved by their Aunts, Elizabeth and Caitlin. A world of careless, everyday growing up, laughter and squabbles and tears, kisses and nursery cuddles amongst a tumble of kittens and puppies and ponies and would not unduly miss her, she told herself, whilst she applied her scheming self to the acquiring of Miles Hamilton, future Earl of . . . where the divil was it? . . . as a husband and when she had him she would send for them.

So she told herself, as she watched her sister-in-law settle herself by the blazing fire whilst she waited for tea to be brought. But even Mara who was not the most sensitive of women, particularly where one of her own sex was concerned, could sense that Elizabeth was not the usual calm and tranquil woman they were all used to having about them.

'What's wrong?' she asked abruptly since she wanted nothing to spoil her own plans for the future.

'Nothing at all,' Elizabeth answered, smiling, doing her best to show an unruffled face to her sister-in-law for how could she tell Mara the true reason why she was unable to call on Ellen O'Shaughnessy? How could Elizabeth go to Fdge Lane and the home where the O'Shaughnessys lived, the home which now included Ellen's son Michael, and his baby daughter, his motherless baby daughter Cliona? How could she and Michael meet for the first time, indeed at any time with the undying, tormented love which had flourished, despite its lack of nourishment, for all these years? It would be unthinkable, impossible to enter that house even at this sorrowful time and see him there amongst his own people, greet him just as though he meant no more to her than any of the others.

It was almost twelve months since they had parted in the woods at the back of Woodall Park. Christmas, the day she had taken Alex and Charles for a walk there, the walk no more than a pretext to allow Michael to see the boy, his boy, known as Alexander Woodall. They had met on the path for a brief agonising moment, the boy unaware that he was talking to his true father as he and Michael gravely discussed the pine cone Alex held in his baby hand. Charles had demanded the stranger's attention as well and had been patiently given it before the two small boys had darted away along the path, high-spirited, unthinking, one so fair, the other dark. Dark like his father, like all the O'Shaughnessys but without, thank God, the O'Shaughnessy eyes.

They had said goodbye, she and Michael, desperately aware that in all probability they would never meet again. The war was killing men in their hundreds and thousands and why should Michael O'Shaughnessy be spared? Three years he had been fighting in the devastation which was France so surely it was time for the gods to look the other way and let Lieutenant Michael O'Shaughnessy fend for himself? Surely it was his turn, when he went back to the trenches to take that step along the road to death with the rest of them?

But he had come back. Like Harry. Like Jack, undamaged as they were, at least where it showed. It was over three weeks now since he had returned to Edge Lane just in time to hold his young wife in his arms as she died and in those three weeks he had made no attempt to see Elizabeth.

Mara was studying her sister-in-law with suspicion, puffing nervously on her cigarette, her eyes narrowed against the drifting smoke. She had flung herself into the sofa by the fire, lounging there with one arm along its back but now she stood up and began to move about the room as though she could not sit still for a moment longer. She picked up one delicate object after another, a silver-framed photograph of Elizabeth and Harry on their wedding day, a Minton pot-pourri vase, a tiny clock set in a mother of pearl and tortoiseshell case, handling each one before carelessly replacing them on the polished table. She pushed a hand through the mop of her hair, fluffing it up with restless fingers then, throwing herself down again in a deep chair, stubbed out her half-finished cigarette in a marble ashtray. She was very evidently bored and fretful and both her sister and sister-in-law knew she was longing to get back to the 'bright lights' wherever they happened to be and as soon as was decently possible she would climb into her fast little roadster and roar off to wherever there was some fun.

'Well, I don't understand you at all,' she said peevishly, 'an' neither will the Mammy when I tell her you can't call on her.'

'Your mother can come and visit me here at any time, you know that, Mara. She would be most welcome, as any of your family are. We are related after all and now that ... well, now there is only Harry and myself to ...'

'You'll be meaning since your mother died?'

'If you want to put it like that, yes. She was very old-fashioned and set in her ways ...'

'An' would sooner burn Beechwood Hall to the ground, as your mother-in-law would this place, than let some Irish mick and his wife over the threshold,' but Mara was smiling in that impudent way she had, taking no offence from the words, her good humour suddenly restored. 'I suppose times have been changed by the war, so they have, but you'd never have got your mother to change with them, Elizabeth, nor mine. There's no chance you'd get her into this place, you know that. My Daddy works for yours, or at least he did.' She looked awkward and confused for a moment or two but was saved the need to go on as the elderly parlourmaid, supervised by Wilson, who would never admit to change of any sort, especially if it meant the lowering of standards, *his* standards, brought in the tea on a trolley.

'Leave it, thank you, Wilson. I will serve myself.'

'Very good, m'lady,' bowing, leaving the room, the maid unobtrusive as she had been trained to be, going before him.

'It makes no difference now, Mara,' Elizabeth continued the conversation which had been interrupted by the butler and the maid. She poured Mara a cup of tea and passed it to her, then another to Caitlin who had yet to speak, waiting until they were both sipping their tea before going on.

'Your father will have a job at Hemingways until he is ready to retire, surely he knows that. My father's death changes nothing in the way the business is run though who will . . .' She stopped, turning her head to stare blindly into the fire, the matter of visiting Ellen O'Shaughnessy and the difficulties it might cause temporarily forgotten.

'Who will run it all, Elizabeth?' Caitlin's voice was gentle, not probing, merely putting into words what was in Elizabeth's mind. There were managers, of course, men who had always been in charge of the vast holdings owned by the Osborne family, but who was to look after the Beechwood estate, see to the farms, the woodland, the stocking and rearing of game, the park, the house, now that Serena and Johnny Osborne were gone and only the almost mindless boy who had been their son remained, the crippled Teddy Osborne who had not been out of his room for nearly three years.

Elizabeth bent her head, then lifting it again looked steadfastly into the eyes of Caitlin Templeton.

'I rather hoped it might be Jack.'

'Jack!' Caitlin reared back in shocked amazement.

'Jack?' Mara echoed but she leaned forward, perhaps sensing some benefit to herself in the suggestion.

'Why not? He comes from . . .'

'. . . the same background as yourself?' Caitlin's voice was mocking.

'I did not mean that, but yes, he has been brought up in similar circumstances and besides,' Elizabeth's voice was resolute but soft, 'what else will he do?'

Her meaning was plain. Jack Templeton had been a soldier since he left school twenty-one years ago. A regular who knew nothing but soldiering and before it the life of the son of a landed gentleman. When he came back from France he had stayed at Woodall – at Harry's insistence for he had taken a great liking to Caitlin's husband – where Caitlin and her daughter had lived for the past two years. The hospital Caitlin ran would take weeks to wind down, its occupants being moved to other facilities as men were discharged, and Jack could be of enormous help with the arranging of the transfers of the more serious cases, the removal of the beds and hospital equipment, the bringing out and restoring of the beautiful Woodall furniture. Harry, still inclined to be jumpy over what seemed nothing at all to others, had a tendency to forget what they were doing and wander away in search of Elizabeth. In the circumstances Jack would be invaluable and Elizabeth wondered what she would do without him and, more importantly, how she would manage when he and Caitlin moved away, as they were bound to do. She had a sick husband and a disabled brother, three children, two vast estates and a lively shipping business in her care and only herself to manage them all.

'I need him, Caitlin, and you,' she said quietly. 'I'm doing neither of you a favour if that's what you're thinking. The other way round, in fact.'

Mara was hanging on her every word. It had occurred to her more than once that, with her son Christian as the heir of Beechwood Hall and the accompanying Osborne wealth, the appalling task of running Beechwood would be flung in her lap but here, or so it seemed, was the perfect answer. If Caitlin and Jack could be persuaded to move into the Hall, become its custodians and manage the whole thing, lock, stock and barrel, until Christian came of age, it meant that she could take herself off to wherever she pleased, whenever she pleased knowing that it was all in good hands. And not only that, Caitlin would be near the Mammy and Daddy which, with her other sisters, would take any responsibility which might have been hers from Mara. The London season would be starting in a few months' time and surely, as it was the first since the end of the war would be the most splendid ever. They said that in the four years before the war staid King George V had set a somewhat dull and sombre stamp on his court but things would be different now and Mara Osborne meant to be there to see it. She had, she told herself, suffered wartime austerity and now she intended to enjoy peacetime plenty. She wanted gaiety, music, dancing, champagne. She was filled with nervous energy which must be spent in the syncopated jazz which was all the rage, as they said. Rag-time, the Twinkle, the Vampire, the Camel Walk and the other wonderful and exciting dances with which she meant to 'wow' – another word which had sprung up during the war – all those who would soon migrate to the capital city. The dust sheets would be coming off in the great London houses, Devonshire House, Spencer House, Lansdowne House, all owned by noble families and surely Mara Osborne, darling of the smart set, loved by dozens of pedigreed young officers since her gallant husband had been killed, would be included? There would be court balls, the Derby, the royal meeting at Ascot, Goodwood, Wimbledon, the new shows, dinner parties and dances, to mention but a sample of the fun to be had, and all thronged with what remained of the noble and upper class sons of polite society. Mara had remained at home for nearly a month now and the strain of living at Beechwood Hall on her own except for her children with ... with himself upstairs like some dark spectre forever hanging over her was becoming quite unbearable. It was not that she ever saw him, none of them did apart from Elizabeth and Harry who went to sit with him every day, reading the newspaper him, but the very idea of this ... this deformed creature, this dreadful apparition of a man being in the same house as herself and her children was enough to crack the steadiest mind. He had a male nurse to look after him, to see to his ... his physical needs, to carry up food from the kitchen and for all anyone else saw of him, of Teddy Osborne, he might just as well not be there. Dead! Forgotten for the most part by everyone but his sister. No sound came from the room where, it was said, he sat from dawn until dark staring out across the gardens only being moved when it was necessary for the maids to clean his rooms. It gave you the creeps, really it did, and if someone other than Mara could live permanently at Beechwood and see to it all, then Mara would be vastly relieved.

'It seems a good idea to me, so it does,' she said eagerly. 'You an' Jack have no home of your own to go to and as Elizabeth says, what's Jack to do now that the war is over? Without a tail to his shirt, so he is, an' it seems to me ...'

Caitlin turned an icy stare on her sister and Mara realised she had gone too far. It was true Jack had no home to offer his wife and child but he had a small and quite adequate private income, settled on him from the estate of his maternal grandmother and though he was trained to be nothing but a soldier he was far from destitute.

'An' wouldn't it just suit yourself to leave me an' Jack doing what you should be doing, Mara O'Shaughnessy? That place, the house and the estate, the businesses which are held by the Hemingways and the Osbornes will, apart from what Elizabeth gets, come to Christian one day so it seems to me that you, as his mother, should be guarding it for him. James was Teddy's brother after all an' you were James' wife an' if you had a spark of decency in you, or humanity, you'd be making an effort to help Elizabeth and to try and do something for Teddy.'

'Please, Caitlin, there is really nothing Mara can do for Teddy and as for looking after the estate ...' Elizabeth had

653

been about to say what good would her flighty, thoughtle
self-absorbed sister-in-law be in the management of wh
would one day come to Christian. And the badly damag
young man who had once been Elizabeth's light-heart
brother would see no one but herself and the ex-sold
who looked after him, himself a veteran of the Somm
Ypres and Cambrai and therefore, because he had kno
what Teddy had known, acceptable to her crippled broth
In some way, how she did not know, Teddy had to
reached, to be dragged from the self-destroying shell in
which he had crawled but Mara was definitely not the pers
to do it. Nor was she capable, had she been willing,
running the estate as Elizabeth's father had done, nor t
house which had been Serena's province. Mara had be
trained to perform neither of these duties as young lad
and gentlemen in Elizabeth's world were. She had taken
the life, the social life of the upper classes, with an enthu
asm and élan which had, after a certain settling in perio
allowed her to become an accepted member of the ran
who had been born to it. But that was all she was capab
of. Both Caitlin and Elizabeth were sadly aware of what sh
was and when Mara stood up, moving huffily to the windo
where she lit another cigarette, they exchanged glance
sighing in resignation. Then Elizabeth smiled and put a har
on Caitlin's arm.

'You don't have to make up your mind at once, darlin,
she said quietly. 'Talk to Jack and please, don't think yc
are beholden to me in any way. I can put an agent in to ru
the estate and see to the farms, you know that. Andre
Brown is a good man and Teddy is well looked after. M
Pritchard and Eaton have been with us for years and a
loyal and trustworthy so the house will run as it always ha
And as for the business,' she went on, 'there have alwa
been splendid managers to look after it and I can see r
reason why they should not continue to do so.'

Caitlin did not answer but she was well aware that wh

izabeth proposed to do was more than any woman should e asked to do, even one as strong, as patient and generous Elizabeth. Holy Mother of God, hadn't she enough with er own unstable husband clinging to her hand like a child, ith three children in the nursery – and the distinct possibil-y of Mara's five as well – the management of this enormous ld house and its servants and the overseeing of the running f the estate of Woodall Park? There was a man, Jethro Petch, ho was the land agent and who took Harry round with im, supposedly easing his employer back into the task of ooking after his own land but Sir Harry, after half an hour a the saddle or in the middle of a discussion with a keeper n the stocking of his game, would dash off with an apolo-etic wave and a strained smile, hurrying back home to look or his wife. Winter was a trying time for him. His lungs, logged with the debris left by that whiff of mustard gas, ound it difficult to function as they should, to force a pass-ge through which the pure air of Woodall might travel. He ad high temperatures, a hacking cough which drained and xhausted him and he was often forced to keep to the armth of the bedroom he shared with his wife. Half a man as Harry Woodall, sweet-natured and devoted to his family.

man who, in kinder circumstances, would have been a trong and supportive husband, a benevolent father, a wise rotector of the inheritance left him, lion-hearted, good-umoured and dependable. The war had destroyed all that nd almost destroyed him. Caitlin was lucky. Her husband, erhaps because of his years of training and campaigning n the regular army, had come through relatively unscathed. Ie had nightmares, but then who didn't? He saw dead com-ades standing on street corners or smiling ruefully at him rom across his own fireside but that would pass with time. hey had their child and the prospect of others and Mara vas right. They had no home. They had talked about it, vhere they should settle, what Jack should do but they had ome to no decision. Perhaps this was the answer.

'You have a kind heart, Elizabeth Woodall,' she said softl then stood up in her usual brisk manner before her frien could deny it, 'and I promise to think about it. I'll talk Jack and ... well, we'll see. Now then, Mara my girl, yo can run me over to the Mammy's in that ghastly thing yo call a motor car though to be sure it wouldn't look out place on the racetrack at Brooklands, oh, and I'll be bac later on this afternoon if Jack should ask. He went off som where with Harry.'

Giving me a break. The thought went through Elizabeth head as she watched Mara and Caitlin go off up the ha followed by the discreet butler who, though he had no been rung for, seemed to know when a visitor was to leav and was there to see them off the premises. Jack is givin me half an hour to myself, she thought gratefully. Dear Jac ... Dear Caitlin ... pray God they decide to stay for reall I do not think I can go on alone.

Drawing a deep breath she left the room in search of he son, her lovely boy, hers and Michael's and therefor though she would admit it to no one, dearer to her tha her other children. Alex had gone to the stables to talk Mr Jackson, she was sure of that. That was where she woul find him and where she would find peace and sanity in th company of her son and his puppy, the two remainin horses and the dour common sense of the old groom wh would be cleaning out the tack room and the stables as h did every day just as though they were to be filled at an moment with the splendid thoroughbreds which had live there before the war.

They were deep in earnest conversation, their heads clos together, the old man and the boy, even the dog taking keen interest in what they said, it seemed. A square of sur shine in the corner of the yard had been taken over, tw upturned buckets used as handy seats. The groom had pipe clamped between his teeth, a bridle in his hand whic he appeared to be mending, the scene one of indescribabl

656

anquillity. Over the half door of the nearest stable hung
e inquisitive head of Jenny, the pony the boys rode, snort-
g her pleasure at the boy and in the next stable was the
estnut mare which was Harry's mount. A gentle old lady
lled Garnet and a far cry from Monarch, the wild black
unter he had ridden before the war. He and the mare were
omfortable with one another her husband said, when he
de over his lands, and in her heart Elizabeth wept for the
ashing young man who had urged his magnificent hunter
higher and higher jumps on that last glorious hunt in the
rly part of 1914.

Alex heard the sound of her footsteps on the cobbled
rd and looked up at once. He grinned and her heart
rned over in her breast as Michael O'Shaughnessy looked
ut from his son's face. There he was, the man she loved,
ger, lively, breathless with something he must tell her,
eeding her immediate attention and seeing no reason why
e should not have it. In some way it was as though Alex
as her only child, the child of her heart not of her womb
nce he had been conceived in a moment of joy so blinding
ere were no words to describe it. The boy, the man, they
ere one person and her eyes blazed their message of love
r them both.

'Mother, Mr Jackson says...' Most of Alex's sentences
egan that way for in his eyes the old man could do no
rong. He was patient and wise and dependable, something
e boy missed in Harry. Alex had known no men except
e servants until the man who was thought to be his father
ad come home from the war. In his frail state the man had
o time for the boy, indeed he had not the strength. Willing,
es, if he had been capable of it, to play, to talk, to have
n, to sing and romp and be a father, to share the small
onfidences the boy shared with Mr Jackson but Harry's
esh and mind were weak and he had not yet forged the
ond his sons needed to be close, as sons and fathers should
e close.

And so, when he could, when he felt the need, Alex Woodall turned to the old man who could have been his grandfather, since the boy had none of his own now. Mr Jackson had been at Woodall when Harry had been no bigger than Alex was now and indeed had worked for the old Sir Charles, Harry's father. No one knew exactly how old he was, nor had they the temerity to ask but for the past fifty years he had worked in these same stables. He had, for as long as Elizabeth could remember, been called Mr Jackson and not just by his surname as the other male servants were.

'Good afternoon, Mr Jackson.'

'Good afternoon, m'lady.' The groom creaked to his feet removing his pipe and his cap. The boy ran to his mother and the puppy, excited as all young animals are over nothing and everything, leaped about chasing his own tail.

'Give over, daft dog,' the old man commanded and it did, standing patiently beneath the gnarled hand on its head.

Elizabeth picked up her son, holding him with both arms about his waist, whirling him round in a spinning game all children love until he shrieked with laughter before setting him down again on his feet. She brushed back his heavy curling hair, her hand hovering at the satin skin of his cheek and chin. If Mr Jackson had not been there she would have hugged him to her, kissed him and called him darling but in front of the groom it would, she knew, have offended her son's male pride. Though he was only four years old he was already being guided in the ways a young gentleman of his class should go but the passionate Irish blood of his father often battled with the pedigreed upbringing of Woodall.

'Mother, Mr Jackson says...'

'What does Mr Jackson say, Alex?' She smiled at the old man.

'That when he was a boy like me father rode a huge black hunter...'

658

'Nay, Master Alex, give over. What I said was that when thi' father was a lad, but I meant goin' on sixteen, not four years old like thissen.'

'Yes of course.' Four years old or sixteen, what did it matter to a big boy like him? 'But mayn't I ride father's mare now, Mother? Charlie can have the pony and I'll take Garnet and that way we'll both be able to ride at the same time,' and save all that squabbling over who's turn it is, Elizabeth thought with amusement.

'Nay, Master Alex, tha's not big enough yet, tha' knows, but when t' time comes I'll put thee on her back, don't thee fret.'

'Will you, Mr Jackson, promise?' There was implicit trust in the boy's voice. He stretched his sturdy frame, already working on the daunting task of being big enough to ride his father's mare and certainly a huge black hunter one day.

'That I will, lad, an' now I must get on. I've things to do so if your ladyship'll excuse me.' The groom touched the peak of his cap respectfully.

Elizabeth's son put his hand in hers as they wandered down the long paddock where, years ago, Harry Woodall had asked Johnny Osborne's permission to marry his daughter. There was the smell of the frozen black earth, the sound of the birds, the chatter of a jay in the bright, clear air and the flash of a robin's red breast against the hedge. A blackbird called and a thrush sat on the gatepost and watched with bright eyes the antics of the dog. The sky was turning to a pure, luminous gold behind the black tracery of the trees as the afternoon drew towards closing and a crackle of frost was beginning to touch the rungs of the gate through which she and Alex had just passed. The dog circled about them, mad as a March hare, Elizabeth was inclined to believe, explaining the meaning of the words to Alex.

'He's just daft,' Alex said tolerantly and as if to complete the intense pleasure of this moment alone with her son, Michael's son, a rare occurrence in the uproar of a nursery in which nine children played side by side, her own retriever bitch flew like a yellow flag down the length of the field to join them.

The mongrel went crazy with delight and, infected by the dog's excitement, the more placid bitch began to run, her tail and ears flat, in a wild figure of eight, just as though she knew and understood the special link which bound the woman and the boy to one another, and to the man who had fathered him.

Alex pulled away from his mother's hand and, unable to resist the joy of the two animals, ran with them.

'Scruff ... Tawny ... heel, boy ... heel, girl ...' but the dogs were well beyond the confines of his orders, of any one's orders, racing off in search of the exciting smells which they knew they would find in the wilder corners of the paddock and among the trees which led down to the lake and the boy went with them.

Elizabeth followed more slowly and from the warm and loving depth of her heart her son's father rose to embrace her, speaking in that lilting Irish way of his, just as she remembered, just as she knew she always would.

'Nothing can touch us, my darling,' he had said to her and she listened to him now with her heart. 'We are indestructible, you and I. What we have cannot be destroyed ... and the living proof of his words could be heard calling to his dogs.

'Don't despair,' Michael had whispered to her, 'I will always be here with you ...' and he was.

She continued on towards the trees, her heels digging into the hard and sloping ground of the paddock. She drew near to the high pitched yelping of the two young dogs and her son as he called to them and then, from behind her came the deeper voice of a man. She turned, startled, for she had thought herself to be alone.

'Wait for me, darling,' the man at the top of the paddock called and even from where she stood, half-way down the

660

slope, Elizabeth could see the broad, engaging grin on her husband's face. The sun, sinking behind the bare trees of the spinney was shining through the faint beginnings of a December mist directly into his eyes and he lifted his hand to shade them. The golden winter glow put colour into his thin face and in it his strong white teeth gleamed. He had not been to the barbers for several weeks and his thick fair hair fell in a boyish tumble over his brow. As he drew near he lowered his hand and in his gentle brown eyes was the warm constant depth of his love for her.

He started to run in that awkward and at the same time strangely graceful way he had, favouring his injured leg and yet not hindered by it. Her heart turned over with love for him. He wore an old tweed jacket he refused to part with, one going back to the days before the war, with leather gun pads at the shoulders and large game pockets. To please her under it he had put on a warm woollen sweater with a polo neck, smiling as he did so, saying she was like a mother hen with an extra chick to cluck over. Corduroy breeches, highly polished boots and a scarf flying back from his neck completed the outfit. He refused absolutely to use a walking stick.

'I thought I heard Alex's voice,' he called, holding out his hand in readiness to take hers. 'I was with Petch up in the far field when I heard him shout to Scruff so I thought I would come over to see what he was up to,' and of course, where Alex was so might his mother be. Peace. Tranquillity. Love. Safety. Elizabeth!

'We were going to find the others.' Her hand was there waiting for his.

'Are they misplaced?' and his folded neatly about hers.

'No more than usual.'

'Well then.'

'Well then,' smiling.

They fell into step, Elizabeth and Harry Woodall, and if the spirit of Michael O'Shaughnessy was present it was folded tenderly and quietly away again in the heart of the woman who had loved him.

From the spinney the voice of his son lifted into the winter sky.

AUDREY HOWARD

A DAY WILL COME

When Miles Thornley rides into her life, everything begins to change for Daisy Brindle. For the first time she catches a glimpse of a very different life to the one she has always known.

Daisy is a field girl, tramping the roads of Lancashire in a gang of women and children, hired out by a brutal master for stone picking, harvesting, winter work down the pits.

But Miles, heir to a great estate, arrogant and spoilt, who teaches her to love, seduces her and casually casts her aside. He teaches her to hate.

Driven onto the streets of Liverpool, Daisy is rescued by a man of honesty and restless energy, sea captain Sam Lassiter.

First as his mistress and then as his wife and business partner, Daisy comes to enjoy the better things in life. But her unrelenting drive for revenge on the dissolute Miles begins to threaten the destruction of everything she has worked for and achieved. Begins finally to threaten her relationship with Sam Lassiter himself . . .

HODDER AND STOUGHTON PAPERBACKS

AUDREY HOWARD

A WORLD OF DIFFERENCE

Cosseted heiress Jenna Townley is used to getting her own way. And when she meets ambitious young Conal MacRae, she soon knows that this is the man she must marry, despite her father's disapproval.

Their courtship is fiery and their marriage passionate. But their happiness is threatened by tragic and sinister family secrets which refuse to be buried. Is Jenna destined to repeat her mother's tragedy, or can she triumph over the past and keep both the Townley legacy and the man she was meant to love?

HODDER AND STOUGHTON PAPERBACKS